SPANISH MUSIC IN THE AGE OF COLUMBUS

ROBERT STEVENSON

University of California
Los Angeles

SPANISH MUSIC IN
THE AGE OF COLUMBUS

MARTINUS NIJHOFF — 1960 — THE HAGUE

ML
315.2
.S74

PRINTED IN THE NETHERLANDS

I have seen dawn and sunset on moors and windy hills
Coming in solemn beauty like old tunes of Spain.

JOHN MASEFIELD (*Beauty*)

Contents

List of Musical Examples

Preface

FOR AID in preparing the present résumé of Spanish music to 1530 I am indebted to so numerous a company of friends that I must content myself in this preface with no more than a token alphabetical list. In an earlier article – "Music Research in Spanish Libraries," published in *Notes of the Music Library Association*, sec. ser. X, i (December, 1952, pp. 49–57) – Richard Hill did kindly allow me to itemize my indebtednesses to the Spanish friends whose names make up two-thirds of the following list. The reader who has seen that article already knows how keenly felt are my *gracias*.

Fernando Águilar Escrich, Norberto Almandoz, H. K. Andrews, Higinio Anglés, Jesús Bal y Gay, Robert D. Barton, Gilbert Chase, R. Thurston Dart, Exmos. Sres. Duques de Medinaceli, Charles Warren Fox, Nicolás García, Julián García Blanco, Juan Miguel García Pérez, Santiago González Álvarez, Francisco Guerrero, Ferreol Hernández, Macario Santiago Kastner, Adele Kibre, Edmund King, Luisa de Larramendi, Pedro Longás Bartibás, Marqués de Santo Domingo, Marqués de Villa-Alcázar, Juan Montejano Chico, B. Municio Cristóbal, Ricardo Nuñez, Clara L. Penney, Carmen Pérez-Dávila, Gustave Reese, Francisco Ribera Recio, Bernard Rose, Samuel Rubio, Adolfo Salazar, Francisco Sánchez, Graciela Sánchez Cerro, Manuel Sánchez Mora, Alfredo Sixto Planas, Denis Stevens, José Subirá, Earl O. Titus, J. B. Trend, John Ward, Ruth Watanabe, J. A. Westrup, Franklin Zimmerman.

Miss Mary Neighbour, who had placed me under obligation by preparing the typescript of two previous books (*Music Before the Classic Era* [London: Macmillan and Co., 1955 and 1958]; *Shakespeare's Religious Frontier* [The Hague: Martinus Nijhoff, 1958]) again graciously returned to my aid when I asked her to undertake the much more difficult typescript of the present volume.

Finally, I thank the Del Amo Foundation (1952), the Ford (1953–54) and Carnegie

(1955–56) Foundations, the American Philosophical Society (1956), and the Comisión Fulbright de Intercambio Educativo in Peru (1958) for generous financial aid while not only *Spanish Music in the Age of Columbus* but also its companion studies – "Cristóbal de Morales: A Fourth Centenary Biography" (*Journal of the American Musicological Society*, VI, i [Spring, 1953]), "Cristóbal de Morales" (*Grove's Dictionary of Music and Musicians*, Fifth Edition [1954]), "Cristóbal de Morales" (*Die Musik in Geschichte und Gegenwart*), *La Música en la Catedral de Sevilla: 1478–1606* (Los Angeles, 1954), *Cantilenas Vulgares puestas en Música por varios Españoles* (Lima, 1958), *Juan Bermudo* (Lima, 1958), and *Spanish Cathedral Music in the Golden Age* – were in preparation.

United States Educational Commission in Peru   R. S.
Lima, Peru
February 1, 1959

Political Synopsis

c. 500 B.C.	First Punic and Greek colonies.
210	P. Cornelius Scipio dispatched to drive out the Carthaginians.
197	Spain divided into two Roman provinces, *Citerior* and *Ulterior*.
1st cent. A.D.	Seneca (3 B.C.), Lucan, Martial, Quintilian, Trajan, Hadrian born in Spain.
409 A.D.	Spanish provinces overrun by Vandals, Suevi, and Alans.
419–507	Visigothic Kingdom of Toulouse, incorporating Spain during Euric's reign (466–485).
507–711	Visigothic Kingdom of Spain, with capital at Toledo.
568–586	Reign of Leovigild. Visigothic power reaches its summit.
587	Reccared I converted from Arianism to Roman orthodoxy. Rules till 601.
672–677	Wamba strengthens the state against the growing menace of the Saracens.
711–715	Moslem conquest.
718–737	Pelayo, a Goth, preserves Christian independence in the mountains of Asturias.
756–1031	Omayyad dynasty at Cordova.
777	Charlemagne's invasion. Routing of his rear guard at Roncesvalles (778).
791–842	Reign of Alfonso II (*the Chaste*), King of Asturias and León. Erection of the first church at Santiago de Compostela over the reputed bones of St. James the Apostle.
912–961	Abdurrahman III, during whose caliphate the Omayyads reach their zenith. Cordova (population 500,000) becomes the leading European intellectual center.
1037	Ferdinand I of Castile conquers León.
1085	Alfonso VI of Castile recovers Toledo from the Moslems.

1086	Almoravids, a Berber dynasty, invited from Africa to subdue rising Christian forces. Alfonso defeated at Zallaka.
1087–1099	The Cid (Rodrigo [Ruy] Díaz of Bivar) fights on one side and another, eventually becoming the ruler of Valencia. (*Cantuar de mio Cid*, c. 1140.)
1137	Union of Catalonia and Aragon under Ramón Berenguer IV, Count of Barcelona.
1144–1225	Almohades, dynasty at Cordova.
1158–1214	Reign of Alfonso VIII, King of Castile (married to Eleanor of England). After various preliminary defeats at the hands of the Almohades, he triumphs at the decisive battle of *Las Navas de Tolosa* (1212).
1179	Portugal recognized by Pope Alexander III as an independent kingdom.
1217–1252	Ferdinand III, King of Castile and León (1230–1252). Recovers Cordova (1236), Jaén (1246), and Seville (1248).
1232–1315	Ramón Lull, foremost Catalonian intellect of the Middle Ages.
1252–1284	Alfonso X (*the Savant*), King of Castile.
1213–1276	James I (*the Conqueror*), King of Aragon. Reconquest of Valencia and Murcia. Addition of Balearic Islands.
1350–1369	Peter the Cruel, of Castile, struggles with his bastard half brother, Henry of Trastámara. Allies himself with Edward the Black Prince, 1363–1367.
1386	John of Gaunt (1340–1399), Duke of Lancaster, conquers Galicia in pursuit of his title to the Castilian crown. Retires to England two years later.
1416–1458	Alfonso V (*the Magnanimous*), King of Aragon. His conquest of Naples (1435) recognized by the pope (1442). Italian Renaissance ideals control his court. At his death, Naples passes to his son Ferrante (1458–1494), Aragon to John II (1458–1479).
1454–1474	Henry IV of Castile, whose reign is marked by prolonged civil disorder. Isabella, his stepsister and heir, marries Ferdinand, heir to Aragon, 1469.
1474	Isabella succeeds to the throne of Castile.
1479	Ferdinand becomes king of Aragon.
1492	Fall of Granada. Discovery of America. *Ea iudios a enfardelar.*
1504	Death of Isabella, who is succeeded by Joanna (consort of Philip the Fair, Archduke of Austria).
1506	Philip's death, followed by Joanna's retirement to Tordesillas, 1509 (d. 1555). Ferdinand takes control of Castile.
1509–1511	Campaigns in Africa, organized by Cardinal Ximénez de Cisneros.
1515	Spain annexes Navarre.
1516	Death of Ferdinand. Regency of Cisneros.
1516–1556	Charles I (b. 1500), son of Philip and Joanna, king of Spain.
1519	Charles elected Holy Roman emperor.
1520–1521	Revolt of the *Comuneros* in Castile.
1521–1529	War between Spain and France. Francis I captured at battle of Pavia (February 24, 1525) and forced to sign Treaty of Madrid, the terms of which he at once breaks on being released.

Spanish Orthography

No present-day European tongue, when purely spoken, shows a more logical correlation between uttered and written forms than Spanish. But this regularity did not yet prevail during the centuries under survey in this book. Not only did usage fluctuate with the passing of time, but spellings conflicted within even the same decade. When the fricative consonants z and ç, s and ss, j and x, were differently pronounced in 1578 at centers so close together as Ávila and Toledo, it is not surprising that spellings took equally various forms throughout las Españas during the Age of Expansion.

Because of these variants, some such introduction as Ramón Menéndez Pidal's "El lenguaje del siglo XVI" (Cruz y Raya, September 15, 1933) will well repay the attention of students seriously interested in Spanish Renaissance music set to vernacular texts. Among the books that can serve as guides, Jaime Oliver Asín's or Rafael Lapesa's Historia de la Lengua española (Madrid, 1941 and 1942), may prove as useful as any.

Several courses are open to a musical historian. He can imitate Asenjo Barbieri, who in his 1890 edition of the Palace Songbook normalized the spellings of his c. 1500 source to conform with modern usage and added accents throughout. Or he can take Isabel Pope's 1954 transcriptions of the Spanish song-texts in Monte Cassino MS 871 N for his model, diplomatically reproducing the originals. Or he can steer Higinio Anglés's middle course (Monumentos de la Música Española, V and X), adding accents but not attempting to modernize the spelling.

The Solomon's judgment which we have adopted has been to follow Anglés insofar as Palacio is concerned, but to omit accents and to strive for diplomatic fidelity in copying all other texts. For place-names we prefer the English forms (Saragossa for Zaragoza, Cordova for Córdoba). For other well-known names (Ferdinand and Isabella) and titles (Duke of Alva) we likewise prefer traditional English usage.

Ancient and
Medieval Beginnings

Iberian Music in Antiquity [1]

AS EARLY as the first century of our era, the music of Spain had gained a reputation elsewhere throughout the Mediterranean world for its frenzy. Strabo (c. 63 B.C.–21 A.D.) describes the vigorous mountaineers of northern Spain who danced to the sound of *aulos* and trumpet, leaping wildly into the air and then crouching low (*Geography*, III, iii, 7). Silius Italicus (26–101 A.D.) alludes in his poetical account of Hannibal's invasion to the noisy Galicians who enjoyed "howling the rude songs of their native language," meanwhile "stamping the ground and clashing their shields to the beat of the music" (*Punica*, III, 346–349).

Martial (c. 40–102 A.D.) – a Spaniard from Bilbilis (near Saragossa) – remembered the grave music of the *choros Rixamarum* along the upper banks of the Ebro (IV, lv, 16). But in Rome he heard nothing Spanish except the castanets of dancing-girls from Cádiz (V, lxxviii, 26; VI, lxxi, 1–2). Both Pliny the Younger (*Epistolae*, I, xv) and Juvenal (*Satura XI*, 162–176) echo his disapproval of their dancing. Juvenal readily enough admits, however, that the tremolo of their hips to the wail of a chorus and the rattle of castanets always excited wild applause.

QUINTILIAN (c. 35–95 A.D.), the best known Empire authority on education, not only was born in northcentral Spain – at what is now Calahorra – but also spent his early manhood teaching in his native province. Perhaps because of what he had heard at home, he carefully distinguishes the art of music from the spontaneous musical ex-

---

[1] On the pre-history of Iberian music, see José Subirá, *Historia de la música española e hispanoamericana* (Barcelona: Salvat, 1953), pp. 30–40. Also Adolfo Salazar, *La Música de España* (Buenos Aires: Espasa-Calpe, 1953), pp. 20–21; plate opposite p. 17. The rôle of music in Iberian culture is discussed in Ramón Menéndez Pidal, *Historia de España: España Prerromana* (Madrid: Espasa-Calpe, 1954), I, iii, 333.

pression of the uninstructed (*Institutio Oratoria*, II, xvii, 10). Though every people, even the most barbarous, has its own repertory of indigenous song, only civilized nations cultivate music as an art. Essentially, the art is founded on the science of numbers (*musica ratio numerorum* [IX, iv, 139]), whether applied to leaps in dancing (*saltationi*) or the size of melodic intervals (*modulationibus*).

He continues with the warning that music can easily enough degenerate. Traditional instruments are to be preferred, rather than twanging importations from Asia such as *spadicas* (I, x, 31). The Greeks perfected the art. But numerous prominent Romans have cultivated it – from Numa Pompilius, second king of Rome, to Gaius Gracchus, the great tribune. Both Cicero and Plutarch assure Quintilian that

Gaius Gracchus, the foremost orator of his age, had a musician stand behind him during his speeches with a pitchpipe, or *tonarion* as the Greeks call it. The musician's duty was to sound the tones (*modos*) in which the voice was to be pitched (I, x, 27).

Music, the noblest of the arts (I, x, 17), is also the most useful for the orator to study (I, x, 30). If the greatest warriors and statesmen from Achilles to Gaius Gracchus have studied it (I, x, 9–30), and if Cicero wished every citizen the ability to play at least one instrument (I, x, 19), then the ideal orator should have passed beyond the elements to musical theory as taught by Pythagoras and Aristoxenus. Such an orator would be able to recite the notes of the cithara and tell the intervals between them (*citharae sonos nominibus et spatiis distinxerit* [I, x, 3]).

THE MANUFACTURE of musical instruments was a recognized profession in Roman Spain – at least at Cordova, birthplace of the two Senecas and of Lucan. A funeral tablet from Quintilian's century designates a certain Syntrophilus of Cordova as *musicarius*.[2] Another slightly later memorial tablet (found near Saragossa) preserves the names of four different stringed instruments: *chelys*, *fides*, *pecten*, and *cithara*.[3]

Isidore of Seville (c. 570–636): "Father" of Hispanic Music

WHETHER OR NOT the Apostle Paul redeemed his intention of visiting Spain, Christianity had already taken vigorous root in the coastal cities before 100. Side by side with the corybantic excesses of Priscillian, bishop of Ávila (d. 385), the early Spanish church gave birth to the still-sung hymns of Prudentius from Saragossa (348–c. 410). The cultural life within the church naturally suffered when the Vandals and Alans overran Spain. But in Spain as around Carthage it must have flourished if Augustine could have so regretted the silencing of the *hymnos Dei et laudes* which Possidius reports in his *Vita Sancti Augustini* (XXVIII).

Isidore of Seville, the first peninsular author who delved deeply into the liberal arts, flourished two centuries later. Only he and Augustine among western church fathers

---

[2] *Corpus Inscriptionum Latinarum*, ed. E. Hübner (Berlin: G. Reimer, 1869), II, 314 (no. 2241).
[3] *Corp. Insc. Lat.* (Berlin, 1892), II, Supp., 939 (no. 5839).

wrote anything of treatise-length on music. Born at Cartagena on the Mediterranean coast and educated at Seville where his brother Leander was bishop, he assimilated not only the scriptures but a remarkably wide store of classical learning as well. Unlike Jerome and Gregory he seems to have welcomed all pagan knowledge not in conflict with Christian dogma. In the paragraphs which he was to write on music he, for instance, invokes the authority of Virgil, Juvenal, and Propertius.

Sisebut, the Visigothic king who died in 621, commissioned him to gather summaries of learning in the various fields recognized by classical Roman educators. Two years after this king's death his erstwhile pupil Braulio – who was now bishop of Saragossa – asked for a copy. Taken up with the cares of administering the Sevillian diocese in which he had been elected bishop after his brother's death (599), he delayed sending the collected summaries until 631: even then forwarding only an unemended copy. The year after his death Braulio divided these summaries into seven books. About 650 a new edition divided *sub titulis* was undertaken at King Recesvinth's request. Three centuries later the same material was divided first into 17 and then into 20 books (whence the present title, *Etymologiarum sive Originum libri xx*).[4]

Since he believed that etymologies give the best clues to word-meanings he compiled the terms used in the various arts and sciences with a view to studying their derivation. His method came to enjoy such a vogue during the Middle Ages that every encyclopedist quotes him – often so slavishly that for a millenium his learning can be said to have circumscribed the bounds of Christian knowledge. Even before his Etymologies were divided into the 20 books known today, the Carolingian encyclopedist Hrabanus Maurus (776–856) copied everything that he had to say concerning music directly from him. Four centuries later the Etymologies were still the quarry from which the influential thirteenth-century encyclopedist, Bartholomaeus Anglicus, extracted all the musical information to be found in *De proprietatibus rerum* (c. 1250). Bartholomaeus – an English Franciscan who studied at Oxford and taught at both Paris and Magdeburg – lived during the century of "Sumer is icumen in" and almost certainly was acquainted with the music of the Notre Dame masters. Yet he still chose to copy his every musical dictum from Isidore, transposing a paragraph here and omitting a sentence there, but always hewing close to his source.

Almost a thousand medieval copies of the Etymologies survive today.[5] Isidore's continuing influence in the late fifteenth century can be assessed not only by counting the number of times the *Etymologiae* were reprinted, but also Bartholomaeus's recension. *De proprietatibus rerum*, as translated into English by John of Trevisa (1398), was printed c. 1495 by Wynkyn de Worde. Reputedly the first book printed on English paper, it was also the first in English to give any systematized musical information. Not until 1562 was it replaced by an English imprint[6] containing any other musical lore than

---

[4] Eduard Anspach, *Taionis et Isidori nova fragmenta et opera* (Madrid: Imp. de C. Bermejo, 1930), p. 55. Anspach proved that much of the information concerning Isidore in present reference manuals needs revision.

[5] *Ibid.*, p. vi.

[6] Sternhold and Hopkins's *The whole booke of Psalmes* (London: John Day, 1562) contains an "Introduction into the Science of Musicke"; their *The first parte of the Psalmes* (Day, 1564) has a 13-page "Introduction to learne to sing" beginning at fol. A. ii.

Isidore's, as transmitted by Bartholomaeus. What is more, *De proprietatibus rerum* was turned into Castilian and published at Toulouse as early as 1494.[7] In the original Latin, Bartholomaeus was reprinted at least fifteen times before the century ended.

As if the number of such reprints did not clinch the proof, testimony to Isidore's continuing influence from 1460–1600 can be taken from the numerous Renaissance theorists who admiringly quote him. Even his fellow-Andalusian, the iconoclastic Bartolomé Ramos de Pareja for whom Guido was a dead letter, reserves a respectful niche for him.[8] Domingo Marcos Durán, whose 1492 *Lux bella* was the first music instructor published in Spanish, names him as the third decisive musical authority of antiquity – Aristotle and Boethius making the other two.[9] Miguel de Fuenllana, in the "Prólogo al lector" which prefaces his *Orphénica lyra* (Seville, 1554), still bows to *el diuino Ysidoro* as the ultimate musical doctor. Both he and Juan Bermudo take their cue from him when they continue to type all musical instruments as either *harmonica*, *organica*, or *rhythmica*. In the first 40 leaves of his *Libro primero de la declaración de instrumentos* alone (1549), Bermudo rests his case on an Isidorean dictum no less than seven times (fols. 10v., 11, 13v., 17, 17v., 29, 38v.).

Not only in Spain but abroad also, he continued to be approvingly cited by theorists from Franchino Gaffurio the Italian to Andreas Ornithoparcus the German. In his *Theorica musice* (Milan, 1492), Gaffurio contends for music as a crucial subject in any liberal arts curriculum because Isidore gave it so prominent a place in his scheme.[10] When arguing for the science of number as the only secure foundation on which to rear any theory of music, he again appeals to Isidore's higher authority.[11] He can find no better definition for dissonance than Isidore's (who called it a mixture of sounds that reaching the ear together cause discomfort).[12] Ornithoparcus in his *Musice actiue micrologus* (Leipzig, 1517) still looks to Isidore for a correct definition of accent.[13] He moreover calls him for his star witness when advocating a melodically inflected – rather than monotone – delivery of the psalms, epistles, and gospels appointed to be read in churches.[14]

In England, even after Reform, he continued to be cited as a prime authority in such a book as John Case's *The Praise of Musicke* – the earliest Oxford imprint (1586) to deal specifically with music. This book, dedicated to Sir Walter Raleigh, was written by a fellow of St. John's College who was simultaneously canon of Salisbury. Case cites Isidore first among the church fathers quoted in his central chapter: "The necessitie of Musicke."

---

[7] Fray Vicente de Burgos, *El libro delas propriedades delas cosas trasladado de latin en romançe* (Toulouse: Heinrich Meyer, 1494). The section dealing with music (*Delos instrumentos* and *Delos sones*) appears in Book XIX, chapters 131-146.

[8] Ramos de Pareja, *Musica practica* [Bologna: Baldassarre da Rubiera, 1482], ed. Johannes Wolf (Leipzig: Breitkopf & Härtel, 1901), p. 78n. Also p. 45.

[9] Domingo [Marcos] Durán, *Lux bella* [Seville: Quatro alemanes compañeros, 1492], facs. ed. (Barcelona: Ediciones Torculum, 1951), p. 16.

[10] Franchino Gaffurio, *Theorica musice* (Milan: Philippus Mantegatius, 1492), fol. a vj recto.

[11] *Ibid.*, fol. d i recto.

[12] *Ibid.*, fol. c iiij verso.

[13] Andreas Ornithoparcus, *Musice actiue micrologus* (Leipzig: Valentin Schumann, 1519 [2nd ed.]), fol. I ij verso.

[14] *Ibid.*, fols. I ij verso and I iij recto.

His Isidorean catena links passages from both the *Etymologiae* and the *De ecclesiasticis officiis:*

The custome of singing in the church, was instituted for the carnall, not for the spirituall, that they whome the wordes doe not pierce might bee moued with the sweetnesse of the note [15] ....
Of the auncient custome of singers in the old church of the Jewes, the primitiue church tooke example, to noorish singers, by whose songs the minds of the hearers might be stirred up to god [16] .... Isidorus Archbishop of Hispalis in Spaine ... maketh a difference betweene Anthems and Responsories .... Responsories hee sheweth ... were vsed in the Churches of Italy, and were so called because when one sang, the quire answered him singing also[17].

At the end, as at the beginning, Case appeals to one authority: "For conclusion of this point, my last proofe shall bee out of Isidore." [18]

Isidore's Sources

FAUSTINO ARÉVALO, his eighteenth-century editor, found among his musical dicta (*Etymologiae*, III, xv–xxiii) borrowings from no less than twenty such late Latin authors as Augustine and Martianus Capella.[19] After even more careful sifting, Karl W. Schmidt concluded in his 1899 doctoral dissertation that both Isidore and Cassiodorus copied what they had to say on music from the same no longer extant Christian source.[20] W. M. Lindsay's edition of the Etymologies in 1911 and R. A. B. Mynors's of Cassiodorus's *Institutiones* in 1937 stimulated further quest for their common sources. Mynors in particular took the trouble to list at p. 193 of his edition 65 parallel passages (bks. 1–3 of the Etymologies and bk. 2 of the *Institutiones*). The musical parallelisms extend to approximately 30 printed lines among the 209 in the *De musica* chapters (Lindsay's edition).

The evidence gathered in the 1911 and 1937 critical editions absolves Isidore of the "crude and misleading paraphrases" imputed to him by H. E. Wooldridge at the turn of the century. For that matter, it also proves that he did not pillage the *Institutiones*, II, v, 6, for the names of all 22 musical instruments described in his *De musica* section – to say nothing of those others mentioned in the *De bello* section of the Etymologies.[21] What Cassiodorus's *De artibus ac disciplinis liberalium litterarum* did provide him with was a basic pattern over which to embroider in bks. 1–3 of his *Etymologiae*.

Both place music among the four mathematical disciplines in the upper half of the seven liberal arts. Cicero and Quintilian had of course associated it with grammar and

[15] John Case, *The Praise of Musicke* (Oxford: Joseph Barnes, 1586), p. 70.
[16] *Ibid.*, p. 93.
[17] *Ibid.*, p. 108.
[18] *Ibid.*, p. 116.
[19] *S. Isidori Hispalensis Episcopi Opera Omnia* (Rome: Antonio Fulgoni, 1797–1803), III [1798], pp. 132–143.
[20] Karl Wilhelm Schmidt, *Quaestiones de musicis scriptoribus Romanis, imprimis de Cassiodoro et Isidoro* (Darmstadt: G. Otto, 1899). See especially p. 51.
[21] *Oxford History of Music*, I (1901), 33n. *New Oxford History of Music*, II, ed. Dom Anselm Hughes (1954), 270.

rhetoric in the three lower disciplines. The Carthaginian educator, Martianus Capella, had in his *De nuptiis philologiae et Mercurii* (c. 439) lifted it to the apex of a new grouping. Cassiodorus, slightly varying Martianus's new order, places it second (rather than last) in the mathematical group. Isidore places it third. His arrangement (arithmetic, geometry, music, and astrology or astronomy) became standard in all medieval universities.

At the very outset of his musical sentences, Cassiodorus names his authorities: Gaudentius, Mutianus, Clement of Alexandria, Censorinus.[22] In the last of his ten chapters on music he invests himself with the authority of another five: Alypius, Euclid (= pseudo-Euclid), Ptolemy, Albinus, and Apuleius of Madaura. Isidore, on the contrary, begins with a definition followed by an etymology. He next invokes the names of those who invented music and then launches into an exordium praising the art. Like Cassiodorus he calls it a divine science, a mirror of the Eternal Mind, and a source of healing. Both agree that "without music there can be no perfect knowledge." For both, music comprehends harmonics, rhythmics, and metrics. But they disagree in their classification of musical instruments. Cassiodorus divides them under three headings: percussion, stringed, and wind. Isidore divides instruments other than the human voice under two types: those sounded by wind blowing through pipes (*organica*) and those sounded by the impulse of the fingers (*rhythmica*).

Musical Instruments mentioned in the Etymologies

JUST AS he gives more definitions of music than any previous Latin author,[23] so also Isidore provides a fuller list of instruments. Not all their names can be translated with any assurance of accuracy. Hints can be gleaned, however, from John of Trevisa's 1398 English translation, amended by Batman in 1582; from Alfonso de Palencia's *Vocabulario en latin y en Romance* (1490); and from Fray Vicente de Burgos's Spanish version (1494). The accompanying table shows the equivalencies to be found in these earlier translations. Where an equivalency is italicized, some such modern Latin-English dictionary as Lewis and Short's or Latin-Spanish as Terreros y Pando's has been consulted.

acitabulum (III, xxii, 1)	*cup-shaped instrument of bronze or silver* *struck with a small spade-like hammer*	
barbitos (III, xxii, 3)	*lyre of Asiatic origin, not mentioned in* *Latin literature before the Augustan age,*	rabel

[22] *Cassiodori Senatoris Institutiones*, ed. R. A. B. Mynors (Oxford: Clarendon Press, 1937), pp. 142–143.

[23] Ernest Brehaut, *An Encyclopedist of the Dark Ages* (New York: Columbia University Press, 1912), p. 135, n. 1. From this wealth, medieval encyclopedists could take their pick. Medieval theorists such as Odo and Guido dissented, however, from his definitions of *symphonia* (= consonance, agreement of sounds [*Etym.*, III, xx, 3]) and *diaphonia* (= dissonance, jarring of sounds). Charles Burney as long ago as 1782 (*A General History of Music*, II, 133) presciently observed that Isidore was the last before the Dark Ages to understand these terms correctly, i.e. as opposites. F. J. Fétis understood Isidore by symphonia and diaphonia to mean the consonance and dissonance of harmonic, rather than melodic, intervals (*Biog. univ. des musiciens* [Paris: Firmin-Didot, 1874], IV, 404).

probably with strings of deeper pitch than other lyres, and suited for the accompaniment of tearful songs

buccina (XVIII, iv, 1)	war-trumpet, of horn, wood, or brass: properly the "token" of the wild northern barbarians who blew it as a signal for assembly	bozina (1494); *trompeta*
calamus (III, xxi, 5)	general name for any pipe made of reed	flauta (1494); *flauta pastoril, zampoña*
cithara (III, xxii, 2)	lyre, with outlines shaped like the human breast, strung classically with seven strings	guitarra, solia aver siete cuerdas (1494)
classicum (XVIII, iv, 5)	signaling-trumpet used in battle	*trompa*
cornu (XVIII, iv, 5)	bugle, made of horn	*corneta, serpentin*
cymbala (III, xxii, 11)	cymbals, hollow round metal plates, struck together	çinbalos, campanas (1494)
fides (III, xxii, 4)	*lyre*, especially one of the classical type	corde instrumentorum ([L.] 1490)
fidicula (III, xxii, 4)	small stringed instrument belonging to the lyre family	cithara: et fidicen citharedus dicitur ([L.] 1490)
fistula (III, xxi, 6)	soft pipe, especially one blown by hunters to charm unsuspecting harts	*flauta compuesta de muchas cañas*
indica (III, xxii, 3)	*Indian zither*	
lyra (III, xxii, 3)	*lyre*, originating as a hollow tortoise-shell, over which strings were stretched	guitarra se dixo por la diuersidad delas bozes (1490); arpa (1494)
organum (III, xxi, 2)	general name for any instrument sounded by blowing wind	*órgano*
pandura (III, xxi, 8)	*syrinx*, not bandores (like both Martianus and Cassiodorus he classifies *panduria* or *pandura* as wind instruments)	apud gentiles instrumentum pulsationi aptum ([L.]1490)
pecten (III, xxii, 3)	*a harp, with twenty or more strings*	

phoenice (III, xxii, 3)	*Phoenician zither*	
psalterium (III, xxii, 3)	psaltery, an instrument with latten or silver strings stretched horizontally, struck not plucked	psalterio (1494)
sambuca (III, xxi, 7)	pipe made of hollow elderwood branch	sanbuga (1494)
sistrum (III, xxii, 12)	a bronze tambourine, an instrument of Egyptian origin; a *rattle*	tuba ([L.], 1490); laud [24] (1494)
symphonia (III, xxii, 14)	hollow piece of wood enclosed in leather beaten with small sticks: a favorite of mendicant musicians	sanphonia (1494)
tibia (III, xxi, 4)	bone-pipe, an instrument frequently played in lamentation or mourning	*flauta*
tintinnabulum (III, xxii, 13)	small bell, giving a tinkling or ringing sound	cascauel (1494)
tuba (III, xxi, 3; XVIII, iv, 3)	straight trumpet, *as opposed to curving trumpets such as the cornua*, ending in a flaring bell	trompeta (1494)
tympanum (III, xxii, 10)	drum with leather head and sieve-like belly, played with two small sticks	atabal (1494)

Isidore's References to "Contemporary" Practices

THOUGH ISIDORE abstained from describing contemporaneous musical practices, his writings have been ransacked for dicta from which inferences could be drawn. Because he said, *Nisi enim ab homine memoria teneantur soni, pereunt, quia scribi non possunt* (For unless sounds are held in man's memory they perish since they cannot be written down),[25] some historians have contended that no system of musical notation had as yet been invented in Visigothic Spain.[26] Ramos de Pareja when taking note of this dictum as long ago as 1482 interpreted it to mean that for certain sounds, such as that of an

---

[24] Isidore classified the sistrum as a percussion instrument but instead of describing it merely said: "The sistrum is named from its inventress, for Isis, a queen of the Egyptians, is considered to have invented this species of instrument" (tr. Oliver Strunk, *Source Readings in Music History* [New York: W. W. Norton, 1950], p. 99). Fray Vicente with no more information than this to go on, guesses sistrum meant lute, possibly because he thinks that the lute was originally an Egyptian instrument imported into Spain at the time of the Moslem invasion.

[25] Cf. Strunk, p. 93, n. 2.

[26] Higinio Anglés, *El Còdex Musical de Las Huelgas* (Barcelona: Institut d'Estudis Catalans, 1931), I, 10, n. 4.

aeolian harp, no written symbols exist; and that therefore these sounds must be carried in the memory.[27] Gaffurio in 1520 took Isidore's statement to mean that the mere notation of a musical sound cannot "preserve" it unless the significance of the written symbols is remembered also.[28] However interpreted, the dictum loses its relevance to the question of Visigothic notation when other early manuscript evidence is brought into the picture. The Azagra Codex, a late ninth-century manuscript in the Madrid National Library,[29] contains laments on the deaths of a Visigothic king, Chindasvinth (d. 652), and queen, Recciberga (d. 657). Both laments are ascribed to St. Eugenius of Toledo who died in the same year as Queen Recciberga. The music has not yet been deciphered; but neums can be seen above several lines of poetry.

A second quotation often brought forward does, however, unequivocally refer to contemporaneous musical usage:

In North Africa it is not the custom to sing Alleluias every day of the year, but only on Sundays and on weekdays from Easter to Pentecost, to signify joy in the thought of a future resurrection. But on the other hand here in Spain we follow a long-established local tradition when we sing Alleluias avery day of the year, except fast-days and during Lent. For it is written: *His praise shall continually be in my mouth* [Ps. 33(34). 2b].

De ecclesiasticis officiis (1, xiii, 3) [30]

Isidore in the same passage draws an analogy between Spanish usage and the ancient Jewish custom of singing alleluias at the ends of psalms. If the Hebrew psalmist could sing alleluias because of his joy in contemplating the church to come, should not we now rejoice in being members of it? he asks.

No Visigothic liturgical practice more excites the astonishment of the musical historian than the frequency of alleluias in both Office and Mass. Because Isidore played so dominant a rôle in the councils which framed the liturgy his eagerness to justify local custom suggests that he fully recognized the regional peculiarities of the rite but wished to retain them.

Music in the Visigothic Church (589–711)

IN THE DOZEN decades between the recovery of Spain from Arianism (589) and the Moslem invasion (711) the other principal leaders in the Visigothic church are nearly always represented by their biographers as having composed chants. Leander, personal friend of the future pope Gregory during their sojourn together in Byzantium (579–582), *multa dulci sono composuit* (composed many fine-sounding things).[31] He added to th

---

[27] Ramos de Pareja, *op. cit.*, 78n. He gave Sibylline utterances as a sample of sounds for which no written symbols are known. But he believed any conventional musical sound could be "written down."

[28] Gaffurio, *Apologia ... adversus Ioannem Spatarium ...* (Turin: Agostino de Vicomercato, 1520), fol. A iii.

[29] H. Anglés and J. Subirá, *Catálogo Musical de la Biblioteca Nacional*, Vol. I (Barcelona: Instituto Español de Musicología, 1946), pp. 3–4 (MSS 10029).

[30] J. P. Migne, *Patrologiae Cursus Completus* [Latin fathers], LXXXIII (Paris, 1862), cols. 750–751.

[31] *Ibid.*, col. 1104. (*De viris illustribus*, caput xli.)

musical repertory of both Office and Mass, composing with great skill and taste, said his own younger brother, Isidore.

At the head of the Toledan school of composers stood Eugenius II (d. 657). This school included as its two other most illustrious representatives Ildephonsus (d. 667) who composed two masses,[32] and Julian (d. 690), who wrote a songbook containing hymns and threnodies.[33] Conantius (d. 639), bishop of Palencia, *melodias soni multas noviter edidit* (newly recast many tunes).[34] In Saragossa, Joannes and Braulio – two brothers like Leander and Isidore – similarly succeeded each other as bishops. Like Leander, Joannes was a composer. Like Isidore, Braulio was a scholar. Joannes, the composer, *in ecclesiasticis officiis quaedam eleganter et sono et oratione composuit* (skilfully composed both words and music for certain portions of the office).[35]

Literary evidence bearing on the musical abilities of prominent Visigothic churchmen is by no means the only kind which survives. The Antiphoner of León contains chants ascribed to Isidore (fols. 172 and 200), to Ildephonsus (fol. 88), to Julian of Toledo (fol. 116v.), and to Rogatus of Baeza (fol. 281). Since the texts in each instance were written previously, these ascriptions must therefore refer to the melodies.

THE EARLIEST extant Visigothic liturgical manuscript is a *Libellus orationum*. Containing prayers and collects to be said in the office as recited at Toledo (but with certain local variants appropriate to Tarragona) it was probably copied around the year 710 and then carried out of Spain by some ecclesiastic fleeing before the Moslem invaders. Eventually it was deposited at Verona. It does not contain music. But it so perfectly tallies in every other respect with the Antiphoner of León that the music of the latter must be presumed – like its prayers, readings, and calendar – to embody traditions of the pre-Conquest period.[36] Indeed this Antiphoner, which is the most imposing Spanish musical monument antedating 1100, is today invariably regarded as a Visigothic relic, even though copied towards the end of the Mozarabic period. For that matter, nearly all Mozarabic manuscripts hark back to the Visigothic past.

Mozarabic Music (711–1089)

SOME THIRTY CODICES containing Mozarabic neums have been inventoried.[37] At least five are conserved in Toledo cathedral, four each at the Benedictine Abbey of Santo

---

[32] *PL*, XCVI, col. 44: *duas missas in laudem* [sanctorum Cosmae et Damiani], *quas in festivitate sua psallerent, miro modulationis modo perfecit, quas missas notatas habemus.*

[33] *Ibid.*, col. 449: [Conscripsit] *librum carminum diversorum, in quo sunt hymni, epitaphia, atque de diversis causis epigrammata numerosa.*

[34] *Ibid.*, col. 203.   [35] *Ibid.*, col. 201.

[36] Dom Louis Brou, "Antifonario visigótico de la Catedral de León" (review), *Hispania Sacra*, VII, No. 13 (1954), p. 229: "C'est donc l'une des gloires de l'Antiphonaire de León de pouvoir offrir une correspondance aussi parfaite que possible avec un livre liturgique écrit près de deux siècles plus tôt: aucun autre antiphonaire latin ne peut revendiquer un tel privilège."

[37] Casiano Rojo and Germán Prado, *El Canto Mozárabe* (Barcelona: Diputación Provincial, 1929), pp. 18–39. In "Mozarabic Melodics," *Speculum*, III, ii (April, 1928), at p. 224 Prado gives the total of "Mozarabic

Domingo de Silos, the Madrid Biblioteca Nacional, and the British Museum, three at the Madrid Real Academia de la Historia, two at the Paris Bibliothèque Nationale, and one each at the university libraries in Saragossa and Santiago de Compostela, the cathedrals of León, Cordova, and Coimbra, the Madrid Royal Palace Library, and the Ruskin Museum in Sheffield. Two Bibles, one formerly belonging to the Castilian monastery of Cardeña, the other to the monastery of Oña, contain Mozarabic neums. In 1915 three leaves of an antiphoner were found in the Toledo parish church of Saints Justa and Rufina.

Since the Roman rite officially displaced the Mozarabic during Alfonso VI's reign,[38] all of these surviving manuscripts very probably antedate 1100. Mozarabic neums were already thought hard to read at so important a center of liturgical music as León in 1069. The author of the rhymed preface to the Antiphoner of León (the music of which was copied considerably earlier) admits as much. Why should they have been considered so difficult? The Spanish Benedictines, Casiano Rojo and Germán Prado, suggest an answer. In their 1929 publication, *El Canto Mozárabe*, they contend that Mozarabic notation contained a greater variety of forms for each neum-type than any other known system of plainsong notation.[39] The *scandicus* of the four-note type was written some 9 different ways, the *punctum*, a single note, 10 ways, the *podatus*, a two-note type, 13 ways, the *clivis*, a two-note type, 17 ways, and the *torculus*, a three-note type, 28 ways. The Toledan neums, moreover, look as basically different from the notation used in León and elsewhere in northern Spain, as does Pitman shorthand from Gregg.

The variety of forms for identical neum-types found in one and the same manuscript gave Rojo and Prado the right to believe that Mozarabic neums indicated much more than merely pitch. Perhaps the different forms designated rhythmic distinctions. Certainly when an effort was made around 1500 to revive Mozarabic chant the tradition still alive in Toledo called for pronounced rhythmic distinctions.

THE ROSETTA STONE which should have opened the secrets of Mozarabic notation was a *Liber ordinum* owned formerly by the renowned monastery of San Millán de la Cogolla and now by the Madrid Real Academia de la Historia (Codex 56). In this manuscript the Mozarabic neums for 21 melodies – 18 for use in burial ceremonies and 3 for use in Maundy Thursday foot-washing ceremonies – have been scratched out and Aquitanian neums (staffless) substituted in the resulting empty spaces. A comparison of the two neum-systems thus becomes possible insofar as some half of these melodies are concerned – they being found with their original Mozarabic neums in the Antiphoner of León, presently to be discussed, and in the *Liber ordinum* of Silos. Even so, many difficulties remain unresolved. Only a limited number of neums are represented, the

liturical manuscripts known today" as 38. Obviously not all contain music. For an index of the "manuscrits avec notation musicale" see Dom Marius Férotin's *Le Liber Mozarabicus Sacramentorum* (Paris: Firmin-Didot et Cie, 1912), col. 1061. Cf. also *New Oxford History of Music*, II, 83–84.

[38] For an account of the "practical difficulty brought about in Spain in the eleventh and twelfth centuries by the substitution of the Roman for the Mozarabic liturgy," see Casiano Rojo, "The Gregorian Antiphonary of Silos and the Spanish Melody of the Lamentations," *Speculum*, V, iii (July, 1930), pp. 306–307.

[39] Rojo-Prado, p. 40.

Aquitanian version sheds extremely dim light on the problem of clefs, no rhythmic inferences can be securely drawn, and the Aquitanian transcript only partially solves the most tantalizing mystery of all – what pitch-distinctions to make within any given Mozarabic compound neum or between any two disjunct neums.

If the melodies in question reveal no strikingly individual traits, at least their transcription into Aquitanian neums proves that the monks of San Millán de la Cogolla still hankered after the old Mozarabic burial melodies rather than new ones introduced along with the superimposed Roman rite. This favoring of the old burial antiphons and responds is not to be wondered at, however, since funeral customs in any culture are among those which most stoutly resist any sudden changes.

The 21 melodies which alone of the extensive Mozarabic repertory can be brought with confidence into modern notation include: 16 antiphons, 3 responds, and 2 *preces*. The pair of penitential preces exemplify a litany-type peculiar to Spain. Since the verses in the first start successively with the letters a, b, [c,] d, e, f, and g, this preces appropriately bears the title *Abecedarium* in the San Millán manuscript. The same preces – though with small musical variants and not as rigorously alphabetical in its arrangement of verses – recurs in an eleventh-century French manuscript formerly conserved at Albi in southwestern France and now at the Paris Bibliothèque Nationale (B.N., lat. 776). Monks travelling from one monastery to another perhaps carried abroad still other chants of Mozarabic provenience if only they could now be identified.

The two preces in the San Millán *Liber ordinum* were to be sung "at the door of the church" just before the body was brought inside.[40] Other preces to be sung not in the burial office but on the Sunday before Ash Wednesday, on Good Friday, and at other penitential times, have been partially reconstructed. In every case *preces* meant not just "prayers," but a musical type in which each strophe sung as a solo by the officiant was answered by a short group-refrain. As such, the form has given rise to an extensive scholarly literature beginning with studies published in 1913 and 1914 by Wilhelm Meyer. He attempted to show that the Mozarabic *preces* were not an indigenous form but were borrowed from France, just as was the St. Gall sequence.[41] His thesis lost favor when it was discovered that both Julian of Toledo (d. 690) and Vicente of Cordova (fl. 820) had composed *preces* long before Notker Balbulus met any monk fleeing from Jumièges.[42]

Thirteen antiphons and three responds bring the number of burial pieces in the San Millán manuscript to 18. Interestingly, the sentiment of the words is nowhere morose or fearful, but on the contrary confident and robust. They show none of the stark dread of penal fires so often found in later Spanish religion. Rojo and Prado classify ten of these burial antiphons as Mode II and three as Mode III. They transcribe the foot-washing antiphons in phrygian or hypomixolydian. According to them, none of these melodies

----

[40] *Ibid.*, pp. 74–75. Anglés cites the first of these as an example of a *preces* sung in the Mozarabic Mass (*New Oxford History of Music*, II, 87). He also reads the 13th and 14th notes of the source-melody differently from Rojo-Prado, p. 74, who give A–B instead.

[41] W. Meyer, *Die Preces der mozarabischen Liturgie* (Berlin: Wiedmannsche Buchhandlung, 1914), p. 9. In his introduction to this monograph he summarizes his previous article, 'Über die rythmischen Preces der mozarabischen Liturgie' (1913).

[42] Rojo-Prado, p. 64.

was written in either lydian or hypolydian modes – these two being the modes which with an added flat most often sound like modern major.

The Antiphoner of León (1069)

SCHOLARS of all nationalities – Anglés, Brou, and Peter Wagner, to name only representative Catalonian, French, and German scholars by way of example – have unanimously declared the León Antiphoner to be the most important monument of Spanish music produced before the reconquest of Toledo in 1085.[43] The text, without neums, was published in 1928 by the Benedictines of Santo Domingo de Silos (Burgos). A facsimile of the original manuscript was issued at Madrid in 1953. The manuscript, which reaches 306 leaves, contains music over every page except those in the preface and calendar. The main body was written c. 950, if the dedication to Abbat Ikilanus (917–960) is to be taken seriously.[44] A miniature on the back of the first leaf shows a scribe handing the completed antiphoner to the dedicatee. The manuscript contains 18 other miniatures, that at fol. 271v. of a royal consecration being one of the earliest of its class known. The preface, which includes 130 lines of inflated Latin poetry, bears a much later date: 1069.[45]

This poem, like many of the chants in the León Antiphoner, is ascribed to a definite author: in this case Eugenius III of Toledo. Like most Mozarabs, he hankers after a vanished past. According to him the old customs were always better than new ones. In former times three choirs alternated in the singing of chant, one located at the altar, a second by the pulpit, a third in the nave. This threefold division of the whole body of singers accorded with St. Paul's division of the repertory into hymns, psalms, and spiritual songs. The art of singing has decayed in these present times, singers now inclining to sloth and other vices. Formerly singers respected their holy orders, but not now. They sing discordantly and have forgotten how to interpret properly the neums in their books.

ACCORDING to our poet, no single individual endowed the Spanish church with its numerous beautiful chants. On the contrary, many holy men inspired by God made up its dowry. "In that former age many individuals, enjoying a common inspiration, composed chants in honor of the Almighty." His testimony is, of course, confirmed by evidence scattered in the margins throughout the main body of the León Antiphoner.

[43] See the *Antifonario visigótico mozárabe de la Cathedral de León: Edición facsimil* (Madrid: Consejo Superior de Investigaciones Científicas, 1953), "Proemio," unnumbered pages. See also H. Anglés, "La música medieval en Toledo," *Gesammelte Aufsätze zur Kulturgeschichte Spaniens*, 7. Bd. (Münster in Westfalen: Aschendorffsche Verlagsbuchhandlung, 1938), pp. 11–12.

[44] The dedicatory epigram at fol. 1v, and the phrase *Librum Ikilani abbati* at fol. 6v. prove that Ikilanus once owned the antiphoner. See Zacarias García Villada, *Catálogo de los Códices y Documentos de la Catedral de León* (Madrid: Imp. Clásica Española, 1919), pp. 38–40. The musical tradition of the León Antiphoner may be as old as King Wamba (662); Wamba's antiphoner is cited in the León (fol. 25 vb.) as its model. See García Villada, p. 40.

[45] Latin poems at fols. 2v.-3 printed in Férotin, *Le Liber Mozarabicus*, cols. 918–921.

Allusion has already been made at page 10 to those chants which carry ascriptions in the manuscript margins to such pre-Conquest fathers as Isidore, Ildephonsus, Julian of Toledo, Rogatus of Baeza, and Balduigius of Ercávica. The case for their authenticity is strengthened by the fact that the same scribe who jotted the ascriptions copied both text and neums. Medieval glossators elsewhere throughout Europe attributed the whole body of Roman chant to Gregory I (d. 604) and of Ambrosian chant to Ambrose (d. 397). Mozarabic traditions of authorship deserve the more credence because famous names are not constantly invoked. Indeed, several of the *plurimis sacris virorum* to whom chants in the León Antiphoner are ascribed were obscure persons, even by Spanish standards.

With his eye ever on the past, our Antiphoner poet complains not only that the threefold division of the choir has died out, but – worse still – that the whole body of singers *connexi nunc psallant exules a docmatu* (now stand together when singing praises, departing from right tradition). But he hopes for the return of better days, when singers who carefully meditate on every word they sing will win back many wandering minds from vain things. Certain other of his preliminary injunctions compare inter- estingly with the early medieval performance-ideals mentioned by S. Van Dijk of Oxford in his two articles, "Saint Bernard and the *Instituta Patrum*" and "Medieval Terminology and Methods of Psalm Singing." [46] The following lines from Eugenius III's poem can be pitted against Ekkehard II's prose injunctions in the *Instituta Patrum*.

> Remove from the choir those with raucous voices,
> Those who refuse to apply what they have been taught,
> Those who burst their lungs and strain their throats,
> Those whose breath miserably gives out,
> Those who make an ugly noise like the braying of donkeys,
> Those whose wretched voices sound like the howling of wolves.
> Leave off such sounds and banish such voices,
> For be assured that no sound abhorred by man can please God.
> But seek after artistry so that you may please Christ,
> And at the same time be found well pleasing in sight of men.

Throughout the main body of the León Antiphoner such performance-directions as the following appear: *Dicentes voces praeconias* (fol. 133); *Imponit arcediaconus voce clara hanc antiphonam* (fol. 153v.); *Imponit episcopus hanc antiphonam subtili voce decantando: Ecce venit hora ut dispergamini* (fol. 164v.); *Imponit episcopus voce tremula* (fol. 166v.). In the first rubric, the deacons giving instruction to an assembly of catechumens (not those to be confirmed, since confirmation in the Mozarabic rite was administered immediately after baptism, and by a priest, not a bishop) are required to sing in a loud, town-crier's voice. In the second, the archdeacon is advised to sing a Palm-Sunday an- tiphon in a clear voice. In the third, the bishop chanting the following antiphon with words from the Passion narrative: "Behold the hour cometh, yea is now come, that ye

---

[46] *Musica Disciplina*, IV, 2, 3, 4 (1950), pp. 99–109; *MD*, VI, 1, 2, 3 (1952), pp. 7–26.

shall be scattered, every man to his own, and shall leave me alone" (John xvi. 32), is enjoined to sing this particular text sotto voce – doubtless for dramatic effect. In the fourth, the bishop who sings *Popule meus* ("O my people, what have I done unto thee? and wherein have I wearied thee" [Micah vi. 3]) is directed to begin the *Improperia* with a tremolo in his voice – again surely with deliberate dramatic intent.

Fortunately, the León Antiphoner is preserved complete. Beginning with November 17, the first day in the Mozarabic church year (St. Acisclus's Day), it carries through without interruption to the following November 17, providing certain additional chants at the end for the dedication of a basilica, consecrations of bishops and kings, marriages, the ministry to the sick, and committals. Because it is not mutilated after the fashion of other Mozarabic monuments the liturgiologist can go through it, making a comparative study of "forms" in Mozarabic music. Such a study is the more necessary because certain Mozarabic chant-types are uniquely Spanish while others, if not uniquely so, bear names which can cause confusion. For instance, *prolegendum* = introit; *psallendum* = gradual; *laudes* = alleluia; *sacrificium* = offertory; *trenos* = tract. The two uniquely Spanish chant-types would seem to be the already mentioned *preces* and the *sono*. But *sono* like *selah* in the Hebrew psalms is a term still too imperfectly understood to permit of secure definition.

The Antiphoner not only contains chants for the entire church year but (unlike modern antiphonaries) for Office as well as Mass. Such ramifications of any chant-type as the following can therefore be studied: (1) comparative position in the Hours and in the Sacrifice; (2) choice of text – different or the same in Office and Mass; (3) syllabic versus melismatic treatments of the text; (4) formal structure of the melodies; (5) use of borrowed musical material.

THE *laudes* are one Mozarabic chant-type that has been exhaustively studied with just such criteria as the above in mind. Dom Louis Brou, the Benedictine of Quarr Abbey (Isle of Wight) who made the study, finds that *laudes* were omnipresent in the Mozarabic Office and Mass: always occupying a climactic position. In the Office, *laudes* came at the end, followed only by a hymn and closing benediction.[47] The words were invariably taken from either Psalm 148 or 150, the typical "alleluia" psalms. After the psalm-verse of the *laudes*, set syllabically, the singers erupted into flaming melismas on the postscript-word always reserved for the ends of *laudes* (except in Lent), the word *alleluia*. Moreover this jubilus, insofar as the Mozarabic Office is concerned, always flared on the second rather than last syllable – the "e" rather than "a".[48] As a rule *laudes* in the Office were durchkomponiert, each carrying a notably individual stamp. Their individuality needs stressing. Though often the words of one *laudes* were repeated in another office, the music seems always to have differed. Perhaps the composers wished to give each saint's office its own unique tinge.

As for their place in the eucharist, *laudes* climactically closed the Mass of the Cate-

---

[47] Dom Louis Brou, "L'Alleluia dans la liturgie mozarabe," *Anuario Musical*, VI (Barcelona: Instituto Español de Musicología, 1951), p. 8.

[48] *Ibid.*, p. 11.

chumens. They provided a musical coda to the homily expounding the Gospel for the Day. But if their position made of them an *Ite missa est* closing the Mass of the Cate-chumens, they also served as a transition into the Mass of the Faithful.

Though the word *alleluia* came after the scriptural verse in Office-*laudes* it preceded the verse in Mass-*laudes*. What is more, the scriptural texts of Mass-*laudes* – though still of a laudatory type – were not invariably chosen from Psalms 148 or 150, or even for that matter from any psalm.[49] The jubilus in the *alleluia*, to make a further contrast with Office-*laudes*, came always on the last syllable, the "a". In 68 of the 76 Mass-*laudes*, the luxuriant melisma on the final "a" in allelui*a* was again repeated on the final (or penultimate) syllable of the scriptural verse which follows the alleluia.[50] As in the Roman use, the Mozarabic composer on these occasions therefore worked out a musical rhyme-scheme.

Fifty-two Mass-*laudes*, outside Lent, can be grouped according to several well-defined musical types.[51] One of these, the *Ecce servus* type of *laudes*-melody, appears in Masses honoring masculine saints: Andrew, Eugenius, Cucufatus (Cugat), Cyprian, Cosmas and Damian. Another, the *Lauda filia* type, appears in Masses honoring feminine saints: Eulalia, Justa and Rufina. A third type, the *Lauda Hierusalem*, is again dedicated to masculine saints: John the Baptist, Columba, Emilianus. Twenty-four *laudes*-melodies cannot, however, be classified under types.

If in the Visigothic liturgy the word *alleluia* dominates Mass- as well as Office-*laudes*, it appears even more frequently elsewhere in the liturgy as an interjection. A study of its use shows that the single word *alleluia* was considered equally appropriate in an Office for the Dead and in an Easter Mass. The alleluia outside *laudes* was always melis-matically treated. Occasionally it stretched to spectacular lengths. Vocalises in the León Antiphoner reaching such an extravagant number of notes as 300 are by no means rare. On the very first page of the facsimile (fol. 29) such a melisma can be seen. The scribe copied it in the outer margin, beginning the neums at the bottom of the page and carrying them up to the top. In the first hundred leaves the margins of 34 pages have been so used.

OBVIOUSLY neums that can be written from bottom to top of a page lack any heighted implications. But patterns of neums occur. In the marginal alleluia copied at fol. 60 the following musical structure can be easily enough detected: AA', BB', CC', D ... (the vocalise appears here over the second syllable of the word). This same melody recurs elsewhere in the Antiphoner fitted syllabically to a text beginning *Sublimius diebus*. Brou has found three other Mozarabic sequences based on such AA', BB', CC', DD' alleluia-melismas [52] – a significant discovery since the Mozarabic codex, *Toledo 35.7*, in

[49] *Ibid.*, pp. 23–26. Six out of 76 alleluiatic verses sung at Mass (not in Lent) came from the New Testament.

[50] *Ibid.*, p. 30. Mozarabic practice duplicated Roman but differed from Ambrosian in recapitulating the jubilus-melisma.

[51] *Ibid.*, p. 33.

[52] *Ibid.*, pp. 57–58; see also pp. 80–81. Brou's article, "Séquences et Tropes dans la liturgie mozarabe" (*Hispania Sacra*, IV [1951], pp. 27–41), contains texts of all the sequences (pp. 28–37) together with facsimi-

which he discovered the *Alme Virginis* sequence (fol. 45, line 15) belongs to the ninth century. The sequence was therefore an established form in Spain a century before Notker Balbulus.

Because long melismas of the AA′, BB′, CC′, DD′ ... type so frequently occur in the Mozarabic books it is not surprising to find that repeat-signs were sometimes used to lighten the labor of copying. In the León Antiphoner a stylized letter *d* looking like a backward 6 with the ascender crossed (abbreviating *denuo* or *dupliciter*) is used 128 times as a repeat-sign.[53] In the Toledo manuscript-group a plus-sign at the end of an incise indicates a repeat. Plainsongs incorporating such frequent doublets violate the spirit of primitive Roman chant. Wherever they occur in manuscript collections of Roman chant they usually discover themselves as late-comers of non-liturgical origin. According to Brou:

In France, Spain, England, and elsewhere, all the *sequelae* (alleluia-vocalises) which can be found seem not to belong to the original Gregorian repertory. Melismas extending to hundreds of notes do not occur with the word *Alleluia* in the oldest Gregorian manuscripts, but on the contrary the alleluia was always rather short. Outside Spain, then, not only were the sequence-texts a manifestly late development but so also was the melodic scaffolding (the *sequelae* of alleluias) to which the texts were added. In Spain, quite the contrary obtained. Mozarabic liturgical manuscripts show a very considerable number of extended melismas (whether in the case of the *Alleluia* or of any other word) and these melismas were an *integral part of the liturgy:* they cannot be cut out without denaturing the liturgy .... Moreover, we have every right to believe that they belong to the most primitive stratum of the ancient Spanish liturgy.[54]

Music in Mohammedan Spain (712–1492)

CHRISTIAN SPAIN during the so-called Dark Ages produced in Isidore a scholar of universal renown whose musical dicta were to be respectfully repeated a millenium later. Music moreover in the Visigothic church enjoyed extraordinary prestige, even the principal bishops priding themselves on being composers. Finally, a system of notating Visigothic chant the complexities of which still baffle scholars was developed. What was to be the status of the art in Moorish Spain? If one considers the other arts – architecture, for instance – it is of such Moorish rather than Christian monuments as the Cordova Mosque (finished c. 1000 and at that time second in size only to the Kaaba in Mecca itself), the tower in Seville called the Giralda (erected c. 1196), and of course the Alhambra in Granada (built between 1248 and 1354), that one thinks first. These abiding proofs of Moorish cultural genius have inevitably caused historians of the other arts to seek out similar evidences of accomplishment in literature and music. So long ago as the eighteenth century such an effort was made by an exiled Spanish Jesuit, Juan Andrés.

les of the manuscript sources. He continued his discussion of sequences in a review-article, "Le joyau des antiphonaires latins" (*Archivos Leoneses*, VIII, no. 15 [1954], pp. 32–34). The melisma which served as a model for the sequence *Sublimius diebus* (fol. 1v. of the León Antiphoner) forms part of the "Sono" of the office *Ad matutinum* found at fol. 60 in the León Antiphoner.

[53] Brou, "L'Alleluia ...", p. 50.
[54] *Ibid.*, p. 62.

In his *Dell' origine, de' progressi e dello stato attuale d'ogni letteratura* (1782–99) he advanced the then new theory that Provençal lyric poetry, notably that of the troubadour period, flowered over a bed of Moorish precedents.[55] The theory that such a Moorish poetic type as the *zajal* (= zejel) seeded a cognate Spanish type – the *villancico* – is one which still finds strong adherents today.[56]

Since music and poetry were twin arts in the Middle Ages, such prominent Arabists as Ribera and Farmer have contended that not only Moorish poetry but also Moorish music exercised a decisive influence throughout Christian Spain. Clinching proof of musical influence is, however, difficult to assemble. In the first place, no Moorish music antedating 1492, the year in which Granada was captured, survives. Quite possibly the Spanish Moors did not practice notating their music but contented themselves instead with improvising around traditional patterns. The earliest notated music extant anywhere in the Islamic world for that matter cannot be dated earlier than 1250 – and even it is nothing but a set of examples introduced into a theoretical treatise by the inventor of "systematist tuning," Ṣafī al-Dīn (c. 1230–1294), a native of Baghdad.[57] His examples are written in letter-notation with numerals to indicate time-values. In contrast, four-line staff notation was already used in Galicia at Santiago de Compostela (the most famous of medieval shrines) as early as 1140. To carry the contrast further, Islamic music whether in Mesopotamia or Morocco never knew independent two-part writing; but the 1140 Codex Calixtinus from Santiago de Compostela already contains two-part melismatic organum.

WANT of written examples, then, is the first deterrent to our study of medieval Moorish music. This lack is not remedied by an appeal to modern Moroccan music, which both Ribera and Farmer reject as bastardized. The best that can be done in their absence is to study the treatises either copied or composed in Spain. The most famous of such treatises was written by the Turk, Al-Fārābī (c. 872–950), who as a youth was taken to Baghdad, there to learn Arabic and to study under a Christian physician, Yūḥannā ibn Ḥaylān. He read through Aristotle's extant works "more than one hundred times, but said he could never read them sufficiently." After lecturing for a time at Aleppo he died in Damascus. One of the most important extant copies of his masterpiece on musical theory, the *Kitāb al-Mūsīqī*, was made c. 1120 at Cordova and is now preserved (MS 906) at El Escorial, the monastery near Madrid founded by Philip II in 1563.

Al-Fārābī early gained a name among Christian as well as Mohammedan scholars as the foremost interpreter of Greek philosophy. His "Grand Book on Music," though written in Arabic, utilizes Greek terms throughout. Even the word *mūsīqī* in its title shows that the art discussed is not to be an indigenous Arabian one: for the Arabic word

[55] Juan Andrés, *Dell' origine* ... (Venice: Giovanni Vitto, 1783), II, 297–298. Esteban Arteaga, another exiled Jesuit, counterblasted Andrés's Arabian theories. See *Le rivoluzioni del teatro musicale italiano*, sec. ed. (Venice: Carlo Palese, 1785), I, 162n.–171n.

[56] Ramón Menéndez Pidal, *Poesía árabe y poesía europea*, 2nd ed. (Buenos Aires: Espasa-Calpe, 1943), pp. 17–18.

[57] Henry George Farmer in "Arabian Music," *Grove's V*, I, 186a, wrote: "The earliest Arabian composer who has given us notated compositions is Ṣafī al-Dīn. They are mostly examples to illustrate his theories ..."

denoting "song" or "music" indifferently was *ghinā'*. His influence can be proved not only from the dissemination of manuscript versions, but by the more important fact that when a Spanish Muslim such as Abū'l-Ṣalt (1068–1134) [58] came to write his own music treatise he paraphrased and re-arranged the "Grand Book." Abū'l-Ṣalt's treatise survives in a Hebrew translation (Paris, Bibliothèque Nationale, *Fonds Hébreu No. 1037*). If possible, Abū'l-Ṣalt, the Spaniard from Andalusia, leaned more heavily on Aristotle than Al-Fārābī, the Turk. Particularly is this shown in the arrangement of material. Al-Fārābī disposes his material into three books, preceded by an introduction. Book I treats of the Elements, Book II of Instruments, Book III of Composition. Abū'l-Ṣalt takes Al-Fārābī's twofold division of music into theory and practice as his starting-point, but subdivides each of these according to the *materia-forma* dichotomy recognized as the root of all Aristotelian philosophical concepts. If the *materia* of theoretical music is notes and intervals, the *forma* is the groupings of these within scale-systems. If the *materia* of practical music is musical instruments, the *forma* is the shaping of melodies and rhythms to conform with the natural possibilities of such instruments as the *qānūn*, *barbaṭ*, *ṭanābīr*, and *rabāb*.

Hanoch Avenary of Tel Aviv thus summarizes Abū'l-Ṣalt's contribution to musical theory:

[His] arrangement does not agree with that of other Arabian scholars; it is rather in contradiction to it. But it seems to have been the intention of the author when grouping his subject in such a manner .... Abū'l-Ṣalt obviously endeavours to follow more closely Aristotle's scheme of classification.[59]

The existence of a Hebrew translation shows that this late eleventh-century treatise was appreciated in medieval Jewish circles; as does also the fact that in 1403 a Hebrew philosopher, Profiat Duran, quoted a sentence from Abū'l-Ṣalt's treatise.[60]

Al-Fārābī wrote at least one, and possibly two, other treatises which left a mark in medieval Spain.[61] The first of these, *Iḥṣā' al-'ulūm*, exists in only one Western manuscript copy. Conserved at El Escorial (MS 646), the unique copy is dated c. 1310 (i.e., after Cordova and Seville had been retaken and the Moors driven back into the Kingdom of Granada). This particular work was twice translated into Latin by linguists in the employ of Raymund, archbishop of Toledo (d. 1151). John of Seville (d. 1157?) and Gerard of Cremona (d. 1187) produced the two independent versions, both called *De scientiis*. John of Seville's version, the older, was in turn incorporated, almost entire, in a university text compiled by an archdeacon of Toledo, Dominicus Gundissalinus (= Gundisalvus). His text – entitled *De divisione philosophie* – reached England, and Robert Kilwardby, archbishop of Canterbury (d. 1279) quoted it. Kilwardby, who had taught at Oxford in Roger Bacon's time, begins a section in his compend, *De ortu et divisione philosophie*, thus: "Musicam autem sonoram sic difinit *Gundissalinus* ...." [62]

[58] Farmer, *A History of Arabian Music* (London: Luzac & Co., 1929), p. 221.

[59] "Abūl–Ṣalt's Treatise on Music," *Musica Disciplina*, VI, 1–3 (1952), p. 31.   [60] *Ibid.*, p. 29.

[61] H. G. Farmer, *Al-Fārābī's Arabic-Latin Writings on Music* (Glasgow: The Civic Press, 1934), pp. 6, 37.

[62] Dominicus Gundissalinus, *De divisione philosophiae*, ed. Ludwig Baur (Münster [Beiträge z. Geschichte der Philosophie des Mittelalters], 1903), p. 161.

The second of Al-Fārābī's two minor treatises, if indeed it be his, descends to us with the title *De ortu scientiarum*. In this smaller work only four mathematical sciences are treated, arithmetic, geometry, astrology, and music. But in the *De scientiis*, which is indubitably Al-Fārābī's, seven sciences are treated: optics, statics, and mechanics being added to the other four.

The influence of Al-Fārābī, or Alpharabius as his name was latinized, can be shown to have traveled over all Europe between 1200 and 1500. In France Vincent of Beauvais (c. 1190–1264) in his *Speculum doctrinale*, Jerome of Moravia (fl. 1240) in his *Tractatus de musica* [63] and pseudo-Aristotle (fl. 1270) in his like-named work,[64] all quoted him not only in short snatches but at substantial length. A century later Al-Fārābī's influence was still so strong in England that the author of *Quatuor principalia musicae* (1351) [65] could repeat the whole blocs from Al-Fārābī (via Gundissalinus) already used in pseudo-Aristotle's *Tractatus de musica*. In Germany as late as 1503 Gregor Reisch (1467–1525) still cited Al-Fārābī in his *Margarita philosophica* (Freiburg ed., fol. n viij), especially deferring to him in Book V, chapter ii. As if these citations were not enough, his is still brought forward as a name to be conjured with in the culminating Spanish treatise of the sixteenth century, Juan Bermudo's 1555 *Declaración de instrumentos*,[66] Osuna in Andalusia being its place of publication. The influence of Al-Fārābī thus at the end came full circle and stopped in the very heart of what had for more than five hundred years been Moslem territory.

Al-Fārābī deservedly overshadows all other Arabian theorists – of whom Al-Kindī (d. 873) would be the earliest and Ibn Sīnā (= Avicenna [980–1037]) the most widely known. Even so, these others merit the attention of anyone concerned with the progress of musical thought in Mohammedan Spain. In the century between Al-Fārābī and Ibn Sīnā, the second of whom treats of music in his *Kitāb aš-Šifā'*, several new rhythmic schemes had come into vogue. The "possible" rhythmic patterns allowed by both were, it is true, complex, extending to patterns of seven's (3 + 4 or 4 + 3), ten's (3 + 3 + 4), and eleven's (3 + 4 + 4), with accents sharpened by staccatissimo marks. But the "traditional" rhythms of Arabian music carried to Spain by such early virtuosi as Ziryāb (d. 880?) were, according to Al-Fārābī, limited to seven distinct groups. These can be studied in Baron Rodolphe d'Erlanger's *La musique arabe* (II, 40–48). The rhythmic patterns recorded by Al-Fārābī and Ibn Sīnā were always built up as combinations of indivisible beats, often fast enough to warrant transcription as quavers in a brisk allegro. Le-

---

[63] E. de Coussemaker, *Scriptorum de musica medii aevi*, Vol. I (Paris: A. Durand, 1864), pp. 4b, 10a.
[64] *CS*, I, p. 253a, lines 9–15, 21–28. See Farmer, *Al-Fārābī's Arabic-Latin Writings*, pp. 22–24, 27–29.
[65] *CS*, IV, p. 205a, lines 7–14, 22–30.
[66] Bermudo, *Declaración* (Osuna: Juan de León, 1555), fol. viii verso (col. 1).

gato and staccato "notes" were sharply differentiated, as were also accentuated versus unaccentuated "beats." The light *ramal* involved, for instance, unaccentuated patterns in fives, such as are shown on page 20.[67] The heavy *ramal* called, on the other hand, for pronounced accents. Al-Fārābī supplies examples which can be equated with the following note-values:[68]

SUCH HEAVILY ACCENTED PATTERNS as these last naturally inclined the Moors in Spain to prefer plucked and percussive rather than suave instruments. The forty miniatures[69] in Alfonso X's *Cantigas de Santa María* (c. 1280) show 72 instrumentalists playing every variety of instrument from organistrum to clackers. But when a Moorish player is pictured he plays a plucked instrument, not a bowed or wind instrument: even though the rebec, the *albogón*, and *añafil*, all shown in the miniatures, were as surely introduced into Spain by the Moors as was the lute. Moreover Juan Ruiz, Archpriest of Hita, explicitly affirms in his *Libro de buen amor* (1343) – a poem in which he shows himself the most musically knowledgeable of medieval Spanish poets – that the Moors preferred plucked and percussion instruments above all others.

The preference for bright and sparkling rhythms in their festive music gave the Moorish *zambra* the reputation of being the liveliest music in the Spanish peninsula, even after Granada was captured and the Moors were placed under rigid surveillance. When López de Gómara, an Andalusian and Cortés's personal chaplain, wished for instance to call the music of a certain Aztec dance the liveliest and most exhilarating that one could possibly hear, he was able to think of only one equivalent – the music of the Moorish *zambra*, it being the most exciting music stay-at-home Spaniards could have heard.[70]

As for the repertory of instruments introduced into Spain by the Moors, the list extends to more than twenty named types. Seville became the center of instrument-manufacture during the eleventh century, and a proverb had it that when a Cordovan musician died his instruments were sold in Seville but when a Sevillian scholar died his

---

[67] d'Erlanger, *La musique arabe*, Vol. II (Paris: Librairie orientaliste, 1935), pp. 42–43.

[68] *Ibid.*, II, 43–44.

[69] Reproduced in Julián Ribera, *La música de las Cantigas* (Madrid: Tip. de la Rev. de Archivos, 1922), on seven plates following p. 152.

[70] Francisco López de Gómara, *La conquista de Mexico* (Saragossa: Agustín Millán, 1552), fol. xliii: "Todos los que an visto este vayle dizen que es cosa mucho para ver. Y mejor que la zambra de los moros, que es la mejor dança que por aca sabemos."

books were sold in Cordova. [71] Al Shaqandī, a Sevillian (d. 1231), drew up the following
list of 20 instruments in contemporary vogue: [72]

abū qurūn = large drum; *bandair* = tambourine; *būq* = metal shawm; *dabdaba* = drum;
duff = tambourine; *ghaiṭa* = bagpipe; *juwāq* = flageolet; *kaithāra* = guitar; *khullāl* =
kettledrum; *nafīr* = trumpet; *nīra* = recorder; *qānūn* = psaltery; *rabāb* = rebec;
rūṭa = rotte; *shabbāba* = small flute; *ṣun ūj* = metal clappers; *ṭabl* = small drum;
ṭunbūr = bandore; *'ūd* = lute; *zulāmī* = shawm.

These, he said, were manufactured in Seville for export to North Africa, as well as for
the Spanish market. The emphasis on Sevillian instrument-construction is especially
interesting because Seville was the first city after the Reconquest to enact an elaborate
set of *ordenanzas* regulating the manufacture of instruments, a set published as early as
1502 and repeatedly thereafter.[73] Sevillian rules were in turn copied by those who framed
the first municipal ordinances in Mexico City.[74] According to Ibn Sa'īd al-Maghribī (d.
1280), already in the thirteenth century there were available in Seville rule-books
explaining in precise detail how each instrument should be constructed.

However little else the Spanish Christian may have borrowed from Moorish music, he
certainly took such instruments as the lute, the rebec, and the naker. Their very names,
though indigenized in the English language before Shakespeare, are indisputably of
Arabian origin. Other instruments borrowed by Spanish Christians during the Moorish
occupation included these: [75]

> adufe = *al-duff* = square tambourine
> ajabeba (exabeba) = *al-shabbāba* = transverse flute
> albogón = *al-būq* = metal cylindrical instrument with reed-mouthpiece and seven
>   finger-holes
> añafil = *al-nafīr* = straight trumpet four feet or more in length
> atabal = *al-ṭabl* = drum
> atambal = *al-ṭinbāl* [Persian] = drum
> canón [Ruiz, 1343] = *qānūn* = canon, a psaltery
> panderete [Ruiz, 1343] = *bandair* = tambourine
> sonajas de azófar [Ruiz, 1343] = *ṣunūj al-ṣufr* = metal castanets

The Spanish for "fret" (as of the lute) comes also from the Arabic: traste = *dastān*.

MOORISH VIRTUOSI were prized by Spanish Christian monarchs. Sancho IV of Castile
(1284–1295) employed Fate as his chief trumpeter, Maomet as a player of the *añafil*,

[71] Eleanor Hague, *Music in Ancient Arabia and Spain* [trans. of J. Ribera's *La música de las Cantigas*]
(Stanford: Stanford University Press, 1929), p. 116.

[72] Ahmed Ibn Mohammed Al-Makkari, *Mohammedan Dynasties in Spain*, trans. by Pascual de Gayangos
(London: Oriental Translation Fund, 1840), I, 59; also I, 365, n. 17. Corrections by H. G. Farmer in *GD V*,
V, 872b.

[73] José Subirá, *Historia de la música española e hispanoamericana*, p. 219.

[74] Francisco del Barrio Lorenzot, *Ordenanzas de Gremios de la Nueva España* (México: Dir. de Talleres
Gráficos, 1921), p. 85.

[75] Miguel Asín Palacios, "Etimologías Árabes," *Al-Andalus*, IX, i (Madrid-Granada, 1944), pp. 15–41. See
also Julián Ribera, *Disertaciones y opúsculos* (Madrid, 1928), II, 143–144.

Rexit as a player of the *axabeba* (cross flute), and in addition eight other named Moorish musicians.[76] Pedro III (1276–1285) of Aragon employed Moorish trumpeters, as did also such royalty as Jaime II (1291–1327), Juan I (1387–1395) and Juan II (1406–1454). *Shabbāba, qānūn,* and *rabāb* players attended Alfonso IV (1327–1336) and Pedro IV (1336–1387), kings of Aragon. According to Menéndez Pidal, an organized Moorish school of minstrelsy existed in Játiva during the fourteenth century.[77] Pedro IV's favorites, Ali Eziqua, player of the *rabeu* (= rabāb), and Çahat Mascum, player of the *exabeba* (= shabbāba), were both summoned from Játiva.[78]

Moorish instrumentalists even enjoyed a temporary vogue in Christian churches, if the 1322 legislation against further employment of Mohammedan musicians is accepted as evidence.[79] The 1322 Council of Valladolid censured the prevalent custom of engaging them to enliven vigils, and invoked severe penalties against churches which allowed them to make a *tumultum.* Their vogue is the more interesting when one considers the fact that never has there existed any such thing as "mosque" music – the only approach to it being the long wailing call to prayer of the muezzin. When at Master Peter's puppet-show in *Don Quixote* the Interpreter ignorantly refers to the *"bells* that sound in the high towers of the Mesquits [mosques]," Don Quixote reproves such foolishness: "Master Peter is very improper in his bells; for amongst the Moors you have no bells." [80] (During his Algerian captivity Cervantes came to know Moslem music at first hand.)

Though Mohammed himself did not proscribe music, his immediate followers and exegetes banned it. In consequence, music in Islam has always been a profane art. The Valladolid fathers who sought to ban Moorish musicians from Christian churches knew, of course, that no Spanish mosque would have tolerated their presence.

THE "PROOFS" of Moorish musical influence thus far cited can now be summarized: (1) Arabian theoretical treatises were translated at Toledo and disseminated in the peninsula and abroad; (2) Moorish instruments were borrowed by the Spanish Christians and reached France and even England; (3) Spanish Christian sovereigns patronized Moorish virtuosi. With these lines of evidence no one takes issue.

Much more strenuous claims have, however, been made. Briefly they run as follows:

I *Organum was taught at Cordova in the eleventh century.* This claim is founded on a passage in the *Philosophia* of Virgilius Cordubensis, putative eleventh-century Cordovan philosopher, which reads: [81] "Seven masters taught grammar every day at

---

[76] Ramón Menéndez Pidal, *Poesía juglaresca y juglares* (Madrid: Tip. de la "Rev. de Archivos," 1924), p. 249.

[77] *Ibid.,* p. 139.

[78] *Ibid.,* p. 264.

[79] *Ibid.,* p. 138. For the pertinent decree of the Valladolid Council see Joseph Sáenz de Aguirre, *Collectio maxima conciliorum omnium Hispaniae et Novi Orbis* (Rome: J. J. Komarek, 1694), III, 567 (paragraph 68).

[80] Cervantes Saavedra, *Segunda parte del ingenioso cavallero Don Quixote de la Mancha* (Madrid: Juan de la Cuesta, 1615), fol. 101r. (cap. xxvi): "Esso no, dixo a esta sazon don Quixote, en esto de las campanas anda muy improprio maesse Pedro; porque entre Moros no se vsan campanas, sino atabales, y vn genero de dulzaynas que parecen nuestras chirimias."

[81] Latin original in Gotthilf Heine, *Biblioteca anecdotorum, sive veterum monumentorum ecclesiasticorum collectio novissima* (Leipzig: T.O. Weigel, 1848), pp. 241–242.

Cordova, five taught logic, three natural science, two astrology, one geometry, three physics; and two masters taught music, that art which is called organum ..." Specific though this quotation sounds, its authority is suspect. The text of Virgilius's *Philosophia* from which the passage is excerpted survives only in a 1290 Latin translation.[82] The reputed author makes errors so crude as to cast a shadow over all he wrote.[83] No one can be sure he was describing the curriculum in an eleventh-century Moslem rather than Christian school. The phrase *Et duo magistri legebant de musica* may be genuine but *de ista arte quae dicitur organum* a translator's gloss. No other "evidence" that the Moslems knew polyphony has been produced.

II *The music of Alfonso X's* Cantigas, *the great medieval collection of Spanish monodies, shows pronounced Moorish traits.* Since the Arabian literary type known as the *zejel* resembles the *estribillo-estrofa* of the *Cantigas* [84] and since music and poetry were admittedly interdependent in the Middle Ages, it is therefore asserted that the tunes of the *Cantigas* must exhibit Arabian influence. This conclusion is drawn from a syllogism with a distributed middle.

III *The Spanish Moslems invented guitar tablature.* This claim is founded on a passage from a 1496–1497 manuscript preserved in a Gerona *convento*, which ascribes to a "certain Moor" in the Kingdom of Granada the invention of an alphabetic system designating finger-position.[85] The MS is in Latin, and the "anonymous" author purports to have received his information from a Barcelona Dominican, Jaime Salvá.

The Cantigas of Alfonso X

PROGRESS in our understanding of Mozarabic music has been painfully achieved, and will continue to be slow, until the neums in which it is written are better understood. The study of Moslem music in Spain poses even more serious problems because no contemporary examples survive to guide the investigator. But the student of thirteenth-century

---

[82] *Ibid.*, p. 211.

[83] H. G. Farmer, *Historical Facts for the Arabian Musical Influence* (London: W. Reeves, 1930), pp. 342–343.

[84] The evidence linking the zejel with the Cantiga-poetry is brilliantly set forth in R. Menéndez Pidal, *Poesía árabe y poesía europea*, pp. 18–66.

[85] Latin text in Rafael Mitjana, "L'Orientalisme musical et la musique arabe," *Le Monde Oriental* (Uppsala: Akademiska Bokhandeln, 1906), pp. 210–212. Also in Marcelino Menéndez [y] Pelayo's *Historia de las ideas estéticas en España*, rev. edn. (Santander: Aldus, s.a., 1940), I, 525–526. For the original text, both Mitjana and Menéndez y Pelayo had recourse to Jaime Villanueva's *Viage literario á las iglesias de España*, XIV [Gerona] (Madrid: Imp. de la Real Academia de la Historia, 1850), pp. 176–178. In our century, no scholar seems to have seen the MS from which Villanueva copied his text.

Although I follow both Mitjana and Menéndez y Pelayo in citing the Latin *Sequitur ars de pulsacione lambuti, et aliorum similium instrumentorum* as "anonymous", Villanueva himself seems to have considered the Latin to have been written by a Benedictine monk, Michael de Castellanis, who dwelt at San Marsal hermitage atop a peak in the Montseny mountain range (province of Barcelona). See Villanueva, *op.cit.*, XIV, 175, 178. Further on Michael de Castellanis below at p. 66.

Castilian and Galician music encounters less formidable hurdles. An abundant repertory of monodic song survives; and even though the transcriptions made by such reputable scholars as Pierre Aubry (*Iter Hispanicum* [Paris, 1908], pp. 37–56) and Higinio Anglés (*La Música de las Cantigas de Santa María* [Barcelona, 1943], II) differ,[86] especially in details of rhythmic interpretation, still the issue of 423 monodic songs in the latter's stout 1943 publication[87] now brings within reach a body of Castilian music which in extent and in variety compares favorably with the total surviving repertory of Provençal song.

The ostensible author, as well as composer, of the entire collection, is Alfonso X, "the Sage" (1221–1284), king of "Castilla, Toledo, León, Compostela, Córdoba, Jaén, Sevilla, Murcia," and other parts of Spain (reigned 1252–1284). Alfonso – reputed author of books on astronomy, precious stones, games, of a history of the world since Creation, a Spanish history, not to mention a famous legal code, *Las siete partidas* – was obviously aided in his various literary tasks by a corps of paid assistants. Even so, the *General estoria* contains an explicit statement that the plan, conception, and supervision were always Alfonso's.[88] He was an accomplished versifier from youth, as his thirty-odd love lyrics in the Vatican Portuguese-Galician *Cancioneiro* testify. One will do well, then, to believe his avowal that he wrote the texts of the 420–odd *Cantigas de Santa María* (Canticles of the Virgin). Even the music may have been his. A miniature at the head of the first cantiga in Escorial MS B. i.2 shows him dictating the music to a professional scribe. Meanwhile seven singers – three clergy and four laymen – make ready for a trial performance. Behind the laymen stand two string players, one in the act of bowing, the other of tuning. On the opposite side (behind the clerics) stand two players of *peñolas*, small five-course plucked instruments.[89] If the evidence of the illumination is taken at face value, Alfonso "composed" the music and prescribed the performance-media as well – which involved male voices accompanied by bowed and plucked string instruments.

A comparison with the troubadour repertory can usefully be made, though of course the Provençal poets treated of an earthly and Alfonso of a heavenly love. Speaking at the outset in the first person, Alfonso says he wishes to be the *trobador* of the Virgin Mary, and to recount all the miracles accomplished through her intervention. He does not consider his task complete until he has recounted 353 first-class miracles. To some 23 of these he or another member of the royal family had been personally a witness.[90]

He initially committed himself to a scheme of only a hundred cantigas. The earliest collection, finished c. 1275, ended with a line mentioning *cen cantares*.[91] The manu-

[86] The problems of transcription are exposed in F. F. Lopes, "A música das 'Cantigas de Santa Maria' e o problema da sua decifracão," *Brotéria*, XL, i (Lisbon, 1945), pp. 49–70.

[87] Actually only 414, subtracting the nine cantigas which are musical duplicates. See Anglés, *La música de las Cantigas*, II, *31* (Introduction).

[88] Antonio G. Solalinde, "Intervención de Alfonso X en la redacción de sus obras," *Revista de Filología Española*, II (1915), p. 286.

[89] Or *péndola*. See Ruiz, *Libro de buen amor*, line 1229d.

[90] Frank Callcott, *The Supernatural in Early Spanish Literature* (New York: Instituto de las Españas, 1923), p. 29 (number of miracles), and p. 31, n. 6 (miracles personally witnessed).

[91] Alfonso el Sabio, *Cantigas de Santa María*, ed. Marqués de Valmar (Madrid: Real Academia Española, 1889), I, [34].

script of this first collection, though now in possession of the Madrid Biblioteca Nacional (*MS 10069*) formerly belonged to the Toledo capitular library, and is therefore customarily referred to as the Toledo version (*Tol*). Two later versions, one containing 200 cantigas, the other 417, are conserved at El Escorial (*T. i. 1* [*E 1*] and *B. i. 2* [*E 2*]).[92] A fourth version containing 104 cantigas exists, but is obviously incomplete, the spaces for musical notation having been left empty. This unfinished copy belongs to the Biblioteca Nazionale (*MS Banco Rari 20*) at Florence (*F*). E 1 is perhaps the most lavishly illuminated of the group with a whole page of miniatures illustrating the action in each cantiga. E 2, more complete than any of the other three collections, contains every cantiga in E 1 and 100 of those from F; but is less sumptuously illuminated than E 1 or F.

The chronology of E 1, E 2, and F has been determined from internal evidence, E 1 dating after 1275, F after 1279, and E 2 probably after 1281.[93] Thus, the final version – the one considered by the Marqués de Valmar in his 1889 two-volume critical edition of the texts and by Anglés in his 1943 musical edition to be the most authoritative – must be accounted a work of Alfonso's last years. That he ascribed supernatural powers to the manuscripts in which his cantigas were written is proved by the fact that when he lay sick in Vitoria during the winter of 1276–1277 he ordered an unfinished copy (perhaps *Tol*) to be placed on the affected part of his body with the result that he immediately recovered (*Cantiga 209*).[94]

The cantigas are so grouped that every tenth is a *loor* (praise of the Virgin), and the intervening nine, narratives of *miragres* (miracles). In direct answer to prayer the Virgin restores the dead to life, cures bodily ailments, wards off threatened physical harm, and recovers lost possessions. At times she even works such miracles as these without waiting to be asked. Similarly, her very relics, image, or name occasionaly work miracles without the necessity of her personal intervention. Sometimes the miracles border on the extravagant, as when an unfaithful abbess is vindicated though still unrepentant, or an unnatural mother saved from condign punishment (*Cantigas 7* and *17*).

The locale of the miracles stretches from Syria (*265*) to Scotland (*108*). The most interesting of those set in England are Cantiga 6, retold by Chaucer as *The Prioress's Tale*, Cantiga 226, recounting the legend of the engulfed cathedral, and Cantiga 85, in which the Virgin plays the Good Samaritan to a Jewish traveller stripped by highwaymen. Echoes of Cantiga 155 can be heard in Thomas Moore's *Paradise and the Peri* and of Cantiga 103 in Longfellow's *The Golden Legend*. The earlier cantigas, especially those in the Toledo MS, tend to range through more distant territory than the latter ones added in the Florentine version. Every cantiga the composition of which can be dated after 1275 deals with some local miracle, and preferably with one in Alfonso's own ken.

THE LANGUAGE is a literary form of the Galician dialect.[95] Since Alfonso was the first Spanish king to use Castilian for all internal state dispatches, he perhaps wrote his poetry

---

[92] Evelyn S. Procter, *Alfonso X of Castile* (Oxford: Clarendon Press, 1951), pp. 24–26. Anglés's E 1 is Procter's E 2 and vice versa.

[93] Procter, p. 46.

[94] Copied in F, fol. 119v.

[95] Valmar, I, [171].

in Galician (nearer Portuguese than Spanish) in deference to literary fashion. Galician and not Castilian was the language of poetry. Indeed the only poet aside from Alfonso whose name occurs in any manuscript of the *Cantigas* was the Portuguese, rather than Castilian cleric, Ayras (= Arias) Nunes; [96] the latter's nationality being known because of his contributions to the Vatican Cancioneiro (*MS 4803*). Nunes's name, apparently written in Alfonso's own hand, occurs between columns of Cantiga 223 in E 2. On the contrary, when a painter is mentioned (*Cantiga 377*), he is a Castilian, Pedro Lorenzo. Moreover, the copyist whose name appears at the close of Cantiga 402 (*E 2*, fol. 361v.) is also a Castilian, Juan Gonsález. The latter's couplet imploring the Blessed Virgin to remember him must be quoted because it is the only bit of Castilian poetry in the MSS:

> *Virgen bien Auenturada*
> *Sey de mj Remenbrada*
> . Johñs gundisaluj.

The metrical scheme of the Cantigas is extremely varied, with lines ranging in length from four to seventeen syllables. Long and short lines are sometimes mixed in the same stanza, Cantiga 300 offering an instance. Stanzas range from four to ten lines. Such exceptions as Cantiga 401 (ten strophes of 20 lines each) are very rarely enountered. If the metrical scheme is prodigally varied, so also is the rhyme-scheme. Rhyme is occasionally replaced by assonance. Each cantiga, whether a *loor* or a narrative, begins with a short refrain in the form of a couplet or quatrain. (Cantiga 139 begins with an eight-line refrain; but no line contains more than a brief snatch.) The refrain (= *estribillo*) is repeated between each stanza (= *estrofa*) and at the close.

The narrative poems move rapidly, at least by medieval standards,[97] and the music is similarly taut and well-paced throughout the collection. A legend which Gautier de Coincy may have told in 753 lines and Chaucer in 203, Alfonso tells in 136 lines (*Cantiga 6*). The drastic cuts to speed the action are interestingly paralleled in the classic Spanish *romances* of the fifteenth and sixteenth centuries – likewise intended to be sung. Alfonso by no means considered his collection to be a private venture but rather a public treasury, freely available to the various *joglares* (= jongleurs) who were ubiquitous in Spain as in France during his century. Above all, he emphasized that his cantigas were to be sung by the *joglares*, not said or read.[98] In his own words (*Cantiga 172*), "we made this song for the joglares to sing":

> *Et d'esto cantar fezemos*
> *que cantassen os iograres.*

THE MUSIC can usually be barred in triple meter. Triple and duple sometimes mix in the same cantiga. The notation of E 2 is mensural throughout; and whatever the differences in interpretation, the neums always imply accented rhythms. Julián Ribera's transcriptions in *La música de las Cantigas* (Madrid, 1922) differ from Anglés's

[96] *Ibid.*, I, [148].
[97] *Ibid.*, I, [115].
[98] *Ibid.*, II, 245 (last couplet of Cantiga CLXXII).

not so much because he preferred the Toledo manuscript and Anglés E 2, but rather because Ribera was an Arabist without any special training in musical notation. He moreover added accidentals with reckless abandon. The sources show only one accidental – B♭, which appears in 96 cantigas as a "key-signature," not counting its frequent use as a temporary accidental in the other 327 cantigas.

Alfonso's favorite modes are quite obviously not the E-modes which Spanish folklorists nowadays consider typical of peninsular music. By actual count he uses them (E-final, or A-final with flat) in only 4 out of 100 cantigas. Instead, his favorite modes are those with finals on D, G, and F. He affirms the modality of each cantiga twice: at the final note of the opening refrain and at the final in the stanza. These two finals are always identical. The following table shows the finals in 100 cantigas.[99]

D (42) without flat 35, with 7;
G (28) without flat 23, with 5;
F (22) with flat 18, without 4;
A (5)   with flat 3, without 2;
C (2)   without flat 1, with 1;
E (1).

As for range, the melodies rarely go beyond an octave, In less than a tithe of the cantigas does the range exceed a minor ninth and in none does it go beyond an octave and a fourth. In almost half, the range does not even reach the octave.[100]

The most usual melodic intervals are seconds and thirds. Fourths and fifths occur but rarely. The estribillo frequently inhabits a lower range than the estrofa. Between estribillo and estrofa a dead interval of a major sixth or minor seventh sometimes intrudes. Within phrases the downward fifth seems to be the most frequently used "wide" interval. Telling instances of its use at ends of phrases can be found in Cantigas 15, 54, and 200.

The musical structure often proves to be more tightly knit than a mere *da capo* sign might suggest. In the typical cantiga, Alfonso – or whoever else was the composer – repeats the music of the refrain unaltered or with slight variants during the second half of the stanza. Phrases are invariably clearcut, and are often symmetrically balanced. Just as medieval Spanish saints'-tales deal only rarely with visions and dreams (though with flesh-and-blood appearances frequently): so the cantigas as a rule choose a brisk and strictly matter-of-fact mood. Neither as poet nor musician does Alfonso ever become a dreamy Eusebius.

Since the poetry contains a number of conceits, such as the ingenious play on the words *Ave* and *Eva* in Cantiga 60 and the acrostic on the Virgin's name in Cantiga 70, the music may well exhibit similar feats. These still await revelation. But the length of time which elapsed before modern scholars discovered the acrostic made on Alfonso's name in *Las siete partidas* counsels patience while the search continues for musical conceits to match the already known literary feats in the Cantigas.

---

[99] Cantigas 1–59 and 160–200 tabulated in this summary.
[100] Ribera, *La música de las Cantigas*, p. 127 (Introduction). Cantiga 127 in Anglés's edition spans an octave and a fourth.

The familiar subject-matter of Cantigas 6 and 226 – shown as accompanying examples – has already been mentioned. The first tells *The Prioress's Tale* of the child who sang praises to Mary after his throat was slit, the second the story of the church engulfed one Easter and lifted out of the sea the next.

Cantiga VI

Madrid:
Bibl. Nac. MS 10069, fol. 14.

* El Escorial B.i. 2 inserts another A (quaver-value in transcription).

Cantiga CCXXVI

Escorial MS B.i.2., fol. 206.

Thirteenth-Century Secular Monody

AT LEAST THREE laments for Spanish kings and one for an abbess survive from the twelfth and thirteenth centuries. The kings thus commemorated were Sancho III of Castile (d. 1158),[101] Ferdinand II of León (d. 1188),[102] and Alfonso VIII of Castile (d. 1214).[103] The abbess was María González (fl. 1325) of the Royal Convent of Cistercian Nuns known as Las Huelgas (Burgos).[104] Each is in Latin. In none does the style markedly differ from that of contemporary French monodic threnodies. No thirteenth-century secular music with Castilian text survives. But the case is better in Galician. The half-dozen secular pieces with Galician texts which survive combine words and music by the *trovador*, Martín Codax. Long known as a poet because of his contributions

[101] Anglés, *El Còdex Musical de Las Huelgas*, III, 390–391 (Item 172).
[102] *Ibid.*, I, 356–357.
[103] *Ibid.*, III, 388 (Item 169).
[104] *Ibid.*, III, 389 (Item 171).

to contemporary *cancioneiros*, he garnered added fame as a composer when musical settings of six authenticated poems were discovered by a Madrid bibliophile in 1915.[105]

Though of course their use of literary Galician unites them, Codax's poetry as well as music differs sharply from Alfonso's. Instead of varied stanza-lengths Codax without exception chooses a three-line stanza. Instead of beginning with a refrain Codax repeats the third line of each strophe. Instead of a varied rhyme-scheme, he alternates double i-o or a-o rhymes (or assonances) in the initial couplet of every strophe. Not only does the third line of every tercet serve as a refrain, but also the second line becomes the first of the second tercet following. This chain-repetition scheme places Codax's poetry in the literary genre known as the *cosante* (= *cossante*).[106]

His poems seem to tell a connected love-tale. On the other hand, he writes his verse not for himself but for his lady-love to sing. In the opening poem of the cycle she apostrophizes the sea at Vigo: "Waves of the ocean that have borne him at his departure, return him safely home again." In the second she asks her mother to join her at Vigo – because he now returns, safe, and what is more a trusted friend of the king. In the third she invites her beautiful sister to attend the church located beside the sea at Vigo, and there to meet her beloved. In the fifth she urges all who truly know the art of loving to come to Vigo and bathe in the sea with their *amigos*. The sixth, which lacks music in the copy Pedro Vindel discovered in 1915, is a dance-song. In the seventh the cycle is completed. Her lover has again departed and she stands desolately looking at the waves that have borne him from her.

Some annotators have seen in this earliest of song-cycles only the joys and sorrows of a Galician maiden whose lover must make his livelihood at sea. Others have read more specific meanings into the series. José Joaquim Nunes, who edited the set in 1926–28, feels that a mere mariner would not have returned from a fishing-trip "a friend of the king" (second poem in the cycle). Instead, Codax may have been a retainer of Ferdinand III's in the expeditionary force which retook Seville from the Moors (1248).[107] Nunes cites contemporary evidence to show that this king was as great a patron of troubadours and jongleurs as was Alfonso X, his son. Codax could well have been one of the *omes de corte que sabien bien trovar e cantar* (men at court who could worthily recite and sing) and no mere *joglar*.[108]

HIS MUSIC, though the pitches are easily enough read, poses more difficulties than Alfonso's because the rhythmical scheme never becomes quite clear. According to

---

[105] For details of its discovery in the wrappers of Cicero's *De officiis*, see Pedro Vindel, *Las siete canciones de amor: poema musical* (Madrid: Pedro Vindel, 1915), pp. 5–8.

[106] José Romeu Figueras, "El cosante en la lírica de los Cancioneros musicales," *Anuario Musical*, V (Barcelona: Instituto Español de Musicología, 1950), pp. 17–21. See also W. J. Entwistle's chapter in Bell-Bowra-Entwistle, *Da Poesia medieval portuguesa*, 2nd ed. (Lisbon: Ed. da Rev. "Ocidente," 1947), entitled "Dos 'Cossantes' às 'Cantigas de Amor'," pp. 75–99.

[107] José Joaquim Nunes, *Cantigas d'Amigo* (Coimbra: Imp. da Universidade, 1928), I, 201n.

[108] Isabel Pope in "Mediaeval Latin Background of the Thirteenth-Century Galician Lyric," *Speculum*, IX (1934), p. 15, identified Codax as a "jongleur probably connected with the court of Don Dinis of Portugal." He may have attended both kings. She shows a non-metrical transcription of *Ondas do mar* in "El Villancico Polifónico," *Cancionero de Upsala* (Mexico City: El Colegio de México, 1944), p. 30.

Anglés: "The six *Cantigas d'amigo* of the Galician troubadour Martin Codax conserved with their music survive in a notation intermediate between square and mensural; the copyist knew something, but not much, of mensural practice in his epoch and transcribed in such a confused way that he gives no clear idea of the [intended] rhythm." [109] The modern transcriber encounters another obstacle: the lacunae which exist, not merely because the forgetful copyist omitted filling in the black musical notation on his red five-line staff (as in the sixth of the seven cantigas), but also because the Vindel manuscript through centuries of use as a wrapper for Cicero's *De officiis* became so worn at creases that the musical notes were occasionally obliterated (third and fourth cantigas).[110]

What can be clearly established are these musical traits: (1) as in Alfonso's cantigas, the G- and F-modes rather than E-mode (now popularly typed as Spanish) are used; (2) as in Alfonso's cantigas, the melodic range is restricted – indeed even more so, since a major sixth or minor seventh proves to be Codax's maximum; (3) phrases are clear-cut, and cadences correspond exactly with line-endings in each strophe; (4) the lowest point in the melodies occurs regularly in the refrain-line; (5) the caesura in the refrain-line is clearly marked by some such change of musical stance as a shift from a lower to a higher tetrachord.

The melody of *Ondas do mar* (Cantiga 1) slightly resembles that of Alfonso's Cantiga 73. Since no agreement can be reached on the rhythms, the best that can be shown below will have to be the pitches. So that they may be read more intelligently, those which join each other in ligature have been italicized. Pitches shown as superscripts end plicas. Empty space has been left after each pitch which in the original copy seems to be intended for a note longer than the usual quaver. As will be at once seen, the music for line 2 of each tercet recalls that for line 1. Only in the refrain-line does he make any use of the flat. Since this one flat sets an exclamation, he may even have introduced it here for its *Affekt*.

$$G \; A \; c \quad B \; c \; d \; c \quad c \; B \; A \; c \quad B \; c \; d \; c \; B \; A \; B^A \; A \; G$$
On-das do   mar de   Vi-   go,

$$A \; c \quad B \; c \; d \; c \quad c \; B \; A \; c \quad B \; c \; d \; c \quad d \; c \; B \; A \; B^A \; A \; G$$
se vis-tes   meu   a- mi-   go!

$$GA \; B(\flat) \; A \; A^G \; G \; F \quad G \; A \; c \quad B \; c \; d \; c \; d \; c \; c \; B \; A \; B^A \; A \; G$$
e   ai   Deus, se ve- rrá   ce-   do!

Though *Ondas do mar* extends to only four tercets, *Mandad' ei comigo* (Cantiga 2) reaches six. The melodies of both prove similarly melismatic, even if no ligature in Cantiga 2 combines more than four notes. Again, he only slightly varies the music for lines 1 and 2.

---

[109] Anglés, *La música de las Cantigas*, II, 39 (Introduction).

[110] R. Mitjana in "Cancionero poético y musical del siglo XVII," *Rev. de Fil. Esp.*, VI, i (January, 1919), p. 18n., said the parchment was indubitably thirteenth-century. He owned it in 1919.

BG AB B*d* *c*B A   BA G
Man-dad' ei   co-   mi- go,

AG   AB   B*d*   *c*BAG   GF
ca   ven   meu   a- mi- go:

G*A* B   AG AG F   G   AB *c* B   A   B   G
e   i-   rei, madr'   a   Vi-   go.

The Beginnings of Polyphony in the Spanish Peninsula

THE EARLIEST two- and three-part music conserved in Spain consists of 21 short pieces with Latin text copied at folios 131 and 185–190 of the twelfth-century *Codex Calixtinus*.[111] This codex, one of the best known Spanish MSS, belongs to the cathedral of Santiago de Compostela (Galicia). Easily accessible transcriptions by Walter Muir Whitehill (text) and Dom Germán Prado (music) may be found in the three volume-publication, *Liber Sancti Jacobi: Codex Calixtinus* (Santiago de Compostela: Seminario de estudios gallegos, 1944).

The polyphonic rather than monodic pieces give the codex its reputation in musical circles – though actually more than nine-tenths of the chants in the MS are monodic. Insofar as the polyphonic numbers are typed, they bear the following titles: *Benedicamus*, *conductus*, or *prosa*. At fol. 185 is to be found the most famous of these, *Congaudeant catholici*, by "Master Albert of Paris." [112] Friedrich Ludwig in 1905 and again in 1924 pointed to this three-part work as one of the earliest in existence.[113] It does not purport to be Spanish, nor as a matter of fact need it be accepted as having been originally written for three voices. Still its occurrence in the oldest polyphonic source in the peninsula gives it special claims to attention. In *The New Oxford History of Music* (II, 305–306) two transcriptions are printed, the first by Ludwig, the second by Hughes. The latter version has been recorded in *The History of Music in Sound* (ii, side 14).

The Calixtine Codex lists the names of 15 pilgrims who composed specific chants. Only one of these composers can however qualify as Spanish. Even he is but vaguely referred to as a "Galician doctor." His contribution is a monodic *Benedicamus*, reworked polyphonically by another composer elsewhere in the codex.[114] All the other contri-

---

[111] The music is copied (both monody and polyphony) on the four-line staff. A transcription made by a pilgrim who visited Santiago, Arnaldus de Monte (monk of Ripoll in Catalonia), bears the date 1173. Arnaldus wrote the Calixtinus monodies in staffless neums. Anglés thinks the present Codex Calixtinus a later copy of the book Arnaldus transcribed. See *Huelgas*, I, 60–62.

[112] Jacques Handschin in "The Summer Canon and its Background," *Musica Disciplina*, V (1951), p. 95, identified Albertus as precentor of Notre Dame, 1147–1173. He bequeathed a missal, lectionary, antiphoner, gradual, *psalterium cum hymnis*, two tropers, and two versaries to his cathedral.

[113] *Huelgas*, I, 60.

[114] *Regi perennis* (*Codex Calixtinus*, 1944 ed., II, 67). A monody at fol. 139r., *Regi perennis* earns a descant by Gautier of Châteaurenault at fol. 187r.

butors came purportedly from Chartres, Troyes, Bourges, Soissons, Châteaurenault, not to name more distant and unlikely spots such as Jerusalem.[115]

The musical contents are therefore more a subject for international study than for local investigation. Some of the melismas at the ends of phrases in such a two-part *Benedicamus* as the one entitled *Ad superni regis decus* (fol. 186) [116] have been said to show peculiarly Galician traits.[117] But the very purpose of the codex precluded much emphasis on locally Spanish customs or music. Designed as a panegyric of the Apostle James, an apologia for the location of his shrine in Galicia, and a guide-book for tourists coming like Chaucer's Wife of Bath from foreign lands, its whole atmosphere is essentially cosmopolitan.

When the compiler stops to dwell on merely local matters he never describes the chants which the pilgrim will hear but insists instead on being useful by giving phrases in the Basque tongue or up-to-date information on travel routes.[118] A brief account of Santiago and its cathedral is given, it is true,[119] but none of the cathedral music. Such a description would have been however most valuable, especially if its sumptuousness matched that of the Romanesque building (begun in 1078) in which it was heard. Moreover by rights it should have been if Santiago, as the compiler declared, was the third great shrine of Christianity, Rome and Ephesus being the others.

Both monody and polyphony appear in the codex on four-line staves. In Albert of Paris's three-part *Congaudeant* the scribe wrote the two slower-moving bottom voices on the same staff, distinguishing them however with different-colored inks. As for the plainchants, they are more often notated in F- than in C-clef. In the polyphonic pieces G-clef is used in addition to F- and C-clefs, changes of clef within a line being rather frequently called for. In one instance a single melodic line carries two clefs a third apart.[120]

The compiler of the codex made a careful attempt to cover the complete cycle of eight church modes in his selection of plainsong antiphons. The polyphonic pieces, however, are cast predominantly in the D-mode (9 examples) and G-mode (5 examples). What is assuredly a mixed signature with B♭ in the lower voice occurs once (*Annua gaudia*).[121] Three instances of the B♭ as an accidental have been found in the polyphonic and ten in the plainsong repertory. The plainsongs in Modes V and VI sound strongly "major." Nine of the ten flats occur in plainchants labelled one or the other. Neither Peter Wagner (*Die Gesänge der Jacobsliturgie zu Santiago de Compostela* [Freiburg, 1931]) nor Germán Prado (1944) attempted to solve the baffling rhythmic problems. These still

---

[115] *Codex Calixtinus* (1944 ed.), III, 51.

[116] *Ibid.*, II, 71.

[117] *Ibid.*, III, 50. Item 291 in Felipe Pedrell, *Cancionero musical popular español* (Valls: E. Castells, c. 1922), II, 207–208, a Galician dance-song to the bagpipe, reminded Dom Germán Prado of *Ad superni regis decus* (*Codex Calixtinus*, II, 71). The top parts do tally.

[118] *Codex Calixtinus* (1944 ed.), III, 38–39.

[119] *Ibid.*, III, 41–42.

[120] The chant in question, *Ad honorem regis summi* by Aiméry Picaud de Parthenay-le-Vieux, may have been sung in thirds after the fashion of *cantus gemellus*, thinks Prado (*Codex Calixtinus*, III, 54). On the other hand, the scribe may have changed his mind, erasing the C-clef rather carelessly.

[121] Fol. 186v.

await the kind of convincing solution that William Waite gave the *Magnus liber organi* of Léonin in his *The Rhythm of Twelfth-Century Polyphony* (1954).

AFTER THE *Codex Calixtinus* – with its impressive bishops, archbishops, a patriarch, and even a pope (Calixtus II) listed as composers of the music, with its *Alleluia* in Greek and its *Prosa S. Jacobi* in a mixture of Latin, Greek, and Hebrew, and with its glamorous repertory extolling the Apostle James, patron saint of Spain – the next principal polyphonic source preserved in the peninsula may appear somewhat drab by comparison. Actually, however, the *Huelgas Codex*,[122] which was labelled simply an early fourteenth-century Troper when first discovered in 1904, is as important a document in its kind as is the older and more spectacular codex.

The Huelgas Codex takes its name from Las Huelgas, the *monasterio* for Cistercian Nuns founded c. 1180 on the outskirts of Burgos by the warrior-king Alfonso VIII ("de Las Navas"). Lacking any famous relics, this convent never became an international shrine drawing revenues from vast hordes of pilgrims. But it did become enormously wealthy, largely because of royal donations. Alfonso VIII and his wife, Eleanor of England (daughter of Henry II), were but the first of a long line of patrons who enriched it beyond any religious house in Castile.

In such a convent one would expect to encounter relics of the highest musical culture. Fortunately the French armies which sacked it during the Napoleonic era and the greedy hirelings of Mendizábal during the later wave of expropriation left Las Huelgas its codex – which now enjoys the distinction of being "the one great monument of medieval music still preserved in its identical place of origin."

The codex which reaches 168 leaves, has been transcribed, annotated, and its music compared with examples from other contemporary polyphonic sources by Higinio Anglés in his three-volume publication now recognized as a scholarly classic, *El Còdex Musical de Las Huelgas* (Barcelona: Institut d'Estudis Catalans, 1931). The following statistics may prove a useful introduction.

I The 186 items in the Huelgas repertory comprise 87 compositions *a 2*, 49 monodies, 48 compositions *a 3*, one *a 4*, and one without music. Two-part compositions, then occupy almost half the manuscript.

II These items are broken down in Anglés's edition under the following headings: 59 motets, 32 conductus, 31 *Benedicamus* (usually troped), 31 proses (= sequences), 30 organa (for the Mass), a Credo (same as that of Tournai), an exercise in solfège (no. 177), and a textless monody (no. 11).

III As for the 136 polyphonic pieces in Huelgas, Anglés himself printed alternate versions of some 46 from other MSS, besides listing concordances for 30 more. At least 38

[122] Discovery was first announced by Dom Luciano Serrano in *¿Que es canto gregoriano?* (Barcelona, 1905), p. 140. See Anglés, *Huelgas*, II, xiii.

of the 59 Huelgas motets appear in other contemporary sources. The high incidence of *Hu* music in MSS copied abroad certifies the international character of the *Hu* repertory.[123] Motets of French provenience are the rule, but Handschin has advanced reasons for believing that at least four may be of English origin (Items 101, 107, 121, 133).[124]

IV   As befits a source containing a predominantly international repertory, *Hu* proves to have been copied in the main by scribes who had fully mastered the principles of *ars antiqua* notation.[125]

V   Though the one composer actually mentioned by name in *Hu*, a certain Johan Rodrigues, was obviously Spanish, not many of the polyphonic pieces can have been peninsular in their origin. The weight of manuscript evidence proves that the *ars antiqua* repertory radiated out from Paris and other French centers to such "peripheral" areas as Spain and England.

VI   When crossing the Pyrenees the *ars antiqua* motets underwent a "sea-change," the bones becoming coral and the eyes pearls: i.e., not one voice-part was suffered to retain its originally profane text, but all were new-furbished with decorous Latin.

VII   In other ways besides substituting sacred for profane texts the compilers of *Hu* showed their staid disposition. Their favored rhythmic mode was, for instance, the conservative first mode.[126] The repertory, especially if much of it was copied as late as the death of the abbess María González (c. 1335), seems old-fashioned by French standards. Though such feats as opening a conductus in canon (Item 149), organizing over a "ground bass" (Item 133), voice-interchange in a three-part *Benedicamus* (Item 40), mutation of identical melodic material by a change of rhythmic mode (Item 154),[127] and use of borrowed material in a supposedly "original" conductus (Item 156),[128] along with others, can be found in *Hu*, still no feat can be localized as either typically Castilian or a new departure at the time the manuscript was copied.

FOUR *Benedicamus* (Items 173, 174, 178, 183) and an *Ave Maria* (Item 156)[129] are ascribed to the Spanish composer, Johan Rodrigues (fl. 1325),[130] in *Hu*. Two of the Benedicamus are monodic, the other three pieces being for two voices. From a parochially Spanish viewpoint the lively jottings of one of the anonymous scribes in upper and

---

[123] *Hu*, I, 233–235.

[124] Handschin (*Musica Disciplina*, V [1951]), p. 105.

[125] *Hu*, II, xviii.

[126] *Hu*, I, 232.

[127] M. F. Bukofzer, "Interrelations between Conductus and Clausula," *Annales Musicologiques*, I (Paris: Société de Musique d'Autrefois, 1953), pp. 98–100. The modal transformation to which Bukofzer calls attention will be seen if bars 37–44 on *Huelgas*, III, 358 are compared with bars 71–84 on *Hu*, III, 360–361.

[128] Bukofzer, *op. cit.*, p. 98.

[129] Anglés doubts Rodrigues actually wrote the *Ave Maria* ascribed to him (*Hu*, I, 325).

[130] For Rodrigues's date, see *Hu*, II, xviii.

lower margins of *Hu* are perhaps more interesting than the few pieces assigned to Rodrigues.

The copyist in question admired Rodrigues, quoted him as an authority, and even went to unwarranted lengths: ascribing to his idol the tenor of the last motet in *Hu*, *Mellis stilla* though Anglés proves it cannot have been his.[131] Rodrigues was a paragon of wisdom according to the scribe; and if he edited a motet (Item 112) [132] it could be sight-sung with confidence that its parts would fit. He evidently specialized in editing tenor-parts, and taught his singers that upper parts sung without their tenor [i.e., lowest voice-part] were of no more value than a company of soldiers without a captain (*mas sin tenura non valemos mas que valen las compannas sin cabdiello o tanto*).[133] If doubt arose concerning the proper tenor – sometimes the tenor part is separated several pages from the upper parts in *Hu* or missing altogether (Items 157 and 109) – the singers could turn to him for aid: "sing this with the tenor which Johan Rodrigues corrected," says the copyist at the bottom of fol. 106v. (Item 108). Though his identity is not disclosed by such remarks, he must surely have been music director in Las Huelgas. The tenors which he "corrected" were not thereby improved according to Anglés.[134] However if the *Hu* scribe may be believed, Rodrigues could do no wrong.

The copyist on one occasion turned rhymester. With poetic license he caused the conductus *O gloriosa Dei genitrix Virgo* (Item 151) to speak thus in the first person: [135]

> Those with little knowledge should not sing me.
> Let them not cause offense by their errors,
> For I am a conductus and difficult to sing.
> The ignorant who try me cannot avoid mistakes,
> But first practice me, for none can successfully sing me at first sight.

As for Rodrigues's music, it must be immediately confessed that Anglés discounts its value, not considering it the equal of contemporary foreign models.[136] But "poor and ill-favoured a thing" though Rodrigues's music may be, still a Touchstone might say "it is mine own." The second of the *Benedicamus* (Item 174), a festive piece, is clearly divided into eight four-bar phrases. What the upper voice sings in the first four bars the lower sings in the next four, and vice versa. Since the first eight bars are exactly repeated four times, the structure is pellucid. The piece is C-Major music, despite its date; and the tunes could be easily change-rung on English bells. The fourth *Benedicamus* is shown as an accompanying example.

The voice-parts in Rodrigues's four *Benedicamus* never climb higher than e above Middle C nor do they descend lower than $B_1\flat$ on the third line of the bass-clef. Since in

---

[131] *Hu*, I, 345. But Anglés thinks the two upper voice-parts may be by Rodrigues ([*triple*] *segurament obra del susdit*).

[132] *Hu*, III, 211.

[133] *Hu*, III, 205 (Item 109).

[134] *Hu*, I, 265, 270.

[135] *Hu*, III, 331 (fol. 140v. in original manuscript).

[136] *Hu*, I, 112, 265, 325.

Benedicamus XXVIII
Virgini matri

Huelgas Codex, fols. 163v.–164.   JOHAN RODRIGUES

1. Be————ne————di—ca—mus Vir————gi—
2. Ip————si————a——ga—mus di——vi—

—ni ma————————tri, Que nos con—ci————li—at De—
—ni—ta————————ti, No—stre con—iun————cte hu—

—o Pa————tri In hac san—cta na-ti-vi-ta—te Do-mi————————no.
—ma-ni-ta————ti, In hac san—cta so-lem-ni-ta—te Gra-ci————as.

Let us bless the Virgin Mother who in this holy birth reconciles us with God the Father.
Let us give thanks during this holy festival to her through whom our human flesh is joined to the Godhead.

Hu are found a number of motets known elsewhere in versions a fourth or fifth higher, Anglés suspects that the musical examples copied in *Hu* under Rodrigues's direction were intended for men's chorus.[137] The Las Huelgas choir in such a case would have enrolled only adult male voices. By contrast, Santiago de Compostela cathedral choir boasted boys' voices at least a century earlier – on the evidence of those *Codex Calixtinus* rubrics which designate *pueri* as singers of specific chants.[138] It is interesting that this distinction between the choirs of *monasterios* (Las Huelgas) and *catedrales* (Santiago de Compostela) began to be made so early in Spanish music history.[139]

[137] *Hu*, I, 231–232.
[138] *Codex Calixtinus*, III, 49, n. 4.
[139] This same distinction held during the sixteenth century. The amount of music for equal voices in the Morales and Guerrero repertories proves that choirs entirely composed of *voces mudadas* were prevalent. When Charles V retired to Yuste monastery, his choir though containing the finest voices in Spain was entirely adult. The Escorial Jeronymite choir to which Philip II listened in his later years was similarly adult.

The *Benedicamus* shown as an example is by no means as square-cut as Rodrigues's *In hoc festo*. But a pair of four-bar phrases (the second answering the first) divides the first half. Both monodic *Benedicamus*, like the example *a 2* here shown, are in dorian mode. The monodies do differ because of their larger proportion of bold skips, a rising minor seventh occurring in one and a descending octave in the other.

Still another composition, a two-part *Ave Maria*, appears as Rodrigues's in Anglés's edition (Item 156). A conductus, it ends with a melisma (bars 66–76 in *Hu*, III, 375) borrowed outright from the two lower voices of another conductus in *Hu*, the three-part *Mater patris filia* (bars 89–99, *Hu*, III, 362). As a rule, a conductus implies newly composed music. But as Bukofzer has shown, rare examples did incorporate borrowed material. The *Ave Maria* conductus ascribed to Rodrigues contains just such a borrowed section.

Llibre Vermell ("The Red Book")

ONLY A FEW scattered polyphonic items survive in Catalonian MSS copied before 1300. At the Paris Bibliothèque Nationale lat. 5132 (fol. 108v.) shows one such polyphonic piece – a conductus *a 2* copied during the late twelfth or early thirteenth century. Entitled *Cedit frigus hiemale*, this joyous salute to Easter in virelai form was copied into a *Collectaneum* at the Ripoll monastery of St. Mary's around 1200. Hans Spanke published it in 1932 (*Neuphilologische Mitteilungen*, XXXIII, 20–22) and Anglés again in 1935 (*La música a Catalunya fins al segle XIII*, p. 257). Anglés also at pp. 227–230 in his 1935 volume published the two sequences *a 2* which survive at fols. 17v. and 20 in Orfeó Català MS 1, *Marie preconio* and *Potestati magni maris*. The MS from which these two Marian sequences were drawn is a vellum *Troparium* of 27 leaves, copied shortly before 1300. From the same source he extracted two troped Osanna's *a 2*. The first of these (at fol. 5) begins *Sospitati dedit mundum*. The second (at fol. 5v.) begins *Ad honorem Virginis* (*La música a Catalunya*, pp. 243–245). Both belong to Marian masses.

The most important of medieval Catalonian musical sources was however discovered a century earlier by the industrious Dominican savant, Jaime Villanueva. He it was who in his *Viage literario a las iglesias de España*, VII (Valencia: Imp. de Oliveres, 1821), first advertised the existence of MS 1 at the Montserrat monastery library. What is more, he dated the MS correctly when he assigned it to the middle of the fourteenth century. He also understood at once that the *varios tratados curiosos* in this MS were gathered for but one purpose, the edification of pilgrims visiting Our Lady's shrine at Montserrat. The various songs, some with Latin, some with Catalonian, texts were meant to be sung and danced by those who had climbed the steep 2910-foot ascent to this most famous of Catalonian shrines; the formulas and prayers were meant to be said by them; and the *sermones y exhortaciones* preached to them (*Viage literario*, VII, 152–153).

The *Llibre Vermell* (as the MS is now commonly called) breathes throughout not only an air of popular piety, but also would seem to contain nothing but homegrown musical bouquets. Montserrat, though an ancient enough shrine, never drew such large numbers from abroad as Santiago de Compostela. Quite appropriately, then, the devotional songs in the *Llibre Vermell* do not pretend – as do those of the Calixtine Codex – to foreign authorship. Whereas some dozen Calixtine musical items are ascribed to contributors from such French cities as Bourges, Chartres, Soissons, and Troyes, none of the ten *Llibre Vermell* musical items is ascribed to any foreign author (or to any named author whatsoever, for that matter). Two of the ten *llibre* pieces set Catalonian-language texts. The rest set Latin texts. Whether in Catalonian or in Latin, every text in the *llibre* either praises the Virgin, whose carved image St. Luke purportedly brought from Galilee to Montserrat (some few miles above Barcelona), or "purges" the pilgrim about to worship at her shrine.

Again, unlike the Calixtine musical items, the ten *llibre* pieces are not heterogeneously scattered throughout the whole codex, but on the contrary are grouped together (at fols. 21v.–26v.). With the exception of the first *llibre* item, all the rest – monodic and polyphonic pieces alike – are cast in measured rhythms. Otto Ursprung – who in 1921 published transcriptions of the entire *llibre* music at the close of his article, "Spanisch-katalanische Liedkunst des 14. Jahrhunderts" (*Zeitschrift für Musikwissenschaft*, IV, 136–160) – elected to use no less than five diverse time-signatures. For the polyphony he employed C (*Laudemus Virginem* and *Splendens ceptigera*, both of which are rounds, for three voices); $\frac{2}{4}$ (*Stella splendens*, a dance-song *a 2*, in virelai form); $\frac{6}{4}$ (*Inperayritz de la ciutat ioyosa*, a strophic 2-part song the seven stanzas of which celebrate Mary's attributes in Catalonian); and ¢ (*Mariam matrem*, a virelai *a 3*, only the upper voice-part of which is texted). For the monody he used C (*Los set gotxs*, a responsorial dance-song, the leader singing of Mary's seven joys *en vulgar cathallan*, the replying pilgrims singing the Hail Mary in Latin); and $\frac{3}{4}$ (*Cuncti simus, Polorum regina*, and *Ad mortem festinamus*, each of which is again a responsorial dance-song).

AT THE HEAD of the ten musical items preserved in the *Llibre Vermell* stands an "antiphona dulcis harmonia." Entitled *O Virgo Splendens* (fols. 21v.–22), this antiphon differs radically from any of the nine successor pieces in the *llibre*. The differences are worth naming. (1) Only *O Virgo Splendens* is listed in the MS as an antiphon, and therefore, properly speaking, a liturgical item. *Laudemus Virginem* and *Splendens ceptigera*, the rounds *a 3* which immediately follow at fol. 23 in the MS, are each listed as a *caça* (= chace [Fr.], caccia [It.], caza [Sp.], canon [Eng.]). *Stella splendens*, the Latin virelai at fol. 22v. is listed in the MS as a *cantilena omni dulcedine plena* ("song filled with every kind of sweetness"). *Los set gotxs* at fol. 23v. is called a *Ballada* (= ballata [It.]). Nothing but *O Virgo* is classified however under a liturgical type. Other unused liturgical types would be hymns, responsories, and sequences. (2) Only *O Virgo* is cast in unitary rhythm. Each incise consists of 15 notes transcribable as quavers, followed by a last note worth a crotchet. (3) In *O Virgo*, each of the dozen incises halts invariably on a D-A incomplete chord.

O Virgo is the earliest known canon composed in the peninsula. To the left of the opening four-line staff appears at fol. 21v. this notation: *Caça de ij[obus] vel tribus* (two-in-one, or three-in-one canon). When viewed as a canon *a 2*, leader-and-follower voices always produce these harmonic intervals – unisons, thirds, fifths, sixths, octaves (except for one fourth and two seconds). Since out of 192 harmonic intervals only 3 are fourths or seconds, and even these three are introduced in conjunct motion, the composer must be presumed to have disliked fourths or seconds when writing two-part counterpoint. The rubric however reads, *Caça de ij[obus] vel tribus*. Not only does performance as a two-in-one canon, but also as a three-in-one, therefore fall within the composer's purview. Realized in a three-in-one canon, the leader and his second follower do freely wander about in parallel fourths. They also collide in sevenths and ninths. Then again, they often move in parallel unisons. Either the solution of the canon *a 3* suggested by Ursprung (and earlier by Dom Gregori Suñol in his article, "Els Cants dels Romeus," *Analecta Montserratensia*, I [1917], at pp. 119–120) must be presumed at fault insofar as the third voice is concerned, or the composer considered that his rules for harmonic intervals between first and second voices did not apply to harmonic intervals between first and third voices. It should perhaps be noted in passing that Ursprung often disregarded the ligatures of the MS. His plainsong transcription (*ZfMW*, IV, 151) contains material errors at "vir"-go and "cel"-so. The straitjacketing of such a melody in classic neums gives it, moreover, a quite deceptive appearance. By comparison with *O Virgo splendens* (which because of its length cannot have been readily memorized by pilgrims) the anapestic *Laudemus virginem* and *Splendens ceptigera* are such elementary canons that an overnight guest could have learned words and music of both. Even when sung *a 3*, only two notes ever sound at once – so elementary is the canonic concept. Ossia texts appear below each of the two Marian texts in the MS. These optional lyrics voice the pilgrim's sorrow for his sins. Clearly, these rounds are to be thought of not as art but rather as "teaching material." Because they are part-music that the uninstructed can have sung, *Laudemus* and *Splendens* enjoy at least however the merit of being the two provably *volkstümlich* polyphonic items in the "Red Book."

Interestingly enough, all the polyphonic pieces in the *Llibre Vermell* adhere to the D-mode. No accidentals appear anywhere throughout the polyphony. Flats are needed, however, in the upper of the two voices at the ninth note in *Stella splendens;* and in the lowest of the three at the third note in *Mariam matrem*. The stitching of the phrases throughout both *Stella splendens* and *Mariam matrem* produces a virelai pattern. On the other hand, *Inperayritz* divides otherwise: abcd ecef. In *Inperayritz* every phrase, except "b" and "d," extends to five bars of $\frac{6}{4}$ (Ursprung's transcription); "b" and "d" extend to only four bars. Each of the eight phrases ends on an octave, preceded by a sixth (with flatted leading-tone in the top voice). In succession, the finals of the eight phrases read thus: DAED; AEAD.

Mariam matrem is according to Gregori Suñol *el més notable* piece in the *Llibre Vermell*, and *de major vàlua*. Ursprung's transcription has been corrected by Anglés. The treble should, for instance, enter not on the fourth but on the second beat in meas. 23 of his version. His time-values go askew in meas. 27, during which he omits a beat. But that the upper two voice-parts were composed to fit the tenor can by no means be doubted. A virelai-pattern emerges in each part; cadences synchronize in all voices. Probably the slow-moving tenor was a cantus prius factus: though it is not likely to have been a branch pruned from an elderly Gregorian vine. Or at least Suñol, whose acquaintance with the Gregorian repertory was exhaustive, could find no plainsong prototype (*Analecta Montserratensia*, I, 167).

THE FOUR already-cited monodies in the *Llibre Vermell* have attracted more critical attention as a group than the part-music. All are dance-songs. *Los set gotxs, Cuncti simus,* and *Polorum regina* are each headed in the MS, "*aball redon*." Each was therefore meant for singing while joyous pilgrims danced about the Virgin's image. Both Trend and Reese have pointed to an interesting likeness between the first incise of *Polorum regina*

Mariam matrem *

Biblioteca de Montserrat: MS 1, fol. 25.

* *Praise and extol the Virgin Mother Mary together with Jesus Christ.* Mary, sanctuary of the ages, protect us; Jesus, secure refuge, hear us. Be now for us scattered abroad an effectual shelter spread over the whole world.

and the tune with words, *Yo me yua mi madre,* to be found at p. 306 in Salinas's *De musica libri septem* (Salamanca, 1577). Possibly, then, *Polorum regina* was nothing but another traditional folktune baptized, like the Reading rota, with Latin words. Reese noticed the unusual form of *Los set gotxs* – aaB for the introduction, and aa ‖ :b: ‖ B for each of the seven stanzas, that, like the telling of a rosary, recount the Virgin's seven joyful mysteries. Since "B" in *Los set gotxs* is the Latin Ave Maria, this one item in the *Llibre Vermell* should be classed as macaronic. *Cuncti simus* divides into symmetrical four-bar phrases. Such symmetry, for that matter, can be discerned in all the *llibre* dance-songs.

Reese not only prints the final monody from the *llibre* – *Ad mortem festinamus* – at p. 375 in his *Music in the Middle Ages;* but also stresses its importance as the "oldest known surviving example with music of a 'Dance of Death', that curious and mysterious outgrowth of the period of the Black Death which ravaged Europe from 1347–48." The Dance of Death took its origin in Spain, according to Anglés – who in his "El *Llibre Vermell* de Montserrat" (*Anuario Musical,* X [1955], p. 68) calls attention to a fragmentary Latin example, without music, conserved at Toledo in an eleventh-century Visigothic manuscript. In the *Llibre Vermell*, a skeleton lying in an open coffin has been drawn after the ninth and last strophe of the poem. The music itself, for all its dancing rhythms and vaunting sequences, is not likely to have been intended for a jest in the presence of death. As in the morality, *Danza de la muerte* (composed in twelve-syllable octaves around 1400 on the theme of Death, the Great Leveller), the purpose seems rather to preach terror and penitence.

In clearcut four-bar phrases, *Ad mortem festinamus* everywhere implies heavy footfalls on first beats. The first bar of four always starts with a trochee. Each third bar ends with a skip, or breaks into a running rhythm.

Nascent "Spanish" Style

THE HUELGAS CODEX in addition to containing the marginal comments of a scribe who was perhaps an overzealous admirer of Rodrigues, contains three extremely interesting annotations written below the notes of the tenor part on folios 147v., 148, and 148v., *manera francessa, hespanona, manera francessa*. In these three passages, then, one finds first "French style," then "Spanish," then "French" again, definitely prescribed. The exact differences between these national styles c. 1325 is a problem not yet solved. Handschin and Bukofzer argue that the French at that date preferred the more advanced rhythmic modes, whereas the Spanish clung to the first mode. But however the national differences manifested themselves, it cannot be doubted that some sort of distinction existed.

Still earlier (c. 1280) the English theorist, Anonymous IV, knew of a distinction between Spanish and French methods of notation. The French notated rhythmic patterns with considerable precision, whereas the Spanish, and also the English, were content to let the singer's good sense and experience dictate the rhythmic mode (*sed solo intellectu procedebant semper cum proprietate et perfectione operatoris in eisdem, velut in libris Hispanorum et Pompilonensium* [Pamplona = northernmost Spain], *et in libris Anglicorum*).[140]

Within Spain, especially where Moslem clashed with Christian, the Castilian was fully aware of the musical differences separating his style from that of the Arab. Our best fourteenth-century evidence for this assertion comes from Juan Ruiz, Archpriest of Hita, who in quatrains 1513–1519 of his poem *El libro de buen amor* listed instruments which were unsuited for Arab music, and by contrast those which suited the music of the Christian Spaniard.

Instruments in Fourteenth-Century Usage

RUIZ, who occupies a place in medieval Spanish literature similar to that held by Chaucer (d. 1400) in English letters, left a comparable source of musical allusions in his *El libro de buen amor* (c. 1343). According to Clair C. Olson's study, "Chaucer and the Music of the Fourteenth Century" in *Speculum* (XVI, 64–91 [January, 1941]), Chaucer preferred vocal rather than instrumental music,[141] and mentioned no more than 21 [142] of the at least 50 instruments [143] current in England during his epoch. The instruments mentioned by Chaucer are listed below in alphabetical order so that they can be conveniently compared with Ruiz's list:

bell, beme, clarioun, cornemuse, doucet, floute, giterne, harpe, horn, lute, naker, organ, pype, rede, rote, rubible, sautrye, shalmye, simphonye, tabour, trompe.

---

[140] *CS*, I, 345. Anonymous IV also tells (*CS*, I, 350a) of a "certain Spaniard" who composed the hocket *a 3, In seculum* (copied in Madrid MS 20486 [facs. publ. by Luther Dittmer in 1957], fol. 122v.; cf. Yvonne Rokseth, *Polyphonies du XIIIe Siècle*, II, 2).

[141] Olson, p. 91.   [142] *Ibid.*, p. 74.   [143] *Ibid.*, p. 66.

Ruiz, though he left a poem reaching only 6912 lines, and therefore a much smaller body of verse than Chaucer, named almost twice as many instruments. Some notion of their variety can be obtained from the next list (line-numbers from *El libro de buen amor* are given in parentheses):

albogue, pastoral recorder (1213b, 1517a)
albogón, large recorder (1233a)
añafil, Moorish trumpet (1096c, 1234a)
atanbal (= *atabal*), kettledrum (1234a)
atanbor, drum (894c, 895c, 898b, 1227d)
axabeba, transverse flute (1233a)
baldosa, zither played with a plectrum (1233b)
caño entero, large canon (1232a)
    medio caño, small canon (1230a)
canpana, bell (383d, 623d, 1222c)
çanpõna, syrinx (1213b, 1517a)
caramillo, pipe made of reed (1000c, 1213c, 1517a)
cascabel, sleighbell (723a)
çitola, citole (1019d, 1213d, 1516c)
dulçema, shawm (1233a)
flauta, recorder (1230c)
gaita, cornemuse (1233a)
galipe francisco, small French recorder (1230b)
guitarra latina, guitar, probably akin to a lyre (1228d)

guitarra morisca, guitar, probably in the modern sense (1228a)
harpa, harp (1230a)
laúd, lute (1228c, 1511c)
mandurria, bandore (1233d, 1517a)
odreçillo, bagpipe (1000b, 1233c, 1516c)
órgano, organ, portable (1232c)
pandero, tambourine (470d, 705d, 1003b, 1212c)
    panderete, small tambourine (1232a)
rabé, rebeck (1229a)
    rabé morisco, Moorish rebeck (1230a)
rota, rote (= rotte) (1230c)
salterio, psaltery (1307c, 1554c)
sinfonía, symphony (1233b, 1516b)
sonajas de açófar, metal clappers (1232b)
tamborete, side drum (1230d)
trompa, trumpet (1234a)
vihuela de arco, bowed fiddle (1231a, 1516a)
    vihuela de pendola, stringed instrument, played with quill plectrum (1229d)

As if the mere naming of 37 different instruments were not enough, he goes on to characterize each instrument: the *mandurria* as "silly" and "whining," the *rabé* as sufficiently "noisy" for such a traditional Arab tune as *Calvi garabi*,[144] the *tamborete* as the "indispensable" time-beater when instruments play in ensemble. He praises the versatility of the *vihuela de arco*, whose sweet sounds lull us asleep at one moment but whose commanding voice awakens us to lofty thoughts at the next.

WHEN A CHORUS in an Easter procession sang motets (1232c), they did not perform a cappella but were instead accompanied by portable organs, says Ruiz. Though the marchers did not yet sing their chanzonetas in the *vernacular*, still he insists that they *played* as well as sang such chanzonetas as *Mane nobiscum, Domine* (1241d). Almost invariably – even in the golden age – Spanish religious music has been "played" – not just sung. So closely have voices and instruments been associated from the beginning that already in Gonzalo de Berceo (1180–1246) the verb *organar* can mean *to sing*: "las aves que *organan* entre essos fructales" (the birds singing amid those fruit trees [*Los Milagros de Nuestra Sennora*, 26a]).[145]

---

[144] Salinas cites this tune in *De musica libri septem* (Salamanca: M. Gastius, 1577), p. 339; but with *Calui vi calui/Calui araui* for its title.
[145] On the meaning of *organar* in Gonzalo de Berceo see Rufino Lanchetas, *Gramática y Vocabulario de las obras de Gonzalo de Berceo* (Madrid: Sucs. de Rivadeneyra, 1900), p. 535. For *violero*, see p. 787. The poem

RUIZ'S POEM, though the most conspicuous, is by no means a unique fourteenth-century source. In the anonymous *Poema de Alfonso XI* (lines 407a–409d), the "blandishing" lute, the bowed fiddle, rebeck, psaltery, guitar, the "Moorish" *exabeba* (= axabeba), the small canon, cornemuse, harp, and "otros estromentos mil" [146] resound through chamber, hall, and chapel of Las Huelgas – the medieval Westminster Abbey of Castile – during the coronation ceremonies of Alfonso XI (1311–1350). In the neighboring kingdom of Aragon, John I (1350–1395), a composer [147] as well as patron of poets and performers, lavishly rewarded his instrumentalists. He not only sent favorite players as far afield as Germany to study, but did his best to lure prominent foreign virtuosi to his court. His retinue included players on such instruments as organs, harp, rote, *xelamia* (shawm), *bombarda*, and *cornamusa*.[148] He himself described the new *exaquier* as an "instrument like an organ (i.e., keyed) but sounding with strings" (*semblant d'orguens que sona ab cordes* [1388]).[149] In correspondence of the same year he mentioned *Johan dels orguens*, the Fleming who played the *exaquier:* the latter was to bring along to Saragossa "the book in which are noted the *estampies* and other things he knows how to play on the *exaquier*" (*lo llibre on te notades les estampides e les altres obres que sab sobrel exaquier e los orguens*).[150] A poem written to celebrate the birth of John II (at Barcelona, 1397) contains allusions to *escaques* (a cognate word for exaquier) and to the *monicordio*.[151] At the baptism, these instruments (with harps) accompanied the singers.

A still more diversified list of instruments than any thus far alluded to can be found in the *Cancionero de Ramon de Llabia* published c. 1490 by John Hurus at Saragossa. The catalogue occurs in the poem by Fernan Ruyz of Seville, "Una coronacion de Nuestra Señora." [152] Because he mentions hocketing as a still current practice, he probably lived in the fourteenth rather than in the fifteenth century. He names 35 different instruments, including the *monicordio* and *escaquer* (= exaquier). A half dozen instruments mentioned in this source are not to be found even in the *Diccionario histórico*, which

---

Los Milagros is printed in *Bibl. de Autores Españoles: Poetas Castellanos anteriores al siglo XV*, ed. Tomás A. Sánchez (Madrid: Suc. de Hernando, 1921), Vol. LVII. The quoted line occurs on p. 104; the poet imagines that the birds sing in organum: "No one could ever hear better tuned organum, or more harmonious sounds; some sang the fifth above while others doubled [below]; still others sang the tenor which governs all the parts, all moving when it moves."

[146] *Bibl. de Aut. Esp.*, ed. Sánchez, Vol. LVII, p. 489.

[147] Felipe Pedrell, "Jean I d'Aragon, Compositeur de Musique," *Riemann-Festschrift* (Leipzig: Max Hesses Verlag, 1909), p. 240. John I wrote a letter January 4, 1380, in which he mentioned having composed a rondeau *a 3* and said he hoped to write a virelai and a ballade.

[148] *Ibid.*, p. 239. Further on the *cornamusa* (1357), *laut* (1392, 1402), *rebeba* (1313) = *rabeu, rota* (1383), *arpa* (1384, 1385, 1382), *naffiler* (1371), *guitarra* (1424, 1429), *exabeba* (1338), *xilimia* (1308) = *xalamia* (1418), at the Aragonese court in Francisco de P. Baldelló, "La música en la casa de los Reyes de Aragón," *Anuario Musical*, XI (1956), p. 43. The rote-player Walter previously had served the king of England, p. 50; the lutanist Salomó Çaçon was Jewish (fl. 1392–1413).

[149] *Riemann-Festschrift*, p. 233.

[150] *Ibid.*, p. 232. For his other musical correspondence, see Walter Salmen, "Iberische Hofmusikanten des späten Mittelalters auf Auslandsreisen," *Anuario Musical*, XI, 55.

[151] Juan Alonso de Baena, *El Cancionero de J. A. de Baena* (Madrid: Imp. de la Publicidad, 1851), p. 209 (No. 227: "Este desir fiso el maestro Fray Diego de Valençia de la orden de Sant Françisco").

[152] R. Isnard, "Anciens instruments de musique," *Revue hispanique*, XLIII (June-August, 1918), pp. 559–560. See also *Cancionero de Ramón de Llavia* (Madrid: Soc. de Bibliófilos Españoles, 1945), pp. 302–303.

began publication at Madrid in 1933 with the intention of registering every known word in the Spanish language.

Music and Learning in Medieval Christian Spain

SALAMANCA UNIVERSITY, though not as ancient as the Universities of Paris and Oxford by half a century, was nevertheless the first medieval university with a chair of music.[153] Established by a royal rather than a papal charter, Salamanca received its letters patent from Ferdinand III in 1243. Eleven years later his son, Alfonso X, extended its charter and set the salaries of its professors in law, medicine, and the liberal arts. The chair of music at Salamanca thus antedates the formal endowment of chairs at Oxford (1627) and Cambridge (1684).

Alfonso X must himself have originated the idea of establishing such a chair, since there was no foreign precedent for him to have followed. Juan Gil of Zamora (= Aegidius Zamorensis), his biographer and close personal associate, said that he "composed many exceptionally beautiful *cantilenas*." [154] If he was as creative as the Cantigas suggest, the idea of endowing a chair rightly occurred to him first, even though none existed as yet in Italian, French, or English universities. He set the annual value of the chair at 50 *maravedis* (those of canon law and medicine were valued at 300 and 200 respectively). The original deed of the William Heather music lectureship at Oxford provided a correspondingly low sum, only £17.6.8 a year.

In 1411 the reigning antipope, Benedict XIII – a Spaniard (Pedro de Luna) – granted Salamanca unusual privileges. In listing its 25 endowed professorships he specifically named the chair of music. Though the full list of thirteenth- and fourteenth-century *maestros en órgano* has yet to be reconstructed, the earliest occupants whose names and dates are known held cathedral appointments simultaneously.

OF THE THEORY texts by medieval Spanish clerics which survive one is a *Breviarium de Musica*, by Oliva (fl. 1065),[155] monk of Ripoll, the principal center of early Catalonian musical culture; the other an *Ars musice* by Juan Gil of Zamora (fl. 1265), the Franciscan who tutored Alfonso X's son and heir, Sancho IV (1257–1295). Oliva wrote at the request of a fellow-monk who wished instruction in the art of dividing the monochord. Juan Gil, "doctor" but of what faculty is not known, wrote his treatise to comply with a request made by the head of the Franciscan order, John of Parma. The latter adjured him to write "briefly and simply" (*brevius et puerilius* [*GS*, II, 370a]).

Gil is the earliest Spanish writer to dwell on the "affects" of the church modes.[156] But

---

[153] Enrique Esperabé Arteaga, *Historia [pragmática é interna] de la Universidad de Salamanca* (Salamanca: Imp. y Lib. de F. Nuñez Izquierdo, 1914–1917), I, 22: "Otrosi mando e tengo por bien que ayan vn maestro en organo e yo que le [de] çinquenta maravedis cada anno."

[154] Marqués de Valmar, I, 126, n.1: *ad praeconium Virginis gloriosae, multas et perpulchras composuit cantilenas, sonis convenientibus et proportionibus musicis modulatas.*

[155] On Oliva see Anglés, *La música a Catalunya fins al segle XIII* (Barcelona: Institut d'Estudis Catalans, 1935), pp. 64–66.

[156] Gerbert, *Scriptores*, II, 387–388.

if the first peninsular to read an exact emotional meaning into each mode, he on the other hand but follows in Isidore's footsteps when he describes at length the *tuba, buccina, tibia, calamus, fistula, pandorium, sambuca, symphonia, tympanum, cithara, psalterium, lyra, cymbala, sistrum,* and *tintinnabulum* – to list their Latin names in his order. Half-apologetically he adds the names of three instruments of "recent" origin (*postremo inventa*): [157] the canon, guitar, and rabel. He distinguishes the canon under two types, full and half size (*caño entero* and *medio caño*). He perhaps differentiates canon from psaltery and guitar from cithara because he knows the canon, guitar, and rabel to be Arabian instruments. In any event he does not confound them with Isidore's ancient prototypes.

Unlike many medieval treatises, Juan Gil's can be closely dated. He says in his introduction that he writes at his minister-general's request. Since John of Parma served as head of the Friars Minor during only the decade from 1247–1257 Gil must obviously have completed the *Ars musice* before being summoned to the royal household as tutor to the future Sancho IV. John of Parma visited Spain on a tour of inspection late in 1248. His commissioning Gil's treatise, and the preservation of the manuscript in Roman rather than Spanish archives, would both indicate that in the *Ars musice* we are dealing with a treatise that epitomizes the best peninsular opinion on musical issues at approximately the date the Salamanca chair was founded.

Though Gil claims only the merits of a compiler, he quotes his various sources – from Aristoxenus [158] to John of Afflighem [Cotton] [159] – accurately and with discrimination. His treatise may mean that Zamora – only 40 miles above Salamanca – enjoyed an even older tradition of theoretical studies. Gil at the time of writing called himself "lector insufficiens Zamorensis" but the *insufficiens* should be understood only as a token of modesty. Not perhaps by chance did one of the most "learned" of Spanish Renaissance composers arise also from Zamora, the celebrated papal singer, Escobedo.

JUST AS GIL's treatise is preserved in a foreign archive, so an occasional foreign treatise hints at Spanish practices. The *Quatuor principalia*, which is conventionally attributed to the Oxford Franciscan, Simon Tunstede (d. 1369),[160] embodies such hints. According to both the *Quatuor principalia* (CS, IV, 257) and *Anonymous I* (CS, III, 337) the minim as a note-value was first used in Navarre, a kingdom which then lay south of the Pyrenees with Pamplona as its capital.[161] The notational puzzles in music composed by Jacomi de Sentluch (served John I of Aragon c. 1378–1382) and Gacian Reyneau (in the royal chapel at Barcelona, 1398–1429) still today confound all but a handful of specialists.[162] The *ne plus ultra* of notational complexity was reached according to Gilbert Reaney in the two-voiced ballade of S. Uciredor (= Rodericus) copied into the Chantilly

---

[157] *Ibid.*, II, 388b.

[158] Aristoxenus cited at 382b and 384b. In addition to Boethius and Isidore, Gil cites Solinus (375a) and Constantinus Africanus (392b).

[159] *Ibid.*, II, 376a, 377b.

[160] Gilbert Reaney, "The MS Chantilly, Musée Condé 1047," *Musica Disciplina*, VIII (1954), p. 73, n.51.

[161] On *minoratas* and *minimas* see also Regula XII, *CS*, I, 397b (Regula XII).

[162] Reaney, p. 74. "The name Senleches is obviously a corruption of Sentluch . . ."

manuscript (item 77) with the title *Angelorum psalat tripudium*.[163] Rodericus – identified as the *Rodriguet de la guitarra* who served Alfonso V (1396–1458) before 1416 – posed such rhythmical conundrums in his *Angelorum psalat tripudium*, though only cantus and tenor are involved, that accurate transcription in modern note-values is probably not possible.[164] For its epoch it is unusual, because the signature includes E♭ and A♭. In ionian mode, it might even be called a piece in E♭ Major.

How high the level of musical erudition rose in late medieval Spain can also be gauged from the foreign treatises circulating in the peninsula. Anglés extracted two from a miscellany of treatises bound together as MS 5-2-25 at the Biblioteca Colombina in Seville, and published them in an article entitled "Dos tractats medievals de música figurada" (*Festschrift für Johannes Wolf* [Berlin: Martin Breslauer, 1929], pp. 6–12). The first treatise concords with so much of a *Tractatus* ascribed to Philippe de Vitry as Coussemaker printed in his *Scriptorum*, III, 29–35; the second is a treatise copied at Verona about 1420 by a Venetian Dominican, Bernardo di Santa Croce, from an original by Nicolaus of Siena (with seven sentences at the end from Egidio de Murino [*CS*, III, 128]). Peninsular singers needed all the theoretical information that treatises such as these could yield – and much more – if they were to cope with such difficulties as are posed by the ballades of Jacomi (*Fuions de ci* [1382]) and Trebor (*En seumeillant* [1389]) commemorating events in the reign of John I of Aragon; or if they were to sing the sacred pieces copied in the Barcelona-Gerona MSS that Hanna Harder and Bruno Stäblein analyzed in their "Neue Fragmente mehrstimmiger Musik aus spanischen Bibliotheken" (*Festschrift Joseph Schmidt-Görg zum 60. Geburtstag* [Bonn: Beethoven-haus, 1957], pp. 131–141).[165]

---

[163] *Ibid.*, p. 79.

[164] *Ibid.* "Rodrigo de la guitarra" still served at the Aragonese court in 1424. See Baldelló, pp. 40, 43. Menéndez Pidal quotes a letter of Alfonso V recommending Rodrigo to Juan II of Castile in 1417. A native of Castile, Rodrigo returned home in August of the next year, but stayed only temporarily. Later (1421) Alfonso made him *Consol dels castellans* at Palermo, with the right to collect imposts from Castilian vessels touching that Sicilian port. For other details of Rodrigo's career, see *Poesía juglaresca* (Madrid: Instituto de Estudios Políticos, 1957), pp. 223–224; for names of Spanish guitarists contemporary with Rodrigo, p. 222.

[165] The Apt composers, Taillandier and Pellisson, are represented in these *neue Fragmente*; also, Johannes Alamanus (serving Pedro IV of Aragon in 1351).

Foundations of
Spanish Musical Theory:
1410-1535

Vernacular versus Latin Treatises

JUST AS the most famous Spanish Renaissance scholar, Juan Luis Vives (1492–1540), wrote exclusively in Latin, so the two best-known Spanish Renaissance theorists, Bartolomé Ramos de Pareja (fl. 1482) and Francisco Salinas (1513–1590) published exclusively in Latin. Also like Vives, they both spent much time abroad. Their choice of Latin brought them recognition – not only in their own centuries, but later – which peninsular theorists who wrote in Spanish have missed.

Only they, for instance, are mentioned in John Hawkins's five-volume *General History of the Science and Practice of Music* (1776) or in Charles Burney's *General History of Music* (1776–1789). Again a century later Hugo Riemann in his *Geschichte der Musiktheorie* (Leipzig, 1898) mentioned Ramos and Salinas, but no others.

The vernacular treatises enjoy one advantage, however, that is denied the classics of peninsular musical scholarship. They bear witness to music culture as it existed, not the ideal culture of savants. When Martínez de Bizcargui (1508) contended that singers should know how to read neums written on a one-line staff he gave the very best of reasons: choirbooks except in cathedrals were – as a rule – copied on a one-line staff. When Juan Bermudo (1555) described the various methods of conducting a group of singers, with the hand alone, with a baton, or by a method he execrated, stamping one's foot, he gave not always a pretty picture but at least a graphic one of music conditions as they existed. When Luys de Villafranca reprinted a choice group of plainchants with constant accidentals, he was not perhaps invoking a style that would be favored by present-day plainsong specialists, but at least he was describing the highly chromaticized readings which Sevillian singers gave the traditional repertory in 1565.

Fernand Estevan (fl. 1410)

LIKE MANY of the vernacular theorists, Estevan was a practical church musician without the university connections of a Ramos or Salinas. He lists himself in his *Reglas de Canto Plano è de Contrapunto, è de Canto de Organo* (Toledo Provincial Library, MS *R 329*) as sacristan of St. Clement's Chapel at Seville – a chapel later incorporated in the newly rising cathedral as the Capilla del Sagrario. He gives an exact date for the completion of his treatise: March 31, 1410. His title promises more, however, than the now-extant section actually performs. The unique copy preserved at Toledo shows no signs of maltreatment, except that the fourth of 51 numbered leaves has been removed. At the end Estevan writes: "finished in the very loyal and noble city of Seville on the last day of March in the year 1410 after Our Lord Jesus Christ's nativity." But even so, it can be but Part I of the larger work advertised in the title, the first dealing with plainsong, the second with counterpoint, the third with polyphony in the more general sense.

Plainsong theory did not remain static but on the contrary made considerable progress between Gil and Estevan. The theoretical range was extended to include e^1 in in the top space of the treble clef.[1] Meantime the gamma ut lost its prestige as the lowest note in the Guidonian hand, the retropolis F_1 (space below bass clef) taking its place. Only those hexachords built over G_1, G, g ("hard"), C, c ("natural"), and F, f ("soft") belonged to the systems of the classic Guidonian theorists. As a result B♮ and b♮ could be "sung" but not E♭, A♭ (or G♯), F♯, and c♯: because to have sung these other accidentals would have required the enlargement of the solmization system to include those hexachords built over $B_1♭$, E♭ (or E♮), D, and A, respectively. But it was precisely these "forbidden" hexachords which won acknowledgment in Spanish plainsong theory sometime between Gil and Estevan. In the *Reglas* these "forbidden" hexachords are called *conjuntas* (singular, *conjunta*).

In approving the frequent use of degree-inflection in plainsong, which in a practical sense is what Estevan's ten *conjuntas* amount to (hexachords over F_1-retropolis, A_1, $B_1♭$, D, E♭, A, B♭, d, e♭, a), he goes exactly counter to the learned opinion of foreign theorists who treated the subject. Jacques de Liège, author of the most exhaustive of all medieval musical encyclopedias, the *Speculum Musicae* (c. 1330), does mention, but reprobates, the introduction of the C♯ or F♯ into plainsong (*CS*, II, 293). According to Jacques, who had studied at Paris and had travelled at least as far as the south of France,[2] the introduction into mensurable music of an f♯ (*cantus*), if above B♮ (*tenor*), is right and necessary (*CS*, II, 294, c. 1); but never in plainsong. He calls any shifting to such hexachords as the *conjuntas* "irregular or false mutation" (*irregularis vel falsa mutatio*), and denounces the use of F♯ or C♯ in plainsong as "improper" license (*CS*, II, 294, c. 1).

If such license was "improper" Spanish plainsong during the fifteenth and sixteenth centuries – on the explicit testimony of every theorist from Estevan (1410) to Villafranca (1565) – became licentious in the extreme.[3] Estevan not only acknowledges these other

---

[1] Jerome of Moravia included e^1 (*CS*, I, 21). Gil implied its existence (*GS*, II, 381).

[2] Roger Bragard, "Le Speculum Musicae," *Musica Disciplina*, VIII (1954), 16–17.

[3] Estevan's tables of hexachords occur at fols. 6v and 38r.

accidentals but exemplifies their use at Seville in the singing of such plainsongs as *Sancta et immaculata, Emendemus in melius, Gaude Maria, Beatus servus, Jesu, Redemptor omnium, In manus tuas, Domine,* and *Ad te levavi animam meam,* in 1410. (Since all of these plainsongs were to be at one time or another set in a polyphonic frame by such Andalusian masters as Morales, Guerrero, and Navarro, knowledge of the long-estab-lished local tradition of accidentalizing can prove most advantageous to the student of their works.)

Estevan himself realizes that classic plainsong theory ignored all accidentals except B♭ and its various octave duplicates. With rare historical acumen, he points to the transpositions out of proper range which the codifiers of Roman chant had made in order to avoid writing theoretically banned E♭'s. Two examples which he mentions can be seen in the 1950 edition of the *Liber Usualis*: *Hodie scietis* (short resp., p. 359) and *Haec dies* (p. 783). The latter ends on A and – as Estevan observes – both have been transposed up a fifth simply to avoid E♭'s. He thinks it far better to square theory with practice, and argues thus:

Without these [additional accidentals] many plainsongs do not sound well nor are they melodious; and there is no way to remedy the situation even though using accidentals runs contrary to plainsong usage. If someone protests that they were invented for counterpoint and do not belong in plainsong, let it be replied that they do suit plainsong and are not only appropriate but often necessary .... Many say also that such additional accidentals do not properly exist and that they are "fictitious" music. Yet look at organs; you will find on them these very accidentals because they are constantly called for in written [mensurable] music. Accidentals, however, are not to be introduced into plainsong merely at random, but only when manifestly needed. In accidentalizing, moreover, the singer ought not to continue using the same accidental indefinitely, but should naturalize as soon as possible [fol. 12r.].

ESTEVAN follows Gil in assigning an "affect" to each of the eight modes. His list of authorities begins with the inevitable Boethius; but continues with such fresher names as Albertus de Rosa,[4] Philippe de Vitry (1291–1361), Guillaume de Machaut (c. 1300–c. 1377), Jean de Muris (c. 1290–c. 1351), and Egidio de Murino (fl. 1389). The latter, an Augustinian, wrote the principal treatise on late *ars nova* notation, *Tractatus de diversis figuris.*[5] He on the other hand claims to owe the better part of his knowledge not to any of these foreigners but to his own Spanish mentor, Remon (= Ramón) de Caçio. This person – probably a Sevillian predecessor – "advanced the art considerably, without derogating from the authority of former masters."

He made many new discoveries which he communicated to me out of kindness. In these he was not anticipated by others, but demonstrated his own entire originality (fols. 21v.–22r.).

Estevan sets down his rules for reading plainchant written on one line, clearly and succinctly. His clues are those now conventionally accepted: look to see where the chant

---

[4] According to Anglés, "La notación musical española en la segunda mitad del siglo XV," *Anuario Musical,* II (1947), 154, Albertus de Rosa was a fourteenth-century Spanish theoretician. Durán also mentions him.

[5] *Die Musik in Geschichte und Gegenwart,* III, columns 1169–1172.

ends and where the semitone occurs. The finalis lies on the line in Modes II, VI, VIII, and one step below in Mode IV. The confinalis (dominant) lies a third above in Modes I, II, IV, V, VI, and VII, and a fourth above in Modes III and VIII. His rules take up considerable space, because he gives them twice, first in Latin, then in *rromançe*. No other peninsular theoretician succeeds better in clarifying the rules, except perhaps Martínez de Bizcargui, who gives a full list of the neums peculiar to single-line chant (several neum-types were found only in one-line chant, as Durán and Bizcargui both attest). An accessible résumé of Estevan's rules will be found in Gregorio Arciniega's monograph, "Un documento musical del año 1410" (June and July issues of *Tesoro Sacro-Musical*, XVIII [1934]). Since as Solange Corbin has shown in her *Essai sur la musique religieuse portugaise au moyen âge* (Paris, 1952), the surviving medieval Portuguese repertory consists almost entirely of one-line music, such rules as Estevan gives can profitably be studied by others, as well as by Spanish investigators.

His treatise even if it does not go beyond plainsong is thus a genuinely interesting document. The numerous musical examples further enhance its value. These extend to 69 staves, and without exception are copied on five lines. Other than a few Saragossa liturgical books, Spanish Renaissance sources – in manuscript or in print – almost always show plainsong on five-line (red) staves. As a result, Spanish plainsong rarely changes clef in the middle of an example – an expedient frequently necessary in plainsong copied or printed abroad on the four-line staff. In one other respect Estevan anticipates later use. Since he already writes the accidentals F$\sharp$, C$\sharp$, E$\flat$, and A$\flat$ (fols. 9v. and 38r.), he sets a precedent for the numerous printed accidentals to be found in Spanish liturgical incunabula.

Ars mensurabilis et immensurabilis cantus (c. 1480)

ESTEVAN repeats his own name almost to excess in his *Reglas*. By contrast, the next treatise still remains anonymous – though it can be dated with considerable assurance. Conserved at El Escorial library (C. iii. 23), the manuscript reaches 50 unnumbered leaves, and ends with a statement that it was finished at Seville July 7, 1480. But on the other hand the anonymous author cites 11 fifteenth-century composers at fol. 3 who improved and advanced the art of music more in the forty years preceding 1482 than all previous composers had done from Jesus Christ's birth to 1440. The discrepancy between the dates in first and last chapters forces us to believe that chapter one – which is manifestly introductory – was (like many prefaces) written after, rather than before, the rest.

The anonymous author does not name his own personal teacher as did Estevan. But if he did not study with the most celebrated of fifteenth-century theorists, Johannes Tinctoris (c. 1435–1511), he certainly shows the latter's influence. Bukofzer in his "Über Leben und Werke von Dunstable" (*Acta Musicologica*, VIII, iii–iv [1936], 104–105) pointed out such close verbal similarities to Tinctoris's *Liber de arte contrapuncti* – the manuscript of which is dated October 11, 1477 – that contact between our anonymous Sevillian and Tinctoris can hardly be doubted. Tinctoris at that time was of course residing in Naples as chaplain and singer to Ferdinand I (= Don Ferrante: 1423–1494) of the house of Aragon.

Instead of the eleven composer's names listed by our Sevillian anonymous, Tinctoris in his *Liber de arte contrapuncti* (*CS*, IV, 77) gave the names of eight whom he considered to have advanced music spectacularly during the previous forty years. Common to both lists are the names, Dunstable, Dufay, Binchois, Busnois, Ockeghem and Guillaume Faugues. But whereas Tinctoris completed his list with Regis and Caron, the Sevillian anonymous completes his with Constans [de Languebroek (d. 1481)], Jehan Pullois (d. 1478), Johannes Urrede [= Wreede (d. 1481?)], Johannes Martini (d. 1492?), and an Enrricus who seems to have been the highly praised Henry Knoep of Liège (d. 1490?) chosen to succeed Gaspar van Weerbecke in the Milanese court chapel c. 1473 [6] (Eitner, *QL*, III, 341). At all events, both Tinctoris and the Sevillian anonymous unite in lauding John Dunstable (d. 1453) as the English fountainhead from which gushed a "revivifying" school of Franco-Flemish masters. Urrede, one of the composers found in the Sevillian's list but not in Tinctoris's served the first Duke of Alva in 1476 and composed music for his poem, *Nunca fué pena mayor* (see below, pp. 203, 228). Later – 1477–1481 – he became chapelmaster to Ferdinand V of Aragon. But no other composer of those added by the Sevillian anonymous can be connected with Spain. The better inference then has it that our anonymous visited the Spanish court at Naples c. 1480. He brought back to Seville if not the music of Faugues, Pullois, and Martini, at least a boundless enthusiasm for the music of the Franco-Flemings who flourished in Italy c. 1480. His eager zest for novelty presages the sixteenth-century Sevillian musical outlook. Bermudo, the greatest Andalusian theorist, treads in his exact footsteps when he compares "old" music to the "old" law, and "new" music to the "New" Testament (*Declaración* [1555], 66r., 84v.).

The Sevillian anonymous quotes Isidore – as did everyone. His also quoting Nicholaus de Capua (fl. 1415) strengthens the theory of a Neapolitan sojourn. From the latter's *Compendium musicale* [7] he extracts three lines of poetry on the "great gulf that separates a mere performer from the schooled musician who knows the theory of his art" – an idea as old as Boethius. From Nicholaus he also probably takes the couplet on the "bestiality" of singers who learn by rote instead of from the book. The rules on singing b♭'s are not credited to Nicholaus in our Sevillian anonymous – but so exactly resemble his as to suggest further borrowing.

At fol. 20v. our anonymous lists rules for copying one-line chant *en cinco reglas* (on five lines), and warns against the drastic errors an ignorant scribe can compound. At fol. 23v. he ranges himself on the side of those who call the semitone from A–B♭ the large rather than small semitone. Only the maligned Martínez de Bizcargui among his immediate successors dared follow him on the "size" of the A–B♭ as compared with B♭–B♮ semitone. At fol. 34v. our anonymous cites the custom, peculiar to Spain, of singing

---

[6] Emilio Motta, "Musici alla Corte degli Sforza," *Archivio storico lombardo*, XIV, ii (June, 1887), pp. 330–332.

[7] Adrien de la Fage, *Essais de Diphthérographie musicale* (Paris: O. Legouix, 1864), p. 310 *seq.* The Sevillian anonymous cites Nicholaus de Capua at fol. 5r.

all the canonical hours not only in monastic houses and in cathedrals, but also in the smaller parish churches – a custom, he declares, which "makes necessary our knowing the proper intonations for the beginning, middle, and end, of every canonical hour." [8]

Bartolomé Ramos [9] de Pareja (fl. 1482)

RAMOS DE PAREJA, the most renowned of fifteenth-century Spanish theorists, not only made his reputation in Italy but stayed there long enough to publish *Musica practica* (Bologna, 1482), and to gather about him a coterie of admiring disciples – headed by Giovanni Spataro [10] – who upheld his reputation during the protracted controversy aroused by his novel doctrines.

That he was from Baeza in the diocese of Jaén,[11] and therefore an Andalusian like so many of the other principal Spaniards of his century, is known from the colophons to the two issues of his *Musica practica* – both of which appeared in 1482.[12] His first teacher *qui me musices imbuit rudimentis* [13] was the Spaniard, Juan de Monte (papal singer, 1447–1457),[14] whom he dared cite as the equal of such celebrities as Ockeghem,

[8] For further information concerning the Sevillian anonymous and printed excerpts, see Luis Villalba Muñoz, "Un tratado de música inédito del siglo XV," *La Ciudad de Dios*, LXX (Madrid, 1906), pp. 118–123, 531–543.

[9] Variants: *Ramis* is the form Spataro adopted in his *Tractato di musica* (Venice: Bernardino de Vitali, 1531), chapters vi, xiv, xvi, xix. In ch. xiv, for instance, he alluded to *mio optimo preceptore B. Ramis*. Ramus is the form he used, however, in his *Honesta defensio in Nicolai Burtii parmensis opusculum* (Bologna: Plato de Benedictis, 1491). In this *Honesta defensio* Spataro was, moreover, consistent in spelling the name *Ramus* (*il fonte delli musici il mio Ramus*, fol. c ii). Occasionally, however, Spataro (1491) left out the Ramus, *mio Pareia fonte delli musici*, (fol. d viii verso). Domingo Marcos Durán, the only fifteenth-century Spanish theorist who refers to Ramos called him simply Bartholomé de Pareja. Ramos (= "boughs") is adopted in the present text because it is nowadays the preferred Spanish spelling. "Ram*is*" does not occur in Castilian.

[10] Spataro's jousting with Burzio and Gaffurio in behalf of his *optimo preceptore* lasted almost thirty years. For chronology of his dispute with Gaffurio see Knud Jeppesen's article, "Eine musiktheoretische Korrespondenz," *Acta Musicologica*, XIII (1941), p. 21.

[11] For a history of Baeza see Fernando de Cózar Martínez, *Noticias y documentos para la historia de Baeza* (Jaén: Est. tip. de los Sres. Rubio, 1884). Of special interest will be found the information at pp. 154–156 and 481. Ramos was evidently proud of his Baeza origin. Spataro (*Honesta defensio* [1491], fol. d Vr.) alludes to Ramos's birth in Biatia (= Baeza), "two days' journey distant from the ancient Roman settlement of Italica."

[12] For a discussion of the two editions see Albano Sorbelli, "Le due Edizioni della 'Musica practica' di Bartolomé Ramis de Pareja," *Gutenberg Jahrbuch*, 1930, pp. 104–114. The colophon of the "original edition" begins thus: *Explicit feliciter prima pars musice egregii et famosi musici domini bartolomei parea* ...; of the "second edition" thus: *Explicit musica practica Bartolomei Rami de Pareia* ... Ramos originally intended to publish his musical theories in three parts (1) Musica practica (2) Musica theorica (3) Musica semimathematica (Sorbelli, p. 109). When he discovered that he would not be appointed Bolognese music professor he abandoned such an ambitious scheme: as the difference in colophons testifies. That his disappointment was intense may be inferred from Spataro's testimony (*Honesta defensio*); who said he had spent a decade preparing *Musica practica*. Ramos preferred to dictate to his students and then to discuss his theories in class sessions before resorting to the printed word, according to Spataro. See Federico Ghisi, "Un terzo esemplare della 'Musica Practica' di Bartolomeo Ramis de Pareia alla biblioteca nazionale centrale di Firenze," *Note d'archivio*, XII, 3–5 (May-Oct., 1935), p. 226.

[13] *Musica practica*, ed. Johannes Wolf, p. 88.

[14] Fr. X. Haberl, *Bausteine für Musikgeschichte*, III (*Die römische "schola cantorum" und die päpstlichen Kappelsänger* [Leipzig: Breitkopf und Härtel, 1888]), pp. 37, 39.

Busnois, and Dufay.[15] That he lectured at Salamanca and there disputed with the celebrated Pedro de Osma [16] on the meaning of the diatonic, chromatic, and enharmonic *genera* as defined by Boethius can also be learned from his own testimony (Pars I, Tract. II, cap. vi).[17] Before leaving Spain he wrote a now-lost music treatise in the vernacular.[18] In Spain or in Italy he became intimately acquainted with Tristano de Silva,[19] who served for a time as *maestro* in the chapel of the Portuguese king, Affonso V (1432–1481), and who wrote two treatises.[20] Ramos also knew Urrede, Ferdinand V's *maestro*, and called him *carissimus . . . magister* (dearly-beloved master).

He journeyed to Italy before 1472, perhaps first settling in Florence.[21] *Musica practica*, on the authority of Spataro, took ten years to write. Sometime before 1480 he removed to Bologna. There he lectured publicly without however actually occupying the chair which Pope Nicholas V (d. 1455) had sought to create.[22] He found the mathematical faculty – which was jealously opposed to the very existence of such a chair – ranged against him. While *Musica practica* was still in the press (or shortly after publication) he departed for Rome where he was still residing during 1491,[23] a year when Spaniards rode high in the saddle and Castilian was a fashionable language among the upper classes. Spataro says that he was highly regarded in Rome, and that learned men in every faculty resorted to him, esteeming him *maestro delli maestri*. His date of death cannot be ascertained but probably belongs around 1500. Gaffurio in his 1520 *Apologia* referred to him as long dead.[24] His doctrines remained a focus of controversy as late as Salinas's *De musica libri septem* (1577).

[15] *Musica practica*, Wolf ed., p. 84.

[16] Pedro de Osma, cited as a musical authority in Marcos Durán's *Comento sobre Lux bella*, enjoyed considerable academic distinction if he was the Pedro Martínez de Osma who was a member of San Bartolomé College in 1444, a leading professor of theology in Salamanca University for fifteen years (1463–1478), and author of a famous commentary on Aristotle's *Ethics* (*Liber Ethicorum*, published at Salamanca in 1496). Because of "errors" in his book on confession he was required to retire from his professorship to Alba de Tormes where he died in 1480.

[17] Wolf ed., pp. 42–43.

[18] *Ibid.*, p. 42.

[19] *Ibid.*, p. 86. Silva is incorrectly identified as Portuguese (Tristão da Silva) in Joaquim de Vasconcellos's *Os musicos portuguezes* (Oporto: Imp. Portugueza, 1870), II, 177. Ramos (*op. cit.*, p. 14) distinctly says that Silva was a Spaniard: *Tristano de Silva Hispano familiarissimo nostro et acerrimi ingenii viro disputatione.* If the evidence of Fernando del Pulgar's letter *Para el maestre de la capilla del rey de Portogal* (*Epistolario Español*, I, 58 [Letter 27]) be applied to Silva, he was a restless spirit who had roamed from royal chapel to chapel throughout Europe while his mother remained in Spain. He had written Pulgar several times without getting a reply. Though Pulgar addressed him as "Dearest Sir," he advised him to remain in Portugal, and to quit hankering after a still better place.

[20] Vasconcellos, II, 177. According to Vasconcellos, Silva's *Amables de música* was in João IV's Lisbon library. Cf. Diogo Barbosa Machado, *Bibliotheca Lusitana*, III (Lisbon: Ignacio Rodrigues, 1752), p. 765, c. 1.

[21] Albert Seay, "The *Dialogus Johannis Ottobi Anglici in arte musica*," *Journal of the American Musicological Society*, VIII, 2 (Summer, 1955), pp. 91–92.

[22] Sorbelli, pp. 106–107.

[23] Spataro, *Honesta defensio* (1491), fol. c vii: "tu sai che lui e a Roma doue assai piu sonno. . . ."

[24] *Apologia* (Turin: Agostino de Vitomercato, 1520), fol. A v recto [lines 22–23]: ". . . quanquam culpare *mortuos* leue sit non responsuros. . .". The *Diccionario de la música Labor* (Barcelona: Editorial Labor, 1954 [II, 1831b]), states that Ramos was still alive in 1521, but Gaffurio's *Apologia* bears the colophon date, April 20, 1520. In a letter to Pietro Aron written in 1532, Spataro said that when Ramos moved to Rome he fully intended to finish the theoretical portions of his treatise but that instead he gave himself up to wanton

Ramos opposed tradition in the following several respects:

I He rejected the method of tuning the diatonic scale which plainsong theorists since Odo of Cluny (*Enchiridion musices*, c. 935) had taught.[25] This older method enjoyed the advantage of uniformly tuning all fourths (G–c, A–d, B–e, c–f, d–g, e–a, f–b♭, etc.) in the stringlength-ratio 4:3, and all fifths in the stringlength-ratio 3:2. In order to achieve these uniform ratios, earlier theorists were however constrained to sacrifice the 5:4 ratio for the major third in favor of 81:64, and the 6:5 ratio for the minor third in favor of 288:243. All whole steps vibrated meantime in the 9:8 ratio but the sung semitone in the 256:243 ratio.

Ramos altered the older method in order to tune the major thirds c–e, f–a, g–b, and their octaves in the 5:4 ratio. He also managed to work out his tuning system in such fashion that the minor thirds A–c, d–f, e–g, and their octaves, conformed to the 6:5 vibration-ratio. What is more, he arranged his scale so that the semitones e–f, a–b♭, and b♮–c¹ would vibrate in the 16:15 ratio rather than the Pythagorean 256:243 ratio.

In order to make these improvements, he was however himself forced to sacrifice certain advantages inherent in the older system, taught by conservatives from Guido to Gaffurio. In the first place, he was obliged to vary the size of his "perfect" fifths and fourths. While A–e, c–g, d–a, e–b♮, f–c¹, and their octaves all conformed in his system with the 3:2 stringlength-ratio required in classic theory, he on the other hand tuned the remaining fifth in the diatonic scale, g–d¹, slightly flat (40:27). As for fourths, he tuned all of them in the 4:3 ratio except d–g – which in his system became a trifle larger (27:20) than a mathematically perfect fourth.

Secondly, he was forced to vary the size of his major seconds. In his new system A–B, d–e, f–g, and their octaves still conformed with the 9:8 ratio prescribed by the Pythagorean tuning theory and accepted by Guido. But not c–d, g–a, and their octaves. These two major seconds were tuned in the 10:9 ratio, and were therefore smaller seconds.

Thirdly, he was not quite successful in making all his minor thirds conform with the 6:5 ratio. Though A–c, d–f, and e–g did fit the 6:5 ratio in his new system, B–d and g–b♭ were a trifle smaller (tuned in the ratio 32:27).

Lastly, though his semitones e–f, a–b♭, and b♮–c¹ were tuned in the very desirable ratio 16:15, his b♭–b♮ semitone could not escape being tuned smaller (in the ratio 135:128). According to the overtone series b♭–b♮ ought, however, to be slightly *larger* (15:14) than the b♮–c semitone (16:15).

In summary: Ramos in order to obtain three 5:4 major thirds and a like number of 6:5 minor thirds abandoned the centuries-old symmetry of the Guidonian hexachord system. In his system the two major triads, c–e–g and f–a–c¹, reached mathematical perfection (though not the g–b–d¹ triad). Likewise the three minor triads,

---

habits that brought on his death before he could ever finish: "andò a Roma et portò con lui tute quelle particole impresse con intentione de fornirla a Roma; ma lui non la fornite mai; ma lui atendeva a certo suo modo de vivere lascivo el quale fu causa de la sua morte" (quoted in Sorbelli, p. 107).

[25] For a description of Odo's method, see Strunk, *Source Readings*, p. 106.

A–c–e, d–f–a, and e–g–b♮ (though not g-b♭–d¹). Excellent as he felt his new system to be, an adventurous singer tuning to his monochord, instead of Odo's or Guido's, would necessarily have formed a small major second followed by a large major second when singing *ut-re-mi* of the natural hexachord built on C; and exactly viceversa when singing *ut-re-mi* of the soft hexachord built on F.

II Ramos himself realized that his novel tuning of the monochord [26] – which he professed to have devised for the benefit of the unlearned, but according to principles set down by Boethius – laid the axe at the root of the Guidonian system. His second assault against classic plainsong theory followed inevitably. He proposed (Pars I, Tract. I, cap. vii) that the time had now come to do away with the whole tiresomely intricate solmization system, and to devise new syllables. These should cover not the hexachord but the octave instead. They should begin with C_1 (second ledger-line below the bass clef). From this C_1, the lowest note on keyboard instruments, they should rise to c^1 (middle space on the treble clef). The syllables suggested, and which were to be repeated from octave to octave, included these eight: *psal-li-tur per vo-ces is-tas*. The notes C or c would, according to his new system, be sung with either *psal* or *tas*, depending on whether the melody ascended or descended afterwards.

The "Guidonian" hand (Pars I, Tract. II, cap. vii), as revised by Ramos, still served to denote pitches; but the bottom of the index finger stood for C, the bottom of middle and ring fingers for c (Middle C), and the bottom of the little finger for c^1. Both sides of the thumb served for the seven notes in the lowest octave.

In the older system *mi* always signaled that a semitone came next if the melody ascended, and *fa* a semitone if it descended. In his new solmization system, no such pair of syllables as *mi-fa* existed to herald the semitone. John Hothby (c. 1415–1487), the famous English Carmelite theorist who studied Ramos's theories before returning from Lucca to the service of Henry VII (1486), dictated his *Excitatio quaedam Musicae artis per refutationem* in order to show the dangers of such a newfangled solmization system and to expose Ramos's "errors." He objected to *psallitur per voces istas* on the grounds that the semitone is sung the first time in the octave with *tur – per* (E–F) but the second time with *is – tas* (B♮–c).[27]

Ramos, perhaps anticipating such an objection, claimed for his system a compensating advantage. Those two places in the octave where at the singer's discretion a semitone might, or might not, occur (A–B♭ and B♮–c) were each signaled by syllables ending in "s" (A = *ces*, B = *is*).[28] He also liked his system because the singer changed from one octave into another on syllables with the same vowel (the note C = *psal* or *tas*).[29] As for the *number* of syllables – the Guidonian system calling for six and his for eight – he thought eight numerologically just as "good" if not "better" than six.

Ramos, however, was not so sanguine as to fancy that solmization through the whole

[26] Ramos's method: Strunk, pp. 201–204.
[27] Wolf ed., p. 109.
[28] *Ibid.*, p. 20.
[29] *Ibid.*, p. 21.

octave would catch on quickly. Meanwhile he suggested that students ease their task by singing A–c♯–d with the syllables re-fa-sol rather than the proper syllables belonging to the A–*conjuncta*: ut-mi-fa.[30] Similarly he recommended singing g–f♯–g with the syllables sol-fa-sol, even though a semitone was involved.[31] He invoked the authority of Johannes Gallicus, a Carthusian residing at Mantua, for the suggestion that singers abandon overt mutation from one hexachord to a "conjunct" when sharping at cadences – the *semitonium subintellectum* being secretly understood instead.[32]

III As if the lèse-majesté of opposing both the Pythagorean tuning system and the Guidonian solmization system were not enough, Ramos was so daring as to challenge still other established musical doctrines. He, for instance, decreed that tritones were not necessarily improper. In order to lend weight to so airy a dictum he again appealed to the same Johannes Gallicus of Mantua mentioned above – this Carthusian being the only Renaissance theorist in Italy whom he seems to have respected. Even so, he found it necessary to wrest Gallicus's "corroborating" statement from its proper context when he wrote as follows: "To make a tritone, as Brother John the Carthusian observed, is not the mortal sin that many believe it to be" [33] (*Tritonum facere, ut frater Johannes Carthusinus dicit* [CS, IV, 372a], *non est peccatum mortale, ut multi credunt*).

Another statement that similarly showed his daring because of its radical novelty was the dictum that "consecutive fifths can be tolerated if one be a diminished fifth and the other perfect: examples can be found in the song, *Sois emprantis* [by Tristano de Silva] and in other old songs; such consecutives are permitted when the parts move swiftly though not when the motion is slow." [34] The music of Tristano de Silva, like that of such other fifteenth-century Spanish polyphonists mentioned by Ramos as Juan de Monte and Luis Sánchez, is lost. The extant music of Pedro de Escobar, Martín de Rivafrecha, and Juan de Anchieta, all of whom flourished in the immediately succeeding generation (1500–1510) shows, however, that he breasted current practice in permitting fifths, even when only two parts were sounding. But no other contemporary theorist dared put such licenses as those for tritones and fifths in print.

RAMOS's sturdy originality must not, however, be so stressed that simultaneously one loses sight of the more conventional teachings in his treatise. Indeed he would not have drawn about him a group of devoted disciples headed by Spataro, nor would he have won Aron's accolade of having been "a most estimable musician, truly worthy of veneration by every learned person" (*Bartholomeo rami musico dignissimo, ueramente da*

---

[30] *Ibid.*, p. 43.

[31] *Ibid.* Even Gaffurio later admitted that in solmization many articulated "sol" below "la" when singing a semitone (*Practica musice* [Milan, 1496], fol. ee iij).

[32] Wolf ed., p. 44; see also p. 31.

[33] *Ibid.*, pp. 50–51.

[34] *Ibid.*, p. 65. Pietro Aron in his *Lucidario in musica* (Venice: Girolamo Scotto, 1545), Libro secondo, opp. VIII (fol.7v.), quotes Ramos's dictum concerning fifths and cites Tristano de Silva's *antico canto chiamato Soys emprantis*. However, it is not clear that Aron quotes Silva's *canto* in the accompanying music example. The example would, in fact, seem to be an excerpt from Verdelot's *Infirmitatem nostram*.

ogni dotto uenerato) [35] had he been merely a rebel against convention. *Musica practica* even contains such formal bows to convention as the following: "But since we do not wish to depart from ordinary practice, we do not allow the counterpoint to remain static, even though it concords with the *cantus firmus*" (*Sed quia ab usu communi discedere nolumus* ... [p. 67]).

As good a proof as any of his effectiveness when teaching conventional doctrine can be seen in his *Secunda pars idest contrapunctus*. He begins (Tract. I, cap. 1) with six rules for writing note-against-note counterpoint. He cites these rules – which he ascribes to the "ancients" – just as succinctly and precisely as does his archenemy, Franchino Gaffurio. Here are Ramos's rules: [36] (1) begin and end with an octave, perfect fifth, or unison; (2) avoid parallel octaves, perfect fifths, and unisons; (3) two, or even more, successive thirds or sixths are acceptable; (4) if the *cantus firmus* repeats a note, the counterpoint moves; (5) a major sixth should resolve to an octave, minor sixth to a fifth; major third to a fifth, minor third to a unison; (6) insofar as possible the voices should move in contrary motion.

Gaffurio in his *Practica Musice* (Milan, 1496, fol. dd i) extends the rules slightly: (1) begin with a perfect interval; (2) if both voices are moving in the same direction, two perfect intervals of the same kind cannot succeed each other; (3) up to four successive thirds or successive sixths may be used; (4) perfect intervals, when not of the same kind, may succeed each other: for instance an octave followed by a fifth; (5) two perfect intervals of the same kind may succeed each other, if the voices cross; (6) regardless of the type of intervals, contrary motion should be preferred to constant similar motion; (7) perfect intervals are best approached in contrary motion, especially at cadences; (8) an exercise should not only end with a perfect interval, but – if the Venetian school of composition be followed – in a unison.

Comparison of the two theorists, one a progressive, the other a conservative, redounds to Ramos's advantage when any problem so thorny as the use of *musica ficta* in counterpoint arises for discussion.[37] The forthright Spaniard never hesitates to pull the bud off the prickly bush even if he must get scratched while doing so. The cautious Italian usually waits until he can find a pair of gloves. But when nothing of a controversial nature is under discussion, Ramos willingly enough echoes the past.

Though Johannes Wolf who ably edited *Musica practica* did not call attention to the borrowing, Ramos in Pars I, Tract. III, cap. iii,[38] echoed word-for-word everything that Juan Gil of Zamora had more than two centuries earlier written on the emotional connotations of the eight church modes (*GS*, II, 386-388). For his source in this particular instance, Ramos named Luis Sánchez. But obviously Sánchez was only a link in a long transmission chain. Swept away by his enthusiasm for astrology Ramos argued a little later in the same chapter that the stars actually settle the character of each of the

[35] Pietro Aron, *Toscanello in musica* (Venice: Marchio Sessa, 1539), fol I (= 33) v. (lines 25–26). In the context Aron is discussing the use of the sharp-sign. He quotes Ramos as having called it *b quadro*.

[36] Wolf. ed., p. 65.

[37] *Ibid.*, pp. 66–67.

[38] *Ibid.*, pp. 56–57.

eight modes. In his opinion the dorian received its character from the sun, the hypodorian from the moon, the phrygian from Mars, the hypophrygian from Mercury, the lydian from Jupiter, the hypolydian from Venus, and the mixolydian from Saturn.[39] Their astral influences accounted, he thought, for such diverse emotional effects as anger (phrygian), punctillious tears (hypolydian), joy (lydian), and melancholy (mixolydian).

Neither can he be accounted very original in what he wrote concerning *musica mundana*, the authorities which he cited in discussing the music of the spheres being Cicero, Martianus Capella, and Macrobius. As for numerology, he was heir to the fancies of his time when he argued the relative merits of 8 and 6. Even his division of *Musica practica* into three parts, the first part into three tractates, the first two tractates into eight chapters and the third tractate into three chapters, shows a highly schematic mind laboring to make the formal plan reflect his theory of "good" and "bad" numbers.

He also reveals an old-fashioned streak when he delights in puzzle canons and volubly lauds musical enigmas. Dufay's only achievement singled out for praise is his *Missa Se la face ay pale* – because it contains the enigmatic direction: *Crescit in triplo et in duplo et ut iacet*. He admires Busnois for having written a canon that can be sung backwards as well as forwards. When he himself composes a canon he takes pride in having illustrated a literary programme. He remembers canons of just such sort which he had inserted both in a mass composed while he was lecturing at Salamanca and in a magnificat (in one verse of which he had constructed a three-in-one "programmatic" canon).

ALTHOUGH *Musica practica* does not contain such a programmatic canon, Albert Seay has recently found one bearing the legend, *Mundus et musica et totus concentus Bartholomeus Rami*, and has published it in his article, "Florence: The City of Hothby and Ramos" (*Journal of the American Musicological Society*, IX, 3 [Fall, 1956], p. 195). In this case he wrote a perpetual canon to illustrate the idea: "Singers all share the vice of never acceding to the request of friends when they are asked to sing and of never stopping when they have not been asked" (*Omnibus hoc vitium est cantoribus inter amicos ut nunquam inducant animum cantare rogati iniussi nunquam desistant*). To enforce the "perpetual" idea, Ramos's copyist even makes a circle of the staff and pictures the four winds blowing at the successive entering-notes in the canon *a 4*.[40]

With characteristic lack of modesty he praises not only his Salamanca mass but admires his own Bologna motet, *Tu lumen*, because it can be sung with the tenor moving chromatically and enharmonically as well as diatonically. Ramos's predilection for such highly intellectualized feats was too much for Hothby, who reminded him that the time

---

[39] For a translation of Ramos's remarks on the lydian and hypolydian modes see Edward E. Lowinsky, "The Goddess Fortuna in Music," *Musical Quarterly*, XXIX, i (January, 1943), p. 72.

[40] See plate 61 in Sandra Vagaggini, *La miniature florentine aux xive et xve siècles* (Milan-Florence: Electa Editrice, 1952). Gherardo (1445–1497) and Monte (1448–1528) di Giovanni del Fora did the miniatures.

Mundus et musica et totus concentus

Circular Canon a 4

Florence: Bibl. Naz. Cent.
Banco Rari 229, fol. 111v.*

BARTOLOMÉ RAMOS DE PAREJA

* inside the circular staff on which this clefless canon is copied appears the following legend:
Siue lidi/um in sinemēon | siue ypolidiū diaçe/ugmenon p *quatuor | quartaˢ ducaˢ renouādo | dulcem harmoniam | intra diapason sēti/es melodiā bene | modulādo*

when composers deliberately confused performers had long passed. Gaffurio returned to Ramos's *Tu lumen* motet as late as 1520, criticizing its unsoundness.[41]

A MEASURED APPRAISAL of Ramos is difficult to come by. His fame rests on the novelties in *Musica practica*. Yet, as can be more abundantly demonstrated than we have attempted, some of his views were so traditional as to seem old-fashioned to his contemporaries. He vituperated his enemies while at the same time extravagantly lauding his friends, especially if Spaniards. He condemned Guido as unlearned ("a better monk than musician")[42] and scoffed at the ignorance of Guidonians in one paragraph but in the next made an embarrassing number of grammatical blunders in his own use of the

[41] Gaffurio, *Apologia*, fol. viii verso: *dum Bononiae (illiteratus tamen) publice legeret adnotauit tenoris hoc ordine* ... (while he was publicly lecturing at Bologna, though he was himself an ignoramus, he notated the tenor of his riddle-canon in the following way ... [fol. ix verso] but incorrectly, for he was never able to grasp the true meaning of the chromatic and enharmonic genera). The following additional quotations from the *Apologia* clarify Gaffurio's objections: "Truly the diligence of antiquity overlooked nothing; yet you [Spataro] seem ready to imitate the petulance and ingratitude of that teacher of yours, Ramos, who is just as bad as you ... If Ramos, as you claim, borrowed the 5 : 4 and 6 : 5 consonances from Ptolemy, then he was a thief since he did not acknowledge his debt .... Ramos railed against even Boethius; but that Boethius was a skilled practitioner as well as theorist was acknowledged by Cassiodorus." For Cassiodorus's testimony on Boethius's ability as a practical musician see his *Epistola 40*, in Migne, *PL*, LXIX, 570.

[42] Wolf ed., p. 11; also pp. 39–40.

Latin tongue. The paradoxes revealed in his own disposition explain why equally intelligent theorists such as Aron and Gaffurio have extolled and denounced him.

What can be said of him when both the pros and cons are balanced, however, is that he showed courage bordering on foolhardiness; that his mind was always agile; that he relished controversy; that he never failed to make his own dicta as incisive as possible; that he never soft-pedaled criticism of his foes, however well intrenched; that he indulged in name-calling; and that his attacks on Guido dead four hundred years, often as not preluded bombardment of his immediate contemporaries. If he showed little of the conventional piety found in other Spanish treatises of the fifteenth and sixteenth centuries, it is on the other hand probable that only in such a rebellious spirit as his would there have fermented the novel theories that made him famous. Had he been more docile, he would not have been denounced by Gaffurio as an overweening and vulgar upstart. But he also would not have been praised by Aron as "most worthy of the respect of every learned scholar" nor would Fogliano and Zarlino have made his divisions of the scale their own.

Perhaps no one has ever yet better defended him than his compatriot Antonio Eximeno. At one time a professor of mathematics, Eximeno was himself adept enough to understand not only the problems that Ramos undertook to solve but also the arguments of his opponents. He wrote thus: "Before Zarlino the Spaniard Bartolomé Ramos had already foreseen the necessity of sacrificing the perfection of certain fifths and fourths in instruments of fixed tuning. This alteration of fifths and fourths was to be the first step in the direction of modern temperament .... Although for his pains he was attacked by both Burzio and Gaffurio ... still in time the opinions of this Spaniard – this 'author of paradoxes,' this 'prevaricator of the truth' – were to prevail over those of his most embittered foes." [43]

Domingo Marcos Durán (fl. 1492)

DURÁN, author of a 28-page Castilian plainsong instructor published at Seville in the most famous year of Spanish history (1492), listed his name in the first edition of his *Lux bella* as Domingo Durán: but in his next two publications as Domingo Marcos Durán. In consequence, Otto Kinkeldey when discussing the earliest Spanish imprints in his useful essay, "Music and Music Printing in Incunabula" (*Papers of the Bibliographical Society of America*, XXVI [1932], 96), suggested that two different Duráns were active during the decade after 1492. This supposition was a logical one; because in Spanish the second name of three usually has the same significance as the last in English. But *Lux bella*, originally printed by *Quatro alemanes compañeros* at Seville in 1492, was reprinted in 1518 by Jacob Cromberger of Seville – this time with the author's name given in full: Domingo Marcos Durán. Only one Durán can therefore have been re-

---

[43] Antonio Eximeno, *Dubbio ... sopra il saggio fondamentale pratico di contrappunto* (Rome: Michelangelo Barbiellini, 1775), p. 85. Eximeno was as bold and restless a spirit as Ramos. But he was at the same time enough of a scholar not to call Ramos the inventor of equal temperament.

sponsible for *Lux bella*, the *Comento sobre Lux bella* (Salamanca, 1498) and the *Súmula de canto de órgano* (Salamanca, c. 1507).

His biography like Ramos's, must be pieced together from his writings. His father was Juan Marcos and his mother Isabel Fernández. Both were natives of Alconetar (Garro-villas) – which lies thirty miles west of the Portuguese border along the Tagus river. Like the famous New World conquerors, Cortés and Pizarro, he was thus an Estremaduran. Born c. 1465, he may well have received his early musical instruction in the cathedral choirboys' school at Coria (the diocese includes Alconetar). In any event, he dedicated his first publication – *Lux bella* – to the bishop of Coria, Pedro Ximeno.

Already in 1492 he held the bachelor's degree from Salamanca. When six years later he published his second treatise, the *Comento sobre Lux bella*, he was a *licenciado* – the intermediate grade between bachelor and doctor. In his preface to the *Comento sobre Lux bella* (Salamanca, 1498) he remarks on the many years which he had spent at Salamanca University studying not only music but the other liberal arts and philosophy. Because he had found the pathway to knowledge strewn with pitfalls and impeded by crags, he had published *Lux bella* and now publishes a commentary in order to fill in low places and level off precipices for the benefit of novices who may follow. His *Comento* is dedicated to Alfonso III de Fonseca (1475–1534) – distinguished patron of learning, founder of colleges at both Salamanca and Santiago de Compostela, archbishop of the latter see from 1506–1524, and during his last ten years Spanish primate.[44]

His chef-d'oeuvre, the *Súmula de canto de órgano*, cannot be as exactly dated as *Lux bella* and the *Comento*, the reason being that its colophon contains only the following statement: "This work, after being seen and examined, was ordered printed by the very reverend, noble, and virtuous Alfonso de Castilla, rector of studies in the very noble city of Salamanca." Since however Alfonso de Castilla did not become rector until the academic year, 1502–1503,[45] the *Súmula* certainly ought not to be classed as an incunabulum – despite its listing as such in the *Catálogo Musical de la Biblioteca Nacional de Madrid* (Barcelona, 1949), II, 119. A still more obvious clue to its date ought to be its dedication to Alfonso de Fonseca, arch-bishop of Santiago and "mi señor," were it not that two Alfonsos de Fonseca succeeded each other in the see of Santiago. The 1498 *Comento* can only have been dedicated to Alfonso III; for had Alfonso II been intended, Durán in 1498 would inevitably have called him archbishop. He did not do so; therefore he meant Alfonso III. In the case of the *Súmula*, the dedicatee was still in all likelihood Alfonso III – who inherited the see at the close of 1506 but remained three years longer in Salamanca before formally entering Santiago (November 30, 1509). Even if not an incunabulum the *Súmula* must

---

[44] Alfonso III de Fonseca was always a munificent patron of music. Like his successor in the primacy, Juan de Tavera, he maintained his own private chapel, which included some of the best singers in Spain. See Antonio López Ferreiro, *Historia de la santa a. m. iglesia de Santiago de Compostela* (Santiago: Imp. y. enc. del Sem. Conciliar Central), VIII (1906), p. 42. For details concerning his elevation to the Santiago archiepiscopate see López Ferreiro, VIII, 9–14. He became archbishop at the same time that Alfonso II de Fonseca became Patriarch of Alexandria, i.e., towards the close of 1506.

[45] Enrique Esperabé Arteaga, *Historia pragmática é interna de la Universidad de Salamanca*, II (1917), p. 7.

be one of the very earliest Spanish imprints containing polyphony, its only certain predecessor having been Diego del Puerto's *Ars cantus plani ... siue organici* (Salamanca, 1504). All circumstances considered, 1507 seems as likely a date as any for the *Súmula*.

Durán is next caught sight of in 1518 when he issues a second edition of his *Lux bella*. This reprint carries not only a new dedication to Don Bernaldino Manrique de Lara, but also a notice on the reverse of the title page stating that it has been "corrected and amended." New paragraph headings and a *prohemio* increase its practical utility. The issue of a second edition does not, however, reflect on the sufficiency of the original. Rather, it proves the popularity of the first. Less than a half-dozen of the very numerous Spanish Renaissance instructors won the testimony to their popularity of a reprint or an enlarged edition.

Durán spent his later years as *phonascus* (choirmaster) at Santiago de Compostela Cathedral. Alonso Ordoñez succeeded him in 1530. He died around the latter year. Paul Hofhaimer's pupil, Dionisio Memo, sometime organist of St. Mark's, Venice (1507), and to Henry VIII (1516–1519), was paid 1000 silver *reales* on June 12, 1528, for fixing the old large organs at Santiago de Compostela Cathedral and for starting the construction of new ones. Memo resided in Santiago throughout 1529. Early in the following year his task was nearly enough completed for Diego de Béjar, organist of Astorga, to deliver it as his professional opinion (on April 19, 1530) that one of Memo's new big organs was an excellent instrument. (Further details concerning Memo's interesting term at Santiago de Compostela can be read in Antonio López Ferreiro's *Historia de la santa a. m. iglesia de Santiago de Compostela*, VIII [1906], p. 200. After lavish gifts from Henry VIII, Memo – a Crutched Friar – had been accused of betraying the royal confidence, and to save his life had fled to Portugal.)

Summaries of Durán's Publications

I. *Lux bella* (1492 edition) contains nine pages of highly compressed text followed by a page on which appears an ingenious circular diagram of the hexachord system. In all three extant copies of *Lux bella* a 14-page tonarium showing the melodic formulas appropriate to each of the eight church modes appears immediately after the text of *Lux bella*. The music in the *tonarium*, like the music examples shown in the preceding textual portion, was obviously not printed from movable type; all the examples would appear to have been printed from metal or wooden blocks.

Durán though offering only a beginner's manual lists his eighteen authorities with scrupulous care. Moreover he always prints the appropriate name in the margin to show the source of each dictum. Guido, and especially the *Micrologus*, serves as his most frequent source. Among his other authorities Boethius, Franco of Cologne, Philippe de Vitry, Jean de Muris, Marchettus of Padua, and Franchino Gaffurio are of course easily enough identified. Arnaldus – his most frequently-cited authority after Guido – may have been the Arnaldus de Monte of Ripoll whose copy of the Calixtine Codex is dated 1173. He is less likely to have been the Arnaldus Villanovanus (d. 1312) credited with having been Ramon Lull's teacher.[46] "Durandus of Paris" cannot easily have been the liturgiologist, Guillaume Durand (d. 1296), who was dean of Chartres. But Magister Vincentius may quite well have been Vincent of Beauvais (d. 1264), whose *Speculum doctrinale* (XVII, 10–35) enjoyed considerable vogue as late as 1500. Guillermus, cited once in connection with the ambitus, finals, and dominants of the modes, may have been Guillelmus Monachus (fl. 1460) (*CS*, III, 273–307) – or even Guillermo Despuig (though the latter's *Ars musicorum* was not printed until 1495).

Of the two other theorists cited in *Lux bella*, Goscaldus and Michael de Castellanis, only the latter has been identified. Castellanis (fl. 1490) wrote a *Tractatus de musica* that survived in MS (at the Capuchin convento in Gerona) as late as 1821: in which year the Valencian littérateur, Jaime Villanueva (1769–1824), saw it.[47] Castellanis, a Benedictine educated at a house in the Toulouse province, completed part I of his now lost *Tractatus* at a hermitage atop a peak in the Montseny range on December 29, 1496. In part I he treated of vocal music, in part II of instrumental. For a codetta he added his translation into Latin of a *tratadito* by Fernando Castillo, a Castilian cutler then dwelling in nearby Barcelona. Though a monk, Castellanis did not scruple at inserting remarks on notes of smaller than minim-value by Rabbi Samuel Judah of Morocco. It is he also who paid Moorish musical genius generous tribute in the preface to the *Sequitur ars de pulsacione lambuti* (see above, p. 24, n. 85).

The text of *Lux bella*, which runs 36 lines to a page, is printed in Gothic with frequent abbreviations. The style is cryptic and difficult to follow unless the reader has studied other analogous Spanish treatises. The manual provides more of a list of "things to remember" than an explanation of items in the list. But on the other hand for what was probably a small sum Durán was able to offer a booklet which contained an astoundingly full list of subject-headings. If it is true that in such tightly compressed space he restricted himself to no more than sentence-definitions, music students purchasing *Lux bella* at least possessed a skeleton of musical knowledge. Those who wanted meat on the bones could after 1498 buy the 76-page *Comento sobre Lux bella*.

Adequately to appreciate *Lux bella*, one should compare it with similar plainsong instructors issued in Italy and Germany before 1500. Otherwise, its idiomatic traits can be easily missed. Two manuals of equivalent size, one, Michael Keinspeck's *Lilium musice plane* in the Ulm edition (Johann Schaeffler, 1497), and the other, Bonaventura de Brixia's *Regula musice plane* in the Brescia edition (Angelus Britannicus, 1497), suggest themselves for comparison. As in *Lux bella* the plainsong examples in each of these foreign manuals are xylographically printed. The elements of music in all three manuals are presented in as succinct and abbreviated a style as possible. The Keinspeck

---

[46] Anglés, *El Còdex Musical de Las Huelgas*, I, 22–23, alludes to a music treatise by Arnaldus Villanovanus, which he however had not seen. Villanovanus's works were condemned at Tarragona on November 6, 1316. See Roque Chabas, "Arnaldo de Vilanova," *Homenaje á Menéndez y Pelayo*, II (Madrid: Lib. de V. Suárez, 1899), p. 368. Anglés on the other hand also mentions Arnaldus de Monte (*Hu*, I, 60–62). Since Durán identifies his Arnaldus as "de Alpes" in his 1498 *Comento sobre Lux bella* it seems all the likelier that his theorist was "de Monte" rather than the Villanovanus whose works had been publicly condemned.

[47] *Viage literario á las iglesias de España*, XIV: Viage á Gerona (Madrid: Imp. de la Real Academia de la Historia, 1850), pp. 175, 178.

is in Latin. So for that matter is the only previously published plainsong manual of German authorship, the *Flores musice* (1488) by Hugo von Reutlingen. The Bonaventura is in the vernacular. But Keinspeck does not therefore write a more learned manual. Actually, Durán covers more ground than either Keinspeck or Bonaventura. He also shows his university background even when treating the most elementary topics.

Neither foreign manual cites authorities. The number of pages of music examples in each is distinctly less. Somewhat more than 15 pages, or better than half of *Lux bella* is taken up with music. But less than a quarter of the Keinspeck or Bonaventura is given over to music examples. The foreign manuals use four lines; the Spanish five. Keinspeck specifies flats, but no other accidentals; Bonaventura flats and naturals. Durán calls for flats, naturals, and sharps.

The three most striking differences are these: (1) neither foreign manual recognizes the existence of *conjunctae* [conjuntas]; (2) neither foreign manual supplies a large repertory of intonations in each mode to cover the various classes of church festivals; (3) neither foreign manual tells the singer how to read chant written on a one-line staff.

(1)   Neither of the foreign plainsong instructors mentions any system of 13 ancillary hexachords nor attempts to rationalize the use of *subintellectas*. Durán on the other hand constructs a circular diagram with all 13 conjunct hexachords clearly numbered, from F_1-*retropolex* (hexachord starting on F below bass staff) to $e^1\flat$-*retromedius* (top space in the treble staff). He states, however, that ten of the thirteen suffice for the ordinarily required sharps and flats in plainsong. Odd-numbered *conjuntas* (F_1-retropolex, $B_1\flat$, $E\flat$, $B\flat$, $e\flat$) provide the needed $E\flat$'s and $A\flat$'s; even-numbered *conjuntas* (A_1, D, A, d, a) supply $F\sharp$'s and $C\sharp$'s. Durán's four rules telling when to shift into *conjuntas* repeat much information already found in Estevan's 1410 *Reglas*, although in more concise form. He ends with this singularly interesting statement: in order to allow for accidentalizing, one ought to play [*tocar*] [48] without transposing – the obvious reason being that an already accidentalized plainchant, if it were to be transposed, might easily call for more sharps or flats than those available on contemporary Spanish keyboard instruments: $B_1\flat$, $B\flat$, $b\flat$; $C\sharp$, $c\sharp$, $c^1\sharp$; $E\flat$, $e\flat$, $e^1\flat$; $F\sharp$, $f\sharp$, $f^1\sharp$; $G\sharp$, $g\sharp$, $g^1\sharp$. The foreign plainsong instructors of the period, failing to mention the higher accidentals, also omit any allusions to the instrumental accompaniment of plainsong.

(2)   As for the repertory of psalm intonations, Keinspeck of Nuremberg gives five in Mode I, one in Mode II, three in Mode III, three in Mode IV, two in Mode V, two in Mode VI, four in Mode VII, and four in Mode VIII; or a total of 24 for ferial use. He adds one in each mode for festal use. Bonaventura provides one in each mode for ferial use, and another in each for festal use. In contrast with this parsimony, Durán begins with eleven variants of the Mode I intonation formula alone, and correspondingly raises the number of formulas in the other modes. He also provides "regular" and "irregular" *Gloria Patri* formulas for use with *responsorios* and *responsetes*, and for use

[48] *Lux bella*, fol. 6: "Iten para que se faga coniunta: ha de tocar por la mayor parte en el signo do se señala."

during the various hours. This prodigality can perhaps best be explained by referring again to the Sevillian anonymous of 1480 who first mentioned the custom of singing hours even in small parish churches as a peculiarly Spanish habit.

(3)   Spanish parish churches c. 1492 still made use, moreover, of choirbooks in which the plainchant was noted on only the one-line staff. Durán implicitly acknowledges widespread use of such choirbooks when setting down rules at fol. 3 for reading neums written on the one-line staff – rules which he later expands in his 1498 commentary on *Lux bella*.

Some other Spanish idiosyncrasies spring to view when Durán is compared with his foreign coetaneans. According to him, b♭ and b♮ (also b¹♭ and b¹♮) are different notes. They bring the number used in plainsong to 22, not 20 as Keinspeck (fol. A iii v.) and Bonaventura (fol. a ii v.) count them. Then again, he thinks that Modes I, II, IV, and VI should be notated in F-clef (fol. 3): but Modes III, V, VII, and VIII in C-clef. Bonaventura, however, chooses F- instead of C-clef for Mode V. Keinspeck indulges in double-clefs. He throughout prints both F- and C-clefs simultaneously – except at times when one or the other would fall on a ledger-line.

II.   In the *Comento sobre Lux bella* (Salamanca, 1498) Durán, after praising his dedicatee and listing his own credentials, cites these reasons for the "worthiness" of music: (1) it is the only art that accompanies us to heaven; (2) all except men of meaner passions acknowledge its appeal; (3) the greatest philosophers of the past appreciated it; (4) music has powers to heal the sick, exorcise evil spirits, and even to soothe savage beasts. Throughout this commentary we constantly see the schematic mind at work organizing all musical knowledge under numbered headings.

He for instance lists 30 reasons why there are seven letters in the musical alphabet. To prove the virtue of the number seven he cites the existence of seven (1) planets (2) habitable climes (3) baptismal gifts (4) mortal sins (5) works of charity (6) joys of the Virgin (7) sorrows of the Virgin (8) sacraments (9) articles of faith (10) Athenian philosophers (11) celestial spheres (12) bodily members anointed at extreme unction (13) orders culminating in the priesthood (14) petitions in the Lord's Prayer (15) days of the week – and we have exhausted only half his list (fol. a iiij v.).

The lowest note used in plainsong is the *gamma ut* (Γ): to commemorate the *G*reeks, *G*regory, and *G*uido. The notes in plainsong are divided into *graves*, *agudas*, and *sobre agudas* (low, middle, and high): to commemorate the "threeness" in the Godhead. The solmization syllables commemorate the virtues of the number six. The vowels in the hexachord, *ut*, *re*, *mi*, *fa*, *sol*, *la*, are different except for *fa* and *la*, the "a" being twice used in order to commemorate the virtues of the first letter in the alphabet, the name of *A*dam, and the first vowel in *Ma*ria, *Pa*ter, *A*ve, and *A*lpha. The entire system of hexachords, including *deduciones* and *conjuntas* can be reduced into the diagram of a circle because *O*mega represents perfection and completion, and because the hexachord system when carried through the entire hand doubles back on itself, like a circle.

These examples of his "reasoning" do not necessarily belittle the quality of his mind.

Rather they show how ardently he believed that everything, even the most inconsequential musical fact, could and should be rationalized. Now and then his rationalizations become sufficiently ingenious to serve as mnemonic aids.

The *Comento* for the most part deals with "practical" music. Some 21 exercises in *mutanças* (shifting between the hexachords on G, C, and F) appear at fols. 8 and 9. Though not always graceful as melody, these exercises do show how carefully students were drilled in singing B♭'s and B♮'s in close succession. He believed in frequently attacking a difficult musical problem and if necessary from a changed field position. He struggled to define terms such as tones, modes, tropes, *constituciones*, and *ptongos* (fol. 10); and from fols. 17r. to 20r. grappled with the problems inherent in reading chant written on only the one-line staff. His *Comento*, prolix as the *Lux* is concise, shows the zeal of an infinitely conscientious pedagogue – one, moreover, who must footnote every assertion.[49]

As for notation on the five-line staff, he repeats his dictum from *Lux bella* that the square note in plainsong with tails on both sides enjoys double the length of the ordinary punctum, and adds that the two notes in a descending oblique ligature, if without left-hand tail, should be sung in what would now be called dotted rhythm: ♪· ♪
with the second note in the pair enjoying only a third of the time-value allotted the first. Such rules as these show how strongly mensural theory influenced the singing of plainsong in Renaissance Spain.

III.   His *Súmula de canto de órgano* (c. 1507) ranks not only as the earliest Spanish-language treatise entirely devoted to polyphony, but also as the finest treatment published before Juan Bermudo's epochal *Declaración de instrumentos* (1555). In his prologue he remarks that he has spent the twenty-five best years of his life in the arduous pursuit of musical knowledge (fol. 5r. [pencil numbering, Biblioteca Nacional copy, sign. I 2185]). His treatise justifies the labor of a quarter-century.

In previewing its contents (fol. 5r.) he promises that his *Súmula* will contain a discussion of polyphonic writing in all its various branches. He will give a set of rules for writing counterpoint or for improvising it at sight – organized according to the different *species del contrapunto*.

[These rules] apply to playing as much as singing. For playing is the equivalent of singing. In each case the written or improvised notes are the same, and there is no difference except that at one time the music is sung and at another time played on an instrument (fol. 5r.).

At fol. 6v. he says that the *alfado* (oblique ligature)[50] with a left-hand descending tail equals a breve followed by a breve. He adds that any ascending two-note ligature

---

[49] His authorities in addition to those cited in *Lux bella* include Albertus de Rosa, Avicenna, *Catholicon de Musica* (by Hugo of Pisa, bishop of Rouen [1249], d. 1268: see Roger Bragard, "Le Speculum Musicae," *Musica Disciplina*, VIII[1954], p. 3), Egidio de Murino, *Flores musice* (by Hugo von Reutlingen[1286–1360]), Guillaume de Machaut, John "of London," Pedro de Osma (theological professor at Salamanca, 1463–1478, d. 1480), Peter of Venice, and Bartolomé [Ramos] de Pareja.

[50] Guillermo Despuig called this ligature an *alpha;* see H. Anglés, "La notación musical española," *Anuario Musical*, II (1947), pp. 167–168.

with or without a left-hand descending tail equals the same. These rules duplicate those Thomas Morley was to give in *A Plaine and Easie Introduction to Practicall Musicke* (1597).[51] They conflict with Tinctoris's. The ascending *alfado* without tail should be rendered as a long followed by a breve, according to the latter's *Tractatus de notis et pausis*, Lib I, cap. x, regula iv (*CS*, IV, 43b). Durán, on this disputed point, as on others, always prefers in his *Súmula* to side with Gaffurio (*Practica musice* [Milan, 1496], Lib. II, cap. v).[52]

Just as his conscientious explanation of the notes in and out of ligatures deserves praise, so also does he prove especially valuable when discussing ligatures with dots, dots of augmentation, and dots of alteration; setting forth as he does the basic principles and then illustrating them with no less than 32 examples (fols. 10v.–11v.).[53]

Sometimes his tarrying over a matter such as *compás llano* and *compás partido* not only enables him to differentiate the lengths of bars but also to offer valuable information on so practical a point as the correct method of beating what would now pass for $\frac{4}{4}$ (*compás llano* = four minims in the bar) and $\frac{2}{4}$ (*compás partido* = two minims in the bar). As for *compás llano*, the singer begins on *1* when the conductor's hand touches bottom, on *2* when the hand starts to rise, on *3* when it reaches top, on *4* when it begins to fall (fols. 11v.–12r.). *Compás llano*, because more difficult, finds less favor with singers than *compás partido*. In the latter the conductor's hand-motion, touching bottom on *1* and top on *2*, is easier for most singers to follow.

Similarly in his chapters on counterpoint (III–VII) the asides are often as useful and revealing as the main argument. The rules for written counterpoint combine Ramos's and Gaffurio's (see p. 60), and are therefore familiar enough. But his last aside in Chapter IV has an individual ring: "When two, three, or four voices improvise counterpoint [above a *canto llano*], the conterpointing singers ought carefully to avoid clashes of a second, seventh, ninth, eleventh, and so forth,[54] except when moving in passing notes on weak beats (*en diminución*), or when creating a suspension (*síncopa*) or preparing cadences (*cláusulas*)." In Chapter V he tells the proper degrees on which to cadence: final or *confinalis* in authentic modes, final or the fourth below in plagal. In the next two chapters he proceeds with rules for improvising either above or below a *canto llano*, and at the close of Chapter X sets out a table for the use of the beginning singer who wishes to add counterpoints at sight. According to him, the singer ought always to remain within the confines of a single hexachord while so improvising. Therefore his table groups the possible notes under three headings: notes possible when singing in hard, in natural, and in soft hexachords. The singer presumably picks the hexachord which best suits his voice-range. The table on fol. 18r. then acts as a mechanical note-finder, and can be memorized just as a modern multiplication-table.

---

[51] Morley, ed. by R. Alec Harman (London: J. M. Dent, 1952), pp. 20–21; see especially n. 2 on p. 21.

[52] Fol. aa iiij verso.

[53] For a facsimile reproduction of cap. xix, see José Subirá, *Historia de la música española e hispano-americana*, p. 169. The date, 1498, given by Subirá, cannot however be accepted.

[54] The interval of a fourth is not mentioned in this list of prohibited intervals, although the eleventh is interdicted.

But the point which he insists upon (and now deserves underlining) is expressed in his own words thus:

In this style [improvised counterpoint] the singer must rigorously adhere to his hexachord; for even if the *canto llano* were to circle the entire hand [Guidonian hand = two octaves plus a major sixth], the counterpoint should never on any account go outside the six notes of its chosen hexachord [fol. 17r.].

He of course adds that when one plainsong ends and another begins the contrapuntist is free to change hexachords.

Beginning at fol. 20v. he assumes the rôle of vocal coach, setting down six pages of vocalises in contrasting rhythms and on various vowels. Infinite practice is his watchword to success. His exercises proceed from scales through only the six notes of a hexachord to the fifteen notes in a double octave. He expects all men-singers [fol. 22r.] to vocalize from low G_1 up to at least g (two octaves). On the other hand, they do not vocalize below G_1. He also emphasizes the necessity of practicing distinctive rhythms, and at fol. 22v. sets down examples using such galloping patterns as these (sung to a six-note scale):

To sing a *discante*, according to him, means singing a rhythmic (or rhythmic and melodic) variant of a plainsong. For an example he contents himself with a natural hexachord sung up and down in minims, ending on D. His *discantes* immediately follow. Each plainsong minim suffers fracture into either two crotchets, or a dotted crotchet and quaver, or a crotchet and two quavers. Thus, a *discante* of a minim, C, means something such as a crotchet C followed by two quavers at the same pitch. Though the pitch in a *discante* may on occasion rise a step above or descend a step below the plainsong original, still a *discante* as illustrated in his examples never flowers into a counterpoint above a given *cantus firmus*. At best, he allows it to become no more than embroidery stitched over the plainsong original. As vocal embroidery it belongs with the other vocal exercises in the *Súmula*, and not in the sections on *contrapunto y composición*.

At fol. 25r. he passes to a discussion of proportions. The proper mensuration sign for three minims in a bar [*compás*] would be C3; for three semibreves in a bar ₵; and for three breves in a bar $\frac{2}{6}$, according to the *Súmula*.

AS AN EXAMPLE of their simultaneous use in a three-part composition, he gives the following excerpt, the *tiple* (superius) being directed to sing three semibreves in the bar, the *tenor* three minims, and the *contra* three breves. Since no source is listed for the excerpt, Durán himself must be accepted as the composer. The modality and even disposition of note-values resemble Urrede's *Nunca fué pena mayor*, to whose generation he obviously belonged, even if there is no evidence that the two ever became personal friends.

Cum Sancto Spiritu

Súmula de canto de órgano, fol. 25.

DOMINGO MARCOS DURÁN

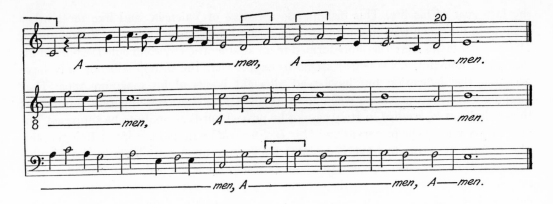

Guillermo Despuig (fl. 1495)

GUILLERMO DESPUIG (= Guillermus de Podio), though at present somewhat neglected, exerted far more influence on his immediate Spanish followers than did his notorious contemporary, Ramos de Pareja. Aside from Durán, no Spanish theorist before Salinas (*De musica libri septem*, 1577) even so much as mentions Ramos. But the list of those who extol Despuig reaches great lengths. Beginning with Francisco Tovar (*Libro de música prática*, Barcelona, 1510), and continuing with Gonzalo Martínez de Bizcargui (*Arte de canto llano e contrapunto e canto de órgano*, Saragossa, 1508), Juan Bermudo (*Declaración de instrumentos*, Osuna, 1549 and 1555), Luys de Villafranca, *Breue instrución de canto llano*, Seville, 1565), Martín de Tapia Numantino (*Vergel de música*, Burgo de Osma, 1570) [55] – not to proceed still further with such distinctly baroque theorists as Andrés de Monserrate (*Arte breve, y compendiosa*, Valencia, 1614) and Antonio de la Cruz Brocarte (*Medula de la música theorica*, Salamanca, 1707),[56] Despuig wins nods of approval from a continuing succession of peninsular authorities. Martínez de Bizcargui in 1528 summarizes their attitude: "He was a scholar expert in every field, but especially in music." [57]

Despuig differs from Ramos in several crucial respects. Insofar as biography is concerned, Ramos's is better known because Despuig – not so vainglorious – tells very little about himself in either his *Ars musicorum* printed at Valencia,[58] or his *In Enchiridion de principiis musice discipline* preserved in manuscript at the Bologna Liceo Musicale (Cod. 159, fols. 134–190). However, the *Ars musicorum* clearly enough reveals him to have been no mere underling but a personal friend of the dedicatee, Alfonso of Aragon (c. 1440–1514), bishop of Tortosa from 1475–1513 and archbishop of Tarragona during

[55] See Anglés-Subirá, *Catálogo Musical de la Biblioteca Nacional*, II (Barcelona: Instituto Español de Musicología, 1949), pp. 220, 219, 164, 233.

[56] *Ibid.*, II, 128, 243.

[57] "... tan experto hombre en todo y especial en la musica ...." Cristóbal de Villalón (*Ingeniosa comparación entre lo antiguo y lo presente* [Valladolid: N. Tyerri, 1539; repr. Madrid: Sociedad de bibliófilos españoles, 1898], p. 178) was another who extravagantly praised Guillermo.

[58] Jaime de Villa, a "molt pia" local Maecenas of Valencia, paid the expenses of printing; he paid also for the printing of the 1493 *Istoria de la Passió* by Bernat Fenollar and the 1494 *Hores de la Setmana Sancta* – both in the Valencian tongue, but neither relating to music.

the last year of his life. This bishop was a native of Valencia, and like most other bishops of his epoch was of noble birth, his father having been Duque de Villahermosa. His musical tastes were therefore formed in an aristocratic environment. Despuig in his last paragraph (fol. LXV verso) seems to expect that the bishop will not only have accepted the dedication but have read all eight books of his magnum opus. That Despuig was a mature scholar when he wrote his *Ars musicorum* is apparent throughout the work. That he studied in Italy cannot be proved but is strongly to be supposed, not only on account of the preservation of his *In Enchiridion* in manuscript at Bologna, but also because it seems to have been intended for use among students in the Spanish college at Bologna. Juan de Vera, to whom *In Enchiridion* was dedicated, was one of the more erudite Spanish clergy of the epoch, rising from a mere precentor's dignity in the cathedral at Valencia to the episcopate – and eventually cardinalate, after Rodrigo Borja (his fellow-townsman) became Pope Alexander VI.

From external sources a few further biographical hints can be gleaned. A second copy [59] of his 1495 *Ars musicorum* preserved in the Madrid Biblioteca Nacional but overlooked in the 1949 *Catálogo musical* begins with a marginal notation (probably antedating 1600) which states that de Podio (= Despuig) was descended from a distinguished Tortosa family. Tortosa, on the eastern coast of Spain between Barcelona and Valencia, seems then the likeliest place of his birth. As for ecclesiastical preferment, Jaime Moll Roqueta discovered a notice in the *Liber Collationum*, LXXII (fols. 115–116v.) of the Barcelona *obispado* showing that a Guillermo Molins de Podio, priest and prebendary of Barcelona Cathedral, was on 20 June 1474 beneficed in the royal chapel of John II of Aragon.[60] This assignment probably lasted five years. The discovery of one further proof of ecclesiastical preferment was made by José Ruiz de Lihory and published in his *La música en Valencia* (1903).[61] His evidence, found at the Valencian Archivo del Reino, showed that a Guillermo Puig held a benefice in the parish church of Santa Catalina at Alcira sometime between 1473 and 1483. Curial records made him the son of Pedro Puig who was in 1477 a notary public at Valencia; and showed that because he was only in minor orders, he had been temporarily forced out of his benefice in 1479 by a competitor.

THE *Ars musicorum*, printed in Gothic, two columns to the page, and reaching 68 leaves, chooses a more learned audience than any other treatise published in Renaissance Spain, excepting that of Salinas. Proof is found in the fact that the 1495 *Ars musicorum* and the 1577 *De musica libri septem* were the only two published in Latin, while all others are in Spanish. Despuig was not a little proud of his own ability to write correct

[59] The two copies at the Biblioteca Nacional are listed under call numbers I 1947 and I 1518. This latter copy bears on its first leaf the following notation: *Guillermo Despuyg, familia antigua, y noble de tortosa.* No copy bore I 1564/1 as its call number in 1954.

[60] Anglés, "La notación musical española de la segunda mitad del siglo XV," *Anuario Musical*, II (1947), p. 158, n. 3. On the flourishing state of music at John's court see *MME*, I, 37.

[61] *La música en Valencia: Diccionario Biográfico y Crítico* (Valencia: Est. tip. Domenech, 1903), p. 378. The anonymous author of the article on Despuig in the *Diccionario de la música Labor* (Barcelona: Editorial Labor, 1954 [I, 714b]) discounts this evidence.

and elegant Latin. Indeed after the usual compliments to his patron and formal bow to the authority of Boethius he next strikes out against "other theorists" who dare write on music but know so little Latin that they assign *diatessaron*, *diapente*, and *diapason* to the feminine gender. This error in gender is of course exactly the mistake that Ramos de Pareja made repeatedly in his *Musica practica* of 1482.[62] Since on every disputed point Despuig sides with tradition against Ramos, it seems quite probable that he has the latter in mind when he lashes out against ignorant Latinists: especially if Despuig's manuscript *In Enchiridion* conserved at Bologna be taken as evidence that he travelled in Italy while the fires lit by his compatriot were still raging at full blast.

His *Ars musicorum*, on account of its learned language and of its length (eight books), at once impresses the reader as having been an attempt at a definitive and exhaustive treatise. Book I – comprising eighteen chapters – works systematically through such topics as the origin of music, its proper definition, the meaning of consonance and dissonance, the divisions of music (*mundana*, *humana*, *et instrumentalis* [I, vii]), the proper classification of musical instruments (strings, keyed woodwind, brass and wind without keys [I, viii]), typology of vocal music (plainsong, counterpoint, and polyphony [I, ix]); and eventually reaches the topic which because of the space devoted to it manifestly interests him more than any other in Book I: namely the proper size of such controversial intervals as the semitone, the whole step, major and minor thirds, and major and minor sixths (I, xvi–xviii). If one sentence were to be extracted as typical of his attitude it might be this from I, vi: [63]

The size of musical intervals can be judged by two distinct faculties: first, by that of hearing, which recognizes the distances between high and low sounds; second, by that of reason which measures such intervals by mathematical and scientific criteria.

Despuig throughout his entire treatise ranges himself beside those who believe that music can be properly understood only by skilled mathematicians.

Book II begins with the question: shall the diatessaron (perfect fourth) be accounted a consonance? After arguing the matter through three chapters he decides the case affirmatively. In so doing, he anticipates Salinas (*De musica libri septem*, 1577, p. 56) – although it must be confessed without displaying any of the latter's vast erudition in the arguments which he advances. Despuig's best reason for accepting the perfect fourth as a consonance seems to be merely the fact that it completes the octave. Counting intervals from the tenor, the fourth above obviously does complete the octave when a fifth is used below. But even so, Cornago, Madrid, and Torre, not to mention any other of Despuig's contemporaries, conscientiously avoided the interval of a fourth between outer voices

---

[62] Wolf ed., pp. 8, 49–50, 100–101.

[63] Passage beginning: *Musice igitur facultas duas habet iudicij partes*. Andrés de Monserrate in his *Arte breve, y compendiosa* (Valencia: Pedro Patricio Mey, 1614), p. 14, cites with approval another passage of like tenor (III, 21) beginning *Nisi de fonte Geometriae, Arithmeticaeque gustaueris, perfectus Musicus esse non poteris*. Monserrate – who always cites the name as Guillermo de Podio (not Despuig) – seems to have been a fanatical admirer. See other citations in his *Arte breve* at pp. 26 ("el grande Musico Guillermo de Po-dio"), 40–41, 54, 66–68, 78, 90–91, 95, 97. Monserrate's opinion is all the more interesting because he was himself so well read in theoretical texts.

and the tenor: as reference to their examples in the Palace Songbook at once discloses. Salinas in 1577 adduced an example from Josquin des Prez's *Missa L'Homme armé Sexti toni*, in the *Et resurrexit* of which the bare fourth between only two voices is sounded at the very beginning.[64] Whether Despuig could have found a Spanish example after sufficient looking is, however, an irrelevant point. He differs from Salinas no more conspicuously than in his willingness to rely upon reason, and reason alone, in deciding all moot questions in musical theory. Not here nor at any other place does he feel it necessary – as did Ramos and Salinas writing in Latin, and Bermudo, Santa María, Tapia, and Montanos writing in Spanish – to buttress theory with examples from respected composers.

In Book II, chapters iv, v, vi, he defines the diatonic, chromatic, and enharmonic genera. For once his definitions do not materially conflict with Ramos's (*Musica practica*, Pars I, Tract. II, cap. vi). But he accepts none of his rival's tuning innovations, preferring instead the Pythagorean system endorsed by all *Guidonis sequaces* (as Ramos called the conservatives). When therefore in Book III he turns arithmetician, telling in what proportions to divide the monochord, he merely repeats the ratios prescribed by all orthodox theorists.

Like Gaffurio,[65] or any other Pythagorean tuner for that matter, he accepts "ten as the symbol of truth." The significance of the number ten in Pythagorean theory was widely understood in Despuig's generation. Indeed Raphael in his celebrated painting, "The School of Athens," identified Pythagoras perfectly when he showed an elderly man in the foreground with no more than a tablet in hand on which is inscribed the perfect number 10 – the fundamental numbers 1, 2, 3, 4 being written beneath. So significant were these fundamental numbers adding up to ten that Pythagoreans were willing to accept surprisingly complicated ratios for all other intervals if only octaves $(2:1)$, fifths $(3:2)$ and fourths $(4:3)$ were in every case exactly tuned. Ramos, as we have already seen, willingly sacrificed the fourths, D–G and d–g, and the fifth, G–d, in order to obtain three major thirds in the $5:4$ ratio, three minor thirds in the $6:5$ ratio, and all diatonic semitones in the $16:15$ ratio. This sacrifice Despuig, Gaffurio, and other conservatives for that matter, categorically refused to make.

As a result Despuig's major and minor thirds and diatonic semitones must be expressed in the following ratios (fols. xix *verso* – xx *recto*):

> major thirds $= 81:64$ (C–E, F–A, G–B♮, B♭–d)
> minor thirds $= 32:27$ (A₁–C, B₁♮–D, D–F, E–G, G–B♭)
> diatonic semitones $= 256:243$ (B₁♮–C, E–F, A–B♭).

As for the chromatic semitone (B♭–B♮), his ratio of $2187:2048$ [66] results in a distinctly larger interval than his $256:243$ diatonic semitone. The Sevillian anonymous of 1480 and

---

[64] *Werken van Josquin Des Prés*, ed. A. Smijers (Leipzig: Fr. Kistner and C. F. W. Siegel, 1931), V, 118, bar 82 (Salinas, p. 56, lines 5–8).

[65] *Theorica* (1492), Lib. II, cap. viii.

[66] On Gaffurio's use of the 2187 : 2048 semitone see Giovanni Spataro, *Dilucide et probatissime demonstratione* (Bologna, 1521), facs. ed., Johannes Wolf [Berlin: Martin Breslauer, 1925], fol. a 5 verso.

Ramos in 1482 had, of course, decreed the chromatic semitone to be the smaller. Despuig, when he recites orthodox Pythagorean tuning doctrine, establishes a precedent to be followed by all Spanish theorists of the next generation, except Martínez de Bizcargui.

In Book IV he discusses the eight modes, at first abstractly. Only in Book V at chapter xii does he actually recite the notes which may be used in plainchant, carrying them up to f¹. His decision to reduce the number of *graves* from the customary eight to seven (thus equalizing the number of *graves*, *agudas*, and *sobre agudas*) caused the same Martínez de Bizcargui who dared to disagree on the relative size of the chromatic and diatonic semitones to censure him for a fault that he can be but rarely accused of – reckless innovation (*Arte de canto llano* [Burgos, 1528], ch. 2).[67]

Among Despuig's musical examples in Book V there is one plainsong (chapter xviii [fol. 41v.]) the crucial fifth note of which he decrees must without fail be sharped (i.e., naturalized). The chant in question is a Mass-introit sung on such days as February 5 (St. Agatha), August 15 (Assumption), November 1 (All Saints), and December 29 (St. Thomas) – *Gaudeamus omnes in Domino, diem festum*. In all presently-used liturgical books, the fifth note in this extremely ancient (perhaps third century) introit is on the other hand flatted (B♭), the first incise reading thus:

Whether the fifth note is to be flatted or naturalized poses a by no means academic question. It was the first incise of this identical *Gaudeamus*-introit which Cristóbal de Morales was to use in 1538 as a tenor ostinato in his festal motet *a 6* composed for the Nice peace parley between Charles V and Francis I, *Jubilate Deo omnis terra*.[68] In turn, Morales's motet was transcribed for vihuela by Enríquez de Valderrábano in *Silva de sirenas* (1547). Every time the latter could transcribe the tenor ostinato with B♮ instead of B♭ he did so. When Victoria later parodied Morales's *Jubilate Deo* in his six-voiced *Missa Gaudeamus* (1576) he called, however, for only the B♭. Despuig commemorated ancient Spanish custom when signalizing the B♮ – a custom still strongly observed in 1547 by Enríquez de Valderrábano. Victoria turned to the Roman tradition of accidentalizing this same chant when he composed his *Missa Gaudeamus*.

In Book VII, chapters x – xxxiii (with the exception of xviii, xxiv, and xxvii), Despuig translates into Latin [69] the very material already available in Spanish at the end of his *In Enchiridion*, the manuscript treatise now conserved at Bologna.[70] Were it not fully known from other sources, a comparison of the two versions, Latin and Spanish, would reveal at once that *cantus mensurabilis* (Book VII, ch. xxxvi [f. LV *verso*]) is the

---

[67] "... donde el dicho guillermo no tuvo razon de diminuir las ocho graues en siete y quitar la costumbre segun de mucho tiempo aca sea enseñado..."

[68] Actually *quintus*-part (*Il primo libro de motetti a sei voce* [Venice: Scotto, 1549]).

[69] Or viceversa. The Latin may just as well have been composed first.

[70] Gaetano Gaspari, *Catalogo della Biblioteca del Liceo Musicale di Bologna* (Bologna: Lib. Romagnoli dall'Acqua, 1890), I, 159.

Latin for *canto de órgano*.[71] The examples in the Spanish manuscript version show a greater number of notes in ligature, nine to be exact, than those in the printed *Ars*, where five notes are the upper limit. The oblique ligature which Durán called *alfado* is referred to as an *alpha* [72] in Despuig's Spanish text. Despuig follows both Tinctoris and Gaffurio when he declares that the first note in a descending *alpha* (= *alfado*) without left-hand tail properly should be a long and the second a breve; but disagrees with Gaffurio when he says the two notes in an ascending *alpha* without left-hand tail should likewise be rendered as a long followed by a breve. Despuig calls the ascending *alpha* old-fashioned and a ligature "all moderns have rightly discarded." [73]

He disagrees with Gaffurio not only on time-values in the ascending *alpha* but also on a more important issue in mensural theory. Gaffurio taught that a note of ternary time-value can be "imperfected" (i.e., diminished in time-value) by more than a third of its original time-value. To be more specific, he claimed that a breve ordinarily equalling nine minims in *prolatio perfecta in tempore perfecto* can by a clever flanking arrangement of minims be robbed of almost half its ordinary time-value and reduced to the equivalent of a mere five minims. A diagram from his *Practica musice* (Milan, 1496, fol. bb i *verso*) will clarify his doctrine. Ordinarily with a mensuration sign of the dotted circle (*prolatio perfecta in tempore perfecto*)

or in modern terms the breve equals

But at fol. bb iiij he asserts that a breve "imperfected" by minims flanking it in the following arrangement (still presuming *prolatio perfecta in tempore perfecto*):

will lose one-third of its total ordinary time-value to the first pair of minims and a further ninth to the last minim.[74] In consequence, the modern equivalent of the above four notes cannot be

but has to become instead

With Gaffurio, Despuig agrees that the second minim of such an initial pair doubles

---

[71] Anglés, "La notación...", p. 171.

[72] *Ibid.*, p. 167.

[73] *Ibid.*, p. 168: "... porque meritamente [asçendientes] son fuera lançadas por los modernos." Ramos and Despuig both adhered to the *LB* rule for the *alpha* without left-hand tail. See Wolf ed., p. 79.

[74] *Practica musice* (1496), fol. bb iiij: "... si duae ipsae minimae praecedentes imperficerent ipsam breuem quo ad totum: cuius ipsae sint tertia pars per alterationem secundae minimae: tunc sequens minima imperficiet ipsam quo ad tertiam partem propinquam a parte post: & secunda pars propinqua perfecta est. Atque ita breuis ipsa integra nouem minimas continens: huiusmodi detractione: quattuor propriae quantitatis minimas relinquit."

in time-value. He also agrees that such a pair "imperfecting" such a breve will rob it of one-third its ordinary total value. But he vehemently denies Gaffurio the right to diminish the value of any imperfected note beyond the limit of one-third its recognized perfect value. Gaffurio subdivided such notes as maximas, longs, and breves into components. The *pars propinqua* was the component of next lower value (i.e., *pars propinqua* of a breve would be a semibreve). Going down the ladder he spoke of a *pars remota*, then *remotior*, and, lowest of all, *remotissimus*. With Gaffurio's right to imperfect the whole *or* any pars, Despuig does not disagree. What Despuig does violently contest is Gaffurio's right to imperfect the whole *and* any of the residual *partes*.

To make his objection stick, he goes so far as to protest in both Latin and Spanish: *Porque aquella regla que ellos dizen: Omnis figura ternaria, quantum ad totum et quantum ad partes, potest imperfici, ita copulatiue sumpta, falsa est; disiuncte autem, id est, secundum totum uel secundum partes, es verdadera.*[75] (For that rule which they repeat: "Every ternary note-value can be imperfected both in the whole *and* in its parts," using the conjunction *and*, is false; but using the disjunctive *or*: ". . . [imperfected] in the whole *or* in its parts," the rule holds true).

Purely academic though such a distinction between the doctrine of Gaffurio and Despuig may seem, it would yet be worth recalling, because it indicates: (1) that Spanish singers were accustomed to contending with all the notational intricacies of fifteenth-century music; (2) that peninsular theorists never blindly followed the lead of foreign theorists, even when so traditionally minded as Depuig; (3) that Ramos was by no means the only fifteenth-century Spaniard who grappled with difficult problems.

Despuig in the last book of his *Ars musicorum* discusses proportions. Here again he dares match wits with Gaffurio,[76] even when treating of admittedly treacherous topics. He lucidly explains and illustrates not only the easier proportions (2:1; 3:1; 4:1; 6:1; 8:1; 16:1) but also the more complex juxtapositions such as 3 against 2 and 4 against 3.[77] José Subirá in his ambitious *Historia de la música española e hispanoamericana* (Barcelona: Salvat, 1953, p. 170) reproduces in facsimile fol. 59v. from Despuig's *Ars*. The first example transcribed below is a modern solution of the rhythmic problem to be seen on the page reproduced by Subirá. The other four excerpts illustrate certain of his more complex proportions. But Despuig's examples, cleverly constructed though they always are, show him to have been more than an ingenious puzzle-maker. He somehow manages to write music and not merely proportions, even when pitting a melody that must be rendered in $\frac{9}{8}$ (upper part) against one that must be transcribed in $\frac{4}{4}$ (lower part). Both he and Gaffurio compose all their *exempla proportionum* a 2, with the proportions in the top voice. Gaffurio is the more catholic in choosing his modes, and the more adventuresome in changing proportions within an example. To show his Spanish devotion to plainsong, Despuig insists on paraphrasing a chant even in the "proportioned" voice of such examples as the first and fourth below (*Nunc Sancte nobis* "for ordinary Sundays").

[75] Anglés, "La notación ...", p. 166.

[76] Gaffurio's entire Book IV of the *Practica* deals with proportions.

[77] Despuig, *Ars*, fols. LVIII v. – LXI v. (easier) and LXII r. – LXIII r. (harder).

Exemplum quadruple proportionis

Ars musicorum (1495), Lib. VIII, cap. vi, fol. 59v.   GUILLERMO DESPUIG

Exemplum octuple proportionis

Ars musicorum, fols. 60v.–61r.

Exemplum sedecuple proportionis

Ars musicorum, fol. 61 v.

Exemplum sesqualtere proportionis

Ars musicorum, fol. 62 r.

** = DF.

Exemplum sesqualtere sub proportione dupla institue

Ars musicorum, fol. 62 v.

Cristóbal de Escobar (fl. 1498)

NOT BECAUSE its intrinsic value exceeds that of every other early Spanish treatise but because the unique copy was sold to the Prussian State Library in 1924 – and therefore attracted the attention of Johannes Wolf – Cristóbal de Escobar's eight-page *Introduction muy breue de canto llano* (Salamanca, c. 1496) came out in a modern reprint as long ago as 1925, a quarter-century before any other Spanish treatise of its time was reprinted.[78]

Wolf in the 1925 reprint of the *Introduction* disavowed any attempt at analysis. He did however remark that Escobar hews closely to convention. In Escobar's defense it must at once be said that he would have defeated his own purpose had he tried to be original. His aim (plainly stated in his first sentence) was purely didactic; his subject, the generally accepted principles of plainchant. But even though his ambition was quite modest, his few pages do at least reveal what were the most basic and fundamental elements in the Spanish plainsong tradition just at the moment when the great century of church music was opening.

In his tract he identifies himself as a *bachiller*. Since it was published at Salamanca he probably was a bachelor of Salamanca University. Like Durán he insists on listing his authorities by name, even though his plainsong manual can have been intended only for beginners. Guido, as one might expect, serves as his classic authority. To identify each of his ten Guidonian citations he offers this marginal comment: *Guido prima parte* (each time adding an appropriate chapter-number). Once he adumbrates: *Loduuicus de Barcelona. in introductione latina Guidi prima parte*. None of the chapter-numbers cited after "prima parte" corresponds however with chapters in the *Micrologus* nor with divisions in any other Guidonian work printed by Gerbert or Coussemaker. Did he perhaps use some now-lost edition – or revision – of Guido made by Louis of Barcelona? and was the latter the same theorist whom Ramos in 1482 cited as Luis Sánchez, an authority on the emotion-producing qualities of each mode (see above, p. 60)? Escobar does not cite carelessly. His references to Boethius tally exactly, for instance, with the conventional book-and-chapter divisions. Perhaps therefore he quoted his "Guidonian" source just as accurately – but used a Catalonian recension.

Johannes Goscaldus [79] is the authority whom he cites oftenest after Guido. When invoking Goscaldus's authority he refers to first, second, and fourth parts of an unnamed treatise: giving in each case a chapter-number. These numbers show that there must have been at least six chapters in each part – but parts of what treatise one cannot now discover, the very name of Goscaldus being apparently unknown outside Spanish

---

[78] *Gedenkboek aangeboden aan Dr. D. F. Scheurleer* ('s-Gravenhage: Martinus Nijhoff, 1925), pp. 383–391. The unique copy of the *Introduction* passed through the hands of the Madrid antiquarian, Pedro Vindel. For date and place of imprint see Francisco Vindel, *El arte tipográfico en España durante el siglo XV: Salamanca, Zamora, Coria y el reino de Galicia* (Madrid: Relaciones Culturales, 1946), p. 116.

[79] Goscaldus may be a corruption of Godescalchus (= Gottschalk). Escobar does not record Goscaldus's first name, but the Sevillian anonymous of 1480 gives it on fol. 1r., in the following context: "Boecio, Guido, Johannes Goscaldi, Philippus de Bitriaco ..." See Anglés-Subirá, *Catálogo Musical* (Barcelona, 1946), I, 167.

fifteenth- and sixteenth-century sources. Peninsular theorists cite him as an authority
of stellar magnitude. As to what he taught, and even in what order, something can be
inferred from Escobar's citations. Thus, one discovers that Goscaldus broached the
favorite Spanish topic of *conjuntas* (f♯, c♯, e♭, a♭) as early as chapter 2 in his "prima
parte." [80] According to him, the reason for sharping and flatting in plainsong is "neces-
sidad de consonancia." [81] But Goscaldus reserved for *parte quarta capitulo quinto* his
differentiation of the genera: diatonic, chromatic, and enharmonic. As for chromatic
genus Rubinetus said it ought no longer to be defined in Boethius's terms, but rather
taken to mean the *intensiones* (sharps) and *remissiones* (flats) which occur in plainsong
without Guidonian sanction. Relying on such authority, Escobar declares that the singer
who ascends through five scale-degrees in f–g–a–b♮–c^1 sequence, but starting elsewhere[82] (for example, c–d–e–*f*♯–g; d–e–f♯–g♯–a; g–a–b–c^1♯–d^1) makes use of the chromatic genus. Or if the singer widens a diatonic semitone (for example, e–f [e♭–f]; a–b♭
[a♭–b♭]) he also makes use of the chromatic genus.

Besides Goscaldus, Johannes Wolf calls three other authors cited by Escobar *un-
bekannten*; Blasius de Ro., Rubinetus, and Johannes Illarius. [83] As for the easily
identified half-dozen, these include in addition to the familiar trio – Boethius, Gregory,
and Guido, the following three: Remigius, Jean de Muris, and Marchettus. Interestingly
enough, half his sources after Pope Gregory I are theorists whose names do not crop
up in writings outside the peninsula. Evidently, numerous treatises circulated in Spain
c. 1500 which no longer survive. Salamanca or Alcalá de Henares university lecture-
rooms provided the milieu in which they found users.

Escobar resembles Durán when he cites his authorities – even though writing only a
beginner's manual. He also follows in his footsteps when he stresses the importance of
conjunctas (= conjuntas).[84] He even names specific chants in which the first (*Dicit
Dominus*: *Ego cogito* [*Liber usualis*, 1950 edition, p. 1074]), third (*Haec dies* [*LU*, p. 783]),
fourth (*Beatus servus* [*LU*, p. 1203]), seventh, and eighth conjuntas should appear.
True, the *LU* versions of *Haec dies* and *Beatus servus*, now omit the E♭ and F♯ which his
third and fourth conjuntas require. But the *LU* vesions, classified respectively as Modes
II and III, end on "improper" finals. Transposed back so that they end not on the note
A but on the proper finals of D and E, the notes E♭ and F♯ appear just as Escobar
said they would.

Again he resembles Durán (1) in giving a complete set of rules for reading plainchant
written on only the one-line staff [85] and (2) in codifying the rules for intoning at various
classes of festivals. He goes beyond Durán in recognizing the possibile use of other
accidentals than E♭, A♭, F♯, and C♯. The conjuntas which would yield these others

---

[80] *Gedenkboek*, p. 388.

[81] *Ibid*. In discussing the ten conjunctas Escobar foreshadows our "circle of keys" concept.

[82] *Ibid*., p. 387.

[83] Bermudo cited Rubineto as an authority in his 1549 *Declaración*, fol. 12v. (Introduction). Illarius =
the composer *Ylario* who is represented by two four-part motets (*Conceptio tua* and *O admirabile commercium*) in Tarazona Cathedral MS 2, fols. 286 v. – 287 and 274 v. – 275.

[84] *Gedenkboek*, p. 389.

[85] *Ibid*., p. 390. Rules in Latin on p. 391.

would have to begin on E and B. Since these are not yet received into plainsong theory, he prescribes a remedy: "The lack [of a sufficient number of conjuntas] is compensated for by using the fourth diapente-type [f–g–a–b♮–c¹]." [86] Beginning on D the fourth diapente-type does of course yield G♯ just as beginning on A yields d♯.

Alonso Spañon (fl. 1500)

ALONSO SPAÑON, a *bachiller* and therefore a university graduate like both Marcos Durán and Cristóbal de Escobar, published his twelve-page *Introducion muy vtil: y breue de canto llano* at Seville, probably in 1500.[87] Half of his booklet comprises text, the other half plainsong intonations printed on pentagram in a single impression. In chapter x Spañon tells how to read chants copied on only the one-line staff. In his last two chapters he briefly expounds the differences between intonations for psalms, canticles, gospels, epistles, lessons, readings from the prophets, and prayers.

Spañon's instructor, the second published at Seville, is dedicated to Juan Rodríguez de Fonseca, bishop of Cordova; one infers that Spañon enjoyed some dignity in Cordova cathedral. The dedicatee – first president of the Council of the Indies – is known by every student of American history as the archdeacon of Seville who in 1493 helped Columbus prepare for his second voyage, though he later opposed the discoverer. Fonseca's name also figures prominently in the lives of Cortés and Magellan. What the crusading Las Casas did not say of Fonseca but what Spañon's dedication as well as Martínez de Bizcargui's later dedication (1517) reveals is that Fonseca was an intelligent and enthusiastic patron of music. Rivafrecha was another musician who profited from his bounty.

Diego del Puerto (fl. 1504)

THE *Ars cantus plani portus musice vocata siue organici* of Diego del Puerto, whatever its imperfections, at least enjoys the distinction of being the first dated Spanish publication which contains printed polyphony. A booklet of twelve unnumbered leaves, it appeared at Salamanca on August 31, 1504.

In his introduction the author tells the names of his parents, Pedro Derrada and Catalina Martínez del Puerto, describes himself as a sometime student in St. Bartholomew's – the oldest *colegio mayor* (1401) at Salamanca University, calls himself at present a college chaplain and singer, qualifies himself as *sacerdos* and holder of a benefice not requiring residence in Burgos diocese (St. Mary's at Laredo), and submits his booklet to his dedicatee – Alfonso de Castilla, rector of studies in the university (1502–1503) –

---

[86] *Ibid.*, p. 389.

[87] Pedro Bruns was the printer. The year 1498 is too early since Juan de Fonseca, the dedicatee, did not become bishop of Cordova until October 12, 1499. See Pius Boniface Gams, *Series Episcoporum Ecclesiae Catholicae* (Regensburg: G.v.J. Manz, 1873), p. 28.

with an extravagant expression of gratitude for favors already bestowed. He gives two reasons for publishing his book: (1) he feels obliged to his "dear university for manifold benefits" and therefore issues his compendium in testimony of his singular gratitude; (2) after turning over the writings of numerous ancients and moderns he has prepared a summary in parallel columns, Latin and Spanish, that he believes can be mastered in *breuissimo tempore*.

Laudable as are his intentions, the author attempts more than he can reasonably expect to accomplish in so restricted a space. Because he burdens himself with parallel Latin and Spanish text his printer moreover is forced to use almost microscopic type. Some idea of his widely dispersed interests can be gained from his opening sentence, in which he promises to treat the following subjects: plainsong, counterpoint, polyphonic composition in three and four parts, intonations of psalms and responds, method of finding the date of Easter or any other movable feast in a given year, and even the times when marriages may properly be celebrated. As if this were insufficient, he adds an unadvertised page (fol. 12v.) on which he shows a diagram of the *vihuela* and gives directions for tuning it. For a codetta to the coda he then tacks on an 8–line original Spanish poem.

Puerto cites only one modern authority, Gaffurio. He arrives at *conjuntas* as early as fol. 3. He follows Cristóbal de Escobar in citing examples of plainchants requiring E♭'s and F♯'s. At fol. 4 he tells how to read plainchants written on the one-line staff. On fol. 4v. he treats another favorite topic: when to sing B♭ and when B♮ in a passage linking *befabemi* with the note F. At fol. 5 he hurriedly recapitulates the rules for intoning psalms and responds, and gives examples of intonations in each mode. A charming mishap unseats him just here. He or his printer forgets to include examples for Mode VII. Two pages later someone blushes, and confesses: "Mode VII [intonation] was left out by an oversight, but you will see it below" (*Septimus tonus pro obliuionē dimissus fuit, sed infra videbis* [fol.6]).

The differences between his 1504 intonations and Durán's 1492 formulas can be found chiefly in the qualifying accidentals. In Mode IV Puerto adds sharps before the note B: to remind the singer that it must be naturalized. In two Mode VI Glorias – the first, "regular de responsorios," the second, "de oficios" – he inserts the flat-sign before the note B. In his first Mode V *Gloria de oficios* he twice changes the first three notes A–B–c, called for by Durán, to read F–A–c.

These variants are so minute as to be in themselves quite insignificant. But since they are so small, they demonstrate the basic uniformity of the plainsong tradition taught by Durán, Puerto – and for that matter by Escobar, Spañon, Molina, and Águilar. If one compares their intonation-formulas with those set down in Gaffurio's 1496 *Practica musice* printed at Milan, really notable differences begin however to show. The formulas listed by Gaffurio[88] (Book I, chapters 8–15) never once exactly duplicate Durán's or Puerto's. Often they are quite distinct. Gaffurio's Mode VII intonation, for

---

[88] Cf. John Hawkins, *A General History of the Science and Practice of Music* (London: Novello, Ewer, and Company, 1875), I, 132–133.

instance, begins on d [89] instead of G, is much more melismatic at the mediation, and ends on the note d instead of A.[90] Moreover none of his formulas provides for a flex in the middle of the half-verse. The Spanish formulas on the other hand always show a melodic dip at the flex. As a general rule, Gaffurio's are more melismatic both at mediations and at endings. He himself called attention (fol. b iiij *verso*) to the peculiarities that existed in Ambrosian intonations. His *Practica musice* formulas were not Ambrosian, he said, but Roman. If so, the Spanish differed as much from the Roman c. 1500 as did the Ambrosian formulas.

JUST AS Puerto closely follows his peninsular predecessors when treating plainsong, so his doctrine resembles Durán's when he turns to counterpoint and mensurable music. He scores his four-part polyphonic example for *tiple* (= soprano), *contra altus*, *tenor*, and *contra baxo* (= bass). The movements in the bass continuously imply "harmonic" thinking. Of the 13 skips, for instance, eight are of a fourth or a fifth. The example is clearly divided into two halves, the first a "chordal" prelude the second a "fugal" exposition. The bipartite structure is emphasized not only by a double-bar and a change of texture, but also by a shift from C to ₵ in the middle of the example.[91] Both halves continue in the same mode (III). Puerto does indulge in one old-fashioned mannerism. He requires his bass to jump up an octave at cadences, crossing the tenor. He thus avoids the appearance of consecutive fifths.

Bartolomé de Molina (fl. 1506)

A *bachiller en santa theologia* and a friar minor, Bartolomé de Molina published his *Arte de canto llano Lux videntis dicha* (Valladolid: Diego de Gumiel, 1506) [92] not so much for the general welfare but, so he says in his introduction, for the benefit of the clergy in a particular diocese – that of Lugo in the northwestern corner of Spain. In dedicating his 24-page plainsong instructor to the bishop of Lugo, Pedro de Ribera, he makes a strong appeal to local pride. He writes:

Since ignorance is the parent of every error, it ought stoutly to be resisted by all the faithful and especially by the clergy whose duty it is to guide and enlighten those entrusted to their care. Much more ought this city and diocese to combat ignorance both because of its ancient glory as a metropolitan see and the regard in which it is held elsewhere throughout the realm. Knowing your zealous desire that the humblest clergy should be informed and all faults corrected, and realizing moreover that not knowing how to sing is a grievous fault – God Himself having commanded that singers should inhabit the church and stand before the altar, making sweet melody (*Ecclesiasticus 47*) – . . .

---

[89] Gaffurio gives an alternate beginning note: *c*. His Mode VII intonation appears on fol. c iij (*Practica*, 1496).

[90] Gaffurio likewise gives a different ending for Mode I intonation from that given by Durán or Puerto.

[91] Ornithoparcus in *Musice actiue micrologus* (Leipzig, 1519), explained: "hoc signum ₵, huius C, duplum est" (fol. F5v.), an explanation in agreement with Puerto's.

[92] Copy in British Museum (k. 8. f. 2.), but not in Madrid.

His gesture was not made in vain, for at the close (fol. 12v.) the bishop added a commendation in the following terms: "Venerable father, having received and read what you have written, we order it printed at our expense and freely given to all needy clergy in our diocese; a candle is not to be hid but set on a hill, and yours burns brightly." [93]

Molina's instructor follows the conventional division already noted in the Durán and Spañon instructors – six leaves of text and an equal number of music. His authorities include not only Augustine, Bernard, and Guido, but also Arnaldus, Goscaldus, Rubinetus, Peter of Venice, and John of London [Hothby]. The latter five names are invoked elsewhere in Spanish treatises – in Durán's or Escobar's, for instance. Only Hothby's name has on the other hand been often met with in foreign manuals.

Gonzalo Martínez de Bizcargui (fl. 1508)

THE *Arte de canto llano e contrapunto e canto de organo* of Martínez de Bizcargui – first published at Saragossa in 1508,[94] reprinted in a corrected edition at Burgos in 1511,[95] at Saragossa in 1512 and 1517,[96] at Burgos in a revised and enlarged edition in 1528 and 1535,[97] and at Saragossa in five successive printings of the enlarged dated 1531, 1538, 1541, 1549,[98] and 1550 [99] – was by all odds the most successful plainsong instructor published in sixteenth-century Spain. In addition to the ten issues listed above, the Burgos revised edition of 1528 was counterfeited in a replica edition: a copy of which is now in the Madrid Biblioteca Nacional.

At its 1508 maiden appearance in Saragossa it comprised but a modest quarto booklet (printed in Gothic) reaching a dozen unnumbered leaves. Already in the Burgos 1511 imprint it comprised 19 leaves and in the *añadida y glosada* Burgos 1528 imprint it reaches 36 leaves, thrice its original size. From the moment it first appeared, moreover, its popularity extended beyond Burgos diocese. In the introduction to his 1528 *añadida y glosada* edition the author refers to the popularity of his *arte*:

Many times I was importuned to write an instructor, and these frequent requests emboldened

---

[93] Ferdinand Columbus, son of the discoverer, bought a copy of Molina's *Lux videntis* for only 8 *maravedís* in Valladolid. He listed 25 November 1506 as its date of imprint: not as the date of purchase. Cf. *Anuario Musical*, II, 29. Columbus's own entry can be seen in *Catalogue of the Library of Ferdinand Columbus*, facs. ed. (New York, 1905), Item 3321.

[94] Subirá in his *Historia de la música española* mentioned a "primera edición del año 1504 o 1505" without giving any bibliographical references (p. 279). A note in the British Museum copy of the 1508 edition, for which £95 was paid (sign. k.8.f. 22), refers to that edition as having been the first. Moreover there is nothing in the text to support the idea that the 1508 was a reprint or revision. Its colophon reads: "Esta obra fue emprimida enla muy noble y leal cibdad de Carragoça: por George Coci aleman. a.xxiij. dias del mes de Mayo. Año del nascimiento de nuestro saluador Jesu christo de mill y quinientos y ocho años."

[95] Copy in Biblioteca Nacional, Madrid (see Anglés-Subirá, *Catálogo*, II, 218).

[96] For whereabouts of the Saragossa imprints see Juan M. Sánchez, *Bibliografía Aragonesa* (Madrid: Imp. Clásica Española, 1913), I, 126, 241, 275, 292, 389, 399.

[97] 1528 edn. at Madrid (Anglés-Subirá, *Cat.*, II, 220). Also a copy in the British Museum (k. 8. f. 21). 1535 edn. at Washington, D. C. (Library of Congress).

[98] Data concerning 1538, 1541, 1549 editions in Madrid Bibl. Nac. MS 14035.254.

[99] 1550 edition in British Museum (k. 8. f. 7).

me to write an *Introduction to plainsong, counterpoint, and mensurable music* which has now these nine or ten years been read everywhere in Spain.

As if the evidence of the frequent editions and the author's own testimony were not sufficient to prove its immediate and widespread success, the attacks which the author had to suffer from Juan de Espinosa of Toledo would clinch the proof. Espinosa's *Retractaciones de los errores et falsedades que escriuio gonçalo martinez de biscargui* (Toledo, 1514) listed Bizcargui's "mistakes" one by one; but proved nothing so devastatingly as the vogue that these "errors" already enjoyed in Toledo archdiocese.

There must obviously have been reasons for such success. One therefore asks (1) who was Bizcargui? (2) how did his *arte* differ from its competitors? (3) why did it become so popular?

HE BOASTS neither of his ancestry nor of his schooling. His dedications, first to Fray Pascual de Fuenpudia and then to Juan Rodríguez de Fonseca, successive bishops of Burgos, are couched in terms implying that he was chapelmaster in Burgos cathedral. Since he flaunts no bachelor's degree, he cannot be presumed to have attended Salamanca or Alcalá de Henares universities. Nevertheless he had read widely, as his citations from Aristoxenus, Ptolemy, Macrobius, Boethius, Isidore, and Guido show. He does not, however, cite the recurring group of theorists invoked by Durán, Escobar, and Molina. His late medieval authority is Jean de Muris. His modern one is Guillermo Despuig, whom he cites with such constancy as to suggest that he had studied with Despuig. His attitude towards the Tortosan, though not as reverential as Spataro's towards Ramos, is nevertheless extremely appreciative. He moreover seems to have known certain writings of Despuig in addition to those still extant. After seven references to Guillermo in the 1511 edition he adds *Liber* and *caput* numbers, not mentioning a title. Only two of these book-and-chapter references, however, correspond with the printed version of the *Ars musicorum*. Some other work by Despuig (he mentions a *comento* of Guillermo in his 1528 enlarged edition) may therefore have served him as a source. Gaffurio's name is conspicuously absent from any of Martínez de Bizcargui's citations.

As for his dates, he was still alive in 1541 when he published an octavo *tonero* of 23 leaves, the music being printed in black notes over red lines instead of xylographically. The title-page of the exemplar in the Biblioteca de la Real Academia Española is missing, but the first sentence is self-explanatory: *Intonationes segun vso delos modernos*: || *que hoy cantan y intonan enla yglesia romana.* || *Corregidas y remiradas por Gonçalo mar* || *tinez de Bizcargui*: || *Imprimidas enla noble* || *ciudad de çaragoça. Año de M. D.xlj.*

HIS *arte* differs from other Spanish theory texts not because the topics are novel. Indeed the subjects are conspicuously the same. But in almost every instance he carries his explanations much further than any predecessor had attempted. Moreover he gives not only clear, precise, and full sets of rules, but also he coaxes the student by giving reasons for studying the more difficult topics: such as plainchant written on only one line. Since chapter 34 in the 1528 edition provides as good an example of his "coaxing" as any, and since also the information is historically valuable, this chapter is abridged below in a one-paragraph summary.

Not a few singers resent the effort that learning to read plainchant written on the one-line staff involves. Granted chant copied on five lines is easier to read, still the principles of one-line notation should be studied; for if a singer can read chant copied on one line he can certainly read it off five lines. The reverse is by no means true. Indeed a singer is no more able to read chant on the one-line staff after a year spent exclusively with five-line notation than he was before he began. Even ten years with five lines will not help him. But those who have started with one-line necessarily become masters of five-line notation. This is true because no one can learn to read chant on one line without mastering the whole theory of plainsong. There is an added reason for studying one-line notation. Everywhere in Spain from the southern tip to the northern boundary there is not a parish church but owns books written on the one-line staff, while five-line books are found only in cathedrals, some collegiate churches, and most exceptionally in a parish church. Bishops and their deputies who examine candidates should therefore insist upon ability to read one-line chant. It is too much to hope that parish churches will soon replace their old chant books; most are too poor, especially here in the diocese of Burgos. I admit that I prefer to teach the five-line staff, because it is easier to learn; but I also believe in doing my duty.

Bizcargui differs from contemporary theorists not because he knows more but because he gives fuller explanations of difficult topics and constantly coaxes the laggard pupil. He does not disdain to substitute an easier term such as *grados* for a harder traditional term, *deduciones*. He does not, moreover, disdain to give example after example illustrating the same point, if only clarity be achieved. Then again he is bold where other writers are timid. Escobar in 1496 wanted to say that other accidentals were used in plainsong besides e♭, a♭, f♯ and c♯ (in addition, of course, to the traditionally added b♭). But he buried the statement at the end of a paragraph, and even then avoided giving examples. Bizcargui, on the other hand, says in so many words: accidentals up to d♭ and d♯ are used. To drive home the point, he shows examples with e♭, a♭ and d♭ as printed accidentals.

His directness and circumstantiality gained him readers and at the same time provoked enemies. He offended his learned contemporaries most by asserting with Ramos de Pareja that the diatonic semitone is actually larger than the chromatic. He pleaded his own experiments with the monochord in justification rather than any statement by Ramos. He knew that he disagreed with Guillermo Despuig on this controversial issue, but had the courage of his convictions, founding them on *la practica que es la esperiencia dela cuerda.*[100]

If he seems to have been exceptionally honest and forthright, he was not on the other hand contentious and truculent. He did not elevate his own convictions founded on personal experience to the level of dogma – as did Ramos de Pareja. Instead, he invited his critics to visit him in Burgos and to confer and test his experiments. For once, then, popular success was the reward a theorist who insisted on retaining his own integrity, who disdained the arts of the demagogue, and above all, who refused to water down his doctrine for the sake of the indolent student.

[100] 1511 (Burgos) edition, fol. 12v.

Francisco Tovar (fl. 1510)

IN THE *Libro de musica pratica* (Barcelona: Johan Rosembach, 1510) [101] of Mosen Francisco Tovar the scholastic tradition with its ingenious system of rationalization reasserts itself with full vigor. As for Tovar's biography, he calls himself in the colophon of his book a native of the small village of Pareja in the diocese of Cuenca. At fol. 33 v. he mentions having many times disputed publicly in Sicily and also at Rome and Saragossa. Since he now holds minor office in Barcelona Cathedral, he dedicates his treatise to the bishop and chapter. Soon thereafter he was to become chapelmaster in Tarragona Cathedral (1510), where he seems to have remained six years. His successor, Juan de Alcalá, was appointed in 1516.

Either in Rome or elsewhere – if homonyms do not play us false – he grew to such terms of friendship with Francisco de Peñalosa that he was chosen by the latter to present to the Seville chapter Pope Leo X's 1518 brief, *Dudum vos* (entry in the Sevillian *Actas Capitulares*, IX [1517–1519] at fol. 137 [May 26, 1518]). During the next two years a Francisco de Tovar was *cantor* in Granada Cathedral; he became chapelmaster in 1521 and died at Granada on May 22, 1522.

His treatise at once makes it plain that he admires Guillermo Despuig as the prince of "modern" theorists but despises Martínez de Bizcargui, *criado del obispo de Burgos* (the bishop of Burgos's servant) as nothing but a vulgar upstart who offends every learned musician by pretending that the diatonic semitone is larger than the chromatic.[102] In Tovar's opinion Guido must still be called *sapientissimo*. Like a true scholastic, he therefore seeks a suitable reason for enlarging the Guidonian staff to include ten lines (the double five-line system). Not the necessity of accommodating 20 letter-name notes from G_1 to e^1, but rather the desirability of commemorating the Ten Commandments, accounts for the expansion of the great staff to a double five-line system, says Tovar. Plainsong begins on G to commemorate the Greeks. The interval from A to e is a perfect fifth, the most consonant of intervals, in commemoration of the consonance joining *A*dam and *E*ve.

On the practical side he proves more helpful. He declares that upper voice-parts in Modes I and II, VII and VIII *tienen necesidad de acidencia en sus clausulas* (necessarily accidentalize at cadences).[103] Upper voice-parts in any of these four *modos traen el ssemitono sub intellecto* (utilize the unwritten semitone). At cadences in Modes I and II the written notes d–c–d must be performed d–c♯–d. The written notes g–f–g similarly must be sung g–f♯–g. *Sub intellectas* being universally used, one cannot at cadences

[101] This small folio contains 35 numbered leaves preceded by four unnumbered. The British Museum copy shows handwritten music examples over the printed five-line staves, but in the Biblioteca Nacional (Madrid) copy these staves remain empty. For further bibliographical details, see H. Anglés, *La música española desde la edad media* (Barcelona: Bibl. Central, 1941), p. 56.

[102] Francisco Tovar, *Libro de musica pratica*, fol. 12. Lest however Tovar be thought unduly harsh it should be here added that even the progressive Bermudo joined him in excoriating Bizcargui. In his *Declaración* (1555) at fol. 68 he wrote: "If you think you can learn anything about the subject from reading Bizcargui and other barbarous authors who call themselves theorists you are mistaken." Bermudo is here discussing the size of semitones.

[103] Tovar, fol. 34v. For criticism of Tovar's cadences see Bermudo, *op. cit.*, fol. 87v.

write B–c–B in counterpoint against d–c–d, nor e–f–e in counterpoint against g–f–g. Although on paper the second interval in each group would appear to be a unison, in actual performance it will sound as a dissonance (augmented unison). Tovar's injunctions confirm the thesis advanced by Charles Warren Fox in his paper on Spanish vihuela transcriptions of polyphonic music: namely, that sharps were used much more frequently than modern editors might suggest.

When categorizing Tovar's contribution to Spanish musical theory, his successor, Martín de Tapia (*Vergel de música* [Burgo de Osma: Diego Fernández de Córdova, 1570], fol. 79v.), called him *vno de los principales que en musica en nuestro lenguage scribieron* ("one of the most important writers on music in our language"). Tovar's *Musica pratica* did not go through ten editions but Tapia's allusions show it was still regarded as an anthoritative text sixty years after publication. In the latter's opinion Tovar was a mensural authority equal in rank with Tinctoris and Ornithoparcus.[104]

Juan de Espinosa (fl. 1514)

THREE TREATISES by Juan de Espinosa survive: (1) *Retractaciones de los errores et falsedades* (Toledo: Arnaldo Guillermo de Brocar, 1514), an attack on Martínez de Bizcargui; (2) *Tractado de principios de musica practica e theorica sin dexar ninguna cosa atras* (Toledo: Brocar, 1520), a text covering the same ground as Despuig's 1495 *Ars musicorum* but in Spanish; (3) *Tractado breue de principios de canto llano*, a plainsong instructor of uncertain date printed in Toledo. The latter (copy in the British Museum) reaches 24 leaves in small octavo. Like Escobar's and Molina's instructors, it contains no music notation. In his dedication to Martín de Mendoza, archdeacon of Talavera and Guadalajara, he claims to have hit upon a new method (*nueva manera*) that has proved uniquely successful at Toledo. The actual substance cannot however be rated as novel.

Espinosa in his 1520 *Tractado* reveals his first patron to have been the son of the famous Marqués de Santillana – Archbishop Pedro González de Mendoza of Toledo. This ecclesiastic was primate of Spain from 1483-1495. After Cardinal Mendoza's death he transferred from Toledo to Seville in order to serve another scion of the same family, Diego Hurtado de Mendoza (archbishop of Seville, 1486-1502), in whose household he remained until the latter's death. "All that I am I owe to the illustrious Mendoza family," gracefully acknowledges Espinosa in his 1520 *Tractado*. Among his later protectors he seems to have counted Francisco de Bobadilla, bishop of Salamanca, 1511–1529. Bobadilla stirred him to write against Martínez de Bizcargui, he claims in chapter 63 of his *Tractado*. Espinosa in 1520 was archpriest of St. Eulalia, a dignity in Toledo Cathedral. Still later he occupied a canonry at Burgos.[105]

---

[104] Tapia, fol. 105v.: "Segun tres doctores ... touar, jo. tintor.andrea." At fol. 12v. Tapia cites "Tobar, Lux bela, Ciruelo" (for information concerning Pedro Ciruelo see note 141 below). The theorists who still cited Tovar in the next century include: Pedro Cerone (*El melopeo y maestro* [Naples, 1613]), Andrés de Monserrate (*Arte breve* [Valencia, 1614]), and Manoel Nunes da Sylva (*Arte minima* [Lisbon, 1685]).

[105] Tapia, fol. 76v.: "Si algunos porfiaren a cantar siempre estos dos modos [V, VI] por B mol, quiten la tercera specie de el Diapente que es de Fa, a Fa, Como pareze quitarla el reuerendo Ioan de espinosa,

Because he was such a conservative in matters theoretical it is difficult to believe that he was the same Juan de Espinosa who composed two plaintive villancicos conserved in the great collection of secular song belonging to the reigns of Ferdinand and Isabella, the Palace Songbook (nos. 4 and 202). On the other hand his dates and aristocratic connections do not forbid such a supposition. Whether the composer and theorist were one, the theoretical treatises deserve attention because his learning equals that of any writer of his generation. He broke lances in contentions over adiaphora and fell off his charger into the mire of name-calling, but he had mastered his Boethius.

Gaspar de Águilar (fl. 1530)

THE ONLY known copy of the *Arte de principios de canto llano: nueuamente emendado y corregido por Gaspar de Aguilar* is preserved in the Biblioteca Colombina (sign. 15-2-4) but without date or place of imprint. Its date of publication must however be fixed between 1530–1537 [106] because of its dedication to Pedro Manrique, bishop of Ciudad Rodrigo. (The latter's dates in the see obviously fix the outer limits of publication.)

The unique surviving copy of this 32-page *arte* cannot be a first edition since Águilar calls it "newly emended and corrected." In his dedication he expresses the hope it will win his patron's favor, and that he will thereby receive encouragement to commence a larger work. Probably, then, the author at the time of writing held a prebend in Ciudad Rodrigo, some sixty miles southwest of Salamanca towards the Portuguese border.

He cites several Italian theorists, two of them not mentioned in prior Spanish treatises – Niccolo Burzio (fol. 12) and Lodovico Fogliano (fol. 7). The latter's experiments may possibly have attracted his attention before any account was published. But since Fogliano published nothing until 1529 (*Musica theorica*) it is more probable that Águilar became acquainted with his theories after that date. Not only Gaffurio but also the less likely Marchettus of Padua fills up his Italian list. He gives unusually accurate citations of all sources that he quotes. Since he is one of the few who seems to have read Juan Espinosa's 1520 *Tractado* with care and since his allusions to Espinosa are unusually complimentary, he may have been the latter's pupil.

His treatise contains a number of conventionalities. The diatonic (sung) semitone is the smaller, he declares – thus siding with the traditionalists. He tends to oversimplify Cristóbal de Escobar's comments on chromatic genus. The following abridgment of a paragraph on fol. 13v. shows a sample of his teaching. In his opinion any accidental, even the time-honored B♭, implies chromatic genus.

The diatonic genus is used when singing in the hard or natural (G or C) hexachords. The chromatic genus is used when singing in the soft (F) hexachord. All eight modes are sung in either

Canonigo de Burgos ..." Tapia here complains that Espinosa always added ficta B♭'s when singing lydian and hypolydian plainsong melodies, thus destroying the individuality of those modes. Except for the last three words, Tapia here – as throughout most of his *Vergel* – copied Bermudo verbatim. Cf. *Declaración*, 1555, fol 39v., col. 2.

[106] Anglés's suggested date of publication (c. 1500) must be rejected. For Pedro Manrique's dates in the see of Ciudad Rodrigo, see Gams, *op. cit.*, p. 66.

diatonic or chromatic genus. Modes I, II, III, IV, VII, and VIII require diatonic genus since no accidentals regularly appear. Modes IV and V require chromatic genus because they regularly make use of the soft hexachord with B♭.

This and several other passages of like tenor show that he believed in denaturing Mode IV and V melodies: not simply to avoid tritones, but because he thought that these modes could not exist without continuous use of the B♭. The doctrine that B♭'s should always be sung was not, however, generally taught in Spain. It does correspond with the Ambrosian treatment of these modes at Milan in the early sixteenth century.

Águilar's merits include: (1) accurate citations from authorities; (2) unhackneyed quotations; (3) interest in simplifying the vocabulary of musical theory.[107] His defects counterbalance his merits: (1) overcompression; (2) lack of musical examples; (3) an occasional tendency towards provincialism or particularism.

Juan Martínez (fl. 1532)

JUAN BERMUDO, the best informed Spanish theorist to write in his native tongue, did not begin publishing until 1549. During the intervening two decades between Gaspar de Águilar's just described *Arte* and Bermudo's *Libro primero de la declaración de instrumentos* (1549) some four Spanish-language instructors were published in the peninsula.[108]

To 1532 (January 16) belongs a 20-leaf quarto printed in Gothic at Alcalá de Henares — Juan Martínez's *Arte de canto llano puesta y reducida nueuamente en su entera perficion: segun la practica del canto llano.*[109] The popularity that it was to gain at home and abroad caused it to be at least six times reprinted within 93 years. It was reissued in octavo by the Sevillian printer Juan Gutiérrez in 1560, "corrected and emended" by Luys de Villafranca. It appeared at Barcelona in 1586 with a new title, *Compendio de canto llano.* A Salamanca sixteenth-century reprint, of which only a fragment survives, was discovered by Salvá.[110] Three reprints were published at Coimbra during the first quarter of the next century – in 1603, 1612, and 1625. The last of these was augmented with various *cousas muyto necessarias* by Antonio Cordeiro, succentor in the Coimbra Cathedral. Fortunately Cordeiro separated his additional "many necessary things"

---

[107] At fol. XIV (cap. XXIV), Águilar for instance proposes that *divisiones* be substituted for *conjuntas.*

[108] The only new Spanish treatise published between 1535 and 1549 seems to have been Melchior de Torres's gothic-print, 46-leaf instructor in plainsong and polyphony (dedicated to Gutierre de Carvajal, bishop of Plasencia, 1524–1559) entitled *Arte ingeniosa de Musica con nueua manera de auisos breues y compendiosos sobre toda la facultad della.* First published at Alcalá de Henares in 1544, it was reissued in 1559 and in 1566 (Pedro de Robles and Juan de Villanueva). Torres was chapelmaster at Alcalá. The title-page of the 1566 edition carries the sentence, *Agora nueuamente reformada y corregida por su mesmo autor* ("Now newly revised and corrected by the author of the same").

[109] Bibliographical details in Eitner, *Quellen-Lexicon,* VI, 354, conflict with those given in Antonio Palau y Dulcet, *Manual del librero hispanoamericano,* VIII (Barcelona: Libreria Palau, 1954–1955), p. 268 (item 154416). Because of the reprints, it is hard to guess which edition entered the library of the creole architect, Melchor Pérez de Soto, haled before the Mexican Inquisition in 1655. But its presence in his library proves in what esteem it was held in the New World more than a century after its first appearance.

[110] Palau y Dulcet, VIII, 268.

from Martínez's original text. Each of these Portuguese baroque reprints bears for its title *Arte de Canto Chão, posta e[t] reduzida em sua enteira perfeição, segundo a pra[c]tica delle, muito necessaria para todo o sacerdote, [e] pessoas, que hão de saber cantar*.[111] His name is spelled "Ioão Martinz" on each Coimbra title-page. No claim is made however that he was of Portuguese nationality.[112]

On September 1, 1525, the chapter appointed him master of the *moços de coro* (altar-boys) in Seville Cathedral.[113] Unlike the singing-boys in numerous lesser cathedrals, those at Seville were during the century divided into two groups: each ruled by a different maestro. *Moços de coro* sang plainsong, *seises* polyphony. He was hired to teach the former, not the latter.[114] As a reward for merit his salary was on December 9, 1536, raised from 9,000 maravedís and one cahiz of wheat to 12,000 and two cahizes.[115] The Sevillian capitular act of this date denominates him *racionero de los niños de canto llano* (prebendary in charge of the children singing plainsong). His successor was the same Villafranca who edited his *Arte* when it came to be republished at Seville in 1560. Villafranca, however – as his own later publication record teaches us – was not for long to remain content with the humble rôle of any mere editor. In 1565 he issued his own original plainsong instructor.

MARTINEZ'S *arte* – even if six reprints were not known – could be proved to have enjoyed both a wide and a long-continued vogue. Pedro Cerone at Naples in 1613 (*El melopeo y maestro*, p. 336), Andrés de Monserrate at Valencia in 1614 (*Arte breve, y compendiosa de las dificultades que se ofrecen en la musica practica del canto llano*, p. 15), and Pedro Thalesio at Coimbra in 1628 (*Arte de Canto chão, com huma breve instrucção . . . segunda impressão*, pp. 35, 39) each recognized his authority. Thalesio, appointed to the chair of music at Coimbra on January 19, 1613, but himself probably of Spanish origin,[116] quarreled with him for claiming that so many as ten different accidentals can be intruded in plainsong; namely, $B_1\flat$, C$\sharp$, E$\flat$, F$\sharp$, A$\flat$, c$\sharp$, e$\flat$, f$\sharp$, a$\flat$, and c$^1\sharp$. According to

---

[111] Manoel de Araujo printed the 1603 Coimbra edition; Nicolao Carvalho the 1612 and 1625. Copy of the latter at the Library of Congress.

[112] Fétis in his *Biog. univ. des musiciens* (Paris: Firmin-Didot, 1875), V, 479, criticized Diogo Barbosa Machado (*Bibliotheca Lusitana*, II [Lisbon: Ignacio Rodrigues, 1747], p. 692, c. 2) for making of Martinéz a Portuguese. Barbosa Machado cited the Portuguese imprints but said nothing concerning Martínez's origins.

[113] Seville Cathedral, *Autos Capitulares años de 1525–1526*, fol. 66: Este dia sus merçedes resçibieron para maestro para enseñar moços de coro desta santa iglesia a juan martinez clerigo desde primero de setienbre deste año en adelante con el salario que tenia.

[114] Fétis, *op. cit.*, V, 479, again erred when he proposed that Martínez for a time was *maître de chapelle à l'église cathédrale de Séville*. Anglés claims (*DML*, II, 1484) that Martínez held the title of *maestro de los seises* at Seville Cathedral.

[115] Seville Cathedral, *A.C., 1536–1537–1538*, fol., 71v. As reason for the increase, the chapter noted *lo mucho que ha seruido en esta santa yglesia*. The increase was to become effective January 1, 1537. Since the new *salario* was to last *durante su vida e no mas* (during his life and no longer) he was already old – one may suppose – and surrounded with heirs who hoped for "consolation payments" from the cathedral after his death. The original Spanish for this and all other Sevillian *actas capitulares* cited in the present volume may be seen in my collection, *La Música en la Catedral de Sevilla, 1478–1606: Documentos para su estudio* (Los Angeles: Raul Espinosa, 1954).

[116] Joaquim de Vasconcellos, *Os musicos portuguezes* (Oporto: Imp. Portugueza, 1870), II, 191. Thalesio's "chapelmastership at Granada" seems however to have become confused by Vasconcellos with his chapelmastership at Guarda (northeast of Coimbra in Portugal).

Thalesio, only the following accidentals are actually used: B₁♭, C♯, E♭, F♯, G♯, and c♯. He denounced Martínez's octave duplicates on the ground that no chant covers so wide a range. Thalesio furthermore claimed that, in Portugal at least, not A♭ but G♯ was the needed plainsong accidental. For still another matter, Thalesio emphatically disapproved of his raising the controversial fifth note to B♮ in the _Gaudeamus omnes in Domino_ introit – even though Guillermo de Podio, Gonzalo Martínez de Bizcargui, and Juan de Espinosa had sided with him.[117] For Thalesio, such a B♮ contravenes _toda razam, & arte._

Matheo de Aranda (fl. 1533)

MATHEO DE ARANDA published two treatises, both at Lisbon but both in Spanish. The first (1533, 38 leaves) deals with plainsong,[118] the second (1535, 36 leaves) with mensurable music.[119] Like Diego Ortiz, he therefore made his reputation with theoretical literature published in Spanish but in a foreign capital. Somewhat more is known at present concerning Aranda's early life in Spain than Ortiz's. He received his university education at Alcalá de Henares where, sometime before 1524, he studied music theory with the "learned Doctor Pedro Ciruelo."[120] It was Ciruelo who redacted the _Cursus quattuor mathematicarum artium liberalium,_ used throughout the century as a standard university text. Upon finishing at Alcalá de Henares, he studied "practical music" in Italy. Sometime before 1530 he emigrated to Portugal. In 1870 Vasconcellos, with his usual abandon, gave the faulty impression that when Aranda published his treatises he was serving as chapelmaster of Lisbon Cathedral.[121] Actually, however, the royal printing privilege at fol. iv., of each _tractado_ plainly states that he held the chapelmastership not of Lisbon but of the cathedral (erected c. 1200) at Évora,[122] 72 miles east of Lisbon. The dedicatee in each instance was the young cardinal-infante, Dom Affonso (1509–1540), King João III's third brother.

Affonso had studied humanities with the celebrated Portuguese classicist, Ayres

---

[117] Pedro Thalesio, _Arte de Canto chão,_ 2nd edn. (Coimbra: Diogo Gomez de Loureiro, 1628), p. 39. For Martínez's B♮, see the Portuguese edition of 1612 (enlarged by Antonio Cordeiro), fol. B6v.

[118] _Tractado d' cāto llano nueuamente compuesto por Matheo de arāda maestro en musica. Dirigido al muy alto y illustrissimo señor don Alonso cardenal Infante de Portugal. Arçobispo de Lixboa. Obispo Deuora. Comendatario de Alcobaça.&c._ The colophon reads: _Fue impressa la presente obra en la muy noble ciudad de Lixboa por German Gallarde: a veynte y seys de Setiembre año de mil y quinientos y treynta y tres._

[119] _Tractado de canto mēsurable: y contrapūcto: nueuamēte cōpuesto por Matheo de arāda maestro ē musica. Dirigido al mui alto y illustrissimo señor dō Alōso Cardenal Infante de portugal. Arçobispo de Lixbōa. obispo Deuora. Comēdatario d' Alcobaça._ Colophon: _Fue impressa la presente obra de Cāto mensurable y Contrapuncto. En la muy noble y semp̃ leal ciudad de Lixboa por German Galhard Empremidor. Acabose alos quatro dias del mes de Setiēbre. De Mil & q̄nientos: y treynta y cīco._

[120] _Tractado,_ 1533, prologue (fol. 2). Ciruelo held the chair of Thomist theology at Alcalá. He was succeeded by Miguel Carrasco in 1524. See Antonio de la Torre y del Cerro, "La Universidad de Alcalá. Estudio de la enseñanza ...", _Homenaje ofrecido a Menéndez Pidal,_ Tomo III (Madrid: Ed. Hernando, 1925), p. 362. Further on Ciruelo below at p. 100, n. 141.

[121] _Os musicos portuguezes,_ I, 11. Anglés echoes Vasconcellos (_DML,_ I, 94). He also falls prey to Vasconcellos's factitious title-pages (cf. _Os musicos portuguezes,_ II, 246–247, with I, 11, lines 26–30).

[122] Manuel II, _Livros antigos portuguezes, 1489–1600_ (London: Maggs Bros., 1929), I, 514.

Barbosa.[123] In 1517 he was named a cardinal by Leo X,[124] at the request of his father, King Manuel I "the Fortunate" (d. 1521). In 1523, two years after his father's death, Dom Affonso was consecrated bishop of Évora. At twenty he was in addition invested with the archbishopric of Lisbon. Meantime, however, he continued to reside at Évora.[125] An energetic ecclesiastic, he convened the important synod at Lisbon on August 25, 1536, during which the vestiges of the Sarum rite (introduced in the twelfth century by Bishop Gilbert of England) [126] were at last swept away – thenceforth to be replaced by a uniform use modeled on the Roman rite.[127]

Affonso early during his Évora episcopate insisted that those whom he patronized must bear fruit. Aranda's 1533 *prologuo* plainly shows that he was working for a prelate who expected results: "Many times the thought has struck me, most puissant and illustrious prince, that no one can call himself an expert in any art or science, nor for that matter consider himself even a teacher of the first rank, unless he writes; and by his publications proves his competence in his field." Fortunately, Affonso was generous with his protégés who did publish. So Aranda testifies in his 1535 *prologo*: "Your great zeal that all shall study and become learned in music as in every other science, together with your lordly favor and support of the art, have encouraged me to compose this other treatise concerning music." Since (insofar as is now known) no previous theoretical works had been published in Portugal, both must be considered works of major historical importance.

IN THE PLAINSONG instructor Aranda argues that the sung semitone is the *menor*, not the *mayor*. He naturally despises Bizcargui. Doubtless he refers to him when he says that in 1527 someone had again published a treatise who could not compose a note. "Every year a new edition appears, each worse than its predecessor, the emendations being poorer than the original." At fol. 35v., he quotes admiringly, on the other hand, Bizcargui's archenemy, *el reuerendo Joanes d'espinosa racionero en la yglesia de Toledo*. He couples Juan Espinosa's name with that of *el reuerendo ribaflrecha* [128] [sic] *racionero en la iglesia de Palencia*. Such *maestros en musica* as Espinosa and Rivafrecha *reprehendiesen aquellas personas: que careciendo de musica hablasen en ella* ("reproved those who, lacking any musical ability, presume to talk about it").

---

[123] Antonio Caetano de Sousa, *Historia Genealogica da Casa Real Portugueza* (Lisbon: Joseph Antonio da Sylva, 1737), III, 419. Ayres Barbosa, a fellow-student at Florence with the future Pope Leo X, became the most renowned Portuguese classicist of his generation. Both studied simultaneously with Politian. Appointed master of rhetoric at Salamanca University in 1495, Barbosa rose to a professorship of Greek and Latin from which he was called home by Manuel I to tutor the two princes, Affonso and Henrique. According to Caetano de Sousa, Affonso early became a *favorecedor dos eruditos a quem premiava con merces*.

[124] Damião de Goes, *Chronica do felicissimo Rei dom Emanuel da gloriosa memoria*, reprinted from the original edition of 1566–1567 (Coimbra: Acta Universitatis Conimbrigensis, 1949–1955), II, 142.

[125] Dom Affonso continued to reside at Évora until just before his death. See Frei Luiz de Sousa, *Anais de D. João III*, ed. M. Rodrigues Lapa (Lisbon: Livraria Sá da Costa, 1938), II, 143 (pte. seg., cap. 2): "Viera de Evora curar-se de certa infirmidade...".

[126] Manuel II, *op. cit.*, I, 531.

[127] Pedro de Mariz, *Dialogos de Varia Historia* (Lisbon: Antonio Craesbeek de Mello, 1672), p. 418: *em todo o Arcebispado se rezasse o officio Romano, & se deixasse o de Sarisbea, que de Inglaterra trouxera ...*

[128] Concerning Martin de Rivafrecha (= Rivaflecha) see below, pp. 190–193.

He does not so slavishly ape the learned discourse of others as to say nothing original in his two treatises. At the close of his 1533 *Tractado* he, for instance, declares that ligatures in plainsong must on occasion be broken, and that mere "use" is no excuse for such "abuse" of the Latin language as is frequently to be found in Gregorian books. With this complaint he anticipates the loud humanist outcry for revision of chant that was to call forth a century later the now-deplored Medicean gradual (1614). Among the more familiar features are the inevitable table – this one with numbers carried to seven digits, expressing interval ratios;[129] and several examples showing what accidentals should be added in plainsong. Like most Renaissance Spanish plainsong theorists, he calls for copious sharps, as well as flats.

THE MUSICAL EXAMPLES in his 1535 *Tractado de canto mensurable: y contrapuncto* begin at fol. 15 with four counterpoints against a Mode I given melody. These four note-against-note *contrapunctos* exemplify such rules as the following: begin with 5ths, 8ves, or unisons; avoid similar motion to perfect intervals (violated once);[130] use no more than two repeated notes (violated once);[131] no more than three parallel 3rds or 6ths; hold the counterpoint within the range of either the authentic or the corresponding plagal mode; end the exercise with opposite stepwise motion to an 8ve or unison. At fol.

Counterpoint a 4

Tractado de canto mensurable y contrapuncto (1535), fol. 16v.   MATHEO DE ARANDA

* in original: | ♩ ♩·♪| ♪♪♪|

129 *Tractado*, 1533, fol. C iiij verso.
130 Tenor, mm. 11–12.
131 Tenor, mm. 24–36.

15v. he offers still another four examples. These move in "fifth species" against a Mode II c. f. His licenses in this "species" include an unprepared dissonant suspension (7–6) at the cadence, the 7th having been approached stepwise from below. Once, he dissonates with a passing-note 4th on the second half of the "bar." [132] His bass counterpoint descends frequently to D_1.[133]

At fol. 16v. he graduates to four-part counterpoint. The c.f. closely resembles the Mode V Agnus Dei of Mass XVII (*LU*), beginning after the intonation. As mm. 8–9 in the accompanying transcription disclose, he likes the escaped-note leaping up a fourth to a syncope, thence resolving with a dissonant ornament. He holds the "subdominant" in reserve for meas. 12. At the close, the upward octave leap in the bass (crossing the tenor) perpetuates a bygone fashion.

ARANDA continued as chapelmaster of Évora Cathedral until 1544 when, by a royal *alvará de nomeacão* dated July 26, he was elevated to a professorship of music at the University of Coimbra (with an annual salary of 60,000 *reaes*).[135] Founded at Coimbra in 1308, this university had moved back and forth between Lisbon and Coimbra until finally placed by João III at Coimbra in 1537. Aranda held the post of *lente de musica* during the last year spent at the university by the national poet, Luiz de Camões. His official duties included two hours of lecturing each day, one in plainsong, the other in counterpoint. On February 12, 1546, by an *acta do conselho universitario*, certain music books (costing 7,000 reis) and another containing 20 masses (costing 2 cruzados) were bought for use with his choir.[136] His death during early February of 1548 was six months later attributed to insults that he was forced to endure because he was a foreigner.[137] His successor, Pedro de Trigueiros, was named April 16, 1548.[138] A year later, Aranda's body was carried back to Évora, and there buried by a fraternal religious organization on June 2, 1549.[139] (It was perhaps his brother who was the Diego de Aranda that

[132] *Contrapuncto para voz de tiple*, meas. 8.

[133] Mm. 2, 4, 7, 8, 12. Aranda does not balk at using sequences and repetitions. See *tiple*, mm. 1–2 = 5–6; *tenor*, mm. 2₃–4 = 5₃–7; *baxo*, mm. 2–3 = 4–5.

[134] For a three-part example, Aranda adds alto and bass beneath a Mode VII c.f. The contour of the c.f. strongly resembles, however, that of the Mode I plainsong hymn, *Ave maris stella*. In the penultimate measure, he ascends stepwise in the altus to a syncope. This note at the outset dissonates with both the other voice-parts.

[135] *Documentos de D. João III*, ed. Mário Brandão, II (Coimbra: Universidade, 1938), pp. 190–191. Dated at Évora, the alvará speaks of Matheus de Aranda as *mestre da capella da see desta cidade*.

[136] Francisco Marques de Sousa Viterbo, *A Litteratura Hespanhola em Portugal* (Lisbon: Imprensa Nacional, 1915), p. 23.

[137] *Ibid.* Juan Fernández, a compatriot who had occupied the chair of rhetoric in Coimbra University since 1529, complained on August 11, 1548 *d'insultos q̄ lhe tinham dirigido e nessa occasião se declarou q̄ o facto não era novo e que por caso similhante morrera de pura paixão o mestre de musica Matheo de Aranda* ("of insults which he had received, and declared that this was not the first time such had been received, and that Matheo de Aranda, master of music, had died of pure vexation because of a like incident").

[138] Francisco Leitão Ferreira, *Noticias chronologicas da Universidade de Coimbra, segunda parte: 1548–1551*, Vol. III (Tomo I), ed. Joaquim de Carvalho (Coimbra: Universidade, 1944), p. 801. In *GD* (5th edn.), I, 188, Trend gave May, 1548, as the month during which Aranda died. Since his successor took office after his death, he cannot have been alive during May.

[139] Sousa Viterbo, p. 23. The supporting documentation was discovered by Gabriel Pereira who published it in *O Archivo da Santa Casa da Misericordia d'Evora* (Estudos Eborenses, Pte. 2), (Évora: J. J. Baptista, 1888).

beginning in 1531 served as organist first in Santo Antonio Monastery, Lisbon, and then in Santa Justa; only to be readmitted as *tangedor dos orgãos* of Santo Antonio in June of 1551.) [140]

Summary

I In the half-century between 1482 and 1535, some fourteen competent Spanish theorists published treatises.[141]

II No one center attracted them all; but rather their treatises were issued in at least eleven cities: Alcalá de Henares, Barcelona, Bologna, Burgos, Lisbon, Salamanca, Saragossa, Seville, Toledo, Valencia, and Valladolid. Their own spheres of activity were even more widely dispersed.

III Comparison of texts published in Spain with those abroad shows that an independent and consistent Spanish plainsong tradition existed, stemming perhaps from earlier peninsular theorists whose works are now lost (e.g. Albertus de Rosa, Arnaldus, Goscaldus, Lodovicus of Barcelona (= Luis Sánchez [?]), etc.

IV Unlike university-trained theorists abroad, Spanish university graduates wrote numerous plainsong instructors.

V Among the topics which they made peculiarly their own, *conjuntas* [142] and *tonos de una regla* stand out prominently.

---

[140] Eduardo Freire de Oliveira, *Elementos para a historia do Municipio de Lisboa, 1.ª parte*, I (Lisbon: Typographia Universal, 1882), p. 562. ("Carta regia de 7 de junho de 1551.")

[141] The count could be augmented were one to include such borderline theorists as Pedro Ciruelo (d. 1548) of Daroca, whose *Cursus quattuor mathematicarum artium liberalium* was published in 1516. See above, p. 96, n. 120. This university textbook of the liberal arts was reprinted at Alcalá in 1526, 1528, 1577, and was still in standard use at Salamanca University in 1593 when Bernardo Clavijo was a candidate for the music chair. The four mathematical disciplines in Ciruelo's order culminate in music: arithmetic, optics, geometry, and music.

At fol. 72 Ciruelo begins somewhat as follows. "Boethius was himself a redactor who brought together many things from various authorities. Let us ask ourselves first whether the theories of these authorities concord with the common practices of musicians who sing and play instruments. To answer without involving ourselves in useless argument: the theorist and the practical musician use a different language. The theorist for instance speaks of a diatessaron, diapente, or diapason; the practical musician on the other hand refers to these same intervals, as a fourth, a fifth, or an octave .... Music does not include disputes concerning the physical properties of sound or of audible voice; does not attempt to find out whether music is a substance in the air or something travelling through the air and colliding with another body; nor does it seek to discover whether sound consists of an unbroken stream or of successive particles. These disputes belong to physics; or better, to metaphysics .... Music, on the contrary deals with such ascertainable facts as the proportions which determine intervals."

At fols. 72–93 he reprints the *Elementa musicalia* of Jacques Le Fèvre d'Étaples, a work first published at Paris in 1496 and reprinted there in 1503 and 1514.

[142] This emphasis on *conjuntas* distinguishes early anonymous Spanish treatises (e.g., *R 14610* at the Madrid National Library, an imprint antedating 1534, but without author, publisher, or place of issue) just as much as the ascribed treatises. For a contemporary foreign plainsong manual that endorses *conjuntas* with true "Spanish enthusiasm" see Pietro Cannuzio's *Regule florum musices* (Florence: Bernardo Zuchetta, 1510), a copy of which is bound in with Biblioteca Colombina MS 5–5–20 at Seville.

VI In the mensural treatises, Spanish theorists showed themselves at home with the more intricate problems of the epoch, often propounding solutions which were original and even epoch-making.

VII In the same treatises, Guillaume de Machaut, Dunstable, Dufay, Ockeghem, and later composers of international repute are familiarly mentioned.

VIII Such fifteenth-century Spaniards as Juan de Monte, Tristano de Silva, Ramos de Pareja, Domingo Marcos Durán, Guillermo Despuig, and Diego del Puerto, can be proved from evidence in the mensural treatises to have been not merely theorists but competent composers as well.

Liturgical Music:
1470-1530

Early Liturgical Imprints Containing Music

THE EARLIEST Spanish book on the date of which incunabulists agree – the *Manipulus curatorum* printed by Matheus Flandrus – appeared at Saragossa in 1475. Only a decade later the first Spanish imprint containing music appeared in the same city. Since but a single copy of the 1485 *Missale Caesaraugustanum* printed by Paul Hurus survives, and since the unique exemplar in the Saragossa Cathedral Library was not brought to light until 1917, the existence of such an early Spanish liturgical imprint containing music has not been as widely advertised as it deserves.[1]

A total of at least fourteen Spanish liturgical incunabula survive containing music. Half of these are found in unique copies. That still others which contained music were printed before 1501 can hardly be doubted. Data concerning one missing incunabulum that must have included music – a *Missale Compostellanum* printed by Juan de Porras in an edition of 750 copies at Salamanca in 1496 – has been for instance gathered from the contemporaneous diary of events in Santiago de Compostela Cathedral kept in the *Actas Capitulares* of 1495 and 1496.[2] If not a single copy of an edition of 750 survives then it is hardly surprising that other liturgical imprints are found in unique copies.

Of these fourteen extant liturgical incunabula containing music only one, moreover, is described in the *Catálogo Musical de la Biblioteca Nacional de Madrid*, II.[3] On the other hand, some forty liturgical books printed in sixteenth-century Spain are described

---

[1] For data concerning its discovery see Franciso Vindel, *El arte tipográfico en Zaragoza durante el sigle XV* (Madrid: Dirección general de relaciones culturales, 1949), pp. 59–60.

[2] Francisco Vindel, *El arte tipográfico en las ciudades de Salamanca, Zamora, Coria y en el reino de Galicia* (Madrid: Relaciones culturales, 1946), p. 117.

[3] Anglés-Subirá, *Catálogo*, II, 28–29.

in the same catalogue. The present review of Spanish liturgical incunabula containing music can therefore serve as its supplement. Among the other cogent reasons for now undertaking such a review these can be advanced: (1) the earliest imprints set the pattern for those to follow; (2) printed at the expense of local bishops, these books show what was considered the basic, irreducible musical minimum in local parishes; (3) these books reveal the variants in local musical traditions which prevailed from diocese to diocese; (4) they prove that Holy Saturday was the most important day, musically speaking, in the church year; (5) in isolated instances early Spanish liturgical books contain printed naturals or sharps as well as flats, a somewhat surprising fact since only plainsong was included; (6) where diamond-shaped notes (not in descending series), single square notes with two stems, and single squares with right-hand descenders combine to make rhythmic patterns – as in the Toledo books – measured chant rather than plainsong in free rhythm must have been sung.

Missale Caesaraugustanum (Saragossa, 1485)

ALFONSO of Aragon, who underwrote the expense of the first Spanish imprint containing music, boasted royal blood – his father being Ferdinand V. His rearing conformed with the precepts in Ruy Sánchez de Arévalo's *Vergel de los Principes*, a treatise on the education of princes written by the dean of Seville Cathedral in 1455. From early adolescence he surrounded himself with virtuoso instrumentalists and singers.[4]

For the task of editing the music he selected Martín García Puyazuelo (1441–1521), a canon of Saragossa Cathedral who had started life as only a shepherd boy, had learned the alphabet from travellers through his native valley of the Ebro, and music as a boy-chorister in the cathedral.[5]

The missal, which reaches 350 leaves, contains 16 pages of music (fols. 191–198v.). Only punctum, clivis, podatus, and *strene* enter the scribe's repertory. He copies the neums over printed red four-line staves. The printed liturgical text underlines the staves. One page of the music is reproduced in facsimile in Francisco Vindel's *El arte tipográfico en España durante el siglo XV: Zaragoza* (p. 58); quite evidently the words were printed without much forethought for the spacing of the neums. The rest of the music consists of eight Gloria-intonations, a lesser number for the Credo, three settings of the *Sursum corda* for various degrees of solemnity, two Lord's Prayers, nine prefaces (Easter, Ascension, Pentecost, Christmas, and other feasts), and a tenth for all Lady Masses. The last leaf lists seven formulas for the *Ite missa est* and three for the *Benedicamus Domino*. Not only the order, but also the music itself shows close resemblances to that in use contemporaneously at Barcelona – if the music at fols. 211 and 212 in a handsome, handwritten fifteenth-century missal *scd'm vsum barch'n* now owned by The Hispanic Society of America sufficiently attests Barcelona use.

Immediately preceding the music section can be seen printed texts of 16 sequences – three for Christmas Masses, one each for Circumcision, Epiphany and its octave, Easter, Ascension, Pentecost, Trinity Sunday, Corpus Christi, Transfiguration, and four others for use between

[4] Félix de Latassa, *Bibliotheca antigua de los escritores aragoneses* (Saragossa: Medardo Heras, 1796), II, 374: "Tubo novilisima Casa, Varones sabios de diversas facultades; ... Capilla de estremados Musicos, y Cantores..." This Alfonso de Aragón (1470–1520) was not the same person as the Alfonso de Aragón to whom Despuig dedicated his 1495 *Ars musicorum*.

[5] *Ibid.*, II, 379–380. Born at Caspe, he rose from humblest origins to a canonry at 39. In 1512 he was named bishop of Barcelona.

Easter and Ascension. In the Huesca missal of 1488, to be described next, music not only for the still current *Victimae paschali* but also for the now obsolete Ascension and Pentecost sequences, *Omnes gentes plaudite* and *Sancti Spiritus adsit nobis gratia*, has been copied on parchment leaves pasted at the beginning and end of the exemplar owned by The Hispanic Society.

Missale Oscense (Saragossa, 1488)

THE HUESCA of 1488 is identical with the Saragossa of 1485 in every respect except these: (1) ten new preliminary leaves of Huesca calendar have been substituted for the ten old leaves of Saragossa calendar; (2) a new pastoral letter by Juan of Aragon and Navarre, [6] bishop of Huesca, has been inserted in place of the old letter of Alfonso of Aragon; (3) a new final leaf with a colophon dated June 1, 1488, and mentioning John Hurus of Constance rather than Paul Hurus as printer replaces the previous colophon dated October 26, 1485.

Antiphonarium et graduale ad usum ordinis S. Hieronymi (Seville, 1491)

THOUGH it has usually been said that *Lux bella* of 1492 was the first Sevillian musical imprint, the present 166-leaf combination antiphoner and gradual precedes it. In both cases the printers were the same four-man group, *Quatro compañeros alemanes* ("Four German associates" – Paul of Cologne, John Pegnitzer of Nuremberg, Magnus Herbs de Fils, and Thomas Glockner). Only one copy of this book printed on vellum for use among the Jeronymite order survives; [7] and it is defective. Conserved at the Paris Bibliothèque Nationale, it differs from the usual Spanish liturgical incunabulum in showing music on nearly every page. Only one other contains as much – the 1494 *Processionarium ordinis praedicatorum*. These two imprints also invite comparison because of the similar appearance of the music on the page (red tetragram, infrequent use of compound neums), because both were printed at the behest of powerful Spanish orders for use in religious houses rather than for secular use, and because both testify to the elaborate musical routine which was a part of the daily life in those houses. Both were printed at Seville, but the *Processionarium* by a different printers' association, Meinard Ungut and Stanislaus Polonus.

Processionarium ordinis praedicatorum (Seville, 1494)

MORE COPIES of this *processionarium* survive than of any other Spanish incunabulum of whatsoever kind. Over 100 copies were discovered in one Dominican house in 1912,[8] placed on sale, and disseminated throughout the world. Any student of Spanish music printing has therefore in all likelihood seen at least one copy. In respect of its preser-

---

[6] Juan de Aragón y Navarra (1457–1526), son of Charles Prince of Viana, and grandson of John II, king of Aragon, took possession of the Huesca see in 1484. The lineage and upbringing of most fifteenth- and sixteenth-century Spanish bishops was princely. The art and music with which they surrounded themselves reflected their own personal tastes. See Latassa, *Bibliotecas antigua y nueva*, additions by Miguel Gómez Uriel (Saragossa: Imp. de Calisto Ariño, 1884), I, 118–119.

[7] F. Vindel, *El arte tipográfico en España durante el siglo XV: Sevilla y Granada* (Madrid: Dir. Gen. de Relaciones Culturales, 1949), p. 110.

[8] *Ibid.*, p. 181.

vation, the *processionarium* is therefore in a different class from its companion musical incunabula.

This *processionarium* can be usefully compared not only with the Sevillian 1491 antiphoner, but also with an exactly contemporaneous (1494) processional [9] for the use of the same order, the Dominicans – but of the Lombard congregation – published in Venice by Joannes Emericus, a German printer. The Seville processional reaches 114 leaves,[10] quarto-size; the Venice 122, octavo-size. As for differences, the Seville music is much more opulently printed, with more space between the lines of the red tetragram, bigger neums, fewer ligatures, and with more careful spacing of the words. Then again, the rubrics telling what is to be done at such and such a moment tend to be more explicit.

The Seville processional inaugurates a printing custom observed in nearly all later Andalusian musical imprints: bar-lining of the words. The double bar-line in this processional indicates a shift from cantor to chorus. Neither of these refinements captures the fancy of the Venetian printer. Instead of the double-bar, the Venice copy contains printed directions, *cantor*, *chorus*, and occasionally *duo cantores*. In the Huntington Library copy of the Venice processional a contemporary hand has also written *orga* (organ) and *cho* (chorus).[11]

The Seville begins with Purification, then skips to Palm Sunday, after which it follows the major events of the church year through Assumption (August 15), omitting however Corpus Christi. Music for the latter is included in the Venice processional. Holy Saturday is much more largely treated in the Seville book, only two leaves being devoted to this day in the Venice book. Seville also contains a *Liber generationis* for both Matthew and Luke, various responds for feasts not found in Venice, and a respond to be sung "in time of war against the enemies of the faith," *Congregati sunt*. The martial spirit still current in Spain, where the Moors had been finally subjugated only two years previously, required a type of military expression in the Seville *processionarium* which is significantly absent from its Venice coetanean.[12]

Manuale Toletanum (Seville, 1494)

THE FIRST dated Toledo incunabulum of any dimension – the *Confutatorium errorum* printed by Juan Vázquez – came out as late as 1486. In Seville, on the other hand, a sizable *Repertorium quaestionum super Nicolaum de Tudeschis* (237 leaves) reached print as early as 1477. The tardiness in luring a first-class *impresor* meant that the first liturgical book for use at Toledo which contains music, the *Manuale seu baptisterium secundum vsum alme ecclesie Toletane*, had to be printed at Seville (by Tres compañeros alemanes).

[9] *Processionarium ordinis fratrum predicatorum.* The Seville processional lacks a title-page.

[10] Vindel, p. 178, cites 114 as the number of leaves. But the Huntington Library copy once owned by the Dueñas de Zamora seems to be complete with two less.

[11] Although portatives were also in constant use at Seville during processions, none of the three copies which we have seen of the Sevillian *processionarium* shows such hand-written annotations.

[12] Venice has the complete music for a *Missa pro defunctis* not in Seville; also a hymnary (fols. 52v.–64) missing from Seville. Both include an *Officium sepulture fratris defuncti*.

A copy is preserved at El Escorial, apparently unique.[13] The manual, which according to the preface was printed for the benefit of local diocesan clergy, is a miscellany of 76 leaves designed to satisfy the parish priest's most basic needs. The music printed on red tetragram is, like the primer of the Christian faith in the same manual, extremely simple. This manual does, however, precede all other Spanish imprints in providing music for a nuptial Mass.

Missale Auriense (Monterrey, 1494)

OSTENSIBLY, Juan de Porras and Gonzalo Rodrigo de la Passera printed the Orense missal at Monterrey, a Galician hamlet lying just above the Portuguese border. Two copies survive – one at the Madrid Biblioteca Nacional [14] and the other in Orense Cathedral. This 278-leaf Gothic-type missal is however so sumptuous a printing achievement that almost certainly the major part of the work on it was done in Salamanca rather than in Monterrey.[15] Since all Porras's other books were printed in Salamanca, since no other book with Monterrey as its place of imprint survives, and lastly since Porras was definitely at Salamanca when in 1495 the Santiago de Compostela *cabildo* commissioned him to print 750 missals, it seems likely the Orense missal was also printed, except perhaps for a few leaves, in Salamanca where printing began as early as 1480.

Though the music is too small to be read easily from any distance, at least the neums are actually printed and not merely hand-copied over a printed set of staves – in this case red pentagram rather than tetragram. Words are usually bar-lined, except in the case of monosyllables. *Puncta* with two tails and the clivis with the second note a diamond frequently occur. Neums first appear as late as the verso of folio clxx. The fourteen pages of music include chants for the Lord's Prayer, various prefaces, *Ite missa est*, and *Benedicamus*.

Missale Caesaraugustanum (Saragossa, 1498)

PRINTED by Paul Hurus like the 1485 Saragossa missal already described, this 1498 missal [16] heads a large family of handy quarto-size missals issued at Saragossa before 1550. Indeed so distinctive of Saragossa did the small portable missal become that the bibliographer can now safely guess the place where any such Spanish missal was published before 1550. The Madrid Biblioteca Nacional alone owns seven such handy Saragossa missals: [17] 1498, Paul Hurus (*I 323*); 1511, George Coci [18] (*R 929*); 1522, Coci (*R 6096*); 1531, Coci (*R 14465*); 1532, Coci (*M 218*); 1543, Coci (*R 6118*); 1548, Coci (*R 6643*). Of these the 1498 and 1522 form a pair since they are "local use" missals, so designated in their title and confirmed in their contents. The quintet of 1511, 1531, 1532,

---

[13] Vindel, *El arte . . . Sevilla y Granada*, p. 194.

[14] Signature: I 1128.

[15] Vindel, *El arte . . . Salamanca . . .*, p. xxvii. One other liturgical book was reputedly printed in Monterrey – a *Manuale Bracarense* (1496, Joannes Gerlinch) for use in Braga diocese (Vindel, *op. cit.*, p. 285). No known copy, however, survives.

[16] Size: $9\frac{1}{4}'' \times 6\frac{3}{4}''$ ($\times 2\frac{1}{4}''$).

[17] The Anglés-Subirá *Catálogo*, II, refers to the 1552 *Missale Caesaraugustanum* (sign. M 557) as the earliest Saragossa missal containing music.

[18] On Coci see Henry Thomas, "The Printer George Coci of Saragossa," *Gutenberg Festschrift* (Mainz: Gutenberg-Gesellschaft, 1925), pp. 276–278.

1543, and 1548, are each entitled *Missale Romanum*. Fray Pedro de la Vega, editor of the "Roman" missals, belonged to the Jeronymite order. He came to Saragossa in 1510, was elected prior of Santa Engracia *convento* in 1522, again in 1528, and general of his order in 1537. In his "Roman" missals he succeeded "so admirably with the size, print, and a hundred other niceties that they were eagerly bought throughout all Spain," reports José de Sigüenza in his *Tercera parte de la Historia de la Orden de San Geronimo* (1605 [bk. 2, ch. 41]).

The 1498 missal reflects again the personality of Alfonso of Aragon, archbishop of Saragossa. At his expense the first folio-size missals of 1485 had been printed. These being evidently exhausted he entrusted the revision and reissue of the missal to Domingo Tienda. The impression took some ten weeks, 11 September–23 November. The music, on red tetragram as is the rule in Saragossa books, everywhere bespeaks careful printing: the neums are always beautifully registered, words bar-lined, and ligatures so spaced as to avoid any misinterpretation of the beginning- and ending-notes for a specific syllable.

The Madrid copy of the 1498 missal reaches 359 leaves, of the 1522 missal 326 leaves. Proportionately, more music fills up the latter. The music carried over from 1498 to 1522 is printed identically except that in 1522 right-hand tails are added to indicate accented syllables. Liberal flats (as accidentals) have been added in both. The importance of music in the Saragossa use is inferred from the decision to print 101 pages of music in the 1522 missal.[19] The 1498 missal shows but 72 of music.

The relative importance of Holy Saturday can be judged from the fact that 15 pages of music are included in the 1498 missal for that one day alone. Good Friday, for purposes of comparison, is musically less important – only ten pages being allowed. Easter itself is in the 1498 book, for that matter, less important (as always in Spanish books, musically speaking) than Holy Saturday.

Missale Toletanum (Toledo, 1499)

THE 324-leaf *Missale mixtum alme ecclesie toletane* [20] issued by Peter Hagenbach on June 1, 1499, survives as the earliest Toledo liturgical imprint. But its preface witnesses to an earlier printed missal, the copies of which were all destroyed by order of the archbishop to whom it was dedicated, Francisco Ximénez de Cisneros. Absent in Granada when the earlier issue appeared, he immediately called for a revision when he saw a copy on his return.

This missal therefore illustrates a classic bibliographical principle: the dedicatees determined the character of these liturgical imprints. Ximénez de Cisneros was a scholar of the first order, but an ascetic. The 1499 missal, as we now know it, exactly mirrors his character. In the first place, it carries marginal references, not to be found in any other Spanish missal of its generation and anticipatory of usage after the Council of Trent.

[19] Total number of leaves in B.N. (Madrid) exemplar: 326. The reason for reprinting the 1498 missal was its "disorder" and lack of index, states the author of the 1522 colophon (fol. ccc iii).

[20] Copy in Madrid Biblioteca Nacional: sign. I 1137 (*olim* I 978).

These marginal references tell in each case the precise scriptural locations for gospels and epistles read at Mass. Moreover this is the first Spanish missal with an adequate index. The printing refinements obviously cost considerable sums, not to mention the use of vellum. Yet this Toledo missal, unlike others of its epoch eschews illuminations. In the lone picture adorning it, the Virgin confers special graces on Isidore. A half-century later when Juan Martínez Siliceo ruled as Spanish primate (1546–1557), a Toledo-use missal not nearly so carefully executed insofar as text or music is concerned was printed at Alcalá de Henares (1550).[21] It, by way of contrast, was filled with pictures of undraped adult angels. They may be correctly pictured as far as theology is concerned. But they do not add an ascetic tone to the missal.

The 1499 editors seek by every means to ensure correct performance of the printed chants. Exceptionally wide spacing between lines of the pentagram and correspondingly large neums make for a new legibility. The following musical refinements call for notice: (1) printed flats; (2) right-hand stems to designate accented syllables; (3) words half bar-lined; (4) sentences bar-lined; (5) changes from cantor to chorus double bar-lined; (7) diamond-shaped notes (not in descending series) used to denote rapid utterance; (8) punctum with two stems, both up or both down, used to denote double time-value.

Neums appear at a total of 107 pages, one-sixth of the book, with the chants for Holy Saturday taking up 34 of these 107 pages.

Missale Giennense (Seville, 1499)

PRINTED by Ungut and Polonus, this missal for use in Jaén diocese [22] contains 262 numbered leaves. Again the most "musical" day in the church year proves to have been Holy Saturday. For this one day 19 pages of music are printed [23] in the Jaén missal. Of these 13 are full pages of music. That this emphasis on Sabbato Sancto was distinctively Spanish is proved by comparing the Jaén 1499 missal with the 1498 Braga missal, the latter printed in Lisbon by Nicholaus de Saxonia.[24] Four staves are provided on one page [25] for Holy Saturday music in the Braga missal: no more. Indeed the textual

---

[21] *Missale secundum ordinem primatis ecclesie Toletane* (Bibl. Nac. Madrid: sign. R. 6052).

[22] *Incipit missale secundum morem et consuetudinem sancte ecclesie Giennensis;* printed by order of Diego de Deza, bishop of Jaén. The latter, a Dominican, was the principal opponent of Pedro de Osma, and succeeded him as Salamanca theological professor in 1477. The copy seen by the present author, apparently unique, belongs to the Huntington Library. Karl Haebler in his *Bibliografía Ibérica del siglo XV, segunda parte* (Leipzig: Karl W. Hiersemann, 1917), pp. 125–126, wrote: "Not a single copy of this book is known, but that it was printed cannot be doubted." In the Archivo de Protocolos at Seville was found the will of the printer, Meinard Ungut (d. December, 1500), in which he deposed that the bishop of Jaén still owed him 100,000 maravedises (= 267 ducats) for 400 copies printed on paper and 12 on vellum. See *Archivo hispalense,* t. II (1886), pp. 297–298, for further details concerning the careers of Ungut and Polonus in Seville.

[23] On ten of these pages the four-line red staves have been left blank for the Litany (fols. lxxxix–xciii verso).

[24] For bibliographical data see Haebler, *Bibliografía Ibérica* (The Hague: Martinus Nijhoff, 1904), pp. 207–208. A copy of the *Missale Bracarense* is in the Huntington Library.

[25] The exemplar at the Huntington Library unfortunately shows only empty staves. This missal was the first published in Portugal. Like the Jaén, it ends with a "manual" partly in the vernacular.

matter for the whole day consumes only 8 pages. But the Jaén missal assigns 36 pages to this one day. Both books contain a like total number of leaves: Jaén 262, Braga 230.

As for Sundays, Palm Sunday towers musically above all others in the church year as observed at Jaén.

Missale Tarraconense (Tarragona, 1499) and Missale Benedictum (Montserrat, 1499)

TWO MISSALS were printed in Catalonia in 1499. The first, issued by John Rosembach in Tarragona – one of the most ancient of all Catalonian sees, contains printed staves over which music was to have been copied by hand.[26] The other, a *Missale secundum consuetudinem monachorum congregationis Sancti Benedicti de Valladolid*, was printed by John Luschner at Montserrat. [27]

Processionarium ordinis S. Benedicti (Montserrat, 1500)

ISSUED like the preceding by Luschner, this Benedictine processional bears as its full title, *Processionarium secundum consuetudinem Monachorum congregationis sancti Benedicti de Valladolid*. A total of 130 copies on vellum and 300 on paper are known to have been printed, but of these only three vellum and one paper seem to have survived – the solitary paper copy having come into possession of The Hispanic Society in New York. Music printed over red tetragram is to be found at 108 of the 112 numbered leaves (front and dorse).

Comparison of this processional with, for instance, the 1494 and 1519 Dominican processionals published at Seville, or the Jeronymite 1526 processional published at Alcalá de Henares [28] reveals many illuminating differences: (1) in the arrangement of the contents; (2) in the relative importance attached to various events of the church year; (3) in methods of notating the chants; (4) in the exclusion or admission of certain melodies of peninsular origin such as, for instance, the Spanish melody for St. Thomas Aquinas's *Pange lingua gloriosi;* (5) in the actual notes prescribed even when the chants prove to have been essentially the same; (6) in the addition of accidentals. Certain of these differences can be ascribed to the religious orders themselves for which the books were printed. Others may even reflect the liturgical variants that flourished from diocese to diocese in which the books were respectively printed. The differences which

[26] A copy is in The Hispanic Society, New York City. Further on Rosembach's activity as a music printer, see Jordi Rubió, "Una carta inèdita catalana de l'impressor Joan Rosenbach de Heidelberg," *Gutenberg Festschrift* (1925), pp. 408–411. In The Hispanic Society paper exemplar (parts 1 and 2) two short chants have been actually notated – the *Ecce lignum crucis* in pt. 1 at fol. XCII verso (Good Friday) and the *Venite et accendite* in pt. 2 at fol. XII verso of the *Sanctorale* [February 2]. As in the other Spanish missals, Holy Saturday (with 11 full pages of red four-line staves) musically outranks all other days in the church year. *Exultet iam angelica turba* consumes fols. XCIIII verso-XCV verso in pt. 1. *Dominica in ramis palmarum* also outranks all other Sundays (8 pages).

[27] For further details see F. Vindel, *El arte tipográfico en Cataluña durante el siglo XV* (Madrid: Relaciones culturales, 1945), pp. 228–230.

[28] *Incipit liber processionum secundum ordinem fratrum predicatorum* (Seville: Jacob Cromberger, 1519); *Incipit liber processionarius secundum consuetudinem ordinis sancti Patris nostri Hieronymi* (Alcalá de Henares: Miguel de Eguía, 1526). Copies in The Hispanic Society.

are most enlightening for our purposes have to do with points (3), (4), (5), and (6) in the above enumeration.

Luschner's processional introduces ligatures sparingly and knows no way of showing a held punctum of double time-value. Moreover his processional does not trouble to distinguish parts for soloist or soloists. Like Cromberger he bar-lines his words, but the correct placement of syllables proves trickier because of his infrequent recourse to ligatures. Luschner's chants, even when fundamentally the same, tend toward longer melismas, wider ranges, and more profuse embellishment. As a typical example the *Collegerunt pontifices* (Luschner, fol. 24; Cromberger, fols. 9v.–10) deserves study. No melisma of the extravagant kind concluding the *Benedicamus* for Trinity Sunday (Luschner, fol. 56v.) with its 36 notes on one syllable is anywhere to be encountered in the Cromberger. Furthermore Luschner abhors *recto tono* recitation; and in a chant such as *Ingrediente Domino* (fols. 24v.–25) introduces inverted mordents on such a word as "resurrectionem" to escape repeating the same note six or seven times (Cromberger, fol. 13v.). Because Luschner's melodies, even when fundamentally the same, tend to stray out of bounds he frequently finds himself forced to change clef in the middle of a chant. If his melodies range more widely and freely, and if his book devotes much more impartial attention to the different feasts of the church year than do either Cromberger's or Eguía's, Luschner's on the other hand omits such characteristically Spanish melodies as the "more hispano" *Pange lingua* (Cromberger, fol. 48, and Eguía, fol. 36v.) and *Sacris solemniis* (Cromberger, fol. 48v.; Eguía, fol. 39), both of which figure largely in the works of Spanish sixteenth-century polyphonists from Peñalosa to Navarro. If, lastly, comparison be made of the Luschner with the Eguía, such added refinements as these are to be found in the 1526 processional: (1) mensural notation of hymns; and (2) rather frequent use of the natural as a precautionary accidental.

Hymnorum Intonationes (Montserrat, 1500)

OF THE 406 copies of this 48-leaf hymnary known to have been printed, only one exemplar seems to have survived; and it was conserved in the private library of D. Pablo Font de Rubinat (Reus, Catalonia) when last studied.[29] The *hymni dominicales* take up the first 15 leaves, the *hymni sanctorales* the rest. Even the melodies associated with such familiar texts as the *Ave maris stella* and *Verbum supernum* depart from any found in contemporary Andalusian or Castilian liturgical books. The collection is stripped of accidentals; then again, the jaunty triple meter in which hymns were sung elsewhere throughout Spain is nowhere hinted at in the notation.

Missale Abulense (Salamanca, 1500)

JUST AS THE 1499 Toledo and Jaén missals were printed at the order of bishops newly introduced into their sees and eager to improve liturgical standards, so also the Ávila missal of 1500 was printed at the express order of Alfonso Carrillo de Albornoz, newly

---

[29] *El arte tipográfico en Cataluña*, p. 240.

translated to the see of Ávila in 1498. But in contrast with the sobriety of the Toledo and Jaén books, one printed for the austere Franciscan, Ximénez de Cisneros, and the other for the Dominican champion of orthodoxy, Diego de Deza, the Ávila missal spills precious spikenard on every page. Not much is known of the personality of Carrillo de Albornoz, who was bishop of the Sicilian see of Catania before translation to Ávila. But his name suggests that he belonged to the noble Carrillo de Albornoz clan which had produced a primate and numerous other prelates.

The printing, executed on vellum in the Madrid Biblioteca Nacional copy (sign. I 1044 [*olim* I 2016]) by the Salamanca printer, Juan de Porras, reaches a level not exceeded in any other Spanish liturgical incunabulum under present survey. Even so, the bishop in his introductory letter to the dean and chapter of Ávila Cathedral complains that the printing had been negligently done and that time had been wasted in assembling vellum. If many copies of this 265-leaf missal, the dimensions of which are 15 inches by 10 by 5, were printed on vellum it is not surprising that the assembly of sufficient *membranas* took time. The coloring of the border designs, which include as diverse elements as griffins, unicorns, turbaned Moors, and full-blown roses, would also have taken time. Indeed the last 50 leaves of the surviving exemplar in the Madrid Biblioteca Nacional lack coloring, though the designs have been executed and gilding added.

As for the music: words are bar-lined, neums are printed over red pentagram, F-clef is used preponderantly, clef position changes in the middle of a staff where necessary to avoid ledger lines. But what is novel in the music is the frequent use of the natural-sign. The sign is given in the shape of a modern natural,[30] not as a sharp, and is placed directly before the note to which it refers. Only one other early Spanish printer of liturgical books, Miguel de Eguía of Alcalá de Henares, added more natural signs than Porras. The naturals added in the Porras 1500 missal and the Eguía *Processionarium secundum consuetudinem Ordinis Sancti Hieronymi* (1526) [31] occur usually in dorian or lydian chants. The printing of naturals in supposedly unaccidentalized plainsong would not be so noteworthy were these naturals mere "cancellations" of previous flats in the same chants. Such is not the case in either the Ávila missal of Porras or the Jeronymite processional of Eguía.

Printed naturals or sharps do not characterize plainsong books published c. 1500 outside Spain. Perhaps only the Spaniards sang *bemol* so habitually that naturals were needed to correct the habit.[32]

[30] Lacking, however, the right descender.

[31] For bibliographical references see P. Benigno Fernández, *Impresos de Alcalá en la Biblioteca del Escorial* (Madrid: Imp. Helénica, 1916), p. 24 (Item 26). The defective copy of this vellum processional now conserved in the New York Public Library lacks the last 62 leaves. These are found in El Escorial library: see Fernandez, *op. cit.*, p. 24. The Colombina French chansonnier affords another more famous example of a MS which must be completed with leaves conserved in a foreign library.

[32] The Spanish theorists were not the only ones who recognized the national tendency to "weep in flats." Even poets made mention of the national flatting habit. As early as 1405 the poet Alfonso Alvares wrote this quatrain (*Cancionero de Baena* [Madrid: M. Rivadeneyra, 1851], p. 115):

> Los ynoçentes canten chanzonetas
> Dando loores á Ssanta Marya
> En musyca fyna, dulçe melodia,
> Mudando bemoles en primas ó quintas.

Musical Variants in Spanish Liturgical Incunabula (Roman Rite)

TO APPRECIATE the monodies found in these various Spanish incunabula, and to assess their musical distinctions, some one chant common to several books should be studied. The Holy Saturday chant *Exultet iam angelica turba* sung at the blessing of candles can be found in these five different Spanish incunabula: (1) Dominican processional published at Seville, 1494; (2) Saragossa "local use" missal published in 1498; (3) Toledo missal, 1499; (4) Jaén missal published at Seville, 1499; (5) Ávila missal published at Salamanca, 1500. Despite the variants, these five different versions at once reveal themselves as essentially the same melody. If its peninsular origin cannot be proved, at least it can be called a distinctively *more hispano* chant. The melody to which these words were sung in Italy, as shown in the 1497 *Missale Romanum* published by John Hertzog at Venice, is on the other hand an entirely different chant. To make the case as clear as possible, the 1497 "Roman" melody for *Exultet iam angelica turba* is here shown immediately below the five Spanish incunabula melodies. The "Roman" melody is austere, restrained, syllabic. The Spanish melodies are florid, expansive, more richly hued. Not until after the Council of Trent did the "Roman" version replace the Spanish version in peninsular local use missals. The earliest missal printed in Spanish dominions, but reproducing the Roman version of this chant, may possibly be a *Missale Romanum* printed for local use in the archdiocese of Mexico by Antonio de Espinosa in 1561. The seventh melody shown below is therefore extracted from the Espinosa missal (fols. 104v.–105r.), the earliest printed in the New World.

The first lesson learned from studying Spanish liturgical incunabula is, then, the independence of the peninsular musical tradition. Secondly, one learns that within the national tradition there was room for individual variation from diocese to diocese. The two melodies published at Seville show, for instance, very close resemblance. The Toledo melody, however, pursues its own way at cadences. The Ávila version is the only one prescribing b♮'s each time the high note of the chant is reached. Were it possible to give an interpretation of the semimensural notation on which all scholars would agree, the comparison of local variants could be pushed much further. All scholars will at least accept this premiss: the notation in the Toledo 1499 and in certain later Saragossa missals [33] does imply measured rhythm.

IN CONSIDERING local Spanish variants from diocese to diocese we should remember that not only music but also text itself often differed. Even the wording of the canon of the Mass differed at Toledo, Salamanca, and Saragossa. As an example, the wording of the first sentence after the consecration of the wine differs in early books published for each use.[34] At Toledo, moreover, the Agnus Dei preceded the mixing of *corpus cum*

---

[33] The Saragossa *Missale Romanum* published by Coci in 1543 deserves special attention. It can hardly be doubted that such notation as that found on the last two staves of fol LXXVII implies measured rhythm.

[34] In the Toledo missals of 1499 and 1512, the first published at Toledo, the second at Burgos, the word *eiusdam* is inserted between *sancta* and *Christi* but is not to be found in the Salamanca missal of 1562 nor in the missals printed at Saragossa in 1511, 1531, or 1532. The Salamanca missal omits *Dei* between *domini* and *nostri*; the Toledo and Saragossa missals include *Dei*.

Exultet iam angelica turba

sanguine, while it came after the mixing at Salamanca and Saragossa. If differences are found in the canon, then obviously they are present to an even greater degree elsewhere in these uses. In the Toledo calendar, for instance (and the Mozarabic rite restored by Cardinal Ximénez de Cisneros is not here under consideration, but rather the Roman rite), Sundays were numbered after the octave of Corpus Christi. But in the books examined from Salamanca and Saragossa Sundays were numbered after Pentecost.

The saints who received special honors also differed notably. The feast of Ildephonsus (January 23) was, for instance, celebrated at Ávila with the same degree of solemnity as Circumcision and Ephiphany, but was omitted entirely in the Saragossa calendars of 1511 and 1531. In compensation Saragossa diocese observed April 16 (Eighteen Martyrs of Saragossa) and November 3 (*Passio martyrum Caesaraugustanorum*) as major feast days.

The differences are emphasized not for their own sake, but to show how real the variants

* B♮ though not specified except in the 1500 Salamanca print should be sung, the rules of the Spanish plainsong theorists requiring the natural when in a descending scale passage ♭fa ♮mi is succeeded by repeated a's.

** E is misprinted in the original.

were until uniformity was achieved through the decrees of the Council of Trent. Each local center nursed its local traditions, each needed its own books, each proudly observed certain local liturgical and musical customs. The central national tradition was the theme on which each local diocese constructed, as it were, its own canonic variation.

AS FOR THE RUBRICS found in connection with such a chant as the *Exultet iam angelica turba,* they differed also. These variants will not be recapitulated here; but the rubrics never failed to prescribe a dramatic rendition. One instance only: at Ávila just before the singing of this chant the officiating deacon entered the choir and announced in a low voice: "Behold the Light shed by Christ." All replied: "Thanks be to God." Then a second time the deacon repeated: "Behold the Light shed by Christ," but louder. The chorus replied, "Thanks be to God." A third time the deacon repeated: "Behold the Light shed by Christ," this time with maximum force. The chorus replied a third time, and then broke into the jubilant chant: "Now the whole angelic host of heaven exults in

the divine wonder, and the trumpet sounds for such a kingly victory and deliverance; Earth rejoices in the bright rays of such a Light ...". This tendency to dramatize the chant may ill accord with present-day plainsong doctrine, but also may explain why Spanish Renaissance composers favored plainsong themes as did composers of no other nationality.

Missale Mozarabe (Toledo, 1500)

FRANCISCO XIMÉNEZ DE CISNEROS (1436–1517), Queen Isabella's confessor, archbishop of Toledo after 1495, and sponsor of the most ambitious publishing venture undertaken in his generation – the six-volume *Complutensian Polyglot* (Alcalá de Henares, 1514–1517), has often been credited with a gesture which he actually did not make: namely, the restoration of the Mozarabic rite in Toledo. What he did do was to sponsor publication of a 480-leaf *Missale mixtum secundum regulam beati Isidori dictum Mozarabes* (Toledo:

Peter Hagenbach, 1500), [35] to endorse the copying of various *cantorales*, and to endow the Mozarabic chapel in Toledo Cathedral.

The Mozarabic rite though generally discontinued after 1085 had never wholly died, six parishes in Toledo having been permitted to continue using the Mozarabic liturgy. In the introduction to the 1500 *Missale Mozarabe* Alfonso Ortiz, canon of Toledo to whom Ximénez de Cisneros had entrusted the editing, specifically mentions the rectors of three of these Mozarabic parish churches as his "editorial aides." The three churches were those of Saints Luke, Justa and Rufina, and Eulalia, and their parish priests were Gerónimo Gutiérrez, Antonio Rodríguez, and Alfonso Martínez.

Ortiz claims to have availed himself of help "from those most learned in the rite [Gutiérrez, Rodríguez, Martínez] here in Toledo." He furthermore promises that what he has gathered from dispersed sources he has collated; that he has expunged errors, and has carefully considered all doubtful points in order to ensure an accurate missal. Anyone who is familiar with the *Complutensian Polyglot* or even with the 1499 *Missale*

---

[35] Biblioteca Nacional Madrid exemplar: I 15. The Hispanic Society in New York also possesses a copy.

Toletanum will agree that Ximénez de Cisneros was the most painstaking scholar among the hierarchy of his century. Such an inflexible perfectionist as he would have demanded no less accuracy, finish, and care in the Mozarabic missal than he expected in every other publication that he endorsed.

Since it was through his initiative that the Mozarabic chapel was founded in the primatial cathedral,[36] the music in the 1500 missal (and in the Mozarabic *cantorales* copied at his instigation) doubtless reflects the tradition still alive in the Mozarabic parishes c. 1500. Was this tradition contaminated with such a variety of outside influences as to be wholly corrupt? This question has been argued extensively. Any final answer must necessarily be delayed until more is known concerning Mozarabic chant in its golden age.

---

[36] Ximénez de Cisneros provided an endowment for 13 chaplains, a sacristan, and two acolytes, his intention being that the Mozarabic Mass and office should be sung daily. An interesting contemporary account of a Mozarabic Mass in Toledo Cathedral beginning at six on Monday morning, June 27, 1502, is preserved in an account of Philip the Fair's first Spanish tour. See Edmond Van der Straeten, *La musique aux Pays-Bas* (Brussels: G.-A. Van Trigt, 1885), VII, 155–156.

ONE principal objection taken against the music of the 1500 missal is its excessive amount of arabesque. In no other Spanish liturgical book of its date do we encounter so much *fioriture*. The embellishments follow such unmistakable rhythmic patterns as these:

The copyist in his endeavor to record rhythmic distinctions finds that he must use crotchets and quavers, as well as diamond-shaped notes without tails, single squares, and oblique ligatures. He also resorts to the long-outdated plica.

The *tessiture* of the solo melodies in this Mozarabic missal differ radically, moreover, from what is required in other Spanish missals printed c. 1500. In the Song of the Three Children (*Benedicite*) shown below, the soloist sings high *a*'s frequently and high *g*'s constantly. Only a virtuoso tenor can have met the overweening vocal demands.

On the other hand, a chant in which the congregation participates, such as the Lord's

Benedicite omnia opera *

Missale mixtum secundum regulam beati Isidori dictum Mozarabes

(Toledo, 1500), fol. ccxxii verso.

* In the transcriptions ■ = ♩; ♦ = ♭; ♪ = ♪; ♪♪♪ = ♪♪♪

Deo ac Domino nostro

Missale mixtum ... Mozarabes, fol. ccxxvii verso.

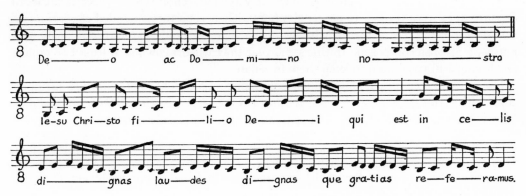

Prayer (fol. CCXXVI) traverses a comfortably medium range. The *Pater noster* with its congregational *Amen* after each petition differs from such solo chants as the *Benedicite* not only by its range but by its syllabic simplicity. A still lower range, indeed a range suitable for *basso profondo*, characterizes chants which the presbyter rather than deacon is to sing. For instance at fol. CCXXVII (verso) the "officiating priest with folded hands bowing towards the middle of the altar" sings a chant, *Deo ac Domino nostro*, which hovers around low B's, A's, and G's. From gamma G the melody rises only to b a major tenth above. Even its lower range does not however interdict arabesque. Again a much more highly trained soloist would be required than in the case of chants printed in any other early Spanish missal.

The skips never bridge a wide gap. A fifth is unusual, and a fourth rare. Accidentalizing is unheard of. Scalar runs up to a fifth are common. Distinctive rhythmic and melodic patterns recur frequently enough in the solo chants to impose a strict unity. The tracery of the embellishments soon becomes as stylized as a Mudéjar initial.

In summary, the solo chants in this Mozarabic missal show the following traits: (1) arabesques (2) rhythmic vitality (3) contrasting *tessiture* (4) diatonicism, especially as exhibited in short scalar runs (5) extremely obvious repetition of rhythmic and melodic patterns. Finally, marked contrast is to be observed between the simple syllabic music when congregational participation is expected and the difficult melismatic music for soloists.[37]

Cathedral Polyphony in the Fifteenth Century

NO MASSES or motets by Spanish composers who flourished before mid-century have

[37] The Lord's Prayer "according to Mozarabic use" has been reprinted in the *New Oxford History of Music*, Vol. II (1954), p. 82. The response to the fifth petition should be, however, not "Amen" but "Quia Deus es." Cf. the 1500 Mozarabic Missal, fol. CCXXVI. The recorded version (*The History of Music in Sound*, ii, side 3) belies the original by omitting all responses but the last Amen.

thus far been inventoried.[38] Nevertheless, evidence can be brought forward proving that polyphony flourished, at least in the major centers, throughout the entire century.

At Toledo, for instance, there existed as early as 1418 a choir school where at cathedral expense boys were trained to sing polyphony. Their repertory included *chançonetas de sancta maria e de Ihesu christo* with words in Spanish, and therefore obviously with music by Spanish composers. In this same year the cathedral owned at least two organs, employing a Fray Giraldo to keep them in repair.

(1) As for the choir school in which polyphony was taught, the following document copied from the *Libro de gastos del año de 1418* conserved in the *Archivo que fué de la Obra y Fábrica* (Bibl. Nac. MS 14033.74) states the case plainly enough:

On Wednesday, May 18, 1418, Alfonso Martínez, cathedral treasurer, paid Brother John, Franciscan, the sum of four florins due him for a book of polyphonic music, purchased for the use of the cathedral boys in the [choir] school who are learning to sing polyphony. Each gold florin equals 51 *maravedís*. [39]

(2) As for the *chançonetas* which were sung in the cathedral, the same *Libro de gastos* yields the following information (Bibl. Nac. MS 14043):

Pedro Sánchez, singer, music copyist, and illuminator of books, received 720 *maravedís* on December 24, 1418, due him for a book in which he copied both text and music of [Christmas] songs honoring the Virgin and Christ, and *misereres*, for the choir to sing.[40]

(3) As for the organs, the same *Libro de gastos* records payment on July 4, 1418, of 1000 *maravedís* to Fray Giraldo "que tiene de auer del adobo que fizo delos dichos organos" (due him for fixing the organs).

IF FOR ONE YEAR, such concrete proof that polyphony flourished can be found, equally convincing proof can be brought forward from the same Toledo *Libros de gastos* for later years in the century. Information from these account books has not yet, however, been assembled in any really systematic fashion. When it is brought together, the historian of Spanish fifteenth-century polyphony will perhaps begin his account with names of peninsular composers who stayed at home rather than with records of those who like Cornago made their reputations in Italy.

---

[38] Cornago, at least at the present moment, seems the earliest Spanish composer from whom so large-scale a work as a mass survives (incipits printed in *Denkmäler der Tonkunst in Österreich*, VII, 43).

[39] Miercoles diez e ocho dias de mayo de 1418 años dio e pago alfonso martinez rracionero a frey Johan frayle profeso dela orden de sant francisco quatro florines del cuño de aragon que ouo de auer por rrazon de vn libro de canto de organo que del conpro puntado para por donde aprendan los moços cleriçones el canto de organo en la escuela, por los quales dichos quatro florines de oro le dio e pago a rrazon de a cinquenta e vn maravedis por cada florin que montaron docientos e quatro maravedis.

Earlier choirboys' schools at Santiago de Compostela and at Barcelona are noticed below on p. 235 (note 80).

[40] Pero sanchez ... que ouo de auer por rrazon de vn libro que escriuio e fizo e punto de chançone[n]tas de sancta maria e de Ihesu christo e misereres para el choro....

Johannes Cornago (fl. 1466)

THE EARLIEST SPANISH monarch to patronize arts and letters with true Renaissance enthusiasm and bounty was Alfonso the Magnanimous (1416–1458), king of Naples, Sicily, Sardinia, and Aragon. On October 12, 1455, this Maecenas sent an Aragonese noble residing at his Neapolitan court on a confidential mission to Rome. The commissioning document refers to Johannes Cornago as a Franciscan residing in Rome on a 300-ducat annual pension granted by Alfonso.[41]

After his death, Cornago became the chief almoner of Don Ferrante, Alfonso's son and successor to the Neapolitan crown (ruling with interruptions from 1458–1494). As holder of this office, he dispensed royal charity. On April 3, 1466, he received 10 ducats and a tari to pay for the cost of altering certain garments in the royal wardrobe which Ferrante proposed to give away on Maundy Thursday to 34 poor persons. On the same April 3 he also took in trust 25 ducats to bestow as alms during the king's adoration of the true cross on the following Good Friday.[42]

Like most Spaniards from Martial to the present, Cornago after his Italian sojourn seems to have yearned to spend his later years in Spain. At all events, his name crops up in a list of Ferdinand V's court chapel singers during 1475.[43]

HIS THREE-PART MASS conserved in Trent Codex 88, a folio of 422 paper leaves, bears this heading: *Frater Johannes Cornago la missa: Signum: de lo* mapa mundi *Apud Neapolim: et la missa de nostra domina Sancta Maria* (fol. 276v.). In this mass he exploits both parody and tenor techniques. Kyrie I, Et in terra pax, Patrem omnipotentem, Sanctus, Agnus I and Agnus II movements illustrate his use of the first technique. He threads both cantus and contra in the duets which begin each named movement with identical melodic material. What this repeated melodic material consists of is shown in the first two bars of the accompanying example, a transcription of Kyrie I. With slight changes of time-values this duet reappears in identical pitches at the beginnings, then, of every major section of his mass. It shares also the character of a tenor mass, however, because in every movement in which the tenor sings,[44] this voice-part quotes the same tune. The ditty that goes with the tune reads: *Ayo* (= aggio) *visto lo* [or *la*] mappa mundi *et la carta de navigare ma chi chi me pare la la piu bella la piu bella de questo mondo* (I have seen the map of the earth and mariner's chart, which seem to me the most beautiful things in the world). These very words are themselves written beneath the tenor part towards the close of both the Qui tollis and Et resurrexit

[41] Camillo Minieri Riccio, "Alcuni fatti di Alfonso I. di Aragona," *Archivio storico per le province napoletane*, VI (Naples: Stab: Tip. del Cav, Francesco Giannini, 1881), p. 437.

[42] Nicola Barone, "Le Cedole di Tesoreria dell' Archivio di Stato di Napoli dall' anno 1460 al 1504," *Archivio storico per le province napoletane*, IX (Naples: Federico Furchheim, 1884), p. 209.

[43] *MME*, I, 24. This date needs reconciliation with the year to which his *mappamundi* Mass is credited, 1480. Trent Codex 88 places him in Naples at the time of writing it.

[44] The tenor does not sing in the *Pleni* or *Benedictus* movements, both of which are marked "duo" in the manuscript.

movements. Though the words are not written below in any Kyrie,[45] Sanctus, or Agnus movement – only the Gloria and Credo movements being actually polytextual – still the same *Ayo visto* melody is itself everywhere alluded to by the tenor in the less wordy movements as well.

The title of the mass yields a clue to its date. On November 18, 1480, a certain Giovanni di Giusto received two-and-a-half yards of Holland linen on which to trace a *mappamondo*.[46] The age of discovery was dawning, and already navigators had sailed far enough beyond the Azores to discover the Cape Verde islands (1456). This flush of explorer's enthusiasm accounts for the commission given Giusto by Don Ferrante. The popularity of such a song as *Ayo visto* shows how widespread must have been the enthusiasm which later found vent in the discovery of the New World. Coupled with this zest for exploration a real missionary zeal seems always to have fired the courts which patronized navigators. This mass itself bears a twofold title, the second stamping it as a mass of the Virgin.

Cornago has set the two Osannas with different music, the first in triple the second in duple meter. He also has polyphonically set all three parts of the Agnus. For a variety of reasons this mass seems an altogether remarkable performance and one well worthy of being published at the earliest possible moment.[47] His other extant liturgical work, *Patres nostri peccaverunt* (Monte Cassino MS 871 N) should also be published – especially since it is the earliest Spanish polyphonic lamentation, *threni* being a genre of liturgical music in which the Spaniards were to excel during the next century.[48] The text is from the Prayer of Jeremy (Lamentations 5:7). This would be not only one of the very "earliest polyphonic settings of a passage from that source" [49] by a composer of any nationality, but would also be Cornago's only work originally for four voices still extant.

WHERE in the Palace Songbook, the Colombina *Cancionero*, and Monte Cassino MS

[45] In *Denkmäler der Tonkunst in Österreich*, VII (1900, ed. by G. Adler and O. Koller), the words "Ayo iusto" were printed in roman beneath the tenor-part of the Kyrie; this was an editorial error. The second word, moreover, should have read "visto".

[46] N. Barone, *op. cit.*, p. 406. See also André Pirro, "Un manuscrit musical du XVe siècle au Mont-Cassin," *Casinensia: Miscellanea di studi Cassinesi* (Montecassino, 1929), I, 206.

[47] This cannot be well done from microfilm because of the seepage of the ink from one side of the paper to the other.

[48] Andreas Ornithoparcus repeated the opinion voiced by most sixteenth-century theorists when he wrote thus (1516): "diuers nations have diuers fashions, and differ in habite, diet, studies, speech, and song. Hence is it that the English doe carroll; the French sing; *the Spaniards weepe*; the Italians, which dwell about the Coasts of Ianua [Genoa] caper with their Voyces; the others barke: but the Germanes (which I am ashamed to vtter) doe howle like Wolues." (*Liber IV*, *cap.* 8 [quoting Gaffurio], p. 88 of John Dowland's *Ornithoparcus* [1609]; fol. M 2 of Valentin Schumann's 1517 Leipzig edition.)

A confirming opinion was given by Paride de Grassi (*Il Diario di Leone X*, ed. by Pio Delicati and M. Armellini [Rome: Tip. della Pace di F. Cuggiani, 1884], p. 66) when he described Tenebrae during Holy Week of 1518. He said: "Three lamentations were sung, the first by the Spanish singers being filled with pathos, the second by the French being learnedly sung, and the third by the Italian singers being sweetly sung."

The best known work by Morales is a "lament", *Lamentabatur Jacob*. Of Victoria, *O vos omnes* (Lamentations 1.12) if not the most famous is certainly performed as often as anything that he wrote. Morales's Lamentations were still sufficiently in vogue in 1564 to make simultaneous commercial publication by two Venetian printers feasible.

[49] Gustave Reese, *Music in the Renaissance* (New York: W. W. Norton, 1954), p. 576.

Missa mappamundi
Kyrie I

Trent Codex 88, fols. 276 v.–277.

JOHANNES CORNAGO

* Because of the deterioration of the MS the next eight notes in the cantus cannot be clearly discerned.

871 N, canciones *a 4* ascribed to Cornago seem to survive the fourth voice-part has been added by some other composer. The other composer in the Colombina example was Triana; in the Monte Cassino example, Ockeghem. The popularity of *Qu'es mi vida* was doubtless considerable if so celebrated a master as Ockeghem (c. 1420–c. 1495) could

have become interested in adding a fourth voice. In alphabetical order Cornago's eleven surviving secular songs are listed below as a complement to his biography. His poets – insofar as they are known – were fellow countrymen (Diego de Castilla and Mossen Pedro Torrellas) active at Naples shortly after mid-century either at Alfonso V's or Ferrante's court. Although musical analysis must be deferred to pp. 218–225 below, the wide vogue of his songs can be inferred from the geographic spread of the manuscript sources: (1) Florence: Biblioteca Nazionale Centrale, Magliabechiana XIX, 176; (2) Madrid: Biblioteca Real, sign. 2–1–5; (3) Monte Cassino: MS 871 N; (4) Paris: Bibliothèque Nationale, MS f. frç. 15123 [*Pixérécourt Chansonnier*]; (5) and (6) Seville: Biblioteca Colombina, sign. 5–1–43 and 7–1–28.[50]

The numeral (or numerals) after each item in the following list refers to the source (or sources): *Donde stas que non te veo* (3) and (6); *Gentil dama non se gana* (2) and (6); *Moro perche non dai fede* (1) (3) (4) and (5); *Morte merce gentile* (3); *Non gusto de male estranio* (3); *Qu'es mi vida preguntays* (3) [51] and (6); *Porque mas sin duda creas* (6); *Pues que Dios* (2) [52] and (6); *Segun las penas me days* (3); *Señora qual soy venido* (6); *Yerra con poco saber* (3).

Bernardo Icart (fl. 1480)

EDMOND VAN DER STRAETEN, the first to collect documented data concerning Icart, suggested that he originated in Belgium. Icart's name (spelled *Hycart*) occurs in a list of chapel singers at Ferrante's Neapolitan court in 1479 immediately above Tinctoris's;[53] it appears again in 1480, on October 27 of which year he received an allowance of approximately three-and-a-half yards of blue cloth for a choir gown.[54] Tinctoris was certainly a Fleming. Icart's national origin was unknown, but since other evidence showed him to have become an eminent artist Straeten inferred that he came from a strongly musical environment. *Huickart*, close enough to *Hycart*, occurs as a Flemish family name.[55]

Actually, however, no evidence, other than the fact that Icart and Tinctoris follow each other in Neapolitan lists and that Huickart is a Flemish family name, has been brought forward. He may quite as well have been Catalonian. Certainly the name Icart, as Anglés has pointed out,[56] is common enough in Catalonia, the most distinguished

[50] Bibliographical details, except for items (1) and (5) in *MME*, I, *95–103, 117, 118, 103–106*.

[51] Anglés suggests that Ockeghem added the fourth voice (found in both sources) during his Spanish visit of 1469. See *MGG*, II, 1681. But *Preguntays no vos la quiero negar* should not figure as a separate item in Cornago's repertory. The text lacks the first three words, *Qu'es mi vida*. Ockeghem threw out Cornago's contra, adding two of his own in its place.

[52] *Palacio* shows two versions, the second "arranged" by Madrid. Like Ockeghem, he expunges Cornago's contra and adds a new voice in its place.

[53] *La musique aux Pays-Bas avant le XIXᵉ siècle*, IV (Brussels: G.-A. Van Trigt, 1878), p. 25.

[54] *Ibid.*, p. 29.

[55] *Ibid.*, p. 63. Straeten would have Icart specifically from Brabant.

[56] *MME*, I, *24* and *136*. Isabel Pope, though well aware of Anglés's suggestion, does not yield to it in her definitive study, "La musique espangole à la Cour de Naples dans la seconde moitié du xvᵉ siècle," *Musique et Poésie au XVIᵉ Siècle* (Paris: Centre National de la Recherche Scientifique, 1954), p. 42.

carrier of the name probably having been the Barcelona Jesuit, Francesc Icart (1572-1610), who wrote various devotional tracts.[57]

Ferrante's court musicians were oftener Spanish than Flemish, as Straeten admits.[58] Francesco Florimo asserts that he rose from being a mere singer to *maestro di cappella* at the Neapolitan court.[59] Florimo also supposes him to have been five years younger than Tinctoris; and considers the theoretical work of both to have been more important than their few compositions that survive.

Icart's theoretical knowledge gained him the respect of even the exacting Gaffurio, who in the company of the exiled doge of Genoa had settled in Naples at the end of November, 1478. Some years later Gaffurio supervised the preparation of a short sketch of his personal life. In it he mentions his reasons for settling at Naples, his efforts towards preparing his first theoretical book for the press, and also the famous men whom he had met at Naples. The *clarissimi musici* with whom he consorted were Tinctoris, Icart, and Guarnier.[60]

A pair of lamentations *a 3* ascribed to "Ber: ycart" were published in 1506 at Venice by Petrucci in his *Lamentationum Jeremie prophete Liber primus*, the Icart pair coming immediately after one by Tinctoris. His other extant sacred works are found in the so-called Bonadies Codex, preserved at the Biblioteca Comunale in Faenza (*Cod. 117*). This manuscript contains six items by Icart: three Magnificats (even verses) [61] — one *a 3*, the rest *a 4*; and three movements of a Mass *a 4* (Kyrie, Et in terra pax, Qui tollis). [62]

In the *Pixérécourt Chansonnier* (which also contains Cornago's *Moro perche non dai fede*) can be seen a picaresque item at fols. 62v.–63 entitled *Non toches a moi car son trop*. The composer's name is spelled thus: "b. ycart." The *chapurrado* text, a gibberish of French, Italian, and nonsense phrases, is copied under all four voice-parts. The structure resembles that of a villancico, with the nonsense phrase "nichi, nichi, nioch" recurring at the end of both the estribillo and the coplas.[63]

[57] *Diccionari Enciclopèdic de la Llengua Catalana* (Barcelona: Salvat, 1931), II, 929. This Icart was a novice-master at Tarragona and Gandia.

[58] Straeten, IV, 31. See the musicians hired, for instance, in 1481. At least six of the nine were Spanish.

[59] *La scuola musicale di Napoli* (Naples: Stab. tip. di Vinc. Morano, 1881), I, 67; also p. 74.

[60] Alessandro Caretta and others, *Franchino Gaffurio* (Lodi: Ediz. dell' Archivio Storico Lodigiano, 1951), pp. 21 and 22. Gaffurio's reference to Icart occurs in the Latin *Vita* written by Pantaleone Malegolo and revised by Gaffurio in March of 1514.

[61] Gino Roncaglia, "Intorno ad un codice di Johannes Bonadies" (Reale Accademia di Scienze, Lettere ed Arti, Modena: *Atti e Memorie*. Series V, 4 [1939]), pp. 35–36, reported two; but there are three (fols. 6v.–7, 7v.–8, 44v.–45). In the first, Icart's tenor follows the outline of the plainchant verse, *Et misericordia eius* for Assumption. See the Jeronymite processional (Alcalá de Henares, 1526), fols. 99v.–100, for the florid original. In all three of Icart's magnificats the music for verses 2 and 8 is the same; also for verses 4 and 10, 6 and 12. Throughout the first magnificat, the tenor for every polyphonic verse is identical: thus in effect serving as a 26-note ostinato. In the third, the tenor for verses 2 = 8 substantially duplicates that for 6 = 12.

[62] The two other composers of vocal polyphony in this codex were John Hothby, the celebrated English Carmelite theorist (d. 1487), and Joannes de Erfordia, a fourteenth-century Franciscan. Icart's Kyrie, Et in terra pax, and Qui tollis not only share a common modality (VI), but a tenor cantus firmus that recalls the Kyrie of Mass XIV, transposed down one step (*Jesu Redemptor*). In both Gloria movements the tenor enters so late at the second half ("Domine Deus" in Et in terra; "Tu solus" in Qui tollis). Fermatas crown the block chords to which "Jesu Christe" is sung in the Et in terra. Not only are these Gloria movements bicinia during their first halves; but the texting of the top part alone suggests that Icart intended them as instrumentally accompanied sections.

[63] Cf. Alonso's *La tricotea*, mentioned below at p. 286, n. 198.

Johannes de Yllianas

YLLIANAS (= Hillanas, Llanas, de ylianas, lanas, llanes), a native of Aragon – whence his name, Johannes de Aragonia [64] – was, prior to his reception into the papal choir, "chapelmaster to the bishop of Barcelona." So reads the citation after his name in October, 1492, one month after his entrance into the choir. Which bishop of Barcelona, however, is uncertain. González Fernández de Heredia, bishop from 1479 until the middle of 1490, was followed by Pedro Garcia. Later Roman documents refer to him as an Augustinian canon;[65] probably he was already an Austin canon before leaving Spain.

When he entered the papal choir it comprised twenty singers, among whom the most illustrious was Josquin des Prez. The productive composers – aside from Josquin – were Bertrandus Vaqueras (= Beltrame Vacqueras) and Marbriano de Orto. The next Spaniard to enter following Yllianas was Alfonso de Troya (c. 1500),[66] a composer however of whom only three short part-songs now survive. At least another pair of Spaniards entered before the death of Alexander VI, last of the Spanish popes.

Yllianas joined in September of 1492, one month after Rodrigo Borja's election, and was the first Spaniard to be added to the papal choir in more than a decade. Indeed at the moment he entered there was none other among the twenty singers who can un-equivocally be so claimed. Vaqueras's name is Spanish, and the *bassca* (*basco?*) after his first name in a St. Peter's register of 1482 [67] means possibly that he like Anchieta was a Basque. But leaving aside Vaqueras, the papal choir immediately prior to Alexander's VI's accession contained no identifiable Spaniards. At Alexander's death in 1503 it enrolled at least three. Yllianas in 1509 stood not only third in seniority but also found himself one of six Spaniards in a choir of twenty-one members.[68]

Five years later he had become so senior as to be dean. In the same year (September 22, 1514), Leo X permitted him to cede a 24-gold-ducat pension which he currently enjoyed on the fruits of St. John of Casteneto monastery in Calabria to a 17-year-old relative named Michaeliangelo de Yllanes, who was already in orders.[69] Pope Leo, always so generous to his singers, also exerted himself to obtain absentee benefices for Yllianas in Cuenca (August 5, 1513) and Osma (September 11, 1516) dioceses. His

---

[64] Fr. X. Haberl, *Bausteine für Musikgeschichte*, III (*Die römische "schola cantorum" und die päpstlichen Kapellsänger bis zur Mitte des 16. Jahrhunderts* [Breitkopf und Härtel, 1888]), p. 68.

[65] Herman-Walther Frey, "Regesten zur päpstlichen Kapelle unter Leo X. und zu seiner Privatkapelle," *Die Musikforschung*, VIII/2 (1955), pp. 184–185.

[66] Haberl, *Bausteine*, III, 59.

[67] *Ibid.*, p. 50 n. (1482.2). In 1918 Mitjana definitely identified Vaqueras as Spanish. See *Estudios sobre algunos músicos españoles del siglo XVI* (Madrid: Sucs. de Hernando, 1918), p. 203, n. 2. *Grove's Dictionary*, 5th edn., VIII, 649, follows suit. Bukofzer alludes in a posthumous article, "Three Unknown Italian Chansons of the Fifteenth Century," *Collectanea Historiae Musicae*, II (Florence: L. S. Olschki, 1957), to a composer whose nickname – in two Italian MSS of late fifteenth-century origin – was *Le petit Basque* or *Le pitet basque* (p. 109).

[68] Haberl, *Bausteine*, III, 60 (1508).

[69] *Leonis X. Pontificis Maximi Regesta*, ed. Joseph Hergenroether (Freiburg i/B: Herder, 1884–1891), V–VI [1888], p. 731.

income from the Cuenca rectorate (and probably from other sources) enabled him to retire early in 1518, after a quarter-century in the papal choir.

He is the earliest assured Spaniard whose music still survives in the papal archive. But his untitled *Missa* a 4 in Capp. Sist. MS 49 at the Vatican Library awaits publication. [70]

Juan de Anchieta (c. 1462–1523)

Part I: Biography

THE LIVES of only a few Spanish composers have been as assiduously investigated as that of Juan de Anchieta. This interest in his biography has of course been stimulated by the eminence which he achieved in his lifetime and the fame that he enjoyed for at least a century thereafter. He was music master to the son of Ferdinand and Isabella, Prince John, who until his untimely death in 1497 was the bright hope of the newly united nation. Both as singer in Isabella's court chapel and as music master to the young prince he travelled widely, in the meantime extending his reputation throughout the whole peninsula. So solidly did he ground it that in 1577, a half-century after his death, Salinas in *De musica libri septem* could still refer to him (VI, vii [p. 312]) as "a composer of no mean repute," and could think it worth his while to cite the tune on which his *Ea iudios a enfardelar* Mass had been based. Even more lasting was the popularity of Anchieta's villancico, *Dos ánades*, which Francisco de Quevedo (1580–1645) cited in his *Cuento de Cuentos* [71] as still frequently sung in 1626, though then regarded as old-fashioned. Cervantes himself paid tribute to this same villancico when he mentioned its being sung by Carriazo in his comic tale, *La ilustre fregona*.[72]

But it is by no means Anchieta's musical reputation alone which has stimulated research in his biography. Rather it is the fact that he was closely related to so famous a personage as Ignatius Loyola – his mother and the grandfather of the saint being sister and brother – that has decisively influenced research. What is more, Adolphe Coster was able to show in an article published in 1930, "Juan de Anchieta et la famille de Loyole" (*Revue hispanique*, LXXIX, 175 [June, 1930], 322 pages) that the relationship between Anchieta and the founder of the Society of Jesus was a dramatic and important influence in the latter's early life. Many of Coster's discoveries bear on Anchieta's career after he retired from court, to be sure. Yet they all help to illumine the character of a composer whose importance in his epoch can scarcely be overstressed.

---

[70] *Bausteine*, II (*Bibliographischer und thematischer Musikkatalog des päpstlichen Kapellarchives im Vatikan zu Rom*), p. 142. The only two named composers in this codex of 138 leaves are Vaqueras with two masses and Yllianas (Hillanas) with one. The other eight masses are anonymous. This codex dates from Julius II's pontificate (1503–1513). See *Bausteine*, II, 21.

[71] Francisco de Quevedo Villegas, *Obras completas*, ed. Luis Astrana Marin [2nd edn.] (Madrid: M. Águilar, 1941), I, 793, col. 2: "¿Y aquellos majaderos músicos que *se van cantando las tres ánades, madre* ..." This reference occurs in Quevedo's introduction; but see also I, 794, col. 2: "se iria con él cantando las tres ánades, madre ...".

[72] Cervantes Saavedra, *Novelas exemplares* (Brussels: R. Velpio y H. Antonio, 1614), p. 357.

Since the whole body of biographical discoveries has now swollen to unusual size, the basic facts must here be digested into a chronological table.

1413 Marriage of Lope García de Lazcano and Sancha Yañez de Loyola,[73] grandparents of Juan de Anchieta the composer, and great-grandparents of Ignatius Loyola, the founder of the Society of Jesus.

c.1442 Birth of Urtayzaga, seventh daughter of preceding couple.

c.1460 Marriage of Martín García de Anchieta and Urtayzaga, parents-to-be of Juan de Anchieta.

c.1461 Birth of Pedro García de Anchieta,[74] elder brother of the composer.

c.1462 Birth of Juan de Anchieta, probably at Urrestilla,[75] a small village one mile south of Azpeitia.

c.1463 Birth of his sister, María López de Anchieta.

1489 Engagement as chaplain and singer to Ferdinand and Isabella, February 6, with annual salary of 20,000 *maravedís*.[76]

During summer composes a 4-part topical romance, *En memoria d'Alixandre*,[77] celebrating the military prowess of Ferdinand and Isabella.

c.1492 Composes a mass based on a popular ditty, *Ea iudios a enfardelar*, now lost but known to have existed in 1577 when Salinas made allusion to it.

1493 Salary raised from 25,000 to 30,000 *maravedís* by a royal cedula dated August 30; [78] tutors Don Juan.

1495 *Maestro de capilla* (musical director) in newly erected household of the crown prince, Don Juan, aged 17.[79]

[73] Adolphe Coster, "Juan de Anchieta et la famille de Loyola," *Revue hispanique*, LXXIX, No. 175 (June, 1930), p. 51. The birthdate of Urtayzaga (c. 1442), Lope García de Lazcano's posthumous daughter, and also the presumed date of her marriage to Martín García de Anchieta are given on p. 54.

[74] *Ibid.*, p. 58.

[75] *Ibid.*, pp. 57–58. Further information concerning Juan de Anchieta's birthplace is found in Bibl. Nac. (Madrid) MS 14020.170 ("Biografía del Reverendo Señor Johannes de Anchieta, Rector de Azpeitia, Abad de Arbas, Prestamero de Villarino, Canónigo de la Santa Iglesia de Granada, Capellán y cantor de sus Altezas los muy católicos Reyes Don Fernando y Doña Isabel y Maestro de capilla del Principe Don Juan," a 43-page biography assembled from various archives by P. Eugenio de Uriarte at Asenjo Barbieri's expense in 1884), p. 6.

[76] Francisco Asenjo Barbieri, *Cancionero musical de los siglos XV y XVI* (Madrid: Real Academia de Bellas Artes de San Fernando, 1890), p. 21.

[77] During the spring of 1489 Ferdinand while besieging Baza entertained an embassy of two Franciscan monks sent from Palestine by the reigning sultan. The words of Anchieta's romance express the Spaniards' faith in their sovereigns' ability eventually to retake the Holy Sepulchre itself.

[78] Barbieri, p. 21, states: "se le aumentaron otros 5,000 maravedís," which would lead one to suppose his new salary was only 25,000. However the accounts gathered by Barbieri from Simancas ("Quitaciones de Casa Real" [Legajo 85]) show that before 1493 his salary had already been raised to 25,000.

[79] Coster, p. 67.

1497   Marriage of Don Juan in the spring; death in early autumn.

c.1497 Appointed a canon in the newly established cathedral of Granada, but without obligation of residence, holding this dignity approximately two years.[80]

1499   Named an absentee benefice-holder in Salamanca diocese: with the title of *prestamero de Villarino* (worth 180 ducats annually); [81] takes possession during June, by proxy.[82]

c.1500 Named Rector of San Sebastián de Soreasu parish church in his home town of Azpeitia, this appointment being in the gift of his 61-year-old cousin, Beltrán de Oñaz,[83] the lay patron (father of Saint Ignatius Loyola [b. 1491]); but continues to reside at court, discharging his parish duties through a vicar.

1503   Given a five-months' paid leave of absence from the court (receiving 12,500 *maravedís* for his time spent on leave).[84]

1504   Death of Queen Isabella, November 26; Anchieta remains in the household of Doña Juana, her daughter and heir, probably travelling as far as Flanders [85] with Joanna and her husband, Philip the Fair (d. 1506).

1506   Acting within his rights as rector of San Sebastián parish church, Anchieta intervenes in a local Azpeitia affair during March,[86] continuing however to employ a vicar, Domingo de Mendizábal, to discharge ordinary parish duties.

       Philip the Fair dies suddenly, September 25, aged only 28.

1507   Continues presumably in Doña Juana's household after Philip's death; salary raised to 45,000 *maravedís* [87] at which level it remains through the year 1515; Ferdinand becomes regent of Castile on account of his daughter's incapacity and rules both Castile and Aragon until his death on January 23, 1516.

1508   Anchieta's brother, Pedro García de Anchieta, acts as intermediary in collecting certain sums due from the Villarino *prestamera*.[88]

1510   Anchieta tries to overstep his rights as Rector of San Sebastián,[89] and comes into sharp conflict with Martín García de Loyola, elder brother of Inigo = Ignatius, and lay patron after the death of Beltrán de Oñaz, their father (d. 1507).

       Royal cedula of October 30 [90] issued in Madrid requires Anchieta to resign his pre-

---

[80] Bibl. Nac. MS 14020.170, pp. 7–8. Coster, *op. cit.*, p. 66.

[81] Coster, p. 86.

[82] *Ibid.*, p. 68.

[83] *Ibid.*, p. 70. Coster fixes the approximate date as 1498.

[84] Barbieri, p. 22. Coster, *op. cit.*, p. 71.

[85] Bibl. Nac. MS 14020.170, p. 13.

[86] *Ibid.*

[87] Barbieri, p. 22.

[88] Bibl. Nac. MS 14020.170, p. 13.

[89] Coster, p. 92.

[90] Eugenio de Uriarte in his manuscript biography (Bibl. Nac. MS 14020.170, pp. 15–17) quotes this royal cedula in full; Coster seems not to have had access to it, although it throws abundant light on Anchieta's character. Anchieta had first complained at the local level, then in Valladolid, always determined

tensions at naming a successor, controlling all parish revenues, accepting the vows of all professing nuns.

1512   Pay voucher signed by Ferdinand in Burgos, April 15, names him *capellán y cantor de la reyna Juana nuestra señora*.[91]

1515   Two younger Loyola brothers, Pedro López and Inigo, join in an assault on Anchieta during the carnival season (February 20).[92] Inigo attempts to save himself from punishment by flight but is detained in an ecclesiastical prison at Pamplona.

1518   Juan de Anchieta's nephew, García de Anchieta, named his successor in the San Sebastián de Soreasu rectorate by Martín García de Oñaz y Loyola, the lay-patron; [93] shortly afterwards, however, the nephew is assassinated by unknown hands and Pedro López, brother of Martín García de Oñaz and Inigo, succeeds as rector.[94]

In this year Juan de Anchieta, composer, is mentioned for the first time as "abbat of Arbas" (or Arbos),[95] his proudest title during his remaining years.

1519   On August 15, the young king Charles issues a cedula at Barcelona, declaring Juan de Anchieta too old (57 years of age) to reside at court, but confirming him in his former annual salary of 45,000 *maravedís*, paid until Ferdinand's death in 1516; Anchieta is henceforth permitted to reside wherever he pleases.[96]

1520   Court pay voucher, October 23, lists him as "ill in his house" at Azpeitia.[97]

1521   In April Anchieta secures a rescript from Pope Leo X permitting him to transfer the income from the Villarino benefice to a new foundation of Franciscan sisters in Azpeitia; [98] they respond by naming him manager of business affairs and assuring him a privileged burial location in their convent church.

On 27 August Martin García de Oñaz, lay-patron of S. Sebastián parish church, offers

---

to vindicate his "rights". But the cedula accommodated him in no way. His claims to a fourth of the parish tithes, half of the altar collections, right of choosing both clergy who actually discharged parish duties, right of receiving vows of friars and nuns, were all dismissed: "en el qual dicho pleyto los dichos presidente e oydores dieron sentencia en que absoluieron al dicho martyn garçia de oñez de las / p. 16 / demandas contra el puestas sobre lo susodicho por el dicho juanes de ancheta." Anticipating further trouble the cedula ended thus: "si algund derecho el dicho juanes de ancheta o otra persona pretende thener a lo susodicho lo venga a pedir e demander ante los del consejo a quienes pertenesçe el conosçimiento dello. los quales vos oyran breuemente en cumplimiento de justiçia. fecha en la villa de madrid a treynta dias del mes de otubre de mill e quinientos e diez años.

Yo el rrey."

[91] *MME*, II, *4*.
[92] Coster, pp. 94–95.
[93] *Ibid.*, p. 113.
[94] *Ibid.*, p. 120.
[95] *Ibid.*, p. 112. Coster's contention that Anchieta obtained his Arbas dignity before the rectorate of San Sebastián is not supported by the document quoted on the same page (footnote 1). He equates Arba*s* with Arb*os*. But in the codicil to his will Anchieta mentions Jorge de Valderas, living in León, as collector of the revenues. Arbos lies between Barcelona and Tarragona in Catalonia, geographically remote from León.
[96] *Ibid.*, pp. 123–124..
[97] *MME*, II, *16*.
[98] Coster, p. 141.

them a gift of land, but they in thanking him warn that he cannot secure privileges exceeding those promised to Juan de Anchieta.[99]

1522 Juan de Anchieta, having outlived both his brother and sister, signs his will on February 19;[100] in it he leaves specific directions concerning his interment in the convent church of the *concepçionistas* which he has so richly endowed; he also establishes annual Masses for the souls of his principal benefactors, Ferdinand and Isabella; he mentions Don Juan *cuyo maestro de capilla yo fui* (whose chapelmaster I was); he leaves 400 ducats in trust for his namesake, another Juan de Anchieta,[101] such sum to be used for the expenses of the latter's education and marriage; after payment of all debts, the remainder of his estate is willed to his niece, Ana de Anchieta, still a minor.

1523 On July 26 he adds a codicil[102] itemizing various debts he still owes in the total amount of 189 *doblas de oro;* he lists among his liquid assets 188 *doblas de oro*, which he says are kept in a chest in the house where he lies sick;[103] he tallies up the sums still owed him by various debtors: 24 *doblas de oro;* he names among those who still owe him money a certain Acelayn to whom he had advanced *dos doblones de oro que son quatro doblas que le empreste en flandes*[104] (two gold doubloons, which equal four doblas, loaned to him in Flanders).

On July 30 he dies, and his body is carried to the parish church where he was formerly the rector;[105] the Franciscan sisters dispute his burial in the parish church, because his

[99] Coster did not know of this transaction. As copied in Bibl. Nac. MS 14020.170 (pp. 20–22) the *Escritura de donación y concordia* between Martín García de Oñaz y Loyola and Fray Bernardino de Salcedo, provincial of the Franciscan order and director of business affairs for the *Religiosas Beatas de la Tercera Orden*, reads in part as follows: "la dicha Reuerenda señora [head of the house at Azpeitia] con su conuento le hazian gracias por el benefiçio tan grande e donaçion ... eçepto que si el Reuerendo señor Johanes de Anchieta Abad de Arbas se quisiese enterrar delante el altar mayor se le sera conçedida y tenga bien de aqui una sepoltura ynsigne delante el dicho altar mayor ... por razon de la dotacion de la primera rrencada, pero el resto de las sepolturas que quedasen de la dicha rrencada primera a la man derecha e man izquierda de la dicha sepoltura del dicho Reuerendo sēnor abad dauan al dicho martin garçia pa su enterramiento con sus desçendientes perpetuamente ...". Anchieta was not the only aggressor in the conflict.

[100] Coster, *op. cit.*, p. 153. The will is reprinted in full at pp. 287–291, but unfortunately not the codicil.

[101] Concerning this *hijo natural* of his last years, see Coster, *op. cit.*, pp. 161–162, 290. Concerning an elder son, Martín García de Anchieta, see Coster, pp. 95 (n. 2), 115 (n.), 118, 162 (n. 1).

[102] *Ibid.*, p. 160. The codicil – twice the length of the will – must be read in the manuscript biography (Bibl. Nac. MS 14020.170, pp. 27–37).

[103] The value of the *dobla* = *castellano* was fixed at 480 *maravedís* in 1480, but rose in apparent value with the influx of gold from the New World. In cash "en mi arca" Anchieta possessed on July 26, 1523, the equivalent of at least 100,000 *maravedís*. In 1526 when Morales accepted the chapelmastership at Ávila his annual pay was fixed at 37,500 *maravedís* (= 100 ducats). See also note 22 above for a suggestion concerning the purchasing power of 100,000 *maravedís*.

[104] Probable dates for the Flanders journey: 1504–1505. Joanna rejoined her husband in Brussels during March, 1504. Queen Isabella died November 26, 1504. Ferdinand immediately dispatched Juan de Fonseca, the same bishop to whom Spañon and Martínez de Bizcargui dedicated treatises, with a message of recall to his daughter in Brussels. Anchieta's service to Queen Isabella having ended with her death, he would have continued with the chapel singers of the House of Castile, and therefore may very well have accompanied Fonseca. Joanna gave birth to Mary in Brussels on September 15, 1505, and sailed with her husband on January 8, 1506. Their entourage included 1500 armed knights and a brilliant array of singers (including such celebrities as Pierre de la Rue and Alexander Agricola). After Philip's death in September the only official document which she could be induced to sign was a pay voucher for her husband's Flemish musicians.

[105] Coster, p. 161.

will is thereby violated; but Pedro López (rector and brother of the future saint) carries the day against them.[106]

On August 1 Ana de Anchieta formally takes possession of her uncle's house, she and her mother (widow of Juan de Anchieta's elder brother) having already resided in it for over a year; the inventory of movables itemizes two bound song-books, another parchment-bound song-book, three history-books, a dictionary, and a devotional book,[107] none of these having been specifically mentioned in the will of the preceding year.

c.1530 Death of Pedro López de Oñaz y Loyola,[108] rector of San Sebastián (brother of Inigo).

1535 Return of Inigo to Azpeitia; final settlement of strife between the clergy of San Sebastián and the *concepçionistas*. By terms of the agreement which Inigo persuades both parties to sign on May 18, Juan de Anchieta's gift of his Villarino pension to the Franciscan sisters is confirmed, but they in turn give up all claim to his body.[109] Against Anchieta's will his body is thus allowed to rest forever in the parish church of San Sebastián, close to the very spot where his nephew had been assassinated in 1518.

THE DATA thus far assembled does not however tell anything concerning his own early education. How he obtained sufficient background to prepare him at the age of 27 for one of the most coveted musical posts in the kingdom, that of a singer in Queen Isabella's chapel, can only be guessed. Coster surmises that he may have studied at the University of Salamanca,[110] though admitting that he can find no documentary prop to support such a guess. Certainly Anchieta never used either of the titles that had he completed a university course he would have acquired – *bachiller* or *licenciado*.

Still, this is an interesting surmise. The Salamanca music professor (*catedrático*) from 1481 until 1522 was Diego de Fermoselle, an elder brother of the famous dramatist, poet, and musician, Juan del Encina. The latter was himself a university student c. 1484, graduating *Bacchalarius in legibus* (see below, pp. 254, 264). Anchieta if a Salamanca student in the 1480's would have been surrounded with the best musical talent in Spain. Or if another guess is desired, one might enroll him as a youthful chorister in the palace choir of Henry IV of Castile and presume that he received instruction from some royal

---

[106] Not only did he nullify Anchieta's will by refusing him burial in the convent church of Anchieta's choice, but also he refused any special honors at his interment. He even went so far as forcibly to eject Anchieta's residuary legatee, Ana de Anchieta, from her uncle's house. St. Ignatius was not proud of his priestly brother, whose other misdeeds were numerous, and never once mentioned him by name nor told that he had been a priest. See Coster, *op. cit.*, p. 163, n. 1; p. 196.

[107] Bibl. Nac. MS 14020.170, p. 40: "Yten, dos libros enquadernados de canto, y otro libro de canto cosido en pergamino: otros tres libros, donde hauia las tres partes historiales: otro libro, que se llame vocabulario: otro libro, que se llame Suma Rosela."

[108] Coster, p. 169.

[109] *Ibid.*, p. 210.

[110] *Ibid.*, p. 59. The only two fifteenth-century Salamanca music "professors" whose names are preserved in university archives were Fernando Gómez de Salamanca (1464–1465) and Martín Gómez de Cantalapiedra (1465–1479), neither of whom seems to have been a composer. See Enrique Esperabé Arteaga, *Historia pragmática é interna*, II, 249 and 262.

chapelmaster.[111] But without documents, any guessing is as hazardous as the oft-repeated attempts to unravel the life story of his famous literary contemporary, Fernando de Rojas.

When Isabella married Ferdinand she did not give up her queenship in Castile. Her own household remained always separate and distinct from her husband's. Anchieta was not to become a singer on Ferdinand's Aragonese rolls, even after her death. The greatest honor conferred upon him by Isabella was of course the appointment as *maestro de capilla* to the crown prince, Don Juan, c. 1495.[112] Even if easily available elsewhere [113] a famous contemporary account of Anchieta's services to the young prince must here be repeated.

My lord, the Prince Don Juan, was naturally fond of music and well versed in it, though the quality of his voice was not as remarkable as his persistent desire to sing: to gratify which desire, Juan de Anchieta, his music master, and four or five youths, members of his chapel choir with beautiful voices, one of which with a fine high voice was named Corral, used to join him in the afternoons, especially during summers, and the Prince would sing with them two or three hours, or longer if he cared to; he sang the tenor part and was very skilled in the science of music. In his own quarters he had a hand organ, other organs, *clavicordios*, virginals, plucked vihuelas, viols, and flutes, and he actually knew how to play all these instruments.[114]

This interesting extract comes from the *Libro de la cámara real del príncipe Don Juan* by Gonzalo Fernández de Oviedo (1478–1557) – who was one of the five boy chamberlains chosen by Queen Isabella to serve in her young son's mimic court (1493). Since the adolescent prince sang tenor Anchieta would have sung bass. To have taught Don Juan how to play such a variety of instruments as Oviedo lists, Anchieta must obviously have been himself something of a performer on most of them. Long after Don Juan's death he remembered the blue-eyed, red-haired, oval-faced young prince with devoted affection, as the 1522 reference in his will testifies.

While chapelmaster to the prince, and while chapelsinger for Queen Isabella until 1504, he travelled constantly. The court journeyed to Santafé in 1491, Granada in 1492, Barcelona in 1493, Valladolid, Segovia, and Madrid in 1494, Alfaro and Tortosa in 1495, Burgos in 1496, Granada in 1499, Seville and Toledo in 1502, Alcalá, Segovia, and Medina del Campo in 1503. Queen Isabella died in the latter city on November 26, 1504. After attending her remains to Granada he was in all probability dispatched with other members of the Castilian royal household to Flanders, there to attend the new sovereign, Joanna, whose consort was the handsomest king in Europe, Philip the Fair.

[111] The constitutions of Henry IV's royal chapel are reprinted in *MME*, I, 57–58. The corps of singers included both clergy and laity. A lay singer who came to the choristers' desk wearing his sword was fined twice and the third time cut off the payroll. Henry IV's chapelmaster in 1465 was Joanes Curiel, but the latter's length of service is not known. See E. Van der Straeten, *op. cit.*, VII, 187.

[112] Coster, p. 67.

[113] Gilbert Chase, *The Music of Spain* (New York: W. W. Norton, 1941), p. 36.

[114] Spanish original in *Libro de la camara real del prínçipe Don Juan ... compuesto por Gonçalo Fernandez de Ouiedo* (Madrid: La Sociedad de Bibliófilos Españoles, 1870), pp. 182–183. Oviedo composed this account for the young prince, later to be crowned as Philip II. "Menistriles e diuersos musicos" from which the extract is taken was written in 1548.

The codicil to Anchieta's will testifies to a Flemish sojourn. If 1505 is accepted as the probable year, then he spent at least a few weeks in Southern England during the return journey (January 15–April 15, 1506).[115] At all events, his pay vouchers prove him to have been chaplain and singer from Isabella's death onwards not in Ferdinand's household, but in that of his eldest daughter, Joanna, heir to the Castilian kingdom.

This "mad" queen, like her brother, Prince John (d. 1497), ardently loved music. It is not to be doubted that Anchieta accompanied her husband's catafalque from Burgos where he died, September 25, 1506, on its famous journey that ended in Tordesillas. Moreover, it was in 1507 that his salary was raised from 30,000 to 45,000 *maravedís*. The obvious conclusion must be that he continued in her entourage when she retired into virtual seclusion to mourn her husband. All who have written on her mental condition agree that she was troubled by an obsession, but one which did not prevent her from conversing in Latin when she chose,[116] or from continuing to enjoy music which was from childhood "una de sus distracciones favoritas." [117]

The chronicler Alonso de Estanques describes her condition from October, 1506, onwards thus:

After the death of her husband she began to lead a very sad life, withdrawing into solitude and obscure retirement. She brooded without saying a word and without wishing any company, except that at various times she took delight in performances of music, to which art she had been extremely addicted since early childhood.[118]

In this removed world Anchieta must be thought of as having brought such solace as music offers. His Ash Wednesday motets, one for three male voices, *Domine, non secundum peccata nostra*, the other for four, *Domine, ne memineris*, cannot be dated, but by virtue of their musical content epitomize Joanna's bereaved world after her husband's death. From February, 1509, until her own death at the age of 75 she remained in Tordesillas, near Valladolid. Here he must surely have served, if the evidence of such a pay voucher as that of April 12, 1512, [119] is accepted. Ferdinand, her father, governed as regent until 1516, and distributed salaries; but Anchieta was "cantor de la reyna Juana nuestra señora."

No more remarkable tribute can be brought forward than the royal cedula Charles, son of Joanna, issued at Barcelona on August 15, 1519, confirming the composer in his salary of 45,000 *maravedís* for life. After Ferdinand's death some official had proposed that Anchieta was worth only 25,000. Charles ordered his salary restored to its former level on account of "los muchos e buenos servicios que el dicho juanes nos ha hecho" (the many and excellent services which the said Juan has rendered [our royal house]).

[115] Antonio Rodríguez Villa, *La Reina Doña Juana la loca: Estudio histórico* (Madrid: Lib. de M. Murillo, 1892), pp. 133, 138.

[116] Juan Luis Vives, *A very frutefull and pleasant boke called the Instruction of a Christen Woman*, tr. Richard Hyrd (London, T. Berthelet, c. 1529), fol. E: "dame Joanne, the wyfe of kynge Philippe, mother vnto Carolus, that now is, was wont to make answere in latyn and that without any studie..."

[117] Rodríguez Villa, p. 10.

[118] *Ibid.*, p. 225.

[119] *MME*, II, 4.

At 57 Anchieta according to this royal cedula was "too old" to reside at court. But Charles was only 19; he had arrived from Brussels speaking only a few words of Castilian and came surrounded, as was his father while in Spain, by Flemish favorites. Anchieta's age need not have kept him from playing Falstaff so much as chronic illness. In any event, the pay vouchers for 1520 list him as ill in his house at Azpeitia.[120]

Though crowded with local events the rest of his life may be conveniently summarized as a series of vain attempts at raising his own family to equal dignity with the Loyola clan. He died hoping that the provisions of his will would be respected. But once his own forceful and commanding presence was removed the fortunes of the Anchietas declined, his legatee was moved out of his house, and even his burial wishes were flouted. Such luster as was later to be added to the name was shed by a collateral descendant, José de Anchieta (1533–1597). Ironically, José made his reputation as a member of the very society which the most illustrious of the rival Loyola clan was to found in 1534.

Part II: Checklist of Juan de Anchieta's Compositions

O bone Jesu, one of the five motets attributed to Anchieta in the *Cancionero musical de Segovia* (a manuscript discovered by Higinio Anglés in 1922) was printed in Ottaviano Petrucci's 1519 *Motetti de la Corona*, Libro tertio, as item 14, Petrucci attributing it however to the better-known French composer, Loyset Compère (c. 1450–1518). If this motet actually belongs to Anchieta, then it would be his first printed work. But if not, then he would seem to have gone unpublished in his lifetime.

Asenjo Barbieri was the first modern editor to bring out any of his works, sacred or secular, when in 1890 he published the *Cancionero musical* generally known as the *Cancionero de Palacio*, this collection containing four of his Spanish part-songs. Juan B. de Elústiza and Gonzalo Castrillo Hernández in 1933 were the first to print any of his sacred music with Latin text, publishing in that year two motets and a *Salve Regina* as the opening works in their *Antología musical*. Higinio Anglés followed suit in 1941 with his *La música en la corte de los Reyes Católicos: Polifonía Religiosa*, a collection which begins with a complete *Missa* by Anchieta, followed by the Kyrie, Gloria, and Credo of a *Missa de beata Virgine*.

Anglés was the first who called attention to the wide peninsular distribution of manuscript copies; several of Anchieta's extant compositions are preserved in more than one source. Alphabetically listed according to the places where conserved, the known sources are as follows: (1) and (2) Barcelona: Biblioteca Central MS 454 and MS 681; (3) Coimbra: Biblioteca Geral, MS de musica 12; (4) Madrid: Biblioteca Real, sign. 2-1-5; (5) Segovia: Archivo musical, MS without signature; (6) Seville: Biblioteca Colombina, sign. 5-5-20; (7) and (8) Tarazona: Archivo musical, MS 2 and MS 3;[121] (9) Valladolid: Parroquía de Santiago, MS s.s.

---

[120] *Ibid.*, II, *16*.
[121] Bibliographical details in *MME*, I, *112–115, 134–135, 118–122, 95–103, 106–112, 129, 122–123, 124.*

Works with Latin text

Conditor alme siderum, 3 v. (Segovia, fol. 169.) [122]

Domine Jesu Christe qui hora diei ultima, 4 v. (Coimbra, fols. 191v.–192; Segovia, fols. 94v.–95; Seville, fols. 18v.–19 [123]; Tarazona MS 2, fols. 279v.–280; Valladolid, fol. 95.) [124]

Domine, ne memineris, 4 v. (Segovia, fols. 97v.–98.) [125]

Domine, non secundum peccata nostra, 3 v. (Segovia, fol. 168v.) [126]

Libera me, Domine, 4 v. (Tarazona MS 2, fols. 218v.–219.)

Magnificat, Tone I, even verses, 3 v. (Segovia, fols. 146–147v.; Tarazona MS 2, fols. 24v.–26.) [127]

Magnificat, 4 v. (Tarazona MS 2, fols. 55v.–58.)

Missa [quarti toni], 4 v. (Tarazona MS 3, fols. 171v.–181.) [128]

Missa Rex virginum [*De beata Virgine*], 4 v. Only the Kyrie, Gloria, and Credo movements. (Barcelona MS 454, fols. 38v.-41; Segovia, fols. 63v.–67 [Credo and Gloria]; Tarazona MS 3, fols. 209v.–215.) [129]

[*O bone Jesu*, 4 v. (Segovia, fols. 100v.–101.) [130]]

Salve Regina, 4 v. (Barcelona MS 454, fols. 60v.–62, MS 681, fols. 77v.–79; Seville, fols. 7v.–11; Tarazona MS 2, fols. 232v.–234.) [131]

Virgo et mater, 4 v. (Segovia, fols. 95v.–97; Seville, fols. 11v.–12; Tarazona MS 2, fols. 277v.–278.) [132]

Works with Spanish text

Con amores, la mi madre, 4 v. (Palace Songbook, no. 335 [fol. 231].)

Donsella, madre de Dios, 3 v. (*Palacio*, no. 404 [fols. 265v.–266].)

Dos ánades madre, 3 v. (*Palacio*, no. 177 [fol. 107].)

En memoria d'Alixandre, 4 v. (*Palacio*, no. 130 [fols. 76v.–77].)

[122] Four-bar fragment transcribed in Rudolf Gerber, "Spanische Hymnensätze um 1500," *Archiv für Musikwissenschaft*, X, 3 (1953), p. 171. The composer Marturià, whose setting of *Conditor alme siderum* (*a 3*) appears in the Segovia MS below Anchieta's at fol. 169 would have been a Spaniard, according to Gerber.

[123] Transcriptions: Elústiza-Castrillo Hernández, *Antología musical* (Barcelona: Rafael Casulleras, 1933), pp. 1–4; present text, pp. 142–144.

[124] The index in *Antología musical* (p. XXIII) erroneously describes item 53 in the Valladolid codex as *Pasiones*, and lists Anchieta as the composer. Unfortunately, however, the sole Anchieta item in this MS is the *Domine Jesu Christe* motet at fol. 95, and even it is incomplete for want of the leaf on which were copied cantus and tenor. The composer's name appears at the head of fol. 95 thus: ф ancheta.

[125] Transcription in the present volume at pp. 140–142.

[126] Transcription in Albert Cohen, "The Vocal Polyphonic Style of Juan de Anchieta," New York University Master's Thesis (May, 1953), pp. 81–82.

[127] Cohen, pp. 86–92. For a facsimile of the first Tarazona opening, see *MGG*, I, cols. 1383–1384.

[128] *MME*, I, 1–34 (parte musical).

[129] *Ibid.*, I, 35–54.

[130] Ottaviano Petrucci, who in his *Motetti de la Corona*, Libro tertio, No. XIIII (Fossombrone, 1519), attributes this motet to Loyset Compère (repr. *Van Ockeghem tot Sweelinck*, ed. A. Smijers [Amsterdam: G. Alsbach, 1942], pp. 116–118), inserts an extra measure (74). The last three measures (79–81) differ, the "Anchieta" closing on C, rather than G, chord. Otherwise the versions are identical. H. E. Wooldridge (*OHM*, II, ii, 95 [1932 edn.]) highly praises this motet. He likes it precisely because it looks forward to tonic-dominant harmony.

It again comes up for discussion in Ludwig Finscher, "Loyset Compère and his Works," *Musica Disciplina*, XII (1958), pp. 123–124. Finscher discovers its appearance in Barcelona MS 454 (fols. 135v.–136) with an attribution to Peñalosa; and in both Orfeón Catalán MS 5 (fol. 69) and Coimbra MS de música 12 (fols. 190v.–191) as an anonymous item.

[131] Elústiza-Castrillo, pp. 8–15.

[132] *Ibid.*, pp. 5–7.

Part III: Anchieta's Musical Style

ACCORDING TO Juan Bermudo (1549) indigenous Spanish style implies not profound learning but rather "graciosidad, y sonoridad." [133] Anchieta's music aptly confirms this dictum. None of it vaunts any extremely clever devices. When he quotes a secular melody as for instance the *L'Homme armé* in the Agnus of his *Missa* (which for convenience will be called "quarti toni" to distinguish it from the *Missa Rex virginum*) he allows the tenor to sing the tune in perfectly straightforward fashion, and surrounds it with only simple counterpoints that "tell" in performance. He imitates, but never in a recondite way, nor at intervals other than the unison, octave, fourth, or fifth. He rarely inverts, writes no cancrizans (or at least none that has been thus far discovered). He is not interested in puzzles, but in sound.

The most famous of the works, a mass based on the secular tune *Ea iudios a enfardelar*, has been lost. That he wrote such a mass, not to mention the Agnus from the *Missa "quarti toni,"* sufficiently proves that he – like his more dazzling Spanish contemporary, Peñalosa – entertained no prejudices against secular tunes. The foundation of his other extant works, however, would always seem to have been some melody from the plainsong repertory.

In the two Ash Wednesday motets, *Domine non secundum peccata nostra* and *Domine ne memineris* (which belong together liturgically [134] though separated in the Segovia manuscript), the plainsong always goes in the tenor, never peregrinating to other voices. In the Glorias of his two masses, on the other hand, the honor of singing the plainsong is shared,[135] discantus alternating with an interior part in the opening sections and bassus enjoying his opportunity in the closing sections. As for the *Magnificat a 3* and *Salve Regina a 4*, he confides the plainsong principally to the top voice. But at phrase-beginnings he does often thread it through the lower parts before its entry in the upper voice. If it were possible to know the Spanish shape of the plainsong melodies which he used, then we could perhaps make other useful generalizations concerning his plainsong technique. Even in comparing his adaptations with the *Liber usualis* versions, we at once see extremely close fidelity in pitches, his deviations at cadences representing perhaps Spanish plainsong variants rather than individual caprice.

He does, as a rule, allow himself great latitude in choosing a rhythmic pattern within which to fit a plainsong melody. Only once does he bind himself rigidly to the set iambic scheme of a given plainchant: and that once in his hymn *Conditor alme siderum* (the two lower parts disport themselves in lively instrumental play). His more usual practice, that of rhythmic transformation, can be seen in the richly hued motet, *Domine, ne memineris*, which is shown as a second accompanying example.

Unity within such a plainsong motet is imposed by obvious repetition of a chordal and rhythmic complex: measures 2–4 corresponding with 9–11, for example. He never shies at repeating rhythmic or melodic figures. His *Missa quarti toni* is, for instance,

---

[133] *Libro primero de la declaración de instrumentos* (Osuna: Juan de León, 1459), fol. x verso [introduction].

[134] See *Liber usualis*, (1947 edn.), pp. 422–423.

[135] Plainsong for the Gloria of the *Missa quarti toni* in *LU* [1947], pp. 62–63 (*Dominator Deus*, Mass XV); for that of the *Missa Rex virginum* in *LU*, pp. 43–44 (*De Beata Virgine*, Mass IX).

welded together by a "motive" riveted not only at the beginning of each major movement (except the *Gloria*, where it is reserved for bar 14) but also frequently inside movements – his "motive" being the three-note figure, e–f–g, with the first two related in a dotted rhythm.

The formal balance of such a motet as *Virgo et mater* [136] can be discerned even at first hearing, his method for securing such balance being the same that he uses throughout the extremely successful Credo of his *Missa Rex virginum*. In both instances he swings with pendulum-like regularity from duos, usually involving imitation, to four-part chordal passages. Since the Credo [137] of the *Rex virginum* is all one movement, his method not only gives the singers an opportunity to breathe but also insures clarity of text. In succession the sections run as follows: (1) "Patrem": upper pair of voices; (2) "visibilium": lower pair; (3) "Et in unum": four parts; (4) "Et ex Patre": contratenor and bassus; (5) "Deum de Deo": discantus and tenor; (6) "Genitum": four parts; (7) "Et incarnatus": discantus and tenor; (8) "ex Maria": contratenor and bassus; (9) "Et homo": four parts; (10) "Et ascendit": two lower; (11) "sedet": two upper; (12) "vivos et mortuos": four; (13) "Et in Spiritum": lower pair; (14) "qui ex Patre": upper pair; (15) "Qui cum Patre": four; (16) "unum baptisma": upper pair; (17) "in remissionem": lower pair; (18) "Et expecto": four. Every third change of voice-texture brings forward a passage for the full chorus. The intermediate two changes involve pairs of voices. The number of measures in each vocal registration induces a formal balance that, even if obvious, must be admired.

As for his treatment of text: Anchieta in conformity with contemporaneous usage occasionally inserts a rest in the middle of a word. But he never fails to bring the general mood of the music into agreement with the overall sense of the text. Now and then he singles out a poignant word for special emphasis, as at the close of the motet *Domine, Jesu Christe* when he ascends to his highest pitch on the climactic word, "ardentissimo." Here the preparation for the climax is carefully thought out, both rhythmically and harmonically. In the Gloria of the *Missa quarti toni* at the words "Jesu Christe" (mm. 57–60) and in the Gloria of the *Missa Rex virginum* at the words "Mariae Virginis" (mm. 125-127), he writes block-chords, with obvious intent at emphasizing the words.

Not only is he possessed of a fine instinct for rhythmic variety, but also of a well developed harmonic sense. There can be no mistaking the harmonic implications of such a bass-line as that found in measures 177–206 of his *Salve Regina* where sixteen skips of a fourth or fifth follow in quick succession. A tabulation of the other bass-intervals during these same bars gives twelve seconds, three thirds, and one octave. His fondness for harmonic as well as melodic sequence shows at measures 99–104 of the same Marian antiphon. Though no extended count has been attempted, he seems less enamoured of the nota cambiata – complete or "incomplete" – than the Flemings who

---

[136] Printed in Elústiza-Castrillo, pp. 5–7. But the two middle parts must sound an octave lower than printed and certain accidentals must be added. The Elústiza-Castrillo version of Anchieta's *Salve Regina* similarly stands in need of correction.

[137] No plainsong original has been thus far located, although one probably exists. This Credo forms one large movement; Anchieta's other Credo is divided into three movements (*1* Patrem omnipotentem *2* Qui propter nos homines *3* Crucifixus).

Conditor alme siderum *

Segovia MS [s. s.], fol. 169.   JUAN DE ANCHIETA

* Bountiful Creator of the heavens, eternal Light of the faithful, Christ, Redeemer of all, give ear to the prayers of Thy suppliants.

** F in *Liber usualis*.

Ash Wednesday Versicle

Liber usualis (1947 edition), p. 423.

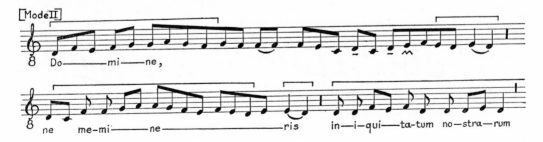

Domine, ne memineris *

Segovia MS [s. s.], fol. 97 v.–98.

JUAN DE ANCHIETA

* Lord, remember not the iniquity of our forefathers: let thy mercies speedily relieve us, for we are grown very miserable. [Ps. 78 (= 79 A.V.), 8].

Domine Jesu Christe *

Segovia: MS s.s., fols. 94v.–95;

JUAN DE ANCHIETA

Seville: Bibl. Colombina, sign. 5-5-20, fols. 18v.–19.

* O Lord Jesus Christ who the last hour of the day wast laid in the sepulchre, and wast mourned and lamented by Thy most sorrowful mother and other women, make us here present overflow with tears in compassion for thy suffering and, deeply moved, make us bewail Thy passion and remember it, as if recent, with most heartfelt grief. Amen.

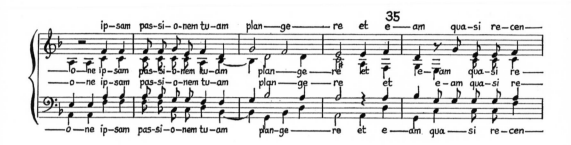

visited Spain in Philip the Fair's entourage – La Rue and Agricola. His "chords" are overwhelmingly in root position. If he uses "first-inversion chords," the bass is approached stepwise (with very rare exceptions). Passages of parallel first-inversion chords are more frequent in his *Magnificat a 3* than in any other of his works. Because by way of exception he uses the Landini-type cadence in the last section of this *Magnificat;* and because the final chord in the concluding section is built not over F (although this is the chord with which every previous section ended) but instead over G, the Sicut erat poses a stylistic problem. Perhaps it replaces another now-lost Sicut erat. At all events it seems an incongruity in its present position in the Segovia manuscript – which as we have already seen gives him a motet elsewhere attributed to Compère. Certainly he in no other instance except this *Magnificat* strays out of mode at a last crucial moment.

THROUGHOUT his *oeuvre* he showed an instinct for drama. Always however he turned resolutely away from anything that smacks of mere cleverness. After diligent search one might press the claim that he alludes to this or that contemporaneous motet in his

Missa quarti toni – Brumel's *Mater Patris et Filia* [138] in the first incise of the *Christe eleison*, for instance, or Busnois's *Quant j'ay au cueur* in the first incise of Kyrie I. Actually, however, such resemblances as these can be dismissed as purely fortuitous. At best they last no longer than a few notes. Until further evidence is brought forward, Anchieta's masses cannot be labelled erudite or even involute.

For their proper effect he depended on extraordinarily large choral groups. Unlike the choirs which attended monarchs abroad, Ferdinand and Isabella carried in train choirs numbering from 60 to 80 singers. Such for instance was the size of the Spanish royal choir which sang on Sunday, May 8, 1502, when the peninsular sovereigns joined their daughter, Joanna, and son-in-law, Philip the Fair, at Mass in Toledo Cathedral.[139] In such surroundings and with such forces his music must be created anew if it is to be appreciated as it deserves. If he lacks Peñalosa's subtlety and contrivance, his music on the other hand reflects a personality as direct and forceful as that of Bartolomé Bermejo (fl. 1474–1498), the first master in the peninsula to endow each figure in his oils with distinct individuality.

Francisco de Peñalosa (c. 1470–1528)

Part I: Biography

PEÑALOSA was an acknowledged favorite of Ferdinand V and of Leo X, king and pope respectively. Personal letters written in his behalf were, moreover, dispatched by both in an endeavor to conserve his rights to a canonry in Seville Cathedral while he sang at their courts. His music is the most virtuostic written by any Spaniard before Morales. Six masses and part of a seventh, a half-dozen magnificats, at least thirty motets and a set of lamentations survive, in addition to ten secular part-songs in the Palace Songbook. His merits were so generally recognized that when Cristóbal de Villalón wrote his dialogue, *Ingeniosa comparación entre lo antiguo y lo presente* in 1539, he adduced Peñalosa as his first example when citing modern musicians who could worthily vie with the ancients. Even Josquin des Prez was in his opinion inferior to Peñalosa, of whom he wrote:

A very short time ago died that celebrated master, Francisco de Peñalosa, he who was director of music for His Catholic Majesty, Ferdinand; both because of his prowess as a composer and as a singer he exceeded even Apollo, the inventor of music.[140]

---

[138] Brumel's *Mater Patris* (*a 3*) occurs in the Biblioteca Colombina source (sign. 5–5–20) immediately after Anchieta's *Domine Jesu Christi*. Anglés lists *Mater patris* as anonymous (*MME*, I, *129*), but Brumel is the composer.

[139] Antoine de Lalaing, "Voyage de Philippe le Beau en Espagne en 1501," *Collection des Voyages des Souverains des Pays-Bas*, ed. Louis Prosper Gachard (Brussels: F. Hayez, 1876) I, *176*. The narrator was obviously surprised to encounter so large a choir.

[140] Villalón's dialogue was published in 1898 (Madrid: Sociedad de Bibliófilos Españoles). Original reads (p. 175): "Muy poco há que murió aquel famoso varón don Francisco de Peñalosa, Maestro de capilla del cathólico Rey don Fernando, el qual en la Música en arte y boz escedió á Apolo su inuentor." The footnote giving Peñalosa's date of death is a modern editorial guess and must be corrected.

Yet despite the attentions paid him by king and pope, the survival of a greater quantity of music than by any other Spanish contemporary, acknowledged versatility in sacred and secular styles, and the highest plaudits from a discerning critic who a decade after his death rated him above Josquin, not to mention Morales, Peñalosa is today but poorly known in English-speaking countries.[141]

Of his early life no record seems to survive, but Anglés would have him born about 1470 in Talavera de la Reina.[142] Like the virtuostic painter, Master Alfonso whose technical skill in his 1473 panel, *The Martyrdom of Saint Medin* (= Emeterio),[143] leads art historians to predicate a youthful apprenticeship in Italy, Peñalosa may well have enjoyed just such an advantage. His immediate success in Rome when summoned to the court of Leo X c. 1517 gives reason for supposing that he was returning to familiar ground.

The earliest record makes of him in May of 1498 a singer in the household of Ferdinand V. Isabella's household all through their joint reigns was kept separate. Had Peñalosa been her singer, as was Anchieta, his name would of necessity appear in Simancas *quitaciones* of the House of Castile. It does not; therefore he belonged always to the Aragonese royal household throughout his eighteen years at court, 1498–1516. His last thirty years run in this vein:

1498 On May 11 he is appointed a singer in the Aragonese royal chapel.[144]

c.1500 A certain Francisco de Peñalosa, an *hidalgo*, is by royal decree named one of 29 members of the newly formed *cabildo* at Granada.[145]

1505 On December 15 the Seville Cathedral chapter accedes to the royal request that he be named to a vacant canonry. He takes possession by proxy.[146]

1506 On January 12 the Seville chapter receives bulls transmitted in behalf of another contender for the canonry, the powerful but corrupt Italian cardinal, Raffaele Riario.[147]

Four days later (January 16) Peñalosa appeals to the chapter, again through a proxy,

[141] *Grove's Dictionary*, Fifth Edition (1954) confuses him with Anchieta when it makes him chapelmaster to Prince John by Queen Isabella's appointment. *GD* makes of him a Cappella Giulia singer during his Roman sojourn – and doubts his authorship of several motets conserved at Toledo. But because found elsewhere in earlier MSS these cannot well be the work of a mid-century organist, Juan de Peñalosa. *The International Cyclopedia of Music and Musicians*, Sixth Edition (1952) gives him a mere six lines, naming 1535 as his year of death, though in 1933 was published the document from Seville Cathedral archives which shows that he died in Seville on April 1, 1528 (Elústiza-Castrillo, p. XLI).

[142] *MME*, I, 7.

[143] Local Catalonian saint, martyred c. 330 in company with San Severo. For information concerning Master Alfonso, the painter, see Oskar Hagen, *Patterns and Principles of Spanish Art* (Madison: University of Wisconsin Press, 1943), pp. 124 and 130.

[144] *MME*, I, 7.

[145] Francisco Bermúdez de Pedraza, *Historia eclesiastica, principios, y progressos de la ciudad, y religion catolica de Granada* (Granada: Andrés de Santiago, 1638), fol. 200. This reference occurs in cap. xxviii, "La forma que el primer Cabildo de Granada tuuo."

[146] Seville Cathedral, *Autos capitulares. 1505. 1506. 1507. 1510. 1523. 1524.*, fol. 143 (Anglés signalizes the year as 1506, but by an oversight).

[147] Elústiza-Castrillo, p. XXXVI. For identification of the *Cardenal de S. Jorge* see Alfonso Chacón, *Vitae et res gestae pontificum Romanorum* (Rome: P. et A. de Rubeis, 1677), III, 70–75.

countering the claims of Cardinal Riario, the latter having enjoyed such wealthy sinecures as the bishoprics of Cuenca and Osma but without ever having set foot in Spain.

On September 13 the chapter decides to nullify Peñalosa's appointment, giving the canonry to the pluralist cardinal.

On September 28 Pedro Diaz de Segovia, Peñalosa's father, appears personally before the Seville chapter in defense of his son's rights, the latter not yet having transferred residence to Seville. Subsequent events will show that the chapter decides to favor Peñalosa's suit, even though his competitor for the canonry is a cardinal.[148]

1510 On November 8 the chapter orders a book of polyphony in Peñalosa's possession appraised, the inference being that he is at that moment in Seville.[149]

1511 He becomes chapelmaster in the new household set up by Ferdinand V [150] for his grandson, the youthful Ferdinand (brother of the future Charles V, and after the latter's resignation, Holy Roman Emperor).

1512 He meets Lucio Marineo, Sicilian humanist and Latin scholar residing at court, and persuades the Sicilian to write a gloss on the Angelic Salutation; [151] an exchange of letters in Latin survives showing Peñalosa to have been residing with the court in Burgos,[152] and moreover proving him to have been a competent Latinist. Marineo addresses Peñalosa as "prince of musicians"; among Peñalosa's chapel singers at this

---

[148] Elústiza-Castrillo, p. XXXVI, n. 1: "If it should seem strange that a cardinal should seek a mere canonry, let this passage from Peraza's *Historia de Sevilla* (Colombina MS) be remembered: 'Pope Clement VII said that when one sought a canonry in Seville Cathedral, he sought [the equivalent of] a bishopric'."

[149] *A.C., 1505. 1506. 1507. 1510. 1523. 1524.*, fol. 325v.

[150] *MME*, I, 7.

[151] Lucio Marineo [Siculo], *Ad illustrissimum principem Alfonsum Aragoneum Ferdinandi regis filium ... epistolarum familiarium libri decem et septem* (Valladolid: A. G. Brocar, 1514), fol. h ii [Liber IX, ep. 8]. Letter begins: "In regii palacii sacello cum essemus nuper Pignalosa musicorum princeps: a me petisti familiariter ut angelicae salutationis ad Virginem deiparam binis dictionibus binas alias uel plures partes adiungerem. Quas in uirginis ipsius: cui maxime deditus es: laudes et honorem: sicut omnia soles: deuotissime concineres" (When recently we were in the palace chapel you, Peñalosa, foremost of musicians, asked me as your particular friend to pair added phrases with those of the Angelical Salutation so that you might sing them as is most mete in honor of the Blessed Virgin, very devotedly after the fashion of all your singing). Marineo, one of the most cultured Italians of his day not only called Peñalosa *musicorum princeps* but filled his letter with phrases of personal warmth and admiration, at its conclusion adding the gloss to the *Ave Maria* which Peñalosa had requested. The latter acknowledged Marineo's kindness in a well-phrased Latin reply, printed in Marineo's *Epistolarum* at fol. h ii verso: "... Ita ut ad nostram compositionem nihil potuerit addi aptius nihil dulcius: eoque magis quod duplex est salutatio et altera Siculi .... Vale probitatis exemplum" (... no added text could be more apt or more delightful for us to set, and it proves the more so because the Salutation has been paired with other phrases by our Sicilian .... Farewell, you example of uprightness).

[152] The Peñalosa letter bears no date, but Caro Lynn from internal evidence deduced that it must have been written in 1512 or 1513 while Marineo served as tutor to the sons of the *contador mayor* of Castile, Juan Velázquez de Cuéllar. Marineo began tutoring these five sons in the autumn of 1511. During the next year he frequently accompanied one or another son when visits were paid at the royal monastery of San Pedro de Cardeña just outside Burgos, this monastery then being the residence of Prince Ferdinand. It was during 1511 that Peñalosa became chapelmaster in the prince's household. See Caro Lynn, *A College Professor of the Renaissance* (Chicago: University of Chicago Press, 1937), p. 241.

time is Juan Ponce,[153] famous as composer of a dozen part-songs in the *Cancionero Musical de Palacio*.

1513   On January 3 Peñalosa attends a meeting of the cathedral chapter in Seville.[154]

On March 7 a letter from court requesting that his salary and other perquisites be sustained at their top level, even though he remains constantly absent, is read in chapter meeting at Seville Cathedral; this letter denominates him "chaplain and singer of His Majesty, and chapelmaster of his grandson, the illustrious Ferdinand, son of His Serene Highness Philip [d. 1506] and Queen Joanna." [155]

1515   On February 12 he again attends a Seville chapter meeting.[156]

1516   On January 23 Ferdinand V dies; while awaiting the arrival of the new king, grandson Ferdinand's household remains intact, but late in the year is dissolved, thus ending Peñalosa's eighteen years of court service.

1517   On February 4 the Seville cathedral chapter orders its archivists to search for the deed bestowing Peñalosa's dignities upon him.[157]

On March 6 Peñalosa, having arrived in Seville, is entrusted with cathedral business. He and another canon are directed to survey the curriculum set up for youthful ex-choristers, who having lost their voices are being educated at cathedral expense. He is also requested to report on the teaching of the *maestro del estudio de la gramatica* (grammar master) who instructs the younger boys still in active cathedral service.

Sometime between March 6 and autumn he transfers to Rome. He at once makes so favorable an impression that already in early November papal secretaries are busy drafting requests to the ordinaries at Cordova, Segovia, and Seville, for non-residential preferments that can be accepted by his brother acting as proxy.[158]

On November 4 Pope Leo X, patron of art and music, writes a brief asking the Seville cathedral chapter to dispense him from his obligation of residence: *Dearly beloved sons* [formula of the papal benediction]: *Among the singers in our chapel on solemn occasions is our beloved son, Francisco de Peñalosa, canon of Seville, who acting as chamberlain and musician extraordinary displays such exquisite art coupled with such discretion and probity that we fervently desire his continuing presence. He is moreover exceedingly welcome on account of other virtues which cause us to wish that he remain in our service. Since those whom we select ought not to suffer impairment of their other privileges whatever favors we bestow, and since your devotion to the Holy See is well known, we request and adjure you to continue him in all the salaries and privileges of his canonry and prebend* [in Seville Cathedral] *while he continues in our service, requesting furthermore your reply by return messenger, granting him all the rights, salaries, and privileges he would enjoy if he were present daily in your cathedral. That you may the more expeditiously and conveniently act in his favor, we absolve you from all promises made to us or our predecessors to guard the*

[153] Marineo, Liber XIV, ep. 3 (fol. m iiij verso). See pp. 184–189 of the present volume for futher details concerning Ponce.

[154] *A.C., 1513. 1514. 1515.*, fol. 1.

[155] Elústiza-Castrillo, p. XXXVII.

[156] *A.C., 1513. 1514. 1515.*, fol. 110v.

[157] *A.C., 1517. 1518. 1519.*, fol. 7.

[158] Frey, "Regesten zur päpstlichen Kapelle [Nachlese]," *Die Musikforschung*, IX/4 (1956), pp. 414–415.

canonical obligations of residence; we suspend the statutes requiring residence for this one time only, and request you to observe their suspension. Given at Rome under the Fisherman's seal, November 4, 1517, the fifth year of our pontificate.[159]

On December 26 (1517) Leo X's secretary, Pietro Bembo, writes a letter in the pope's name to Diego de Muros, bishop of Oviedo (Spain), asking further favors for Peñalosa: *To the Bishop of Oviedo: In other of my letters to you I have written in what high regard I hold my singer, Francisco de Peñalosa, and how I make frequent and intimate use of him – almost daily – in offerings of the Holy Sacrifice and in numerous other ceremonies; and so we will not any longer dwell on this fact, already known by you. But since he would very much like you to order that the Archdeaconate of Carmona which you hold in Seville Cathedral be given him; and since he himself wishes to exchange for the fruits of the archdeaconate other emoluments which are reckoned of equal value; and since others well known to you have requested the same thing of you, I ask that you accommodate him in this matter (at my behest), he being a man who is obviously industrious; and you will give me cause for gratification. I by no means see why he himself so vehemently desires this thing but if you can serve him it will please me very greatly.* [160]

1518 On January 13, not yet having received Pope Leo X's brief of the preceding November 4, the Seville cathedral chapter passes a rule requiring all absentee canons in Rome to return before January 1, 1519, under pain of forfeiting their dignities.[161]

On February 8 Pope Leo's November 4 brief arrives, is read, and voted upon; the chapter decides to deny the pope's request and to supplicate from the young king, Charles, a royal cedula against absenteeism.[162] On March 22 Charles during his stay in Valladolid accedes, issuing a cedula in which he bids the cathedral chapter to stand firm.

On Good Friday Peñalosa sings the passion *more hispano* (Spanish manner) in the pope's chapel at Rome. The pope's diarist, Paride de Grassi, records that Peñalosa sings alone, whereas formerly three singers were always accustomed to intone the Johannine narrative. Moved evidently by the beauty of Peñalosa's singing Pope Leo dedicates the large sum of 50 gold ducats and 100 julios "to the Cross." [163]

On May 26 another papal brief arrives from Rome renewing in still stronger terms

---

[159] Elústiza-Castrillo, p. XXXIX.

[160] Pietro Bembo, *Epistolarum Leonis Decimi Pontificis Max. nomine scriptarum libri sexdecim* (Venice: Apud Gualterum Scottum, 1552), pp. 510–511 (Liber XVI, ep. 5): Episcopo Ouetensi. Alteris meis ad te litteris scripsi; quo in loco Franciscum Penalosam cantorem meum haberem; quamque eo nostris in sacris et ceremoniarum celebritate familiariter ac prope quotidie uterer. Itaque non erimus nunc quidem ea in re tibi ostendenda longiores. Verum cum is magnopere cupiat, ut Archidiaconatus Chermonaeus, quem obtines in Ecclesia Hispalensi, sibi mandes ut conferatur: tibique ipse reponere fructus Archidiaconatus uelit alijs in sacerdotijs, quae tantidem aestimentur: petantque idem abs te alij perfamiliares tui: uelim des ei te facilem ea in re hortatu meo, hominique plane industrio et mihi grato commodes. Omnino cur ipse tantopere id cupiat, non uideo. Sed si ei satisfeceris; erit mihi ualde gratum. Septimo Cal. Ian. Anno quinto. Roma.

[161] Elústiza-Castrillo, p. XL.

[162] *A.C., 1517. 1518. 1519.*, fol. 110.

[163] Paride de Grassi, *Il diario di Leone X ... dai volumi manoscritti degli archivi Vaticani della S. Sede, con note di Mariano Armellini* (Rome: Tip. della Pace di F. Cuggiani, 1884), p. 66. The MS entry on fol. 306 reads thus: "In die veneris majoris ebdomadae, habitum fuit officium per cardinalem agenensem majorem poenitentiarum. Passionem cantat solus cantor Pignalosa hispanus more hispano cum alias semper tres cantores consueuerint cantare. Papa cruci obtulit quinquaginta ducatos auri et centum julios."

Leo X's request. This brief is presented by Francisco de Tovar, "resident of Seville," and in all likelihood Peñalosa's personal friend.[164]

On May 31 the dean and two canons are instructed by the assembled chapter to write Peñalosa in Rome in the name of the chapter, offering him 120 ducats annually (in gold) in partial payment, while he continues to reside in Rome.[165]

On June 9 the chapter reverses itself and decides to appeal its case against him to the highest ecclesiastical court, if necessary (the Roman Rota).[166]

On August 30 he relinquishes his former canonry in exchange for the Archdeaconate of Carmona, one of the richest dignities in Seville Cathedral, a new creation. His proxy in accepting the new dignity is Diego Méndez, singer in the previous archbishop's household (Diego Hurtado de Mendoza, d. 1502), and currently a prebendary in the cathedral.[167]

1521   On December 1 Pope Leo X dies.

1525   On March 24 Peñalosa, again in Seville, presents bulls entitling him to the added dignity of *Tesorero* (treasurer).[168]

1527   On April 2 his nephew, Luis de Peñalosa, becomes a canon of Seville Cathedral.[169]

1528   While residing in the Calle de Abates ("Street of Abbots") at Seville he dies, April 1. His body is interred in the nave of San Pablo (St. Paul), and over its resting place is affixed this inscription: *Aqui yace el Muy Iltre. Sr. Francisco de Peñalosa, Arcediano de Carmona, Canonigo de esta Sta. Iglesia, que murio en 1. de abril de 1528* ("Here lies the very illustrious Francisco de Peñalosa, Archdeacon of Carmona and canon of this cathedral church, who died on April 1, 1528").[170]

1554   On February 9 Luis de Peñalosa, nephew of Francisco, dies, having enjoyed his Seville canonry 27 years.

SOME FEW notices may have escaped students who have read the Sevillian capitular acts, 1505–1528, in search of data concerning Peñalosa. But the notices thus far recovered prove his presence in Seville during the following years only: 1510, 1513, 1515, 1517, 1525, 1528; and even during these years the capitular acts reveal that he was

---

[164] *A.C., 1517. 1518. 1519.*, fol. 137.

[165] *Ibid.*, fol. 139v.

[166] *Ibid.*, fol. 142. On the same day a document was drawn up at Rome authorizing Peñalosa's resignation of benefices worth 300 ducats in Cordova and Seville dioceses in exchange for the Archdeaconate of Carmona (which the bishop of Oviedo was at last willing to abandon). See Frey, "Regesten zur päpstlichen Kapelle," *Die Musikforschung*, VIII/1 (1955), pp. 69–70.

[167] Elústiza-Castrillo, p. XLI.

[168] This is the year in which he may well have taught the rising young Cristóbal de Morales. The Sevillian *A. C. años de 1525.1526* record at fol. 45 the chapter's decision on June 26 that "Gonzalo Pérez substitute for Morales as organist of the Antigua [Chapel] while he is busy with the marquis." The next year Morales began as chapelmaster at Ávila.

[169] Like Alonso Mudarra, Luis de Peñalosa rose to the dignity of cathedral majordomo. As such, he controlled housekeeping expenses, took charge of the structure, and looked after purchases of such items as music books and organs (see *A. C., 1536, 1537, y 1538*, fols. 25v. and 74 [Apr. 24 and Dec. 13, 1536]).

[170] Elústiza-Castrillo, p. XLI.

oftener absent from chapter meetings than present. The same *actas* show that the chapter reluctantly granted him leave upon leave only because of royal request, and then solely because Ferdinand was willing to break his own strict rule of 1488 against such cathedral absenteeism.[171] When Pope Leo X later asked an extension of the same absentee privileges, the chapter denied two successive papal appeals, dragging – or at least threatening to drag – the case through the highest ecclesiastical court at Rome rather than acceding to his earnest requests.

Part II: Checklist of Peñalosa's Compositions

HIS WORKS are scattered in the following locations, arranged in alphabetical sequence: (1) and (2) Barcelona: Biblioteca Central, MS 454; Biblioteca Orfeón Catalán, MS 5; (3) Coimbra: Biblioteca Geral, MS de musica 12; (4) Madrid: Biblioteca Real, sign. 2–1–5; (5) Seville: Biblioteca Colombina, sign. 5–5–20; (6) (7) and (8) Tarazona: MS 2, MS 3, MS 4; (9) and (10) Toledo: Biblioteca Capitular, MS 18 and MS 21.[172]

Works with Latin text [173]

Adoro te Domine Jesu Christe, 3 v. (Tarazona MS 2, fols. 249v.–250.)
Aleph. Quomodo obscuratum est [Lamentation for Holy Saturday], 4 v. (Tarazona MS 2, fols. 294v.–297.)
Aleph. Quomodo obtexit caligine, 4 v. [Good Friday Lamentation] (Tarazona MS 2, fols. 291v.–294.)
Ave Regina coelorum, 4 v. (Tarazona MS 2, fols. 269v.–270.)
Ave vera caro Christi, 4 v. (Tarazona MS 2, fols. 267v.–268.)
Ave vere sanguis Domini, 4 v. (Barcelona MS 454, fols. 65v.–66; Tarazona MS 2, fols. 268v.–269.)
Ave verum corpus natum, 4 v. (Tarazona MS 2, fols. 255v.–256.)
Deus qui manus tuas, 4 v. (Tarazona MS 2, fols. 262v.–263.).
Domine Jesu Christe, 4 v. (Tarazona MS 2, fols. 264v.–265; Tarazona MS 4, fols. 86v.–87; Toledo MS 21, fols. 73v.–75.)
Domine, secundum actum meum, 4 v. (Tarazona MS 2, fols. 265v.–266.)
Emendemus in melius. 4 v. (Tarazona MS 2, fols. 253v.–254; Toledo MS 21, fols. 67v.–69.)
Et factum est postquam, 4 v. [Maundy Thursday Lamentation] (Tarazona MS 2, fols. 288v.–291.)
Gloria, laus et honor, 4 v. (Tarazona MS 4, fols. 26v.–27.)
In passione positus, 4 v. (Barcelona MS 454, fols. 139v.–140; Tarazona MS 2, fols. 266v.–267; Toledo MS 21, fols. 75v.–78.) [174]
Inter vestibulum et altare, 4 v. (Tarazona MS 2, fols. 257v.–258; Toledo MS 21, fols. 94v.–96.)
Jesu nostra redemptio, 4 v. [Ascension hymn] (Tarazona MS 2, fols. 5v.–6.)
Kyrie, 3 v. (Barcelona: Orfeón Catalán MS 5, fol. 62.)

---

[171] *Ibid.*, p. XXXVII.

[172] For bibliographical details see *MME*, I, *112–115, 115, 119–122, 95–103, 129, 122–123, 124, 125, 131, 130–131.*

[173] Trend adds a *Missa pro defunctis* (*Grove's* [5th edn.], VI, 617, col. 1, lines 35–36). He locates the MS in Granada Cathedral. The titling of the hymns in our list follows Gerber, "Spanische Hymnensätze", p. 175. Scored excerpts from *Sacris solemniis* and *Jesu nostra redemptio* in Gerber, at pp. 182 and 183.

[174] Toledo version printed in Hilarión Eslava's *Lira sacro-hispana*, I, 37–42.

Magnificat, Tone I, odd verses, 4 v. (Coimbra MS 12, fols. 161v.–166; Tarazona MS 2, fols. 29v.–32.)

Magnificat, Tone IV, even verses, 4 v. (Tarazona MS 2, fols. 32v.–35.)

Magnificat, Tone IV, even verses [another setting], 4 v. (Tarazona MS 2, fols. 35v.–39.)

Magnificat, Tone VI, even verses, 4 v. (Tarazona MS 2, fols. 39v.–42; Toledo MS 18, fols. 95v.–101.)

Magnificat, Tone VIII, even verses, 4 v. (Tarazona MS 2, fols. 42v.–46.)

Magnificat, Tone VIII, even verses [another setting], 4 v. (Tarazona MS 2, fols. 46v.–49.)

Memorare piissima, 4 v. (Barcelona MS 454, fols. 162v.–163; Coimbra MS 12, fols. 201v.–203; Toledo MS 21, fols. 78v.–82.) [175]

Missa Adieu mes amours, 4 v. (Tarazona MS 3, fols. 134v.–144.)

Missa Ave Maria peregrina, 4 v. (Tarazona MS 3, fols. 94v.–104.) [176]

Missa El ojo, 4 v. (Coimbra MS 12, fols. 37v.–42, 43v.–53; Tarazona MS 3, fols. 114v.–124.) [177]

Missa L'Homme armé, 4 v. (Tarazona MS 3, fols. 124v.–134.)

Missa Nunca fué pena mayor, 4 v. (Tarazona MS 3, fols. 144v.–152.) [178]

Missa Por la mar, 4 v. (Tarazona MS 3, fols. 104v.–114.)

Missa Rex virginum (De Beata Virgine), 4 v. Only Gloria and Credo movements. (Tarazona MS 3, fols. 201v.–206.)

Nigra sum, 3 v. (Tarazona MS 2, fols. 248v.–249.)

Ne reminiscaris, 3 v. (Tarazona MS 2, fols. 250v.–251.)

[*O bone Jesu*, 4v., spurious; see above, p. 136, n. 130 (Barcelona MS 454, fols. 135v.–136.)]

O Domina sanctissima, 4 v. (Tarazona MS 2, fols. 260v.–261; Toledo MS 21, fols. 64v.–67.)

O lux beata, 4 v. [Trinity hymn] (Tarazona MS 2, fols. 8v.–9.)

Pater noster, 4 v. (Tarazona MS 2, fols. 252v.–253; Toledo MS 21, fols. 71v.–74.)

Precor te Domine Jesu Christe, 4 v. (Barcelona MS 454, fols. 66v.–67v.; Coimbra MS 12, fols. 34v.–35; Tarazona MS 2, fols. 261v.–262; Toledo MS 21, fols. 87v.–95 [expanded version].)[179]

Sacris solemniis, 4 v. [Corpus Christi hymn] (Tarazona MS 2, fols. 10v.–11.)

Sancta Maria, succurre, 3 v. (Tarazona MS 2, fols. 251v.–252.)

Sancta mater, istud agas, 4 v. (Seville, fols. 12v.–13; Tarazona MS 2, fols. 254v.–255; Toledo MS 21, fols. 62v.–65.) [180]

Sanctorum meritis, 4 v. [Several Martyrs hymn] (Tarazona MS 2, fols. 19v.–20.)

Transeunte Domino, 4 v. (Tarazona MS 2, fols. 263v.–264.)

Tribularer si nescirem, 4 v. (Barcelona MS 454, fols. 138 bis v.–139; Toledo MS 21, fols. 69v.–71.) [181]

Unica est columba mea, 3 v. (Tarazona MS 2, fols. 243v.–244.)

Versa est in luctum, 4 v. (Toledo MS 21, fols. 82v.–84.) [182]

Works with Spanish text

A tierras agenas, 3 v. (*Cancionero de Palacio*, no. 362 [fol. 246].)

Alegraos, males esquivos, 3 v. (*Palacio*, 307 [fol. 214v.].)

[175] *Ibid.*, I, 42–49.

[176] *MME*, I, 62–98.

[177] Kyrie I (first 13 bars) printed in Mario de Sampayo Ribeiro, *Os Manuscritos Musicais nos. 6 e 12 da Biblioteca Geral da Universidade de Coimbra* (Coimbra: Atlântida, 1941), p. 80.

[178] *MME*, I, 99–124.

[179] Eslava, I, 53–60.

[180] *Ibid.*, I, 29–33; Elústiza-Castrillo, *op. cit.*, pp. 16–19. The latter (transcribed from Seville, sign. 5–5–20) pitches both interior voices an octave too high.

[181] Eslava, I, 33–37.

[182] *Ibid.*, I, 50–53.

De mi dicha no se spera, 3 v. (*Palacio*, 315 [fol. 220].)
El triste que nunca os vió, 3 v. (*Palacio*, 125 [fol. 74].)
Lo que mucho se desea, 2 v. (*Palacio*, 382 [fol. 254].)
Los braços traygo, 3v. (Barcelona MS 454, fol. 144)
Niña, erguídeme los ojos, 3 v. (*Palacio*, 72 [fols. 50v.–51].)
Por las sierras de Madrid [quodlibet], 6 v. (*Palacio*, 311 [fol. 217v.].)
Pues vivo en perder la vida, 3 v. (*Palacio*, 127 [fol. 75].)
Que dolor mas me doliera, 3 v. (*Palacio*, 290 [fol. 206].)
Tu que vienes de camino, 3 v. incompl. (*Palacio*, 447 [fol. 291v.].)

Part III: Peñalosa's Musical Style

BECAUSE Anchieta and Peñalosa were almost exact contemporaries, and because both held high court appointments, one as chapelmaster to the son of Ferdinand and Isabella, the other as *maestro de capilla* to their grandson, a comparison of their styles ought to throw light on a number of important problems. First, their treatment of borrowed material may be studied. Neither felt any qualms when using secular source material, nor in braiding together sacred and secular tunes in the same mass. Anchieta treats *L'Homme armé* as a cantus firmus in the Agnus of his *Missa quarti toni*; Peñalosa weaves strands of the Gloria from Gregorian Mass XV (Dominator Deus) and of the superius from the secular part-song, *Nunca fué pena mayor*, into the same mass-movement. Peñalosa, the more prolific composer, seems perhaps readier to quote a secular tune than Anchieta, but such an impression might not hold if a larger number of Anchieta's works survived.

Fortunately for purposes of comparison both used the plainsong Gloria of Mass XV as the basis of polyphonic Glorias – Anchieta's use of it occurring in his *Missa quarti toni*, Peñalosa's in his *Missa Ave Maria peregrina*. Both polyphonic Glorias are almost equal in total length, Anchieta's in modern transcription occupying 176 bars, Peñalosa's 165. Both composers use the same group of voices: four; both quote the entire plainsong Gloria; both divide their polyphonic Glorias into two movements of roughly equal length, "Et in terra pax," and "Qui tollis peccata mundi." Both set off the words *Jesu Christe* with block-chords; both end with an *Amen* in triple meter. A few other less important resemblances can be found.

The differences, however, are more instructive. Anchieta adheres to the original plainsong mode, hypophrygian. Peñalosa shifts the mode from IV to II, his reason being sufficiently obvious: his desire to preserve modal unity throughout his entire mass (which elsewhere quotes the *Salve Regina* Mode I melody). [183] Anchieta assigns the plainsong sometimes to the *discantus*, sometimes to an inner voice, and once to the *bassus* (bars 110–122). Peñalosa confides the entire plainsong melody to the contratenor. But at the same time he manages to weave much imitation of the plainsong into other voices. Anchieta contrives imitative entries at no more than three places – though actually he should be freer to do so since he does not in this instance allow any single voice the privilege of singing the plainsong entire. Peñalosa devises eight imitative

[183] Cantus firmus in Sanctus, Hosanna, Agnus I, Agnus II.

entries with the plainsong of the contratenor acting the rôle of either *dux* or *comes* as the case may be. He even manages to write an eight-measure canon between bassus and contratenor at one place (bars 94–102). In addition he makes at least a half-dozen braids between discantus, tenor, and bassus out of melodic strands that are not related to the contratenor plainsong. But Anchieta never once even tries to surround the plainsong with a tapestry of imitative entries woven from extraneous material. As for intervals at which imitation is attempted, Peñalosa favors the fourths, fifths, or octaves which Anchieta uses exclusively; but does not eschew other intervals – using for instance imitation at the ninth in bars 109–111 (bassus and discantus).

Peñalosa uses imitation, however, not just for its own sake but to bind together sections that might otherwise show seams. Whereas Anchieta arrives at every cadence in his Gloria with long notes in all the parts at once, Peñalosa when arriving at a close of a plainsong phrase as often as not surrounds the long final note in the plainsong cantus firmus with a shimmering veil made of some discantus or tenor melisma – then uses this same melisma transferred to another voice as counterpoint for the first few notes in the next plainsong entry (the plainsong initium in turn inspiring imitation of itself). This artful procedure can best be understood by reference to an example. At bars 91–95 in

Missa Ave Maria peregrina
Qui tollis

MME, I, 71 (mm. 91–102).

FRANCISCO DE PEÑALOSA

Peñalosa's "Qui tollis" the plainsong comes to rest on a long *d*, the under parts supply held B♭'s, and the top part weaves a moving figure, which the tenor canonically answers two and a half bars later.[184] No sooner has the tenor begun its canonic answer at the lower octave than the bass enters with an anticipation of the plainsong theme. One bar after the bass's anticipatory entry the contratenor – to which the plainsong regularly belongs – takes up its usual rôle. Throughout the next six bars he contrives a bass part which exactly anticipates the plainsong in the contratenor, making the latter appear to be a canonic answer.

His use of imitation to hide seams contrasts strongly with Anchieta's willingness for them to show. In this same Gloria Anchieta writes 15 cadences during the first 60 breves, 13 of which end on the A minor chord and the other two on the incomplete E chord. Peñalosa, on the other hand, while using just one more breve to set the same amount of text, writes only six cadences in 61 breves – the first being of a "deceptive" type (mm. 10–11), the second of a "half-cadence" type (mm. 15–16), three others of the "VII⁶–I" variety (mm. 21–22, 53–54, 60–61), and another of the "authentic" type (mm. 36–37). Whereas Anchieta's cadences stop the motion every fourth or fifth breve, dividing the music into a series of short, pithy, newspaper sentences, Peñalosa's much more widely spaced cadences round off Ciceronian sentences of the compound and complex types.

Anchieta's cadences are all of approximately equal weight, and involve this rhythmic formula or a slight variant: ‖ ♩ ♩ ♩ | ○ ‖ in an upper voice. Peñalosa touches intermediate ones lightly; but at the ends of sections extends them so that five or six bars are spent in confirming final cadences. Thus, when Anchieta arrives at the culminating words, "Tu solus Altissimus, Jesu Christe," he ends with a cadence of no greater weight than any previous one in the movement; but Peñalosa makes a sweeping gesture lasting six measures, all to confirm the V–I cadence – which he uses so much more sparingly but at the same time emphatically than Anchieta.

Useful contrasts between the *Dominator Deus* Glorias of these two masters can also be made by touching on such matters as voice-range: wider in Peñalosa than Anchieta;[185] melodic repetition: more artfully contrived in the younger than the older composer;[186] use of large intervals such as the fifth and octave: more expressively handled by one than the other.

BUT LEST further comparisons of this particular type have the undesired effect of exalting one composer at the other's expense, we turn next to a comparison that involves only Peñalosa's own work: namely, a study of differences between his style in masses and in motets. The predominating virtues of the two published masses can be classified as follows: (1) skilful blending of disparate source-materials that are introduced simultaneously oftener than consecutively; (2) invention of highly characteristic motives

---

184 Reference is to the Anglés transcription, *MME*, I, 71 (parte musical). Wherever the anachronistic term "bars" is used, the modern transcription must be understood.

185 The Peñalosa contratenor, carrying the c.f., does not illustrate this generalization; the bass does (B₁♭–f in Peñalosa; A₁–A in Anchieta).

186 Peñalosa's discantus in bars 145–151 aptly illustrates this point.

which, because constantly repeated throughout a movement in counterpoint to the borrowed themes, unify material that would otherwise run the danger of sounding like a mere quodlibet; (3) division of larger movements into neatly balanced units; (4) a well-developed sense of climax, manifesting itself within individual movements as well as in the masses as wholes.

I In the Gloria of his *Nunca fué pena mayor* Mass he expounds two borrowed themes: the Urrede villancico in triple meter, the treble of which he lifts note-for-note; and the plainsong Gloria from Mass XV, which he deftly contrives for the bassus to sing simultaneously (with occasional anticipating imitation in the tenor). The only Spanish composer to make much of proportions, he arranges for the triple-meter villancico and the duple-meter lower voices to shake hands by writing the top part in "moode perfect of the lesse prolation" [187] but the lower voices in C2. Or for a more dazzling example: in the last Agnus of his *Ave Maria peregrina* Mass he combines the reversed tenor of Hayne van Ghizeghem's extremely popular chanson, *De tous biens plaine*, with the plainsong of the *Salve Regina*, verses 2 and 4. Peñalosa has been considered since Barbieri's publication in 1890 of the Palace Songbook as unique among "palace" composers because of his ability to collect several tunes of independent origin in a smooth quodlibet. Study of his masses now shows that his 6–part quodlibet *Por las sierras de Madrid* was not an unusual feat but one which he performed frequently in his larger liturgical works.

II If during the diastole of his creative process alien strains flow into his music, he on the other hand strongly unifies them at the systole. In *Por las sierras* he unifies with an original top melody that moves more rapidly than the other five, and exploits this rhythm 𝄽 ♩ ♪♪♪♪ │ ♩ five times in 19 bars. In the final Agnus of the *Ave Maria peregrina* Mass he begins with imitation between first contratenor and bass. When four breves later the Hayne chanson tenor (*canon per antiphrasin*) enters in duet with the *Salve Regina* plainsong, the second contratenor at the same moment takes up the theme already stated during the opening play of imitation between contratenor and bass. Again four breves later the second contratenor sings this same imitated theme. For that matter, if he starts a theme or melodic figure anywhere in a surrounding part he almost invariably "develops" it by a considerable amount of melodic repetition and sequence, as well as by imitation. In the *Christe eleison* of this mass he invents a particularly winsome tune to serve as counterpoint to the *Ave Maria* plainsong in the tenor voice. First heard in the discantus, it is imitated immediately in the bass, then contratenor.

But not done with it, he now proceeds to repeat it again in the discantus, then to sequence it twice, the first time one step lower and the second time two steps lower.

[187] Thomas Morley, *A Plaine and easie introduction to practicall musicke* (London: H. Lownes, 1608), p. 18.

During these sequences the bass sings a fragmented version of the same tune, still further dramatizing its importance. Because of such imitations, repetitions, and sequences, his surrounding voices make an extraordinarily unified continuum in all his movements quoting plainsong.

III Profoundly interested in balance and symmetry, he wrote movements which can be analyzed not only in such measure counts as 21 + 21 + 4,[188] 7 + 8 + 7,[189] 13 + 11 + 13,[190] 14 + 14 + 14,[191] 10 + 10 + 11,[192] but also organized the cadences within movements so that they occur at fairly regular intervals. Thus if the first cadence occurs at bars 6–7, the next will probably occur five or six bars later, followed by others at regular intervals throughout the movement. But if the first cadence is long delayed, as often for instance in certain Gloria and Credo movements, then the second will also be delayed. This is to say that the larger harmonic rhythm of his movements is well conceived, and by no means haphazard.

IV Not only does he constantly strive for balance and symmetry, but also for well-spaced climaxes. The most learned and complex movement in the *Ave Maria peregrina* Mass comes last. Moreover it is fullest, with five voices. A reiterated figure such as the scale descendlng from Middle C which he repeats five times in the bassus of his *Nunca fué* Gloria is climaxed by a descending scale from e above Middle C to a tenth below.[193] Cadences at ends of sections or movements are always extended much beyond the length of intermediate cadences. Melodically and harmonically then – as well as contrapuntally – he reserves his best effects for culminating moments.

IN HIS MOTETS, he allies the same exquisite beauty of melodic line, the same firm control of structure, with a heightened expressiveness. Those published by Eslava set texts that are uniformly penitential in character. For once he therefore eschews all learned contrivance, clearing the texture so that the words can always be understood. Such texts as *Precor te* (which in the Toledo source runs to half as many breves as in the Coimbra source), *In passione positus*, and *Sancta mater, istud agas* are non-liturgical and possibly by Peñalosa himself, he being known from other evidence to have been a poet as well as composer. When he does use Scripture as in the four-voiced *Versa est in luctum* – shown as an accompanying example – he gathers his text by a process of centonism. By careful control, he assures himself that only one mood is suggested by the words. He

[188] Christe, *MME*, I, 63–65. The last two bars in the transcription are however defective; the antepenult and penult in the contratenor should read semibreve-semibreve (= minim-minim), thus bringing the movement to a close one bar earlier.

[189] Sanctus, *MME*, I, 84–85.

[190] Benedictus, *MME*, I, 90–91.

[191] Christe, *MME*, I, 100–101.

[192] Pleni, *MME*, I, 120–121 (Hosanna not included). These measure-counts are not offered as the final word in analysis. Though dividing on the basis of cadences, the author is aware that a bar can often be counted as the last of a preceding section or the first of a new section, thus shifting the count. Enough will have been gained if the reader sees how strongly Peñalosa was devoted to the principle of symmetry.

[193] *MME*, I, 103–109, mm. 35–38, 42–44, 48⁴–50, 51–53, 54–59, 62–65.

then unifies still more strongly by pitching his music in the same emotional key throughout. Like Morales – whom he no doubt influenced profoundly, he reserves his learning for his masses, and concentrates on intense expressiveness in his motets.

He seems to have been the first Spaniard to understand the expressive implications of a drooping fifth, an interval Victoria later exploited to perfection. An example can be seen between bars 4 and 5 of *Versa est in luctum*. To tell most strongly, the fifth should be placed in outer parts. But its effect is still potent in the tenor between second and third beats of bar 6. Though this occasion cannot be taken for melodic or harmonic analysis, no sensitive listener will miss the "slow tears" that fall in such a cadence as that between bars 7–8, in such a melodic line as the tenor sings in bars 8–9, in such a shift of harmony as that from d minor to E♭ Major between bars 23–24. Even in this smallest of his motets he proves himself a master of all those expressive devices which were to become the peculiar glory of the sixteenth-century Spanish school.

Part IV: Missa Nunca fué pena mayor [194]

IF ANCHIETA's style can be contrasted with Peñalosa's and segments of his own output compared, a significant work of his can also be pitted against one by a foreign master working with identical materials. Pierre de la Rue's mass based on the Urrede villancico and his of the same name make an instructive pair. La Rue visited Spain twice, in 1502 and in 1506, both times in the entourage of Philip the Fair. *Nunca fué pena mayor* had already however become such a popular item in the international repertory before 1503 that La Rue's splendid parody need not necessarily date from the first visit.[195]

Again comparisons can be the more easily made because the source material in each instance is identical, the framework in which the borrowings are set is identical, and the vocal resources are the same – four voices. La Rue's mass is divided into 14 movements, seven in triple and an equal number in duple meter; Peñalosa's contains a dozen movements, eight in duple meter. Both masses alternate movements ending on A, G, and C with those closing on E, phrygian being the predominant modality of the Urrede villancico and of the two masses. La Rue and Peñalosa both take care to use the tenor of the borrowed villancico in occasional movements. Various likenesses can be found in the

[194] Both Matthaeus Pipelare (*Hymnus de septem doloribus dulcissimae Mariae Virginis* [pr. R. van Maldeghem, *Trésor musical: Musique religieuse*, XI, 31]) and Peñalosa follow the Odhecaton version of the tenor rather than the *Palacio* version (see m. 6). On the other hand, the discantus in Peñalosa's Sanctus seems different from Urrede's only because the transcriber has read the first note as a rest; this same mishap occurs in the discantus at m. 10. The accented and unprepared dissonance at m. 88 in the "Qui tollis" of the *Nunca fué* Gloria similarly results from a defective transcription. The discantus ought to read semibreve c (= minim in transcription) followed by breve (= semibreve tied across bar-line). Cf. m. 9 (p. 103) with m. 88 (p. 106). Similar mishaps mar the *MME* transcription of the *Ave Maria* Mass. For example, the tenor begins a bar too soon in the Christe (pp. 63–65) and remains a bar previous to itself through meas. 38. Instead of two tied semibreves in mm. 38–39 the tenor should read C–G (semibreves). In view of such faults, any analysis of his dissonance-technique founded solely on the *MME* transcriptions would have to remain tentative. What appears to be exceptional dissonance-treatment in the Christe of the *Ave Maria* Mass disappears, for instance, as soon as the tenor is remedied.

[195] First published by Petrucci, October 31, 1503, in the *Misse Petri de la Rue* issued at Fossombrone in four part-books, this mass cannot be dated later than the first Spanish tour. Harvard University Library owns a complete set of part-books.

Versa est in luctum *

Toledo: Bibl. Cap. MS 21, fols. 82v.–84.   FRANCISCO DE PEÑALOSA

* My harp is turned into mourning: and my organ into the voice of those that weep. Spare me for my days are nothing. My skin has become blacker than coals and my bones are dried up with heat. O that my sins whereby I have deserved wrath and the calamity that I suffer were weighed in the balance. [Job 30:31; 7:16b; 30:30; 6:2].

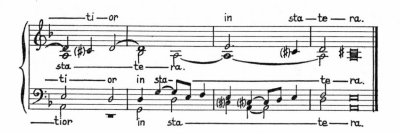

treatment of text, both composers for instance shifting into homophony for the words "Et homo factus est" in the creed.

The differences should however be studied if the musical personalities of the Fleming and the Spaniard are to be individualized.

La Rue, though like Peñalosa availing himself of both Urrede's treble and tenor for cantus firmus quotations, makes occasional changes in the borrowed themes to suit the harmonic or contrapuntal exigencies of the moment;

Peñalosa on the other hand quotes his sources exactly, never allowing himself any "convenient" licences when borrowing Urrede's treble or tenor for a cantus firmus;

both composers surround the borrowed themes with a play of imitation, but La Rue rarely repeats a melodic figure in the same voice;

Peñalosa, by contrast, makes a practice of repeating melodic figures until they become motives;

La Rue exercises himself less to make the inner voice-parts singable, often requiring successive wide leaps in minim motion;

but Peñalosa writes inner parts which can be as easily vocalized as the outer parts;

the Fleming alternates passages in long and short notes within a single voice-part in the same movement;

the Spaniard after setting his voices in motion tends to keep them going at the same general gait till the end of the movement;

La Rue does not prolong his cadences, even at ends of movements;

Peñalosa's final cadences are so elongated that they become much more decisive;

La Rue's "chord-changes" more frequently involve triads on adjoining scale-degrees;

Peñalosa's oftener involve shifts that can be analyzed as IV–I or I–IV (= V–I);

La Rue, though in the Flemish main stream, seems much less interested than Peñalosa in symmetry on a broad scale;

Peñalosa symmetrically divides so large a movement as the Gloria into 69 measures of duple music ("Et in terra pax"), 12 of triple ("Domine Deus"), 66 of duple ("Qui tollis"), and finally 13 of triple ("Cum Sancto Spiritu" – in both cases with the triple-meter section treated as an epilogue (*deshecha*) to the preceding duple-meter section.

Obviously, no one movement can illustrate all these distinctions. But the opening Kyrie of each can at least serve as an earnest. Peñalosa's treble is an *ipsissima verba* quotation of Urrede's; La Rue's departures can therefore be at once localized without so much as having to see their model (p. 228 of this book). On the other hand, neither master quotes anything from Urrede's lower parts. Neither specifies more than the one word Kyrie as text, and that word but once at the beginning. In the accompanying examples no attempt is made to fit the text throughout, such an effort not being germane to our purpose. While an open-score transcription would facilitate study of the linear

Missa Nunqua fue pena maior

Kyrie I

Misse (Petrucci, 1503), fols. 13v., 9, 13, 11v.   PIERRE DE LA RUE

motion, a compressed score at least makes possible the printing of the two Kyries on pages that face each other.

Other Composers of Liturgical Music

LITURGICAL music by approximately twenty other composers active during the reigns of Ferdinand and Isabella still survives. These composers can be classified according to

Missa Nunca fue pena mayor
Kyrie I

Tarazona: MS 3, fols. 144v.–145.
(*MME*, I, 99–100).

FRANCISCO DE PEÑALOSA

various schemes. Six were composers of masses – Almorox, Alva, Escobar, Quixada, Ribera, and Tordesillas. Four left as their principal or sole sacred work a *Salve Regina* – Fernández de Castilleja, Medina, Ponce, and Rivafrecha. Five left no extant secular music – Díaz, Marlet, Plaja, Rivafrecha, and Segovia.

Insofar as biography is concerned, the birthdate of not one is known. The exact dates , of death of only four can be given – Alva's, Escribano's, Fernández's, and Rivafrecha's; for perhaps another half-dozen the death date can be conjectured within a margin of two or three years. But for the following quartet no shred of biographical evidence seems to survive: Quixada, Plaja, Sanabria, and Segovia. In the absence of any birth-dates the best that can be done towards classifying the rest chronologically is to list the years in which one first hears of them in some contemporary document or other source. Thus arranged their chronological sequence runs as follows: 1477, Medina; 1478, Triana; 1479, Madrid; 1483, Torre; 1484, Díaz; 1485, Almorox; 1491, Alva; 1498, Illario; [196] 1502, Mondéjar; 1503, Rivafrecha; 1506, Marlet; 1507, Escribano; 1507, Escobar; [197] 1514, Fernández; 1514, Ponce; 1514, Ribera.

Another scheme of classification would be to separate the composers according to their patrons or employers. Three were at one time or another chapel singers in Queen Isabella's employ: [198] Alva, Medina, and Mondéjar. Seven served her husband, Fer-dinand, in similar capacity: Almorox, Díaz, Madrid, Mondéjar, Ponce, Tordesillas, and Torre. Two were papal singers at Rome: Escribano and Ribera. Six held cathedral posts in Spain: Alva, Escobar, Fernández, Marlet, Rivafrecha, Torre, and Triana.

But because of lacunae in our information, no single scheme can be applied with rigor. As the most convenient way, then, of presenting such data as can at the present moment be assembled, a merely alphabetical order has been chosen.

Juan Almorox (fl. 1485)

Listed as a singer in Ferdinand's chapel in 1485, Almorox held appointment until at least 1498.[199] A patriotic part-song *a 4* written to celebrate the 1504 victory over the French and the taking of Gaeta (above Naples) proves him to have been still active in the year of Queen Isabella's death. Publication of his three-voiced Mass, copied at fols. 87v.–94 in Tarazona MS 3, has been promised by the Spanish Institute of Musicology. His three secular songs, each *a 4* are found at numbers 200, 211, and 423 in the *Cancionero de Palacio*, the last celebrating the capture of Gaeta.

Alonso de Alva (d. 1504)

ALONSO PÉREZ DE ALVA (= Alba) – first appointed on April 8, 1491, as a singer in Queen Isabella's chapel with an annual salary of 20,000 maravedís – continued as *cantor capellanus* in her establishment until 1501. On February 6 of the latter year his title was

---

[196] Illario, cited in Cristóbal de Escobar's plainsong treatise of this approximate date, may have flourished several decades earlier.

[197] If Pedro de Escobar = Pedro do Pôrto then 1489 rather than 1507 would be the year from which the first dated information survives.

[198] Similarly, Escobar's name would be added to Queen Isabella's list if Pedro de Escobar = Pedro del Puerto = Pedro do Pôrto.

[199] Anglés-Pena, *Diccionario de la música Labor*, I, 50. Henceforth abbreviated *DML*.

changed to sacristán.[200] As a chaplain, perhaps honorary, his name continues to appear in her payroll until 1505.

The only composition which in a manuscript source seems to bear the full name, A[lons]o Pérez Dalua [= de Alva], is the Agnus Dei of a *De beata Virgine* Mass conserved in MS 3 at Tarazona Cathedral, the composers of the Kyrie, Gloria, and Credo movements of which mass were Escobar and Peñalosa.[201] The half-dozen 4-voiced hymns, five 3-voiced *alleluias*, the three 4-voiced motets, the pairs of 3-voiced Marian antiphons, Eastertide *Vidi aquam*, and the solitary 3-voiced mass in the same Tarazona musical archive are uniformly ascribed to Alonso Dalba, Alonso Dalua, or Alonso de Alua, without the name Pérez occurring in the composer-attribution.[202] In all likelihood, the "Pérez" was a name like the "Marcos" in Domingo Marcos Durán's full name, which the composer used only occasionally.

On January 25, 1503, Alonso de Alva, whom we would equate with Alonso Pérez de Alva, was received as chapelmaster in Seville Cathedral.[203] His predecessor in that portion of his duty which pertained to the care and upbringing of the choirboys was Francisco de la Torre. On February 1, 1503, the cabildo rented Alva a large house close to the cathedral which at the moment was in use as a tavern,[204] the chapter's intention being that the tavern when remodelled should serve as the abode of the chapelmaster and choirboys.[205] On February 8 these boys were still in Torre's charge, and on February 10 the cabildo decided to compensate the latter at the chapelmaster's rate until Alva could receive them.[206] On the same date the cabildo voted to advance Alva three measures of wheat and two of barley to be repaid later in the year.

During the next year, 1504, the capitular acts show that the cathedral organist, Bernaldino de Cuenca, was busy overseeing the installation of new bellows for the organs used at the main altar.[207] Alva's name does not appear until September 6, 1504, on which date he has died and the cathedral succentor, Andrés de Hojeda, is asked to take charge of the choirboys while a new *maestro de capilla* is being sought.[208]

The fact that Alva's name continues to appear in Queen Isabella's list of chaplains

---

[200] *MME*, I, *8* (introduction).

[201] *MME*, I, *124* (item 19).

[202] *MME*, I, *122–124*.

[203] *Autos capitulares. 1503–1504*, fol. 5: "Este dia resçibieron sus mercedes por su maestro de capilla a alonso de alua y le aseguraron que por enfermedad ni por vejez no le quitarian el oficio no caresciendo la iglesia del seruicio a que el es obligado y que sus mercedes le mandaran dar su parte de las pitanzas que se reparten del globo de la mesa capitular" (On this day Alonso de Alva was appointed chapelmaster and the chapter assured him that neither on account of sickness nor of old age would he be dismissed, as long as he remained faithful to his duty; and the chapter ordered that he share in the salaries distributed from the chapter chest).

[204] *A.C., 1503–1504*, fol. 8v.

[205] The remodelled tavern was so large that on January 15, 1505, Alva having died, his successor – Juan de Valera – was requested to share it with the workmen who were preparing the cathedral stained-glass windows (see *A.C., 1505. 1506. 1507. 1510. 1523. 1524.*, fol. 88v.).

[206] *A.C., 1503–1504*, fol. 10v. Torre was on this date a *conbeneficiado*; on September 30, 1504, he was a *compañero* (*A.C., 1503–1504*, fol. 102). The number of Sevillian canons was on the latter date given as 34, of prebendaries as 18, of fellows (*compañeros*) as 14.

[207] *A.C., 1503–1504*, fol. 60v. (January 8, 1504).

[208] *Ibid.*, fol. 98v.

(not singers) during 1503–1505 need cause no embarrassment. Anchieta was another singer who also continued to receive a chaplain's stipend during several years following his retirement from the court. Disbursements were made usually in *tercios* after, not before, the stipulated period of service. The fact that a "third" was stlll due in 1505 would therefore be expected, since he died after the middle of 1504.

At his death he must have possessed something of a library of polyphonic manuscripts. Three weeks after his death these were auctioned off, and the Seville chapter ordered that several be purchased for use in the cathedral.[209] Nothing by him, however, survives in the present cathedral archive at Seville. Indeed all his surviving ascribed liturgical works are found in one location only, the Tarazona cathedral archive.[210]

Alphabetically arranged, their titles read: *Alleluia: Angelus Domini descendit*, 3 v.; *Alleluia: Ascendo ad Patrem*, 3 v.; *Alleluia: Assumpta est Maria*, 3 v.; *Alleluia: O adoranda Trinitas*, 3 v.; *Alleluia: Vidimus stellam*, 3 v.; *Ave Maria*, 3 v.; *Beata nobis gaudia*, 4 v.; *Christe Redemptor omnium*, 4 v.; *Missa*, 3 v.; *Missa Rex virginum* (Agnus movement only: Kyrie by Escobar, Gloria and Credo by Peñalosa, Sanctus by Pedro Hernandes), 4 v.; *O felix Maria*, 4 v.; *O sacrum convivium*, 4 v.; *Stabat mater dolorosa*, 3 v.; *Te ergo quesumus*, 4 v.; *Tibi, Christe, splendor*, 4 v.; *Ut queant laxis*, 4 v.; *Veni Creator Spiritus*, 4 v.; *Vexilla regis*, 4 v.; *Vidi aquam*, 4 v.; *Vidi aquam* (another setting), 4 v. In addition to his Latin pieces, the *Cancionero de Palacio* contains one Spanish item ascribed to A[lons]o d'Alva, *No me le digáis mal, madre* (no. 391).

The Mass *a 3* published in 1941, though not a pretentious work, includes a one-movement Gloria written in canon at the unison. The answering voice follows its leader at a distance of three breves while the bass supplies a freely-moving counterpoint. For men's voices, this mass is unified more by its texture and its recurring cadences than by any thematic carry-over from movement to movement. True, the beginning of the Christe slightly resembles the beginning of the Sanctus. But in these openings the melodic material is too neutral in character for the likeness to be called crucial. The Credo is divided into two parts, the second commencing with the words "Qui cum Patre." Sanctus, Pleni, and Hosanna with Benedictus make three movements; he however sets only one Agnus. Thus the entire mass comprises ten movements, all of which end on an incomplete G-chord. All ten carry a "signature" of one flat, and all but two start on the note G. The prevailing motion is remarkably uniform in all voices. Only 14 bars in the entire mass are in triple meter (beginning of "Qui cum Patre"). Every movement is written for three voices. The voice parts are bounded by an octave and a sixth, the lowest note in the bass being G_1, and the highest in the contratenor reaching only e♭. We are here dealing therefore with less ambitious music than either the Peñalosa or Anchieta masses.

On the other hand, since it is music which more ordinary choristers could have attempted, the use of such large blocs of strict canon takes on added significance. The

---

[209] *Ibid.*, fol. 100v. (Sept. 23, 1504).

[210] Rudolf Gerber in "Spanische Hymnensätze um 1500" [see note 122 above], p. 169, identifies the anonymous *Veni Creator* at fol. 99 in the Segovia cancionero as Alva's through a concordance with Tarazona MS 2, no. 7 (*MME*, I, *107* and *122*). Transcriptions of fragments from Alva's hymns in Gerber, pp. 172, 177, 178.

Latin phrase, *Post triduum me sequeris*, standing at the beginning of the Gloria may perhaps indicate that Alva used continuous canon throughout the movement with symbolic intent, in which case the words could be interpreted as Jesus's to his disciples ("After three days you will follow me," i.e., after the Resurrection). The very fact that the canon runs through so wordy a continuum as the Gloria, but that he divides the Credo and even the Sanctus, makes such an explanation the likelier. At all events, such a lengthy canon left Spanish footprints for Morales to walk in when in 1544 he published a mass in canon throughout (*Ave maris stella*).

Alva's extended canons are matched by his drawn-out chains of sequences. The accompanying 15-bar example (mm. 38–52 of the *Christe*) is perhaps extreme, but at least proves to what lengths he could go in harmonic as well as melodic sequence.

Missa [sine nomine]
Christe eleison

MME, I, 157 (mm. 38–52)

ALONSO DE ALVA

Pedro Díaz (fl. 1484)

Known only as a chapel singer at Ferdinand V's court beginning in 1484,[211] Díaz is remembered as a composer because of an equally solitary item – the motet *a 4*, *Ave sanctissimum et gloriosum corpus*, copied in MS 2 at Tarazona Cathedral (fols. 275v.–276).

Pedro de Escobar (fl. 1507)

PEDRO DE ESCOBAR's early life can only be guessed at and even his seven years at Seville (1507–1514) have not yet been exhaustively explored. Still he can with certainty

[211] *DML*, I, 722–723.

be identified as a close personal friend of both Anchieta and Peñalosa. Two *De beata Virgine* masses survive in Tarazona MS 3. He wrote one cooperatively with Anchieta,[212] the other with Peñalosa.[213] Both introduce the *Rex virginum* trope. In the first of these Anchieta contributed the Kyrie, Gloria, and Credo movements while he wrote the Sanctus and Agnus. In the other, he composed the Kyrie, and Peñalosa the Gloria and Credo movements. Only close personal ties can explain such unusual cooperation.

As for documents, the earliest thus far recovered occurs as an entry in the Sevillian *Autos capitulares. 1505. 1506. 1507. 1510. 1523. 1524*, under May 19, 1507.[214] On that date the cabildo ordered a courier to Portugal at cathedral expense, for the purpose of offering him the recently created post of *maestro de capilla*[215] in Seville Cathedral. During the two previous years this office had been held by Juan de Valera,[216] he having on January 15, 1505,[217] in turn inherited it from Alonso de Alva (d. 1504). Since one of the chapelmaster's most important, yet onerous, chores was the care and upbringing of the cathedral boys, the cabildo particularly charged the courier to come to terms with him on this vexatious matter before making any formal commitments. At the moment the boys were in the care of an adult singer, Fernando de Solís,[218] who had on April 12, 1507, been asked to act as temporary master until a suitable successor to Valera could be engaged.

Political as well as artistic ties closely united Spain and Portugal at this particular moment. Both the first and second wives of Manuel the Fortunate (reigned 1495–1521) were daughters of Ferdinand and Isabella, Castilian remaining their preferred tongue. Gil Vicente, Portuguese "poet laureate," entertained the court with Spanish verses.[219] His acknowledged literary model when he wrote Portuguese as well as Castilian verses was Juan del Encina – who may well have visited the Portuguese court [220] during the 1490 wedding festivities. As for musical ties, they were strong even during the reign of Affonso V (1438–1481) "the African." His chapelmaster was Tristano de Silva, a Spaniard, not a Portuguese. The most important collection of secular part-songs from the early sixteenth century still preserved in Portugal, the *Cancioneiro musical e poético da Biblioteca Públia Hortênsia*, contains 65 songs, 51 in Spanish, 14 in Portuguese. A

---

[212] Fols. 209v.–217 (*MME*, I, *124*, item 20).

[213] Fols. 200v.–209 (*MME*, I, *124*, item 19).

[214] Fol. 229: "Miercoles 19 de mayo 1507.

Scobar. Iten este mismo dya mandaron sus merçedes que pedro de fuentes despache vn mensajero a portogal a llamar a escobar sy pudiere con el que tome los moços que tenia valera e lo que montare el mensajero se lo pague."

[215] The earliest lifetime appointee with the title of *maestro de capilla* seems to have been Alonso de Alva, named on January 25, 1503. See *A.C.*, *1503–1504*, fol. 5.

[216] In Elústiza-Castrillo, p. XLVIII, his name is given Juan de Varela, a form in which it appears once or twice in the Seville *actas*. Metathesis was a commonplace in Spanish pronunciation and orthography during the sixteenth century.

[217] *A.C.*, *1505. 1506. 1507. 1510. 1523. 1524.*, fol. 88v.

[218] *1508*, fol. 223. His full name appears in *A.C.*, *1503–1504*, on fol. 102v. (Sept. 30, 1504). Solis in September, 1504, assumed charge of the boys for a brief period following Alva's death.

[219] See *Four Plays of Gil Vicente*, tr. by Aubrey F. G. Bell (Cambridge [England]: University Press, 1920), pp. xiv ff.

[220] *Ibid.*, p. xiii.

further proof of Spanish musical hegemony so late as 1533 and 1535 is found in the publication at Lisbon in those years of the two first music treatises to appear in Portugal,[221] both by a Spaniard residing at Évora, Matheo de Aranda; and both in Castilian.

Escobar may possibly have belonged to the tradition of Silva and Aranda. Certainly from the evidence of his name alone his nationality cannot be determined: his being a familiar enough family name in both countries.[222] But we can gather other evidence indicative of Portuguese ties aside from the already mentioned notice of May 19, 1507, in the Sevillian capitular acts. Only he and Encina are represented in the *cancioneiro* at the Biblioteca Públia Hortênsia.[223] A mass survives at Coimbra University.[224]The manuscript in which it is copied – MS musical 12, originally belonging to Santa Cruz *mosteiro* in Coimbra – contains in addition his *Clamabat autem mulier Chananea*,[225] the famous motet which Gil Vicente cited in his *Auto da Cananea* (written to be acted in a convent near Lisbon during 1534).[226] Indeed this latter *auto*, composed at the request of the Abbess of Odivelas, can almost be said to have been inspired by the motet, since at the end the action culminates in the singing of it (*E cantando, Clamabat autem se acaba o dito Auto*).[227]

HERE, however, we run into much more interesting evidence: for in Portugal this particular motet, *Clamabat autem*, was in João de Barros's 1549 MS, "Libro das antiguidades" – now preserved in the Lisbon National Library – attributed to Pedro do Pôrto ("Pedro of Oporto"). Copying from Barros, Diogo Barbosa Machado wrote:[228] "Pedro do Pôrto was a native of Oporto, from which city he took his name; he pursued his career in Seville where he was chapelmaster in the cathedral; he also belonged to the chapel establishment of the Catholic Kings [Ferdinand and Isabella] winning general applause on account of his compositions, among which the chief is his motet *Clamabat autem* .... He [later] resided at Évora with the court, and was highly esteemed by João III."

[221] For details concerning Aranda, see above, pp. 96–99.

[222] Esteves Pereira and Guilherme Rodrigues, *Diccionario historico* (Lisbon: João Romano Torres, 1907), III, 171, col. 1 ("Escobar").

[223] Manuel Joaquim, ed., *O Cancioneiro musical e poético* (Coimbra: Instituto para a alta cultura, 1940), pp. 80, 81, 84, 91 (Encina); 37, 43, and 92 (Escobar).

[224] Mário de Sampayo Ribeiro, *op. cit.*, pp. 50–53, 84–86, 95.

[225] *Ibid.*, pp. 70 and 97.

[226] For the exact date, March 1, 1534, see Sampayo Ribeiro, "Sôbre o fecho do 'Auto da Cananeia'," *Brotéria: Revista contemporânea de cultura*, XXVII (1938), p. 387. He adduces the date from the fact that it was presented the second Sunday in Lent.

[227] Gil Vicente, *Copilaçam de todalas obras* (Lisbon: Ioam Aluarez, 1562), fol. 84v. The scriptural incident on which both the *auto* and the motet are based is narrated in Matt. 15 : 22–26.

[228] *Bibliotheca Lusitana*, Tomo III (Lisbon: Ignacio Rodrigues, 1752), p. 611, c. 1. He cited as his manuscript source the "Libro das antiguidades, e cousas notaueis de antre Douro e Minho, e de outras m^tas de España e Portugal. Por Ioão de barros. Composto no año de 1549." This MS, now conserved in the Biblioteca Nacional in Lisbon (Fundo Geral A–6–2), contains a passage at fol. 32v. which reads as follows: *Tãobem foj natural do Porto, Pedro do porto musico excellente, o qual compos o motete Clamabat autem, tido por tão excellente compostura q̃ se chama principe dos motetes* (Also a native of Oporto was Pedro do Pôrto, the excellent musician who composed the motet *Clamabat autem*, considered such fine music that it is called the foremost of motets). Barbosa Machado in quoting João de Barros gave the title as *Clamabat autem Jesus*, but Barros himself left off the "Jesus."

If we now turn to the personnel of Isabella's chapel, we discover that indeed just such a Pedro del Puerto (= Pôrto) was on her chapel roll as a singer from 1489–1499. He entered in the same year as Anchieta and was her only singer listed as *portugués*.[229] Such a ten-year period provides the necessary interval of intimacy with both Anchieta and Peñalosa – the one on Isabella's payroll, the other on Ferdinand's – which is required in order to explain the cooperatively written *De beata Virgine* masses. Here arises his opportunity, if he equals Pedro of Oporto, to contribute 18 of the choicest items in the *Cancionero de Palacio:* and also for him so to win the confidence of the best musicians in Spain that when the chapelmastership at Seville becomes vacant in 1507, Peñalosa, a Sevillian canon since 1505 – or another – can induce the cabildo to hire him, sight unseen, to fill one of the most important posts in Spain.

Before we dismiss as improbable such an identification let us remember that neither Barbieri or Mitjana ever found any information connecting Escobar with the court,[230] neither discovering any other biographical fact than his period as chapelmaster at Seville. Barbosa Machado, who did not err concerning two other Portuguese composers that ended their careers in Seville Cathedral, Francisco de Santiago and Manoel Correa,[231] perhaps can be relied upon in the case of Escobar as well. Pedro do Pôrto will therefore again enter our account after 1514, the year in which his name drops out of Sevillian Cathedral records.

TO CONTINUE with the notices that concern him after his arrival from Portugal: on January 19, 1508, he receives a loan of 100 silver *reales* (= 3400 *maravedís*) and two measures of wheat from the cathedral cabildo.[232] On May 15, 1508, the chapter decides that a certain unpaid balance due the deceased chapelmaster for care of the boys shall not be credited to his account but rather distributed directly to the choirboys whom Valera had supervised.[233] On August 26, 1510, the cabildo arranges to confer upon him another cathedral chaplaincy, thus somewhat augmenting his income.[234] Similarly on September 20, 1510, the chapter finds a way to add still another chaplaincy to his list, he being in the *acta* of this date designated *clérigo de la veyntena*.[235] On January 3, 1513, he and Peñalosa are simultaneously present at a plenary session of the cathedral cabildo,

[229] *MME*, I, 57.

[230] Barbieri despite considerable effort was unable to find any data regarding Escobar. Rafael Mitjana was the first to identify Pedro de Escobar, Sevillian chapelmaster, 1507–1514, as a contributor to the *Cancionero de Palacio* in "Nuevas notas al 'Cancionero musical de los siglos XV y XVI' publicado por el Maestro Barbieri," *Revista de filología española*, V, ii (April–June, 1918), pp. 123–124.

[231] Barbosa Machado, *op. cit.*, II (Lisbon, 1747), p. 274, c. 2 (Fr. Francisco de Santiago) and III (Lisbon, 1752), p. 233, c. 1 (Manoel Correa). He accurately distinguishes between the Manoel Correa, a Carmelite who became chapelmaster at Saragossa, and the prebendary of the same name who was a chaplain at Seville. It is the latter's compositions which are conserved in the cathedral music archive at Seville. Barbosa Machado, who published before the Lisbon earthquake (November, 1755), enjoyed access to the incomparable music library of João IV.

[232] *A.C.*, *1508*, fol. 6v.

[233] *Ibid.*, fol. 30.

[234] *A.C.*, *1505. 1506. 1507. 1510. 1523. 1524.*, fol. 312v.

[235] "Clérigo de la veyntena" (clergyman of the twenty) meant at Seville one on stipend who sang at early services.

he being listed on this date as *magister puerorum* (master of the boys).[236] On August 13, 1514, Pedro Fernández is named his successor in the latter office,[237] no further mention of him appearing in Sevillian records. Significantly, however, no entry in the capitular acts states that he has died, although such references can be found for the former chapelmasters, Alva and Valera,[238] and will be found for Fernández (March 5, 1574), Francisco Guerrero (November 8, 1599), his two immediate successors in the Seville chapelmastership, not to mention Ambrosio Cotes, Alonso Lobo, and the rest of the seventeenth-century chapelmasters.

This fact in itself lends support to the idea that he did not die in Seville, but rather that he departed because of discontent with the financial arrangements made by the cabildo. Certainly he was not satisfied while in Seville, as the attempts at juggling chaplaincies in order to augment his income amply prove.

If like Juan del Encina, whose patronymic was Fermoselle but who preferred to use a place-name,[239] Pedro de Escobar may also have been Pedro do Pôrto, then some additional data concerning his career can be discovered in Portuguese sources. Pedro do Pôrto was in 1521 chapelmaster (*Mestre da Capela*) for Cardinal Dom Affonso (1509–1540), son of King Manuel, and continued as such after the cardinal-infante was invested with the archbishoprics of Évora and of Lisbon.[240]

Gil Vicente (c. 1465–1536) alludes to him in his *Côrtes de Jupiter*.[241] Acted in August of 1521 in celebration of the imminent wedding of King Manuel's daughter, this court play contains lines describing *Pero do Porto* as leader of a band of tiples, contras altas, tenores, and contrabaxas. Vicente's jest at his expense lends support to the idea that he was tall and thin. Also, however, it proves irrefutably that he was considered the leading musician in Portugal.

Like Vicente, he had another source of income. Vicente was goldsmith for the court, Pôrto was scrivener for a Lisbon tribunal (*Casa da Suplicação*) and for a palace court (*Desembargo do Paço*).[242] The latest Portuguese allusion would have him still alive in 1535.[243]

ESCOBAR's extant repertory is scattered through the following nine manuscript sources: (1) Barcelona: Biblioteca Central, MS 454; (2) Coimbra: Biblioteca Geral, MS musical 12; (3) Elvas: Biblioteca Públia Hortênsia; (4) Madrid: Biblioteca Real, sign. 2–I–5; (5) Seville: Biblioteca

---

[236] *A.C., 1513. 1514. 1515.*, fol. 1.

[237] Elústiza-Castrillo, p. XLVIII.

[238] Alva's death: *A.C., 1503–1504*, fol. 98v. (Sept. 6, 1504). Valera's death: *A.C., 1508*, fol. 30 (May 15, 1508). Valera died (*falleçydo*) in 1507.

[239] For further data on Encina, see *infra*, pp. 253–272.

[240] Francisco Marques de Sousa Viterbo, *Os Mestres da Capella Real nos Reinados de D. João III e D. Sebastião* (Lisbon: Of. tip. Calçada do Cabra, 1907), pp. 13–14. Of the three documents which he published, the first two concern Pedro do Pôrto's scrivenerships (March 4, 1521 and December 23, 1524), and the third has to do with the royal pensions granted his two daughters (May 30, 1554).

Further on Cardinal Dom Affonso above at pp. 96–97.

[241] Gil Vicente, *Copilaçam* (1562), fol. 166v., c. 2, lines 15–24.

[242] *Brotéria*, XXVII (1938), p. 329.

[243] *Ibid.*, p. 330, n. 2. His two daughters, Isabel and Caterina Guarcees, were each receiving royal pensions (5000 *rs*) in 1554. See Sousa Viterbo, p. 14.

Colombina, sign. 5–5–20; (6) Seville Cathedral, MS 1; (7) and (8) Tarazona Cathedral: MSS 2 and 3; (9) Toledo: Biblioteca Capitular, MS 21.[244]

Arranged in alphabetical sequence, with a numeral or numerals after each item to show in which of the above mentioned sources each work will be found, his list of presently known compositions with Latin texts reads as follows: [245] *Alleluia: Caro mea*, 3 v. [Corpus Christi] (7) and (8); *Alleluia: Primus ad Sion*, 3 v. [Apostles and Evangelists] (7) and (8); *Asperges*, 3 v. (8); *Asperges*, 4 v. (8); *Ave maris stella* [two settings] (7); *Clamabat autem mulier Chananea*, 4 v. (1) (2) (5) (7); [246] *Deus tuorum militum*, 4 v. (7); *Domine Jesu Christe*, 4 v. (9); *Exultet coelum laudibus*, 4 v. (7); *Felix per omnes*, 4 v. (7); *Hostis Herodes*, 4 v. (7); *Iste confessor*, 4 v. (7); *Jesus Nazarenus* [incomplete] (5); *Memorare piissima*, 4 v. (6) (7); *Missa*, 4 v. (2) (8); *Missa pro defunctis*, 4 v. (8); *Missa Rex virginum* [Kyrie only: Gloria and Credo by Peñalosa, Sanctus by Pedro Hernandes [247] and Agnus by A. Pérez Dalua],[248] 4 v. (8); *Missa Rex virginum* [Sanctus and Agnus by Escobar: Kyrie, Gloria, and Credo by Anchieta], 4 v. (8); *O Maria mater pia*, 3 v. (7); *Salve Regina*, 4 v. (7); [249] *Sub tuum presidium*, 3 v. (7); *Stabat mater dolorosa*, 4 v. (7); *Veni redemptor*, 4 v. (7).

In alphabetical sequence his list of pieces with Spanish texts reads as follows: [250] *Coraçón triste, sofrid*, 3 v. (*CMP*, no. 375); *El dia que vy a Pascuala*, 3 v. (*CMP*, no. 383); *Gran plaser siento yo*, 4 v. (*CMP*, no. 385); *Las mis penas, madre*, 4 v. (*CMP*, no. 59); *Lo que queda es lo seguro*, 3 v. (*CMP*, no. 216; *CMH*, no. 9); [251] *No devo dar culpa a vos*, 3 v. (*CMP*, no. 220); *No pueden dormir mis ojos*, 4 v. (*CMP*, no. 114); *Nuestr' ama, Minguillo*, 3 v. (*CMP*, no. 229); *O alto bien*, 3 v. (*CMP*, no. 124); *Ora sus, pues qu'ansi es*, 4 v. (*CMP*, no. 73); *Ojos morenicos*, 3 v. (*CMP*, no. 263); *Pásame, por Dios, varquero*, 3 v. (*CMP*, no. 337; *CMH*, no. 57); [252] *Paséisme aor'allá, serrana*, 3 v. and 4 v. (*CMP*, nos. 244 and 245); *Quedaos, adiós*, 4 v. (*CMP*, no. 158); *Secáronme los pesares*, 3 v. (*CMP*, no. 199; *CMH*, no. 3); [253] *Vençedores son tus ojos*, 3 v. (*CMP*, no. 286); *Virgen bendita sin par*, 4 v. (*CMP*, no. 416).

---

[244] Bibliographical details in *MME*, I, *112–115, 119–122, 127–128, 95–103, 129*; *Anuario Musical*, II (1947), p. 31; *MME*, I, *122–123, 124, 130–131*.

[245] Hymn-titles in this list are given not as in *MME*, I, *122*, but as in Rudolf Gerber, "Spanische Hymnensätze um 1500" [see note 122 above], p. 175. Fragments of Esocbar's *Exultet coelum*, second and first settings of *Ave maris stella*, may be seen in Gerber's article at pp. 178 ("Vos saecli iusti"), 179 ("Monstra te esse"), and 180 ("Ave Gabrielis").

[246] Faulty transcription of Seville version in Elústiza-Castrillo, pp. 33–36.

[247] Hernandes = Fernández. This composer may be Pedro Fernández de Castilleja. The Sevillian *actas* uniformly refer to the latter as Pedro Fernández, only once adding the identifying "de Castilleja" (= of Castilleja [de la Cuesta], the town between Seville and Huelva in which Cortés, the conqueror of Mexico, died).

[248] Dalua = de Alva.

[249] When in 1941 Anglés edited *La música en la corte de los Reyes Católicos* (*MME*, I) he had found only this one *Salve Regina* ascribed to "P. Escobar" in Tarazona MS 2 (fol. 230): all the other pieces being attributed merely to "Escobar". Unwilling to hazard the statement that Pedro de Escobar of Sevillian fame was necessarily the composer of all the Escobar pieces at Tarazona, he therefore attributed the mass at pp. 125–155 in *MME*, I, to *Pedro* (?) *de Escobar*. Later, however, Seville Cathedral MS 1 – not listed among the Spanish MSS containing early 16th-century polyphony in *MME*, I, 95–136 – came to his attention. In *Anuario Musical*, II (1947), p. 31, he published its table of contents. Fortunately it contained at fols. 31v.–33 the same 4-voiced motet, *Memorare piissima*, already known as Escobar's because of its appearance in Tarazona MS 2 (fols. 283v.–284). But in the Sevillian source this motet was ascribed to Petrus Escobar. No longer could it therefore be doubted that the composer's first name was indeed Pedro, just as Mitjana had said it was when first he brought forward Escobar's name in 1918 (see note 230 *supra*).

[250] From the table of contents given in *MME*, I, *123*, it is impossible to tell whether Escobar's 4-voiced "motet" founded on the popular chanson, *Adieu mes amours*, is in Spanish or Latin.

[251] Manuel Joaquim, *op. cit.*, p. 43.

[252] *Ibid.*, p. 92.

[253] *Ibid.*, p. 37.

AGAIN as in the case of Anchieta and Peñalosa, Escobar's masses, motets, and secular pieces cultivate three separate and distinct styles. The mass transcribed in full by Anglés quotes chanson-treble at the opening of Kyrie I, Et in terra pax, Patrem omnipotentem, and Sanctus; and a tenor in Kyrie II and Agnus II. He brings his mass to a fitting climax in this last movement. In five voices, it discloses a well-made triple canon, the tenor following contra I a fifth down and the bass trailing contra I at the lower octave. The distances between entries are rather close, the tenor entering three breves after contra I and the bass six breves after the tenor. The only "free" voices in this final Agnus are the discantus and contra II. But even between these he contrives much lively imitation.

In contrast with all this rare learning *à la Josquin*, his *Clamabat autem* motet reveals itself as a work of such haunting "simplicity" that once heard it never leaves the listener's memory. What imitation can be found in it is always put to effective dramatic use. The text reads: "And there also cried after Jesus a woman of Canaan, saying, *Lord Jesus, Son of David, help me; my daughter is vexed by an evil spirit.* Replying to her, the Lord said: *I am not sent to any except the lost sheep of the house of Israel.* But she came and worshipped him, saying, *Lord help me.* Jesus replying said to her, *Woman, great is thy faith, be it unto thee as thou has desired."* [254]

In setting this text he entrusts the top voice with the italicized words, that is the direct speech. The *superius* indeed sings nothing but the direct speech, the lower three voices supporting it at its four entries and carrying the entire burden in the intermediate narrative portions. To heighten the dramatic effect the voice-ranges are restricted to major sixths in treble and tenor, and to a minor sixth in the *altus*. This very hovering within a limited compass aptly expresses in musical terms the insistency of the woman of Canaan, who will in no circumstances be dismissed, but instead cries the more continually after Jesus. As for the use of imitation to achieve a dramatic purpose: Escobar in his opening section, a duet, spaces the canon at the fifth (bars 5–16) so that each phrase in the *altus* tellingly echoes the supplication of the *bassus*. When the woman begins her plea (bar 16) she too sings continually in canon, following the lead of the tenor and then the bass. Canon has been often used to illustrate the idea of hunting or pursuing after. This motet makes equally effective use of canon to illustrate the idea of "crying after."

IN 1546 Alonso Mudarra published at Seville his *Tres libros de música en cifras para vihuela*. The third tablature printed in Spain, it contains numerous excerpts from Josquin des Prez, Antoine de Févin, Willaert, and Gombert. Only one peninsular composition, aside from his own pieces, was however included among its 77 different

---

[254] This text in Spanish early sixteenth-century missals allotted to *Reminiscere* Sunday, does not exactly correspond with the Vulgate. Nowadays the gospel selection mentioning the Woman of Canaan is read on a weekday preceding *Reminiscere*. Morales and Guerrero wrote *Clamabat autem* motets. Outside the peninsula the text seems never to have been set by a major composer. The *Clamabat autem* often ascribed to Cipriano de Rore (see *Brotéria*, XXVII, 333–334) is actually the motet by Morales in Toledo MS 17.

items; and that one was this same *Clamabat autem*, arranged for solo voice and vihuela.[255] Whether Escobar is finally accredited to Portugal or Spain, Mudarra could hardly have selected a single piece which more aptly summarizes the virtues of peninsular music at the turn of the century: dramatic intensity, use of learned devices primarily as a means of heightening expression, memorability, clarity of texture and of harmonic intent. Significantly, this motet is the only peninsular one composed during the generation of Ferdinand and Isabella which can be found transcribed in any of the vihuela books published 1536–1576. Its very survival in one of these is as much a cachet of its continuing success in Spain as Gil Vicente's *Auto da Cananea* of 1534 is of its success in Portugal.

Juan Escribano (d. 1557)

ESCRIBANO entered the pontifical choir at Rome sometime between 1501 and 1507,[256] probably late in 1502. He had already earned a master of arts. His biographer, José M. Llorens ("Juan Escribano, cantor pontificio y compositor" [*AM*, XII, 98]), would have us believe him to have hailed from Salamanca, to have been a sopranist in his home town cathedral from 1498–1502, to have earned his degree at Salamanca, and to have left in 1502 to enter the papal choir at Rome. The singer who entered just after him was also a Spaniard, Juan de Palomares. It is extremely likely that both entered before the death of Alexander VI, last of the Spanish popes. Even however if he entered in 1507, four years after Julius II's accession to the papacy, he remained an active member of the choir longer than any other Spaniard who entered before 1520. Only two, Calasanz and Sánchez, bettered his length of service before 1600. He retired in August of 1539,[257] but had been dean since 1527 (on leave eight of these twelve years).

During his long service at Rome he was rewarded with numerous honors and preferments. Already before Leo X named him an apostolic notary on July 5, 1513, he had somehow managed to obtain a Salamanca canonry the income from which he could enjoy *in absentia* (*Leonis X. Pontificis Maximi Regesta*, VII-VIII [1891], p. 55). In 1514 his choir colleagues elected him *abbas* (treasurer). The next year Pope Leo authorized

---

[255] Emilio Pujol transcribed Mudarra's *Tres libros* in *MME*, VII (Barcelona: Instituto Español de Musicología, 1949). See his introduction: p. 48, item 52; and the *parte musical:* pp. 79–83. Mudarra's transcription is no mechanical intabulation, but an independent work of art standing in relation to its source as does, for instance, Busoni's transcription of the *Chaconne* to its original.

[256] F. X. Haberl, *Bausteine für Musikgeschichte*, III (Leipzig: Breitkopf & Härtel, 1888), p. 60. In 1507 Escribano stood fifteenth in a list of 21 singers; his Spanish colleagues included Juan de Yllianas (of Aragon) [no. 5], Alfonso Frias [no. 11], Garcia Salinas [no. 12] and Juan de Palomares [no. 16]. One other Spaniard, Alfonso de Troya, was in 1507 a chaplain with a monthly salary of 10 florins. Further data on Frias and Palomares in Frey, "Regesten zur päpstlichen Kapelle," 1955, pp. 59–60; 1956, p. 152. Frey's data on Escribano is divided between *Die Musikforschung*, VIII, 184 and IX, 152. He documents the careers of the Spaniards who entered the choir during Escribano's second decade at VIII, 62-63 (Antonio de Ribera), 188–189 (Martín Rodrigo Prieto), and 193–194 (Pedro Pérez de Rezola).

[257] On June 12, 1539, Escribano rejoined the choir after extended leave in Spain. But on August 24, 1539, he again asked leave to visit his homeland. See Haberl, III, 79–80. Antonio Calasanz served from 1529–1577, Juan Sánchez from 1529–1572.

the Salamanca chapter to apply the fruits of the Archdeaconate of Monleón (a dignity in the gift of the chapter) to Escribano's canonry. When the chapter demurred, he on June 3, 1516, changed his request to an order sharpened with threats of penalties (*Die Musikforschung*, VIII/2, p. 184).

With papal blessing, Escribano on November 30, 1520, resigned his Salamanca canonry into the hands of his brother – Alfonso – who was to hold it until the day that he should himself come home from Rome. Among Pope Leo's other favors were on November 1, 1517, a canonry in the Oviedo Cathedral; and on October 31, 1521 (if homonyms do not deceive us), a 40-gold-ducat benefice in Sigüenza diocese. Both Adrian VI (1522) and Clement VII (1527, 1530, 1532) showered him with such further favors that he could end his days in Spain (d. October, 1557) a comfortably fixed man. A year after his death an alien generation of pontifical singers attended an anniversary Mass in the Spanish national church of St. James at Rome (October 12, 1558).[258]

HIS six-voiced motet, *Paradisi porta*, is copied in Sistine Codex 46 and his four-part *Magnificat VI toni* in Codex 44.[259] Andrea Antico printed two of his Italian secular songs, one a frottola, the other a mascherata, at Rome in his 1510 *Canzoni nove*.[260]

If his 70-breve *Paradisi porta* can be accepted as a token of his powers, Escribano was as learned a Spanish composer as any between Peñalosa and Morales. Properly to read his many ligatures, the transcriber must for instance observe those rules listed as A. 1, A. 3, B. 5, and B. 7 at p. 92 in Willi Apel's *The Notation of Polyphonic Music* (4th edn., 1949). For a further show of skill, he contrives between two upper parts a rigorous canon at the fifth (antecedent voice enters at meas. 6, consequent at meas. 8) which by omitting any reference to the note B through the antecedent adroitly sidesteps the problems of *befabemi* that usually arise when solving such canons. Only once does he even touch the note B (meas. 63) – and then for but a fleeting crotchet in an ornamental resolution. For a third proof of his powers, he spins the notes in the canonic voices out of a plainsong antiphon: in this case, *Nativitas tua*, an antiphon to be sung at second vespers on September 8 (*LU* [1947], p. 1503). Although there can be no doubt that the under parts were conceived as handmaidens to the canonic pair in this Nativity of Our Lady motet, they too disport themselves in imitations whenever they can so frolic without disturbing the progress of the slower-moving canonic voices: e.g. at mm. 46–47, 56–57.

For still another matter, the proportions of *Paradisi porta* beautifully illustrate the perfections of the number 7. Sectionalized by its cadences, this motet divides into

---

[258] *Ibid.*, III, 121, c. 1, lines 50–54. If he retired at 62 in 1539 he would have died in his eightieth year. Martín de Tapia in his *Vergel de música* (Burgo de Osma: Diego Fernández de Córdova, 1570), fol. 76v., cites him as *el venerando Ioan escribano, Arcediano de Monleon* and claims that Escribano favored the constant use of *ficta* B♭'s when singing plainsong melodies in Modes V and VI: a practice which Bermudo – from whom Tapia plagiarized most of the *Vergel* – had not endorsed.

[259] Codex 44 was copied before 1513, codex 46 probably before 1521. See Haberl, II, 66. A facsimile of Escribano's *Paradisi porta* (Capp. Sist.: Cod. 46, fols. 120v.–121) may be seen in *MGG*, III, at plate 45 (following columns 1567–1568).

[260] Alfred Einstein, "Andrea Antico's *Canzoni Nove* of 1510," *Musical Quarterly*, XXXVII, 3 (July, 1951), p. 332. *Vola il tempo*, second in Antico's collection is classified by Einstein as a frottola; *L huom terren*, seventh, as a mascherata. This latter, according to Einstein, should be thought of as a "Trionfo della Fama" in frottola form.

7 + (14 + 14) + 28 + 7 breves = a total 70 breves. The cadences successively debouch into chords of A minor, D minor, A minor, D minor, D. Such symmetry can hardly have been accidentally achieved. The "portals" of seven breves at each side support an arch comprising the middle group. The significance of the word *porta* as applied to the Virgin is doubly underlined at mm. 8–12, during which he requires altus I to sing "porta" to the notes of the Salve Regina plainsong initium (breves). Viewed in any light, then, this Nativity of Our Lady motet stamps him a virtuoso. He moreover set a precedent to be followed by Morales, Guerrero, and Victoria when he showered his richest learning on a motet composed in honor of the Virgin.

Throughout *Paradisi porta* he stratifies the parts according to the following scheme: canonic voices move in semibreves, breves, and longs; the three inner parts in crotchets, minims, semibreves, and breves; and the bass in semibreves, breves, and longs (with slight exceptions at mm. 14–15 and 32–35). Occasionally, skips intrude in the bass which though singable enough in semibreves suggest that he considered this part a harmonic prop (mm. 48–49). He adheres throughout to Mode I, never once denaturing the dorian with *bemol*. He interdicts ficta flats in two ways. (1) The MS shows "precautionary" sharps (i.e., naturals) before the bass-note B_1 at doubtful moments (mm. 2, 7, 65). (2) When realizing the canon at the fifth, *e* cries for $b\natural$ as its answer in mm. 26–29, 48–50, 53–55, 58–61. As for dissonance-treatment, syncopes occur frequently enough; but a passing minim dissonance on a third minim of four in the bar only once (meas. 103), and the *nota cambiata* never.

Pedro Fernández [de Castilleja] (d. 1574)

NAMED CHAPELMASTER at Seville on August 13, 1514 (in succession to Pedro de Escobar), Fernández held office for sixty years, twenty-five of which were spent in a semi-retired status. Since he is unlikely to have been appointed in 1514 without already having made something of a reputation he must have been at least thirty when named. If so he would, like the Spanish basso in Rome, Calasanz, have reached some such extravagant age as ninety before his death in 1574.

He may well be the Pedro Fernández (= Hernandes) who cooperated with Escobar, Peñalosa, and Alva in writing the *Rex virginum* Mass *a 4* found at fols. 200v.–209 in Tarazona MS 3. His part would have been the Sanctus, Escobar's the Kyrie, Peñalosa's the Gloria and Credo, and Alva's the Agnus.[261] The associations of the other three with Seville make such a conjecture at least plausible. He would in that case be also the composer of the *Alleluia: Nativitas tua* (*a 3*) found at fols. 241v.–242 in the same MS.

At Seville in MS 1 a *Salve Regina* (*a 4*), *O gloriosa Domina* (*a 4*), and *Deo dicamus gratias* (*a 4*), ascribed to Petrus Fernandez occur at fols. 14v.–17, 86v.–87, and 96v.–97.[262]

[261] *MME*, I, *124*.

[262] *Anuario Musical*, II (1947), p. 31. Collet published *O gloriosa Domina* in *Le mysticisme musical espagnol* (Paris: Librairie Félix Alcan, 1913), at pp. 258–261. He printed wrong notes, however, in several places, among them m. 14 (cantus), m. 85 (tenor), m. 64 (bassus); not to mention numerous omissions of rests and ties.

A pair of four-voiced motets ascribed to Pedro Fernández, "chapelmaster of Seville," were published by Eslava, *Dispersit dedit pauperibus* (*a 4*) and *Heu mihi, Domine* (*a 5*). [263] As for secular music, item 101 – *Cucu, cucu, cucucu* (ascribed to Pedro Fernández in both editions of the *Cancionero de Palacio*) cleverly reiterates the same admonition against cuckoldry already sounded at *CMP*, 94, with music by Encina.

But whether any or all of these Pedro Fernández compositions are rightly ascribed to the Sevillian chapelmaster, they uniformly reveal a composer of limited vision. Certainly *O gloriosa Domina*, printed by Henri Collet in *Le mysticisme musical espagnol*, is no great work – though if anything ascribed to Pedro Fernández is the Sevillian's this should be his, coming as it does from a Sevillian MS. True: Guerrero called his defunct colleague *maestro de los maestros de España* [264] (teacher of the masters of Spain). But if Fernández taught Morales, so also did Neefe teach Beethoven and Elsner Chopin.

Juan Illario

Already referred to on page 84 as a theorist whose writings were known to Cristóbal de Escobar c. 1498, Illario seems also to have been a composer. The two extant motets, *O admirabile commercium* and *Conceptio tua*, both of which are conserved in Tarazona MS 2, are for four voices. The first of these is repeated in Barcelona MS 454 at fols. 104v.–105.

[Juan Fernández de] Madrid (fl. 1479)

A THREE-VOICED setting of *Domine non secundum peccata nostra* occurs in Bibl. Nat. Paris, nouv. acq. frç. 4379 (at fols. 78v.–79), the ascription reading "Madrid." Since this psalm-verse (Ps. 102 [103] : 10) belongs liturgically with the verse which follows immediately afterwards in the same MS, *Domine ne memineris iniquitatum* (Ps. 78 [79] : 8) – both verses being sung in direct succession on Ash Wednesday –, "Madrid" is in all likelihood the composer of the second as well as of the first psalm-verse. There is, however, no ascription on fols. 79v.–80.

In the same MS three sections of a polyphonic Gloria by "Madrid" fill fols. 81v.–83. The *Et in terra pax* and *Domine Deus Rex* are both set for three voices, but the *Domine fili unigenite* as a duo. At the beginning of his *Et in terra* Madrid quotes the introit sung on August 15, *Gaudeamus omnes in Domino*. If the remainder of his mass could be found we might possibly have another equally fine *Gaudeamus* mass to add to Josquin des Prez's (1502) and Victoria's (1576). The MS in which these sacred items occur originally belonged to the Biblioteca Colombina at Seville, coming into the possession of the Paris Bibliothèque Nationale as late as 1885. Since the leaves then acquired were but a frag-

---

[263] *Lira sacro-hispana*, I, 157–160 and 161–166.

[264] Francisco Guerrero, *Viage de Hierusalem* (Seville: Francisco de Leefdael [1690]), p. 3. By one of the most unusual agreements in Spanish cathedral history Fernández and Guerrero shared the Sevillian chapelmastership, 1549–1574. Guerrero himself – though he titles Fernández "master of the masters of Spain" – calls Morales, rather than Fernández, his own master.

Et in terra pax *

Paris: Bibl. Nat. nouv. acq. frç. 4379, fols. 81v.–82.   [JUAN FERNÁNDEZ DE] MADRID

* MS contains words through *Benedicimus te* for the middle voice, but none for the other two voices.

ment, it is to be hoped that further search in Spain may one day reveal the rest of this mass.

As the accompanying example shows, he possessed more than a mean talent. His harmonic daring is indeed hardly matched in any fifteenth-century Spanish mass thus far brought forward. Though *Et in terra* is clearly in dorian mode, yet exactly half way through he contrives to reach the foreign chord of A♭ Major and then to hover between it and F minor (in first inversion) for the space of four breves. The harmonies can be no others, since the accidentals A♭ and E♭, are both specified in the MS. The smooth transition from D minor to A♭ Major deserves applause. Each individual voice makes excellent melodic sense when sung alone. Yet together the three accomplish "modulations" that are meaningful and beautiful, even from a much later historical vantage-point. In bars 2_3, 3_1, 4_1, 4_2, 5_3, 6_4, 7_1, 11_2, 13_1, 14_1, 17_4, 20_2, 21_2, 22_4, 23_2, 24_1, 24_4, he suggests "first-inversions." Such a profusion of "sixth-chords" is another mark of his individuality. No Spanish contemporary used them more lavishly.

The Chigi Codex (Vatican Library, Chigiana C.VIII.234) ends with an *Asperges me* (*a 4*) by "Madrid" (fols. 284v.–286). A flyleaf note fixes c. 1490 as the date when these leaves were copied in Spain. His name, in a faint Spanish hand, heads fol. 284v., but is not in the index.

As for his identity, Anglés equates him with the Juan Fernández de Madrid who was in 1479 appointed a singer in Ferdinand V's chapel.[265] He therefore joined only a quadrennium after Cornago became a member of the choir (1475). Their names are linked by the use to which Madrid put the elder composer's *Pues que Dios te fiso tal*. After casting out the old contra, he added a new *tiple* in its place, which far exceeds the former voice in lithesomeness and grace. Cornago's original setting can be seen in the Palacio cancionero at no. 2 and Madrid's arrangement at no. 5.

Antonio Marlet (fl. 1506)

Known only as chapelmaster at Tarragona in 1506, this Marlet would be the composer of a

---

[265] *DML*, II, 1454. See also Herbert Kellman, "The Origins of the Chigi Codex," in *Journal of the American Musicological Society*, XI/1 (Spring, 1958), pp. 7–8.

Magnificat *a 4* (odd verses) conserved in Tarazona MS 2 and of a motet *a 3, O quam pulcra es,* copied in Bologna Liceo Musicale Cod. 159 at pp. 211–212.[266] The Bologna source contains also Despuig's *In Enchiridion* and a Spanish summary of thirty-odd chapters from his *Ars musicorum.*

[Fernand Pérez de] Medina (fl. 1479)

MEDINA, even though enrolled as a singer in Queen Isabella's chapel on November 7, 1477, continued to maintain residence in Seville. To protect him from Sevillian taxation she therefore sent his city fathers on July 28, 1479, a *carta de franquesa* from Trujillo, ordering them to cease and desist from all further levies against *fernard peres de medina mi cantor.*[267] She reminded them that any member of the royal household enjoyed exemption from local taxes. During the same year (1479) she still further favored Medina with a raise in his annual salary from 16,200 *maravedís de ración* to 20,000.[268] Fittingly enough, his *Salve Regina* for *voces mudadas* (men's voices) – his only extant sacred work, is conserved at the Biblioteca Colombina in his hometown of Seville (MS sign. 5–5–20).

The two villancicos by Medina in *Palacio* are both *ernste Gesänge* – the first (*No ay plazer en esta vida,* no. 56) voicing the soul's longing for a better world after death, the second (*Es por vos si tengo vida,* no. 70) a lover's mortal distress while he awaits his mistress's change of heart. The intimate poignancy of *Es por vos,* written for three men's voices, well accords with the fervid inwardness which sounds through his *Salve Regina.*

THOUGH the *Salve Regina* antiphon was, of course, set by many a foreign fifteenth- and sixteenth-century composer, the Spanish polyphonists seemingly made it their national specialty. Over half the settings of the antiphon mentioned in Gustave Reese's *Music in the Renaissance* were, for instance, composed by Spaniards or by those who like La Rue had spent considerable time in Spain. That this antiphon should have been particularly favored in the peninsula seems moreover logical when it is remembered that the reputed author – Pedro de Mezonzo [269] (d. 1003) – was bishop of Santiago de Compostela. Certainly the weight of tradition tips in favor of this Galician bishop, the earliest attribution of authorship in both Italian (Jacopo da Varazze's *Legenda aurea*

---

[266] *MME,* I, *128.*

[267] For a diplomatic transcript of the original royal *carta* see *Archivo hispalense,* tomo II (1886), pp. 355–359. With the usual vagaries of orthography to be found in such documents, his first name is variously spelled "fernard", "fernand", "fernad". Barbieri's "Juan Pérez de Medina" (see next note) is almost certainly the same singer. If the Francisco of Francisco de Medina is an expanded abbreviation (see Barbieri, *op. cit.,* p. 617) he also may be "Fernando".

[268] Barbieri, p. 39.

[269] Name given as *Petrus* (= *Pedro*) *Martínez de Mosoncio* and date of accession to the see as 986 in P.B. Gams, *Series episcoporum,* p. 26. For the correct spelling, and for a biography, see Antonio López Ferreira, *Historia de la santa a.m. iglesia de Santiago de Compostela,* Vol. II (Santiago: Seminario Conciliar Central, 1899), pp. 381–431.

[1255]) [270] and French (Guillaume Durand's *Rationale divinorum officiorum* [1286]) [271] sources giving it to *Petrus vero de Compostella episcopus*. In 1302 at the Council of Peñafiel the bishops of Toledo archdiocese decreed it should be sung after compline every day (*singulis diebus*) in all archdiocesan churches.[272] In 1362 it was throughout Spain sung after every Saturday *De beata Virgine* Mass.[273] The earliest printed Constitutions of the Toledo Archdiocese, drawn up at the 1498 Synod of Talavera, devoted an entire chapter to the Salve. This synod ordered that "after vespers and compline, parish priests every Sunday should cause the Salve to be played and devoutly sung." [274] The singing of the Salve in substitution for the last gospel (*In principio*) not only at the close of *De beata Virgine* Masses but also of other Masses had indeed become everywhere in sixteenth-century Spain so intrenched a custom that the reform decrees of the Council of Trent were scarcely strong enough to break its hold.[275] In 1573 the reform was not yet complete.

The laity had taken it to their hearts as no other piece of religious music. Las Casas tells us that Columbus's sailors gathered on the prow of his flagship the night before the New World was discovered to sing the *Salve*. In the popular devotions of the fighters who followed Cortés and Pizarro, it occupied the same privileged position of *Ein' feste Burg* in immediately contemporary Germany. The first enactments of both Mexican and Peruvian church councils prescribed its universal use in parish and cathedral.

Set in its proper historical background, then, the fact that Medina should be known as a sacred composer exclusively because of a Salve seems not surprising but, on the contrary, appropriate – just as does its occurrence in a MS devoted exclusively to Salves or "motets based on the Salve" (Bibl. Colombina, sign. 5–5–20). One looks in vain for a foreign polyphonic source dated c. 1500 which is so exclusively dedicated to this particular antiphon. Nor can one name French, Flemish, or Italian composers of this period who like Medina and Ponce are today known as sacred composers exclusively because of Salves; or even foreigners whose major work – like Rivafrecha's and Fernández's – was a Salve.

MEDINA's Salve, like Anchieta's, Escobar's, Rivafrecha's, and Ponce's, alternates verses in plainsong with those in polyphony. But Medina's is unique because it expands into five voices during the *Et Jesum* verse. The accompanying example may very well be, as a

[270] Jacobus de Varagine, *Lombardica historia que a plerisque Aurea legenda sanctorum appellatur* (Strassburg: Georg Husner, 1486), fol. G 7v., col. 2 [ch. 176, sect. k].

[271] Gulielmus Durandus, *Incipit Rationale diuinorum officiorum* (Rome: Per Udalricum Gallum Almanum & Simonem Nicolai de Luca, 1473), fol. 71 [pars IV, cap. xxii]. The earliest sermons based on the *Salve Regina* were also preached in Spain – by Bernard of Toledo (1086–1124). The four sermons of this bishop, a Benedictine, are printed in Migne, *PL*, 184, 1059–1078.

[272] Joseph Sáenz de Aguirre, *Collectio maxima conciliorum omnium Hispaniae et Novi Orbis* (Rome: J. J. Komarek, 1694), III, 541 (paragraph 14).

[273] Jaime Villanueva, *Viage literario á las Iglesias de España*, XIV (Madrid: Imp. de la Real Academia de la Historia, 1850), p. 17.

[274] *Constituciones del arçobispado de Toledo* (Salamanca, 1498), fol. 5: "ordenamos ... que todos los domingos despues de visperas y completas luego incontinente los curas o sus tenientes fagan tañer ala Salue. i se cante deuotamente ... la qual cantada luego los dichos curas ... enseñen publicamente ..."

[275] Villanueva, *op. cit.*, XIV, 92.

Salve Regina

Seville: Bibl. Colombina, sign. 5-5-20, fols. 3v.-4.   [FERNAND PÉREZ DE] Medina

matter of fact, the very earliest example of five-part writing by a Spanish composer. Certainly this would be true if Medina's Salve is dated anywhere near his year of appointment in Queen Isabella's chapel. In still another sense this Salve breaks fresh ground. His first line of text reads *Salve Regina mater misericordiae*. This is of course the present reading of the first line. Not so in the fifteenth century. According to Dreves,[276] the word "mater" did not appear in the first line until after 1500. Medina's setting affords not only an extremely early instance of five-part writing but also of *"mater" misericordiae*.

As can be seen in the example, he distributes the rhythmic motion rather evenly among all voices except the bass. He clearly intends the lowest voice to govern the "harmony." To invest him with such authority, he allows the bass fourteen skips of a fourth or fifth, as against nine such leaps in all four of the other voices combined. As in most Spanish Renaissance Salves, the polyphonic sections are all dorian, untransposed.

Alonso de Mondéjar (fl. 1502)

FIRST mentioned in an *albalá* signed at Toledo by Queen Isabella on August 17, 1502,[277] Mondéjar is listed as one of her chapel singers. After her death in November of 1504, he passes into the establishment of Ferdinand. In 1505 his salary is set at 25,000 *maravedís* annually. His extant repertory includes: three Magnificats, two motets with text, a third textless motet; and eleven secular items in the *Cancionero de Palacio*. On the other hand, the assertion that he is also represented in the Colombina cancionero cannot be verified and seems improbable in view of his ascertained dates. The two motets with text are *Ave, Rex noster*, 4 v. (Segovia cancionero, fols. 227v.–228), and *Ave verum corpus in ara crucis*, 4 v. (Barcelona: Bibl. Cent. MS 454, fols. 82v.–83). The textless motet survives at Barcelona in MS 454, coming immediately after his Magnificat.

[Pietro] Oriola

IN COMPANY with Cornago, Damiano, and Icart, Oriola made his mark at the Neapolitan court of Alfonso the Magnanimous. The same Pietro Oriola who held chaplaincies as early as 1444 and 1455 may have returned to Spain with an appointment in Ferdinand V's Aragonese choir.[278] At all events, Monte Cassino MS 871 N contains two sacred pieces: *In exitu Israel* (a 4) and *O vos homines* (a 3). The psalm joins the same text that Alfonso used upon entering battle. A secular part-song *a 3* with Italian text, *Trista che spera morendo*, and textless item *a 3* survive at Perugia in Bibl. Com. MS 431 (G 20), fols. 74 and 76.

---

[276] *Analecta Hymnica*, 50 (Leipzig: O. R. Reisland, 1907), p. 319 (lines 3–5). In the Medina *Salve*, Tenor I intones the first three words as a solo, and is then joined by the other three voices at the word *misericordiae*.

[277] Barbieri, p. 40.

[278] Minieri Riccio, pp. 246, 439. *MME*, I, *116–117*: Pedro Orihuela replaced the recently deceased chorister, Diego Alderete c. 1480. But see also *DML*, II, 1685, which lists dissenting data.

Tommaso Damiano, identified in *MME*, I, *22, 116–117*, as a Spaniard, played flute at Alfonso's Neapolitan court in 1456 (Minieri Riccio, *op. cit.*, p. 444). Anglés does not bring Damiano back to Spain. Rudolf Gerber transcribes his *Ave maris stella* a 4 in "Die Hymnen der Handschrift Monte Cassino 871," *Anuario Musical*, XI (1956), pp. 19–20.

Alonso de la Plaja

A *Regina coeli* for three voices,[279] each carrying the baritone clef, enters Biblioteca Orfeón Catalán MS 5 (fol. 61v.). Aside from the fact that the datable composers in the manuscript are Josquin, Isaac, and Peñalosa, Plaja would himself be known to have belonged to their same generation because of one stylistic mannerism. Throughout the entire antiphon he insists upon concording each of the outer voices with the inner voice. Although extending to 82 breves, the tonality remains everywhere unmistakably F Major (B♭ in signature). The repetition of strongly-marked rhythmic figures (mm. 55–60; 71–79) and the incessant syncopations in the modern sense of that term lend this Easter piece a distinctly popular flavor. The general pause inserted at meas. 71_1 before the climactic Alleluias adds markedly to their effectiveness. Each phrase begins imitatively, but the counterpoint is always as naive as that of the *Frère Jacques* round.

Juan Ponce (fl. 1510)

Juan ponce was a singer in the Aragonese royal household during the latter part of Ferdinand V's reign. He may have served also in Charles V's household until 1521 if the entire text of his villancico *Françia, cuenta tuganançia* (*Cancionero de Palacio*, no. 443) be taken as evidence.[280]

In his youth he was a pupil of Lucio Marineo (c. 1460–1533), the Sicilian humanist whom Fadrique Enríquez, Admiral of Castile, brought back with him from Italy in 1484 to become a private tutor in Spanish noble houses. An exchange of letters between the two survives in Marineo's *Epistolarum familiarium libri decem et septem*, published at Valladolid in 1514. Both pupil's and teacher's letters are in Latin. Ponce writes asking his mentor to look over some Latin verses that he has written in praise of the Virgin, his intention being to set them to music.[281] In his reply Marineo, addressing Ponce as a protégé who has now become a *cantor regius* (royal singer), says that he is delighted to do this; that after looking them over he approves of the verses just as they stand; that they are elegantly composed with nothing amiss; that they cannot be censured even by a severe critic; that indeed they can be both read and sung everywhere with credit to their author. Continuing, Marineo advises Ponce thus: "Compose, then, for your verses music to be sung by the finest human voices, adding your harmony which is nearer

---

[279] Facsimile in Anglés, *La música española desde la edad media hasta nuestros días* (Barcelona: Biblioteca Central, 1941), p. 30⁴ [facs. 21]. The manuscript copy shows a mistake: from mm. 22₃–24₃ a melodic fragment was left out in the lowest voice (*3a vox*). But the copyist has remedied this error with one carat showing just where six notes were accidentally omitted and another inverted carat at the bottom of the page showing the six notes and minim rest which must be inserted.

[280] Barbieri, p. 174. He assigns the original verses to 1513 and a revised version to 1521. Ponce need have had nothing to do with the revision. But the touching up of such topical verses would in any event testify to the popularity of the music.

[281] Marineo, fol. m iiii verso. Ponce approaches Marineo not only as a preceptor but as an old and valued friend. He complains of the many arduous duties which prevent him from suitably polishing his verses and appeals to Marineo as a paragon of learning brought to Spain by Divine Providence.

divine than human, and arranging an accompaniment of sweetest-sounding organs together with plucked string instruments; you who in this art exceed the most skilful musicians of antiquity – Orpheus, Timotheus, and Arion. The verse, the [instrumental] sonority, and the song, will bear threefold witness to your art." [282]

Marineo was somewhat of a flatterer when he addressed high nobility,[283] but there is no reason to suppose that he needed flatter his sometime student. Ponce would not have been a hired singer in Ferdinand's chapel if at the same time he had been independently wealthy. All the more reason, then, for supposing that his fluently-written Latin epistle was entirely his own, and that Marineo's praise was sincere.

PONCE'S dozen part-songs in the *Cancionero de Palacio* take high honors for their musical quality. Among the 458 items in the Palace Songbook only two use Latin texts throughout – an anonymous *Dixit Dominus* and his *Ave color vini*. The Latin lyrics of the latter extol the virtues of wine. Of a class with *Gaudeamus igitur* and *Mihi est propositum in taberna mori*, this medieval student song received its most famous polyphonic setting at the hands of Lassus, who made of it a motet *a 5* in two *partes*. Ponce's setting, which omits a concluding couplet damning teetotallers, was doubtless a product of his own university days. Marineo, his Latin preceptor, occupied the chair of grammar in Salamanca from 1484–1496. One will not go far astray in assuming that *Ave color* was composed while he was himself enrolled as a university undergraduate along with seven thousand others at Salamanca around 1495.[284]

The other eleven Ponce items are all villancicos. *Para verme con ventura* (no. 175) is a mirror canon. Starting an octave apart, the top and bottom voices move in opposite directions throughout the estribillo and coplas. Although *La mi sola, Laureola* (no. 343) does not exploit a soggetto cavato, still the melodic subject is one which he contrived with the same kind of ingenuity. The first four syllables in the opening line are made to serve as solmization syllables sung through both natural and hard hexachords. At the same time however these four syllables do duty as the first three words of the lyrics. The verse, written c. 1492 (the year in which Diego de San Pedro published his novel, *Cárcel de Amor*, with Laureola, princess of Gaul, as a leading character), continued still sufficiently popular for the great Juan Vásquez to reset it (1551 and 1554 [*Orphénica Lyra*, fol. 159]) in a version *a 3* that leans on Ponce's villancico *a 4* for all its most characteristic musical ideas.

Françia, cuenta tu ganançia has already been cited as a patriotic outburst that cannot antedate 1513. One Ponce villancico, *Alegria, alegria* (*a 4*) – celebrating Easter – must surely rank among the best religious pieces in *Palacio*. The rest of the Ponce items tell

---

[282] *Ibid.* The superscription reads: *Lucius Marineus Siculus Ioanni Pontio discipulo & cantori regio.*

[283] Caro Lynn, *A College Professor of the Renaissance*, p. 154.

[284] For Marineo's dates at Salamanca see Lynn, pp. 61 and 108. The *Cancionero de Palacio* was originally gathered for use at Alba de Tormes, the ducal seat of the Alva's located fifteen miles south of Salamanca (see Barbieri, p. 8). *Ave color* is the only Ponce song belonging to the original corpus of the manuscript. Circumstantial evidence therefore makes it not only his earliest song but also points to Salamanca as the place where it was composed.

us nothing more of his biography than that he was often a distressed lover – if indeed there is any personal intent in their "passionate pilgrimages."

An alphabetical list of his contributions to *Palacio* reads thus: *Alegria, alegria* (227), *Allá se me ponga el sol* (431), *Ave color vini* (159), *Bien perdí mi coraçon* (207), *Como está sola mi vida* (328), *Ell amor que me bien quiere* (144), *Françia, cuenta tu ganancia* (443), *La mi sola, Laureola* (343), *O triste que estoy* (405), *Para verme con ventura* (175), *Todo mi bien é perdido* (156), *Torre de la niña* (341). With the exception of *Ave color vini*, all of these were copied into the manuscript after it was first completed, on spaces left empty by the original scribe. This fact corroborates the surmise that Ponce was a decade or so younger than Encina.

Seven of his pieces in *Palacio* are composed *a 4*, four *a 3*, and one *a 2*. His sole surviving sacred work is for three voices and therefore cannot exploit as full sonorities as he customarily preferred. Neither does it contain the clever feats which might be expected from the composer of *La mi sola, Laureola* or *Para verme con ventura*. But as a work for popular devotional usage there is no reason why it should have been. Like most Salves written for Spanish consumption this one alternates plainsong with polyphony. The same breaks in the text are observed by Medina, Anchieta, and Rivafrecha when dividing plainsong and polyphony. Later in the century when Morales and Guerrero write Salves of the alternating type they too observe these breaks – with one exception. At the end, they set all three acclamations (*O clemens, o pia, o dulcis*) polyphonically, rather than requiring the *o pia* to be plainchanted.

Ponce's *Salve* is a treble-dominated work. Certain passages for the two lower voices suggest realization with *dulcissimas Organorum uoces & cytharae cantus*, to quote Marineo, more than with unaccompanied voices (mm. 48–49; 65-67). Verses 2, 6a, and 7c begin with imitation. But elsewhere, imitation is lightly used. Sequences, harmonic as well as melodic, distinguish 29–31: 32–34, 52:53, and 66:67. The cadences are more varied than those in Anchieta's *Salve*, despite the fact that the Basque composer's is a longer work. Anchieta's cadences always move to D or A, with two exceptions, once to F and another time to G. Ponce's cadences end four times on G, four times on an incomplete chord of A suggesting minor, and a dozen times on D also suggesting minor. In addition, he twice feints deceptively at F chord and at E (minor chord).

Salve Regina

Seville: Bibl. Colombina, sign. 5–5–20, fols. 5 v.–7.   JUAN PONCE

1. Salve Regina, mater misericordiae:

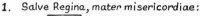

3. Ad te clamamus, exsules, filii Hevae.

4.

5.   Eia ergo, Advocata nostra, illos tuos misericordes oculos ad nos converte.

6ᵇ   Nobis post hoc exsilium ostende.

Quixada (= Quexada)

Though both a three-voiced Mass (Tarazona MS 3, fols. 73v.–80) and a four-voiced Magnificat (Barcelona: Bibl. Cent. MS 454, fols. 152v.–153) survive from this composer, not even his first name has been recovered.

Antonio de Ribera (fl. 1514)

On August 2, 1514, a singer named "Antonius de Ribera" was listed as a newcomer in the papal choir.[285] An "Ant. Rybere" – evidently the same singer – was listed as one among six Spaniards in the 26-member choir on September 3, 1522.[286]

A four-voiced mass by "Antonio de Ribera" fills fols. 152v.–160 in Tarazona MS 3. Another four-voiced mass is attributed to "Ribeira" in Coimbra MS de musica 12 at fols. 90v.–91v. (Kyrie and Gloria) and 81v.–88 (Credo and Sanctus). Three motets a 4, *Ave Maria* (fols. 258v.–259), *O bone Jhesu* (fols. 273v.–274), and *Patris sapientia* (fols. 272v.–273), are found in Tarazona MS 2. Two villancicos, one ascribed to "Antonio de Rribera" (*Nunca yo, señora, os viera* [item 192]), the other to "A. Rribera" (*Por unos puertos arriva* [item 107]), survive in the *Cancionero de Palacio*. This composer may also be the Ribera to whom four items of incidental music formerly sung at Elche (south of Alicante) on August 15, the Feast of the Assumption, are ascribed.[287]

---

[285] Haberl, III, 69. Frey in "Regesten zur päpstlichen Kapelle," *Die Musikforschung*, VIII/1, pp. 62–63, contests this data. He would have him a singer for Ferdinando Cardinal Ponzetto between April, 1518, and April, 1520. On the other hand, he is willing for him to have been a papal singer in 1522.

[286] Haberl, III, 71.

[287] Felipe Pedrell, *La Festa d'Elche* (Paris: Au Bureau d'édition de la "Schola," 1906), p. 33. The Ribera musical excerpts appear on pp. 18–19 (XII), 19–20 (XIII), 21 (XIV), and 22–23 (XVI).

Martín de Rivafrecha [= Rivaflecha] (d. 1528) [288]

THOUGH not many of Rivafrecha's works survive, his biography is known with gratifying fulness. He was appointed chapelmaster in Palencia Cathedral on December 1, 1503, only five days after the post was declared vacant because of the absence without leave of the previous occupant, Fernando de Orgaz. At the moment of his appointment, Rivafrecha held no musical post. He was however already in orders, his home church being one located at Santo Domingo de la Calzada in northcentral Spain (west of Logroño). Within seven weeks of his appointment a Palencia cathedral singer, Gonzalo Gómez de Portillo, was named his aide, the chapter placing the latter in direct control of the choirboys. Ordinarily in Palencia Cathedral responsibility for their physical care and upbringing rested on the chapelmaster's shoulders. The aide's salary was therefore in this case declared deductible from Rivafrecha's. On December 19, 1506, an arrangement more favorable to the chapelmaster was worked out, the aide being transferred into a lifetime cathedral prebend. On June 26, 1521, Rivafrecha resigned, whereupon Gómez de Portillo was declared his successor. On January 3, 1522, García de Baena, formerly organist at León, was appointed cathedral organist at Palencia: an appointment of considerable importance because during the next four years he is credited with having taught the blind youth, Antonio de Cabezón (b. 1510).

On December 12, 1523, the Palencia cabildo advanced Gómez de Portillo to a canonry. A week later Rivafrecha – who upon quitting in 1521 had returned to his home diocese and had held a post as singer in Calahorra Cathedral – was again received as a prebendary in Palencia Cathedral, though without being immediately renamed chapelmaster. This title, which had been his from 1503–1521, was again conferred upon him only on January 27, 1525. But he was at the same time saddled with the load of rearing the choirboys. One month elapsed during which he showed his clumsiness, insofar as this added duty was concerned. At the end of the month he was summarily deposed from the chapelmastership, the title reverting to Gómez de Portillo.

Rivafrecha, bewildered by the turn of events, wrote a memorial on March 29 (1525) reminding the chapter that he had served Palencia Cathedral 22 years, the best of his life, and appealing for fair treatment. In response, the cabildo reinstated him in his prebend – without requiring him henceforth to fulfill the duties of chapelmaster. On the same day that he presented his memorial, these duties (together with the title *maestro de capilla*) fell to a clergyman of Toledo diocese, Diego del Castillo, whom Rivafrecha, Gómez del Portillo, and García de Baena – the three senior musicians in Palencia Cathedral – had unanimously recommended.

Simultaneously, Rivafrecha was granted leave of absence from the cathedral in order to appear before a superior ecclesiastical court, the purpose of his suit being the recovery of certain funds due him on account of his prebend. On December 30, 1526, the chapter authorized him to collect in behalf of Palencia Cathedral 21,000 maravedís bequeathed by the former bishop, Juan Rodríguez de Fonseca, to endow a Salve and a Mass in his

---

[288] All biographical data concerning Rivafrecha is taken from Elústiza-Castrillo, pp. XLIV-XLVII. Castrillo Hernández used Palencia Cathedral *actas capitulares* as source material.

memory. On June 15, 1528, he petitioned the chapter for sick-leave pay. Two weeks later, June 29, he died. Sometimes reluctant to admit his claims while alive, the cabildo at his death drew up a Latin testimonial to his virtues including these phrases: *in arte musica tam practice quam theorice unicus, doctissimus, subtilissimus, sapientissimus.* Not only did the chapter declare him learned, skilful, and wise beyond all others in both the practice and theory of his art, but also praised his acquirements in the humane letters, his character, and his devotion. He was interred in the Chapel of the Holy Cross. A half-dozen years later Gómez de Portillo (d. October 9, 1534) was buried in the same chapel.

THE DUTIES of the chapelmaster at Palencia in 1528 have been extracted from the chapter minutes and printed.[289] Though Rivafrecha's term as chapelmaster lasted from 1503–1521, and though he was not always held to the obligation of rearing the choirboys, nevertheless the later statutes reveal the general scope of his assignment while he was still active. Palencia in 1528 supported twenty boy choristers with prime voices. These were trained to perform antiphonally, half the group singing polyphony in alternation with the other half in plainsong. All were taught to sing improvised melodies above a cantus firmus, as well as how to write counterpoint. But the chapelmaster's duty as an instructor did not end with the choirboys. Every day, morning or afternoon, he was required by the chapter to give one hour's free public instruction in music to anyone desirous of learning to sing – to the canons and prebendaries first, but also to anybody else who wished to study.

The days on which the *maestro de capilla* was required to conduct the cathedral music included all Sundays, Saturdays, and special feast-days such as Christmas, Epiphany, Purification, Easter, Ascension, Pentecost, Trinity Sunday, Corpus Christi, St. John the Baptist, SS. Peter and Paul, and Assumption of the Virgin – together with their respective vigils. His duty-days also included those on which special processions with polyphonic singing were ordered and any day when the entreating Psalm 69 (*Deus in adjutorium meum*) was to be sung in *fabordón*.

To ensure proper discipline the chapter at the same time strictly required all singers, whether canons or choirboys, to obey the *maestro de capilla*'s musical instructions. His was the complete disposition of the music, decreed the cabildo – wisely entrusting him with control of such matters as choice of soloists and singers for polyphony (but not for plainsong),j governing of tempi, decisions concerning accompaniments, and even the selection of repertory (within confines specified by the cabildo). Furthermore, singers whether canons, prebendaries, or unbeneficed clergy, were declared equal in choir rank, and therefore liable to the same penalties for absences and other faults. Anyone who sang was also declared eligible for payment. Thus, no concerted music was performed without fees being paid every singer. Because even the extras such as "graduated" choirboys and other "volunteers" were awarded honoraria, the choir retained at all times its professional character.

The recourse against absences, tardinesses, and other faults committed by "regular"

289 *Ibid.*, p. XLV, n. 1.

choir members was in the 1528 statutes, as always elsewhere in Spain during the sixteenth century, an elaborate system of graded fines. Each hour counted at a stated rate, and the *escritor de horas* therefore kept a complete day-by-day and hour-by-hour record which was to be examined and approved by the cathedral treasurer before any disbursements were made. Sick-leave pay was allowed for certified illnesses, but the cost of substitutes was declared deductible from the regular singer's wages. Forty vacation days with pay were annually allotted, on condition that they be not all taken consecutively and that they be not taken during festival or penitential seasons.

These 1528 *Ordenanzas* are reviewed here, however, not because the musical situation at Palencia was exceptional but because the duties of the chapelmaster at Palencia were duplicated a dozen times over in the principal Spanish churches c. 1528. The Palencia soil was that out of which grew such a famous musical personality as Cabezón, but the Seville soil nurtured Morales in the same epoch, Guerrero in the next generation; and in Ávila Cathedral Victoria was inscribed as a boy chorister after the middle of the century. The Spanish cathedrals provided therefore the ground in which were rooted nearly all the prominent creative personalities of the century.

AS FOR Rivafrecha's extant works, all are "soulful" pieces for four-part chorus. At Barcelona in the Biblioteca Central MS 454 a motet, *Quam pulchra es;* at Seville in the Biblioteca Colombina, sign. 5–5–20, another motet *Vox dilecti mei*, and a *Salve Regina;* at Tarazona Cathedral in MS 4 a *Benedicamus Domino;* have been catalogued.[290] In addition an anonymous *Anima mea liquefacta est* in identical style appears immediately after the *Vox dilecti mei* in the Biblioteca Colombina source, and should probably be assigned to him since the scriptural texts of the attributed and anonymous motets form a single continuous passage of scripture in the Song of Solomon [5:2–8].

His choice of the *Vox dilecti mei* text is not parallelled by any other Spanish composer of his generation. Indeed, nothing from the Song of Solomon seems to have attracted Spanish composers of the fifteenth or early sixteenth centuries, however fond of the Old Testament epithalamium may have been the more allegorically minded Flemings – or later in the century, Victoria. These earlier Spaniards were literalists. Rivafrecha's excision of the lines in the fifth chapter which speak of the beloved putting his hand through the aperture and of the trembling of her regions at his touch proves that he was willing to read allegory into the text only up to a point. Actually, the careful editing results in a text that is entirely decorous.

His music is all liquid sweetness. Especially fine is the motive of the descending fifth which appears at the words, "aperi mihi" (open to me). Nothing could be more convincingly "F Major" than this motet. Its harmonic perspicuity parallels that of *Anima mea liquefacta est*. The phrase structure is also extremely clear, each phrase being set off by decisive cadences. There are a dozen of these, following in this order: C, F, B♭, F, C, F; F, F, F, d, C, F. The measure-count between cadences is quite symmetrical:[291] 5, 5, 6, 6, 5½, 6½; 5, 6, 3½, 2½, 3½, 6½. Every *cláusula* – except the full ones rounding off the

---

[290] *MME*, I, *114, 129, 125*, for bibliographical details.

[291] Resolutions occur at the beginnings of succeeding measures or half-measures.

first 34 and the final 27 bars, and the single "deceptive" cadence into d minor – belongs to the "leading-tone" variety, that is to say, the VII⁶–I type. All but two involve syncopation in an upper part. The contrast of voice-paired sections with full sections becomes something of a structural device in this as in the *Anima mea* motet. Where pairing occurs, the second voice imitates the first.

In the *Salve Regina* – his longest work now available for study – he alternates a ferial version of the Gregorian antiphon with original polyphony. He imposes unity not only by quoting the plainsong in cantus or tenor, but also by making frequent use of a descending scale-motive in this rhythm:

‖ ♩· ♫ | ♩· · ‖ (nine times). He surrounds the tenor cantus firmus in the *O clemens* verse with imitative play on a motive reminiscent of that used by Peñalosa in Agnus II of his *Ave Maria peregrina* Mass.

Juan de Sanabria

OF THIS otherwise unknown composer a hymn *a 4*, *Ad caenam Agni providi*, and a four-voiced motet, *Lilium sacrum*, survive at fols. 4v.–5 and 287v.–288 respectively in Tarazona MS 2.[292] Two secular items, *Mayoral del hato, ahau*, and *Descuidad de ese cuidado*, both for three voices, enter the *Cancionero de Palacio* (nos. 118 and 377), the first of these including spoken dialogue. Sanabria may have been a writer of comedies as well. *Mayoral del hato* is obviously a song to be sung in some farce of the kind that Encina made popular in the 1490's.

Juan de Segovia

A THREE-VOICED Magnificat (even verses) by this composer intervenes between ones by Anchieta and Peñalosa in Tarazona MS 2.[293]

[Alonso Hernández de] Tordesillas (fl. 1502); [Pedro de] Tordesillas (fl. 1499)

INSCRIBED as a singer in Ferdinand V's chapel on November 23, 1502,[294] Alonso Hernández seems to have come from Tordesillas – the town southwest of Valladolid later made famous by Queen Joanna "the Mad." At his appointment he earns the sobriquet of *del ojo* ("of the eye"), which can refer to an abnormal eye, or to a tune used as a cantus firmus in Peñalosa's *Missa del ojo*. At all events, it distinguishes him from Pedro de Tordesillas, appointed a singer in Queen Isabella's chapel on New Year's Day, 1499.

A *Missa a 4* survives at fols. 191v.–200 in Tarazona MS 3 and a Lamentation at fols. 297v.–299 (*Zay. Jherusalem dierum*) in MS 2. This latter also lists two even-verse Magnificats by "Tordesillas" (items 34 and 35). The *Cancionero Musical de Palacio* has for its item 424, *Franceses, por qué rrasòn*. The words allude to a Spanish victory over the French in October of 1503. Both Anglés and Barbieri assume Pedro, not Alonso, to have been the *CMP* Tordesillas.

---

[292] *MME*, I, *122–123*. See also Gerber, "Spanische Hymnensätze," pp. 175 (item 4), 176, and 183 (last paragraph).

[293] *MME*, I, *122*.

[294] *DML*, II, 2130.

Francisco de la Torre (fl. 1483)

A NATIVE of Seville, Torre enrolled in Ferdinand's chapel choir on July 1, 1483.[295] Johannes Urrede, *maestro de capilla* from at least 1477–1481, may still have been director when he entered. After service in the Aragonese choir, he returned home to become a *conbeneficiado* in the Seville cathedral. On February 10, 1503, the chapter raised his income while he temporarily took charge of the choirboys. His immediate predecessor in that duty had been Francisco García, master of the boys from March 30, 1498 until the close of 1502. Torre's additional income for their care was to cease as soon as he turned them over to the new chapelmaster, Alonso de Alva.[296] His supervision ended before the year was out. On September 30, 1504, he was a *compañero*, a rank below that of canon or prebendary.[297] In February of 1515 a certain Fernando de la Torre was dean of the cathedral.[298] Whether this other Torre was related to Francisco cannot be determined until more archival research has been done. But no actual evidence has been uncovered as yet which ever makes of Francisco anything more than a *compañero*.

His sacred works are preserved at Toledo Cathedral in choirbooks 1 and 21. The first contains two motets *a 4*, *Ne recorderis* (fol. 83v.) and *Libera me, Domine* (fol. 87v.). Choïrbook 21 contains these same two motets and another in addition, *Paucitas*. *Libera me* according to F. Rubio Piqueras, was as recently as 1925 in use at funeral ceremonies for high-ranking Toledan dignitaries.[299] He observed, however, that most listeners believed it could be by no other composer than Morales, on account of its unusual exaltation and solemnity.

Torre's secular works are conserved in the Colombina cancionero and in *Palacio*. The first contains a four-voiced *Dime triste coraçon*, and *Palacio* fifteen items.[300] His most famous work is of course the three-part instrumental dance in *Palacio* called *Alta*. Its

---

[295] *Ibid.*, 2132.

[296] *A.C., 1503–1504*, fol. 10v.: "Este dia mandaron sus mercedes que se le acuda a francisco de la torre su conbeneficiado con la rata de la rracion que por su maestro de capilla le mandaron dar contandogela fasta el dia que entregue los moços de coro que ha tenydo a su cargo alonso dalva su maestro de capilla." This notice distinctly states that Alva, not Torre, was chapelmaster during February of 1503. Actually no evidence has thus far been brought forward to show that Torre was at any time Sevillian chapelmaster. Like Peñalosa he seems to have preferred an office involving less arduous duties than that of chapelmaster.

[297] *A.C., 1503–1504*, fol. 101v.

[298] *A.C., 1513. 1514. 1515.*, fol. 110v. (Lunes XXI de hebrero de MDXV años).

[299] *Códices Polifónicos Toledanos* (Toledo: n.p., 1925), p. 44: "The responsory for the dead by Francisco de la Torre, *Libera me*, is a terribly tragic work, and of an otherworldly expressiveness. As often as it is sung there are always those who approach us in order to tell how overwhelmingly it impressed them. It is performed at funerals of archbishops and on All Souls'. Many attribute it to Morales, but incorrectly. One has only to look at the manuscript (Cod. 21) to assure oneself that Torre composed it."

[300] In alphabetical order: *Adoramoste, Señor, Dios y ombre verdadero* (444), *Adoramoste, Señor, Dios y onbre Jhesu Christo* (420), *Alta* (321), *Ayrado va el gentilonbre* (137), *Damos gracias a ti, Dios* (32), *Justa fué mi perdiçión* (42), *La que tengo no es prisión* (48), *No fie nadie en amor* (262), *O quán dulçe serías, muerte* (62), *Pánpano verde* (11), *Pascua d'Espíritu Santo* (136), *Peligroso pensamiento* (43), *Por los campos de los moros* (150), *Pues que todo os descontenta* (331), *Triste, que será de mí* (140). All these belonged to the original corpus of *Palacio*. Items 32, 43, and 420 are repeated in the *Cancionero de Segovia* at nos. 171, 172, and 188, where they are however anonymous. Torre's music with vernacular text includes three religious villancicos (*CMP*, nos. 32, 420, 444).

tenor is the *La Spagna* basse-danse melody used frequently from Isaac to Cabezón as a cantus firmus.

[Juan de] Triana (fl. 1478)

JUAN DE TRIANA held a prebend in Seville Cathedral during 1478.[301] On February 9 of that year he personally appeared before the cathedral chapter, with bulls from Sixtus IV confirming his title. His immediate predecessor had been Ruy González, now dead. He brought in the papal bulls because his right to succeed in the prebend had been contested by Don Lope de Sandoval, dean of Cordova Cathedral (a pluralist who hoped to add a Sevillian prebend to his list of benefices). Since Dean Sandoval's *proçeso* against Triana was signed by a clerical notary of Toledo archdiocese on June 9, 1477, Triana had obviously entered his Sevillian prebend well before that earlier date.

The Sevillian cabildo, presided over by its own dean, favored Triana. In reply to his suit they declared that he never had been dispossessed of his prebend, whatever pressures Dean Lope de Sandoval had exerted. They added that for his greater peace of mind Canon Fernando Gómez, a member of the Seville cathedral chapter, would in their name go through the formality of installing him again in the same prebend, if he so desired. Triana did so desire and the two, Gómez and Triana, therefore went together into the enclosed portion of the cathedral nave which constituted the *coro*. There Gómez formally inducted Triana into his choir stall, after which a certain sum was symbolically distributed among the members of the choir who were at the moment singing the office. The ceremony concluded with Triana's receiving in testimony of his installation a document signed by two clergymen present during the ceremony, Diego de Mendoza and Juan de Quevedo.

Five years later he was serving as master of the boy choristers in Toledo Cathedral. The 1483 *Libro de gastos* (expense account-book) makes him "cantor de musica que tiene cargo de mostrar el arte de canto dela musica a los seys niños cleriçones cantores eligidos por el cabilldo [*sic*] para cantar en el coro dela dicha yglesia" [302] (music-master charged with teaching the six boy choristers selected by the chapter to sing in this cathedral). The Toledo cathedral paid him that year 18,000 maravedís, in three equal instalments.

Certain other biographical bits may be surmised. His triumph over a powerful rival

---

[301] *Autos capitulares del año de 1478 y principio de 1479*, fol. 7v.: "parescio en el personalmente el districto varon juan de triana racionero de la dicha yglesia e presento a los dichos señores vnas bullas de nuestro señor el papa syxto quarto conviene a saber graçiosa e executoria sobre la prouision a el fecha de la dicha raçion quel posee en esta santa yglesia ... e vn proçeso sobre ellas fulminado por el venerable señor don lope de sandoual dean de cordoua ... e luego el dicho juan de triana dixo quel por virtud de las dichas bullas e proçeso continuaua su posesyon de la dicha su raçion que vaco por muerte de ruy gonsales de segouia vltimo poseedor desta ... e luego los dichos señores dean e cabildo respondieron quel syenpre auya estado en posesyon de la dicha raçion e nunca auya sydo despojado della ..."

[302] Biblioteca Nacional (Madrid) MS 14045. The Toledo entry was copied for Asenjo Barbieri at the time he was preparing biographical notes for his edition of the Palacio cancionero. He did not use his Triana information because he was unaware of the concordances between *CMP* and the Colombina cancionero.

for his Sevillian prebend – the dean of Cordova Cathedral – bespeaks the personal favor of Pope Sixtus IV whose bulls Triana presented in Seville in February of 1478. This was the Sixtus from whom the so-called Sistine Choir took its name. An occupant of the throne from 1471–1484, Sixtus perhaps patronized Triana during the early years of his pontificate. Further research must be done in Rome, however, to substantiate such a conjecture. One may also surmise that Triana and Cornago were personally acquainted. In any event the two cooperated in composing a *canción a 3* found in the Colombina cancionero (sign. 7–I–28, fols. 36v.–38) with the title, *Señora, qual soy venido*.

This Colombina cancionero contains all Triana's surviving works, 18 items to be exact.[303] Two of these, *Por beber, comadre* (fol. 102 v.) and *Aquella buena muger* (fol. 103), are repeated in *Palacio* (nos. 235 and 243), and are therefore available in both the Barbieri and Anglés editions for students interested in Triana's secular style. One other work has been printed, the Song of the Sibyl, but in a faulty transcription.

Triana is unique among composers thus far surveyed in this chapter because he alone seems to have left samples of the song-motet. This term, as is now well known, is applied to simple motets in songlike style, usually *a 3*, whose destination was oftenest the private chapel or oratory. Most song-motets were not transcribed in cathedral collections, but in chansonniers of handbook size. Triana's three examples perfectly comply with all these specifications. Two are *Benedicamus*, and the third a *Juste Judex, Jesu Christe*. In the first *Benedicamus* a high e[1] has been scratched out, and the concluding phrase of the middle voice rewritten, in order to contract its range (fol. 94). Another telltale evidence showing that these Triana song-motets were sung by the rankest amateurs before Ferdinand Columbus acquired this particular cancionero for his library in 1534 [304] is the fact that very often some ignoramus unacquainted with mensural theory has blackened voids and ligatures, and added stems to the original notes. The result of such efforts at "correction" is that the two inks must be carefully distinguished on the page by any modern transcriber. [305]

As a rule only the treble of Triana's secular pieces is texted, the other voice-parts carrying no more than an identifying catch-word or two. His three Latin song-motets are however texted in all voice-parts. Imitation is sparingly used. The first *Benedicamus* opens with it between the middle and top voice; the second employs it successively between lower and middle, then middle and top voices at mm. 11–12. It is absent from *Juste Judex*. As can be seen in the accompanying example, the two lower voices often move in parallel motion. The lowest voice is melodically less smooth than the upper two.

He makes his harmonic intentions crystal clear in each song-motet. The first *Benedicamus* cadences into G at mm. 8$_3$, 10, and 22, these being the only *cláusulas* in this

[303] For an alphabetical list of these see pp. 209–213 *infra*.

[304] This date, though accepted by Anglés, was originally put forward as a mere guess by Simón de la Rosa y López in his *Los seises de la Catedral de Sevilla* (Seville: Imp. de F. de P. Díaz, 1904), p. 70n. He says: "The codex appears to have been bought in 1534 at Seville by Ferdinand Columbus." He also offers it as his opinion that the contents were copied after 1500. This last is a most unlikely presumption.

[305] The traps set by the "corrector" caused errors in the transcription of *Juysio fuerte sera dado* at mm. 6–8 (tenor), published opposite p. 298 in *La música a Catalunya fins al segle XIII*.

22-measure piece. The second *Benedicamus* (in dorian) cadences to A minor at m. 7₃, to E minor at m. 11, deceptively to F Major at 14₃, and authentically to D minor at m. 21 (last measure). *Juste Judex* (accompanying example) cadences to D [minor] at m. 7₃, to A [minor] at m. 15, and plagally to D [Major] in the last bar of Part I. The cadences in Part II, *Et cum Sancto Flamine* – if one disregards the deceptive feints at mm. 31 and 39– are to D at m. 29, A at m. 36, and to D again at m. 45. Tonic and dominant discover themselves as his favorite cadencing chords.

The constant crossing of the two upper voices in the accompanying example results in a much more interesting and vivid, even if synthetic, upper line than either voice-part alone produces. Triana so restricts the range of the lowest voice that it never descends below C. This same C is the lowest note in both *Benedicamus* as well. On the other hand, he was not averse to writing G₁ or even F₁ as a low note in his secular pieces.

Juste Judex, Jesu Christe *

Seville: Bibl. Colombina, sign. 7–1–28, fols 95 v.–96.   [JUAN DE] TRIANA

* Righteous Judge, Jesus Christ, King and Lord, Thou who reignest with the Father eternally, and with the Holy Spirit, deign mercifully to receive our prayers.

** g.

Summary

I Despite the valiant efforts of such scholars as Elústiza and Anglés, only a small number of Spanish sacred works dating from the reigns of Ferdinand and Isabella have as yet been published. Almost thirty composers at work between 1475 and 1525 have, for instance, been named in this chapter. Yet sacred music with Latin text of only a half-dozen has been thus far printed.

II That this unpublished material is important as well as copious is instanced by the fact that in one manuscript alone – Tarazona MS 3 – ten unpublished masses by six composers active c. 1500 survive.

III As far as biography is concerned, liturgical masters during the reigns of Ferdinand and Isabella reaped financial rewards and ecclesiastical preferments which seem on the whole to have exceeded those bestowed on such later polyphonic masters as Morales, Navarro, and Guerrero. Certainly Anchieta and Peñalosa enjoyed financial favors beyond the customary level reached later in the century.

IV Though secular themes were indiscriminately introduced into Spanish masses composed in the period, still the learned treatment of such secular material in works with Latin text sharply differs from the untrussed style common in sacred and secular works using vernacular texts.

V Those sacred composers with the fewest international contacts wrote the most clearly "harmonic" music. The stay-at-home group reveled in strong IV–I and V–I cadences at ends of phrases, usually with a syncopated melodic tag in an upper voice.

VI Expressivity was the composer's chief goal in the earliest *Salve* by Medina where fermatas over block-chords at the words *gementes et flentes* permitted the singers to sigh every syllable; it was also the composer's prime goal in the Ash Wednesday motets of Anchieta, the Torre responsories for the dead, the Rivafrecha Song of Solomon motets, the *Clamabat autem* motet of Escobar.

VII The Spanish sacred composers of this period produced their most characteristic music when texts of a poignant nature were set.

VIII Learned devices occur with greatest frequency in the sacred works of composers who like Yllianas, Peñalosa, and Escribano, are known to have spent time in Italy.

IX But into such learned devices – even when encountered in the works of the international composers – a symbolic or emotional significance can almost invariably be read.

X Because of the national bias in favor of *sonoridad*, expressivity, and clear-cut harmonies, the thus-far performed Spanish liturgical music composed c. 1500 has always proved "immediate" music: i.e. has made a powerful impression on its audience at first hearing.

Secular Polyphony during the Reigns
of Ferdinand and Isabella (1474-1516)

Peninsular Sources

MS 2092 at the Madrid Biblioteca Nacional chronicles the acts of the Constable of Castile, Miguel Lucas de Iranzo, who during the civil strife darkening Henry IV's reign sided with his king. Along with the account of the Constable's deeds for 1466 a musical insertion fills fols. 234v.–235, *Versos fechos en loor del Condestable*. This piece (transcribed below at p. 205), takes pride of place as the earliest surviving bit of Spanish secular part-song that can be dated.

Secular polyphony belonging to the reigns of *los Reyes Católicos* appears in five peninsular *cancioneros*. The oldest of these – found in the library brought together by the discoverer's son, Ferdinand Columbus – is frequently referred to as the *Cancionero Musical de la Biblioteca Colombina* [1] (hereafter *CMC*). The others include one at Madrid – the so-called *Cancionero Musical de Palacio* [2] (hereafter *CMP*), one at Barcelona in the Biblioteca Central [3] (*CMB*), one at Segovia in the capitular library [4] (*CMS*), and, lastly,

---

[1] Sign. 7–I–28; the title on front cover of this parchment-bound volume, *Cantilenas vulgares puestas en musica por varios españoles*, cannot be considered contemporaneous with its contents.

[2] Biblioteca Real, sign. 2–I–5; edited by the savant and composer, Francisco Asenjo Barbieri in 1890, and re-edited by Higinio Anglés in 1947–1951. Vol. III of the Instituto Español de Musicología edition (textos literarios) was still *en prensa* in 1957.

[3] MS 454. Fols. 120, 143v.–144, 157v., 171v.–176, and 179v.–180v. (with a total of 22 Spanish part-songs) show music with Castilian texts. Four composers from the period 1474–1516 – Peñalosa, Gabriel, Lope de Baena, and Mondéjar; and three who flourished c. 1550 – Flecha *el viejo*, Morales, and Pastrana; enter this MS.

[4] MS without signature. Only fols. 207–226 (at which are copied a total of 37 Spanish part-songs) show music with Castilian texts. Five composers from the period 1474–1516 – Torre, Encina, Urrede, Gijón, and Lagarto – are represented. All the Spanish items are anonymous in *CMS*. Ten, however, concord with *CMP* attributed items. See *MME*, I, *111–112*.

one at Elvas in Portugal – the so-called *Cancioneiro Musical e Poético da Biblioteca Públia Hortênsia* [5] (*CMH*).

CMP gives by far the largest and most important assortment. Its 458 items include ten in Italian [6] (six of which concord with *frottole* printed in Petrucci's 1504, 1505, and 1507 collections), [7] two items with Latin texts, [8] one in Basque, [9] two without text, [10] and some eight or more macaronic items. [11] Even with these deductions *CMP* still contains more than twice as many part-songs in Castilian as do all of the other four peninsular cancioneros combined. [12]

Manuscript and Printed Sources of Foreign Provenience

OUTSIDE THE PENINSULA only scattered manuscripts containing early Spanish secular part-songs survive. Occasionally a French chanson adapted to a Castilian text crops up – the Odhecaton *Mais que ce fust* adapted to the Castilian text, *Donzella no men culpeys*, in Capp. Giulia MS XIII. 27 at Rome, [13] for instance. But such mere adaptations should be left out of account. [14] Monte Cassino MS 871 N contains seven part-songs by Cornago and an anonymous *canción a 4* acclaiming Don Ferrante (ascended the Neapolitan throne in 1458, but the song dates c. 1464). At Florence in Bibl. Naz. Cent. Magl. XIX, 107 bis, is to be found an anonymous item *a 3*. [15] The Pixérécourt chansonnier at the Bibliothèque Nationale (f. frç. 15123) contains two songs with Spanish

[5] Sign. 11973. Although all 65 part-songs in this collection are anonymous, 14 concord with items in *CMP*, the composer of four of these being Encina (nos. 46, 47, 50, and 56 in *CMH*) and of three being Escobar (nos. 3, 9, and 57 in *CMH*). Fourteen songs in *CMH* are in Portuguese (8, 20, 26, 27, 29, 30, 32, 33, 34, 38, 39, 40, 43, 55). The other 51 are in Spanish but with spellings frequently showing Portuguese influence.

[6] Nos. 78, 84 (macaronic), 91, 98, 105 (macaronic), 190, 258, 317 (macaronic), 435, and 441. *Sagaleja del Casar* (no. 209) and *Fata la parte* (no. 421) contain a *chapurrado* mixture of Italian and Spanish. All these Italian items were later additions to *CMP*. See *MME*, V, *22* (Estranbotes).

[7] Nos. 78 (lib. v, 1505), 84 (lib. i, 1504), 91 (lib. vii, 1507), 98 (lib. vi, 1505 [= 1506]), 105 (lib. iii, 1504 [= 1505]). 190 (lib. ii, 1504 [= 1505]). Nos. 84 and 78 were intabulated in Francesco Bossinensis's lute books (I, xxxviii and II, xli), published by Petrucci in 1509 and 1511.

[8] Nos. 159 and 418. In nos. 41 and 58 the tenor sings a Latin text (plainsong), the treble a Spanish one.

[9] No. 248.

[10] Nos. 321, 358.

[11] Nos. 55, 84, 105, 154, 232, 317, 363, and 400. No. 41 has a Latin tenor, of which only the catch-words are copied in the MS, and No. 311 has a Latin *bassus*.

[12] In *CMC*, *CMB*, *CMS*, and *CMH* occur approximately 78, 22, 37, and 51 Spanish songs respectively, totalling 188. A dozen or so found outside the peninsula brings the grand total to around 200.

[13] Helen Hewitt, ed., *Harmonice Musices Odhecaton*, pp. 40 (n. 28), 113–114 and 165. The Petrequin *Donzella no men culpeys* does not concord with the anonymous *Donçella non me culpeis* in the Pixérécourt chansonnier and in Monte Cassino MS 871 N. Jozef Robyns, *Pierre de la Rue (Circa 1460–1518): Een Bio-Bibliographische Studie* (Brussels: Paleis der Academiën, 1954), p. 171, identifies the Petrequin as a song by La Rue. See his p. 200 for incipits of each of the four parts. Ludwig Finscher, "Loyset Compère and his Works," *Musica Disciplina*, XII (1958), pp. 138–139, admits that only *Odhecaton* ascribes the music of *Mais que ce fust* to Compère, while three MSS give it to La Rue.

[14] For a lengthy discussion of the problems that arise when a foreign piece has been adapted to Spanish text, see *MME*, X, 24.

[15] *Lo che cheda es lo seghuro* (*CMP*, no. 216). *MME*, X, *19*, lists three other items that concord with villancicos *a 4* by Encina: *Caldere et glave*, *Tam buen ghanadigho*, and *Todos los vienes* (*CMP*, nos. 249, 426, 33). On Encina's Italian sojourns, see below, pp. 256–260.

texts.[16] At the Bodleian, MS Ashmole 831 shows on fol. 261v. the top-part (together with a fragment of the contra) of Johannes Urrede's *Nunca fuit* [sic] *pena maior*. The text, though in Spanish, shows such telltale signs of having been copied by an Italian scribe as the substitution of "che" for "que". (No notice of this interesting MS source is taken in *MME*, V, *41*, even though a fine facsimile was published as long ago as 1901 [*Early Bodleian Music*, I, no. CIV]). At Yale University the Mellon chansonnier contains a solitary Castilian part-song by the French composer Vincenet.[17] Thus it can be readily seen that the number of part-songs with Spanish text surviving outside the peninsula in MSS antedating 1500 reaches no more than a dozen.

As for printed sources, both Petrucci's *Harmonice Musices Odhecaton* and *Canti C* (Venice, 1501 and 1503 [= 1504]) contain *Nunca fué pena mayor*.[18]

URREDE's national origins have been disputed. In 1476 he served García Álvarez de Toledo, Duke of Alva (d. 1488).[19] This ducal house had the reputation of maintaining one of the finest musical establishments in the peninsula (outside the royal courts) during the latter years of the fifteenth century. Even though apparently from Bruges Urrede was by no means the only foreigner hired as chief musician in a leading Spanish ducal house during the 1470's and '80's.[20] In 1477 he passed into the royal establishment of Ferdinand V,[21] where he remained as chapelmaster until at least 1481. Aside from *Pange lingua*'s preserved at Barcelona, Segovia, and Tarazona,[22] a motet at Paris,[23] and a Magnificat (Tone VI) at Coimbra,[24] Urrede – or his

---

[16] Urrede's *Numquam* appears at 99v.–100 but in Italian. At fols. 100v.–101 comes the three-voiced anonymous *Donçella non me culpeis si fago mudança alguna*, a concordance with Monte Cassino MS 871 N, fol. 152 (but not with Capp. Giul. MS XIII. 27). Fols. 195v.–196 (Pixérécourt) show the three-voiced *Amat uos con lealdat*; its continuation (*coplas* a 3) fills 196v.–197, *Et si uos me dais la muerte*. Compare *MME*, I, *118*, the particulars of which require correction.

[17] *MME*, X, *23*. See also Manfred Bukofzer, "An Unknown Chansonnier of the 15th Century," *Musical Quarterly*, XXVIII, 1 (January, 1942), 22. Vincenet, according to Anglés, was a singer at Naples in 1479 (*MME*, X, *23*).

[18] *MME*, I, *136*, cites the *Canti C* version as different from that in *CMP*. But *MME*, V, *42*, cites both *Odhecaton* and *Canti C* as sources alongside the *CMP*, *CMC*, *CMS*, Pixérécourt chansonnier, and Bologna Liceo Musical MS 109 versions. For other sources see Helen Hewitt and Isabel Pope, *Harmonice Musices Odhecaton*, pp. 130–131. Also, Otto Gombosi's edition of the Capirola lute tablature, p. LXXXIV (32).

[19] Henry IV named him first Duke of Alva in 1469. Alba de Tormes, his ducal seat, lies fifteen miles south of Salamanca. He wrote the verses of *Nunca fué pena mayor* probably around 1470. See note 226 below. Urrede's duties included in 1476 the instruction of three Negro boys in singing. He was paid 17,000 *maravedís* plus 50 measures of wheat. For his care of the Negro boys he received an additional 78 maravedís daily allowance. Cf. *MME*, I, *126*.

[20] The chief musician in D. Fadrique Enríquez's house was also a foreigner. See Bibl. Nac. (Madrid) MS 14035.45: "Juan Maynete, o de Paris, natural de esta ciudad de Francia ... era el mejor musico de su casa y procuraba D. Fadrique reunir en su capilla los mejores musicos." This Don Fadrique was Admiral of Castile.

[21] *DML*, II, 2166. By royal provision Urrede's annual salary was set at 30,000 *maravedís* on April 1, 1477 (Medina del Campo). He followed the court in 1478 to Seville, in 1479 to Saragossa and Valencia, in 1480 to Toledo, and in 1481 to Saragossa and Barcelona.

[22] As Rudolf Gerber revealed in "Spanische Hymnensätze um 1500," *Archiv für Musikwissenschaft*, X, iii, 182, at least three different Pange Lingua settings by Urrede survive – at Barcelona, Bibl. Cent. MS 454 (fols. 148v.–149); Segovia, *CMS* (fols. 226v.–227); and Tarazona, MS 2 (fols. 9v.–10). Cabezón's *glosa* closely follows the Tarazona, not the Barcelona. Anglés mistakenly assumed in his "El 'Pange Lingua' de Johannes Urreda," *Anuario Musical*, VII (1952), pp. 193–200, that Urrede left only one Pange Lingua (the Barcelona version), and that therefore Cabezón's 1557 *glosa* bears little or no relation to its announced source.

[23] Bibl. Nat., nouv. acq. fr. 4379 (fols. 84v.–86): *Secundum verbum tuum in pace* a 3.

[24] MS 12, fols. 173v.–180. Urrede disputes authorship of this Magnificat with Peñalosa.

double – composed two movements of a *De beata Virgine* Mass copied in Capp. Sist. Cod. 14 at Rome.[25] A notation after his name at fol. 5v. of the latter reads *brugen.* (= of Bruges). Two other secular songs besides *Nunca fué* survive, both with Spanish texts: *De vos i de mí quexoso* (*CMP*, 17; *CMC*, 32) and *Muy triste será mi vida* (*CMP*, 23; *CMC*, 11). Closely associated as he was with Spain, Urrede seems likelier to have become a peninsular by "adoption" as did Domenico Scarlatti, than to have been Spanish-born. His case also foreshadows Scarlatti's because both while resident in the peninsula saw their music published elsewhere.

A printed source which contains a later arrangement of a part-song composed c. 1500, Juan Aldomar's *Ha, Pelayo, qué desmayo* (*CMP*, no. 89), was printed at Venice in 1556. This Venetian imprint, *Villancicos de diuersos authores*, also contains at least three songs with words but not necessarily music by Juan del Encina (1469–1529). The Aldomar and Encina [26] items in the *Cancionero de Upsala* (so-called because the unique part-books are preserved in Sweden) are anonymous. They can however be identified because of concordances with ascribed villancicos in the *Cancionero de Palacio*. A still more interesting and hitherto strangely neglected print which contains music, and not just words, of an Encina villancico remains for notice. In João IV's *Difesa della musica moderna* (Venice, 1666) at pp. 66–67, *Pues que jamás olvidaros* (*CMP*, no. 30) is printed, transposed a fourth below the *CMP* version but in every other respect identical.[27] The royal author includes the Encina item as the second of three *essempi della più antica Musica degni di gran lode* ("examples of the most ancient music, worthy of great praise"). Until an earlier contender can be brought forward, King John IV of Portugal must therefore be called the earliest "rescuer" of a Spanish item in the Palace Songbook, and *Pues que jamás olvidaros* be acknowledged as the only natively Spanish piece, the music of which can be proved to have been printed intact before 1890.

"Versos fechos en loor del Condestable" (1466)

"VERSES composed in honor of the Constable," a 16-line poem in four stanzas, is set for four voices in Bibl. Nac. MS 2092. The copyist has written the text of the first stanza under each of the four voice-parts.[28] The parts are spread on pages facing each other

[25] Haberl, *Bausteine für Musikgeschichte*, II, 174: "*Jo. Wreede brugen.*" Anglés in attempting to make "Urrede'" a corrupted Spanish name (*DML*, II, 2167) has reworked a claim already put forward by Antonio García Boiza in *La Basilica Teresiana*, June, 1919, pp. 186–190. Boiza contended that the name Urrede could be a corrupt reading of *Ubiedo, Uuiedo,* or *Obiedo*. The then Duke of Alva refuted Boiza's claim in his "Disquisiciones acerca del cantor flamenco Juan de Wrede" published in *Boletín de la Real Academia de la Historia*, LXXV (1919), pp. 199–200.

[26] Encina is represented at nos. 7 (estribillo), 10, 25, and possibly 33 in the Upsala cancionero; but his contribution in each case was the poetry, not the music. The claims in Leopoldo Querol Roso, *La poesía del Cancionero de Uppsala* (Valencia: Imp. Hijo F. Vives Mora, 1932), pp. 98, 106–107, 125–127, 140–141, like those in *MME*, I, *133*, must be scaled down.

[27] At mm. 16–17 and 28–29 in the 1666 print, Encina's bass leaps up an octave instead of descending a fifth, as in the *CMP* version. Certain repeated notes in the accompaniment are "tied" in the 1666 print and viceversa. This was the song which Alvares Frouvo admired (see below, note 159). It must, however, be added that João IV thought all three of his *essempi* had lost their appeal in 1649 because of changing taste.

[28] Facsimile on p. 92 in Jose Subirá, *Historia de la música española* (Barcelona: Salvat, 1953).

Lealtat, o lealtat *

Madrid: Bibl. Nac. MS 2092 (olim G. 126), fols. 234 v.–235.   Anonymous, 1466

* Loyalty, o loyalty!   Behold, O king, the Constable
Loyalty, tell me, where do you reside?   And in him you will find it.
The other three stanzas continue in like vein. See J. de Mata Carriazo, *Crónicas Españolas*, III, 328–329.

with top voice and tenor on the left, and two parts (each called *contra*) on the right. The second, third, and fourth quatrains are copied below the tenor as is the standard practice in such later secular collections as *CMC* and *CMP*.

Quite aside from this earliest dated piece, *Hechos del Condestable Don Miguel Lucas de*

Iranzo interests the historian because of its numerous musical references. Vivid descriptions of festivals celebrated *con cantares y atanbores e otros muchos enstrumentos*,[29] with sound of *tronpetas e atabales e duçaynas y cherimías*,[30] and with singing of *cosantas* and *rondeles* [31] enliven its pages. Sallying forth from his seigniorial seat at Jaén, whether to fight Moor or Christian, the Constable was always attended by *ministriles* (instrumentalists) and singers.

Lealtat, o lealtat gives a sample of the music with which he surrounded himself. Although available in Barbieri's edition of *CMP* [32] it is repeated here – in modern clefs, with reduced time-values, and in compressed score. The Landini cadence in the tenor just before the second fermata and the octave skip of the bass before the last fermata are typical enough fifteenth-century mannerisms. So is the mixed signature, only the lowest voice carrying B♭. Although *Lealtat* looks astoundingly chordal, cantus and tenor alone make unexceptionable counterpoint. The tenor, moreover, possesses equal melodic interest with the top part. The bass (second contra) skips about much more than do the other voices, a dozen of its skips being fourths or fifths.

The anonymous composer balances his phrases. The last two are of equal length. The second and third grow by equal increments over their predecessors. He strives for unity in addition to balance: as the repeated-note rhythmic figure at the beginning of each phrase testifies. The simplicity and stateliness of the music, its symmetrical phrases each ending with a fermata, and perhaps also its clear harmonic structure, unite to remind the listener of so alien and posterior a type as the German chorale.

Cancionero de la Biblioteca Colombina

THIS *cancionero*, already many times alluded to, has not been edited and much of the information presently available concerning its contents stands in need of correction. Preliminary lists of its contents have been twice undertaken,[33] the most recent appearing in *MME*, I, *104–106*. But in both instances errors of titling, attribution, and concordancing are rather frequently found.[34]

[29] *Colección de Crónicas Españolas*, ed. Juan de Mata Carriazo (Madrid: Espasa-Calpe, 1940), III, 25. This passage refers to the entrance of king and queen into León during the Spring of 1459.

[30] *Ibid.*, 49 (festivities after the Constable's wedding in 1461).

[31] *Ibid.*, 155 (Christmas festivities in 1464).

[32] Pp. 605–606. Barbieri "corrects" the original at m. 16 in the tenor (his measure-numbering). He also omits the text which in the MS appears beneath the three lower voice-parts. Undoubtedly the fitting of the words is difficult. Instruments as well as voices must obviously have cooperated in the original performances.

[33] Simón de la Rosa y López in *Los Seises de la Catedral de Sevilla* (Seville: Imp. de Francisco de P. Díaz, 1904), pp. 70–71, was the first to make a list. He assumed that the anonymous items should all be attributed to composers whose names are found in *CMC*, an assumption which has of course proved false. Anglés does not mention Rosa y López in *MME*, I, *103–106*.

[34] e.g., errors in titling: no. 25 (for *Bineleda* read *Biue leda*); no. 32 (for *quexose* read *quexoso*); no. 49 (for *es* read *y*); no. 62 (for *se* read *le*); no. 66 (for *advenias* read *adveniad*); no. 74 (for *Vyrgendina* read *Vyrgen di[g]na*); no. 87 (title corrupted from *S'elle m'amera je ne scay*). See also footnotes 106 and 107 below. *Biue leda*, *CMC*, no. 25, concords with item 470 in the *Cancionero de Baena* (fol. 156) where the poem is ascribed to Juan Rodríguez del Padrón. Its subtitle in *CB* reads: "Juan Rodrigues de Padron composed this song of farewell to his lady-love when he became a friar at Jerusalem." Rodríguez del Padrón also wrote the words of *Muy triste será mi vida* (*CMC*, no. 11; *CMP*. no. 23).

The reasons for citing it as the earliest collection are these: (1) its repertory of approximately 95 secular and sacred items [35] overlaps that of *CMP* in 20 instances, but where divergencies exist the *CMC* can usually be shown to have been the primitive version; [36] (2) presently available biographical clues encourage one to believe that everything in *CMC*, except a few manifestly later additions to the MS, was composed before 1490; (3) since Juan del Encina – the dominating personality in *CMP* and the most prolific secular composer in the reigns of Ferdinand and Isabella – is not represented in *CMC*,[37] it seems extremely likely that he had not yet begun his career when *CMC* was in the process of compilation; (4) the emphasis on the *canción* and the absence of all but two or three "open" villancicos from *CMC* show that most of its songs were composed before the "classic" villancico came into vogue.

The earliest composer in *CMC* thus far identified is Johannes Ockeghem (c. 1420–c. 1495), whose four-part *Petite camusette* occurs at fols. 101v.–102. Ockeghem again appears as a contributor at fols. 24v.–26 where *Qu'es mi vida preguntays*, a Spanish four-part *canción* written cooperatively by Cornago and Ockeghem, is copied. Johannes Urrede, whose birthdate is unknown but who may have been Ockeghem's junior by ten or fifteen years, is represented by his ubiquitous *Nunca fué pena mayor* at fols. 16v.–17 and by the less frequently copied *Muy triste será mi vida* at fols. 19v.–21 and *De vos i de mí quexoso* [38] at fols. 51v.–52v. These three songs are for treble, tenor, and contra. He is again represented at fols. 40v.–41 where the top voice-part of his *Nunca fué* becomes the tenor of Belmonte's three-part *Pues mi dicha non consiente*.[39]

An anonymous three-part French chanson with only five words of text copied beneath each voice-part, and those corruptly, appears at fols. 106v.–107. These five words should perhaps read *Le paure amant qui est*.[40] The "key-signature" of all three voices includes both B♭ and E♭. A♭'s, though not written in, are obviously necessary on several occasions. The treble melody line reaches high b¹♭; the contra ranges up to the b♭ above Middle C. No other instances of such extreme upper vocal limits have been encountered in either *CMC* or *CMP*.

Aside from *Le paure amant*, the Ockeghem, and the Urrede items, *CMC* seems to include only works by native Spanish composers. In alphabetical order their names are Belmonte (no. 24), Cornago (nos. 4, 10, 14, 18, 22, 27), Enrique (nos. 2, 30), Gijón (no. 38), Hurtado de Xeres (nos. 40 and 42), Juanes (no. 67), Lagarto (no. 33), León (no. 17), Madrid (no. 20), Moxica (no. 26), Rodríguez (no. 8), Torre (no. 48), and Triana (nos. 5,

---

[35] This number would be reduced if items 83, 84, and 85 were correctly listed as movements of the same Magnificat.

[36] Primitive because for 3 instead of 4 voices: e.g., *CMC*, nos. 4, 11, 59. Only nine secular items in *CMC* are *a 4*. In *CMP* 143 songs are for four voices. The proportions of secular items *a 4* would be in the neighborhood of a tenth for *CMC* and a third for *CMP*. *CMC*, no. 2 is, however, for four voices whereas its concordance, *CMP*, no. 16, is for three.

[37] On the *CMC* and *CMP* versions of *Nuevas te traygo, Carillo* see below at pp. 270–271.

[38] *Muy triste* is in *CMP* (no. 23); *De vos* is in *CMP* (no. 17), Bologna Liceo Musicale Cod. 109 (fol. 127v.), and the same text – but with different music – in *CMH* (no. 5).

[39] In *Pues mi dicha* the Urrede tune is transposed an octave lower, rest-values diminished (in certain instances), and bars 9–13 (Anglés's transcription of *Nunca fué*) altogether omitted.

[40] *MME*, I, *106*, gives *Le pure amant*. But there is another letter between the "p" and the "u".

19, 22, 23, 28, 34, 35, 43, 66, 69, 70, 71, 80, 81, 82, 86, 88, 89, 90, 91). The total number of ascribed items in *CMC* reaches 31, the number of anonymous items being therefore 64. But this latter number is reduced to 54 when concordances in Monte Cassino MS 871 N and *CMP* are used to determine authorship.

As for the languages, the upper voice-part of Ockeghem's *Petite camusette* (no. 87) is written in a *chapurrado* mixture of Spanish and French. The text of *Le paure amant* (no. 94) is, as stated, limited to five words. But if there are no complete or uncorrupted French texts, there are on the other hand a dozen in Latin, all treating sacred subjects.

JUAN DE TRIANA [41] with twenty ascriptions [42] figures as largely in *CMC* as does Juan del Encina in *CMP*. With justice, then, one may begin a detailed study of the contents of *CMC* with Triana's *canciones*. None of his contributions to *CMC* ia a villancico in the classic sense of the word.

Isabel Pope has lengthily shown in her brilliant dissertation on the villancico [43] published in *Annales Musicologiques*, 1954, that this term was not used to designate a lyric form of poetry before approximately 1450, the first who used it having been the celebrated Marqués de Santillana (1398–1458).[44] Even he did not employ it, however, to designate anything but a poetic framework in which he inserted couplets (and one tercet) of folk-poetry. His isolated excursion into "low life" – that of the *villano* – was undertaken for the amusement of his three young daughters. As a musico-poetic term it occurs only once in *CMC*, the earliest musical source containing a villancico, namely at fol. 53r., in the upper left-hand margin of which the copyist has written the identifying word "Villancico" over Pedro Lagarto's *Andad, pasiones, andad*.

Already in *CMC*, as scrutiny of Lagarto's example will show, the word "villancico" meant a musico-poetic type in which the rhyme-scheme of the strophe spilled over into the musical da capo. In consequence, the poetic refrain began later than the musical refrain. This same Lagarto example is again found in *CMP* [45] which has been twice published – and is therefore easily available for study. In it one sees that the musical refrain, which always comes at the beginning of a villancico, comprises 14 bars (modern transcription). The poetic refrain–couplet, however, does not commence until bar 5 of the musical refrain. At the start of his musical *da capo* Lagarto continues instead with a rhymed-line belonging to the stanza. Only after this last rhymed-line does he proceed to the poetic refrain. This asymmetry of music and poetry is a cardinal principle in the classic villancico.

Triana's pieces with a refrain of any kind are in closed form, the musical da capo and poetic da capo coinciding. This fact is perhaps of more interest to literary than to

---

[41] Biographical information above at pp. 195–196.

[42] *Señora, qual soy venido* (*CMC*, no. 22) is ascribed to both Cornago and Triana.

[43] "Musical and Metrical Form of the Villancico," *Annales Musicologiques*, II (Paris: Société de Musique d'Autrefois, 1954), pp. 189–214.

[44] *Obras de Don Iñigo López de Mendoza, Marqués de Santillana*, ed. José Amador de los Rios (Madrid: Imp. de José Rodriguez, 1852), pp. 461–463. Entitled "Villançico," this poem consists of four stanzas of eight lines each, the rhyme-scheme being always *abba acca*. In the strophes a gallant speaks (in the first person) to *tres damas fermosas*. Each strophe culminates with some such line as "I then began to sing this song," after which two or three lines of a popular song are quoted by way of postscript. Santillana's poetry, in other words, sets the stage for the quoted lyrics. Used as here, the word *villançico* is merely a diminutive of *villano*, no more anticipating the classic significance of the term than a Domenico Scarlatti sonata anticipates a Mozart sonata.

[45] *CMP*, no. 279.

musical historians. It does, however, distinguish him from composers in the generation of Encina when the new open-form villancico all but vanquished the older closed-form canción. As for Lagarto's *Andad, pasiones, andad* – the villancico which appears in *CMC*, it obviously was a later insertion into the manuscript, the handwriting of both music and text differing from that in any of the surrounding items. Triana therefore need not even be thought of as old-fashioned at the time *CMC* was originally compiled.

The complete literary text of one canción with which his name is associated in *CMC* is preserved twice elsewhere in purely literary codices, the poetry having been written by Iñigo López de Mendoza, Marqués de Santillana. One can therefore confirm quite independently of *CMC* the fact that Triana did not compose "Barform" canciones (*ballades*), but instead, canciones agreeing with the virelai-pattern. This distinction is rather important. Indeed there is no evidence anywhere to be found that Renaissance Spanish song-composers ever chose the AAB musical pattern.[46] Their choice was always ABA insofar as the music was concerned.

The following is an annotated list of the Triana items in *CMC*.

Aquella buena muger, 3 v., *CMC*, no. 89, fol. 103. Rhyme-scheme: *AB cccb dddb AB eeeb fffb AB*. The music concords with *CMP*, no. 243. So do the literary refrain and four lines of the first strophe. Subject: amusement at the drunken stagger of a formerly attractive but now sottish woman. Musical structure: A‖:B:‖A‖:B:‖A. Imitation between tenor and upper voices distinguishes the opening refrain. Modality of both refrain and strophe: D (dorian). Duple meter (₵).

Benedicamus Domino, 3 v., *CMC*, no. 80, fols. 93v.–94. This is a mixolydian piece lasting only 44 breves (₵). A short point of imitation between middle and upper voices occurs at the opening. An alternate ending for the middle voice, in a lower range, has been copied in by a clumsy "corrector."

Benedicamus Domino, 3 v., *CMC*, no. 81, fols. 94v.–95. Lasting 42 breves (₵), this piece is divided into three phrases, the third of which begins with a point of imitation carried up from contrabaxo through tenor to tiple. Modality: D without flat.

Con temor biuo ojos tristes, 3 v., *CMC*, no. 19, fols. 31v.–32. Rhyme-scheme: *ABBA*. What should be the strophe lacks words, probably through the oversight of the copyist. Subject: dejection because the lover will never more behold his lady. Musical structure: A‖B‖A. Exact imitation at the lower octave occurs at the beginning between upper and middle voices. Modality: G with constant use of the accidental B♭, ficta or written in. Mensuration: ○. The instrumental character of the lower accompanying voice is indicated by its sudden breaking into a complete triad at the final cadence.

De mi perdida esperança, 3 v., *CMC*, no. 23, fols. 38v.–40. Rhyme-scheme: *ABAAB cdcd ABAAB*. Subject: the loss of all hope is the harder to endure because I, your lover, remember the tormenting past. Musical structure: A‖:B:‖A. "Key-signature": mixed – lowest with

---

[46] This fact in itself strongly suggests that Vincenet's *La pena sin ser sabida* should not be classed as a ballade. Rather it ought to be understood as a da capo (A‖:B:‖A), the repeated "B" section of which shows different first and second endings. If it is not a ballade, neither ought it to be classed as an "Encinian" villancico, the reason being that musical and poetic form run parallel in it. It is a canción, analogous in musical and poetic form to Triana's *De mi perdida esperança*.

two flats, middle and upper with one. The accidental E♮ is written into the upper voice-part near the close of the strophe. Modality: aeolian, the ending chord of both refrain and strophe being G and a signature of two flats controlling the lowest voice. Mensuration: ₵ (only the upper voice; the lower two have none).

Deus in adjutorium, 3 v., *CMC*, no. 66, fols. 85v.–86. A macaronic item, triple-meter sections in Latin, duple in Spanish. Eight bars (modern transcription) are in triple meter, then 15 in duple, then four in triple. Musical structure: AB (triple meter)‖C (duple meter) B (triple meter). Mensurations: 3, ₵, 3. Modality: mixolydian.

Dinos madre del donzel, 3 v., *CMC*, no. 90, fols. 103v.–104. Rhyme-scheme: *AA bb cccb*. Subject: in *AA bb* the questioners ask the Virgin to tell how she felt when Gabriel saluted her; in *cccb* Mary sings an unaccompanied solo (measured rhythm) saying she believed the angelic messenger. Musical structure: A (8 bars)‖B (8 bars)‖C (16 bars) – "C" being Mary's solo reply. Modality: D (dorian) without flat in "A" but with flat (in lower voice) in "B." Mensuration: ₵. This composition is unique because of its easy division throughout into four-bar phrases and because it ends with what appears to be an unaccompanied solo.

Juste Judex, 3 v., *CMC*, no. 82, fols. 95v.–97. See *supra*, pp. 197–199.

Juysio fuerte sera dado, 4 v., *CMC*, no. 91, fols. 104v.–105. See pp. 196 (n. 305) and 290.

La moça que las cabras cria, 4 v., *CMC*, no. 71, fol. 87. Rhyme-scheme: *AA bb AA*. Subject: bawdy invitation to a girl who tends goats. This is the first Spanish item thus far listed with a text under any voice except the treble. In this instance another text, not rhymed, is written beneath the tenor, the sense of which is an invitation to the sexual act. Musical structure: A‖:B:‖A. An extra note is found after a rest in the treble at the end of ‖:B:‖. Modality: C Major with authentic cadences at the close of each section. Mensuration: ₵.

Maravyllome, 3 v., *CMC*, no. 69, fols. 86 bis v.–86 ter. Rhyme-scheme: none. Musical structure: A‖B‖A. No text is copied under "B." Subject: I am astounded and cross myself because of the devil possessing you. Imitation between all three upper voices at the opening. Jaunty repeated-note figures give the "B" portion an especially popular flavor. Modality throughout: G (mixolydian). Duple meter (₵).

No consiento ni me plaze, 3 v., *CMC*, no. 43, fols. 64v.–65v. Rhyme-scheme: *ABAB cdcd A'B'A'B'*. An alternate third quatrain for use with the opening musical refrain is given with the remark: *otra* ("other"). Its rhyme-scheme: *EFEF*. Subject: I will not allow the young man who has struck her fancy to live but will seek him out; when I find him, though he be ready to serve her, yet will he never receive her into his arms. See transcription on opposite page. The text is, by way of exception, written under all three voice-parts.[47] Musical structure: A‖:B:‖A‖:B:‖A. Modality throughout: E (phrygian). A "written-in" g♯ appears near the beginning of the treble. Duple meter (₵).

No puedes quexar amor,[48] 3 v., *CMC*, no. 28, fols. 46v.–47v. Rhyme-scheme: *ABAB cdcd A'B'A'B'*. Subject: You cannot protest that you did not know, nor even less that I deserve my sorrow and your dismissal; because never have my thoughts wandered nor have I

---

[47] However: tenor and contra in the strophe ("B" section) are incompletely texted.

[48] Above the treble appears the abbreviated name "Diego "followed by an illegible word: then "Triana el son" (music by Triana). Presumably the copyist meant to give the name of the poet, then that of the composer.

No consiento ni me plaze *

Seville: Bibl. Colombina, sign. 7–1–28, fols. 64v.–65v.   [JUAN DE] TRIANA

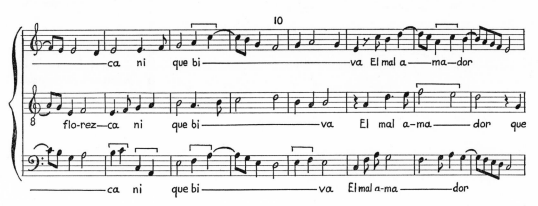

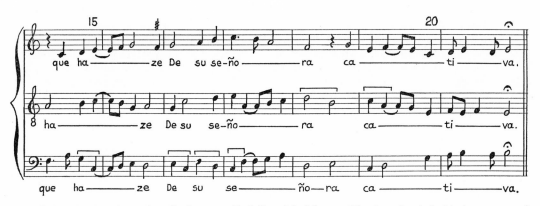

* I do not consent nor does it please me that the wicked lover with whom her ladyship is enamoured should flourish or even live.

On the contrary, when I find him burning to serve her, he will worship her with his hands but never receive her into his arms.

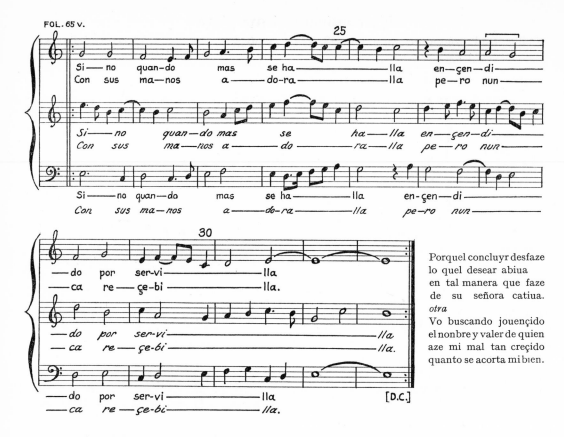

FOL. 65 v.

Si — no quan-do mas se ha — lla en-çen-di—
Con sus ma-nos a — do-ra — lla pe-ro nun

Si — no quan—do mas se ha—lla en-çen-di—
Con sus ma—nos a — do — ra—lla pe—ro nun—

Si — no quan—do mas se ha — lla en-çen-di—
Con sus ma-nos a — do-ra — lla pe-ro nun—

—do por ser-vi — lla
—ca re — çe-bi — lla.

—do por ser-vi — lla
—ca re — çe-bi — lla.

—do por ser-vi — lla
—ca re çe-bi — lla.   [D.C.]

Porquel concluyr desfaze
lo quel desear abiua
en tal manera que faze
de su señora catiua.
otra
Vo buscando jouençido
el nonbre y valer de quien
aze mi mal tan creçido
quanto se acorta mi bien.

desired aught but to serve you. Musical structure: A‖:B:‖A. Light imitation between the two upper voices occurs at bars 24 and 29. Modality: A (aeolian); "B" section ends on an E [Major] chord. Duple meter (₵).

Non puedo dexar querer, 3 v., *CMC*, no. 86, fols. 100v.–101. Different texts in each voice: top voice, "Non puedo"; middle, "Querer vieja yo no"; bottom, "Que non se filar ni aspar." This composition is a quodlibet of which the only other example in the early cancioneros would seem to be Peñalosa's *Por las sierras* (*CMP*, no. 311). Subject-matter: picaresque and amatory; see accompanying example for text and translation (p. 216). Beginning at bar 21_3 Triana introduces a new tune in the lowest voice, *Perdi la mi rueca*. This latter concords with the top voice of *CMP*, no. 253. Although concordances for the *Querer vieja* and *Que non se filar* tunes have not yet been located, the flavor of these is equally popular. The top voice, however, may like Peñalosa's (*CMP*, no. 311) have been freely composed.

O pena que me conbates, 3 v., *CMC*, no. 5, fols. 9v., 11r. (folio 10 is missing). Only top and tenor of the refrain and contra of the strophe are found in *CMC*. Rhyme-scheme of refrain: *ABAB*. Subject: Your beauty slays me.

Pinguele respinguete, 3 v., *CMC*, no. 70, fol. 86 ter. Rhyme-scheme: *aa bbbb a*. This is not a refrain-song, even though bars 4–5 equal 15–16. Subject: jocular report of a woman with five children, perhaps by a priest. Musical structure: three short phrases each ending with a fermata over a G-chord. Phrase I begins with a point of imitation between contra, tenor, and treble; phrase II with light imitation between tenor and treble. Modality: G (mixolydian). Duple meter (₵).

Por beuer comadre, 3 v., *CMC*, no. 88, fol. 102v. Words and music concord with *CMP*, no. 235. Rhyme-scheme: *A bcdc A dcec A*. Subject: give me a drink, barmaid, you who have my skirt in pawn; make my eye glisten and my head dance with your wine. Musical structure: A‖:B:‖A. Short point of imitation between tenor and treble at opening. Modality: E (phrygian). Duple meter (₵).

Quien vos dio tal señorio, 4 v., *CMC*, no. 34, fols. 53v.–54. Rhyme-scheme: *ABBA cdcd ABBA*. Subject: the power of beauty to captivate. See example overleaf (pp. 214–215) for complete text and translation. Musical structure A‖:B:‖A. Modality: D (dorian). Mensuration sign: ○.

Señora, qual soy venido, 3 v., *CMC*, no. 22, fols. 36v.–38. Crowded in above the secular text – of which the author was the Marqués de Santillana – can be seen a sacred text which, though inserted in some contemporary hand, is obviously not the writing of the scribe who copied the music and the secular text.[49] Cornago's name appears at the top of fol. 36v. above the treble voice-part, Triana's at the top of fol. 37 above the contra. Since tenor and treble make a perfect duet, the most obvious explanation is that Triana added the florid contra. His addition would therefore compare exactly with that of Madrid who added a new part to Cornago's duet, *Pues que Dios te fiso tal* (*CMP*, no. 5). The Cornago-Triana music (with secular text, *Señora qual soy*) concords with *CMP*, no. 52. Aside from differences in passing-notes, ligatures, and occasional accidentals, the *CMC* version differs in being longer by two bars (= two breves). Rhyme-scheme of the secular text: *ABBA cdcd A'EEA' [fgfg A'HHA' ijij A'KKA']*. Subject: Lady, just as I came so I depart, heavy-hearted, because you have not rewarded my patient suit; but though I perish of love I am still your humble servitor, hoping against hope. Musical structure: A‖:B:‖A. The first and second phrases of "A" begin imitatively – first phrase at the lower octave with tenor following the treble, second at the upper octave with treble following the tenor. Mixed signature, the contra with B♭, the other voices without flat. Modality: dorian (ending on G). Duple meter (₵).

Ya de amor era partido, 3 v., *CMC*, no. 35, fols. 54v.–56. Rhyme-scheme: *ABAB cdcd ABAB*. Subject: Although love had fled because of your cruelty a single gesture made me return; such charm vanquishes me. Musical structure: A‖:B:‖A. Light imitation distinguishes the second phrase and the close of "A." Mixed signature with B♭ in the contra and no flats in tenor and treble. Modality: G (dorian) in "A"; B♭ (lydian) in "B." Mensuration: ○.

FOURTEEN of these twenty enumerated Triana pieces are secular. Of the fourteen, a dozen are in the closed da capo form typical throughout *CMC* (but not *CMP*). If we disregard *O pena* because one of its leaves is missing, his methods can be thus summarized: (1) for picaresque texts he chooses ionian or phrygian modes, for sentimental lyrics dorian or aeolian; (2) refrain and strophe belong to the same mode, with one exception; (3) although he changes meter at will in through-composed songs, he does not change in da capo pieces; (4) his only mensuration signs are ○, 3,[50] and ₵, the latter occurring thrice as frequently as the others; (5) imitation though frequently used at

---

[49] To the left of the first word in the secular text appears, in another hand, the word "corregida" (i.e. emended). We take this to be an annotation by the scribe who inserted the sacred text above the profane.

[50] "*3*" is used only in *Deus in adjutorium*.

Quien vos dio tal señorio *

Seville: Bibl. Colombina, sign. 7–1–28, fols. 53 v.–54.   [JUAN DE] TRIANA

* Who gave you such dominion that only looking at you enslaved me and makes me yours rather than my own?

Your beauty caused me to desire that I be yours; your grace set the bounds of my imprisonment.

starts never carries far and is never rigorous; (6) he fills the gaps at intermediate phrase-ends in the treble with movement in the accompanying voices; (7) three items out of twenty (two secular and one sacred) are scored *a 4*, the rest *a 3*; (8) he holds the voice-ranges within tight bounds, the contra never descending below G_1 (except in *La moça* to F_1) and only in *Maravyllome* rising to e – the treble never rising above c^1 (except in *No puedes* and *No consiento* where it reaches d^1); (9) two "written-in" sharps invade his *CMC* repertory (twelfth note in treble of *Dinos donsella* [fol. 104] and similarly the twelfth in the treble of *No consiento* [fol. 64v.], both perhaps added by a later hand); (10) sixteen "written-in" accidental flats (B♭ or E♭) [51] on the other hand appear, all of which

[51] *Benedicamus I* (contra, m. 11), *Con temor* (contra, m. 1; treble, m. 2), *De mi perdida* (tenor, m. 3; contra, m. 40; treble, m. 46), *Juste Judex* (contra, m. 25), *Juysio* (contra, m. 6), *Maravyllome* (contra, m. 16), *Quien vos* (treble, m. 8; tenor, m. 18), *Ya de amor* (contra, m. 24; treble, mm. 25, 26, 30; tenor, m. 31).

Non puedo dexar querer

Seville: Bibl. Colombina, sign. 7–1–28, fols. 100 v.–101.   [JUAN DE] TRIANA

* I don't want to love an old woman, Good Lord, no; an old woman like Sarah, her breasts hanging like a guitar. Already because of my burning she gave me a piece of disagreeable skin. Go away, you old hag, with your animal hide. You sigh like a maiden and pretend that love overpowers you. But you haven't a front tooth nor a molar. You eat like a cow[ewe] chewing her cud. Go away, you old hag.

** Because I don't spin nor gather yarn nor reel it and my husband bought me a whole lot of flax, the dogs and cats have made a bed in it.

I lost my distaff and spindle. Have you seen the knob rolling over here? I lost my distaff wound with flax. I found a gut filled with wine. Have you seen the knob rolling over there?

*** [He] I can't stop wanting you and loving you, even though your jealous husband gives me a hard life without any rest. All would turn out happily if you would satisfy my desire. I can't stop wanting you and loving you.

[She] They blame me for a bad one because I loved you, but even though they keep on complaining I will not stop if you want me. Love me with a mad love. I can't repay with less love, for even though they continue complaining I will not stop.

seem to be in the hand of the original scribe; (11) of the four items with mixed signatures, one carries two flats in the contra; (12) he frequently requires the contra to leap up an octave (especially at closes) but uses the Landini-sixth cadence in the treble quite rarely; [52] (13) in the treble wide skips are extremely hard to find, sixths of any kind being unknown, fifths unusual, and even fourths an event; (14) leaps on the other hand of fifths and octaves (though not of sixths) freely appear in the contra; (15) cadences can almost invariably be analyzed as V–I, IV–I, or V–VI; (16) at the final cadence the tenor always sounds an octave with the treble; (17) elsewhere the tenor always makes a consonance with the treble – fourths never separating them on strong beats.

JOHANNES CORNAGO follows Triana as the second most prolific *CMC* composer. Even so, his total reaches only a bare half-dozen.[53] One of these, *Porque mas sin duda creas* seems to be a unicum. The others occur either in *CMP* or in Monte Cassino MS 871 N.

Of the five concording items *Qu'es mi vida preguntays* arouses the most immediate interest, it bearing a double ascription in the Monte Cassino source. That Ockeghem

---

[52] *Benedicamus I*, final cadence; *Deus in adjutorium*, mm. 7–8 and final cadence; *Dinos madre del donzel*, mm. 3–4; *No puedes quexar amor*, mm. 6–7; *Non puedo dexar querer*, mm. 16–17 and final.

[53] This half-dozen includes two songs the authorship of which he shared (*Qu'es mi vida* with Ockeghem; *Señora qual soy* with Triana).

should have had a hand in its composition, as Monte Cassino affirms, can be validated from internal evidence – and need not be believed solely because of the double attribution. Cornago's other songs were composed *a 3*.[54] Moreover the contras in the present instance depart radically from his known style. The lowest voice in *Qu'es mi vida* touches bottom D_1 fourteen times. Such low notes are all but unheard of in the music of the cancioneros.[55] But Ockeghem, composer of *Interemata Dei Mater*,[56] freely called for D_1's, descending on occasion to C_1. Even more to the point, the harmonies change at asymmetrical time-intervals in *Qu'es mi vida* and chords in what would now be called "first inversion" frequently appear on strong beats. Such asymmetry is a known hallmark of Ockeghem's style. It is, on the other hand, alien to the style of any cancionero composer. Certainly it is foreign to Cornago's style as disclosed in *CMP*, nos. 2, 38, and 52, or in the accompanying transcription of his *Porque mas sin duda* (*CMC*, no. 27).

If the range of the bass and the asymmetry of the harmonic flow suggest another composer, what voice-parts can on the contrary be plausibly labeled as Cornago's? First, the treble with its Spanish text. The cadences at mm. 16 and 24–25 exactly duplicate those at mm. 33–34 and 63–64 in *CMP*, no. 38 (an authentic Cornago item). If the treble belongs to Cornago so must also the tenor. The fact that the tenor and treble make a canon at the unison in mm. 27–31 cannot perhaps be called conclusive evidence since the bass has been cleverly made to share in the *Vorimitation*. But with Cornago's duet to suggest the idea, Ockeghem (granted he composed the bass) was too great an artist to have missed improving on Cornago's original idea. More important is the fact that in *Qu'es mi vida*, as in all Cornago's part-songs, the tenor and treble together make a complete harmony at all times. Whatever may be said of the other voices, these were made for each other. A fourth never occurs between them on a strong beat. An octave always separates them at ends of sections.

Having accounted for contra II (bottom voice), treble, and tenor, we are left with contra I. This voice, too, can be credited to Ockeghem on the following internal evidence: (1) treble, contra I, and tenor do not make a satisfactory three-part composition, even though treble and tenor together make a self-sufficient duet; (2) the delayed cadence caused by the last two notes in contra I is typical of Ockeghem's endings but not of Cornago's (which end with all the voices coming to a halt at once); (3) the rest at the end of measure 16 in contra II has obviously been inserted for one reason only – to get contra

---

[54] Anglés in *MME*, I, *105* (line 1) classified *Porque mas sin duda* as a 3- and 4-part composition, probably because in this instance the *CMC* scribe copied the tenor of the "B" part twice – the first time (fol. 45v.) leaving out 21 notes, the second time (fol. 46) correcting the mistake. The omitted notes were those (in our transcription) from mm. 37–42. The scribe's eye doubtless travelled from one phrase over two intervening ones, because of the likeness in phrase-endings (the last three notes before the rest in m. 37 and in m. 42 equal each other). *Olvyda tu perdiçion España* (*CMC*, no. 52) is another piece with a scribal error of the same kind. The copyist in the latter case corrected his mistake not by writing out the tenor-part anew but rather by using a carat at the spot where the notes had been omitted and then another carat at the end of the tenor-part to show where the omitted notes were subjoined.

[55] *CMP* (458 items) shows a lower note than F_1 in only nos. 57 (*Malos adalides fueron* by Badajoz) and 287 (*Todo quanto yo serví* by Baena). Lope de Baena's piece lacks any text beyond the first phrase. The lowest note in the contra of each is D_1.

[56] A. Smijers, ed., *Van Ockeghem tot Sweelinck*, I (Amsterdam: G. Alsbach, 1939), pp. 3–11.

II out of contra I's way at this particular moment; (4) the melodic line in contra I is quite different from the line in Cornago's own authenticated contras – as comparison with the contra in *Porque mas sin duda*, by way of example, soon discloses.

Fortunately external as well as internal evidence clinches the case. Monte Cassino contains Cornago's three-voiced original. Those who catalogued his songs prior to Isabel

Qu'es mi vida preguntays *

CMC, fols. 24 v.–25.   CORNAGO-OCKEGHEM [1469]

* You ask what my life is like: I cannot deny that a life spent in deeply loving and lamenting is what you have inflicted on me.

Who would have served you as faithfully as I during my weary life, or who could so have suffered?

** B₁, C, D, B₁ in *CMC*.

Pope missed it, because the text is defective. She, however, showed that the *canción a 3* formerly credited to him with the title *Preguntays no vos la qu[i]ero negar* is nought else but the superius-tenor duet of *Qu'es mi vida preguntays* joined to his own less suave contra.

Of the visit of *le premier chappellain et maistre de la chappelle du roy nostre sire*, we know that he received a travel grant for a "trip from Tours to the kingdom of Spain in January 1469." [57] Only one Spanish MS, however, preserves anything by him – *CMC*.[58] For every historical as well as esthetic reason, then, *Qu'es mi vida* deserves close study.

[57] Michel Brenet, *Musique et musiciens de la vielle France* (Paris: Librairie Félix Alcan, 1911), p. 39.

[58] Anglés was not aware of the fact that *CMC*, no. 87, *Petite camusette (S'elle m'amera je ne scay)*, is by Ockeghem. (El Escorial MS IV. a. 24 cannot be counted a "Spanish" manuscript.)

Cornago's own disdain of the contra shows up at once in *CMP*, nos. 2 and 38. If he will have his way, the contra exists only to complement the treble-tenor duet. In consequence he endows it with no real interest or beauty of its own. Subtracted from the other voices and played alone, his contras sound angular, humpbacked. He takes no pains to avoid such wide intervals as major sevenths and ninths within a phrase. He outlines tritones which cannot be erased unless one applies an irresponsible number of ficta acccidentals.

In order that the kind of contra Ockeghem added may be conveniently compared with Cornago's, we print the thus-far unedited *Porque mas sin duda*. Ninths and sevenths crop up in the contra at mm. 10, 20, 35–36; but not in the other parts. It is for these other voices that he reserves his imitations (mm. 13–14, 25–28, 40–42). The one time the contra does rhyme (meas. 2), the tenor has already sung the motto (first three notes).

The overall effect of the three voices sounding together is on the other hand quite gratifying. Rhythmic motion is evenly distributed among all the parts. When the song is performed, the likenesses of mm. 19–21₃ and 33–36 are even more apparent than on paper.

The words in *Porque mas sin duda* bristle with the scorned lover's desire for revenge. Like Triana, he seems to have reserved the dorian mode for tender or plaintive songs (*Donde estas, Gentil dama,* and *Pues que Dios* [*CMC*, nos. 10, 4, and 18] and the ionian or phrygian for harsh or bitter ones. Within the limits of his own idiom he knows how to touch the listener's heart. His *Donde estas* ("Where are you?") [59] shows his methods. When the lover protests that each day of his mistress's absence seems ten centuries, he assigns the treble a panting repeated-note figure (setting the words *mill años*), the obvious purpose of which is to express the lover's impatience in musical terms. In both *Donde estas* and *Porque mas sin duda* he interpolates fermatas near the end of each strophe-couplet, doubtless for dramatic effect. Certainly the words after the fermata in *Donde estas* are climactic (*iuventut* = youth; *salut* = health). In *Donde estas* – his only *CMC* canción in which he allows the contra to participate in the imitative play – the imitation is made to serve a dramatic purpose. The treble leads with the cry, "Where are you?" Contra and tenor echo it in succession. Compared with Triana's texts Cornago's may seem to cover a smaller gamut of emotion. But if their subject is invariably *Liebesfreud* or *Liebesleid*, he at least responds to the shades of emotion with musical settings that can be differentiated.

[59] *CMC*, fols. 17v.–19. Concordance in Monte Cassino MS 871 N, fols. 9v.–10. For the texts of Cornago's Monte Cassino songs, see Isabel Pope, "La musique espagnole à la Cour de Naples dans la seconde moitié du xve siècle," in *Musique et Poésie au XVIe Siècle* (Paris: Centre National de la Recherche Scientifique, 1954), pp. 46–50. Her reading of *Qu'es mi vida preguntays* (pp. 49–50) shows corrections from the Bibliothèque Nationale literary concordance. She identifies Don Diego de Castilla, a courtier at Naples c. 1460, as the author of *Donde estás*.

Porque mas sin duda *

CMC, fols. 44 v.–46.   CORNAGO

Porque mas sin du—da cre—as Mi grand
Pues que muer—te me de—seas Sin te—
Porque mas sin duda creas
Porque mas sin duda creas

pe—na la do—lo—ri—da De
ner me—re—sçi—da
—te Dios tan tri—ste vi—da

* In order that you may better appreciate my sorrowful anguish, may God inflict on you the misery of loving and never being loved nor cared for.

And with such a lot I believe that you would appreciate the terrible misery which you cause me without my deserving it.

Since you desire my death without my deserving it, may God inflict on you the misery of loving and of never being loved nor cared for.

** In the MS B♮ appears as "signature" in the first, but is omitted in all succeeding staves.

JOHANNAS URREDE [60] ranks third in *CMC*. Concordances for all three of his *CMC* songs (*Nunca fué pena mayor*, no. 9; *Muy triste será mi vida*, no. 11; and *De vos i de mí quexoso*, no. 32) can be found in *CMP* (nos. 1, 23, and 17, respectively). All are in triple

---

[60] Biographical details at p. 203. Giovanni Spataro commends *Gioanni di Vbrede* in his *Tractato di musica* (Venice: Bernardino de Vitali, 1531) at fols. d i verso and h iv verso for the use of proportions in the Benedictus of *una sua messa*, but without naming the mass. Since Spataro does not know the title of Urrede's mass, though twice referring to the same sequence of "time-signatures" (C followed by ◖) as an admirable

*** Contra in MS shows an extra C after this ligature.

meter (mensuration sign: Æ). In *CMC*, all are for three voices. Lastly, each is a closed-form canción. This last generalization will seem erroneous to a student who consults the literary text of his *Muy triste* printed in the 1890 edition of *CMP*. The faulty transcription of the eleventh line in *Muy triste* there encountered has, however, been set right in José Romeu's revision of the texts for the 1947-1951 edition of *CMP*.

Though their structure allies Urrede's canciones with Triana's or Cornago's, their style and substance show notable divergences. Barbieri himself saw the difference when he wrote: "The style of his three compositions in our cancionero resembles that of the Flemings more than that of the native Spaniards c. 1490-1510; which fact of itself would induce us to support the assertion that Johannes Urrede was in reality a Fleming." [61] What were the qualities that gave Barbieri the right to call his style more

way of indicating proportions (two minims in C equalling three in Ⅽ), he perhaps repeats mere hearsay. Ramos, his mentor, of course knew Urrede personally. Spataro's is the latest printed praise, apparently, that Urrede was to earn in the century after his death. But the memory of his music was kept green by Luys Venegas de Henestrosa who published in 1557 Cabezón's *glosado* version of Urrede's Tarazona Pange lingua (see above, p. 203, note 22); by Juan Pérez Roldán who wrote a Mass c. 1669 on the *Pange lingua de Urreda* (*AM*, VII, 198); and even so late as 1707 by Antonio Martín y Coll who in that year cifered a new keyboard arrangement of the same Tarazona Pange lingua glossed by Cabezón. Copied at fols. 38v.–39 in Biblioteca Nacional (Madrid) MS 1358 (*Flores de Música*, Vol. II), Martín y Coll's *Pange lingua de Urea* is however pitched a minor third below Cabezón's gloss.

[61] *Cancionero musical de los siglos XV y XVI*, pp. 47–48. For a digest of other opinions see Helen Hewitt, *op. cit.*, p. 85 (c. 2).

representative of Flemish than Spanish art? The following several answers may at least prove suggestive.

I His melodic lines in his "Barcelona" *Pange lingua* [62] as in his canciones are always quite supple; he achieves a "moist" quality not only by wandering freely up and down the scale, but also by beginning successive melodic phrases on different parts of the measure, i.e. beat 1, beat 3, beat $1\frac{1}{2}$, beat 2. On the other hand, in indigenous Spanish pieces the lines tend to pivot more around one scale note and to start and stop at symmetrical rhythmic moments. As a result they usually seem less weaving.

II Urrede's chord-changes result from a juxtaposition of melodic lines and not vice versa; only at cadences does he emphasize the IV–I or V–I relationships. Spanish composers are on the other hand constantly aware of the "harmonic function of each bass-note," and within the phrase write many more IV–I or V–I progressions.

III At a cadence Urrede is willing for the bass to drop out just before the resolution. The Spanish composer wants the bass [= contra] to be sounding both on the "V" and the "I" – an insistence which foreshadows the baroque concept of continuous bass.

IV Because of his lithesome melodic lines, the wider spacing of his cadences and his less rigorous harmonic ideas, Urrede's "beats" fall more lightly than in the usual song by indigenous Spaniards of the period.

V The pulse may seem lighter because in all his canciones (as well as his "Barcelona" *Pange lingua*) he chooses a languid triple meter. Three times as many pieces by Triana on the other hand are in duple as in triple meter; only one of the six pieces in *CMC* associated with Cornago's name is in triple meter, the other five being all in duple.

VI Urrede, as would be natural in the case of a Fleming writing music to Spanish texts, seems considerably less sensitive to the meanings of individual words; there are no breathless "mill años" in his settings as in Cornago's. The Spaniards seem, on the other hand, eager to experiment even with harmonic novelties in order to enforce the meanings of important words.

In order that these various comparisons may be tested by the reader, Urrede's *Nunca fué* is here presented on one page, and on the opposite a setting by Belmonte (a *CMC* unicum at fols. 40v.–41). In Belmonte's *Pues mi dicha non consiente* Urrede's superius is transposed an octave lower to become the tenor. Even while working with such an alien tenor, Belmonte however still betrays certain of the "Spanish traits" to which reference has just been made. To enumerate the distinctions: (1) Belmonte in mm. 2–8 hugs e^1, rather than freely divagating. In each *parte* he chooses a small tessitura. (2) In the first 14 measures he writes a chain of "chords" that when analyzed in terms of root-progression shows 23 movements of a fourth or fifth in the root. But in Urrede's "harmonization" of exactly the same melody-notes only nine such movements

[62] Printed in *Anuario Musical*, VII (1952), pp. 199–200.

Nunca fue pena mayor *

CMC, fols. 16v.–17.   JOHANNES URREDE [.jo. Vrede]

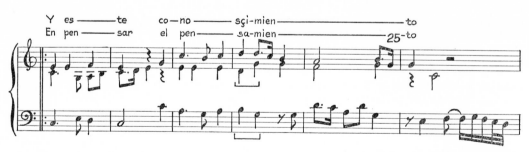

* Never was there greater sorrow nor wilder torment than the pain which I have suffered because of [your] deceit.

     This knowledge makes my days so gloomy while I consider how you requited my affection that I am made to believe death itself would be less of an evil than the torment and pain which I have suffered because of [your] deceit.

Fa-se mis di——as tan tris——————tes.
Que por a—mo——res me dis——————tes.

[D.C]

Pues mi dicha non consiente *

CMC, fols. 40 v.–41.

BELMONTE

FOL. 40 v.
5

Pues mi di—cha non con-sien——te que es-te
Mas mi pues de vos ab—sen—te

TENOR   FOL. 40 v.

Pues mi dicha

CONTRA   FOL. 41

Pues mi dicha

10

do os pue————da ser-vir No cum-ple si—no
ten-go tris————te de bi—vir

* Since my lot will not permit me to be where I may serve you naught remains for me save death.
Neither patience nor prudence alleviate the sad life caused by your painful absence.
With you gone, I lead such a sad life that naught remains for me save death.

of a fourth or fifth in the root are found to occur.[63] (3) Belmonte is so determined to have his contra sing through every cadence that he even writes parallel fifths (measure 7) in order to insure that the V–I progression be heard in the bass. Urrede at the analogous moment in the progress of his melody also writes a V–I cadence, but excludes the contra from participating in the resolution (see mm. 7–8). (4) If it is conceded that skips in the bass result in strong "beats," then we can easily prove that the beats in Belmonte are stronger than those in Urrede. Though Belmonte omits a phrase and therefore writes 14 measures before his first double-bar, whereas Urrede writes 20; in 14 measures he writes 25 skips but Urrede in 20 measures only 17 skips. As with Cornago's contras, Belmonte places the top of every contra leap involving a seventh or ninth on a strong beat. (5) The Spanish preference for duple meter as against a languid triple meter cannot be proved by reference to Belmonte's setting. But only one of Urrede's Spanish coetaneans made much use of the $\bigcirc[=\frac{3}{2}]$ mensuration — Francisco de la

---

[63] "Harmonic" analyses would be anachronistic, but root-movements of a fifth or fourth occur at these locations in Belmonte: 2_1–2_2; 2_2–2_3; 3_1–3_2; 3_2–3_3; 3_3–$3_{3\frac{1}{2}}$; 4_3–5_1; 5_1–5_2; 5_2–5_3; 6_1–$6_{1\frac{1}{2}}$; $6_{1\frac{1}{2}}$–6_2; 6_2–6_3; 7_1–$7_{1\frac{1}{2}}$; $7_{1\frac{1}{2}}$–7_2; $7_{2\frac{1}{2}}$–7_3; 7_3–8_1; 8_1–8_2; 8_2–8_3; 9_2–9_3; 10_1–10_2; $11_{3\frac{1}{2}}$–12_1; 12_1–$12_{1\frac{1}{2}}$; 13_1–$13_{1\frac{1}{2}}$; 13_2–$13_{2\frac{1}{2}}$.

They occur at these places in Urrede: 1_3–2_1; 3_1–$3_{1\frac{1}{2}}$; 5_3–6_1; 6_3–7_1; 7_3–8_1; 15_3–16_1; 16_2–16_3; $17_{1\frac{1}{2}}$–17_2; 17_2–$17_{2\frac{1}{2}}$. The Urrede count could be slightly extended by considering 7_2–$7_{2\frac{1}{2}}$ and $7_{2\frac{1}{2}}$–7_3 as "chord-changes." The reader is reminded that only melody-notes used by both composers are considered in making the count.

Torre, the others all neglecting it. (6) Belmonte writes an extremely interesting G♯ at measure 16. In consequence, the next note must be D♯ in the superius (underpinned with G♯ in the contra). This G♯ is no impossibility. If one questions it, then the validity of the C♯ in m. 14 and of the F♯ in m. 18 would also have to be questioned: the more reason to believe that the G♯ is intentional. It does match the "tal vida y tristura" of which the poet complains. If Belmonte's treble just here

> sings so out of tune
> Straining harsh discords and unpleasing sharps
> *(Romeo and Juliet*, III, v, 27–28)

he has but given the poetry the kind of musical setting that Shakespeare's most famous young pair of lovers thought they heard at their first moment of separation.

The composers thus-far named – Triana, Cornago, Urrede, and Belmonte – account for 29 songs in *CMC*. Ten other Spaniards account for another dozen items.[64]

Enrique

TWO four-part songs, *Pues con sobra de tristura* (*CMC*, no. 2; *CMP*, no. 16) and *Mi querer tanto vos quiere* (*CMC*, no. 30; *CMP*, no. 29), seem to be Enrique's sole pair to have entered the Noah's Ark of the cancioneros. Barbieri in 1890, and following him Anglés in 1947, did, it is true, claim for him one other song, *Pues serviço vos desplase* (*CMP*, no. 27). But this third song has been shown by Manfred Bukofzer[65] from a concordance at Perugia to have been composed by the English singer in Burgundian service, Robert Morton, who died in 1475. As for Enrique's two authenticated songs, both are anonymous in *CMC*. Both must be classed as closed-form canciones rather than classic-type villancicos. In both he chooses duple meter and dorian mode. The one voices a lover's lament, the other a lover's entreaty.

The only Enrique who now seems a likely candidate for the composer was a singer in the service of Charles, Prince of Viana – the pretender to the Aragonese crown who died at Barcelona on September 23, 1461. From the executors of the latter's estate he received "two books of music which he had composed."[66] Because Enrique = Henry, Barbieri suggested in his 1890 edition that Herry Bredemers of Antwerp (1472–1522), the famous organist who twice visited Spain in Philip the Fair's company, might have composed the Enrique items.[67] Sensing the foreign flavor of the canción which Bukofzer has now shown to have been Morton's, he felt certain that Enrique must have been an

---

[64] If *Nuevas te traigo Carillo* in its three-voiced version (*CMC*, no. 59) be considered as Encina's, then the number of items the composers of which can be identified would be raised to thirteen. See pp. 270–271, for further discussion of this problem.

[65] *MME*, X, *23–24*.

[66] *DML*, I, 819.

[67] Barbieri, p. 32.

extranjero. But the two authenticated canciones lack characteristically Flemish touches. Moreover both were copied into *CMC* at the same time the Cornago and Triana items were transcribed – i.e. before Bredemers's first visit to Spain.

[Juan Pérez de] Gijón (fl. 1480)

PRIOR to enrolment as a singer in Ferdinand's chapel choir Gijón held a canonry in the collegiate church of Saints Justo and Pastor at Alcalá de Henares, his title being *Canónigo del coro del Abad*.[68] On Februray 27, 1480, when appointed a singer in the Aragonese court chapel, he was listed as *Johan Xixon*. In the chapel accounts of 1485 his name is spelled two other ways: *Johan Gigon* and *Johan Perez Gijon*.[69]

Just as two songs are all that survive by Enrique, so *Al dolor de mi cuidado* (*CMC*, no. 38; *CMP*, no. 40; *CMS*, no. 168) and *Ruego a Dios que amando mueras* (*CMP*, no. 41) are Gijón's only extant pieces. *Al dolor* is incomplete in *CMC* because fol. 59, on which should have appeared the contra of the first part and all three voices of the second, is missing. It still enjoyed such wide vogue forty years after he became a royal singer that Gil Vicente could introduce it into his *Côrtes de Jupiter*,[70] written for performance in August of 1521 at the royal palace in Lisbon.

Both of Gijón's songs tell a lover's woes. Imitation is lightly used in *Al dolor*. But *Ruego a Dios* is a cantus firmus composition, the tenor of which intones the responsory for the dead, *Memento mei, Deus*, in the first part and *De profundis* in the second. The phrase-endings in both songs (the cadences subsiding into a long-held note in all the voice-parts at once), the ruggedness of the chord-movements (IV–I and V–I being favorite choices), and the tightness of the two top melody lines (as wide a treble skip as a fifth appearing but once within any phrase of *Al dolor*) [71] are all traits which can justly be called typical – not only of Gijón, but of Spanish secular polyphony in general c. 1490. If Gijón has any individual mannerism it must be his frequent use of the dotted semibreve followed by the minim (unreduced time-values).

Hurtado de Xeres [72] [Jérez]

IN THE TOP margin before the treble of both songs by Hurtado de Xeres a fifteenth-century scribe wrote the word, "buena," [73] i.e. good. Only Hurtado's songs bear this comment in *CMC*. Both are unica. Nothing is known of the composer's life, though he may have come from Jérez (between Seville and Cadiz).

[68] *Ibid.*, p. 36.
[69] *DML*, I, 1067.
[70] *Copilaçam de todalas obras* (Lisbon: Ioam Aluarez, 1562), fol. 168, c. 1, line 31.
[71] Mm. 67–68.
[72] "de Exerea" in *MME*, I, *103* and *105*. "de Exereo" in *DML*, II, 1258. Simón de la Rosa y López, *op. cit.*, pp. 70–71, gave the name correctly (Hurtado de Xerez = Xeres) as long ago as 1904.
[73] The annotation "buena, corregida" precedes his second song.

No tenga nadie sperança *

CMC, fols. 60v.–61.

HURTADO DE XERES

No ten———ga na-die sper———an———ça en
Te-ma sien———pre su mu—dan-ça no

No tenga nadie sperança

No tenga nadie sperança

ha-llar————se muy di—cho———
pre-su————ma de di—cho———

—so que de amor y su mu-dan—ça es lo mas cier————to
—so quen su glo-ria y esper-an—ça es lo mas cier————to

* I have no hope of finding happiness, since your fickleness in love makes uncertainty certain. I used to look diligently to see whom you favored; but to be very favored is to be lost indeed. Always fearing your inconstancy I do not expect to be happy; for your beauty and my anxiety make uncertainty certain.

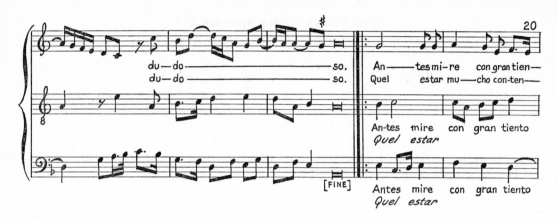

His songs sob lovers' laments *a 3* in phrygian mode. He casts *No tenga nadie sperança* (no. 40) in triple and *Con temor de la mudança* (no. 42) in duple meter. In the first of these he betrays heavy indebtedness to *Nunca fué pena mayor*. His treble, for instance, follows much the same contour as Urrede's during the entire "A" section. The resemblance is the more striking because both composers bring their first phrases to a cadence on identical notes at identical rhythmic moments.[74] In consequence, Hurtado's paraphrase strikes the listener as a "Canción contrahecha a *Nunca fué pena mayor*, letra y punto." [75]

Both Hurtado's songs carry a mixed signature, with B♭ in the contra. In *No tenga* at mm. 4–5 and in *Con temor* at mm. 12–13 chord-successions involving the B♭ major triad and the A minor in close juxtaposition are found. His chords, although he writes only *a 3*, are complete triads in an unusually large number of instances. His tenor creates a fourth with his treble on a strong beat only once,[76] and that one time as a passing-note. The cadence of the under-third or the upward skip of an octave in the

[74] Cadence at mm. 7–8 in both songs. The correspondence is less close between mm. 17–18 of the Hurtado and 18–19 of the Urrede. Urrede uses a chain of first-inversions at mm. 18–19. Hurtado finds another way of ending his "A" section.

[75] To be sure, the exact lengths in bars of the "A" and "B" sections differ in both songs. But the poetic schemes exactly correspond.

[76] *Con temor*, m. 9.

contra does not appear. Frequently, however, Hurtado does use the melodic figure which for want of a better label has been called the "incomplete" nota cambiata.

Like Triana, he holds his voice-ranges within narrow compass. The contra never descends below A_1. Only once does the treble climb to d^1.[77] The tenor in both songs, though not texted, seems equally "melodious" with the treble. It moves just as rapidly, the rests are spaced to come at ends of rational phrases, and the leaps sound lyrical rather than instrumental. Such roughnesses as consecutive fifths do not mar the part-writing. Because of the adept workmanship, these songs well deserve the praise of the word "buena," written by the admiring fifteenth-century scribe.

Juanes

THE COMPOSER of *Tu valer me da gran guerra* (*CMC*, no. 67) is not likely to have been *Juanes de Anchieta capellan e cantor de su alteza*,[78] the reason being that its contra is rough to the point of uncouthness. In the first two bars (= two breves of the original) the contra, for instance, descends in the following ungainly fashion: d–B[♮]–G–C–B_1♭. The piece is, however, so slight that even with a smoother contra it would not add to Anchieta's fame.

The musical structure is the usual da capo one, with the "B" section repeated. Both "A" and "B" are in mixolydian mode. Tenor and treble begin and end on octaves, and in intervening moments make a self-sufficient duet. The lyrics express a wholly conventional tribute to the poet's lady.

Pedro de Lagarto (fl. 1490)

A TOLEDO CATHEDRAL list of prebendaries and chaplains makes Pedro de Lagarto, composer of *Andad, pasiones, andad* (*CMC*, no. 33; *CMP*, no. 279; *CMS*, no. 189), a "claustrero" in that cathedral on June 19, 1490.[79]

The title of claustrero, now obsolete, belonged after 1450 to masters of the boy choristers in Toledo Cathedral. Alfonso Martínez de Fontova, the first chorus-master to be so designated, was named "by virtue of a papal bull" on December 22, 1450.[80] Some

---

[77] *Con temor*, m. 10.

[78] Barbieri, p. 22.

[79] *Ibid.*, p. 36. Nicholas V on August 5, 1448, issued the bull creating the prebend of *claostrero*. One of a total of 50 prebendaries at Toledo, the *magister claostralis* was specifically charged with teaching the boys ritual and music.

[80] Bibl. Nac. MS 14035.289. Rosa y López, *op. cit.*, p. 67, stated that the first papal bull establishing a master of boy choristers in a Spanish cathedral was Eugene IV's *Ad exequendum* of September 24, 1439, addressed to the dean and canons at Seville. Nevertheless, the first Sevillian master whose name he could discover was Pero Sánchez de Santo Domingo, appointed on January 5, 1478. Rosa y López believed that the Spanish cathedrals made formal provision for such masterships in imitation of the cathedral in Florence, where such an office was created in 1433 with an annual stipend of 100 ducats (*op. cit.*, p. 39), the initiator of the office in Florence being Eugene IV himself (pope from 1431–1447).

idea of Martínez de Fontova's duties – and also of Lagarto's – can be gained from studying a letter written by Archbishop Alfonso Carrillo [81] to the dean and chapter of his
cathedral on November 27, 1453. The primate urged that they provide the master of
choristers with a suitable house in which to lodge and board the boys and moreover
that they assign a yearly allowance for the keep of each boy.[82] In 1458 the master's
salary was set at 500 *maravedis*.[83]

A receipt signed by Lagarto on January 21, 1494, shows that the claustrero's salary
in that year had been raised to 1060 maravedís.[84] The receipt reads: "The master of the
boy choristers is entitled to an annual salary of four florins (which equal 1060 mara-
dís) because he teaches reading and singing to the choristers and prepares the
Christmas presentation of the Sibyl's prophecy."

A year later Lagarto obtained a more lucrative post. In February of 1495 the cathedral
singer Alfonso de la Torre having died, the chapter authorities (as the custom was) announced a public examination to fill the vacancy. Two Toledo canons were appointed
judges to decide the contest, they being given instructions to select the most "accomplished and fluent singer." The winner however was to know more than merely how to
sing. He was to be well versed in all branches of music, especially polyphonic composition. Pedro Lagarto, "clergyman of this city," won and was instituted in the vacant
prebend on February 12, 1495.[85] Lagarto was succeeded in the office of claustrero on
February 13, 1507, by a certain Tomás de Morales. He probably had just died.[86]

In addition to *Andad, pasiones, andad* three other songs are attributed to him in
CMP: Callen todas las galanas (no. 226), *D'aquel fraire flaco* (no. 255), and *Quéxome de ti
ventura* (no. 90). He affiliates himself with Encina's generation rather than Triana's
by writing classic villancicos – the rhyme-scheme of the coplas spilling over into the
musical refrain in *CMP*, 226, 255, 279. Only *Quéxome* lacks a poetic or musical refrain.
Callen todas pays graceful tribute to the ladies of Toledo who exceed those of Seville in
deportment, grace, and charm. *D'aquel fraire* is his only four-voiced item. In lively triple
meter (C), it bounces to a C Major chord at every cadence. Since the poem is in eight
stanzas, 34 authentic cadences fall on C-Major pavement in rapid and unremitting
succession. But the dramatic purpose is well served by such insistence. The lyrics voice
a shrill warning against the wickedest friar footloose in Spain, a spoiler of maid, matron,

Already in the thirteenth century *niños de coro* (boy-choristers) are mentioned in Santiago de Compostela
documents, but without details concerning their care and upbringing. See Antonio López Ferreiro, *Historia de la s. a. m. i. de Santiago de Compostela*, Vol. V (1902), p. 175. A choirboys' school annexed to Barcelona Cathedral was functioning as early as 1344. See José M. Madurell and J. M. Llorens Cisteró, "Documentos de archivo: Libros de canto," *Anuario Musical*, XI (1956), p. 219.

[81] Bibl. Nac. MS 14035.289. Alfonso Carrillo de Acuña ruled as primate from 1446–1482.
[82] The annual allowance suggested for each boy was "10 or 12 maravedís" payable to the master.
[83] Bibl. Nac. MS 14035.288.
[84] Barbieri, p. 36.
[85] *Ibid.*, p. 37.
[86] Rubio Piqueras, *Música y músicos toledanos* (Toledo: Suc. de J. Peláez, 1923), p. 68. But on the other
hand the Barbieri MSS in the Madrid National Library contain in folder 14035 a note stating that the name
should be Andreas not Thomas; and that he began as maestro of the boys in 1495 (though not as claustrero
until 1507).

and *monja*. The phrases all divide twelve beats asymmetrically into $3 + 4 + 5$. If Marius Schneider reasons correctly ("Gestaltimitation als Kompositionsprinzip im Cancionero de Palacio" [*Die Musikforschung*, XI/4, p. 415]), no *CMP* item by a named composer better catches the folkish flavor.

Andad, pasiones, andad again inhabits C Major. The greater popularity of this Lagarto item owes something to its lyrics. The music is expressive, but not more so than in his other songs. The lyrics, on the other hand, sound a more distinctive note. The poet cries out to his desires as to a welcome friend. He calls them to swell over him like a wave engulfing him. He wishes to abandon himself completely to passion. The treble melody aptly captures this mood of abandonment with its initial downward swoop of c^1, b, g, e. This descent with slight variants is repeated five times before even the first stanza is done with. Were the villancico with its five stanzas [87] sung straight through this same downward figure would recur 28 times. Schneider sees in these oft-repeated variants (of a "melody-type") a link to such an Arabian composition-principle as the *maqam*.

Juan de León

THE CANCIÓN *a 3* found at fols. 28v.–29 in *CMC* with an ascription to "J. d. leon," *Ay que non se rremediarme*, concords with *CMP*, no. 37, where it is similarly ascribed, and with an anonymous item at fols. 123v.–124 in Bologna Liceo Musicale MS 109.[88] The first name is not expanded in either *CMC* or *CMP*.

Were nothing known of any "J. d. leon," it could still be conjectured from the style of the canción, its manuscript associations with Urrede's two songs, *Nunca fué pena mayor* and *De vos i de mi quexoso*, in the Bologna source, and its having belonged to the original corpus of *CMC*, that León flourished in the 1480's and 1490's. This supposition is borne out by the notices from Santiago de Compostela capitular *actas* summarized at pp. 333–334 in Antonio López Ferreiro's *Historia de la santa a. m. iglesia de Santiago de Compostela*, VII (1905).

According to these, Juan de León was received on August 30, 1480, as *maestro de canto* in Santiago de Compostela Cathedral with an annual salary of 9000 *pares de blancas* (= maravedís). His duties were twofold: (1) he was to teach six beneficed clergymen and six *mozos de coro* (choirboys) of the chapter's choosing; (2) he was to come daily to coro, properly habited, and to sing both Mass and Vespers. His salary equalled three times that of the cathedral organist in 1474 (Álvaro de Castenda) and about twice that of the cathedral organist to be appointed in 1486 (Alonso de Salamanca). The constant recourse of pilgrims made it possible for him to enlist outside aid, as for instance during the summer of 1482 when some French singers performed at the Assumption celebration. These were paid honoraria of 200 *pares de blancas* on August 26 for exception-

---

[87] Only one strophe is copied in *CMC*. The others are omitted for lack of space. *Andad, pasiones, andad* was a late addition copied in a blank space between a Urrede (*De vos i de mi quexoso*) and a Triana (*Quien vos dio tal señorio*) item, both of which belonged to the original corpus of *CMC*.

[88] *MME*, I, *119*.

al musical services. The chapter also encouraged him in his efforts to improve cathedral music by purchasing new medium-size organs in 1483 (payment for which was made on March 15).

León rose to a canonry on January 31, 1487. Like Anchieta's canonry at Granada (c. 1497–c. 1499) and Peñalosa's at Seville (1505–1518), León's seems not to have been strictly residential. On February 17, 1487, his salary as *maestro de canto* was revoked. After an interregnum, a new *maestro* was named by a commission of four on September 19, 1496. León, evidently absent from the cathedral, was not a member of the commission. He did reside, however, during 1499, on March 22 of which year he began to instruct Jácome Alvarez. The cathedral prebendary who took sole charge of the music after León's removal to Málaga Cathedral later in the same year, Jácome de Carrión (Alvarez?), succeeded in the title of *maestro de canto* on August 30.

León may well have selected Málaga because of its bland climate. In any event his name first appears in Málaga cathedral records with an act dated September 6, 1499, naming Juan de León a singer.[89] One month later (October 7) the chapter granted him temporary leave to reside in nearby Granada.[90] At this particular moment the court was dwelling there, this being a year during which thousands of Moors were accepting baptism. The entry in the Málaga capitular acts shows that while in Granada León expected to live in the household of Diego Hurtado de Mendoza, archbishop of Seville (1486–1502) and titular patriarch of Alexandria. The latter was in Granada with Ximénez de Cisneros, primate of Spain, to assist in its massive Christianization. The invitation extended León by the Sevillian archbishop – an enormously rich Maecenas who lived more at court than in his see (and whose patronage of Juan de Espinosa has already been noted at p. 92 above) – suggests that León had long been a familiar palace figure. The chapter required León to promise that he would return if the court should at any time visit Málaga.

Before June 19, 1500, he had returned to Málaga. He and the cathedral succentor, Blas de Córcoles, were on that date fined two months' salary because they had both refused to sing in the Corpus Christi procession.[91] On October 11, 1501, León and two other cathedral singers were granted time off every morning (except Sundays and special feast-days when polyphony was sung) in order to devote themselves more assiduously to their musical practice.[92] On October 12, 1508, he was rewarded by the new bishop of Málaga, Diego Ramírez de Villaescusa, with a lucrative chaplaincy endowed by Pedro Díaz de Toledo, first bishop of Málaga after the reconquest.[93] On March 6,

---

[89] Rafael Mitjana, *Estudios sobre algunos músicos españoles del siglo XVI* (Madrid: Lib. de los sucesores de Hernando, 1918), p. 30.

[90] Mitjana, "Nuevas notas al 'Cancionero musical de los siglos XV y XVI' publicado por el maestro Barbieri," *Revista de filología española*, V, ii (April-June, 1918), p. 127.

[91] Mitjana, "La capilla de música de la Catedràl de Málaga: Año de 1496 al año de 1542," MS dated 1895 in Kungl. Musikaliska Akademiens Bibliotek, Stockholm, p. 7. Córcoles, appointed succentor June 9, 1498, had offended the chapter by openly criticizing the conduct of the canons during High Mass. His independency was the more offensive because he like León was still a layman. He transferred to the royal chapel shortly before January 5, 1505.

[92] Mitjana, *Estudios*, pp. 30–31.

[93] *Ibid.*, p. 31. Pedro de Toledo ruled 1487–1499.

1510, the cathedral records show that he had been appointed succentor, but with a dispensation from the task of teaching music to the choirboys: for two reasons. The work itself was considered too heavy and he was meanwhile prevented from singing in the choir.[94]

On April 20, 1510, the chapter deputized him to visit Seville and there attend to the sale of a house willed to Málaga cathedral.[95] He was certainly absent from Málaga during the summer of 1510, for on July 2 the chapter voted to make Juan de Pedraza cathedral succentor during his prolonged absence and to give his chaplaincy to a substitute named Gonzalo Tamayo.[96] He was still absent on August 20, 1511, when the chaplaincy which he had held was conferred on a new succentor, Cristóbal de Quesada. On September 17, 1511, he was empowered as an agent of the cathedral to pursue a lawsuit against the Nuns of St. Clara in Granada.

Finally on March 17 of the year following, 1512, he returned with a new appointment as cathedral singer. The chapter simultaneously voted him the best salary of any musician on the cathedral rolls – 15,000 maravedís. Later in the same year he asked leave to study in Rome for the priesthood. Though the date of permission was November 10 he delayed his departure for Rome. On June 8, 1513, after waiting seven months, the chapter decided that he should be paid at a prebend's rate and one week later, June 15, he was present to swear his intention of being ordained.[97] He was again in Málaga, or still there (one cannot say which), February 3, 1514, on which date the cathedral acts list him as a *contrabaxo* (bass singer) drawing a salary of 15,000 maravedís.[98] He probably died soon afterwards. His post had been given to Juan de Arévalo temporarily and to Fernando Pérez permanently by 1517.[99] No mention of León has been found in the Málaga acts after 1514.

The most famous secular composer of the early Spanish Renaissance enjoyed a companion dignity in Málaga Cathedral from April 11, 1509, until February 21, 1519: Juan del Encina.[100] Since Encina was not ordained a priest until August of 1519 when he was 50, León may well have reached a similar age when he decided to seek ordination in 1512. If so he would have been born c. 1460. The records at Málaga show that Encina was severely penalized because he was not yet a priest during his decade as Archdeacon of Málaga. León though in a lower status probably suffered like disabilities. Certainly the chapter's requiring him to swear that he would seek the priesthood (June 15, 1513) shows that some valid proof of his intention was thought necessary before an increase in salary could be put into effect.

IF LEÓN of Málaga and "J. de. leon" were indeed the same [101] then it would be pleasant to find some connecting link between the man and his music. The contra in *Ay que non se rremediarme* is much more singable than the contras in Cornago's canciones. Appro-

---

[94] Mitjana, "La capilla de música," p. 15. The chapter appropriated 1000 maravedís to pay a new maestro. Léon's salary was reduced by a like amount.

[95] *RFE*, V, ii, p. 127. [96] *Estudios*, p. 31.

[97] *RFE*, V, ii, p. 128. [98] "La capilla de música," p. 23.

[99] *Estudios*, p. 32. [100] *Ibid.*, pp. 16 and 21.

[101] In *DML*, II, 1401, a "Jorge de León" is offered as a candidate for the composer of *Ay que non se*

priately enough, León was a contrabaxo. In gait, meter, and texture, this canción strongly resembles Urrede's *De vos i de mi quexoso*. The León item cannot have been written under any Encina influence: the musical mannerisms as well as the fitting of poetry to music veto such a presumption.

In *CMC* the León canción lacks any B♭'s in the "signatures" of either tenor or contra, a fact that has particular bearing on the harmony at mm. 7, 24, and 25 where E minor instead of E♭ Major chords become possibilities. The *CMC* scribe carelessly omitted the contra notes between mm. 53–72. But he did place a dot after the penultimate tenor note in the strophe (Middle C tied from mm. 25–26), which reading absolves León from the fault of having written an unprepared seventh between contra and tenor simultaneously with an unprepared fourth between treble and contra. Elsewhere throughout the canción neither unprepared fourths nor sevenths are encountered between tenor and outer voices.

That this song appealed to his generation is to be suspected from its preservation in three sources, one in Italy. Its melodic lines are sinuous. He avoids obvious repetition (melodically or harmonically); and devises no imitations. So old-fashioned a melodic cadence as that of the under-third appears once [102] – at the end of the "A" section. The poet all the while beats his breast. The strophe mounts, for instance, to such ejaculations as "O my secret passion! O my public misery! O key to my prison! O perfection of beauty!" León dramatizes the four long words in these apostrophes to the poet's love. Each long word – *passion, misery, prison,* and *perfection* – is split by a rest in the treble melody that can by no means be edited out of existence.

Juan Fernández de Madrid

IN NEITHER *CMC* (fols. 32v.–34) nor *CMP* (fols. 8v.–9v.) does *Sienpre creçe mi serviros* carry more than "Madrid" for an ascription. Barbieri in 1890 suggested that "Madrid" might have been a self-educated rebeck-player from a village near Madrid (Carabanchel) whose principal occupation was that of a tile-maker.[103] Such an individual made large sums playing before Don Juan, the heir-apparent who died in the autumn of 1497. Anglés has however presciently observed that no humble autodidact performer on the three-string *rabel* is likely to have composed such exquisite works of art as the three-voiced *Sienpre creçe mi serviros*, or the three other Madrid songs *a 3* which are unica in *CMP*: *De vevir vida segura* (no. 66), *Por las gracias que teneis* (no. 31), and *Pues que Dios te fiso tal* (no. 5 [tiple part only]); not to mention the sacred compositions by "Madrid" in the National Library at Paris (nouv. acq. frç. 4379, fols. 78v.–80, 81v.–83). Moreover the style of his vernacular items is rather learned, with

rremediarme. But he did not begin as a singer in the Castilian royal chapel until the year of Queen Isabella's death. In favor of the Málaga León, Mitjana showed his Sevillian connections, his familiarity with the patriarch, his preferential treatment at Málaga. Even as a singer he was better paid than the maestro de capilla (see "La capilla de música," p. 22). His rank posed such a problem that the chapter quit asking him to march in processions after August 24, 1512.

[102] Isabel Pope remarks on the same archaism in a Spanish-text song copied in another Italian MS, *Viva, viva, rey Ferrante.* See her "La musique espagnole à la Cour de Naples dans la seconde moitié du xve siècle," p. 45.

[103] Barbieri, p. 38.

greater use of imitation than characterizes the run of Spanish secular music composed before 1500. Anglés therefore offers as a substitute candidate Juan Fernández de Madrid, singer in the court chapel of Ferdinand V after 1479.

Barbieri may have suspected that Madrid was a mere *rabel*-player because in such a canción as *Sienpre creçe mi serviros* he found – at least in his transcription – unmistakable signs of bungling. The contra in the last phrase of the "A" section and the tenor in the last phrase of the "B" section did not make sense in his transcription. Nor do they for that matter make sense in the *MME* critical edition. On the face evidence of both the Barbieri and *MME* transcriptions, Madrid lapsed into such blunders as chains of consecutive fifths and wrote harsh unprepared dissonances.

Again, as in the case of León, the *CMC* version absolves him from any such faults. In order to see how this may be true, we should compare the part-writing at mm. 57–62 and 90–92 in the *MME* transcription with the better version of these passages to be found in *CMC*. At mm. 57–62 he proves to have written not only intelligent counterpoint but also to have added a smooth contra. This latter point is of some importance if he is to be the same Madrid who knew how to add a smoother third voice to Cornago's already existing treble-tenor complex in *Pues que Dios te fiso tal* than did the original composer.

Sienpre creçe mi serviros

* A "signature" of two flats appears at the beginning of the treble part in *CMC*; but after the first two treble staves only one flat is used.

Madrid starts two phrases with imitation in *Sienpre creçe* (mm. 15–16, 45–46) and three in *Por las gracias* (mm. 1–2, 16–17, 24–26). Significantly the tenor always leads, the treble following. The contra never lends a hand in the imitations at beginnings of phrases but does make a distinctive contribution at phrase-endings in *Sienpre creçe*: at mm. 13–14 and 43–45 the contra moving while the other voices idle. Between phrases he obviously wishes to insert connective tissue of a kind that Spanish secular composers did not frequently provide in *CMC* canciones.

The burden of the text in *Sienpre creçe* is the woes of unrequited love and in *De vevir* of unlucky love. In *Por las gracias* the poet on the other hand sings tenderly and without bitterness or disappointment of his lady's graces. Just as the rhyme-scheme of the "B" section does not spill over into the da capo "A"; so also he will not let the ending-chord of "B" duplicate the final chord of "A". The cadences, as in most Spanish secular music composed c. 1485, always call into play a syncopated melodic tag in some upper part. Tenor and treble resolve into an octave, unison, or third, at the endings of all his phrases. Elsewhere the tenor and treble always make a self-sufficient duet, unprepared fourths on strong beats being consistently excluded. Duple meter is his choice in two instances out of three. It is precisely in the triple-meter canción *De vevir* that he for once forgets to imitate.

Moxica

IF BARBIERI rightly attributed the verse of *Dama, mi grand querer* (*CMC*, fols. 43v.–44; *CMP*, fols. 5v.–6) to Pedro González de Mendoza,[104] then Moxica may have served in the latter's household. Mendoza, cardinal after 1473, was bishop of Sigüenza, 1468–1483, and primate at Toledo, 1483–1495.

Moxica's name – missing from *CMC* – is supplied from *CMP* where it heads two songs: *Dama, mi grand querer*, no. 8, and *No queriendo sois querida*, no. 22. The poetry of both describes the anguish of love. Both are closed-form canciones. In both, sections "A" and "B" end on the same "chord." Moxica is distinctive in one respect: he avoids the syncopated melodic tag ｜♪ ♪ ♪｜° ｜ or a variant of it at cadences. Only once does he use it in his *CMC* canción, and then not at the end of a section but rather at a light intermediate cadence (mm. 28–29), deceptive in nature.

In *Dama, mi grand querer* the contra involves numerous longs and breves. Its melodic intervals never exceed a fifth, except at the end of "A" where it skips up an octave in characteristic fifteenth-century fashion. Or at least it so skips in the *CMP* version.

The obligatory B♮'s in the tenor of *No queriendo* (*CMP*, no. 22) light fires for so many corresponding E♮'s in the contra that modern "C minor" drifts in with the smoke. This song is poetically and musically one of the choicer items in the Spanish song-collections. The "A" section develops this thought: Not wishing to be in love I am in love, to my detriment. The "B" part suddenly shifts poetic mood while simultaneously Moxica moves from "C minor" to B♭ and E♭ Major chords. The lover now all at once declares

[104] *Ibid.*, p. 60.

that the lady whom he admires is – despite his grief – worth his pains: a shift of poetic mood reminiscent of the similar mood-change in the sestet of such a sonnet as "When in disgrace with fortune and men's eyes." Among Moxica's merits is that of having found a simple but effective way of changing musical stance at the beginning of his "B" section.

J. Rodríguez

AGAIN in the case of *Donsella, por cuyo amor* (*CMC*, fols. 14v.–16; *CMP*, fol. 6v.) the composer's name has been omitted by the *CMC* copyist (just as in the Moxica item) and must therefore be supplied from the concordance in *CMP*. But the *CMC* version does enjoy the advantage of bring musically complete. The *CMP*, because of the loss of leaf 7 in the manuscript, lacks a contra, 49 breves of the tenor part, and section "B" of the treble. Though none other of Rodríguez's compositions seems to survive, this closed-form canción in duple meter must have been widely popular, since it was known in Portugal as late as 1521. Gil Vicente introduced it into his wedding compliment, *Côrtes de Jupiter* [105] presented at Lisbon in August of 1521.

Just as in the case of León's *Ay que non se rremediarme* and Madrid's *Sienpre creçe mi serviros*, so also Rodríguez's *Donsella, por cuyo amor* is disclosed by *CMC* to have been less flawed a work of art than might be suspected from the best transcription now available: that found in *MME*, V, 13–14. In the *MME* transcription Rodríguez appears to have bungled his part-writing with consecutive unisons between contra and treble at measure 30 and to have awkwardly skipped up a seventh in his contra at the beginning of measure 55, thus creating an unprepared dissonance between the contra and tenor. But the Colombina source shows, on the other hand, that the note E in the contra at m. 30 should read C, thus obviating any parallel unisons; and that the note c in the contra at m. 55 should read d, thus replacing the contra leap of a seventh with an octave and the unprepared strong-beat dissonance between tenor and contra with a perfect fifth. In view of such discrepancies it would seem that even the humbler Spanish composers active between 1474–1516 were more fastidious than presently available printed editions suggest.

The harmonies of *Donsella, por cuyo amor* clearly belong to C Major. Transient modulations tend towards G Major at mm. $25–26_1$, 75–76, and perhaps at 54–55. The fragrance of the treble melody could not be sweeter. Interestingly enough, the treble notes with active harmonic tendencies move where a much later harmonist would have liked to see them move. The harmonic underpinning seems always right in terms of Rameau's epoch – not merely of Rodríguez's. Moments of repose and tension are admirably balanced. The final cadence can, it is true, be bettered by adopting the *CMC* reading which eliminates the second and third treble notes of m. 66 in the *CMP* version. But elsewhere exactly the right number of notes seems to have been used in each

---

[105] *Copilaçam* (1562), fol. 168, c. 1, line 15.

phrase. Rodríguez does not hesitate to introduce rests into the treble line even in the middle of a word, if thereby the melodic grace will be enhanced (mm. 44, 60, 75).

F. de la Torre

FIFTEEN items by Torre find their place in the Palace Songbook, but only one in *CMC*: and that one proves to be not at all typical when compared with the fifteen in *CMP*. In the first place, *Dime triste coraçon* is his shortest song. Secondly, the rhyme-plan agrees with the scheme that Encina popularized in the 1490's and not with that which Torre himself favored in all his *CMP* songs except *No fie nadie en amor* (no. 262). Throughout the rest of his *CMP* songs furnished with an initial refrain, the rhyme-scheme of "B" musical section is kept rigidly separate from that in "A" section or in the da capo. Only *Dime triste coraçon* and *No fie nadie* can therefore qualify as classic-type villancicos – by reason of their spill-over rhymes.

Torre's *Dime triste coraçon* is today a unicum in *CMC*. It would not be, however, if the manuscript of *CMP* had survived intact. Originally *Dime triste coraçon* appeared at fol. 159,[106] a leaf which has unfortunately been lost from *Palacio* in the course of centuries. Even so, he is one of the better represented composers of his generation in the musical

Dime triste coraçon *

CMC, fol. 69v.   FRANCISCO DE LA TORRE

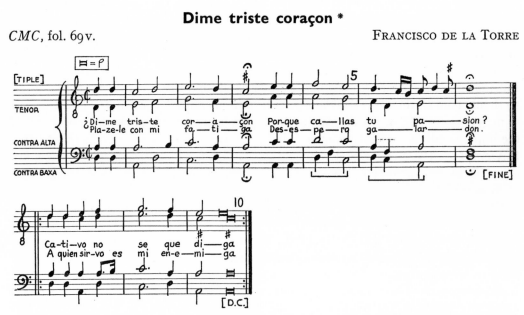

* Tell me, sad heart, why do you conceal your passion? A captive, I know not what to say; she whom I serve is my enemy. She enjoys my distress. I despair of reward.

[106] *MME*, V, 35. Two other concording items originally in *CMP* but later lost from it are the anonymous *Nyña y viña peral* (*CMC*, fol. 72v.) and *Propinan de melyor* [?] (*CMC*, fol. 75v.). See also Barbieri, pp. 52–53, who reads *Propinnan de melion*.

portion of *Palacio* still preserved. By virtue of his fifteen items, he stands fifth among the fifty composers whose contributions have thus far been identified. These fifteen *CMP* pieces are further dealt with below at pp. 281–284.

Anonymous Spanish Songs in the Colombina Cancionero

APPROXIMATELY a third of the secular Spanish items in *CMC* refuse to yield the identity of their composers, directly or indirectly.[107] Two of these anonymous pieces can be dated by their texts. The first, *Muy crueles voses dan* (*CMC*, fols. 11v.–12v.) concords with *CMP*, no. 103. A three-voiced canción, it was composed in 1469 at a moment when Barcelona was in revolt against John II of Aragon. This song affords an extremely early instance of the use of music for political propaganda purposes. It urges the Catalonians to return to their natural allegiance.[108]

The second, *Olvyda tu perdiçion* (*CMC*, fol. 71v.) is a four-voiced romance not belonging to the original corpus of the MS, but added considerably later. Its date on the evidence of its text can be fixed around 1492 – the year in which Granada finally capitulated. It joins Anchieta's *En memoria d'Alixandre*, dated 1489 (*CMP*, no. 130); the anonymous *Sobre Baça estaba el Rey*, also dated 1489 (*CMP*. no. 135); Encina's two romances, one dated c. 1490, *Una sañosa porfia* (*CMP*, no. 126), and the other c. 1492, *Qu'es de ti desconsolado* (*CMP*, no. 74); and finally two romances by Torre, *Pascua d'Espiritu Santo* (*CMP*, no. 136) and *Por los campos de los moros* (*CMP*, no. 150); to form a select group of seven contemporaneously composed romances celebrating Ferdinand's Moorish victories.

The musical utterance in all these – the Anchieta, the Encina, the Torre, the *CMC* and *CMP* anonymous items – is strikingly austere and restrained. The mood never veers to that of the fireworks that were set off at Rome during April of 1492 or the bullfights staged there during the same month to celebrate Spanish military prowess. Rather than paeans the Spanish romances seem to be prayers. Queen Isabella's reaction to the victories is well known. Her first summons after every new advance was always to prayer for the conversion of the vanquished.

At Rome, a gay villancico was sung in April of 1492. Inserted into *Historia Baetica* [109] – a Latin drama by the papal chamberlain and secretary, Carlo Verardi (1440–1500), who wrote it to celebrate the Spanish victory – its mood could not contrast more strongly with that of the Spanish romances in commemoration of the same Granada

---

[107] Twenty-eight secular songs (1, 3, 6, 7, 12–16, 21, 25, 31, 36, 37, 44, 49–54, 56–58, 61, 62, 92, 93, 95) in a total of 95 secular and sacred items remain anonymous. The two lower voices in *Propinan de melyor* (*CMC*, no. 57) suggest a brass fanfare. (Anglés read the title of this piece conjecturally as *Proxima de mejor*, but the first word certainly contains a "p" instead of an "x." The *CMP* title seems a likelier solution.)

[108] See Barbieri, pp. 162–163 for further historical details.

[109] Presented in the palace of Raffaele Riario, April 21, 1492. Printed for the first time in 1493 by Eucharius Silber at Rome. For a modern reprint and for critical comment see L. Barrau-Dihigo, "Historia Baetica," *Revue hispanique*, XLVII (1919), pp. 319–382.

En memoria d'Alixandre *

CMP, no. 130 (*MME*, V, pp. 155–157)   JUAN DE ANCHIETA (1489)

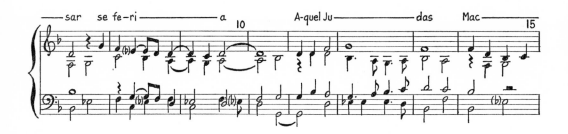

* When they remembered Alexander, Julius Caesar was piqued and Judas Maccabaeus rent his hair.

The remaining 38 lines of the poem declare that if these and other military heroes were outshone by Alexander, Ferdinand exceeds them all. The sultan has sent him an embassy. Soon he will retake the Holy Sepulchre itself.

victory, or of Anchieta's in celebration of the slightly earlier taking of Baza (December 4, 1489). The Spanish pieces play on the theme

> O God, thy arm was here:
> And not to us, but to thine arm alone,
> Ascribe we all! [110]

and the conquerors seem more ready to imitate the "lode-star of virtue" who commanded

[110] *Henry V*, IV, viii, 104–106.

¿ Qu'es de ti, desconsolado? *

CMP, no. 74 (MME, V, pp. 102–103)   JUAN DEL ENCINA

* What misfortune has overtaken you, king of Granada? What has become of your land and your people? Where will you dwell?

The remaining 26 lines urge Boabdil to renounce his faith. The poet congratulates Granada on its liberation.

Olvyda tu perdiçion *

CMC, no. 52 (fol. 71 v.)   Anonymous (c. 1492)

* Forgetting what she lost because of Roderick [last Visigothic king, 711 A.D.] Spain now consoles herself with what Ferdinand has regained.

Viva el gran Rey Don Fernando *

Historia Baetica [Rome: E. Silber, 1493], fols. 39 v.–40.   CARLO VERARDI, 1492

  * Long live the monarchs Ferdinand and Isabella. Long live Spain and Castile, glorious and triumphant. The Mohammedan city, extremely powerful Granada, has been taken and liberated from the false faith, by virtue of the armed might of Ferdinand and Isabella.

  Long live Spain and Castile, glorious and triumphant.

  Three other stanzas continue in like vein.

Let there be sung 'Non nobis' and 'Te Deum' [111]

after so great military successes. But in Rome, Spanish sobriety gave way to the blithe mood of a frottola. To show how real was the difference in national sentiment, four examples are here shown in close succession: (1) Anchieta's, (2) the *CMC* anonymous's, (3) the first of Encina's, and (4) Verardi's musical commemorations of the same Spanish military prowess against the Moors.

The three Spanish romances share the common traits of blood-brothers. Each is a piece of dorian homophony. Each contains four musical phrases starting always in anapest rhythm and ending always with a long-held chord.[112] The *CMC* anonymous and Encina use as "phrase-end" chords the dominant, subtonic, and tonic. Anchieta uses the tonic and mediant. Each of the three romances is a treble-dominated work; yet b♭ is the highest note in each. The vocal ranges, tessiture, rhythmic and chordal practices unite in each to produce a dark and somber mood.

It is of course true that in two of these Spanish 1492 pieces – Encina's *Qu'es de ti* (shown here as an example) as well as his *Una sañosa porfia* (*CMP*, no. 126) – the *romance*-texts condole with the defeated. Not so, however, with the texts set by Anchieta, Torre, or the *CMC* anonymous. Some other explanation for the prevailingly solemn mood in these other *Reconquista* romances is needed. "Battle-pieces" they may well be, but music more strongly contrasting with the most famous of all Renaissance battle-pieces – Janequin's *La Bataille de Marignan* (1515) – could not well be conceived.[113]

Cancionero Musical de Palacio

THE PALACE SONGBOOK, found in 1870 by Gregorio Cruzada Villaamil at the Royal Palace in Madrid (sign. 2–I–5), towers above every other secular monument of Spanish Renaissance musical history. Its distinctions include: (1) its preservation of 458 items;[114] (2) the historical range of its contents; (3) its representative character; (4) the consistently high literary and musical quality maintained throughout the collection.

If no cancionero of its own epoch can match it, it also exceeds every song-collection of

---

[111] *Ibid.*, IV, viii, 121.

[112] The first two notes in the anapest rhythm are always repeated-notes, except at the opening of Encina's third phrase. Anchieta "writes in" the equivalent of a fermata at m. 11. Elsewhere in these romances the corona is used.

[113] Only one *CMP* villancico seems to refer directly to the fall of Granada – Encina's *deshecha* (composed by way of postscript to his *Qu'es de ti*) with the title, *Levanta Pascual* (see pp. 266–267). In this deshecha the two interlocutors are mere shepherds, as far removed from the battlefield as the brilliant folk in Rome. The closer the Spaniard moved to the actual ground of battle the more solemn he became. Miguel Querol Gavaldá confirms this view in his "Importance historique et nationale du romance," *Musique et Poésie au XVIe Siècle* (Paris: Centre National, 1954), pp. 320–321.

[114] *MME*, I, 95–103 and *MME*, V, 25–32 gave the total number of items as 463. But when Anglés actually came to edit the last dozen songs in *CMP* he found that in five instances he had erroneously counted estribillo and coplas as separate songs, viz. at nos. 451 (= 451, 452), 452 (= 453, 454), 454 (=456, 457), 456 (= 459, 460), 458 (= 462, 463). Barbieri in 1890 gave the total number of items as 460. He similarly considered certain coplas as separates.

the next three reigns. The MS, as originally gathered, consisted of some 304 leaves. Even though 56 of these were lost before its discovery in 1870, it still in present truncated form exceeds such a later contender as the *Cancionero Musical de la Casa de Medinaceli* (c. 1560) [115] by fifty leaves. At that, the Medinaceli Cancionero, like the Colombina, is a mixed collection with more than thirty of its items setting sacred Latin words. The so-called *Cancionero de Upsala*,[116] actually a collection printed at Venice in 1556, contains only 54 items. The *Cancionero musical* [117] copied by Claudio de la Sablonara c. 1625 is a stronger competitor, but contains only 78 items.

Outdistancing all other song-collections on account of sheer size, *Palacio* also exceeds its Spanish competitors because of its historical range. *Alburquerque, Alburquerque* (*CMP*, no. 106), an extremely simple piece of dorian three-part homophony, may very well be a musical as well as a poetic product of the 1430's. Its topical verse deals with an event of the year 1430.[118] Certainly the music of *Muy crueles voses dan* (*CMP*, no. 103) cannot be dated later than 1469. *Pues serviçio vos desplase* (*CMP*, no. 27) must obviously have been composed before 1475, Robert Morton the English chaplain who wrote the music [119] being known to have died in that year.

On the other hand *CMP* contains several pieces that can definitely be dated after 1500. Tordesillas's *Françeses por que rrason* (no. 424) describes the French rout at Roussillon on October 19, 1503.[120] Almorox's *Gaeta nos es subjeta* (no. 423) alludes to the capture of an Italian stronghold on January 1, 1504.[121] Ponce's *Françia cuenta tu ganançia* (no. 443) in its original lines mentions events of the year 1513 and in later corrections and additions happenings of 1521.[122] *Palacio* must therefore at the very least cover a time-span of half-a-century.

The Palace Songbook is also the most representative Spanish cancionero. Songs by every major peninsular composer of the period fill its pages. Canciones and villancicos are, for instance, to be found in it by Cornago, Triana, Madrid, Torre, Medina, Anchieta, Peñalosa, Alonso de Alva, Escobar, Encina, Millán, Gabriel, Ponce. As if these were insufficient, it also happens to be the only cancionero with any body of songs by foreign celebrities. Josquin des Prez – in Spain the most admired of all foreign composers throughout the whole of the sixteenth century – is represented by his popular frottola, *In te Domine speravi* (*CMP*, no. 84). Copied no doubt from a Petrucci print, this piece was composed while Josquin was still in the service of Ascanio Cardinal Sforza. The frottola *Io mi uoglio lamentare* by Giovanni Brocco of Verona (Petrucci's *Libro tertio* [1505], fol. 28) is transcribed a whole-step lower in *CMP* (no. 435). The other Italian

---

[115] Edited at Barcelona for the Spanish Musicological Institute in 1949 and 1950 by Miguel Querol Gavaldá (*Monumentos de la música española*, VIII and IX). The source from which the hundred secular items in these volumes were drawn is MS 13230 in the Medinaceli Library at Madrid.

[116] *Villancicos de diuersos autores, a dos, y a tres, y a quatro, y a cinco bozes* ... (Venice: Girolamo Scotto, 1556), ed. by Jesús Bal y Gay (Mexico City: El Colegio de México, 1944).

[117] *Cancionero musical y poético del siglo XVII recogido por Claudio de la Sablonara*, ed. by Jesús Aroca (Madrid: Impr. de la "Rev. de Arch., Bibl. y Museos," 1916).

[118] Barbieri, p. 163, c. 1.   [119] *MME*, X, pp. *23–24.*
[120] Barbieri, p. 173, c. 1.   [121] *Ibid.*, p. 172, c. 2.   [122] *Ibid.*, p. 174.

composers whose frottole have been identified include Giacomo Fogliano (*L'amor donna ch'io ti porto*, no. 91) and Bartolomeo Tromboncino (*Vox clamantis*, no. 105). Robert Morton represents England. When discussing the music, Bukofzer once declared *Pues serviçio vos desplase* to be Morton's only characteristically English song.[123] Evidently its English flavor did not prevent its gaining considerable popularity in Spain. Both music and lyrics were imitated by a later *CMP* contributor (*El bevir triste me haze*, no. 454).

As if these distinctions were not enough, *Palacio* also tends to exceed its near-contemporaries in literary quality. Its poets include such lights as the Viscount of Altamira (*Qué mayor desaventura* [*CMP*, no. 332]), the Count of Cifuentes (*La que tengo no es prisión* [*CMP*, no. 48]), Lucas Fernández (*Di, por qué mueres* [*CMP*, no. 417]), Jorge Manrique (*Justa fué mi perdición* [*CMP*, no. 42]), Juan de Mena (*Oya tu merçed* [*CMP*, no. 28]), Diego de Quirós (*Qué vida terná sin vos* [*CMP*, no. 222] and *Señora después que os vi* [*CMP*, nos. 339 and 450]), Juan Rodríguez del Padrón (*Muy triste será mi vida* [*CMP*, no. 23]), the Marqués de Santillana (*Harto de tanta porfía* [*CMP*, no. 26], and *Señora qual soy venido* [*CMP*, no. 52]), Lope de Sosa (*Alça la vos pregonero* [*CMP*, no. 152]), and Juan de Tapia (*Descuidad d'ese cuidado* [*CMP*, no. 377]). Among the Italian pieces is one with lyrics by Serafino dall' Aquila (1466–1500) – *Vox clamantis*. Were further care taken to search for literary concordances, the above list could doubtless be doubled. Even so, the most famous fifteenth-century Spanish poets have entered the above list. Although it is not claimed that either poetry or music is equally interesting in every *CMP* item, between a third and a half of the songs in *CMP* having been added at blank spaces after the original corpus of the MS had already been copied (175 added items amid a total of 458), still it can be justly asserted that the more one familiarizes oneself with *CMP* the more variety, beauty, and strength does one discern in its contents.

THE FIRST attempt at classifying the contents of *CMP* was made as long ago as the sixteenth century and is in the form of an index prefixed to the main body of the cancionero. The pioneer indexer – who perhaps undertook his task around 1525 [124] – classifies the contents of *CMP* under these four headings: [125] (1) *Villançicos* (2) *Estranbotes* (3) *Romançes* (4) *Villançicos omnium sanctorum*. Certain overlappings however mar the symmetry of his scheme. *Fata la parte* (no. 421) and *Yo me vollo lamentare* (no. 435 [in Italian]) are both listed simultaneously as *villançicos* and *estranbotes*, an evident inconsistency. Moreover only 482 works are tabulated in his classified index.[126] Actually 570 should have been indexed, counting the 92 pieces presently lost from *Palacio*

---

[123] M. F. Bukofzer, "An Unknown Chansonnier of the 15th Century," *Musical Quarterly*, XXVIII (January, 1942), p. 25.

[124] Indexing can hardly have been attempted prior to 1521, the date of *CMP*, no. 443.

[125] *MME*, V, *18–22*.

[126] *MME*, V, *17*, gives a different count – 476 items. Of this total, 389 would be villancicos, 14 estrambotes, 44 romances, and 29 *villancicos omnium sanctorum*. On the other hand, the *tabula* on pp. *18–22* reveals that the number of villancicos should be 396, of estrambotes 13, of romances 44, and of *villancicos omnium sanctorum* 29.

because leaves 7, 83–84, 89–91, 96, 114–116, 123–124, 155–194, 243, and 292 are now missing.

The original indexer calls everything in Spanish with a prefatory refrain a *villançico*. He also gives this name to a Spanish song if any individual section in it, not necessarily the first, is repeated. *Serrana del bel mirar* (no. 71) and *Una montaña pasando* (no. 154) are both, for instance, classed as villancicos in the original index. Yet neither opens with a refrain. Only interior sections are repeated. The indexer does not stop here. He calls even Encina's *A tal pérdida tan triste* (no. 324), Ponce's *Como está sola mi vida* (no. 328), and Peñalosa's *Por las sierras* (no. 311) and *Tú que vienes de camino* (no. 447) villancicos. But these four are innocent of any musical repetition whatsoever – at the beginning, end, or in the middle. For the original indexer, then, the term *villançico* covers a wider class of songs than present-day morphologists would allow. As used by the original indexer, *villançico* means any Spanish song which is not a *romançe*.

The romance was primarily a literary type. It always told some folkish tale. It never contained a refrain. Only the first four lines were set musically. Succeeding quatrains, however many, were sung to the music of the first. Each line contained (usually) eight syllables, with principal stress on the seventh. Every even line assonated. The English equivalent of the romance (texts) is the popular ballad. The original *CMP* indexer classifies 396 songs as villancicos (of the secular type), 29 as sacred villancicos (*villançicos omnium sanctorum*) and 44 as romances.

Estranbote, to judge from its use by the indexer, means any Italian song. Seven Petrucci frottole (*CMP*, nos. 78, 84, 91, 98, 105, 190, 435) become *estranbotes*, for instance. He certainly does not use this term as the equivalent of *strambotto*.[127] Not one of the *CMP* "estranbotes" exhibits any of the crucial literary marks which distinguish the *strambotti* published by Petrucci in his *Frottole … Libro Quarto*.

Having seen that the term *villançico* covers as variegated a song-literature in the mind of the original indexer as the term *frottola* in the thinking of contemporaneous Italian song-editors, the present-day student may therefore decide to follow the original indexer's precedent and to give the name of villancico to every Spanish song in *CMP* that is not a romance. If such a loose classification-scheme is adopted, the student will still find that nearly all his examples begin with a pithy refrain cadencing at a double-bar, proceed to a new musical strain for the first two lines of stanza – which strain is then repeated for the second two lines of stanza. Next will come the musical refrain, commencing simultaneously with the literary refrain in the older specimens and before it in the newer. However to avoid confusion we prefer reserving the term villancico exclusively for Spanish songs with initial musical refrains: not using it for such items as *CMP*, nos. 71, 154, 322, 324, 328, and 447, all of which are called *villançicos* in the original index, while lacking initial refrains. In our opinion a useful distinction can also be made between (1) those classic-type villancicos in *CMP* with "spill-over" rhyme-scheme; and (2) canciones in which literary and musical divisions coincide. Where historical evidence is available all closed-form songs prove to have been composed before Encina became the dominating influence in Spanish secular music. He himself,

---

[127] Concerning the *strambotto* see Gustave Reese, *Music in the Renaissance*, pp. 161–162.

as we shall see, is represented by 62 musical settings in *CMP*. Of these, 54 include a refrain. In 47 of the 54, the rhyme of the coplas spills over into the musical refrain. Only seven violate his rule (nos. 30, 46, 163, 191, 249, 271, 313).

Composers in the Palace Songbook

THE NAMES of 53 composers of songs in *CMP* have been recovered either from the manuscript itself or from concordances. A half-dozen are responsible for twelve or more songs each. Encina's name is associated with 68 songs, he having written the lyrics for all these. Some other composer may however have written the music for six of these 68 items. Millán composed the music of 23 songs. In descending order the others to whom ten or more songs are attributed run thus: Gabriel (19), Escobar (18), Torre (15), Ponce (12) Alonso (11), Mondéjar (11), Peñalosa (10).

Juan del Encina (1469–1529)

ALTHOUGH ENCINA has long been recognized as a literary star of the first magnitude, his early life was wrapped in mist until Ricardo Espinosa Maeso published his findings in the December, 1921, issue of the *Boletín de la Real Academia Española* under the title, "Nuevos datos biográficos de Juan del Encina." In that article he revealed that Encina's father was a mere cobbler named Juan de Fermoselle,[128] but that one brother was Diego de Fermoselle who taught music at Salamanca University from 1478–1522,[129] that another was Miguel de Fermoselle, a long-time prebendary in Salamanca cathedral (died in 1534), that another was Pedro de Hermosilla (= Fermoselle), who took possession of the archdeaconate of Málaga acting as his proxy during 1509,[130] and that in addition there were two other brothers and two sisters in the poet's family.[131]

In the prologue to the edition of Encina's 1496 *Cancionero* published in facsimile by the Royal Spanish Academy in 1928, Emilio Cotarelo admirably summed up all the facts of Encina's life then known.

"FERMOSELLE" is a Galician or Portuguese spelling of the Castilian name, Hermosilla. "Encina" may have been the maiden name of the poet's mother. At all events, one of his sisters bore the name, Catalina Sánchez del Encina.

Juan de Fermoselle enjoyed sufficient standing in the Salamanca community to be appointed one of the twenty-five cathedral tithe-collectors on April 16, 1481, an office which he held until renouncing it on May 30, 1494. He was still alive in 1502. From 1481–1489, and probably until he died, he lived opposite the University Schools.[132]

---

[128] R. Espinosa Maeso, *Nuevos datos biográficos de Juan del Encina* (Madrid: Tip. de la Rev. de Archivos, 1921), pp. 4–5.

[129] *Ibid.*, pp. 5–6 (note 4); also p. 9.

[130] *Ibid.*, p. 6.

[131] *Ibid.*, p. 7.

[132] *Ibid.*, p. 8: "frontero de las escuelas."

Like Francisco Guerrero, another principal figure in Spanish musical history, Juan del Encina probably studied music with his elder brother. He was a boy of twelve when Diego was appointed to the Salamanca chair. Ramos de Pareja can have had nothing to do with Encina's education (he having left Salamanca not later than 1472). Martín Gómez de Cantalapiedra, Diego's predecessor who occupied the Salamanca chair from 1465–1479,[133] may conceivably have influenced Juan. No composition by Cantalapiedra survives. One villancico by Diego is preserved in *CMP*.[134] Another teacher would have been the cathedral master of the boys, Fernando de Torrijos, under whom Encina sat (still using the name of Juan de Fermoselle) in 1484. This was the cathedral singer whom Encina aspired to succeed during 1498.

While an adolescent chorister in Salamanca Cathedral Juan simultaneously pursued an academic course in the university. He read Latin under the most famous Renaissance Spanish master of the tongue, Antonio de Nebrija (= Lebrixa). Although he himself left no Latin publications, Encina revered Nebrija as the fount of all learning.[135] His favorite Spanish poet was Juan de Mena,[136] and his studies in prosody culminated in an *Arte de poesía castellana* (published in 1496) which is still a classic text. To support himself he became a page to Gutierre de Toledo, the university chancellor.[137] In 1490 he began signing himself "de Encina" instead of "de Fermoselle," the evidence being his signature added to a certain cathedral document of that year.

In 1490, having reached the age of minor clerical orders, he gained a better cathedral title, that of *capellán de coro*. The date when he received his bachelor's degree is not known. However, that he did obtain one is certain. On September 25, 1502, for instance, he was named in a papal rescript as *Johannes del Enzina clericus salamantinus Bacchallarius In legibus*.[138] Probably he received the degree before 1492, the year in which he entered the household of Fadrique Álvarez de Toledo, second duke of Alva (and elder brother of Gutierre de Toledo).

The second Duke of Alva, Don Fadrique de Toledo (d. 1531), was no less avid a music lover than his father, Don García Álvarez de Toledo (d. 1488). It was Don García, of course, who wrote the beautiful lament, *Nunca fué pena mayor*, set by Urrede (private chapelmaster in 1476–1477 to the old duke). Don Fadrique's wife, Doña Isabel de Zuñiga y Pimentel, was also well educated musically. Their patronage made possible Encina's rich outpouring of song in the half-decade between 1492 (at the close of which year he joined their household at Alba de Tormes) and 1498. *Triste España sin ventura*

---

[133] Enrique Esperabé Arteaga, *Historia pragmática é interna de la Universidad de Salamanca*, II, 249.

[134] *MME*, V, 113 (*CMP*, no. 88). In his introduction (*MME*, V, 26) Anglés credited this item to Juan del Encina. Since the latter discontinued using the patronymic before 1490 this song – *Amor, por quien yo padesco* – more probably belongs to the Salamanca professor. It is strophic, whereas Encina couched his lover's complaints almost invariably in the form of a villancico. As for musical style, the Fermoselle item shows six instances of a changing-note figure in which the second note dissonates with the other two voices. None of Encina's authenticated songs contains as many cambiatas within so few measures.

[135] *Cancionero de las obras de Juan del enzina* (Salamanca, 1496 [facs. ed. Madrid: Tip. de la Rev. de Arch., Bibl. y Museos, 1928]), fol. 2. Encina calls his teacher "el dotissimo maestro Antonio de lebrixa" and commends him for having resuscitated classical Latin in Spain.

[136] *Ibid.*, fol. 4v.

[137] *Ibid.*, p. 9, c. 2 (see especially note 3).

[138] *Ibid.*, pp. 13 (c. 2) – 14 (c. 1).

(*CMP*, no. 83) may have been written as late as 1504, in November of which year Queen Isabella died. But on Encina's own testimony the bulk of his music as well as poetry dated from 1492–1498.

THE CASTLE at Alba de Tormes was destroyed by the French in 1812. But its appearance during the early years of the sixteenth century was described by Garcilaso de la Vega (1503–1536) in his second eclogue at the lines beginning "En la ribera verde." [139] He praised its location on a slope overlooking the valley of the Tormes a short distance above Salamanca, its lofty towers dominating a plain which remained green the year around, and the admirable proportions of the castle. In these pleasant surroundings Encina served as a "troubadour" for at least five years, entertaining the ducal family with poetic compliments, amorous accompanied solo songs, and playlets into which he invariably introduced part-songs for three and four voices.

THE FIRST such recorded occasion was Christmas Eve of 1492. Encina enters the chamber in which the duke and duchess are hearing matins. Attired as a shepherd he first recites a poem praising such personages. Soon another servant also in the guise of a shepherd enters, playing the rôle of Matthew. A third and fourth, Luke and Mark, join them to reason of the birth of Christ and to end with a villancico *a 4, Grangasajo siento yo,* in which they promise to visit Bethlehem where a Saviour has that night been born. This religious playlet, another for Holy Week with Veronica in the cast, and another for Easter with Mary Magdalene, were all printed at Salamanca in Encina's 1496 *Cancionero*, the publication of which was probably financed by the duke himself. The fifth playlet in this same cancionero deals with so topical a matter as the imminent war with France, the sixth (like the fifth) commemorates Shrove Tuesday, the seventh depicts lovesick courtiers turned shepherds, and the eighth, shepherds returning to their proper status of courtiers. In this last, a courtier-shepherd named Gil presents the duke and duchess with the "complete works of Juan del Encina." Gil was therefore a rôle played by Encina.

In this last playlet, Gil sings and dances. His partner is Pascuala, a shepherdess. They form a foursome with a married shepherd couple, Mingo and Menga. The villancico which they sing between the first and second halves of this "égloga" (Encina calls his playlets "eclogues") enters *CMP* at no. 165 with the title *Gasajémonos de husía*. In order to give each couple an opportunity, he inserts four short duets in this villancico – first for top and bottom, then middle, then upper two, and lastly lower two, voices. The villancico with which this égloga ends is found in *CMP* (no. 167) with the title *Ninguno çierre las puertas*. A third song from an Encina dramatic piece enters *CMP* as no. 174, *Oy comamos y bebamos (a 4)*. Originally written for a Mardi Gras playlet, this last song takes for its theme: Eat, drink, and be merry, for tomorrow we die; and the music marvellously catches the dramatic mood.

Whether designed for characters to sing in one of his playlets or for independent performance, the Encina villancico comments on an "already existing" dramatic situ-

[139] *Biblioteca de autores españoles* (Madrid: M. Rivadeneyra, 1854), XXXII, 15 (c. 1, lines 15–26).

ation. As a rule it reveals the nature of this dramatic situation only indirectly. In his playlets the preceding dialogue of course establishes the situation. Much of the charm in his villancicos is accounted for by their immediacy. The scene having already been set, the song needs be no more than a purely emotional outburst. At that, his villancicos are always youthful outbursts. Much as one may regret his ceasing to compose them after leaving the service of the Duke of Alva, his musical strain might have seemed repetitive had he continued to sound it in middle age. The bold and lusty *Gasajémonos de husía* and the languorously voluptuous *Ninguno çierre las puertas* belong rightly in the quiver of a youthful hotblood but not in that of a fiftyish ecclesiastic.

BEGINNING with 1496, he himself decided to write no more except on commission from his patrons. At least in the last eclogue ot his 1496 *Cancionero* he confesses such an intention through the mouth of Gil. After presenting the duke and duchess with the *copilación de todas sus obras* (his "opera omnia") he promises through Gil's mouth *de no trobar mas salvo lo que sus señorías le mandassen*[140] (not to poetize any more except when their Graces command). The day of rhyming for the sake of rhyming was then long past when in 1498 he applied for the singer's prebend which his old teacher, Fernando de Torrijos, had held until recent decease. When the vote was about to be taken, though, only one cathedral authority spoke in his favor. The others evidently thought the gay troubadour of the 1496 *Cancionero* too secular an individual for the post of a cathedral singer and possible future master of the boy choristers. The post was instead divided between two weaker candidates. Later (January 11, 1499) it was temporarily divided among three, Lucas Fernández, a rival dramatic poet, making the third. Encina, smarting under the rebuff, included in his eclogue *de las grandes lluvias* (for presentation on Christmas Eve, 1498, in the ducal seat at Alba de Tormes) a rather transparent reference to this disappointing episode.[141]

Soon afterwards he left his native region. He may first have visited Portugal if the reference to Estremoz in *CMP*, no. 304, be taken autobiographically. Before the end of 1499 he had reached Rome. On August 12, 1500, Alexander VI named him to a benefice in Salamanca diocese, combining it with a chaplaincy (not requiring residence). Two years later he had so grown in the pope's favor that Alexander called him his closest familiar (*familiaris continus comensalis principalis principaliter*). In testimony of favor the pope conferred upon him in 1502 the very singer's prebend in Salamanca Cathedral which the canons of that cathedral had refused to bestow in 1498. Encina's triumph would seem to have been complete. The bull of September 25, 1502, designated the poet's father and two brothers, Francisco and Antonio, as proxies into whose hands the Salamanca cathedral authorities were to deliver a signed document acknowledging the transfer of the prebend to the absentee Encina.

On December 2, 1502, Francisco appeared in his brother's behalf before the assembled Salamanca chapter. As of that date the singer's prebend had been unified, the

---

[140] *Cancionero* (1496), fol. 113.

[141] Barbieri, pp. 30–31. See *Cancionero de todas las obras de Juan del enzina* (Saragossa: George Coci, 1516), fols. 94v.–95v.

holder now being Lucas Fernández (who served both as organist and singer). The chapter at once agreed to pay the costs of a lengthy ecclesiastical process in Fernández's favor. In 1507 he was no longer cathedral organist and singer. Even so Encina did not follow him. Indeed he never was able to force the chapter's hand, despite his high standing at the court not only of the Spanish Alexander VI but later of the Italian Julius II.

It was Julius who conferred upon him, although he was not yet a priest, the archdeaconate of Málaga – one of the most lucrative dignities in Málaga Cathedral, and certainly a better paying post than any of the absentee benefices bestowed during Alexander VI's pontificate. By a prior papal concession all dignities in Málaga Cathedral had after the Granada wars been placed nominally at the royal disposal. Encina therefore arranged through the papal nuncio at Ferdinand's court that Pedro de Hermosilla, his brother, should obtain the requisite royal document and present it in his behalf to the Málaga chapter. Pedro could the more easily do so since he was in 1509 himself a resident in this Mediterranean haven. The Málaga capitular acts show that Pedro brought in the royal document on April 11, 1509. The first act mentioning Encina's presence is dated, however, January 2, 1510.[142]

On March 20, 1510, the chapter designated him and a fellow-canon as deputies to the court, their commission being to obtain a new royal charter from Ferdinand guaranteeing the cathedral income and setting out certain new rules for the collection of tithes. On the following October 11 the chapter recalled him from the court, but on July 14, 1511, sent both him and Gonzalo Pérez back to pursue the business further. A cloud had already arisen between him and the chapter before his return to court, as is shown by their attempt to diminish his archidiaconal prerogatives (ostensibly because he had not yet been made a priest). The chapter did agree to give him 100 ducats towards the cost of the second trip to court – but reached the decision reluctantly. On August 21, 1511, his fellow-canons voted to reduce his archidiaconal income to one-half, because he was not yet a priest.

With curious vacillation their next step (on January 3, 1512) was to appoint him a delegate to the provincial synod summoned by Diego Deza, archbishop of Seville. He stayed in Seville in company with his own bishop and another Málaga canon from January 11–15. The meetings were held in St. Clement's chapel. Upon returning to Málaga he still did not wish to settle permanently, but instead asked leave from the chapter on May 17 (1512) to revisit Rome. Having reached the city which he loved above all others, he stayed a whole year. The most memorable event of this particular sojourn was the presentation at a Spanish archbishop's palace of his last known dramatic piece, the so-called *Égloga de Plácida e Vittoriano*. The audience included Julius II, Archbishop Jacobo Serra (owner of the palace), the Spanish ambassador, and numerous Spanish and Italian nobility. His play was given the night of January 6, 1513.[143]

---

[142] Mitjana, *Estudios*, p. 17.

[143] The *commedia* began an hour before midnight. The pope sat between Federico Gonzaga and the Spanish ambassador. Gonzaga disliked it, because it was in Spanish. See Alessandro Luzio, "Federico Gonzaga, ostaggio alla Corte di Giulio II," *Archivio della R. Società Romana di Storia Patria*, IX, iii–iv (1886), p. 550.

THOUGH this is his longest and best developed piece, it has been criticized for its pagan atmosphere. The cast includes the goddess Venus. One passage "travesties" the Christian office of the dead. Plácida, the shepherdess who has committed suicide for a carnal love, is restored to life at Venus's instance. The name of Jesus is used, but as an exclamation rather than in a petition. Eritea, an aging female, plies the trade of a Celestina. But if questions of propriety are brushed aside, the play can be applauded for the proof it gives of Encina's ripening dramatic powers. Unfortunately none of the music has been preserved. Before Plácida stabs herself a shepherd named Pascual sings an instrumentally accompanied villancico, railing against the goddess of love. At the end the happy lovers join in dancing to the sound of bagpipes.[144]

ENCINA returned to Málaga before August 13, 1513. In the succeeding autumn he was again chosen to represent the chapter at court. During his absence he also transacted business for Málaga Cathedral in Seville. Early in 1514 he set out anew for Rome, this time without awaiting the chapter's permission. On March 31 his fellow-canons merely heard that he had departed "in conformity with a papal bull." The new pope, Leo X (1513–1521), was to patronize him as enthusiastically as had the two previous pontiffs.

The evidence is first a bull in Encina's behalf which reached the Málaga chapter on October 11, 1514. It read in part: "During the attendance of the Archdeacon of Málaga at the pontifical court he is in no wise to be disturbed nor molested in the enjoyment of his full income, no matter what statutes of Málaga Cathedral may conflict with this provision." The second was the publication at Rome in 1514 of the *Égloga de Plácida e Vittoriano*, a play which on other evidence Leo X is known to have enjoyed. The third proof of Leo's favor is an appointment before May 27, 1517, to be a subcollector of apostolic revenues. For a fourth proof, Encina's ecclesiastical titles were so shifted that in exchange for the archdeaconate of Málaga he received a benefice in the collegiate church of Morón. This exchange took effect on February 21, 1519. To the Morón benefice not requiring residence, was added one month later the priorate in León Cathedral. Encina took possession of his priorate, the final dignity which he was to enjoy, on March 14, 1519. His proxy was a certain canon of León named Antonio de Obregón.

As for Encina's actual whereabouts between 1514 and 1519: he was in Rome during 1515. Early in 1516 he was again in Málaga, briefly. On February 4, 1516, he asked leave to go outside the city, without naming any definite destination. On May 6, 1516, his bishop, Diego Ramírez de Villaescusa, wrote a letter from Valladolid summoning him to appear in that city before May 27. Ferdinand had just died and Charles, the new king, was expected from Flanders. Presumably the bishop, relying on Encina's skill as a negotiator, wished him again to assist in the protracted cathedral suit for financial privileges. On December 30, 1516, the chapter voted to send him twenty ducats while he continued to reside at court. Before March 27, 1517, he had returned to Málaga, but the chapter on that day commissioned him to repair again to court with the purpose of suing for further pecuniary benefits. On April 14, 1517, his fellow-canons received his

---

[144] *Gaitero* = bagpipe-player. See "Plácida y Vitoriano" in *El teatro español: Historia y antología*, ed. Federico Carlos Sáinz de Robles (Madrid: M. Águilar, 1942), I, 183.

letter from court asking for more expense money, a request which they immediately granted. On September 12, 1517, he made his last known appearance at a Málaga chapter meeting, presenting on that date an account of his most recent efforts at court.

Since he appeared at no later session it is likely that he left for Rome immediately. The royal permission which he needed in order to resign his archdeaconate in exchange for a simple benefice at the collegiate church in Morón was given at Saragossa in the names of the titular queen, Joanna [the Mad], and her son, Charles [V], on June 13, 1518. This permission was addressed to the bishop of Málaga, who at that moment was the same Italian cardinal, Raffaele Riario, earlier encountered as a contender with Peñalosa for a canonry in Seville Cathedral (see above, pp. 146–147).

If not in Rome during the whole of 1518 Encina was certainly there on March 14, 1519. The León Cathedral capitular acts for that particular date show that his proxy took possession of the León priorate in the name of *Juan del Enzina, residente en corte de Roma.* At approximately this same date he decided to make a pilgrimage to the Holy Land and to become a priest. The poetical account of this journey, *Tribagia o via sagrada de Hierusalem,* which was to be the last of his published writings, appeared at Rome in 1521.

In 200 eight-line stanzas (written in *arte mayor*) [145] he narrated the events of a round-trip journey from Venice that lasted from July 1 until November 4. He left Rome in late June, passed to Loreto, and thence to Ancona. At Venice he found one of the principal grandees of Spain preparing to make the pilgrimage – Don Fadrique Enríquez de Ribera, Marqués de Tarifa. Don Fadrique's prose account of the same journey contrasts interestingly with Encina's. The grandee offered, for instance, several observations concerning the music of other rites in Jerusalem. He noted that the Greeks did not gather together around a lectern to sing the hours from a large book, but that instead a youth started intoning a psalm.[146] The other singers while remaining at their accustomed place attentively watched his hand rise and fall to indicate the rise and fall in pitch of the psalm-melody. Don Fadrique not only commented on the cheironomy of the Greeks, but added interesting observations on Oriental-rite music in Jerusalem.[147] Encina, by way of contrast, says nothing of the music heard anywhere during the four months' journey. When some seventy years later Francisco Guerrero after taking the same trip wrote his prose account, he too neglected to describe the music which he heard.[148] Both Encina and Guerrero however describe in prolix detail all the sacred sites which they visited.

[145] Encina recognized two standard line-lengths: *arte real* (eight syllables to the line); *arte mayor* (twelve). He allowed an occasional *pie quebrado* (half-line) to break the monotony of whole lines (*enteros*). See his illuminating discussion in the *Arte de poesía castellana* (*Cancionero,* 1496, fol. 4v.) which he dedicated to Prince John, son of Ferdinand and Isabella. His villancicos are written in *arte real* verse.

[146] Fadrique Enríquez de Ribera, *Viage de Jerusalem* (Madrid: Francisco Martínez Abad, 1733), p. 47, c.2: "Las horas Canonicas, i todo lo demas, no cantan en Atril, sino todo lo mas de Coro, è vn muchacho alli con vn Libro, que comiença los Psalmos, que ellos cantan en tono, *i quando suben, i bajan, hacen señal con las manos.*"

[147] *Ibid.,* p. 40, c. 1. The Indian Christians danced and sang on Good Friday.

[148] Guerrero's *Viage de Hierusalem* was published at Seville in 1590, 1592, at Alcalá de Henares in 1605, and elsewhere frequently during the seventeenth and eighteenth centuries.

Encina having but recently been ordained priest celebrated his first Mass on August 6 (1519) in a small side chapel of the Church of the Holy Sepulchre. The "padrino" (= server) on this occasion was Don Fadrique.[149] He was not only served by the *Adelantado de Andalucía* (governor of Andalusia) but also celebrated Mass at the very site on Mount Sion where Jesus was traditionally supposed to have instituted the Sacrament.

After the disembarkation at Venice on November 4 he returned to Rome, to compose his poetical account. At the close of its 200 stanzas he added another dozen urging Christian kings to unite forces for the retaking of Palestine. His zeal for reconquest sounds typically Spanish, and helps to explain why during the trip the Spaniards, and they alone, were warned not to disclose their nationality to Moslem or Jew.[150] The *Tribagia* was published at Rome in 1521, reprinted at Lisbon in 1580 and 1608, at Seville in 1606, and at Madrid in 1748 (1733) and 1786, its popularity during two hundred and fifty years exceeding that of any other poetry which he produced.[151]

After Leo X's death (December 1, 1521) a reforming pope was elected in the person of Adrian VI (January 9, 1522). The succession of Maecenases, interested in art and music, had momentarily ended, and Encina finding Rome no longer a favorable climate, returned to Spain. He was in León at a cathedral chapter meeting on November 20, 1523. On April 14, 1524, he received a certain concession of lands from the chapter. During 1525 he was absent from León, a fellow-canon named Juan de Lorenzana acting as his deputy. On October 2, 1526, he covenanted with the chapter to spend a rather large amount – some 200,000 maravedís – for the remodeling of the piece of cathedral property which he was using as his own residence, and of certain adjoining residences and shops which formed part of the same lot.[152] On May 22, 1527, the chapter appointed two overseers to inspect the buildings which he proposed to remodel.[153] The actual remodeling had not been completed on the target date of October 2, 1528, whereupon the chapter gave him the privilege of delaying completion until the end of the succeeding August.[154]

On January 27, 1529, the chapter named a deputy to exercise the office of prior.[155] According to Cotarelo, the wording of the January 27 act strongly suggests that Encina had been stricken by paralysis or some other incapacitating illness. The deputy named to function in his stead, Salazar, was a fellow-canon. Although an exact date cannot be fixed, the evidence summarized in the next paragraph makes it almost certain that he died late in that year.

First, there is a lengthy entry in the León Cathedral capitular acts dated January 10, 1530.[156] On that day the chapter conferred the priorate upon García de Gibraleón, then

---

[149] Enríquez de Ribera, *op. cit.*, p. 94, c. 2 (lines 49–50).

[150] *Ibid.*, p. 22, c. 1 (lines 24–31).

[151] Further bibliographical details in Encina, *Cancionero* (1496), p. 21.

[152] Eloy Díaz-Jiménez y Molleda, *Juan del Encina en León* (Madrid: Lib. gen. de Victoriano Suárez, 1909) p. 24.

[153] *Ibid.*, p. 27.

[154] *Ibid.*, p. 28.

[155] *Ibid.*, p. 29.

[156] *Ibid.*, pp. 30–32.

residing at the papal court. A proxy took possession of the office in his absence. Gibraleón had preceded Encina in the priorate, and may have resigned with the express understanding that it would revert to him at Encina's death. Although it is not strictly necessary to believe that news travelled to Rome and back again before January 10, still formal possession of the office within a mere week or so of his decease seems hasty. The second document bearing on his death is a capitular act of January 14, 1530 [157] mentioning a bequest by the "late Juan del Encina" to the Dean and chapter of two books of decretals or a thousand maravedís, whichever they preferred.

Francisco Fermoselle del Encina (son of Francisco – Juan's younger brother who was an embroiderer by trade and died in 1504) sought the priorate immediately after his uncle's death. Clement VII eventually gave it to him, nullifying Gibraleón's absentee possession. The papal bull acceding the priorate to the nephew reached the León chapter on July 28, 1531. After a contest lasting some months the nephew made good his claim, and was inducted on February 10, 1532. This uncle-nephew transaction recalls the similar link of Francisco de Peñalosa and Luis de Peñalosa (see above, p. 150).

Juan del Encina stipulated in his will that his body should be moved within five years to Salamanca. Miguel de Fermoselle, his brother, was named his residuary legatee. He had not carried out this provision of the will, however, as late as 1533. The next year Miguel himself died, and an entry in the Salamanca *libro de cuentas* for 1534 shows that in that year the Salamanca chapter received a payment of 500 maravedís to defray the expenses of interring Encina's body beneath the *coro* in the cathedral. Having travelled everywhere else, he wished to rest at last within the choir where he had begun as a singer, from which he had been rejected, and to which he had unsuccessfully intrigued to return. What he had failed to encompass in life, he aspired to do in death.

No portrait is preserved. But an authenticated signature (March 21, 1510) survives in a book of capitular acts at Málaga. It has been twice reproduced,[158] the second time in company with signatures by thirteen other Renaissance composers. Typically enough, Encina strives not so much for the legibility of his signature as for the drawing of a bold and striking picture. A scroll at the left side represents the name "Joan." At the right side a companion scroll with no meaning is added, simply to balance the picture. Above the "del enzina" he has written abbreviations for the Latin words meaning "archdeacon of Málaga." Since "M" is the one capital letter in the superscription, his making the scrolls on either side resemble "M" as closely as possible dresses the picture. His signature seems exactly to express those flamboyant personality traits which his actions and writings have revealed to have been typical of the man.

FORMERLY Encina's position in cultural history was assured almost entirely because of his theatrical pioneering. Such is no longer the case. Within recent years it has come to be realized that his songs are as important and distinctive a contribution as his plays.

On the structural side, only five of his *CMP* pieces are *romances* (nos. 74, 77, 79, 126, and 131). Another three, not easily classifiable, lack a refrain of any sort (nos. 81, 83,

---

[157] *Ibid.*, p. 33.
[158] Mitjana, *Estudios*, p. 40; Reese, *Music in the Renaissance*, opp. p. 62.

and 324). As for the number of those with refrain, 54 of his 62 *CMP* songs open with one. Seven of the 54 are exceptional in that the rhyme-scheme of the strophe (*coplas*) does not carry over into the da capo section (nos. 30, 46, 163, 191, 249, 271, 313). The rest are so constructed that the rhyme-scheme of the *coplas* does always spill over into the *estribillo* (refrain).

Each line of poetry corresponds with a clear-cut musical phrase. He never tries to calk his seams. As a result his villancicos often sound like a string of epigrams. Just as in his poetry he uses a minimum of adjectives and a maximum of nouns and verbs, so in his music he harmonizes his terse melodies with root-position chords related to each other in tonic-dominant or tonic-subdominant senses.

Only once (no. 82) in his 62 *CMP* pieces does he use the mensuration designated with a circle (modern equivalent: $\frac{3}{2}$). Such a signature might do very well for Urrede, who used it in all three of his *CMP* songs (nos. 1, 17, and 23). But not for Encina, who is all nerves and action in triple meter. Instead, he uses two other "signatures" to denote meter in threes: ₵3 and ℂ. The first of these stands at the head of fifteen pieces and is properly understood as the equivalent of $\frac{3}{4}$ (nos. 174, 179, 184, 191, 249, 271, 278, 281, 282, 283, 285, 304, 312, 313, 436). The second urges an even faster gait. In the four instances, it ought probably to be interpreted as the equivalent of $\frac{3}{8}$ (nos. 181, 293, 298, 309). In one isolated instance (no. 421), he omits mensuration signs, but blackens his semibreves and breves, the musical sense being that of a $\frac{3}{8}$ or extremely fast $\frac{3}{4}$. His choice of ○, ₵3, or ℂ, can in every instance be laid to the text. The signature implying the slowest beat matches the most pensive text, that implying the fastest, the most obscene and jaunty texts.

He chooses ₵, however, for the overwhelming majority of his pieces. This "cut-time" signature stands at the head of 39 of his 62 songs (nos. 30, 44, 46, 50, 67, 74, 77, 79, 81, 83, 94, 126, 131, 162, 163, 165, 167, 178, 186, 224, 275, 277, 289, 302, 305, 308, 314, 316, 318, 324, 338, 354, 369, 395, 406, 408, 412, 428, 438). Contrary to the prevalent notion that *CMP* Spaniards favored triple meter, not only Encina, the most fecund of *CMP* composers, but also Francisco Millán, the second most fertile, overwhelmingly favored duple meter. If forty of Encina's 62 pieces are in duple, sixteen of Millán's 23 also use the ₵ "time-signature." As for meter-changes in mid-course, Encina shifts during four of his pieces (nos. 94, 165, 249, and 302). Millán changes meter in the middle of five of his.

Encina and Anchieta belong together in that each uses quintuple meter in two instances. In the Encina pair which ought properly to be transcribed nowadays using the $\frac{5}{8}$ time-signature he designates his meter in these two ways: ₵$\frac{5}{1}$ (no. 102) and 3^2 (no. 426). Anchieta, on the other hand, specifies his quintuple meter: ○$\frac{5}{1}$. This latter "signature" is properly transcribed in both of Anchieta's pieces (*CMP*, nos, 177 and 335) not with the modern $\frac{5}{8}$, but rather with the $\frac{5}{4}$ time-signature.

If the theory that *Palacio* composers especially favored triple meter can no longer be sustained, we should on the other hand stress the novelty of their quintuple-meter experiments. In all, four songs by Anchieta are for instance included in *CMP*. Two are quintuple-meter songs. What is more, *Dos ánades* (no. 177) is the one *CMP* song which retained wide popularity for more than a century [159] – both Cervantes and Quevedo having been familiar with it. Escobar is another who uses quintuple meter, *Las mis penas madre* (*CMP*, no. 59) being written with signature of $\frac{5}{1}$. Still another quintuple-meter exponent is Diego Fernández (*De ser mal casada*, no. 197). The latter's $\frac{5}{1}$,used in conjunction with blackened semibreves and minims, is best represented in modern transcription by the $\frac{5}{8}$ signature.

As for registration, Encina in 30 cases calls for four and in 32 cases for three voices. Although it may be true that in his *Auto del repelón* he introduces a fourth character [160] near the end for the sole purpose of making up a vocal quartet, still he so frequently uses three voices in his extant villancicos that the local availability of another good singer rather than any real preference for the sound of four voices must have been the reason for ending his rowdy playlet of Salamanca student-life with a quartet instead of a trio. He never asks his basses for a lower note than F_1 nor his trebles for a higher note than d^1. The treble is always the leading voice. Its range reaches a major ninth in no. 354, but usually he keeps it to a seventh or less. In the treble he occasionally introduces ascending octave-leaps, but never descending. Skips of a minor or major sixth sometimes separate phrases, but he does not interpolate them within treble phrases. Melodic sequences lend a popular flavor to the treble in such items as *Mas vale trocar* (no. 298), *Quédate Carillo* (no. 304) and *Fata la parte* (no. 421). The faster the gait, the likelier he is to build his treble out of melodic sequences.

HIS FAVORED MODES are the dorian and its cognate, the aeolian. He slights the phrygian and lydian. In the following synopsis his songs are classified according to their lowest ending-notes. The ending-chord comes of course at the close of the estribillo, not the coplas. An asterisk before a number means that the tenor lies a fifth (in nos. 81 and 289, a third) above the contra in the last chord. An italicized number indicates that the tenor sings an ending-note a fifth below the contra, or (if the contra divides into two voices on the last chord) a fifth below the upper of the two notes in the contra. Otherwise the tenor and contra are to be understood as singing the same letter-name note in the final chord.

C: 304, 318, *354*
D: *81, 131, *167, *174, *179, 186, 271, 277, *282*, 298, *302*, 314, *338*, *412*, 426
E: *102, *162, *178, *281, *285*, *369, *436
F: 30, 82, *94, *224*, *283*, 309
G: 44, 50, 67, 74, 83, 184, 249, 278, 305, 308, 312, 324, *395*, *421
A: 46, 77, 79, 126, 163, 165, 181, 191, 275, *289, 293, 313, 316, 406, 408, 428, 438

---

[159] One other song seems to have retained a degree of popularity, at least in Portugal. Alvares Frouvo declared in his *Discursos sobre a perfeiçam* (Lisbon, 1662) that Encina's *Pues que jamás olvidaros* (*CMP*, no. 30) remained "the only piece of 'old' music worth the consideration of 'modern' musicians of his time."

[160] Juan del Enzina, *El Aucto del Repelón*, ed. Alfredo Álvarez de la Villa (Paris: Librería Paul Ollendorff, 1910), p. 274. The fourth in the quartet probably played the *rabel*. The pertinent lines read:

> *Allí viene Juan Rabé.*
> *Muy bien estaria á nos*
> *Cantássemos dos por dos.*

As this synopsis reveals, 17 of his *CMP* pieces end on A, 15 on D, and 14 on G. But of the 14 ending on G, nine should probably be credited to the dorian, since in each of these nine, B♭ prefixes at least one lower voice. The 15 examples ending on D are nearly always pure dorian rather than "natural minor," since in only one does B♭ appear anywhere as a "signature" (no. 298). In that one case B♭ prefixes only the contra voices. Among the half-dozen pieces ending on F, the B♭-"signature" appears in at least a lower voice five times. Among the three ending on C, two pieces carry B♭ in the "key-signature" (all voices, no. 304; contra only, no. 318). Of those ending on A, none shows B♭ anywhere as a "signature."

As for the *deuterus* examples: six must be credited to the hypophrygian – if, following such authorities as Tinctoris and Aron,[161] we allow the tenor voice to determine the mode (nos. 102, 162, 178, 281, 369, and 436). Similarly, one example should be credited to the phrygian (no. 285). As the above synopsis discloses, the *deuterus* examples are his only ones in which he consistently prefers the plagal mode to the authentic mode. The only other plagal mode which he uses more than once or twice is the hypodorian.

He is by no means unique among *CMP* composers in slighting the phrygian and hypophrygian. Millán, the next best represented composer, also slights these modes. Only three of Millán's 23 *CMP* items end on an E-chord, "incomplete" in each case. All three are in hypophrygian – the tenor again serving as the criterion (nos. 295, 336, and 446). No shot misses the mark more widely than the saying that Spanish composers during the 1490's peculiarly favored Modes III and IV.

Encina was a university man, his brother a university professor of music. If any Spaniard should have treated the modes in textbook fashion, Encina ought to have been that composer. Ramos taught that each mode was governed by an astral influence.[162] He often flouted tradition; but not when he propounded this doctrine. Even Burzio, the first to attack him in print, taught that the stars governed the modes. To take an example, Ramos claimed that Mercury controls the hypophrygian mode. If so, then the hypophrygian ought to be peculiarly appropriate for the setting of texts which emphasize mutability or fickleness. Appropriately enough, the texts in Encina's half-dozen hypophrygian villancicos do play upon these very themes of mutability, fickleness, and inconstancy. The first, *Amor con fortuna* (*CMP*, no. 102), adds another example to the already long list of Renaissance songs bewailing the malevolence of fickle Fortune. In the next, *No tienen vado mis males* (*CMP*, no. 162; *CMH*, no. 50) he complains that he can find no way of fording the river of troubles flowing from his lady's fickleness. In *Sy amor pone las escalas* (*CMP*, no. 178) he declares that no one can build high enough walls around his heart but that love will find its way to scale them to the defender's damage. In *Nuevas te traigo, Carillo* (*CMC*, no. 59; *CMP*, no. 281) he sets a dialogue between Carillo and Pascual, two shepherds. Pascual tells Carillo that Bartolilla, his beloved shepherdess, has suddenly married another young man of the neighborhood the

---

[161] See Strunk, *Source Readings*, p. 209 (par. 2 and n. 6). Both Tinctoris (1476) and Aron (1525) unqualifiedly declared that the mode of a polyphonic piece is to be decided by its tenor.

[162] Ramos de Pareja, *Musica practica*, ed. J. Wolf, p. 58.

Sunday just past. Carillo cannot believe such news, she having been his own promised one so recently.

In *Romerico, tú que vienes* (*CMP*, no. 369; *CMS*, no. 169; *CMH*, no. 56), he again writes a dialogue, one speaker being a distraught lover separated from his life, his sweetness, and his hope. This lover implores Romerico, who comes from wherever she is, to tell him how she fares; but he already fears the worst. His manner of questioning betrays the anxiety of an abandoned lover. In *Revelóse mi cuidado* (*CMP*, no. 436), Encina voices the torments of a lover whose mistress has played him false.

All of Encina's hypophrygian pieces, then, play upon the themes of falsehood, perjury, mischance, and sudden change. On the other hand, the phrygian mode is governed – according to Ramos – not by Mercury but by Mars. One song, and one only, in Encina's list is cast in the phrygian mode: *Un' amiga tengo hermano* (*CMP*, no. 285; *CMH*, no. 46). No lyrics could more sharply differ from those in hypophrygian mode. Here Mars has just returned from Venus's bed. The mood is one of triumphal arches and victory garlands. The poet exults because he is in love, and because his future is assured.

ENCINA'S DISSONANCE-TECHNIQUE yields to certain generalizations. He was notably abstemious in his use of the changing-note figure, incomplete or complete. Seventeen instances have been found in the forty songs in duple meter – not a large number. When introduced, it is almost invariably given another voice than the lowest. Four leaps from a dissonant note which properly belongs to the succeeding chord have been inventoried in the same forty songs. His sparing use of the changing- and escaped-note figures is, however, a trait which he shares with other *CMP* composers.

In general, he seems to have counted consonances from the tenor rather than the contra. At the end of six E-pieces, the tenor lies a fifth above the contra in the last chord. In these same six hypophrygian pieces he places the treble a fourth above the tenor in the final chord. Elsewhere he requires the tenor to consonate with the treble in the closing chord. But on the other hand, the interval of a perfect fourth between the tenor and treble will be found at the openings of nos. 83 (*Triste España*, 4 v.), 167 (*Ninguno çierre las puertas*, 4 v.), 271 (*Pues que ya nunca nos veis*, 4 v.), 298 (*Más vale trocar*, 4 v.), 395 (*El que tal señora tiene*, 3 v.), and 436 (*Revelóse mi ciudado*, 3 v.). The first in this list may date from the close of 1504, if the subject of its lament is actually Queen Isabella's death. The second, which brings to a close his égloga entitled *Ah, Mingo, quédaste atrás*, must on the other hand antedate 1496, in which year this égloga was published. He therefore did not begin to write fourths between tenor and treble only after coming under the influence of Italian frottolists around 1500.

The critical edition – again as in the case of León, Madrid, and Rodríguez – does attribute certain passages to Encina that on the surface would seem stylistic lapses. In no. 178 (*Sy amor pone las escalas*, 4 v.) he appears, for instance, to have written parallel octaves between the tenor and treble at measure 11. In his favor, however, is the fact that Barbieri, the earlier editor of *CMP*, did not transcribe this passage in such a way as to produce the offending octaves. What is more, measures 9–12 exactly duplicate 18–21 in every respect other than the conduct of the tenor voice at mm. 11 and 20. No

parallel octaves mar m. 20. Therefore it is likely that Barbieri was right when he transcribed m. 11 without them. According to the critical edition, Encina seems also to have
lapsed in the treble of no. 308 (*Desidme, pues sospirastes*, 3 v.), at m. 12. The second note
reads *f*, thus making it appear that he leapt to dissonances. But if the note is read as *g*
rather than *f*, then no "exceptional" dissonance-treatment is involved.

AS FOR his use of imitation, he employs it neither very frequently nor very rigorously.
Numbers 94 (*Cucú, cucú*, 4 v.), 184 (*Levanta, Pascual*, 3 v.), 249 (*Caldero y llave*, 4 v.), 304
(*Quédate, Carillo, adiós*, 4 v.), and 428 (*Pelayo, tan buen esfuerço*, 3 v.) begin with it; but
these opening imitations always collapse straightway into homophony, once the first
point has been made. All voice-parts of only one example from this "imitative" group
are throughout underlaid with text in the critical edition – *Caldero y llave*. This is also
his only song shown as an example in the *Oxford History of Music* (II, ii [1932], pp. 144–
145). The lyrics under the guise of a tinker's cry border on the obscene. One other of his
songs has gained more lurid notice – *Si abrá en este baldrés*, no. 179. Or at least an early
handler of the manuscript expressed his shock by scratching out a pornographic word.
But *Caldero y llave* (and perhaps also, *Fata la parte*, no. 421) can match it. *Caldero y llave*
differs from the other obscene songs with its imitation. The bawdy ones however are all
of a kind in being set to extremely fast triple-meter music. (*MME*, V and X, print full
texts in only selected instances.)

ENCINA did not anachronistically write any "song-cycles." But *CMP* does contain a few
songs originally conceived in pairs – after the manner of dance and *Nachtanz*, pavane
and galliard, passamezzo and saltarello. The first of such an Encina pair goes slower, and
is in duple meter. The second, insofar as poetry is concerned, takes the name of *deshecha*,
a word which in a dictionary translation means "a genteel departure," or "a polite
farewell," and is also applicable to a dance-step. His three *deshechas* [163] are found at
nos. 178 (*Sy amor pone las escalas*, 4 v.), 184 (*Levanta, Pascual*, 3 v.), and 283 (*Quién te
traxo, cavallero*, 3 v.). Structurally, each antecedent song differs from the deshecha to
follow because it lacks a refrain. The deshechas on the other hand are always villancicos:
that is to say, they begin with a refrain. The "ending-chord" in each antecedent always
serves as the beginning chord in its companion deshecha.

The deshecha of one such pair, *Levanta, Pascual*, is here shown by way of example.
The romance which it follows has already been printed above at page 247, and should be
read through first if the musical effect of their pairing is properly to be appreciated. The
text of *Levanta, Pascual* – as is so frequently the case in Encina's villancicos – forms in
itself a miniature drama, the interlocutors being two shepherds. One brings the other
news of the surrender at Granada. The other cannot believe the news. After eleven

---

[163] *CMP*, no. 178, is the dehecha for no. 79; no. 184 belongs to no. 74; no. 283 belongs to no. 107. See
Encina's *Cancionero*. (1496), fol. 87: "Romances y canciones con sus deshechas". Only the first two lines of
Levanta Pascual and of *Quien te traxo cavallero* are printed at fol. 87, the full texts being reserved for fols.
97 and 99v.

Levanta, Pascual *

CMP, no. 184

JUAN DEL ENCINA

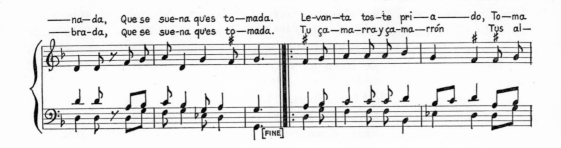

* "Arise, Pascual, arise, let us hasten to Granada which they say is taken. Arise at once, take your dog and knapsack, your suit and cloak, your pipes and shepherd's crook. Let's go see what's happening in that famous city, which they say is taken."

stanzas they then join together in singing a last strophe of thanks to the "Eternal King of glory" for such a victory.

ENCINA'S INDEBTEDNESS to his predecessors has been extensively argued. Formerly it was the fashion to categorize his theatrical achievements as complete novelties in their time. Agustín de Rojas in his *El Viage entretenido* published at Madrid in 1603 indeed flatly declared that Encina's plays were the first acted in Spain. In his way of thinking three events of 1492 shared equal importance – Columbus's discovery, the fall of Granada, and Encina's founding of the Spanish theatre.[164] Nowadays, however, literary scholars tend to see Encina more as the secularizer than as the morning-star of the Spanish stage. Certainly his dramas did not spring, Minerva-like, full-grown from Jove's forehead. As early as 1450 Gómez Manrique's *La representación del naçimiento de Nuestro Señor* was acted during Christmas festivities in a Spanish convent.[165] Neither was the rustic dialect which Encina frequently placed in the mouths of his shepherds (*sayagués*) a novelty.[166] It had been previously used in the *Coplas de Mingo Revulgo*.

As for more direct literary borrowings, J. Wickersham Crawford in his article, "The Source of Juan del Encina's *Égloga de Fileno y Zambardo*," proved that he took the plot and much of the dialogue in his Fileno piece from the second eclogue by Antonio Tebaldeo, a poet of Ferrara.[167] How he gained access to Tebaldeo's eclogue (published in 1499) is immaterial. Encina's piece frequently incorporates passages translated rather than adapted. No mere case of a common parentage or of an accidental similarity is here involved. Encina knew also the poetry of Dante and Petrarch and on occasion borrowed striking images from the latter.[168] That Encina should have read the great Italian poets with approval is not surprising when one recalls that his favorite Spanish poet, the Cordovan Juan de Mena (c. 1411–1456), also visited Italy and enriched Spanish prosody by imitating Italian meter.[169]

The problem of his musical borrowings is, however, somewhat knottier. In the first place, only a few instances have come to view. Following the widespread custom of his time, he on at least one occasion introduced a plainsong theme as a cantus firmus in a secular villancico. In *Mortal tristura me dieron* (*CMP*, no. 44) the tenor repeats the opening incise of a Kyrie sung in Spain at Masses for the Dead.[170] The words of this particular villancico have to do with the death of love. Encina's Spanish text includes the Latin word *circumdederunt*.[171] Alexander Agricola wrote a song in similar vein, *Le*

---

[164] Agustín de Rojas, *El Viage entretenido* (Lérida: Luys Menescal, 1611), fol. 43.

[165] Sáinz de Robles, *op. cit.*, I, 53–54. A still earlier Spanish acted piece descends to us in a brief fragment. An *Auto de los Reyes Magos*, it was written at least two centuries earlier than Gómez Manrique's Christmas play.

[166] M. Menéndez y Pelayo, *Antología de poetas liricos castellanos*, vol. VI (Madrid: Lib. de los sucs. de Hernando, 1921), p. xv.

[167] *Revue hispanique*, XXXVIII, 218–231. Cotarelo argued in rebuttal that Tebaldeo copied Encina (*Cancionero*, fasc. 1496, pp. 24–26). But his rebuttal was weakened by inaccuracies in citing Crawford's data. Cf. the errors in year and volume-number found in footnote 1 on p. 24.

[168] Angel Battistessa, *Poetas y prosistas españoles* (Buenos Aires: Institución cultural español, 1943), p. 225.

[169] *Cancionero* (1496), fol. 5v. On Juan de Mena's meters see Francisco Salinas, *De musica libri septem* (Salamanca: Mathias Gastius, 1577), p. 329.

[170] Francisco Montanos, *Arte de canto llano*, ed. José de Torres (Madrid: Diego Lucas Ximénez, 1705), p. 112. Encina's tenor corresponds with the Kyrie on the fourth staff of this page. He omits the eighth note of the chant (a passing-note) and makes other adjustments at the end of the phrase. The second Kyrie on this staff corresponds with Encina's tenor in measures 15–19.

[171] A villancico expressly entitled *Circumdederunt me* belonged to the Palace Songbook at the time the first index was made (c. 1525). Barbieri showed it to have belonged originally to Encina's *Plácida e Vittoriano* eclogue (1513), transcribing its complete text in his edition of *CMP* at pp. 50–51. The same objection can of course be brought against this Invitatorium of Encina's *Vigilia de la enamorada muerta* that was brought against Garci Sánchez de Badajoz's famous Lessons from Job. The charge of impropriety can be brought against even devout composers in this epoch if one adopts the creed of a Bishop Cirillo Franco.

Mortal tristura me dieron *

CMP, no. 44

JUAN DEL ENCINA

* Maiden, loving you inflicts fatal sorrow and causes me to live amid the pains of death. My sighs and cares and desire to serve you have so crushed me that I have cause to complain to you.

Nuevas te traygo, Carillo

CMC, fol. 77   Anonymous

eure e venue (*Odhecaton*, no. 81). Encina's tenor breves and semibreves and the two repetitions of the first incise (mm. 14–19, 20–26) highlight his borrowed melody, giving it the emphasis that such archaic treatment usually lends a plainsong cantus firmus.

He calls one of his quintuple-meter songs *Tan buen ganadico* (*CMP*, no. 426). In 1577 Salinas quoted the first six notes of a Spanish folksong bearing such a title.[172] He used it to illustrate this metrical pattern in fives: a minim followed by two semibreves, another minim followed by two semibreves. The incipit is unfortunately too short and its melodic contour too commonplace – an upward major third followed by scale-steps downward – to permit conclusive identification of the folksong as the model for the treble-melody in Encina's villancico. On the other hand, the treble certainly does begin with the upward skip of a major third, whereupon it descends a scale-step, then a third, then a scale-step.

Another more interesting case of what seems to be a borrowing from a previous secular source comes up in *Nuevas te traigo, Carillo* (*CMP*, no. 281). In *Palacio* this villancico, set *a 4*, is ascribed to him. In the Colombina cancionero, on the other hand, a three-voiced anonymous song of this title occurs, the music of which strikingly resembles the *CMP* attributed item. The Colombina scribe copied no text beyond the title. For this reason, the *CMP* verses cannot be compared with a corresponding *CMC* poem. Only the music, and not the lyrics, must decide the interrelationship.

In 1941 and again in 1947 Anglés announced that *CMC*, no. 59, is a different piece entirely,[173] and not by Encina. If so, then he should in this case be called a skilful

---

[172] Salinas, p. 337.
[173] *MME*, I, *100* and *105*; *MME*, V, *29*.

Nuevas te traigo, Carillo *

CMP, fols. 200v.–201   Juan del Encina

* "I bring you news concerning your beloved, Carillo." "Tell me the news quickly, Pascual." "Learn then that last Sunday Bartolilla, the daughter of Mari-Mingo, married a youth of the town. I am extremely upset and sorry for your misfortune because you are such a worthy swain."

arranger. The mere ascription of *CMP*, no. 281, does not bear on the paternity of *CMC*, no. 59. Just as Madrid (*CMP*, no. 5) when he added a new voice to Cornago's *Pues que Dios te fiso tal* (*CMP*, no. 2) became in the eyes of the *CMP* copyist the "composer" of the new version, so the *CMP* scribe may have chosen to consider Encina as the "composer" of *Nuevas te traigo, Carillo* (*CMP*, no. 281) even though the latter clearly threaded his needle over the same pattern which had guided the composer of *CMC*, no. 59.

Both the Colombina *Nuevas te traygo* and the Palacio *Nuevas te traigo* are shown as accompanying examples. One or two slight hints in support of Anglés's thesis that the *CMC* piece is not by Encina, strongly as it resembles *CMP*, no. 281, may here be offered. The cadences in *CMC* differ at the end of the first and second double-bars. But in all his *CMP* hypophrygian pieces, on the other hand, the cadence at the close of the estribillo duplicates that rounding off the coplas. For another matter, the first phrase in *CMC*, no. 59, ends with a "deceptive" cadence. No such "deceptive" cadence is to be found in any *CMP* hypophrygian or phrygian example by Encina. Indeed he is very chary of using such "deceptive" progressions anywhere in his entire repertory, always preferring the V–I or IV–I progression at cadences.

To his credit (whether or not he composed both versions) is the added refinement of the four-voiced *CMP* arrangement. Rhythms flow in all voices, and the turgidity that can result from an unrelieved succession of block-chords is carefully avoided. The cadence at the end of his estribillo is more gracefully contrived, both because he assigns the melodic anticipation (end of measure 4) to the treble rather than to the alto and because he avoids bare consecutives between the treble and alto (measure 5).

Rather than diminishing his fame, then, the ascription of *CMC*, no. 59, to some other composer actually enhances Encina's reputation as a self-conscious artist and as one who touched no other man's work without polishing it and giving it his own individual stamp.

Francisco Millán (fl. 1501)

IN CONTRAST with Encina, Millán still remains a shadowy figure. Barbieri discovered him to have been a *capellán cantor* (chaplain and singer) at the Castilian court during 1501 and 1502.[174] Nothing else has been subsequently revealed. Yet he must have been one of the more popular composers at Queen Isabella's court from the number of his pieces in *CMP*. With the single exception of Encina he is the best represented composer, 23 (or 22) [175] songs by him having been copied in *Palacio* as against Encina's 62.

The larger number of these were copied into the manuscript on blank spaces after the original collection had already been completed. Only four of Encina's 62 songs were added after the original collection was gathered (nos. 67, 82, 94, and 102). But 15 of Millán's 23 were so added (nos. 71, 122, 147, 185, 195, 232, 265, 295, 319, 323, 333, 339, 351, 452, 457). Millán was therefore an outlander to the aristocratic Alba de Tormes circle for which the *CMP* nucleus was originally formed.

Strangely enough, not a single sacred villancico enters his repertory. Encina, secularly minded though he was, contributed four (*CMP*, nos. 275, 406, 412, 442). Escobar with 18 items in *CMP*, Torre with 15, and Ponce with 12, are all represented by an occasional sacred villancico. Millán though more prolific is represented by none.

He composed only the scantiest number of his songs *a 4* (*CMP*, nos. 122, 445, and 448). And of these *Temeroso de sufrir* (*CMP*, no. 448) proves to be simply his three-voiced *Porque de ageno cuidado* (*CMP*, no. 319) with a second contra added and with the first five measures changed from duple to triple meter. To show his bent, he set a full score of his songs *a 3* – nine-tenths of his repertory. By way of contrast, Encina is represented in *CMP* with almost equal numbers of items for three and four voices (32 and 30).

Millán shows his individuality in still another way. Ten of his pieces begin with a passage in clearly-intentioned imitation (*CMP*, nos. 71, 122, 185, 232, 265, 319, 323, 448, 452, and 457). Usually the treble enters last, the only exceptions arising in *Míos fueron, mi coraçon* (no. 185), *Sufriendo con fe tan fuerte* (no. 323), and *Temeroso de sufrir*

---

[174] Barbieri, p. 617.

[175] The music of nos. 333 and 351, though not the lyrics, is identical: thus reducing the count by one if music rather than lyrics is counted.

(no. 448), when tenor displaces treble as the final voice to enter. As a rule, the imitation involves only two of the three voices. With two parts, the interval of imitation is always the octave (except no. 323, where the tenor imitates the treble at the downward fifth). In the two cases where the imitation extends through three voices, their order of entry is contra, treble, tenor (no. 185) and contra I, treble, tenor (no. 448). The intervals are octave and fifth in no. 185 but fourth above and second below in *Temeroso de sufrir* (no. 448). In contrast with this display, Encina notably eschewed imitation. Only five of his 62 examples start with it, as compared with Millán's ten among 23 examples. Then again, Encina's points never extend beyond the first phrase, whereas five phrases in Millán's *O dulce y triste memoria* (*CMP*, no. 452) commence with imitation. As a result, this last piece is one of the most continuously flowing to be found in *Palacio*. The recurring caesura is happily avoided. Instead, the phrases interlock. Its madrigalian languor befits Sonnet 30:

> When to the sessions of sweet silent thought
> I summon up remembrance of things past.

In certain other interesting respects his musical style contrasts with Encina's. He never indulges in a mixed signature, whereas Encina frequently combined voices with and without flats in the same villancico (*CMP*, nos. 50, 74, 82, 83, 305, 309). Millán never ends a song on either D-chord or A-chord. In the nine cases where he does close with G-chord, he interdicts B♭'s. What this means is that he never uses dorian mode – untransposed or transposed – nor aeolian. Encina (see pp. 263–264) preferred these modes to all others.

His solitary songs without initial or intermediate refrain are his pair of romances: *Durandarte, Durandarte* (no. 445) and *Los braços trayo cansados* (no. 446). The lower parts in each move as if he had conceived them for agile instruments. Only the trebles preserve a truly vocal character. In common with Encina's four or five romances, Millán's pair show these traits: (1) division of the strophe into four musical phrases of approximately equal length (2) fermatas at the end of each phrase (3) anapest rhythm at the beginnings of most treble phrases. On the other hand, Encina in none of his romances wrote such active or intricate "harmonizations" of his treble melodies. His lower parts instead move in block-chords.

One of Millán's songs, *Serrana del bel mirar* (*CMP*, no. 71) boasts an intermediate refrain. This unique item in his repertory tells a story. A shepherd in the mountains finds a hapless maid. In the musical introduction he accosts her. In the first refrain he describes how he happened to meet her. Next, she sings a short *cantar* bewailing her lot. He then returns with the musical refrain, but set to new words praising her as the belle of the mountains. She responds with another *cantar*, much like the first in sentiment and in musical character. Here for once Millán puts music to a poetic dialogue. Encina, of course, set many such a dialogue – but always as a villancico with initial refrain.

All of Millán's texts, with the exception of his two romances,[176] betray a familial

---

[176] *Ved, comadres* (no. 122) is perhaps another exception, since its lyrics are the confessions of a drunkard.

likeness. Disappointment and lovers' sorrows run though each like a ground bass. In 18 of his 20 songs with opening refrain he cadences to identical chords for the close of both estribillo and coplas. He violates his rule in only *Sufriendo con fe tan fuerte* (*CMP*, no. 323) and *Si dolor sufro secreto* (*CMP*, no. 367). The coplas in each of these mixolydian songs end with the D Major chord (f♯ specified in the treble). Encina – braver by far – closed estribillo and coplas with a different chord some 22 times (*CMP*, nos. 30, 44, 50, 165, 181, 184, 186, 224, 271, 278, 282, 285, 289, 298, 304, 305, 308, 312, 313, 314, 406, 408). A musical reason for Millán's rigid adherence throughout nine-tenths of his refrain-songs to the same ending-chord and even cadential pattern for the close of estribillo and coplas is not far to seek, arising as it does from the nature of his texts. They habitually lack the animal spirits, the lively give-and-take, of Encina's lyrics. Because the moods within his texts shift, Encina can also change his musical stance. But Millán, setting his static and humorless lyrics, even goes so far as to duplicate the two or three last measures of estribillo and coplas in a dozen of his examples (*CMP*, nos. 185, 195, 232, 265, 295, 319, 333, 334, 336, 339, 351, 448).

Indeed, he commits himself so absolutely to texts voicing lovers' plaints that he consents to write a macaronic three-voiced *O vos omnes*, the Latin words of which he excerpted from a Maundy Thursday lamentation and strangely twisted into a lover's sob. The disappointed lover implores all passers-by to stop and consider if there be any woe like unto his. Loyset Compère (d. 1518) also wrote a three-part *O vos omnes*, the bassus singing the Latin text and the upper two parts *O devotz cueurs*.[177] But the French text in Compère's motet-chanson publishes a more appropriate grief, since it is that of a woman bereft of son and father – not of a disappointed swain comparing himself to Christ on Calvary.[178]

Efforts at identifying the poets who supplied Millán with his lyrics have thus far proved rather fruitless. Barbieri could not find any literary source that exactly parallelled even the version of *Durandarte, Durandarte* (*CMP*, no. 445) which he set. For the present, then, all his lyrics except possibly *Señora, después que os vi* (*CMP*, no. 339) [179] must pass as anonymous. Like Encina he may have written his own poetry.

MILLÁN seems to have been the only composer in *CMP* who used the same music for two different poetic texts. The music of *Pues la vida en mal tan fuerte* (no. 333) exactly duplicates that of *Si ell esperança es dudosa* (no. 351), even to the last accidental. As has already been observed, the four-part *Temoroso de sufrir* is musically identical with the three-part *Porque de ageno cuidado*, except that another contra has been added and a rhythmic adjustment made in the first five bars. Curiously enough, *CMP* contains a

---

[177] Ed. by R. J. van Maldeghem, *Trésor musical* (*Musique profane* [1887]), XXIII 23–24. See Reese, *Music in the Renaissance*, p. 225.

[178] Other *CMP* songs which mix the sacred and secular with similar nonchalance appear at nos. 41, 44, 58, 154 (mm. 133–148), 373, 381, 401. To this list can be added the macaronic frottola, *Vox clamantis* (no. 105). For complete texts see Barbieri edition.

[179] The lyrics of no. 339 may have been written by the Valencian poet, Diego de Quirós. See Barbieri, p. 127 (item 219).

dozen poems with alternate musical settings – the exact obverse of Millán's procedure in nos. 333–351 and 319–448.

IN EVERY one of his songs which begins with an initial refrain, except *O dulce y triste memoria* (*CMP*, no. 452) and *Al dolor que siento estraño* (no. 457), he sets poems the rhyme-scheme of which spills over from coplas into the musical da capo. This fact alone strongly suggests that Millán belonged to the generation of Encina rather than to that of Cornago and Triana. He also uses fourths between tenor and treble at the concluding cadences in *CMP*, nos. 295, 336, and 446, his three hypophrygian pieces. Composers of the earlier generation eschewed such tenor-treble fourths. Moreover in *Señora, después que os vi* (*CMP*, no. 339) he writes an unprepared fourth between the tenor and treble on a strong beat – at the beginning of m. 14. No misprint or faulty copy can be blamed at this moment.[180]

On the other hand, the consecutive fifths between contra and treble in *Míos fueron, mi coraçon* (*CMP*, no. 185), last two beats of m. 8, must almost certainly be a copyist's error. If the contra were to move from F_1 to G_1 a mere beat later, the difficulty would be nicely resolved. Some such resolution is required in view of the fact that Millán fastidiously avoided such consecutive perfect fifths everywhere else in his repertory.

Two of his songs adhere to triple meter throughout (*CMP*, nos. 71 and 334). Another five go into it transiently in the estribillo (*CMP*, nos. 122, 295, 319, 339, 448). His signature at the head of nos. 71, 295, and 334 is ₵ 3. The best equivalent time-signature nowadays would perhaps be $\frac{3}{4}$. He did not use ○, which would be the equivalent of a modern $\frac{3}{2}$. In *Ved, comadres* (*CMP*, no. 122), the lower two voices shift into triple meter while the upper two remain still in duple. His mensuration sign for duple meter is always ₵. The fact that he never uses any of the several other "signatures" to be found in Encina's songs (○, ₵, ₵ 5, 3^2) is in itself highly instructive. As was pointed out on page 273, Millán confines himself to a few modes, using less than half as many as Encina. His range of poetic texts is similarly narrow. His fewer "time-signatures" therefore confirms the estimate that he had less arrows in his quiver than Encina.

He casts ten of his songs (*CMP*, nos. 71, 122, 194, 323, 333, 339, 351, 367, 368, 445) in mixolydian. This classification is not left in doubt, since in each the tenor and contra close on the same letter-name note. Even if Millán never heard of Ramos de Pareja, he confirms the elder Spaniard's doctrine of astral influences when he selects Mode VII for each of these songs. "The mixolydian belongs to Saturn, since it induces melancholy," said Ramos.[181] The very titles of Millán's mixolydian songs often suggest those qualities which the astrologically-minded attributed to Saturn – coldness, sluggishness, and gloominess. They read as follows: "Observe what grief I endure" (122), "If you do not intend to assuage my misery" (194), "Suffering with such strong conviction" (323), "Since life in such grievous case is death itself" (333), "If hope is so uncertain and pain so unbounded" (351), "If I suffer secret sorrow" (367), "It is amazing that I am able to survive" (368).

---

[180] Millán was however parsimonious with his fourths if this is his only example.
[181] Ramos, p. 58: *Mixolydius vero attribuitur Saturno, quoniam circa melancholiam versatur.*

One of his songs, the ionian three-voiced *Míos fueron, mi coraçón* (*CMP*, no. 185), was neatly rearranged for three trebles by Mondéjar (*CMP*, no. 294). The lyrics develop a prettier theme than in any of his "saturnine" songs. Still another of his pieces enjoyed more than a merely passing vogue – *Aunque no spero gozar* (*CMP*, no. 336). Gil Vicente alluded to this three-part hypophrygian lover's complaint in his *Dom Duardos* (1525).[182] But on the whole Millán leaves the impression of having been a Jorge Manrique who wrote a few exquisitely beautiful stanzas, his other work trailing in vitality behind the few choice items. These by way of summary would be the songs of the disconsolate mountain maiden, of the girl with the bewitching brown eyes, and the madrigalian one commemorating the "sweet, sad memory of the happy, painful past" (*CMP*, nos. 71, 185, and 452).

Gabriel [Mena] (fl. 1511)

AFTER Encina with 62 and Millán with 23 songs comes Gabriel with 19 items. Eighteen show music as well as text. *CMP*, no. 173, attributed to him, lacks music. None of the ascriptions gives his last name. That it was "Mena" was deduced by Barbieri in 1890 together with the following facts.

Both the *Cancionero general* of 1511 and the *Cancionero general* published at Saragossa in 1554 (by Nágera) contain verses by "Gabriel el músico." The 1511 cancionero refers to him as a singer in the court chapel of Ferdinand V, consort of Isabella. In the Nágera cancionero his verses are headed by this legend: "Gabriel gave his patron, the Admiral [i.e. Fadrique Enríquez who died in 1537], a mule. Having no way to go but on foot himself, he wrote this letter [in verse] to the Adelantado, brother of the Admiral, asking for a sumpter." After this superscription comes the poem. In it he not only asks for a beast of burden so he can get around but also calls himself a singer by profession, reveals that he is married, and speaks of living in Torrelobatón, a small town slightly west of Valladolid.

Still further information concerning Gabriel was discovered by Barbieri in a miscellany of anecdotes collected by the famous knight of Santiago and page at the court of Isabella (wife of Charles V), Luis de Zapata (1526–1595). According to Zapata,

The valorous Admiral, Don Fadrique Enríquez – an extremely small man but a victor in battles and a regent of the realm during the Emperor's youth [i.e. in 1519 during Charles V's absence for his coronation as Holy Roman Emperor in Germany] – was as I have already said, very fond of witty sayings. Now it came about that he sent a friar with whom he was interchanging jests a rather biting bit of verse. The Admiral at this particular time had two servants, one named Coca – his secretary, the other named Gabriel – the famous versifier and courtier. To the Admiral's biting verse the friar thus replied: *"Concerning that poem which you sent me, your only part in it was the paper. I see that Coca wrote it, and I hear the voice of Gabriel dictating it. Though I am very well aware of the fact that you have downed me and that I have no way of getting back at you, still there are three of you against me, or if not three, at least two-and-a-half.*[183]

---

[182] For date see Aubrey F. G. Bell, *Four Plays of Gil Vicente* (Cambridge University Press, 1920), p. xxv.

[183] Luis Zapata, *Miscelánea* (*Memorial Histórico Español*, publ. by R. Academia de la Historia [Madrid-Imp. Nacional, 1859], vol. XI), p. 406.

In calling the three (the Admiral, his secretary Coca, and his troubadour Gabriel) "two-and-a-half persons," the friar was of course alluding to the well-known fact that Don Fadrique Enríquez was only "pint-size." The preservation of the anecdote can be taken as proof that the Admiral liked the friar's clever parry. Elsewhere in his collection of anecdotes Zapata speaks of Gabriel as both a poet and musician, whose full name was *Gabriel Mena*.[184]

More recently Anglés, working with documents in the Archivo del Real Patrimonio at Barcelona, encountered the name *Gabriel de Texerana* in a list of chapel singers employed at Ferdinand's court during 1500.[185] This Gabriel and Gabriel Mena may possibly have been one and the same person.

IF ENCINA and Millán each exhibited certain individual musical traits which when known and understood make it possible to separate their respective styles, so also Gabriel proves to have been something of an individualist.

I. On occasion he includes fleetly running scale-passages. These are by no means restricted to the lower textless voices but also distinguish the singing treble. They sometimes extend through so great a sweep as an octave. Examples of these nimble runs can be seen in *CMP* at nos. 110, 120, 241, 254, 353. Only in one instance did Encina, on the other hand, include a few short scale runs (*CMP*, no. 436); and Millán's trebles never so disport themselves.

II. Gabriel does not overtly change meter in the middle of a piece. He does on a few occasions, however, write syncopations which create strongly-felt cross-rhythms: eight pulses dividing into $3 + 3 + 2$, or twelve pulses (ostensibly to be parsed as $4 + 4 + 4$) regrouping into four sets of threes. Instances of such cross-rhythms occur at *CMP*, nos. 353 (mm. 2–3, 17–18, 20-22), 422 (mm. 12–16), and especially at no. 330 – an item which in the Instituto Español de Musicología edition is credited to "Luchas" meaning "struggles," but which bears the name of Gabriel as its composer, and is so credited in Barbieri's 1890 edition. In this "Luchas" number, the struggle between the apparent meter of $\frac{4}{4}$ and the felt meter of $\frac{3}{4}$ continues throughout the entire estribillo (mm. 1–10). Indeed the constant play of cross-rhythms is one of the principal attractions of this brilliant piece. The "struggles" idea is, moreover, appropriate to the text: which urges smitten swains to fly to the chase of their lady-loves and to capture them, no matter how energetically they should struggle. The *MME* edition gives only a fraction of the whole poem as it appears in the original MS, omitting seven strophes.

III. Gabriel's closing "chords" never rise above E or C, though both Encina and Millán had at least sporadically ended with "chords" built over these notes.

---

[184] *Ibid.*, p. 131 (lines 11–12). The anecdote retailed here as well as at pp. 124–125 shows that Gabriel was never at a loss in repartee. According to Zapata, the Admiral inordinately enjoyed Gabriel's witty sallies.

[185] *DML*, I, 989, c. 1.

IV. Gabriel, in contradistinction to Encina and Millán, occasionally writes what would now be called sequences of parallel first-inversion chords (*CMP*, no. 168).

V. Gabriel – unlike Encina and Millán – leaves no settings of romances. He sets even *La bella malmaridada* (*CMP*, no. 234), one of the most frequently glossed romances in Spanish literature, not as a romance but as an initial-refrain-type song.

VI. All of Encina's and Millán's love-songs were written for the man to sing, but Gabriel places one of his finest love-songs in a maiden's mouth (*CMP*, no. 132).

TO MENTION briefly certain other characteristics of his repertory: *1*. Fourteen of his songs were copied at blank spaces in the manuscript after the original collection had already been completed. Probably he, like Millán, was a stranger to the aristocratic Alba de Tormes circle for which this song-collection was originally formed. *2*. Only two of his songs (*CMP*, nos. 168 and 347) carry a triple-meter "signature." This is in both cases ₵ 3. Fourteen bear ₵; while another pair (*CMP*, nos. 132 and 217) carry C. On the evidence of his unique patter-song, *De la dulce mi enemiga* (*CMP*, no. 217), the "signature" C implies considerably faster minim-motion than does ₵. *3*. The lowest note of the closing chord is in nine instances G (three times with B♭ in the "key-signature"), in four F (always with B♭ in the signatures of at least the lower voices), in three cases D, and twice A. *Mi ventura, el caballero* (*CMP*, no. 153), ending on an A–e–a chord, is his only song classifiable as hypophrygian (transposed). None can be classed as phrygian. A study of his texts in relation to his choice of modes will not be attempted here, but the text of the hypophrygian example sticks throughout to the idea of "evil chances." The final cadence in all his other songs is authentic, the tenor singing the lowest note or its octave in the closing chord.

He threads identifiable folktunes through at least two of his songs, *La bella malmaridada* (*CMP*, no. 234) and *Aquella mora garrida* (*CMP*, no. 254). In each the tenor sings the derived folktune.[186] The rhythm of the tenor in *La bella*, is spondaic, in *Aquella mora* predominantly anapestic. Enríquez de Valderrábano still incorporates the same popular *La bella* tune in the vihuela arrangement which he published a generation later (1547).[187] Identification of the second as of popular origin resulted from a comparison of Gabriel's tenor with the tune of the *Hispanae notissimae cantilenae* shown at page 327 in Salinas's *De musica libri septem* (1577). Fortunately Salinas in this latter case quoted not just a short incipit but twenty notes of *Aquella morica* [sic] *garrida sus amores dan pena a mi vida*. As set by Gabriel the first line of this song begins thus, *Aquella mora* ("That Moorish girl") rather than, *Aquella morica* ("That little Moorish girl"). He therefore needs one less note to set the opening phrase than Salinas. The note added by the latter is of no consequence melodically, it being merely a repeated note. Gabriel inserts a rest

---

[186] Another of Gabriel's songs using a derived tune occurs at *CMP*, no. 422 (*Sola me dexastes*), the tenor being transposed from the treble of *CMP*, no. 223 (a similarly entitled anonymous song *a 3*). In addition to transposing the borrowed melody a fifth down, Gabriel makes minor rhythmic adjustments and also occasionally leaves out passing-notes found in the anonymous treble.

[187] See Barbieri, pp. 609–610, for a transcription of the *Silva de sirenas* setting.

instead of the repeated note. Another minor difference: Gabriel opens with the three notes of a descending major triad, but Salinas with the three notes of a descending major scale passage. Rhythmically they are alike, as well as melodically, both hewing to the same pattern of anapests.

Salinas's tune ends at a point tallying with Gabriel's first double-bar. Because of the exact likenesses up to this point, the rest of the folktune can be reconstructed by adding to the portion quoted in Salinas's treatise its continuation found in the coplas of the *CMP* villancico.

Gabriel wrote a miniature masterpiece when he composed this song. The *Vorimitation* at the beginning of estribillo and coplas charms the hearer without oppressing him. The fleet scales, especially in the instrumental contras, add a delicious shimmer. The words pay tribute to a Moorish girl whose charm has captivated the poet, and every musical touch artfully suggests "moonlight and roses."

Pedro de Escobar

ESCOBAR, who in May of 1507 was summoned from Portugal to assume the Sevillian chapelmastership, may well have been the Pedro of Oporto who sang in Queen Isabella's chapel from 1489–1499 (see pp. 168–171). In any event he is not the only *CMP* composer now known to have spent considerable time in Portugal. Badajoz "el músico," of whom eight pieces survive in *CMP*, was a favorite instrumentalist at João III's court if we are to believe Fray Antonio de Portalegre's report in his *Meditaçã da inocẽtissima morte e payxã de nosso señor em estilo metrificado* (Coimbra, 1547).[188]

Escobar's *CMP* repertory consists of eighteen songs, not less than thirteen of which were copied into the manuscript after the original collection had already been gathered. Like Millán and Gabriel he must therefore be thought of as a stranger to the Alba de Tormes coterie for which the original body of *CMP* was copied. Seven of his songs are for four voices, the remaining eleven for three. His mensuration signs, although not so various as Encina's, include: Φ 3 (nos. 114, 158, 337), Φ $\frac{3}{2}$ (nos. 383, 416), $\mathbb{C}$ 3 (no. 229) and $\bigcirc$ 3 (no. 263), each implying a different triple-meter speed. Like Anchieta, Encina, and Diego Fernández, he on occasion wrote a quintuple-meter song (no. 59), heading it with the "signature" $\frac{5}{1}$. But ten of his songs (nos. 73, 124, 199, 216, 220, 244, 245, 286, 375, 385) are headed by $\mathbb{C}$ – the favorite "signature" of all indisputably peninsular composers in *CMP*.

One song boasts a mixed "key-signature," B♭ being indicated in the second contra but not in the other voices (no. 59). Seven songs show B♭ in all voices. He never went so far as to use two flats, B♭ and E♭, in the same "signature," as did Encina (*CMP*, no. 74). But the second flat appears rather often as a compulsory accidental (nos. 59, 124, 244, 337, and 416). In the pair entitled *Paséisme aor' allá, serrana* (nos. 244 and 245) he

[188] Innocencio Francisco da Silva, *Diccionario Bibliographico Portuguez* (Lisbon: Imp. Nacional, 1858), I, 240–241.

almost certainly wrote the second flat to produce a cross-relation between the C Major chord on one "beat" and the E♭ Major chord on the next (m. 6).

Twice the tenor closes a fifth above the contra (nos. 59 and 375). Classifying these two according to their tenors, we assign the first, *Las mis penas madre*, to hypolydian, the second, *Coraçon triste sofrid*, to hypophrygian. The sentiment of the first is as "venereal" and of the second as "mercurial" as adherents to Ramos's modal theories could desire. The tenor-final lies either at the bottom of the chord or the octave above in all his other songs. Classifying these others according to their tenor-finals, we find that six belong to D (nos. 73, 199, 229, *263*, 383, *416*), four to G (nos. *114*, *124*, 216, 286), three to F (nos. *244*, *245*, *337*), two to A (nos. 158, 220), and one to C (no. 385). The modality of seven of these (italicized numerals) could be disputed because of the presence of B♭ in the "key-signature" of all voices. But the two that are unequivocally mixolydian, *Lo que queda es lo seguro* (no. 216) and *Vençedores son tus ojos* (no. 286), dwell on suitably "saturnine" themes: the poet's detention and death on account of his lady beloved's disdain and coldness of heart.

Encina and Gabriel probably set no lyrics but their own. Millán may also have been his own poet. Escobar, by contrast, definitely set other lyrics. Fortunately, he showed excellent taste in his choice of an author, settling on one of the best poets of his time, Garcí Sánchez de Badajoz (c. 1460–c. 1526). This passionate Andalusian whose *Las liciones de Job apropriadas a sus passiones de amor* was later placed on the Index of prohibited books was not only a literary man but was also recognized as the finest vihuela-player of his generation.[189] Since he was such a consummate musician as well as poet – his reputation as a player being still very much alive as late as 1575,[190] Sánchez de Badajoz may himself have composed the anonymous musical setting of his lyrics, *Lo que queda es lo seguro*, at *CMP*, no. 99. Escobar's name heads the setting of the same verses at *CMP*, no. 216. In Escobar's version, treble and tenor of the anonymous original interchange places. He also rewrites the contra. His setting *a 3* parallels such another *CMP* transcription as Madrid's *Pues que Dios te fiso tal*. That his arrangement soon came to be preferred is attested in the Portuguese source, *O Cancioneiro Musical e Poético da Biblioteca Públia Hortênsia*. At fols. 47v.–48 appears in slightly altered form the Escobar setting – not the *CMP* anonymous.

From Sánchez de Badajoz he took also the lyrics of *Secáronme los pesares* (*CMP*, no. 199). This is again an item carried over from *CMP* into *Hortênsia*, where it appears at fols. 41v.–42. The cadence in the treble at the end of the estribillo differs in *CMP* and *CMH*. In *CMP*, the treble skips from an under-third to the final. But in *CMH* this rather archaic under-third tag is replaced by a more up-to-date melodic formula, indeed the one which Escobar always favors elsewhere in *CMP*, and the one which occurs more frequently than any other ending-tag in Spanish secular music composed

---

[189] Barbieri, *op. cit.*, p. 44.

[190] See F. Hierónimo Román, *Segunda parte delas Republicas del mundo* (Medina del Campo: Francisco del Canto, 1575), fol. 236v. ("Dela Musica y su origen"). After naming various secular musicians of antiquity this chronicler cites "Garci Sanchez de Badajoz, cuyo ingenio en vihuela no lo pudo auer mejor en tiempo de os Reyes Catholicos."

c. 1500. (The treble, starting as a consonant "tied-note" on a weak beat, becomes dissonant on the succeeding strong beat because of the movement of the lower voices, resolves downward stepwise, then returns stepwise upward to the final.) The total number of measures in both the *CMP* and *CMH* estribillos is the same, but mm. 3–5 of *CMP* are compressed into mm. 3–4 of *CMH* and the omitted measure then regained at mm. 8_{3-4} and 13_{1-2} of the *CMH* version. The melodic suppleness of the *CMH* version at mm. 3 and 8 (treble), as well as at m. 18 (treble) in the coplas, would be but one reason among many for preferring the Portuguese version of this Escobar item to the stiffer Spanish. The shape of the contra is also improved everywhere in the Portuguese setting, except possibly at m. 20 in *CMH*, where the return to the dominant seems unduly repetitive.

The poet of *Quedaos adiós* (*CMP*, no. 158) has not been discovered. But the lyrics, cast in the form of a dialogue, mention Seville. A pair of saddened lovers are taking leave of Sevillian acquaintances; meanwhile their bleeding hearts forever drip on the banks of the Guadalquivir. This song, a late addition to *CMP*, may date from those years which Escobar himself spent in Seville – just as Lagarto's *Callen todas las galanas* (*CMP*, no. 226) in praise of the beauties of Toledo is likely to have been composed while the latter was claustrero in Toledo Cathedral.

BECAUSE of the learning found in Escobar's masses the comparative simplicity of his *CMP* songs may cause surprise. Over and over again throughout peninsular musical history it will however be found that composers of great polyphonic contrivance in their masses doff the learned sock and sport it on the green when they turn to the secular field. Peñalosa's *CMP* songs are usually quite simple, though he was perhaps the most learned Spaniard of his epoch. Later in the sixteenth century Morales wrote a villancico *a 3*, a madrigal *a 4*, and a romance,[191] which are all innocent of the contrivance regularly found in his masses. By an anomaly, the named composer in *CMP* who executes the cleverest feats is precisely Ponce whose sacred style, at least as revealed in his Salve Regina (see pp. 186–189), is decidedly simpler than either Escobar's or Peñalosa's.

Francisco de la Torre

THE DATES of Torre's court and cathedral appointments are given above (p. 194). A transcription of his villancico in *CMC* is shown at p. 244.

In contrast with every *CMP* composer thus far studied (even Encina), he wrote nothing that was inserted into the MS as a late addition. Each of his 15 pieces, including his famous instrumental *alta* dance *a 3* (*CMP*, no. 321), belonged to the original corpus of the Palace Songbook. This circumstance agrees well with what is known of his biography, he having reached the summit of his musical career a decade before Encina even began his.

Telltale evidence that he flourished before Encina is embedded in his *CMP* pieces

[191] *Si n'os uviera mirado, Ditimi o si o no, De Antequera sale el moro.*

themselves, quite apart from the dated biographical documents which survive. First, there is the fact that in only one of his 15 pieces (*CMP*, no. 262) did he make any use of the spillover rhyme-scheme which Encina popularized. By contrast, 18 of Millán's 20 refrain-songs, 17 of Gabriel's 18, and 13 of Escobar's 17, are built on the Encinian plan. For a second matter, he wrote a larger proportion of romances (*CMP*, nos. 136, 137, 140, 150) than any of the composers just named. He even on one occasion confounded the initial-refrain-type song with a romance (*CMP*, no. 32). For a third, he is the only composer thus far met in *Palacio* who shows any strong traces of Urrede's influence – a pair of his songs coming so close to *Nunca fué pena mayor*, by every crucial musical test, as to seem almost *contrahechas* rather than independent compositions (*CMP*, nos. 48 and 62).

Those identifying traits which *Nunca fué* shares in common with Torre's *La que tengo no es prisión* (no. 48) and *O quán dulçe serias, muerte* (no. 62) include not only mode, meter, lengths of sections, and literary type, but also the asymmetry of phrase-structure, the perambulating melodic lines, and the frequency of "chord-progressions" with roots related stepwise rather than at a distance of the fourth or fifth. Only one other composer (whose name is known) succeeded so well in echoing Urrede's finer nuances – Madrid [192] (*CMP*, no. 66). Juan Fernández de Madrid began singing in the Aragonese court chapel during 1479. Torre entered the same choir in 1483. Urrede if not still *maestro* when Torre joined had at any rate conducted it from 1477–1481. Since *CMP* contains songs by fifty composers, none of whom more faithfully imitates Urrede's idiosyncratic style than Madrid and Torre, his personal influence may well be the explanation.

Torre's two Urrede-influenced songs are his only ones *1* in perfect time of the less prolation; *2* in phrygian mode; *3* with successive melodic phrases beginning at asymmetrical rhythmic moments; *4* showing many chord-"chains" built over roots related stepwise rather than in the IV–I and V–I relationships.

As for the modality of his other pieces, he never uses the mixolydian. In his one song ending on F (no. 444) he specifies a "key-signature" of one flat in the tenor and allows only B♮'s in the lower contra. Eight of his pieces end on D, the italicized numerals in the following list showing those which carry B♭ in the "signature" of the contra but nothing in the upper voices: *CMP*, nos. 11, *32*, *42*, *137*, *140*, 321, 331, *420*. His *Peligroso pensamiento* (no. 43) ends on G but cannot be classed as mixolydian because B♭ appears as a "signature" in all three voices. The modality of *Pascua d'Espíritu Santo* (*CMP*, no. 136) – a romance commemorating the capture of Ronda in 1485 – is left in doubt, E♭ entering the "signature" of the contra and B♭ that of the tenor, but the treble lacking any flat. For his meter, he usually prefers duple, not triple. The "time-signature" is, for instance, ₵ in each of the following eleven songs: *CMP*, nos. 32, 42, 43, 136, 137, 140, 150, 262, 331, 420, 444 (contra I).

His own personal style is best studied in the four songs which appear both in the Segovia and Palacio cancioneros. His sober piety sounds forth in the first of these, the three-voiced *Damos gracias a ti Dios* (*CMP*, no. 32; *CMS*, no. 171) written in thanks to God

---

[192] León's *Ay, que non sé rremediarme* (no. 37) bears some "Urrede" touches. The anonymous *Quien vevir libre desea* (no. 64) also shows some likenesses.

and the Virgin for Ferdinand's successes against the Moors. The second, *Justa fué mi perdición* (*CMP*, no. 42; *CMS*, no. 164), excites added interest because its verses were written by the famous poet, Jorge Manrique. *Peligroso pensamiento* (*CMP*, no. 43; *CMS*, no. 172), like the Manrique item, is a lover's plaint. *Adorámoste Señor* (*CMP*, no. 420; *CMS*, no. 188) is one of his two fine homophonous laude for men's voices.

His musical personality shows such distinctive facets as the following:

I.　Though like León, Moxica, and Madrid, he obviously counts consonances from the tenor he is on the other hand rather given in his longer canciones to writing chains of parallel tenths between the outer voices. This habit is well illustrated in *Justa fué mi perdición* at mm. 45–51 where 18 successive tenths ride the parallel rails of outer voices and in *Peligroso pensamiento* at mm. 42–46 where 10 succeed. As for chains of thirds between tenor and treble, they are to be found also. The first 20 measures of *Pues que todo* are given up to nothing but parallel thirds between the two top voices.

II.　In his canciones Torre when writing "chord-progressions" that would nowadays be labelled V–I always assigns the root of the "dominant" chord to his lowest voice. Not infrequently, however, he lets the low contra voice drop out in the "chord of resolution." Examples are to be seen at *CMP*, no. 32, mm. 15–16; no. 42, mm. 9–10 and mm. 66–67; no. 48, mm. 4–5 and m. 13_1–2; no. 62, m. 2_1–2, mm. 6–7, and mm. 14–15. This dropping out of the contra on "chords of resolution" contrasts with native Spanish custom during our epoch and is probably to be ascribed to the influence of the foreigner, Urrede. In his romances he is on the other hand *echt Spanier* and never lets the contra drop out of "resolving" chords.

III.　In his canciones he sometimes bodily transfers a cadential passage from one song into another. For an example, mm. 55–60 at the end of the "B" section in *Damos gracias* exactly duplicate, note-for-note (all three voices), mm. 76–82 at the end of the "B" section in *Justa fué* – the only difference being that in this latter song he adds a fourth voice, to the already existing three. For another example, mm. 16–19 of *La que tengo* come very close to being the same as mm. 18_3–21 of *O quán dulçe*. When the resemblances are not absolutely literal, they are often so close that the music of one song "rhymes" with that of another.

IV.　In his canciones (except the phrygian ones) he seems to use the upward melodic skip of a fourth at least as frequently as that of a third. In his *alta* instrumental dance he uses it much more frequently (*CMP*, no. 321). In the treble of this latter he writes 15 upward skips of a fourth (within phrases), but only 8 of a third. All 15 upward leaps of a fourth begin in the treble on "accented" minims (= accented quavers in transcription). But with the upward fourth he reaches the limit of the treble skips which he will allow. Not one of his 15 pieces (including *alta*) shows an upward treble skip of a fifth. One instance, and one only, of a descending fifth is to be found in the treble of *La que tengo* (*CMP*, no. 48, m. 2).

V.   None of his pieces starts with imitation. Indeed he resorts to imitation only once in his entire secular repertory. That he avoids it, except once in the middle of what is by all odds the longest and most ambitious of his songs (*Justa fué mi perdición*, mm. 23–26), should not be wondered at, however. Urrede, learned as he must have been to gain Ramos's esteem, similarly slighted it. *De vos i de mi* (no. 17) and *Muy triste será mi vida* (no. 23) do it is true show spurts of imitation in mid-course. But Urrede never stayed with any point beyond a few head-notes, even then bringing the imitation in so unobtrusively that the eye rather than the ear must catch it.

Juan Ponce

THE FEW external biographical facts thus far discovered (see pp. 184–186) agreeably harmonize with the internal evidence in Ponce's dozen songs. Whereas all 15 of Torre's songs belonged to the original collection, only one of Ponce's was copied by the first scribe: *Ave color vini clari* (*CMP*, no. 159), this being the rollicking Latin student song which is the only such specimen in *Palacio*. Ponce's connections with the Sicilian humanist, Marineo (who taught at Salamanca from 1484–1496), make 1495 a likely date for this particular song.[193] Aside from its Latin, it also enjoys distinction among *CMP* pieces by reason of being *durchkomponiert*. He seeks formal symmetry: (1) by repeating the music (not the words) of mm. 13–17 at mm. 71–75; (2) by prefacing each "full" passage with a short section in which the upper and lower pair of voices answer each other.

Among the Ponce songs which were later added to the manuscript *Françia, cuenta tu ganançia* (no. 443) alludes to events of the year 1521 in the revised lyrics. Quite aside from this late date there are other reasons for assuming that he was somewhat younger than Encina. He for instance reset Encina's poem *Para verme* (no. 175) although it had already been twice put to music. *Torre de la niña* (no. 341) had been once set. Quite possibly *La mi sola* (no. 343) had already been set too: or at any rate, the manuscript shows the telltale rubric "Alias" beneath the title. Both nos. 175 and 341 are more advanced, musically speaking, than the alternate settings of these lyrics in *CMP*.

Ponce's style reveals itself as more "advanced" in several ways. He for example brings his tenor to rest, at least occasionally, on some other note in the last chord than the fifth or octave. In both *Todo mi bien* (no. 156) and *Como está sola* (no. 328) the tenor violates previous custom by ending on a written G♯. At their closes all the other composers thus far studied permitted thirds of final chords to invade only the treble or contra I part. Ponce's break with tradition means that in at least these two cases he can no longer have been thinking of the tenor as governor of the mode. In *Para verme* (no. 175) he obviously was thinking of it as a mere filler. This particular four-part song is written in the form of a mirror-canon between outer voices. The tenor in such a case could not have been conceived separately, much less previously. As for the labelling of parts, it is perhaps significant that the lowest voice not only in *Para verme* but in several other Ponce songs is no longer called "contra."

[193] See above, p. 185.

He also looks to the future in *Como está sola*, a four-voiced song which in the manuscript is subtitled "Lamentación," [194] when he varies the music for the second strophe. The lyrics comprise a pair of quatrains rhyming *abab cdcd*. Those other *CMP* composers thus far encountered were always in such a case content to write a musical setting for no more than the first strophe, letting it do duty for the second. Ponce, although using much the same music for his second quatrain shows that he belongs to an already more sophisticated generation by making certain small changes. He for instance omits the bass anticipation found in m. 13 from the bar in which it should occur during the second quatrain. What is more, three bars in the first strophe (mm. 15–17) fail to reappear at their expected place in the second. To compensate perhaps for this omission he adds to the closing cadence in the second strophe a coda of four bars' length during which he swiftly "modulates" from the G Major chord to the E Major.

The other *CMP* composers thus far studied tended to ignore devices of an especially ingenious or recondite sort. But Ponce in his *La mi sola, Laureola* took advantage of the first four syllables to write a solmization that looks extremely ingenious on paper and in a small way is as contrived as *Scènes mignonnes sur quatre notes* with its *Lettres dansantes*. Only one other late composer in *CMP*, the anonymous who wrote the "canonic" *A los baños dell amor* (no. 149), showed any like-minded interest in using syllables of the Spanish language (Sola m'iré = *sol la mi re*) to determine the contour of a musical line.[195]

Other Composers in CMP

A FRIAR named Francisco de Ajofrin served temporarily as a singer in Toledo Cathedral during 1499 [196] and may possibly have been the composer of the hypophrygian lover's lament *a 3, Por serviros, triste yo* (no. 355). The several fourths occurring between treble and tenor (mm. 13–15) suggest that Ajofrin, whoever he was, cannot have belonged to the eldest generation of *CMP* composers.

Pedro Juan Aldomar, a Catalonian, was appointed chapelmaster in Barcelona Cathedral on January 19, 1506. On March 1, 1508, he was enrolled as a singer in the court choir of Ferdinand *el Católico*.[197] Three songs, each *a 3*, enter *CMP* at nos. 89, 252, 297. The first *Ha, Pelayo, qué desmayo* is the best and was still sufficiently popular a half-century later for a printed arrangement *a 4* to be included in the *Cancionero de Upsala* (Venice, 1556). Both Aldomar's original *a 3* and the Upsala arrangement *a 4* breathe a freshness and charm that are wholly delightful. A smitten swain sighs after the mountains where he saw a beauty in the first of the other *CMP* songs, and the poet advises a swain who wishes not to be forgotten in the other.

---

[194] Other *CMP* songs with subtitles; *O alto bien:* [*Osequia*], no. 124; *Quien tal árbol* [*Endecha*], no. 187.

[195] Alonso in *Sol sol gi gi a b c* (no. 63) brings each refrain to a close with a downward scale, sung to the syllables *la so fa mi re ut*. But on the surface at least these are only nonsense syllables. The context suggests that they probably are meant to be a euphemism for some sexual words.

[196] Barbieri, *op. cit.*, p. 19.

[197] *DML*, I, 40.

Three songs, one of which (*Gaeta nos es subjeta*, no. 423) is dated 1504, survive from Juan Almorox (see above at p. 164). All start in fast triple meter and shift into duple at the coplas. Both nos. 200 and 211 voice the usual lover's woes.

IN *CMP*, eleven songs are ascribed to "Alonso," a name that may be either a first or a last. Songs by at least four composers whose first name was "Alonso" – Alva, Córdoba, Mondéjar, and Toro – appear in *Palacio*. Whether any of these four, or still another, wrote any or all of the eleven songs ascribed merely to "Alonso" remains a matter of conjecture.

One of Alonso's songs, *Niña, erguídeme los ojos* (no. 403), appears twice elsewhere in *CMP*, the first time in a setting by Peñalosa (no. 72), the second in an anonymous setting (no. 108). Aside from the fact that Peñalosa's arrangement belonged to the original corpus of the MS, whereas the anonymous's and Alonso's were later additions, it would still be possible, using stylistic criteria alone, to guess the order in which these three were written. Peñalosa's tenor ends on the root of the final chord, whereas the anonymous's ends on the fifth, and Alonso's on the third. Peñalosa's treble becomes the tenor of the anonymous's setting with the result that fourths between tenor and treble suddenly start cropping up. Alonso borrows Peñalosa's treble for his own top voice, but extends it with codettas at the close of both estribillo and coplas. Melodically Alonso shows daring by writing a skip of a seventh, upwards from an accented beat, in his tenor (m. 4). If this unheard-of skip is not to be discounted as a copyist's blunder, then he would be the first composer thus far met in *CMP* who requires his tenor to leap across any such chasm. On all other counts, however, his is so charming a setting with its added but unaffected *Vorimitation*, its echoing of the Peñalosa treble in the new tenor, and its smooth extension of the cadences, that he at once takes rank as a major *CMP* composer.

Alonso's texts are not usually so sweet and guileless as this Peñalosa one about the girl whose shy glances rouse the lover's hopes. Several are picaresque to the point of brutality. One is about a fool who is cuckolded (no. 387), another infers that a girl is mad if she does not accept the advances of a rich abbot (no. 213), another is a drunkard's song in a frequently incomprehensible jargon (no. 247),[198] another advises each and all to seek pleasure and let the devil take the hindmost (no. 364), while still another warns young girls against wandering procuresses (no. 393). It would not be difficult to read a bawdy meaning into *Tir'allá, que non quiero* (no. 6).

A musical characteristic common to many of his songs is their divisibility into equal phrase-lengths. *Tir'allá* divides as clearly as may be into $3 + 3 + 3 + 3 \,\|3 + 3$. *Gritos davan* (no. 15) separates into $4 + 4 \,\|4$. *Tristesa, quien a mi vos* (no. 18) breaks down into $2 + 4 + 4 \,\|4$. *La tricotea* (no. 247) – his one song without refrain – divides into $4 + 4 + 4 + 4$; $4 + 4 + 4 + 4$; only fracturing during mm. 33–52 into more irregular phrase-lengths. *Plaser y gasajo* (no. 364) divides into groups of three measures,

---

[198] Concerning *La tricotea Sanmartin* Barbieri wrote: "I do not understand this gibberish, which appears to be a drunkard's song" (p. 218, c. 1). The nonsense-words "Niqui niqui don" (*La tricotea*, mm. 35–36) recall the nonsense phrase at the end of both estribillo and coplas in Icart's *Non toches a moi:* "nichi nichi nioch." See above, p. 125.

Pero Gonçales (no. 387) into groups of four measures (indeed Alonso in the coplas of this one condescends to write three successive eight-bar periods that are direct repetitions of each other), *Guardaos d'estas pitofleras* (no. 393) as obviously as possible into 6 + 6 ‖ 6 + 6. In his only religious excursion – *Virgen dina y muy fermosa* (no. 430) – he still exhibits the same passion for phrase-symmetry (dividing the phrases: 4 + 4 + 4 [I] ‖ 4 + 4). None of the previously studied *CMP* composers showed any such predilection for phrase-length symmetry. Instead, they deliberately eschewed such obvious phrase-balancing.[199]

OF THE VARIOUS composers in *Palacio* with Alonso for a first name, the most famous on other counts was Alonso de Alva (see pp. 164–167 above). Only one song enters *Palacio*, however, his setting *a 3* of *No me le digáis mal* (*CMP*, no. 391) [200] – unless we are also to credit him with some or all of the pieces ascribed to "Alonso." Alva's one song is not distinctive enough to warrant any crucial analogies. For what they are worth the following likenesses can be drawn. Alva's song is in mixolydian and the tenor closes on the root, just as in Alonso's *Guardaos* (no. 393). Alva's song was a late addition to the manuscript, and so also were five or six of Alonso's (nos. 6, 15, 63?, 213, 364, 403). Alva's song divides into 6 + 6 [+ 1] ‖ 3 + 3, a scheme similar to that found in *Tir'allá*, the Alva and *Tir'allá* being also alike in their fast triple meter. Alva's lyrics are placed in the mouth of a young girl. She sings the praises of a handsome friar to her mother. But in the last three strophes (omitted from the critical edition) she admits that her delightful friar, though he dissimulates with grave gestures when he first comes in off the street, soon enough begins to unfrock. Alva's lyrics therefore cast unfavorable light on the clergy just as do Alonso's on the ogling abbot (no. 213). Alva's text, if not already folkish property when he composed the music, had become so by 1577. In that year Salinas used the lyrics, *No me digays madre mal del padre fray Anton*,[201] still set in triple meter but apparently to a different tune from that found either in Alva's treble or tenor, in illustration of a dance-measure which he said was then popular in Portugal under the name of *follías*.[202]

JUAN DE ANCHIETA's biography and sacred works are treated of at pp. 127–144. His romance *En memoria d'Alixandre* is shown as an example at p. 246. His use of quintuple meter in two of his four songs (*CMP*, nos. 177 and 335) is alluded to above at p. 262.

Although Salinas does not seem to have quoted any of the tunes to be found embedded in the seven quintuple-meter songs which survive in *Palacio* (nos. 59, 102, 151, 177, 197, 335, and 426) he does, however, print the music of two other quintuple-meter Spanish songs. Concerning the first of these he writes *ex cantilena quadam Hispanica desumptum*

[199] Encina's fast, bawdy songs excepted.
[200] By an error this song is listed as *a 4* in *MME*, V, *31* (item 391).
[201] *De musica libri septem*, p. 309.
[202] *Ibid.*, p. 308. The author of the article, "Folía," in *Grove's Dictionary*, 5th edn., III, 182, shows as his first musical example a melody beginning with the minim note *d*, from Salinas. The tune is, however, incorrectly transcribed. The first note should be not *d* but *B* and the whole line therefore would be read a third lower.

est.[203] The second he similarly declares to have been taken *ex cantilena vulgari Hispanica.*[204] Because he uses both of these folktunes as paradigms to illustrate meter in fives he witnesses unimpeachably to the important part played by quintuple meter in Spanish sixteenth-century folkmusic. The presence in *CMP* of quintuple-meter songs by Anchieta, Encina, Escobar, and Diego Fernández, proves that this meter was also liked by courtly composers – at least at the beginning of the century.

In Encina's, Escobar's and Diego Fernández's songs, quintuple-meter always implies fast, muscular motion. Anchieta's quintuple pair must however be taken slower. He specifies $\bigcirc \frac{5}{1}$ instead of merely the $\frac{5}{1}$ which four of the other quintuple-meter songs in *CMP* carry for their mensuration sign.

EIGHT SONGS attributed to "Badajoz" enter *CMP*. In addition, three poems and a villancico pair ascribed to "Badajoz el músico" survive in the best-known literary miscellany of the epoch, Hernando del Castillo's *Cancionero general* (1511). The first of these three poems is a verse-letter written his lady-love from Genoa.[205] If he does not tell how much else of Italy he has seen he does complain that he has been long anxiously waiting in Genoa for some messenger to carry his letter. "I tell you that my songs and my instrumental music are so many bitter laments distilling the anxieties of my seething soul," one strophe reads. After the accession of João III in 1521 Badajoz served as a chamber musician at the Portuguese court.[206]

Both Badajoz el músico and Garci Sánchez de Badajoz were, then, musician-poets. The two cannot be identified as the same person, however: the reason being that the careful indexer in the 1520 edition of the *Cancionero general* lists them as two separate individuals and ostentatiously distinguishes between the poetry of each.[207]

The disappointed lover's world is the sole orbit within which Badajoz revolves in his *CMP* songs. The most distinctive musically are precisely those cast in the old closed canción mould rather than in the new open mould of the villancico which Encina popularized during the 1490's. Both *Poco a poco* (no. 53) and *Malos adalides* (no. 57) call for three low voices. The contra of the latter descends to the bottom note in *Palacio*, D_1. This contra is not underlaid with text. *O desdichado de mi* (no. 49) is also quite obviously for men's voices alone. In contrast, however, with the preceding, each of the three voice-parts is underlaid with text. *O desdichado* shows his facture at its finest. Patiently and skilfully he threads the openings of each successive phrase with imitation through all three voice-strands. Each is moreover threaded from its first stitch in a "key-area" different from the one sewn at the closing cadence of the preceding phrase. Though it be anachronistic to use the term, still a keen and well-developed "harmonic sense" seems to have been one of Badajoz's most telling assets.

[203] *De musica libri septem*, p. 272.   [204] *Ibid.*, p. 273.

[205] Hernando del Castillo, *Cancionero general nueuamente añadido* (Toledo: Juan de Villaquiran, 1520), fol. CLVIII verso, c. 2. In addition to Badajoz el músico's poetry at fols. 158v.–160, this cancionero contains a villancico by him at fol. 123v., c. 2, entitled *Amores tristes crueles.*

[206] Barbieri, p. 24: "Badajoz." According to Silva (see note 188 above) the title should not however read as Barbieri gave it.

[207] Castillo, *op. cit.*, unnumbered page immediately preceding fol. 1. Garcí Sánchez de Badajoz is listed in c. 2 (line 7) and Badajoz el músico in c. 3 (line 28).

This ability may in turn have been nourished by his constant practice on his instrument. His verse-letter from Genoa mentions not only his *canciones* but also his *música acordada*. Testimony to his playing skill can also be taken from Garcia de Resende's *Miscellania*, a Portuguese poem written about 1532.[208] After lauding a nameless blind player *que gram saber nos orgãos*, Resende next praises those others who play superlatively well: Baena and Badajoz.[209]

LOPE DE BAENA, the most famous among a clan of musicians,[210] was inscribed as a vihuela-player at Queen Isabella's court on May 30, 1493. In 1498 he, Rodrigo Brihuega, and Durán received payment from Castile funds for their joint services as court organists. Baena – still a court organist when she died in November of 1504 – made one of the official mourning troupe which followed her body from Medina del Campo to the royal tomb at Granada. He was perhaps still alive in 1508 when Fray Francisco de Ávila lauded him as a "very knowing vihuela-player, one of the best ... and an excellent composer." [211] Interestingly enough, he and Badajoz – whom the Portuguese Garcia de Resende praised in the same breath – wrote the only two *Palacio* pieces in which the contra touches low D_1. Baena's contra in *Todo quanto yo serví* (*CMP*, no. 287), like Badajoz's in *O desdichado*, lacks a text. For that matter even his top part goes textless. All Baena's pieces are *a 3*. The old-fashioned contra skip of an octave intrudes in two of these at final cadences. In such a passage as mm. 13–15 of *Qué desgraciada sagala* (no. 161) he carries his contra above his tenor in preference to writing a chain of parallel fourths between tenor and treble. Once he forces the tenor to leap an awkward ascending seventh (no. 172, m. 3), to avoid parallel unisons. Written accidentals at the end of the coplas in no. 172 and at the close of the estribillo in no. 287 engender compulsory cross-relations with the immediately succeeding chords. Two of his songs are cast in the phrygian (nos. 161 and 433) and one in the hypophrygian (no. 172). The percentage of Baena's deuterus examples is therefore unusually high. Three of his songs match religious lyrics (nos. 160, 394, and 409). All seven of his *CMP* pieces start with an initial refrain. More often than not he uses a spillover rhyme-scheme.

Bernaldino de Brihuega was keeper of Queen Isabella's organs and *clavicordios* in 1489.[212] He or some other Brihuega composed *CMP*, nos. 69 and 222, the first of which is a triple-meter setting of a pastoral dialogue ("She left Sunday to tend her flocks, but is returning"), the second a lover's lament ("How shall I live without you?").

Giovanni Brocco, Veronese composer of the frottola *a 4*, *Io mi uoglio lamentare* (*CMP*, no. 435; see above, p. 250) is the least known foreign composer in *Palacio*.

Antonio de Contreras, enrolled in Ferdinand V's chapel on August 1, 1485, as chaplain and singer,[213] shows affinities with the older generation of Torre in both his

---

[208] Garcia de Resende, *Chronica dos valerosos e insignes feitos del Rey Dom Ioão II* (Lisbon: Antonio Aluarez, 1622 [first edn. Lisbon, 1545, entitled *Lyuro das obras ...*]), fols. 172v.–173. This poet's chronological survey stops at the year 1531.

[209] *Ibid.*, fol. 164, c. 1, lines 7–8. Antonio de Cabezón may have been the blind player.

[210] *DML*, I, 159. The first names of two others in the Baena family were Alonso and Bernaldino.

[211] Barbieri, p. 24: "Baena."

[212] *Ibid.*, p. 25.

[213] *DML*, I, 576.

CMP songs, *Triste está la Reyna* (no. 148) and *Qué mayor desaventura* (no. 332). The first is a romance *a 4* telling the sadness of a lonely and bereft queen. Among the typical romance-traits are the anapest openings set to repeated-note chords at each of the four phrase-incises, the fermatas over each of the four cadential chords and the simple homophony. His tenor, in long notes, looks like a cantus firmus. The lyrics of the second (a canción of the closed type) were written by a mid-century courtly poet, the Viscount of Altamira.

Alonso de Córdoba, a composer whose biography remains for exploration, contributed two sharply contrasting songs to *CMP*, one being a setting of the solemn Sibylline prophecy sung in Spanish churches on Christmas eve (*Juisio fuerte será dado*, no. 374) [214] and the other a humorous one about a bumpkin who leaves his flock, visits the nearby town, and comes home battered (*Miedo m'é de Chiromiro*, no. 346). His songs are too few and too brief to justify a final judgment, but it could be guessed that he was somewhat older than Encina. Both of his pieces belonged to the original corpus of the manuscript.

Cornago, already discussed at pp. 121–124 and 218–225, is represented in *CMP* by *Pues que Dios* (no. 2) and *Gentil dama* (no. 38). He thus stands between Urrede and Madrid in the original manuscript, a fact which accords well with the historical sequence in which these three probably belong.

Enrique – represented in *CMP* by two songs, *Pues con sobra de tristura* (no. 16) and *Mi querer tanto vos quiere* (no. 29) – is discussed above at pp. 231–232. Juan de Espinosa's biography is summarized at pp. 92–93. Diego de Fermoselle, Juan del Encina's elder brother, is alluded to at pp. 132 and 253–254.

DIEGO FERNÁNDEZ's identity has been disputed. In 1895 and again in 1918 Mitjana brought forward data showing that a composer of this name was appointed chapelmaster of Málaga Cathedral on August 11, 1507, and occupied the post until the middle of 1551 – a period of forty-four years.[215] After reading the capitular acts covering this long interval Mitjana announced that another Andalusian capital – Cordova (ninety miles north of Málaga) – was Fernández's home. His mother's maiden name was probably López, the evidence being the fact that Fernández's brother used López, for a last name. Fernández's immediate predecessor at Málaga, one Juan de Valdolivas, acted as master of the boy choristers from the close of 1499 until 1507. To the upbringing of the boys the cathedral chapter added the duties of the succentorship during Fernández's first two years in Málaga. Towards the end of 1509 Juan de León became *sochantre* in Fernández's stead. In the same year Encina became archdeacon of Málaga.

On August 18, 1512, Fernández's brother, Fernando López, became cathedral organist. As a matter of cathedral bookkeeping this brother was in 1513 allowed to draw chapelmaster's pay, Fernández meantime receiving the salary of a cathedral chaplain.

---

[214] Another transcription in Anglés, *La música a Catalunya fins al segle XIII*, opposite p. 298.

[215] Mitjana, "Nuevas notas al 'Cancionero musical de los siglos XV y XVI' publicado por el Maestro Barbieri," *Rev. de fil. esp.*, April-June, 1918, p. 125. The 1895 discoveries were printed in Mitjana's pamphlet, *Sobre Juan del Encina*, and later reprinted in *Estudios sobre algunos músicos* ... (Madrid, 1918), pp. 32–36.

Not until 1519 was the titular post of cathedral organist created. Although the act of May 27, 1513, naming Fernández to a prebend required him to sing the whole Office, the chapter on January 4, 1516, relieved him of so much of this obligation as pertained to vespers and compline, on condition that he diligently teach the choirboys harmony and counterpoint. This obligation was reimposed in acts dated January 5, 1519, and January 27, 1524. When on January 9, 1523, he applied for leave of absence to visit his home the chapter voted that such leave could not be granted until a competent substitute teacher had been secured. The same condition governed when he asked leave to visit the court on private business during 1525.[216]

In 1528 he and the dean of the cathedral clashed during a Corpus Christi procession. Fernández, wishing to stop at the door of a rich Genoese merchant residing in Málaga and to conduct his choristers in the singing of a specially prepared motet, was prevented by the dean from making any such gesture. Injured by the dean's order, financially as well as socially, Fernández complained to the chapter. Justice was evidently on his side, for the chapter heavily fined the dean. Though he appealed the case, higher diocesan authority sitting on the case did no more than to reduce his heavy fine.

By 1535 Fernández had so lost his vigor (the cathedral act specifically mentions his "advanced age and sicknesses") that he was allowed to stop giving the choirboys their daily lesson in harmony and counterpoint and instead to engage a deputy. He was not so old in 1537 however that the chapter would allow him respite from his duty of composing Christmas music. On December 7, 1537, having heard that he planned to rehearse his choir in only six new chanzonetas instead of the customary nine, the cathedral chapter ordered him to proceed with the usual nine.[217] He died in 1551, probably during the forepart of August. Announcement of a competition to fill the vacancy left by his death was made by the cathedral chapter on August 18. The post was filled on November 27 following by no less eminent a successor than Cristóbal de Morales.

Anglés rejects Mitjana's attempt to equate this Diego Fernández with the composer of the two songs in *CMP*, *Tres moricas m'enamoran* (no. 25) and *De ser mal casada* (no. 197), the first of which is an arrangement *a 3* of a previously existing villancico and the second a nervous quintuple-meter song *a 4*.[218] He contends that the Málaga candidate is too late a person for *CMP*. On the other hand if the Málaga chapelmaster was quite old in 1535 he could easily have been born in 1470. Even Encina was born only one year earlier.

The first of Fernández's songs charmingly describes three Moorish maidens from Jaén who have stolen the poet's heart. Axa, Fátima, and Marien when they draw water at the fountain are even "prettier than any girls from Toledo." The poet swears by the "Koran in which you three believe" that they have collectively thrown him into a lover's frenzy. They courteously reply, "Sir, though your lineage and honor are in high repute, yet to have three lady loves is to have none at all; one man for each maid is what Axa, Fátima,

---

[216] Mitjana, "Nuevas notas," p. 126, adds that the cabildo at first wished to stop his salary while he attended the court but later thought better of the idea and paid him 987 *reales*.

[217] *Ibid.*, p. 126. Another evidence of deterioration in his last years is the notice of December 2, 1541, showing that the cathedral on that date owned practically no polyphonic music books.

[218] *DML*, I, 889, c. 2.

and Marien desire." This sophisticated poem, except for its short refrain, pursues a different course from the lyrics set by some anonymous composer on the upper half of the same manuscript page. The music of the anonymous *Tres morillas m'enamoran*, on the other hand, sufficiently resembles Fernández's *Tres moricas m'enamoran*. The treble, except at cadences, is indeed identical. As for differences, the anonymous's "harmonization" is simpler, the spondaic rhythm of the treble reaching downward into the lower voices as well. In the anonymous setting only one crotchet is to be found intruded anywhere into the steady procession of semibreves and minims (tenor, m. 13) as against fifteen such crotchets in Fernández's arrangement. The closing chords differ; anonymous ends over E, Fernández over C.

By a stroke of fortune these two *CMP* items mentioning Axa, Fátima, and Marien have aroused more literary interest than any other pieces in the whole of *Palacio*. Julián Ribera (1858–1934), the great Arabist, fastened especially on the anonymous version as a prime example of Moorish song.[219] In truth, however, neither harmony nor melody of *CMP*, no. 24, differs in any crucial sense from that found in scores of other *CMP* items. The anonymous's "harmonization" though simple is neither novel nor singular. If one concentrates only on the treble melody, its intervals in both the anonymous setting (no. 24) and in Fernández's *alio modo* (no. 25) must also be conceded to be utterly commonplace – an upward fourth, downward second, two successive downward thirds, followed by stepwise motion upward. As for the contour of the melody, one may call it "Arabian" or not, as he pleases – there being no certified Arabian melodies with which to compare it. But if the shape of the melody is called "Arabian" then Felix Mendelssohn's *Andante con moto* in his Italian Symphony also contains an "Arabian" melody, its opening phrase being a close "transcript" of the treble melody in *Tres morillas m'enamoran*.

THE INITIALS "P.F." standing at the head of *Cucú, cucú, cucucú* (*CMP*, no. 101) have been taken by both editors of *Palacio*, Barbieri [220] and Anglés,[221] to stand for Pedro Fernández. P.F.'s cuckoo-song strongly resembles Encina's (*CMP*, no. 94). As for the lyrics, the opening estribillo in both songs is identical. The coplas differ: but develop the same idea, namely, that husbands should stand guard against cuckoldry. Each song opens with a cuckoo-call in one part which is immediately taken up in a point of imitation by the other three voices. Encina's setting starts in duple but changes to triple meter. P.F.'s version adheres throughout to jaunty triple meter.

Giacomo Fogliano, one of the more prolific frottolists, is known to have composed *L'amor donna ch'io ti porto* (*CMP*, no. 91) – an anonymous item in Petrucci's *Frottole Libro septimo* (fol. 20) – from a concordance at the Bibliothèque Nationale in MS Rés. Vm⁷ 676 at fols. 110v.–111.

---

[219] For a sympathetic discussion of this great Arabist's musical adventures see Miguel Asín Palacios, "La música árabe ..." (in Ribera y Tarragó, *Disertaciones y opúsculos* [Madrid: Estanislao Maestre Pozas, 1928], Vol. 1, pp. LXXXVII–CIII). The part *Las tres morillas* (*CMP*, no. 24) played in setting Ribera off on his spirited chase of medieval Moorish music is mentioned at p. XCII.

[220] Barbieri, p. 40.

[221] *MME*, V, 126. Mitjana suggested that "P.F." might equal Pedro Fernández de Castilleja in "Nuevas notas," p. 129.

GARCIMUÑOZ (= García Muñoz) composed the longest piece of music in the Palace Songbook, *Una montaña pasando* (no. 154). Its nearest competiter is Millán's *Serrana del bel mirar* (no. 71). Both pretend to be autobiographic tales told by a traveller who has journeyed through the mountains. In Millán's piece the wayfarer has encountered a pretty maid who sings him two sad ditties. In Garcimuñoz's, the traveller meets two mountain maids instead of one. Each sings him a single forlorn ditty. Insofar as text is concerned, then, the Millán and Garcimuñoz items not only treat similar subjects but also resemble each other structurally. In each, the lyrics "frame" two sad ditties sung by mountain maids. Millán's entire piece is in triple meter, but Garcimuñoz dramatizes the moment when each maid begins singing her ditty by shifting from duple to triple meter (mm. 17 and 80). Though he stays consistently in F Major throughout (signature of one flat in every voice) Garcimuñoz pleasantly varies his cadences so that phrases will close with every triad except the leading-tone and supertonic. Aside from F-chords (19 times), his most frequent ending-chords are built on C (7 times). It cannot be merely the result of chance that neither at the 33 cadences nor anywhere else in this long piece does an unprepared fourth between tenor and treble obtrude itself. He shows no such qualms when writing intervals between tenor and altus (see mm. 77–79 for a chain of fourths). At the very end of the piece he shifts from Spanish into Latin. In *fabordón*-style his four voices intone this verse: "How shall we sing a new song in a strange land?" (Ps. 136 [137].4), drawing out the cadence on their last word like a long plagal Amen.

Garcimuñoz's two other songs (*CMP*, nos. 166 and 389) are villancicos of conventional length. Both are clearly in major keys: F and C. As in *Una montaña*, he makes gestures towards imitation in each of these. In *Pues bien para ésta* (no. 389) a girl, the youngest of four sisters, hears that soldiers are coming to town and jumps for joy. Since her father is dead she can hope for no better match. In dialogue-fashion her mother begs her to remember that she is the youngest, and pleads with her not to wreck her future. Finally the mother promises to find her a husband before the soldiers arrive. This particular song is one of the choicer in *CMP*, and has proved invariably effective in performance.

JUAN PÉREZ DE GIJÓN, composer of two songs in *CMP*, was also a contributor to *CMC*. Compare page 232 above. Josquin des Prez's *In te Domine speravi* composed while he was in the service of Ascanio Sforza (cardinal after 1484),[222] appears at fol. 56 in our manuscript with this ascription. "Jusquin dascanjo." A later addition to the MS, this frottola was copied in such a small blank space that the scribe could not start each of the four voice-parts on a fresh staff. Reference is made to Pedro Lagarto at pp. 235–236, to Juan de León at pp. 237–240, and to Juan Fernández de Madrid at pp. 177–179 and 240–242.

Lope Martines's three-voiced setting of the border ballad, *Cavalleros de Alcalá* (*CMP*, no. 100), is his only surviving piece. Though sharing many of the conventional romance-

---

[222] Ascanio Sforza (1455–1505), brother to Ludovico il Moro, duke of Milan, lived sumptuously in Rome after being created cardinal. Serafino de' Ciminelli (1466–1500), one of the most renowned poets of the epoch, recorded that Josquin was a fellow-servant in the cardinal's household. See *Le Rime di Serafino de' Ciminelli dall'Aquila*, ed. Mario Menghini, vol. 1 (Bologna: Romagnoli-dall'Acqua, 1894), pp. 34–38. Serafino's sonnet to Josquin (p. 112) should also be read. This poet was himself trained for music as a profession, and was therefore an apt critic.

traits, his setting is distinguished by a larger use of "incomplete" changing-notes, eight to be precise, than is to be found customarily in *CMP* romances. Mention was made of Fernand Pérez de Medina above at pp. 180–183. Six villancicos by Jacobus de Milarte survive (*CMP*, nos. 210, 264, 266, 268, 360, and 398), half *a 4* and the rest *a 3*. One of these, *A sombra de mis cabellos* (no. 360), is an arrangement *a 4* of Gabriel's three-voiced villancico of the same name (no. 132). Milarte skilfully weaves the *Vorimitation* back into his added lowest part. For stylistic reasons, Anglés's guess that he was a peninsular composer [223] seems likelier than Barbieri's that he was a Fleming.[224] "Milarte" does of cf course resemble "Maillart." Pedro Maillart, as Barbieri observed, was a canon of Cambrai and later a singer in Philip II's choir. Moxica, a contributor to both *CMC* and *CMP* is referred to at pp. 242–243.

Alonso de Mondéjar's eleven villancicos (all exhibiting spillover rhyme-schemes) enter *CMP* at nos. 134, 164, 230, 237, 256, 261, 280, 294, 299, 349, and 373. At least ten, and perhaps also the eleventh (no. 237), were added to the original corpus of *Palacio* by some later hand. All are in duple meter throughout. Ten are for three voices, the last (no. 373) being the only one *a 4*. None is in dorian; five end with G-chords, three with F-chords (B♭ in the signature), and two with C-chords. One of those ending on C, *Mios fueron, mi coraçon* (no. 294), is Mondéjar's arrangement for three unchanged voices of the Millán song bearing the same name (no. 185) for three mixed voices. His sole four-voiced exemplar, *Oyan todos mi tormento* (no. 373) starts as if it were to be a psalm instead of a villancico. The last line mentions the *Ne recorderis* sung at matins in the Office of the Dead. But the theme is the gallant's "death" because of his mistress's hardheartedness – and not any sacred subject.[225]

Robert Morton's canción to lyrics by Monsalve, *Pues serviço vos desplase* (*CMP*, no. 27), is his, only in respect of the tenor and outer voices. The clumsy fourth voice was added in the MS by a later hand. Francisco de Peñalosa's contributions to *CMP* are listed above at pp. 152–153. Antonio de Ribera, alluded to above at p. 189, is represented by two items – a rigidly chordal setting *a 4* of Encina's romance *Por unos puertos arriva* (*CMP*, no. 107) and a hypophrygian villancico *a 3* entitled *Nunca yo, señora* (no. 192). This latter vents the suitor's customary sorrows.

J. Rodríguez, contributor to *CMC* as well as to *CMP*, is discussed at pp. 243–244 above. Romá[n]'s first name is not divulged,[226] and his four-voiced piece entitled *O voy*

[223] *DML*, II, 1532.

[224] Barbieri, *op. cit.*, p. 39.

[225] Gabriel's setting *a 4* of the same text (*CMP*, no. 401) must be considered earlier than Mondéjar's for the following reasons: (1) Gabriel's is in simple homophony throughout, Mondéjar's in imitation at the opening of first and second phrases; (2) Mondéjar's is altogether more cursive with its frequent passing notes. The treble of *Oigan todos mi tormento* (Hortênsia cancioneiro, no. 60 [p. 95]), a three-voiced setting, so closely resembles the treble of Gabriel's *a 4* that paraphrase either of Hortênsia or of some other primitive version, will have to be conceded. Mondéjar's setting however is based on Gabriel's rather than the Hortênsia anonymous's version.

[226] Concerning Romá[n] see *El Comendador Roman: Coplas de la Pasión con la Resurreción*, facs. of Toledo print c. 1490 with introduction by H. Thomas (London: British Museum, 1936), pp. 2–3. Román's probable dates: 1430–1500 (p. 4). He was a retainer in the Duke of Alva's household c. 1470 and in about that year wrote a *Glosa suya a una cancion del duque dalua que dize nunca fue pena mayor*. This glosa was commissioned by Doña Juana, wife of Henry IV of Castile ("the impotent") sometime between 1469 and 1474. The glosa

(no. 358) survives textless in all parts. The temptation to consider it a purely instrumental item is however weakened by the vocal character of its melodic lines. Since a bad misprint occurs in the critical edition at m. 18 (contra II), one may hope that the string of four parallel fifths between treble and contra I at m. 14 is also attributable either to a scribe's error or an editorial miscalculation, rather than to the composer's blundering. Salsedo (= Salcedo = Sarzedo), represented by *Que bien me lo veo* (*CMP*, no. 129), was well enough known in Portugal to be called the "fountainhead of singing" (Sarzedo, *Fonte cantar*) by Garcia de Resende in his *Miscellania*.[227] Juan de Sanabria, mentioned above at p. 193, was a composer of more power and versatility than either Román or Salsedo. He contributed an unusual villancico (*Mayoral del hato*, no. 118) when he interspersed spoken text before every refrain. For a *Palacio* piece it again is unusual in containing a chain of parallel fourths between the tenor and treble. As for his other villancico (*Descuidad d'ese cuidado*, no. 377), it also shows a few exceptional touches. He jumps up from one accented crotchet (his time-value) to another, dissonant with both tenor and contra (m. 3). An upward octave-skip in minim-motion would be no rarity in a lower voice, but in his treble it must be classed as such (m. 4).

Sant Juan's grave canción, *El bien qu'estuve esperando* (no. 68), throws into relief an unusual number of "inversions." As a rule, Spanish stylists in both *CMC* and *CMP* preferred root-position chords at all rhythmically emphatic moments, but Sant Juan at mm. 7, 17, 20, 23, 32, 37, 39, 40, 41, 43, 48, 52, 62, 65, 66, 67, and 68, chooses the thinner-sounding inverted triad on strong beats. Even when writing a root-position chord he often thins its sonority by omitting one of the triad-notes. Through the skilful use of imitation, by overlapping his phrases in the three voice-parts, and by carefully distributing motion, he obtains a smoother flow than that running through lover's laments by Encina. Since his closed-form canción belongs to the original corpus of *CMP*, where it interleaves songs by Madrid and Medina (composers who flourished in the 1480's), he ought probably to be grouped with them on external as well as stylistic grounds. Sedano, composer of the young girl's protest against marrying a rich old man with no teeth (*Viejo malo en la mi cama*, no. 455), on the other hand belongs almost certainly in Encina's generation, or even later.

On the two singers named Tordesillas see page 193. Alonso de Toro (nos. 370 and 371) is one of at least four composers in *CMP* bearing the first name of "Alonso." The composer ambiguously called "Alonso" without any identifying "last" name shares his bawdy literary tastes. Toro is however the less technically adroit composer. The second Toro item, *Al çedás*, purports to be the cry of a sieve-vendor trying to "sell" a lady. But as with many of its class the language is throughout sexually connotative. The last four bars of the refrain have an extremely commonplace sound.

proves incidentally that the first Duke of Alva wrote *Nunca fué pena mayor* – a fact that might otherwise not have been certified. See Román's glosa in *Cancionero general nueuamente añadido* (Toledo, 1520), fol. LXXXV, c. 2.

227 Resende, *op. cit.*, fol. 164, c. 1 (line 2). The immediately preceding strophe has to do with events of 1499. Sarzedo (= Salsedo) may have served at Queen Lianor's court. There was also at Charles V's court, 1518–1525, a [Martín de] Salcedo, who was an organist (see *AM*, X, 94). The three-voiced *Que bien me lo veo* contains a tenor which is duplicated in the anonymous setting *a 4* of the same lyrics (*CMP*, no. 139).

Concerning Triana (*CMP*, nos. 235 and 243) see above at pp. 195–199 and 208–218. *Vox clamantis* (no. 105) with lyrics by Serafino dall'Aquila was composed by the celebrated frottolist, Bartolomeo Tromboncino: Petrucci's being the authority for the attribution (*Frottole Libro tertio*, fol. 60).

If Troya, composer of two sacred songs and one secular (nos. 55, 413, and 187), is right-fully to be identified with the Alfonso de Troya who was a papal singer, 1501–1516,[228] he perhaps wrote his two religious pieces before leaving Spain. One reason would be that both were included in the original corpus of the manuscript. For another, the first shows cadential melodic progressions, such as the ascending octave skip in contra or tenor to avoid consecutive fifths, which do not characterize *CMP* songs that can be dated after 1500. Troya's one secular item, *Quien tal árbol pone* (no. 187), is on the other hand a later addition to the MS. Significantly, it exhibits the spillover rhyme-scheme popu-larized by Encina, whereas neither of his sacred pair do. Moreover it lacks the archaic octave-leaps at cadences seen in *O santa clemens* (no. 55: mm. 10, 15, 39). In the MS, the subtitle of no. 187 reads *Endecha* (= dirge).

For references to Johannes Urrede see pp. 203–204 and 225. Concerning Juan de Valera see pp. 168 and 170. Valera is represented by *Ya no quiero aver plaser* (*CMP*, no. 439) – a hypophrygian villancico *a 3* (with several parallel fourths between tenor and treble) set to lyrics constructed on the Encinian plan. On internal as well as external grounds he therefore can be grouped with the later *CMP* com-posers. In chronological order the external facts read as follows. On January 15, 1505, he was appointed maestro in Seville Cathedral in succession to Alva; the choirboys were placed in his charge; and he was permitted to move into the large house formerly occupied by Alva, but on condition that he share it with the cathedral stained-glass window-makers.[229] On April 12, 1507, Fernando de Solís took the choirboys temporarily in charge.[230] On June 7, 1507, Francisco de Troya was named interim organist at the rate which had previously been paid Valera.[231] This particular notice suggests that

---

[228] Haberl, *Bausteine* ..., III, 59–60. Anglés suggests in *MME*, IV, *4*, that "*Troya*" in this case may refer to the Francisco de Troya who was appointed organist of Seville Cathedral on "July *2*, 1507." This identification must however be studied in the light of the following facts. The notice in the *Autos Capitulares*, *1505. 1506. 1507. 1510. 1523. 1524.*, mentioning the latter's appointment on June 7, 1507 (fol. 230v.) reads as follows: "On this day the chapter placed Francisco de Troya, priest, in charge of the organs of the cathe-dral, both those of the *coro* as well as those of the *Antigua* [Chapel] until the chapter can obtain some qualified person (*fasta tanto que el cavildo provea de persona avile para ellos*), the said Francisco de Troya to be paid for his services as from June 1, and at the salary which was paid Juan Valera." Valera, the Sevillian chapel-master, had just died.

Further proof that Francisco de Troya was only an inferior temporary substitute is found in the *auto* dated June 30, 1507 (fol. 233) appointing "Diego Hernandez" player of the cathedral organs. This act specifically states that the cathedral lacked a good player (*vista la avilidad de diego hernandez e quanta mengua tiene esta yglesia de un tañedor*). The Juan Bernal whom Anglés mentions *MME*, IV, *4*, would moreover have been not the cathedral organist but rather the *organero* who repaired and tuned the cathedral organs [*A.C.*, *1505. 1506. 1507. 1510. 1523. 1524.*, fol. 252v. (Nov. 10, 1507) and *A.C.*, *1508.* 41v. (July 19, 1508)].

As for Alfonso de Troya's career in Rome, his salary rose from 8 florins a month in February, 1501, to 10 in September, 1507. Leo X made him a papal notary. He died in December, 1516.

[229] *A.C.*, *1505. 1506. 1507. 1510. 1523. 1524.*, fol. 88v.

[230] *Ibid.*, fol. 223.

[231] *Ibid.*, fol. 230v. (see note 228 above).

Valera had served not only as choirmaster but also as organist. On May 15, 1508, the cathedral acts refer to him as several months dead.[232] That he died prematurely is certain. He could not have been hired in one year if he were so old that his death was expected the second year following. His one villancico is unfortunately all that survives. Copied in as a later addition to the MS, it shows a glaring scribal error. The tenor should have moved from e to f on the final beat of m. 3 rather than on the first of m. 4.

Vilches, the last of those *CMP* composers whose names have been recovered, is represented by a four-voiced villancico, *Ya cantan los gallos* (no. 155). The tenor is quite evidently borrowed. Not only does it proceed in longer values, but also it recurs in the Hortênsia cancioneiro with new outer voices. Vilches's three added voices are infinitely finer, however, than the two added in *Hortênsia*. They are more lithe and supple, they fill their chords more completely, and each line taken alone is independently interesting. The estribillo-text in *Hortênsia* closely enough resembles *Palacio*. But the coplas of the *CMH* version do not match those in *CMP*. As is so often the case when literary variants are studied, the *Palacio* version seems the more polished and graceful from every vantage. In the *CMH* lyrics the maid urges her lover to arise because the cocks are crowing. In the *CMP* expanded version he replies that he welcomes death in her arms. In the third strophe she urges him not to expose himself to peril. In the fourth he counters that death in her arms is victory indeed. In the fifth and last she reminds him that she too is endangered. Just as a mere scene in *CMH* flowers into a miniature drama in *CMP*, so also the rather colorless *CMH* musical setting grows under Vilches's tending into a "trellised garland of morning-glories."

Anonymous Spanish Songs in the Palace Songbook

APPROXIMATELY 178 of the 458 items in *CMP* refuse to yield the identity of their composers, either directly or from concordances. Properly to study these anonymous pieces it would be necessary to begin by drawing up a melodic index of at least all the trebles and tenors in *Palacio*.[233] Just as it was unexpectedly discovered that Millán's repertory includes two songs with identical music though set to different lyrics, and another two with opposing lyrics but with music that differs by the mere addition of a second contra together with some rhythmic adjustments in the first phrase – discoveries not apparently made by any editors of this songbook – so it seems likely that a painstaking survey of the anonymous items might disclose other similarly unsuspected doublets. Already it is known, for instance, that after its time-values were reduced by one-half, the monodic *Reyna y Madre de Dios* (no. 19) was requisitioned by some other anony-

---

[232] *A.C., 1508*, fol. 30.

[233] The tenors are especially important, since it is in this voice that borrowed material is usually to be found. The negative results which Marius Schneider announced after searching *CMP* for traces of folksong influence would not have seemed so conclusive had he taken account of tenors as well as trebles. See "¿Existen elementos de música popular en el 'Cancionero Musical de Palacio'?" in *Anuario Musical*, VIII (1953), pp. 177–192.

Que me quereys [el] cauallero

Salinas, *De musica libri septem* (1577), p. 325 *

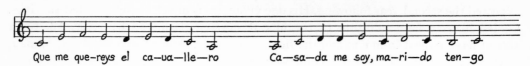

CMP, no. 198 **   Anonymous

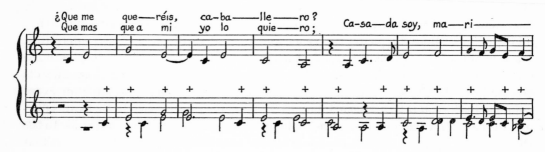

   * What are you seeking, Sir Knight? I am married; I have a husband.

   ** What are you seeking, Sir Knight? I am married; I have a husband. I am worthily matched with an honorable gentleman, good-looking and well-bred. What is more, I love him.

mous composer to serve as the treble of the secular villancico which closely follows, *Yo con vos, señora* (no. 21).

    A melodic index will also expedite the search for concordances with folktunes quoted by Salinas. At present the best that can be done is to search *CMP* and Salinas for items with identical titles. The anonymous *Qué me queréis, caballero* (*CMP*, no. 198) is found after comparison to show affinities with Salinas's *Que me quereys el cauallero* (*De musica libri septem*, p. 325) not only textually, but musically as well. The tenor in the *Palacio* anonymous's setting indeed so closely matches the *cantione usitatissima* quoted by Salinas that folksong paternity must immediately be conceded. If such a literary concordance can lead to the discovery of a parallel musical concordance, it seems at least possible that other tenors in *CMP* matching Spanish popular tunes quoted in Salinas exist, but have thus far defied discovery because the literary texts associated with tenor and folktune differ.

As for anonymous items containing borrowed material other than Salinas's folktunes: I The unknown composer of *Lo que queda es lo seguro* (no. 99) quotes in his middle voice the treble of a song ascribed elsewhere in *Palacio* to Escobar (no. 216).[234] That the anonymous composer was here the borrower – not Escobar – was Barbieri's opinion.[235] Aside from the paleographical evidence that no. 99 was the later setting, two other facts support such a conclusion: (1) tenors were often made out of previously existing trebles; (2) other arrangements for equal voices to be found in *Palacio* have always proved to be of later date than the corresponding material when the alternate setting is for mixed voices. II The tenor in the anonymous *Que bien me lo veo* (no. 139) duplicates the tenor in Salsedo's song of the same name (no. 129). In this instance both songs perhaps embed a pre-existing popular tune. The anonymous *Que bien* could be guessed to be the later setting since it is composed *a 4* whereas the Salsedo was written *a 3*. III Whatever one thinks of *Que bien* it cannot be doubted that the anonymous setting *a 4* of *Tristeza, quien a mí os dió* (no. 112) was composed later than the setting *a 3* of these same *Tristeza* lyrics by Alonso (no. 18). The treble is identical in each instance; but the anonymous composer has contrived an ingenious *Vorimitation* and has broken down Alonso's block-chords – moving in semibreves and breves, into supple counterpoints – running in crotchets and minims. IV The greeting to the nightingale at daybreak *a 4*, with *Dindirindin* for its refrain (*CMP*, no, 359: text in Catalonian), obviously follows the Italian *Dindiridin a 3* in Monte Cassino MS 871 N. The *CMP* arranger switches tenor and treble, and inserts a new contra between them. He retains the same bass. Federico Ghisi has published the Italian original in "Canzoni profane italiane del secondo Quattrocento in un codice musicale di Monte Cassino," *Revue Belge de Musicologie*, II (1948), p. 14. Isabel Pope first drew attention, however, to the *CMP* concordance in her study of Spanish music at Naples (1954).

Secular tunes were not the only ones borrowed. Plainchants were requisitioned as well. *Plega a Dios* (no. 58) quotes, for instance, the antiphon to be sung on Sundays at compline: *Salva nos, Domine*.[236] In the top voice the singer implores God (in Spanish) to wreak revenge on his hardhearted mistress by letting her fall in love with someone who will despise her. Meanwhile the tenor intones an Office prayer (in Latin) for aid through the night, his part proceeding in solemn breves and semibreves. A striking parallel with *Plega a Dios* is found in Gijón's *Ruego a Dios* (no. 41). Both are canciones *a 3*; both are archaically bitextual, the top voice venting a revengeful lover's spleen against his lady, the tenor meanwhile intoning a Latin chant in cantus firmus style.

OTHER PROBLEMS of the anonymous repertory can here be only briefly confronted. The first such problem is that of chronology. Do the anonymous items copied in

---

[234] This is one of the three Escobar songs also in *CMH* (no. 9). See Joaquim, *op. cit.*, p. 43.

[235] Barbieri, p. 102 (item 146).

[236] Chant in *LU* (1939 edn.), pp. 271–272.

the forepart of the manuscript by the original scribe differ in any significant musical ways from those added by later copyists at whatever blank spaces they could find? Does the "musical dating" of an anonymous item tally with the "literary dating" that can be surmised either from the poet's biography or from the circumstantial evidence of spillover rhyme? To both questions an interim answer of yes can be given. Certainly the music of anonymous items 39, 58, 64, 93, 115, 119, and 128 must predate 1490.

Another such problem has to do with the "written-in" accidentals. Less than twenty of the 178–odd anonymous items show any written-in accidentals, other than B♭'s. Only a single written G♯ has been localized in the entire anonymous repertory (no. 133); and only three items carry c♯'s (nos. 133, 270 and 434). In Encina's 60-odd songs are to be found on the other hand not less than eleven "written-in" g♯'s (nos. 79, 162, 178, 275, 281, 289, 313, 406) and twenty-seven c♯'s (nos. 77, 79, 83, 126, 163, 167, 174, 178, 179, 181, 249, 282, 289, 305, 314, 412, 438). In only the dozen songs by Ponce are to be found at least four obligatory g♯'s (nos. 156, 328, 343). Such a difference in statistics must surely be one of the reasons why the anonymous pieces seem on the whole rather colorless.[237]

The anonymous repertory does apparently sound one dramatic clash between an f♯ and an f¹♮ at the same moment. Both notes rest atop B♮ (no. 348, m. 8). This conflict was probably intended; even though it lasts only an instant. The lyrics tell the barnyard fable of a small fox who slips in among the hens, who is however discovered by the watchful cock, and who then pretends that he came to pay only a social call. The cock holds such sly nonsense in derision and reminds the fox that the blood of his own distinguished ancestors is not yet dry on reynard's coat. This droll fable is so aptly set in every other way that the clashing accidentals seem wholly right and proper. [238] There is also reason to believe that the parallel fifths on "Zango-" of the onomatopoetic word, *Zangorromango*, were an intentional, and not a haphazard, stroke.

As for structure: the most artfully organized of all the anonymous pieces – and indeed one of the finest things in the entire Palace Songbook – is the four-part *A los baños del amor* (no. 149). The lyrics voice the complaint of an unwed maiden who has loved not wisely but too well. Treble and first and second contras sing: "To the baths of love I shall go alone, and bathe in them: ‖ in order that I may cure this illness which causes me misery, for this is an affliction so mortal that it ruins my figure. ‖ To the baths of sorrow I shall go alone, and bathe in them." Instead of beginning simultaneously with the other three voices, the tenor rests a *longa*, after which he sings four breves: *so la mi re* (G A E D). Having done, he rests another *longa* before again repeating the four-breve ostinato – G A E D. This goes on throughout the entire song, coplas as well as estribillo. The solmization-ostinato serves not only a musical purpose, but also a literary. The syllables *so la mi re* equal "Sola m'iré" – which in Spanish means: "I [feminine] shall go alone."

Here then virtuosity reaches an unusual height. Poet and composer are completely interdependent. Yet the poetry has the stamp of complete naturalness and sincerity.

---

[237] Significantly, the three anonymous songs with higher sharps (c♯ and g♯) match *via dolorosa* lyrics. In no. 133 the poet paraphrases the *Stabat mater*.

[238] Barbieri, item 442 of his edition, specified d¹♯ rather than f¹.

A los baños del amor

CMP, no. 149

Anonymous

Spanish musical genius always glows brightest when some learned device – such as the unifying ostinato – is made to serve an expressive purpose. Here, even better, a truly Spanish "soggetto cavato" is made to serve both as poetic theme and unifying ostinato.

That this example should appear in *Palacio* is of vital importance for the historian of Spanish sixteenth-century music. Mitjana, as long ago as 1918, called attention to the fact that Morales particularly favored the tenor-ostinato, using it as a unifying device in many of his finest motets. But in so doing, Morales trod no new paths. His conception of "canon" was already current in peninsular tradition. Our *Palacio* anonymous set the stage when he called his tenor-part a *canon*, and thus explained: "[the tenor] will wait through two rests and will then sing *so la mi re*."

Concluding Remarks concerning the Palace Songbook

I. The Palace Songbook is essentially a collection of courtly lyrics set by courtly composers.

II. The most illustrious Spanish poets of the fifteenth century – the Marqués de Santillana, Juan de Mena, Juan Rodríguez del Padrón, and Jorge Manrique, for instance – found composers for their lyrics in *CMP*. But there is no reason to believe the literary taste of *CMP* composers, like that of the frottolists,[239] notably improved as time went on. Indeed the songs composed earliest are often joined to the most distinguished poetry.

III. In *CMP*, a gratifying correlation is to be observed between the literary structure and the date of musical setting (when ascertainable). The older lyrics are stamped, not only externally by the dates of the poets who wrote them, but by reason of their "closed" form: the sense and rhyme of the strophe always ending before the refrain starts. The newer lyrics (after about 1490) are on the other hand in "open" form: the sense and rhyme of the strophe spilling over into the refrain (= da capo). Torre is the most prolific composer of closed-form canciones in *CMP*, Encina of open-form villancicos.

IV. Slightly less than one-tenth (44) of the surviving pieces in *CMP* are romances. The latest generation of *CMP* composers neglected this genre. The musical form conventionally called for four long phrases, each opening in anapest rhythm, each closing with a fermata. Low-pitched homophony was the rule, the dorian mode the most usual. Romances never included a refrain.

V. The older group of *CMP* composers – Cornago, Enrique, Madrid, Gijón, and Torre, for instance – show their age in the archaic cadences which they used, the rigid stratification of their voices, and the hegemony of their tenors as the voice from which consonances were to be counted. The middle group, headed by Encina, used mixed signatures less frequently, avoided the "under-third" cadence, indulged in the contra octave skip upwards much less frequently at cadences, and occasionally allowed unprepared fourths to intrude between tenor and treble on principal beats. The last generation, typified by Ponce, subordinates the tenor still further (requiring him, for instance, to end on another note than the final of the mode), eschews mixed signatures, never writes in slow triple meter, and makes more of a formal principle of imitation.

---

[239] On the literary improvement of *frottole* published between 1507–1520, see Alfred Einstein, *The Italian Madrigal* (Princeton: Princeton University Press, 1949), I, 107.

VI. Taken as a whole, *CMP* composers do not favor triple meter: and more especially the slow kind designated with a circle. In the first hundred items, triple meter governs more frequently than later in *Palacio*. But even in the first hundred songs only 29 instances of triple meter can be found. Of these 29, only thirteen are in perfect time of the less prolation. In the *Pixérécourt Chansonnier*, on the other hand, the first 100 items show 36 instances of triple meter. Of these 36, no less than thirty are in perfect time of the less prolation.

VII. *CMP* composers overwhelmingly favor the $\mathsf{C}\!\!\!\!\mid$ mensuration sign. They also use $\mathsf{C}, \mathsf{C}\,2;\, \bigcirc,\, \Phi,\, \bigcirc\,3,\, \Phi\,3,\, \Phi\tfrac{3}{2};\, \mathsf{C}\,3,\, \mathsf{C}\!\!\!\!\mid 3,\, \mathsf{C}\!\!\!\!\mid\tfrac{3}{1},\, \bigcirc;\,3;\, \bigcirc\tfrac{5}{1},\, \mathsf{C}\tfrac{5}{1};\tfrac{5}{1},\, 3^2$. Some of these seventeen different varieties may be explained as mere whim, no more crucial than a modern composer's choice between C and $\tfrac{4}{4}$. On the other hand, most of the varieties can be rationalized as tempo-indicators. That they do on the whole tell something more than the "number of units in the measure" can be proved by the varieties appearing in the songs of only one composer, Encina. The most unusual meters are those in fives. Both "slow" and "fast" quintuple signatures enter *CMP*.

VIII. All bawdy songs frisk in fast meters – usually triple.[240] Lover's plaints go in slow meters. Even in slow songs, however, strongly accentual rhythm seems usually to be implied.

IX. No song is composed *a 5*. Roughly two-thirds are scored *a 3*, one third *a 4*. Only two duets enter *CMP*, one by Peñalosa, the other by Ponce. But throughout the villancicos, momentary voice-pairing is a common enough event. The more skilful composers vary voice-texture by dropping individual parts from the ensemble.

X. The parts do not range widely. The treble rarely sings higher than e^1 nor the second contra lower than G_1, these being the conventional vocal limits of contemporaneous plainsong. Moreover each individual voice tends to stay within a hexachord. Wide leaps in the treble are virtually unknown.

XI. All the songs are treble-dominated works. Occasionally another voice, or even all the other parts, will be texted – in which case vocal concerted performance is to be inferred. Instrumental accompaniment was probably the rule in songs lacking text in the lower parts.

XII. The following "written-in" accidentals are found: B♭, E♭, F♯, C♯, G♯. But not A♭ nor A♯. Signatures with B♭ in all voices are frequent; and with B♭ in only the contra fairly common in the older pieces. Very occasionally an E♭ is to be seen in a contra signature (though never in that of higher part).

XIII. Short incisive melodic phrases are the rule. Treble melodies always cadence where punctuation is implied in the lyrics. In many instances, successive melodic

---

[240] *Dale, si le das*, one of the most outspoken, is however in duple meter.

phrases rise stepwise to a "central tone." Successive treble phrases in the simpler anonymous items ring changes on melody-types as fixed as a *maqam*. Even the named composers often spin their melodies as a series of variants (unequal in length) on some pungent formula (c^1–b–g–e in Lagarto's *Andad, pasiones, andad*, for instance).[241]

XIV. Although reiteration of coplas and estribillo is the cornerstone of the villancico structural plan, repetition of a melodic bit *within* the estribillo or coplas is resorted to but rarely. Even more infrequently do *CMP* composers repeat a harmonic complex (involving all voices). The baldest example of direct harmonic repetition probably occurs in the coplas of *Çutegón E singuel* (no. 357). A more artistic use distinguishes Encina's *Oy comamos y bebamos* (no. 174). Alonso's *Pero Gonçales* contains blocs of direct repetition. One must search in order to find such examples. Sequence – harmonic as well as melolic – is oftener encountered than direct repetition. But *CMP* composers make no habit of it. They prefer *diferencias*.

XV. Phrase-structure, except in very fast pieces, is usually asymmetrical. Sharp cut-offs between phrases are the rule in all but the oldest *Palacio* songs.

XVI. Tonic-dominant harmony rules in the peninsular pieces, or tonic-subdominant when the more unusual deuterus modes are in use.

XVII. Learned devices do not appeal to *CMP* composers. Those which they do consent to use are made to serve an affective purpose.

XVII. As a rule borrowed material, sacred and secular, goes in the tenor. Types of borrowed material include (1) folksongs (2) plainchants (3) trebles of previously composed courtly songs.

XIX. Subject-matter, literary form, and musical settings do on occasion fall into stereotypes. The literary stereotypes are oftenest seen in the rhymes and the musical at cadences.

XX. The finer composers, however, show truly individual profiles which can be discerned merely for the trouble of looking at their repertories. Generalizations carried too far lose significance in the face of individual variants encountered among men of stature such as Encina, Gabriel, Escobar, Torre, Ponce, and Peñalosa.

XXI. The "national" style of the Spanish songs in *CMP* – like the "national" style in the paintings of Bermejo and Master Alfonso – is more a matter of temperament than of technique. As such it is not always self-vindicating. If it were, the Spanish editors of *CMP* would not have attributed *Pues serviçio vos desplase* (no. 27) to "Enrrique,"

---

[241] See p. 237. Also, Marius Schneider, "Gestaltimitation als Kompositionsprinzip im Cancionero de Palacio," p. 418.

when it is now known to have been composed by an Englishman. Obviously, mere structure and even a Spanish text do not prove the peninsular origin of a *CMP* song.[242] But if not as blatantly national as "Spanish" music of the last two centuries, the *Palacio* repertory compensates by being measurably more aristocratic, subtle, and personally varied. The best songs are instinct with that *peculiar gravedad reposada* for which Isabella herself was so famous.

XXII. Among the qualities of spirit that give *CMP* its national flavor are the gnomic brevity, swift succinctness, and intense fervor everywhere manifest in the native repertory. Juan de Valdés was to aver in his *Diálogo de la lengua* (1536): "All good Castilian speech consists in saying what you want to say in the fewest words you can," and was to praise *refranes* as the epitome of good Spanish style. The *CMP* songs at their finest have all the virtues of *refranes*.

XXIII. During the decades when *CMC* and *CMP* were being compiled, the national Spanish flavor was considered so distinctive that composers abroad could subtitle their calate and ricercari *alla spagnola* (e.g., Dalza in 1508 and Capirola ten years later).

XXIV. Just as the frottole in *CMP* prove the acceptance that Italian music enjoyed at the Spanish court, so also compelling evidence survives to prove the vogue that Spanish canciones enjoyed in Italian courts.[243]

XXV. Although the nucleus seems to have been formed at Alba de Tormes, *CMP* eventually vindicated its right to be known as the most catholic collection of Spanish songs assembled during the era of *los Reyes Católicos* by including representative items from every peninsular center – from Catalonia to Portugal, from the Pyrenees to Gibraltar. On every account, the luster of the composers, their geographic spread, the variety of the songs, and above all, their musical worth, *CMP* deservedly shines as the brightest secular monument of an age when *las Españas* were reaching out to comprehend the world.

---

[242] Morton's song (*CMP*, no. 27) had, previous to the discovery of the *Palacio* concordance, been characterized by Bukofzer as the only characteristically English thing that the *chappelain anglois* ever wrote. See p. 251, note 123.

[243] A ducal singer named Rayner wrote a letter as early as July 3, 1473, to Galeazzo Maria Sforza (Duke of Milan) in which he highly praised *tre canti spagnoli*. He began by saying that he certainly considered these three Spanish songs to be fine and beautiful. He guaranteed that he had copied the parts accurately and promised that if only they were sung sweetly and softly – *sotto voce* – they would be sure to please. The specific songs are not named in Rayner's letter from Pavia, but they could easily have been any of the sad, sweet songs of Cornago or Madrid. See Emilio Motta, "Musici alla Corte degli Sforza," *Archivio storico lombardo*, XIV, iii (Milan, Sept., 1887), pp. 530–531. For further data on the favor shown Spanish music and musicians in northern Italy c. 1490, see Motta, p. 541; also XIV, i, 52.

Bibliography

Only such printed literary sources as are actually cited in our text have been listed in the following short-title bibliography. Standard dictionaries or encyclopedias, modern liturgical books, and musical editions (unless they contain literary matter quoted in our text) are not included. Early liturgical books are listed chronologically by date of imprint under Catholic Church, Roman. First editions of 15th- and 16th-century works have throughout the present volume been cited in preference to later reprints. Except in rare cases, later reprints are therefore not mentioned in the bibliography. The enclosing of the short title of a 15th-, 16th-, or 17th-century work within brackets shows that the short title does not begin with the first word of the whole title.

List of Abbreviations

ActaM	Acta Musicologica
AfMW	Archiv für Musikwissenschaft
AH	Archivo Hispalense
AM	Anuario Musical
BH	Bulletin hispanique
BRAH	Boletín de la Real Academia de la Historia
HS	Hispania Sacra
JAMS	Journal of the American Musicological Society
MD	Musica Disciplina
ML	Music & Letters
MQ	Musical Quarterly
NA	Note d'archivio
RBM	Revue Belge de Musicologie
RdM	Revue de Musicologie
RFE	Revista de Filología Española
RH	Revue hispanique
SFG	Spanische Forschungen der Görresgesellschaft

SIM   Sammelbände der Internationalen Musikgesellschaft
TSM   Tesoro Sacro-Musical
ZfMW   Zeitschrift für Musikwissenschaft

ÁGUILAR, GASPAR DE. *Arte de principios de canto llano: nueuamente emendado y corregido*. n.p.,
     c. 1530.
ALBA, EL [10.] DUQUE DE BERWICK Y DE. "Disquisiciones acerca del cantor flamenco Juan de
     Wrede," *BRAH*, LXXV (1919).
ALBAREDA, DOM ANSELM M. "La Imprenta de Montserrat ss. xvè–xviè," *Analecta Mont-
     serratensia*, II (1918 [1919]).
ALFONSO [X] EL SABIO. *Cantigas de Santa María*, ed. Leopoldo Augusto de Cueto, Marqués de
     Valmar. Madrid, 1889. 2 vols.
ALLGEIER, ARTHUR. "Die Psalmen in der mozarabischen Liturgie und das Psalterium von
     Saint Germain-des-Prés," *SFG*, 3. Bd. (1931).
ALLINGER, HELEN. "The Mozarabic Hymnal and Chant with Special Emphasis upon the
     Hymns of Prudentius." Union Theological Seminary D.S.M. Dissertation, 1953 (unpubl.).
AL-MAKKARI, AHMED IBN MOHAMMED. *Mohammedan Dynasties in Spain*, trans. by Pascual de
     Gayangos. London, 1840.
ALVARES FROUVO, *see* Frouvo, João Alvares.
ANDRÉS, JUAN. *Dell' origine, de' progressi e dello stato attuale d'ogni letteratura*. Venice, 1782
     1799.
ANGLÉS, HIGINIO. "Cantors und Ministrers in den Diensten der Koenige von Katalonien-
     Aragonien im 14. Jhdt.," *Bericht über den musikwissenschaftlichen Kongress in Basel,
     1924* (1925).
——— "Die mehrstimmige Musik in Spanien vor dem 15. Jhdt.," *Beethoven-Zentenarfeier
     Kongressbericht* (1927).
——— "Die spanische Liedkunst im 15. und am Anfang des 16. Jahrhunderts," *Theodor Kroyer
     Festschrift*. Regensburg, 1933.
——— "Dos tractats medievals," *Festschrift für Johannes Wolf*. Berlin, 1929.
——— *El Còdex Musical de Las Huelgas*. Barcelona, 1931. 3 vols.
——— "El *Llibre Vermell* de Montserrat," *AM*, X (1955).
——— "El 'Pange lingua' de Johannes Urreda, maestro de capilla del Rey Fernando el Cató-
     lico," *AM*, VII (1952).
——— *La música a Catalunya fins al segle XIII*. Barcelona, 1935.
——— *La Música de las Cantigas de Santa María*, II. Barcelona, 1943.
——— "La música en la Corte del Rey Don Alfonso V de Aragón, el Magnánimo (años 1413–
     1420)," *SFG*, 8 Bd. (1940).
——— *La música española desde la edad media*. Barcelona, 1941.
——— "La música medieval en Toledo," *SFG*, 7. Bd. (1938).
——— "La musique aux Xe et XIe siècles. L'École de Ripoll," *La Catalogne à l'époque romane:
     conférences faites à la Sorbonne en 1930*. Paris, 1932.
——— "La notación musical española en la segunda mitad del siglo XV," *AM*, II (1947).
——— "La Polyphonie religieuse péninsulaire antérieure à la venue des musiciens flamands en
     Espagne," *International Society for Musical Research, First Congress, Liége, September
     1–6, 1930, Report*.
——— "Un Manuscrit inconnu avec polyphonie du XVe siècle conservé à la Cathédrale de
     Ségovie," *ActaM*, VIII (1936).
ANGLÉS, H. and SUBIRÁ, J. *Catálogo Musical de la Biblioteca Nacional de Madrid*. Barcelona,
     1946–1951. 3 vols.
ANSPACH, EDUARD. (ed.) *Taionis et Isidori nova fragmenta et opera*. Madrid, 1930.

ARÁIZ MARTÍNEZ, A. *Historia de la música religiosa en España*. Barcelona, 1942.

ARANDA, MATHEO DE. *Tractado d' canto llano nueuamente compuesto*. Lisbon, 1533.

—— *Tractado de canto mensurable: y contrapuncto*. Lisbon, 1535.

ARCINIEGA, GREGORIO. "Un documento musical del año 1410," *TSM*, XVIII (1934).

AROCA, JESÚS. (ed.) *Cancionero musical y poético del siglo XVII, recogido por Claudio de la Sablonara*. Madrid, 1916.

ARON, PIETRO. *Lucidario in musica*. Venice, 1545.

—— *Toscanello in musica*. Venice, 1539.

ARTEAGA, ESTEBAN. *Le rivoluzioni del teatro musicale italiano*. 2nd edn. Venice, 1785. 3 vols.

ASENJO BARBIERI, FRANCISCO. (ed.) *Cancionero musical de los siglos XV y XVI*. Madrid, 1890.

ASIN PALACIOS, MIGUEL. "Etimologías Árabes," *Al-Andalus*, IX (1944).

AUBRY, PIERRE. "Iter Hispanicum," *SIM*, VIII and IX (1907 and 1908).

AVENARY, HANOCH. "Abu'l-Salt's Treatise on Music," *MD*, VI (1952).

BAENA, JUAN ALONSO DE. *El Cancionero de J. A. de Baena*. Madrid, 1851.

BAL Y GAY, JESÚS. (ed.) *Cancionero de Upsala*. Mexico City, 1944.

BALDELLÓ, FRANCISCO DE P. "La música en la casa de los Reyes de Aragón," *AM*, XI (1956).

BARBIERI, *see* Asenjo Barbieri.

BARBOSA MACHADO, DIOGO. *Bibliotheca Lusitana*. Lisbon, 1741–1759. 4 vols.

BARONE, NICOLA. "Le Cedole di Tesoreria dell'Archivio di Stato di Napoli dall' anno 1460 al 1504," *Archivio storico per le province napoletane*, IX (1884).

BARRAU-DIHIGO, L. "Historia Baetica," *RH*, XLVII (1919).

BARRIO LORENZOT, FRANCISCO DEL. *Ordenanzas de Gremios de la Nueva España*. Mexico City, 1921.

BATTISTESSA, ANGEL. *Poetas y prosistas españoles*. Buenos Aires, 1943.

BELL, AUBREY F.G. *Four Plays of Gil Vicente*. Cambridge, 1920.

BEMBO, PIETRO. *Epistolarum Leonis Decimi Pontificis Max. nomine scriptarum libri sexdecim*. Venice, 1552.

BERMÚDEZ DE PEDRAZA, FRANCISCO. *Historia eclesiastica, principios y progressos de la ciudad, y religion catolica de Granada*. Granada, 1638.

BERMUDO, JUAN. *Comiença el arte Tripharia*. Osuna, 1550.

—— *Comiença el libro llamado declaracion de instrumentos*. Osuna, 1555.

—— *Comiença el libro primero de la declaracion de instrumentos*. Osuna, 1549.

BISHOP, W. C. *The Mozarabic and Ambrosian Rites: four essays in comparative liturgiology*. Milwaukee, 1924.

BOETHIUS. *Opera*. Venice, 1491–92. 2 vols.

BONAVENTURA DE BRIXIA. *Regula musice plane*. Brescia, 1497.

BRAGARD, ROGER. "Le Speculum Musicae," VII (1953) and *MD*, VIII (1954).

BRANDÃO, MARIO. (ed.) *Documentos de João III*. Coimbra, 1938. 2 vols.

BREHAUT, ERNEST. *An Encyclopedist of the Dark Ages*. New York, 1912.

BRENET, MICHEL. *Musique et musiciens de la vielle France*. Paris, 1911.

BROU, DOM LOUIS. "Antifonario visigótico de la Catedral de León" (review), *HS*, VII (1954).

—— "Fragments d'un antiphonaire mozarabe du monastère de San Juan de la Peña," *HS*, V (1952).

—— "L'Alleluia dans la liturgie mozarabe," *AM*, VI (1951).

—— "Le joyau des antiphonaires latins," *Archivos Leoneses*, VIII, no. 15 (1954).

—— "Le psautier liturgique wisigothique et les éditions critiques des psautiers latins," *HS*, VIII (1955).

—— "Notes de paléographie musicale mozarabe," *AM*, X (1955).

—— "Séquences et Tropes dans la liturgie mozarabe," *HS*, IV (1951).

—— "Un antiphonaire mozarabe de Silos d'après les fragments du British Museum," *HS*, V (1952).

BURNEY, CHARLES. *A General History of Music*. London, 1776–1789. 4 vols.
BUKOFZER, M. F. "An Unknown Chansonnier of the 15th Century," *MQ*, XXVIII (1942).
—— "Interrelations between Conductus and Clausula," *Annales Musicologiques*, I (1953).
—— *Studies in Medieval and Renaissance Music*. New York, 1950.
—— "Three Unknown Italian Chansons of the Fifteenth Century," *Collectanea Historiae Musicae*, II (1957).
—— "Über Leben und Werke von Dunstable," *ActaM*, VIII (1936).
CALLCOTT, FRANK. *The Supernatural in Early Spanish Literature*. New York, 1923.
CANNUZIO, PIETRO. *Regule florum musices*. Florence, 1510.
CARETTA, ALESSANDRO, and others. *Franchino Gaffurio*. Lodi, 1951.
CASE, JOHN. *The Praise of Musicke*. Oxford, 1586.
CASSIODORUS SENATOR. *Institutiones*, ed. R. A. B. Mynors. Oxford, 1937.
—— *An Introduction to Divine and Human Readings*, trans. L. W. Jones. New York, 1946.
CASTILLO, HERNANDO DEL. *Cancionero general nueuamente añadido*. Toledo, 1520.
CASTRO, ADOLFO DE. (ed.) *Poetas líricos de los siglos XVI y XVII* (*Bibl. de autores españoles*, XXXII). Madrid, 1872.
Catholic Church, Roman. [*Missale Caesaraugustanum*]. Saragossa, 1485, 1498, 1522.
—— [*Missale Oscense*]. Saragossa, 1488.
—— [*Antiphonarium et graduale ad usum ordinis S. Hieronymi*]. Seville, 1491.
—— [*Missale Auriense*]. Monterrey, 1494.
—— [*Manuale Toletanum*]. Seville, 1494.
—— *Incipit liber processionum secundum ordinem fratrum predicatorum*. Seville, 1494.
—— [*Processionarium ordinis fratrum predicatorum*]. Venice, 1494.
—— [*Missale Bracarense*]. Lisbon, 1498.
—— *Missale secundum consuetudinem ecclesie Tarraconensis*. Tarragona, 1499.
—— [*Missale Benedictum*]. Montserrat, 1499.
—— [*Missale Giennense*]. Seville, 1499.
—— *Missale mixtum alme ecclesie toletane*. Toledo, 1499.
—— [*Missale Abulense*]. Salamanca, 1500.
—— *Missale mixtum secundum regulam beati Isidori dictum Mozarabes*. Toledo, 1500.
—— *Missale Romanum*. Saragossa, 1511, 1531, 1532, 1543, 1548.
—— *Incipit liber processionum secundum ordinem fratrum predicatorum*. Seville, 1519.
—— *Missale diuinorum secundum consuetudinem sancte ecclesie hyspalensis. Nouiter impressum*. Seville, 1520, 1534, 1537.
—— *Incipit liber processionarius secundum consuetudinem ordinis sancti Patris nostri Hieronymi*. Alcalá de Henares, 1526.
—— *Missale secundum alme Pacensis ecclesie consuetudinem*. Seville, 1529.
—— *Missale secundum ordinem Primatis ecclesie Toletanę*. Alcalá de Henares, 1550.
—— *Missale secundum consuetudinem almę ecclesię Placentinę*. Venice, 1554.
—— [*Missale Romanum*]. Mexico City, 1561.
—— *Missale secundum vsum et consuetudinem sancte ecclesie Oxomensis*. Burgo de Osma, 1561.
—— [*Missale Romanum*]. Salamanca, 1562.
—— [*Missale Pallantinum*]. Palencia, 1567.
—— *Missale Romanum ex decreto sacrosancti Concilij Tridentini restitutum*. Salamanca, 1570.
—— *Missa gothica seù mozarabica*, ed. F. A. Lorenzana. Puebla, 1770.
—— *Antifonario visigótico mozárabe de la Catedral de León*, facs. edn. Madrid, 1953.
CERONE, PEDRO. *El Melopeo y Maestro*. Naples, 1613.
CERVANTES SAAVEDRA, MIGUEL DE. *Novelas exemplares*. Brussels, 1614.
—— *Segunda parte del ingenioso cavallero Don Quixote de la Mancha*. Madrid, 1615.
CHABAS, ROQUE. "Arnaldo de Vilanova," *Homenaje á Menéndez y Pelayo*, II. Madrid, 1899.

CHACON, ALONSO. *Vitae, et res gestae pontificum Romanorum et S. R. E. Cardinalium*. Rome, 1677. 4 vols.

CHASE, GILBERT. "Juan del Encina, Poet and Musician," *ML*, XX (1939).

—— "Origins of the Lyric Theater in Spain," *MQ*, XXV (1939).

—— *The Music of Spain*. New York, 1941.

CIMINELLI, SERAFINO DE'. *Le Rime di Serafino de' Ciminelli dall' Aquila*, ed. Mario Menghini. Bologna, 1894.

CIRUELO, PEDRO. *Cursus quattuor mathematicarum artium liberalium*. Alcalá de Henares, 1516, 1526, 1577.

COHEN, ALBERT. "The Vocal Polyphonic Style of Juan de Anchieta." New York University Master's Thesis, 1953 (unpubl.).

COLLET, HENRI. "Contribution a l'étude des Cantigas d'Alphonse le Savant," *BH*, XIII (1911).

—— "Contribution a l'étude des théoriciens espagnols de la musique au XVIᵉ siècle," *L'Année musicale*, II (1912).

—— *Le mysticisme musical espagnol*. Paris, 1913.

COLÓN, FERNANDO. *Catalogue of the Library of Ferdinand Columbus*, facs. edn., New York, 1905.

CORBIN, SOLANGE. *Essai sur la musique religieuse portugaise au moyen âge (1100–1385)*. Paris, 1952.

COSTER, ADOLPHE. "Juan de Anchieta et la famille de Loyola," *RH*, LXXIX (1930).

COUSSEMAKER, EDMOND DE. *Scriptorum de musica medii aevi*. Paris, 1864–76. 4 vols.

CÓZAR MARTÍNEZ, FERNANDO DE. *Noticias y documentos para la historia de Baeza*. Jaén, 1884.

CRAWFORD, J. WICKERSHAM. "The Source of Juan del Encina's *Égloga de Fileno y Zambardo*," *RH*, XXXVIII (1916).

DESPUIG, GUILLERMO. [*Ars musicorum*]. Valencia, 1495.

DEVOTO, DANIEL. "Poésie et musique dans l'œuvre des vihuelistes," *Annales Musicologiques*, IV (1956).

DÍAZ-JIMÉNEZ Y MOLLEDA, ELOY. *Juan del Encina en León*. Madrid, 1909.

DÍAZ RENGIFO, JUAN. *Arte poetica española*. Salamanca, 1592.

DOORSLAER, G. VAN. "La Chapelle musicale de Philippe le Beau," *Revue belge d'archéologie et d'histoire de l'art*, IV (1934).

DREVES, GUIDO M. *Analecta Hymnica Medii Aevi*, XVI and L. Leipzig, 1894 and 1907.

—— *Hymnodia hiberica. Liturgische Reimofficien aus Spanischen Brevieren*. Leipzig, 1894.

DURÁN, see Marcos Durán, Domingo.

DURANDUS, GULIELMUS. *Incipit Rationale diuinorum officiorum*. Rome, 1473.

EINSTEIN, ALFRED. "Andrea Antico's *Canzoni Nove* of 1510," *MQ*, XXXVII (1951).

—— *The Italian Madrigal*. Princeton, 1949. 3 vols.

ELÚSTIZA, J. B. DE and CASTRILLO HERNÁNDEZ, G. *Antología musical: Siglo de oro de la música litúrgica de España*. Barcelona, 1933.

ENCINA, JUAN DEL. *Cancionero de las obras*. Salamanca, 1496; facs. edn. Madrid, 1928.

—— *Cancionero de todas las obras*. Salamanca, 1509.

—— *Égloga de Plácida y Victoriano*, ed. E. Giménez Caballero. Saragossa, 1940.

—— *El Aucto del Repelón*, ed. Alfredo Álvarez de la Villa. Paris, 1910.

—— *Viage y Peregrinación* [to Jerusalem]. Madrid, 1786.

ENNIS, S. MARY GRATIA. *The Vocabulary of the Institutiones of Cassiodorus*. Washington, 1939.

ENRÍQUEZ DE RIBERA, FADRIQUE. *Viage de Jerusalem*. Madrid, 1733.

ENTWISTLE, W. J. "Dos 'Cossantes' às 'Cantigas de Amor'," in *Da Poesia medieval portuguesa* (with Aubrey F. G. Bell and C. Bowra). Lisbon, 1947.

ERLANGER, RODOLPHE D'. *La musique arabe*. Paris, 1930–49. 5 vols.

ESCOBAR, CRISTÓBAL DE. "Introduction muy breue de canto llano," ed. J. Wolf in *Gedenkboek aangeboden aan Dr. D. F. Scheurleer*. The Hague, 1925.

ESPERABÉ ARTEAGA, ENRIQUE. *Historia [pragmática é interna] de la Universidad de Salamanca.* Salamanca, 1914–17. 2 vols.

ESPINOSA, JUAN DE. *Retractationes de los errores et falsedades.* Toledo, 1514.

—— *Tractado breue de principios de canto llano.* Toledo, n.d.

—— *Tractado de principios de musica practica e theorica sin dexar ninguna cosa atras.* Toledo, 1520.

ESPINOSA MAESO, R. *Nuevos datos biográficos de Juan del Encina.* Madrid, 1921.

EXIMENO Y PUJADES, ANTONIO. *Dubbio . . . sopra il saggio fondamentale pratico di contrappunto.* Rome, 1775.

FABIÉ, ANTONIO M., trans. *Viajes por España [Libros de antaño,* VIII]. Madrid, 1879.

FARMER, H. G. *A History of Arabian Music to the XIIIth Century.* London, 1929.

—— *Al-Fārābī's Arabic-Latin Writings on Music.* Glasgow, 1934.

—— *An Old Moorish Lute Tutor.* Glasgow, 1933.

—— *Historical Facts for the Arabian Musical Influence.* London, 1930.

—— *The Arabian Influence on Musical Theory.* London, 1925.

—— *The Arabic Musical Manuscripts in the Bodleian Library.* London, 1925.

FERNÁNDEZ, BENIGNO. *Impresos de Alcalá en la Biblioteca del Escorial.* Madrid, 1916.

FERNÁNDEZ, LUCAS. *Farsas y Eglogas al modo y estilo pastoril.* Salamanca, 1514; facs. edn. Madrid, 1929.

FERNÁNDEZ DE NAVARRETE, M. *Viajes de Colón.* Madrid, 1922.

FERNÁNDEZ DE OVIEDO, GONZALO. *Libro de la camara real del prinçipe Don Juan.* Madrid, 1870.

FÉROTIN, DOM MARIUS. (ed.) *Le* Liber ordinum *en usage dans l'église wisigothique et mozarabe d'Espagne.* Paris, 1904.

—— *Le* Liber Mozarabicus Sacramentorum *et les manuscrits mozarabes.* Paris, 1912.

FINSCHER, LUDWIG. "Loyset Compère and his Works," MD, XII (1958).

FLORIMO, FRANCESCO. *La scuola musicale di Napoli.* Naples, 1881–83. 3 vols.

FOGLIANO, LUDOVICO. *Musica theorica.* Venice, 1529.

FREIRE DE OLIVEIRA, EDUARDO. *Elementos para a historia do municipio de Lisboa,* 1ª. *parte.* Lisbon, 1882.

FREY, HERMAN-WALTHER. "Regesten zur päpstlichen Kapelle unter Leo X," *Die Musikforschung,* VIII (1955) and IX (1956).

FROUVO, JOÃO ALVARES. *Discursos sobre a perfeiçam do Diathesaron.* Lisbon, 1662.

FUENLLANA, MIGUEL DE. *Libro de Musica para Vihuela, intitulado Orphenica lyra.* Seville, 1554.

GAFFURIO, FRANCHINO. *Apologia Franchini Gafurii musici aduersus Ioannem Spatarium.* Turin, 1520.

—— *Practica musice.* Milan, 1496.

—— *Theorica musice.* Milan, 1492.

GALLARDO, BARTOLOMÉ JOSÉ. *Ensayo de una Biblioteca Española de libros raros y curiosos.* Madrid, 1863–89. 4 vols.

GAMS, PIUS BONIFACIUS. *Series episcoporum.* Regensburg, 1873.

GARCÍA VILLADA, ZACARIAS. *Catálogo de los Códices y Documentos de la Catedral de León.* Madrid, 1919.

GASPARI, GAETANO. *Catalogo della Biblioteca del Liceo Musicale di Bologna.* Bologna, 1890–1905. 4 vols.

GASTOUÉ, A. "Manuscrits et fragments de musique liturgique, à la Bibliothèque du Conservatoire, à Paris," *RdM,* XIII (1932).

GEIGER, ALBERT. "Bausteine zur Geschichte des iberischen Vulgär-Villancico," *ZfMW,* IV (1921).

GERBER, RUDOLF. "Spanische Hymnensätze um 1500," *AfMW,* X (1953).

—— "Die Hymnen der Handschrift Monte Cassino 871," *AM,* XI (1956).

GERBERT, MARTIN. *Scriptores ecclesiastici de musica sacra.* St. Blaise, 1784. 3 vols.

GHISI, F. "Canzoni profane italiane del secondo Quattrocento in un Codice musicale di Monte Cassino," *RBM*, II (1948).

—— "Strambotti e Laude nel Travestimento Spirituale della Poesia Musicale del Quattrocento," *Collectanea Historiae Musicae*, I (1953).

—— "Un terzo esemplare della 'Musica Practica' di Bartolomeo Ramis de Pareia alla Biblioteca Nazionale Centrale di Firenze," *NA*, XII (1935).

GOES, DAMIÃO DE. *Chronica do felicissimo Rei dom Emanuel da gloriosa memoria.* Coimbra, 1949–55. 4 vols.

GOMBOSI, O. *Jacob Obrecht, eine stilkritische Studie.* Leipzig, 1925.

—— "Zur Frühgeschichte der Folia," *ActaM*, VIII (1936).

GRASSI, PARIDE DE. *Il Diario di Leone X*, ed. Pio Delicati and M. Armellini. Rome, 1884.

GUERRERO, FRANCISCO. *Viage de Hierusalem.* Seville, [1590].

GUNDISSALINUS, DOMINICUS. "De divisione philosophiae," ed. Ludwig Baur, *Beiträge zur Geschichte der Philosophie des Mittelalters*, 1903.

HABERL, F. X. *Bibliographischer und thematischer Musikkatalog des päpstlichen Kapellarchives im Vatikan zu Rom.* Leipzig, 1888.

—— *Die römische "schola cantorum" und die päpstlichen Kappelsänger.* Leipzig, 1888.

HAEBLER, KARL. *Bibliografía Ibérica del siglo XV.* The Hague, 1903–17. 2 vols.

—— *The Early Printers of Spain and Portugal.* London, 1897.

—— *Typographie ibérique du quinzième siècle.* The Hague, 1902.

HAGEN, OSKAR. *Patterns and Principles of Spanish Art.* Madison, 1943.

HANDSCHIN, JACQUES. "The Summer Canon and its Background," *MD*, V (1951).

HAWKINS, JOHN. *A General History of the Science and Practice of Music.* London, 1776. 5 vols.

HEINE, GOTTHILF. *Biblioteca anecdotorum, sive veterum monumentorum ecclesiasticorum collectio novissima.* Leipzig, 1848.

HERGENROETHER, JOSEPH CARDINAL, (ed.) *Leonis X. Pontificis Maximi Regesta.* Freiburg im Breisgau, 1884–1891. 8 fascicles.

HERRERO SÁNCHEZ, JOSÉ J. and RODA LÓPEZ, C. DE. *Tres músicos españoles: Juan del Encina, Lucas Fernández, Manuel Doyagüe, y la cultura artística de su tiempo.* Madrid, 1912.

HEWITT, HELEN. (ed.) *Harmonice Musices Odhecaton, A.* Cambridge, 1942.

HÜBNER, E. (ed.) *Corpus Inscriptionum Latinarum*, II. Berlin, 1869.

HUGHES, DOM ANSELM. (ed.) *New Oxford History of Music*, II. London, 1954.

HUGLO, DOM MICHEL. "Les *Preces* des Graduels aquitains empruntées à la liturgie hispanique," *HS*, VIII (1955).

ISABELLA, Queen of Castile. "Carta de franquesa de Fernard peres cantor de la reina," *AH*, II (1886).

ISIDORE, ST. *Etymologiarum sive Originum Libri XX*, ed. W. M. Lindsay. Oxford, 1911.

—— *Opera Omnia*, ed. Faustino Arévalo. Rome, 1797–1803. 7 vols.

ISNARD, R. "Anciens instruments de musique," *RH*, XLIII (1918).

JEPPESEN, KNUD. "Eine musiktheoretische Korrespondenz des früheren Cinquecento," *ActaM*, XIII (1941).

JOAQUIM, MANUEL. (ed.) *O Cancioneiro musical e poético da Biblioteca Públia Hortênsia.* Coimbra, 1940.

JOHN IV, King of Portugal. *Difesa della musica moderna contro la falsa opinione del vescovo Cirillo Franco.* Venice, [1666].

—— *Primeira parte do index da livraria de musica.* Lisbon, 1649; repr. Oporto, 1874.

JUVENAL. *Saturae*, ed. A. E. Housman. Cambridge, 1938.

KASTNER, SANTIAGO. *Contribución al estudio de la música española y portuguesa.* Lisbon, 1941.

—— "Relations entre la musique instrumentale française et espagnole au XVIᵉ siècle," *AM*, X (1955); XI (1956).

KEINSPECK, MICHAEL. *Lilium musice plane.* Ulm, 1497.

KELLMAN, HERBERT. "The Origins of the Chigi Codex," *JAMS*, XI, i (1958).

KINKELDEY, OTTO. "Music and Music Printing in Incunabula," *Papers of the Bibliographical Society of America*, XXVI (1932).

LA FAGE, ADRIEN DE. *Essais de Diphthérographie musicale.* Paris, 1864.

LALAING, ANTOINE DE. "Voyage de Philippe le Beau en Espagne en 1501," *Collection des Voyages des Souverains des Pays-Bas*, I, ed. L. P. Gachard. Brussels, 1876.

LANCHETAS, RUFINO. *Gramática y Vocabulario de las obras de Gonzalo de Berceo.* Madrid, 1900.

LATASSA Y ORTÍN, FELIX DE. *Bibliotheca antigua de los escritores aragoneses.* Saragossa, 1796. 2 vols.

—— *Bibliotecas antigua y nueva ... aumentadas y refundidas por Miguel Gómez Uriel.* Saragossa, 1884–86. 3 vols.

—— *Biblioteca nueva de los escritores aragoneses.* Pamplona, 1798–1802. 6 vols.

LARREA PALACIN, ARCADIO DE. *Nawba Işbahan.* Tetuán, 1956.

—— *Romances de Tetuán.* Madrid, 1952. 2 vols.

LE FÈVRE D'ÉTAPLES, JACQUES. [*Arithmetica et Musica*]. Paris, 1496.

LEITÃO FERREIRA, FRANCISCO. *Noticias chronologicas da Universidade de Coimbra, segunda parte: 1548–1551.* Coimbra, 1944. 3 vols.

LIVERMORE, A. "The Spanish Dramatists and their Use of Music," *ML*, XXV (1944).

LLAVIA, RAMÓN DE. *Cancionero.* Saragossa, c. 1489; repr. Madrid, 1945.

LLORENS CISTERÓ, JOSÉ M. "Juan Escribano, cantor pontificio y compositor," *AM*, XII (1957).

LOPES, F. F. "A música das 'Cantigas de Santa Maria' e o problema da sua decifracão," *Brotéria*, XL (1945).

LÓPEZ DE GÓMARA, FRANCISCO. *La conquista de Mexico.* Saragossa, 1552.

LÓPEZ DE MENDOZA, IÑIGO, MARQUÉS DE SANTILLANA. *Obras*, ed. José Amador de los Rios. Madrid, 1852.

LÓPEZ FERREIRO, ANTONIO. *Historia de la santa a. m. iglesia de Santiago de Compostela.* Santiago, 1898–1909. 11 vols.

LOWINSKY, EDWARD E. "The Goddess Fortuna in Music," *MQ*, XXIX (1943).

LUCAS DE IRANZO, MIGUEL. *Hechos del Condestable* [*Colección de Crónicas Españolas*, III, ed. J. de M. Carriazo]. Madrid, 1940.

LUZIO, ALESSANDRO. "Federico Gonzaga ostaggio alla Corte di Giulio II," *Archivio della R. Società Romana*, IX (1886).

LYNN, CARO. *A College Professor of the Renaissance.* Chicago, 1937.

MADURELL, JOSÉ M. and LLORENS CISTERÓ, JOSÉ M. "Documentos de archivo. Libros de canto (siglos XIV–XVI)," *AM*, XI (1956).

MAGGS BROS. *Books Printed in Spain and Spanish Books Printed in Other Countries.* London, 1927.

MANUEL II. *Livros antigos portuguezes, 1489–1600.* London, 1929. 2 vols.

MARCOS DURÁN, DOMINGO. *Comento sobre Lux bella.* Salamanca, 1498.

—— *Lux bella.* Seville, 1492, 1518; facs. edn., Barcelona, 1951.

—— *Sumula de canto de organo.* Salamanca, c. 1507.

MARINEO [SICULO], LUCIO. *Ad illustrissimum principem Alfonsum Aragoneum Ferdinandi regis filium ... epistolarum familiarium libri decem et septem.* Valladolid, 1514.

—— *De las cosas memorables de España.* Alcalá de Henares, 1539.

—— [*Opus de rebus Hispaniae memorabilibus*]. Alcalá de Henares, 1533.

MARIZ, PEDRO DE. *Dialogos de Varia Historia.* Lisbon, 1672 (= 1674).

MARTÍNEZ, JUAN. *Arte de Canto Chão, posta e[t] reduzida em sua enteira perfeição.* Coimbra, 1603, 1612, 1625.

—— *Arte de canto llano puesta y reducida nueuamente en su entera perficion.* Alcalá de Henares, 1532.

MARTÍNEZ DE BIZCARGUI, GONZALO. *Arte de canto llano y contrapunto y canto de organo.* Saragossa, 1508, 1512, 1517; Burgos, 1511.

—— *Arte de canto llano . . . añadida y glosada.* Burgos, 1528, 1535; Saragossa, 1538, 1541, 1549, 1550.

MATUTE Y GAVIRIA, JUSTINO. *Hijos de Sevilla.* Seville, 1886–87. 2 vols.

MEDINA Y MENDOZA, FRANCISCO DE. "Vida del Cardenal D. Pedro González de Mendoza," *Memorial Histórico Español*, VI. Madrid, 1853.

MENÉNDEZ PIDAL, RAMÓN. *Historia de España: España Prerromana.* Madrid, 1954.

—— *Poesía árabe y poesía europea*, 2nd edn. Buenos Aires, 1943.

—— *Poesía juglaresca y juglares.* Madrid, 1924.

MENÉNDEZ Y PELAYO, MARCELINO. *Historia de la poesía castellana en la edad media.* Madrid, 1911–16. 3 vols.

—— *Historia de las ideas estéticas en España*, 2nd edn. Madrid, 1890–1903. 5 vols.

—— *San Isidoro, Cervantes y otros estudios.* Buenos Aires, 1942.

MEXIA, PEDRO. *Historia del Emperador Carlos V* [*Colección de Crónicas Españolas*, VII, ed. J. de M. Carriazo]. Madrid, 1945.

MEYER, KATHI. "The Liturgical Music Incunabula in the British Museum. Germany, Italy, and Switzerland," *The Library*, ser. 4, XX (1939).

MEYER, WILHELM. *Die Preces der mozarabischen Liturgie.* Berlin, 1914.

MIGNE, J. P. *Patrologiae Cursus Completus* [Latin series]. Vols. 83, 96, 184. Paris, 1862.

MITJANA Y GORDÓN, RAFAEL. "Cancionero poético y musical del siglo XVII," *RFE*, VI (1919).

—— *Estudios sobre algunos músicos españoles del siglo XVI.* Madrid, 1918.

—— "La capilla de música de la Catedral de Málaga: Año de 1496 al año de 1542," MS dated 1895 in Kungl. Musikaliska Akademiens Bibliotek. Stockholm.

—— "La Musique en Espagne," *Encyclopédie de la musique et Dictionnaire du Conservatoire* (ed. A. Lavignac), *Partie 1*, IV.

—— "L'Orientalisme musical et la musique arabe," *Le Monde Oriental.* Uppsala, 1906.

—— "Nuevas notas al 'Cancionero musical de los siglos XV y XVI' publicado por el Maestro Barbieri," *RFE*, V (1918).

MOLINA, BARTOLOMÉ DE. *Arte de canto llano Lux videntis dicha.* Valladolid, 1506.

MONSERRATE, ANDRÉS DE. *Arte breve, y compendiosa.* Valencia, 1614.

MONTANOS, FRANCISCO DE. *Arte de canto llano*, ed. José de Torres. Madrid, 1705.

Monumentos de la Música Española. Barcelona, 1941–.

    I. *La Música en la Corte de los Reyes Católicos: Polifonía religiosa*, ed. H. Anglés, 1941.

    II. *La Música en la Corte de Carlos V*, ed. H. Anglés, 1944.

    V and X. *La Música en la Corte de los Reyes Católicos: Polifonía profana* (Palace Song-book), ed. H. Anglés, 1947 and 1951.

MORLEY, THOMAS. *A Plaine and Easie Introduction to Practicall Musicke.* London, 1597; 1608.

MUDARRA, ALONSO. *Tres libros de musica en cifras para vihuela.* Seville, 1546.

NARVÁEZ, LUYS DE. *Los seys libros del Delphin de musica.* Valladolid, 1538.

NUNES, JOSÉ JOAQUIM. *Cantigas d'Amigo.* Coimbra, 1926–28. 3 vols.

NUNES DA SYLVA, MANOEL. *Arte Minima.* Lisbon, 1685.

OCHOA, EUGENIO DE. (ed.) *Epistolario Español*, I [*Bibl. de Aut. Esp.*, XIII]. Madrid, 1850.

OLSON, CLAIR C. "Chaucer and the Music of the Fourteenth Century," *Speculum*, XVI (1941).

ORNITHOPARC[H]US, ANDREAS. *Musice actiue micrologus*, 2nd edn. Leipzig, 1519.

—— trans. John Dowland, London, 1609.

PALAU Y DULCET, ANTONIO. *Manual del librero hispanoamericano*, 2nd edn. Barcelona, 1948–1957. 10 vols.

PEDRELL, FELIPE. *Cancionero musical popular español.* Valls, 1919–22. 4 vols.

—— *Catàlech de la Biblioteca Musical de la Diputació de Barcelona.* Barcelona, 1908–09. 2 vols.

—— *Diccionario biográfico y bibliográfico de músicos y escritores de música españoles*. Barcelona, 1897.

—— *Emporio científico é histórico de organografía musical antigua española*. Barcelona, 1901.

—— "Folk-lore musical castillan du XVIe siècle," *SIM*, I (1900).

—— *Hispaniae schola musica sacra*. Barcelona, 1894–98. 8 vols.

—— "Jean I d'Aragon, Compositeur de Musique," *Riemann-Festschrift*. Leipzig, 1909.

—— *La Festa d'Elche*. Paris, 1906.

PENA, JOAQUÍN and ANGLÉS, H. *Diccionario de la música Labor*. Barcelona, 1954, 2 vols.

PEREIRA, GABRIEL. *O Archivo da Santa Casa da Misericordia d'Evora (Estudos Eborenses, Pte. 2)*. Évora, 1888.

PIRRO, ANDRÉ. *Histoire de la musique de la fin du XIVe siècle à la fin du XVIe*. Paris, 1940.

—— "Leo X and Music," *MQ*, XXI (1935).

—— "Un manuscrit musical du XVe siècle au Mont-Cassin," *Casinensia: Miscellanea di studi Cassinesi*, I (1929).

PLAMENAC, DRAGAN. "A Reconstruction of the French Chansonnier in the Biblioteca Colombina, Seville," *MQ*, XXXVII and XXXVIII (1951 and 1952).

—— "*La Música en la Corte de los Reyes Católicos*," review, *MQ*, XXXIV (1948).

PODIO, GUILLERMUS DE, *see* Despuig, Guillermo.

POPE, ISABEL. "El Villancico Polifónico," in *Cancionero de Upsala*, ed. J. Bal y Gay. Mexico City, 1944.

—— "La musique espagnole à la Cour de Naples dans la seconde moitié du xve siècle," *Musique et Poésie au XVIe siècle*. Paris, 1954.

—— "Mediaeval Latin Background of the Thirteenth-Century Galician Lyric," *Speculum*, IX (1934).

—— "Musical and Metrical Form of the Villancico," *Annales Musicologiques*, II (1954).

PRADO, DOM GERMÁN. "Mozarabic Melodics," *Speculum*, III (1928).

PROCTER, EVELYN S. *Alfonso X of Castile*. Oxford, 1951.

PUERTO, DIEGO DEL. [*Ars cantus plani portus musice vocata siue organici*]. Salamanca, 1504.

PULGAR, FERNANDO DEL. *Crónica de los Reyes Católicos* [*Col. de Crónicas Españolas*, V and VI]. Madrid, 1943.

QUEROL GAVALDÁ, MIGUEL. "Importance historique et nationale du romance," *Musique et Poésie au XVIe siècle*. Paris, 1954.

QUEROL ROSO, LEOPOLDO. *La poesía del Cancionero de Uppsala*. Valencia, 1932.

QUEVEDO Y VILLEGAS, FRANCISCO GÓMEZ DE. *Obras completas*, ed. Luis Astrana Marín [2nd edn.]. Madrid, 1941.

QUINTILIAN. *Institutio Oratoria*, tr. H. E. Butler. London, 1921–22. 4 vols.

RAMOS DE PAREJA, BARTOLOMÉ. *Musica practica*. Bologna, 1482; ed. Johannes Wolf, Leipzig, 1901.

REANEY, GILBERT. "The Manuscript Chantilly, Musée Condé 1047," *MD*, VIII (1954).

REESE, GUSTAVE. *Fourscore Classics of Music Literature*. New York, 1957.

—— "Maldeghem and his Buried Treasure: A Bibliographical Study." *Notes of the Music Library Association*, VI (1948).

—— *Music in the Middle Ages*. New York, 1940.

—— *Music in the Renaissance*. New York, 1954.

RESENDE, GARCIA DE. *Chronica dos valerosos e insignes feitos del Rey Dom Ioão II*. Lisbon, 1622.

RIAÑO, JUAN FACUNDO. *Critical and Bibliographical Notes on Early Spanish Music*. London, 1887.

RIBERA Y TARRAGÓ, JULIÁN. *Disertaciones y opúsculos*. Madrid, 1928.

—— *La música de las Cantigas*. Madrid, 1922.

—— *Music in Ancient Arabia and Spain*, trans. E. Hague and M. Leffingwell. Stanford, 1929.

RICCIO, CAMILLO MINIERI. "Alcuni fatti di Alfonso I. di Aragona," *Archivio storico per le province napoletane*, VI (1881).

RIEMANN, HUGO. *Geschichte der Musiktheorie im IX.–XIX. Jahrhundert*. Leipzig, 1898.

ROBYNS, JOZEF. *Pierre de la Rue: Een Bio-Bibliographische Studie*. Brussels, 1954.

RODRÍGUEZ VILLA, ANTONIO. *La Reina Doña Juana la loca: Estudio histórico*. Madrid, 1892.

ROJAS, AGUSTÍN DE. *El Viage entretenido*. Lérida, 1611.

ROJO, CASIANO. "The Gregorian Antiphonary of Silos and the Spanish Melody of the Lamentations," *Speculum*, V (1930).

ROJO, C. and PRADO, G. *El Canto Mozárabe*. Barcelona, 1929.

ROMÁN, HIERÓNIMO. *Republicas del mundo*. Medina del Campo, 1575. 2 vols.

ROMEU FIGUERAS, JOSÉ. "El cosante en la lírica de los cancioneros musicales," *AM*, V (1950).

RONCAGLIA, GINO. "Intorno ad un codice di Johannes Bonadies," in Reale Accademia di Scienze, Lettere ed Arti, Modena. *Atti e Memorie*, ser. V, 4 (1939).

ROSA Y LÓPEZ, SIMÓN DE LA. *Los Seises de la Catedral de Sevilla*. Seville, 1904.

RUBIÒ, JORDI. "Una carta inèdita catalana de l'impressor Joan Rosenbach de Heidelberg," *Gutenberg Festschrift*. Mainz, 1925.

RUBIO PIQUERAS, FELIPE. *Códices Polifónicos Toledanos*. Toledo, 1925.

—— *Música y músicos toledanos*. Toledo, 1923.

RUIZ, JUAN, *arcipreste de Hita*. *Libro de buen amor*. Paris, 1901.

RUIZ DE LIHORY, JOSÉ. *La música en Valencia: Diccionario Biográfico y Crítico*. Valencia, 1903.

SÁENZ DE AGUIRRE, JOSEPH. *Collectio maxima conciliorum omnium Hispaniae et Novi Orbis*, III. Rome, 1694.

ST. AMOUR, S. M. P. *A Study of the Villancico up to Lope de Vega*. Washington, 1940.

SÁINZ DE ROBLES, F. C. *El teatro español: Historia y antología*. Madrid, 1942. 2 vols.

SALAZAR, ADOLFO. *La música de España*. Buenos Aires, 1953.

—— "Music in the Primitive Spanish Theatre before Lope de Vega," *Papers read by Members of the American Musicological Society, 1938* (1940).

—— "Poesía y música en las primeras formas de versificación rimada en lengua vulgar," *Filosofía y Letras*, IV, 8 (1942).

SALINAS, FRANCISCO. [*De Musica libri Septem*]. Salamanca, 1577; 1592.

SALMEN, WALTER. "Iberische Hofmusikanten des späten Mittelalters auf Auslandsreisen," *AM*, XI (1956).

SALVÁ Y MALLEN, PEDRO. *Catálogo de la Biblioteca de Salvá*. Valencia, 1872. 2 vols.

SAMPAYO RIBEIRO, MÁRIO DE. *Os Manuscritos Musicais nos. 6 e 12 da Biblioteca Geral da Universidade de Coimbra*. Coimbra, 1941.

—— "Sôbre o fecho do 'Auto da Cananeia,'" *Brotéria*, XXVII (1938).

SÁNCHEZ, JUAN M. *Bibliografía Aragonesa del siglo XVI*. Madrid, 1913–1914. 2 vols.

SÁNCHEZ, TOMÁS. (ed.) *Poetas Castellanos anteriores al siglo XV* (*Bibl. de Aut. Esp.*, LVII). Madrid, 1921.

SÁNCHEZ DE ARÉVALO, RUY. *Vergel de los Principes*. Madrid, 1900.

SARTORI, CLAUDIO. *Bibliografía delle opere musicali stampate da Ottaviano Petrucci*. Florence, 1948.

SCHMIDT, KARL WILHELM. *Quaestiones de musica scriptoribus Romanis, imprimis de Cassiodoro et Isidoro*. Darmstadt, 1899.

SCHNEIDER, MARIUS. "¿Existen elementos de música popular en el 'Cancionero Musical de Palacio'?" *AM*, VIII (1953).

—— "Gestaltimitation als Kompositionsprinzip im Cancionero de Palacio," *Die Musikforschung*, XI/4 (1958).

SEAY, ALBERT. "Florence: The City of Hothby and Ramos," *JAMS*, IX, 3 (1956).

—— "The *Dialogus Johannis Ottobi Anglici in arte musica*," *JAMS*, VIII, 2 (1955).

SÉJOURNÉ, DOM PAUL. "Saint Isidore de Séville et la liturgie wisigothique," *Miscellanea Isidoriana: Homenaje a San Isidoro*. Rome, 1936.

SERRANO, DOM LUCIANO. *¿Que es canto gregoriano?* Barcelona, 1905.

SILVA, INNOCENCIO FRANCISCO DA. *Diccionario Bibliographico Portuguez*. Lisbon, 1858–62. 6 vols.

SOLALINDE, ANTONIO G. "Intervención de Alfonso X en la redacción de sus obras," *RFE*, II (1915).

SORBELLI, ALBANO. "Le due Edizioni della 'Musica practica' di Bartolomé Ramis de Pareja," *Gutenberg Jahrbuch*, 1930.

SOUSA, ANTONIO CAETANO DE. *Historia Genealogica da Casa Real Portugueza*, III. Lisbon, 1737.

SOUSA, LUIS DE. *Anais de D. João III*, II, ed. by M. Rodrigues Lapa. Lisbon, 1938.

SOUSA VITERBO, FRANCISCO MARQUES DE. *A litteratura hespanhola em Portugal*. Lisbon, 1915.

—— *Os Mestres da Capella Real nos Reinados de D. João III e D. Sebastião*. Lisbon, 1907.

SPANKE, HANS. "Zum Thema 'Mittelalterliche Tanzlieder,'" *Neuphilologische Mitteilungen*, XXXIII (1932).

SPAÑON, ALONSO. *Introducion muy vtil: y breue de canto llano*. Seville, c. 1500.

SPATARO, GIOVANNI. *Dilucide et probatissime demonstratione*. Bologna, 1521; facs. repr. Berlin, 1925.

—— *Honesta defensio in Nicolai Burtii parmensis opusculum*. Bologna, 1491.

—— *Tractato di musica*. Venice, 1531.

SPECHTSHART, HUGO *of Reutlingen*. *Flores musice*. Strassburg, 1488; [ed. Carl Beck] Stuttgart, 1868.

STERNHOLD, THOMAS, and others. *The first parte of the Psalmes collected into Englishe metre ... with apte notes to sing them withal*. London, 1564.

STEVENSON, R. (ed.) *Cantilenas Vulgares puestas en Musica por varios Españoles*. Literary Texts. Lima, 1958.

—— *Juan Bermudo*. Lima, 1958.

—— (ed.) *La Música en la Catedral de Sevilla, 1478–1606: Documentos para su estudio*. Los Angeles, 1954.

—— *Music in Mexico: A Historical Survey*. New York, 1952.

—— "Music Research in Spanish Libraries," *Notes of the Music Library Association*, X (1952).

—— "Sixteenth- and Seventeenth-Century Resources in Mexico," *Fontes Artis Musicae*, 1954/2; 1955/1.

STRAETEN, EDMOND VAN DER. *La musique aux Pays-Bas avant le XIXe siècle*. Brussels, 1867–88. 8 vols.

STRUNK, OLIVER. *Source Readings in Music History*. New York, 1950.

SUBIRÁ, JOSÉ. *Historia de la música española e hispanoamericana*. Barcelona, 1953.

—— *La Música en la Casa de Alba: Estudios históricos y biográficos*. Madrid, 1927.

SUÑOL, DOM GREGORI. "El canto español del 'Pange lingua,'" *Revista Montserratina*, III (1909).

—— "Els Cants dels Romeus," *Analecta Montserratensia*, I (1917 [1918]).

—— "La Liturgia dels nostres impresos (segles xv^è–xvi^è)," *Analecta Montserratensia*, II (1918 [1919]).

TAPIA, MARTÍN DE. *Vergel de Musica*. Burgo de Osma, 1570.

THALESIO, PEDRO. *Arte de Canto chão, com huma breve instrucção ... segunda impressão*. Coimbra, 1628.

THOMAS, H. (ed.) *El Comendador Roman: Coplas de la Pasión con la Resurreción*. (Toledo, c. 1490) London, 1936.

—— "The Printer George Coci of Saragossa," *Gutenberg Festschrift*. Mainz, 1925.

TORRE, ALFONSO DE LA. *Comiença el tratado llamado vision deleytable*. Toulouse, 1489.

TORRES, MELCHIOR DE. *Arte ingeniosa de Musica con nueua manera de auisos breues y compendiosos sobre toda la facultad della*. Alcalá de Henares, 1544.

Tovar, Francisco. *Libro de musica pratica.* Barcelona, 1510.

Trend, J. B. "Salinas: A Sixteenth Century Collector of Folk Songs," *ML*, VIII (1927).

—— *The Music of Spanish History to 1600.* London, 1926.

—— "The Mystery of Sybil Cassandra," *ML*, X (1929).

—— "The Mystery of Elche," *ML*, I (1920).

Ursprung, Otto. "Neuere Literatur zur spanischen Musikgeschichte," *ZfMW*, XII (1929).

—— "Spanisch-katalanische Liedkunst des 14. Jahrhunderts," *ZfMW*, IV (1921).

Vagaggini, Sandra. *La miniature florentine aux xive et xve siècles.* Milan-Florence, 1952.

Valderrábano, Enríquez de. *Libro de musica de vihuela, intitulado Silva de Sirenas.* Valladolid, 1547.

Valera, Mosén Diego de. *Crónica de los Reyes Católicos,* ed. J. de M. Carriazo (*RFE, Anejo VIII*). Madrid, 1927.

Van Dijk, S. J. P. "Medieval Terminology and Methods of Psalm Singing," *MD*, VI (1952).

—— "Saint Bernard and the *Instituta Patrum*," *MD*, IV (1950).

Varagine, Jacobus de. *Lombardica historia que a plerisque Aurea legenda sanctorum appellatur.* Strassburg, 1486.

Vasconcellos, Joaquim de. *Os musicos portuguezes.* Oporto, 1870. 2 vols.

Venegas de Henestrosa, Luys. *Libro de cifra nueua para tecla, harpa y vihuela.* Alcalá de Henares, 1557.

Verardi, Carlo. [*Historia Baetica*]. Basel, 1494.

Vicente, Gil. *Copilaçam de todalas obras.* Lisbon, 1562.

Vicente de Burgos, Fray. *El libro de las propriedades delas cosas trasladado de latin en romançe.* Toulouse, 1494.

Villafranca, Luys de. *Breue Instrucion de Canto llano.* Seville, 1565.

Villalba Muñoz, Luis. "Un tratado de música inédito del siglo XV," *La Ciudad de Dios,* LXX (1906).

Villalón, Cristóbal de. *Ingeniosa comparacion entre lo antiguo y lo presente.* Valladolid, 1539; repr. Madrid, 1898.

Villancicos de diuersos Autores, a dos, y a tres, y a quatro, y a cinco bozes. Venice, 1556.

Villanueva, Jaime. *Viage literario á las Iglesias de España,* VII [Vique] and XIV [Gerona]. Valencia, 1821, and Madrid, 1850.

Vindel, Francisco. *El arte tipográfico en España durante el siglo XV: Salamanca, Zamora, Coria y el reino de Galicia.* Madrid, 1946.

—— *El arte tipográfico en España durante el siglo XV: Sevilla y Granada.* Madrid, 1949.

—— *El arte tipográfico en Zaragoza.* Madrid, 1949.

Vindel, Pedro. *Las siete canciones de amor: poema musical.* Madrid, 1915.

Vives, José. (ed.) *Oracional visigótico.* Barcelona, 1946.

Vives, Juan Luis. *A very frutefull and pleasant boke called the Instruction of a Christen Woman,* trans. Richard Hyrd. London, c. 1529.

Wagner, Peter. "Der mozarabische Kirchengesang und seine Überlieferung," *SFG*, I (1928).

—— *Die Gesänge der Jakobusliturgie zu Santiago de Compostela* (*Collectanea Friburgensia,* fasc. XX, Neue Folge).

—— "Untersuchungen zu den Gesangstexten und zur responsorialen Psalmodie der altspanischen Liturgie," *SFG*, II (1930).

Whitehill, Walter M. and Prado, Dom Germán. *Liber Sancti Jacobi: Codex Calixtinus.* Santiago de Compostela, 1944. 3 vols.

Wolf, Johannes. *Geschichte der Mensural-Notation.* Leipzig, 1904. 3 vols.

Zapata, Luis. *Miscelánea* (*Memorial Histórico Español,* XI). Madrid, 1859.

Zarco Cuevas, Julián. *Catálogo de los manuscritos castellanos de la Real Biblioteca de El Escorial.* Madrid, 1924–29. 3 vols.

Index

Religious, academic, and rank distinctions do not enter the index, except when essential to identification. Dates are omitted likewise – unless prerequisite to identification. For a running list of subjects and for the titles of musical excerpts in this book, see the analytical table of contents at pages vii-viii and the list of musical examples at pages ix-x. Italicized entries will be found the more important, when several page references are given. Names and subjects in the footnotes are not indexed, except when especially significant. No systematic attempt has been made to index geographic names that crop up so often as Toledo and Seville. As a rule, titles of the musical works already gathered into alphabetical order at pages 124, 136, 151, 166, 172, 186, 194[300], and 209-213, are not repeated in the index below. Alphabetizing carries through to the first punctuation, regardless of the number of words. Several members of the same family are usually grouped under one entry (e.g., Fermoselle), but not unrelated possessors of a common name (e.g., Fernández).

The printing of this book was completed on December 20, 1960